## *Also by R.W Peake*

### *Marching with Caesar-Conquest of Gaul* Critically Acclaimed

*"Peake, a retired infantry Marine, brings to the familiar story of Caesar's conquest of Gaul the gritty, boots-on-the-ground realism of personal experience, and the results are amazingly compelling...Fans of Roman historical fiction—or military fiction just in general—shouldn't miss what looks to be one heck of a series."*
~ The Historical Novel Society

"The hinge of history pivoted on the career of Julius Caesar, as Rome's Republic became an Empire, but the muscle to swing that gateway came from soldiers like Titus Pullus. What an amazing story from a student now become the master of historical fiction at its best." ~ *Professor Frank Holt, University of Houston*

*R.W. Peake*

# Marching With Caesar
# Civil War

## R.W. Peake

*For Luke*
*Ever Faithful*

## *Foreword*

It's hard to describe the feeling that comes from seeing the results of what was four years of your life so well received as the first book of this series, Marching With Caesar-Conquest of Gaul has been, and to say that it's humbling is an understatement. So before going any farther, I want to thank all of the readers who responded so enthusiastically to this tale of a common Gregarius in the Legions of Rome who, through a combination of luck and skill, managed to survive forty-two years Marching With Caesar.

Because of a choice I made early on in the telling of Titus' story, I hope that there will be a continuity in the pacing and style of all of the books. Very early on, when I recognized that this was going to be more than one book, I was at a point where I could have stopped to get the first book out, then picked the story back up. However, for a number of reasons, none of them adding up to more than a gut feeling, I made the decision to finish Titus' complete story arc first before releasing the first book. What this means in a tangible sense is that the amount and depth of research I did, which has been one of the aspects that has seen the most favorable comments from the readers, is exactly the same. I hope that this holds true for this second installment that covers the Caesarian Civil War.

I want to thank what has turned out to be a great team for helping me turn out a book that is hopefully the best that it can be. Beth Lynne, of BZHercules, has proven to be not only a first-rate editor but a sympathetic ear as I am learning to negotiate what it means to have some success at this, taking the bad with the good as it comes. This cover, like the cover for MWC-CoG, will hopefully turn out to be another great weapon, this time not-so-secret, and Marina Shipova's work will get the kind of notice and acclaim that it deserves. She has made Titus come alive, and as one can see, age and take on the trappings that come with advancement through the ranks in the form of a family. If I have anything to do with it, Marina will be the cover artist for every book of the series, and any other books that I do! Finally, the unending support and love of my family has continued to be the one constant in what has been a rollercoaster ride. Granted, there have mostly been up's, but there have certainly been some dips on this ride that were unforeseen. Knowing that ultimately my success or failure doesn't change the fact that my daughter still views her father as a Grade A knucklehead provides not only a level of comfort, but ensures that I keep my feet solidly on the ground.

So I hope you enjoy this second installment of Titus' story, and that you still feel as if you are Marching With Caesar, along with Titus, Vibius and their friends and comrades.

Semper Fidelis,

R.W. Peake
November, 2012

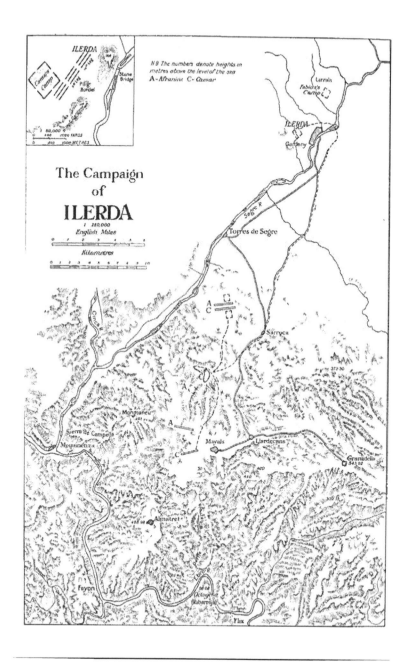

# Chapter 1- Campaign against Afranius and Petreius

These are the words of Titus Pullus, formerly Legionary, Optio, Pilus Prior and Primus Pilus of Caesar's 10th Legion Equestris, now known as 10th Gemina, Primus Pilus of the 6th Ferrata, and Camp Prefect, as dictated to his faithful former slave, scribe, and friend, Diocles.

I am dictating this in my 61st year, three years after my retirement as Camp Prefect, in the tenth year of the reign of Augustus, and 489 years after the founding of the Roman Republic. I have more than 40 military decorations, including three gold torqs, three set of phalarae, two coronae civica, three coronae murales, and a corona vallaris. I have more than 20 battle scars on my body, all of them in the front, and my back is clean, never having been flogged in my 42 years in the Legions, nor have I turned my back to the enemy. Although my record is not as great as the revered Dentatus, I am well known in the Legions, and I have given the bulk of my life and blood to Rome.

My goal is straightforward; with these words, I plan to record all of the momentous events in which I participated as a member of Rome's Legions, during a period that changed the very foundations of Rome itself.

Now that I have recovered and refreshed myself, I pick up my tale where I left off. The conquest of Gaul is over, Caesar and his armies triumphing in the greatest campaign in Roman, or I suspect, world history. However, his success has roused great jealousy by those men, small in every measurable way, who call themselves the *boni*. Using Pompeius Magnus as their stooge, they are doing everything they can to destroy our general, ignoring his popularity with the people of my class. Caesar, given no choice by the *boni*, has crossed the Rubicon with just the 13th Legion. However, the rest of his army, including my own 10th Legion, is preparing to march. Matters between my childhood friend and long-time comrade, Vibius Domitius, are growing increasingly strained because of the situation with Caesar, since Vibius is a strict Catonian in sentiment. Making matters more difficult for me personally, I am forced to leave behind my wife and newborn child, Vibius' namesake, whom we call Vibi. I have been the Secundus Pilus Prior for some time now, but I still have to worry about my nemesis, Secundus Pilus Posterior Celer, who constantly seeks to undermine me. Although none of us are looking forward to facing fellow Romans, we are all prepared to do our duty, even Vibius, if for no other reason than for the men standing next to him in the ranks, and for Caesar and his *dignitas*.

Caesar's army was a mixed lot of veteran and new Legions; there was us, the 7th, 9th, and 14th from the Gallic Army, and also two new Legions that Caesar had raised in Italy, the 21st and 30th, full of raw *tirones*. This army marched west to confront the Pompeian forces, heading through the Pyrenees and sweeping aside the Cohort-sized Pompeian units that guarded the passes through the mountains, suffering few losses. Once across the mountains, we moved towards the spot where our scouts had located Pompey's Legions, in the northeast around the town of Ilerda, on the other side of the Sicoris River. Gathered there to face us was the most veteran of Pompey's army, the 3rd, 4th, 5th, and 6th Legions, veterans all, and from whose ranks our cadre like Crastinus and Calienus had originally come. They were led by two stalwart Pompeians, Afranius and Petreius, one of whom we would have cause to hate with an abiding passion, but that was in the future. However, the Pompeian Legions' veteran status also meant that their discharges were due, just as they had been for Crastinus, meaning there was some question about how steadfast they actually were in their devotion to Pompey and his cause. At least, that was what the Legates and the good young men tried to tell us. Nevertheless, they were Spanish Legions like us and we held little illusion that they would not fight when the time came, a fact that bothered us a great deal, because there were friends and kinsmen across that river that we might have to kill. Little else was discussed around the fires at night, none of us liking the prospect a bit, but also knowing that when the time came, we would do what needed to be done, no matter how distasteful it might be. I could not help wondering if they felt the same way, staring across at us from the other side of the river.

During the period in which we were waiting for Caesar, Fabius put us to work constructing two bridges, about four miles apart. One was on the upstream side of the river from the town, and the other was on the downstream side. The construction of these bridges was contested hotly by the Pompeians, with fierce fighting around the bridge sites, but we managed to get them built despite the resistance. With the bridges built, we waited for Caesar to arrive. He was supposedly coming with about 900 cavalry he had gathered to replace the ones who defected with Labienus. Also, Fabius sent messengers laden with gold across the river and behind the Pompeian positions, bribing the surrounding towns to close their gates and to refuse any aid to Afranius and his troops, instead giving what food they could spare to us. In order to get to what food these towns had to offer, we were forced to send foraging parties out in force across the bridges to get to them.

During one of these forays, a potentially disastrous event struck the 14th and 30th Legions, the former being the reconstituted 14th full of green troops, and the latter being one of the new Legions Caesar had commissioned after crossing the Rubicon. Once they were on the other side of the river, a storm in the mountains higher upriver hit, creating a flash flood downriver. The flood sent a wall of water, accompanied by a maelstrom of wind. It then hit the bridge that the Legions had marched across, sweeping it away and sending the debris downstream. The presence of that debris alerted Afranius that something was afoot, whereupon he sent scouts out who reported to him that there was a part of our force upstream stranded on the Pompeian side of the river. Afranius immediately sent a force out to trap our men on the wrong side, prompting a sharp fight where the Legate in charge of our foraging party, Plancus as I recall, shook his men out into an *orbis* on a small hill, forcing Afranius to reconsider any headlong charge. While Afranius was deploying his men into a standard assault formation, our commander Fabius sent a relief force consisting of the remainder of our cavalry, along with the 9th, across on the remaining intact bridge to come to Plancus' aid. Seeing the standards, Afranius called off his attack after a brief skirmish that claimed few casualties on either side, and once relieved by our force, Plancus marched back across the remaining bridge. It was a close call, and easily could have been a disaster if Afranius was a bolder commander like Caesar and had risked an all-out attack on green troops, but as usual, even by proxy, Caesar's luck held.

A couple of days later, Caesar arrived with his 900 German cavalrymen, and the tempo of our operations immediately picked up. The day after he arrived, he left some Cohorts behind to guard the original camp, marching the rest of us across the nearer bridge to shake us out in a *triplex acies* facing the Afranius camp. This camp had been thrown up a few hundred yards from the walls of the town. Afranius linked the two together by a ditch where supplies could be carried from the town to allow men to move back and forth. Consistent with Roman practice, the camp of Afranius took advantage of high ground and Afranius sent his own forces out to face ours on the slopes of this hill. That was as far as it got, however; he seemed content to let his men stand out in the hot sun, meaning that we had to do the same. The sun moved slowly through the sky, and only through the discipline and experience of countless other days spent in identical circumstances was this day bearable.

There we stood, veterans on both sides, staring across the plain, our men looking up the hill, theirs looking down onto the valley floor, each of us occupied with our own thoughts. It was not lost on any of us that there were men we knew, and indeed may have been related to by blood, standing across from us, waiting for the order to move forward and kill each other. Honestly, despite the boredom, none of us felt particularly eager to head up that hill to start killing men we knew, if not intimately at least by virtue of our common heritage and place of birth. We were all men of Hispania, and professionals and veterans that we may have been, we had no real desire to slaughter or to be slaughtered by such men as these. Consequently, there was little grumbling at the waiting and finally, when the sun had passed over the midday point, it became clear that Afranius was not going to move, whereupon Caesar commanded the back line of the formation to fall out to begin the construction of a camp. Since we marched out in battle order, we did not have the stakes for the palisade, so the men were put to work digging the ditch first. Because our first two lines remained in formation, the work was obscured, meaning that when the order was given to withdraw, we caught Afranius by surprise when, instead of retreating across the bridge to our original camp, we pulled back across the ditch and the earthworks to settle down for the night.

The next day saw a repeat of the same as the day before, except that Caesar kept a part of the army behind in the camp to finish the job of fortifying it. For once, we regretted not drawing the short straw to be left behind in camp, because as monotonous and tiring as fortifying the camp may have been, it was still better than standing motionless in the hot sun. However, this time was a little different, since Caesar allowed us to relax, having taken the measure of Afranius and being certain that he would not take action. At least, it appeared that way on the surface, when he gave the order that either we could sit down or mingle within our immediate area, as long as we were within a few paces of our grounded gear. I believe that he was doing his best to goad Afranius into action by having us appear lax and as if we were ripe for attack, so perhaps Afranius was not as foolish as we thought. It was in this manner that the second day passed uneventfully, and we plodded back into the almost completed camp at least as tired as our comrades working on it. On the third day, Caesar ordered the extra stakes that were gathered brought over from the original camp, along with the baggage, brought under the guard of the Cohorts left behind. This was done, with the three Legions who had worked on the camp the day before now taking their turn out on the plain, while we finished what remained to be done in the second camp. In the same manner as the first two days, this one passed uneventfully as well, with both sides staring at each other, waiting for the other to make their move.

On the fourth day, Caesar grew tired of waiting and decided to act. Taking the 9th, the 14th, and the 21st, he made a move to secure a small mound roughly halfway between our camp and the slopes of the hill that Afranius' camp was occupying. The position of this small hill was such that it would allow us to interpose ourselves between Afranius' camp and the town, thereby cutting them off from resupply. The distance from our camp to the mound was about halfway between the two camps, in the middle of a plain about 300 paces wide. As usual, Caesar was counting on his speed of action and I believe he was emboldened by the seeming hesitance that Afranius had shown over the course of the previous three days. This allowed us to build and fortify a camp on his side of the river, almost literally under his very nose. However, this time Caesar was the one to be caught out because Afranius almost immediately determined what he was up to, and rushed several Cohorts out the gates of his own camp, reaching the mound before Caesar could. There was a brief battle for the mound, and during this skirmish, for the first time, we witnessed the peculiar style of fighting practiced by Pompey's Legions. Cheering at the sight of our men seemingly sweeping the Pompeians off the mound with almost contemptuous ease, we would soon learn that this was nothing more than a ruse. When our men charged to the top of the mound, they were suddenly beset on three sides by the original guard Cohorts, along with some of the other Cohorts that Afranius had sent out. The Pompeians came at our men with a rush, but the moment our men engaged, they broke off and retreated down the hill.

"What in the name of Pluto's thorny cock are they doing?" demanded Priscus with some indignation. "That's not how Romans fight."

"I know," I agreed, with not a little trepidation.

We were watching from the ramparts and, despite being safe, all of us felt as involved as if we were standing in the line on the hill. Before our eyes, the Pompeians darted back and forth at our lines, until finally the Primus Pilus of the 14th, the first Legion to the mound, gave the order to rush after the Pompeians the next time they fell back, exactly what the Pompeians wanted. The instant the 14th charged, they were surrounded, now by at least two Legion's worth of Afranius' troops. In the space of a few heartbeats, the scene was completely obscured by the dust of thousands of feet, a bad sign on its own. Our anxiety increased as we tried to determine what was happening by the sounds, our experienced ears telling us that it was not going well.

The 14th was deployed on the left, with the other two Legions arrayed so they were closer to the Afranius camp, with the 9th on the right and the 21st in the middle, the traditional spot for green Legions. This time it did not work out the way Caesar had hoped, because the men of the 21st started showing signs of panic as the fighting that started with the 14th spread to envelop them. Afranius fed more men into the battle, sensing that he had achieved the rarest of feats: catching Caesar off balance. Even as we watched helplessly, the unease of the 21st turned to panic, the rear ranks beginning to turn for the safety of our camp. At first, their Optios were able to beat them back into the line, then something happened, although I do not know what, but whatever it was triggered a panic. Now the men in the rear were braving the swats of their Optios to push past them, oblivious to anything but the thought of getting back to the safety of the camp. Not all of the men of the 21st panicked, but enough did to cause the center of Caesar's line to start to collapse, and only the sheer bulk of the 21st kept the 14th from being completely surrounded. Now that was about to change, as more men of the 21$^{st}$ began to slip past their Optios to head back towards us in the camp. Caesar then called on the 9th to come to the rescue, which they did, but not before getting into trouble themselves.

From their spot on the right, the 9th had to run parallel across the lines to try to stem the tide of the retreat started by the 21st. By this time, the 21st had crumbled completely, running in a large mass for the camp. Those of us on the rampart hurried to grab our javelins should Afranius' troops be foolhardy enough to get that close in their pursuit. As spirited as their chase was, I have no doubt that some of Afranius' men would have ventured too close, but as it was, their headlong run put them in an untenable position of their own making. By pursuing the 21st, their cohesion was completely gone and that, coupled with the fact that the 9th was now bearing down on their left flank, suddenly put them in mortal danger. The 9th slammed into the Pompeians, who had just a matter of a bare moment to realize the danger, meaning that only a precious few had stopped their pursuit and turned to face the new threat. These men were rolled up like a carpet. In almost a blink of an eye, a disaster of the first proportion turned into at the very least a chance to create a stalemate, depending on how well the Pompeians reacted, and at this point, those tactics that we had witnessed when the 14th took the hill once again showed their effectiveness. Instead of trying to mount a defense, the Pompeians simply melted away in front of the 9th, beginning their own retreat back to the town, which at that point was closer to them than their own camp.

The 9th began a headlong pursuit, but like the 14th, found to their hazard that the retreat of the Pompeians was not a retreat as much as it was a tactic. Once they reached the slope of the hill leading up to the town, the Pompeians immediately turned. Then, with a speed and efficiency at which we could only marvel, they re-formed to launch a countercharge directly into the 9th, who had just reached the lower slopes of the hill. Immediately the tide turned and now the 9th was on their back heels, trying to maintain their formation while fighting desperately. Standing on the rampart, we could only watch the small individual battles break out, as usually two Pompeians would leap forward to try to engage one of our own men before quickly falling back if they did not see an immediate advantage. Soon enough, the dust obscured the fight near the town and we were forced to turn our attention back to the 14th, who had finally extricated themselves from the mound and now were falling back, leaving the small hill littered with bodies.

The 21st had recovered their composure to a degree; at least, they had fallen back into formation, but they too were still moving backwards, although they did not appear to be under that much pressure. However, the retreat of the 21st and 14th further isolated the 9th, and Afranius was quick to see this. He began sending fresh men from the camp through the ditches to the town walls, where they could launch their javelins down onto the heads of the 9th. Now their existence was threatened, and Caesar chose this moment to launch his cavalry in a bid to rescue them.

Despite the slope and the rugged terrain, Caesar's Germans wedged themselves between the lines of the 9th and the Pompeians, allowing the 9th to retreat down the hill. The 14th and 21st had halted their withdrawal to wait in support of the 9th, their presence keeping those Pompeians who took the small hill from turning their back to our two Legions in order to harry the 9th as they withdrew. In this manner, our three Legions managed to extricate themselves. Caesar's attempt to take the small hill had failed; it belonged to the Pompeians.

Our losses were much heavier than any of us had thought they would be; the Primus Pilus of the 14th had fallen. Fulginus was his name, as I recall, a victim of his headlong rush down the hill in the early stages of the battle. In addition, the 14th lost about 70 men, the 9th almost as many, and the 21st about half that. It may not seem like many men when compared to the strength of a Legion. However, it must be remembered that veteran Legions like the 9th, and the 10th for that matter, were nearing the end of our enlistments. We had been fighting and dying for a long time, meaning that every loss at this point whittled us down even further. Our only consolation was that we inflicted at least twice as many casualties as we suffered, so the Pompeian Legions were in much the same state as our own, and could ill afford their losses as well. Still, even with that, the overwhelming topic of conversation that night concerned the strange tactics we had seen the Pompeians employ. The reason for our surprise was that while we expected tribes like the Lusitani to act in such a manner, it was completely unexpected to see men wearing our uniform acting as if they were barbarians.

"It's just not natural," Celer spat into the fire outside my tent where I had called a meeting of the Centurions, and for once I found myself in agreement with my normal nemesis. "Romans shouldn't be fighting like a bunch of barbarian scum."

Heads nodded in agreement, except for Priscus, who merely stared into the fire. Curious that he did not seem to agree, I asked him what he thought. He glanced up, seeing all eyes on him, the color rising to his cheeks. For a moment he said nothing, then shrugged, "I can't say I like it, but it certainly makes them more of a challenge to fight."

This sentiment was met with some agreement, and obviously encouraged, he continued, "Besides, we've always prided ourselves on adopting the tactics of our enemies when they prove to be effective."

"But all that jumping about has never been effective against us," argued Celer.

"That's because they weren't Romans doing it," Priscus replied quietly and I instantly saw that he had gone to the heart of the matter. Despite the fact that Celer was right, that the mad dashing about that we had experienced when fighting Gauls and the like never worked against us, the underlying discipline of fellow Romans was the reason that what we saw that day was so disquieting, because ultimately that discipline was completely lacking with the barbarians. When this fluid type of fighting was coupled with the underlying discipline and training of a Legion, it made for a formidable combination.

"You've obviously been thinking about this," I said, and I could tell that Priscus was pleased at the compliment. "So tell us how we beat them."

His expression changed immediately. His discomfort at being put on the spot in front of his peers obvious to anyone with eyes, but he thought about it for a moment before replying slowly, "Well, I think the only way to counter their tactics is to adopt them for our own."

Priscus' statement was met by a snort of derision and when I turned to look, I was not surprised to see that Celer was now openly sneering.

"As if we would lower ourselves to hop about like grasshoppers on a hot rock."

He looked around to see who appreciated his wit, but I think he was not prepared for what he saw. Instead of laughing or showing any sign of agreement, the others looked more thoughtful than amused.

Seeing an opportunity to take Celer down a peg, I did not hesitate. "I don't know, Celer," I said coolly. "It seems like a good idea to us. Perhaps it's because you're a little too . . . portly to be acting like a grasshopper that's the true cause of your objection?"

Celer's spluttered protests were drowned out by the roar of laughter of the others, and I could tell by the deep red flushing of his face that I had scored a telling blow. Celer was a man who loved his luxuries, and our time in garrison had softened him, despite the training regimen that was part of our peacetime life, and we had all taken notice of his spreading waistline. I had never suffered from this problem; even today, I can still fit into my armor. Neither my baldric nor baltea have had new holes cut in them, so it was and is hard for me to be sympathetic. And when it came to Celer, I was not prepared to show any understanding whatsoever.

The day after the battle for the mound, which by this time Afranius had fortified, it started to rain in a torrential downpour that the locals claimed was the hardest rain in living memory. I do not know if this is true, but I do know that it was strong enough to send a raging rush of debris-choked water downriver, once again sweeping the bridges away

15

from behind us. This time, the damage was such that the work to repair them had to start from scratch; even the pilings had been destroyed this time. Also, the rains lasted sufficiently long that the river overflowed its banks for a number of days, effectively cutting us off from resupply and our foraging parties that had been already sent out were now stranded on the wrong side of the river as well. All in all, it could not have been much worse; the only thing that saved us was our experience, having been through situations like this before. The only bridge remaining was the stone bridge that led into the town, but that was firmly in Afranius' control, and we thought it unlikely that we could dislodge him. Making things even more difficult was the fact that Afranius and his men had already scoured the countryside on our side of the river, snapping up every kernel of grain, pig, chicken, and cow in the region. All we had with us was what we marched in with, augmented by some cattle for which Caesar paid exorbitant prices. Things were definitely looking grim, and they only got worse.

A relief column from Gaul was heading our way; a huge column fully two miles long, with a force of archers, cavalry, and, most importantly, wagons of grain and other supplies. Unfortunately for us, it was a Gallic column, meaning that it was not so much led as it was herded along, with no one man in charge. In other words, it was the normal Gallic chaos rolling at its own leisurely pace, covering barely ten miles a day, on a good day. There is no way to hide such a large number of wagons under the best of circumstances, and it was not long before Afranius learned of the convoy. Late one night, he sent a force of cavalry and three of his Legions across the stone bridge to intercept the wagons. By all logic, the train should have been ripe for the plucking, even with the force of archers and cavalry, but somehow, the Gauls managed to survive more or less intact, with the loss of a handful of cavalry who sacrificed themselves to allow the convoy to withdraw to a hill and take up defensive positions. It was a victory for us, but it was hollow. While the supply train survived, it was still unable to reach us because of the state of the river, keeping any work on reconstruction of the bridges from happening. All in all, we were in a tight spot, and as we were to learn later, both Afranius and Petreius were not shy about letting Rome know that they had Caesar ready for the death blow, that it was just a matter of time. Because of the repulse of our assault on the mound and our supply problems, couriers were issued almost every day from the Pompeian camp, hurrying to Rome with what were undoubtedly highly exaggerated claims of our woes. I will not deny that we were in serious trouble; the problem for the Pompeians was that we had been in trouble before and despite our hunger, we had every confidence in Caesar, and before long, that confidence was justified.

During our time in Britannia, we saw many new and different things. One of those things that we saw on that accursed island, Caesar put to use here. I know not what they are called by the Britons, but they are small, round boats made of hide stretched over a wicker frame. They are extremely light but sturdy craft and are easy to steer. Most importantly, they are easy to make and transport, and these boats proved to be our salvation, thanks to Caesar's ingenuity and willingness to try new things. He ordered a number of these craft built, then using double wagons and under the cover of night, marched out with five Cohorts of the 10th, including mine, making a hard march to the north, slipping past the town and Afranius' camp undetected. We moved to a spot almost 20 miles upriver, finally stopping where the river was narrow enough and would provide a suitable site for a bridge. Unloading the boats, we paddled across, taking position on a small hill overlooking the riverbank, with a good command of the surrounding terrain. Immediately, the rest of the 10th was sent for, along with the 7th, and within two days we had built a new bridge across the river. Word was sent to the Gallic column, and they crossed the bridge. Under escort, they made it to our camp. With this stroke, our supply situation was now solved.

Now that we had regained both sides of the river, Afranius' foragers were in jeopardy. A party of them was captured by our cavalry, and in Afranius' attempt to liberate them, he suffered a sharp defeat, losing a full Cohort of men in the process. Just as quickly as the gods turned their faces from us, they now returned their favor to Caesar. It was almost dizzying how quickly things turned around. Somewhere in this time period, Caesar also received word that Decimus Brutus had succeeded in defeating the combined fleet of Massilia and the personal fleet of Domitius Ahenobarbus. It was clear to all, especially the natives, that Caesar's fortune was restored, thereby making it even more difficult for Afranius to obtain supplies, with all five tribes in the region reaching an agreement with Caesar to supply only us. After the capture of the foraging party, it was almost impossible for Afranius to find volunteers for that duty, and soon men were being turned out of the camp gates at the point of a sword to go forage. Naturally, their hearts were not in it, most of them immediately deserting to us, never returning to Afranius. Still, all was not perfect with our lot. In order to keep the pressure up on Afranius' foragers, Caesar was forced to run the cavalry ragged; the fact that they had to travel 20 miles to the bridge was a hardship on the men and the horses. To remedy this, Caesar contrived to engineer a crossing of the river by creating an artificial ford at a spot about a mile and a half up the river from the stone bridge. Since Afranius was unable to stop us, he and Petreius realized that their position was now untenable, because the creation of that ford would effectively shut off all foraging attempts by the

Pompeians, whose own supply situation had become dire. This move by Caesar convinced them that it was time to shift operations, and accordingly they chose the region south of the Iber River.

It took some time to create the ford; a series of channels had to be cut that diverted the flow of the Sicoris, lowering its normal level in order to allow both horses and men to cross without fear of drowning. While Caesar was working, Afranius sent word to the natives south of the Iber to make ready to receive the Pompeian army. Unlike the region we were in now, the natives south of the Iber were still firmly in the Pompeian camp, and it was this support that Afranius counted on to help prepare the way. He ordered the native tribes to gather a number of small boats at a point on the Iber where they would be strung together to make a bridge for his army to cross. Although the area was friendly to Pompey, such an endeavor was not going to go unnoticed by our scouts. Once the location of the boat bridge was identified, it was a simple matter of plotting Afranius' line of march from Ilerda to the bridge. Knowing where the enemy is going is always a huge advantage in warfare, and this occasion was no exception. To prepare for the evacuation, Afranius sent two of his Legions across the stone bridge, where they built a fortified camp. It became a race; Caesar doubled the workforce on the ford, but after a day, it was still just barely suitable for horses to cross and still too risky for the Legions. It would take us too long to march to the bridge upriver, because by that time, Afranius' evacuation would be complete. Attacking the enemy when they tried to cross the stone bridge was out of the question due to the position of the two Legions already dug in on the eastern bank. Deciding that what was created at the ford would have to suffice, Caesar ordered his cavalry across the river even as Afranius' men marched across the bridge, forming up in marching order to begin their trek south.

We stood on the ramparts watching our cavalry dart in and out, looking for vulnerable spots in the enemy's formation. Despite their best efforts, the Afranius column began marching, although they left a string of bodies behind as they moved slowly across the level plain by the river. It looked very much like the Pompeians would escape and that the fighting would continue.

I am not sure who started it, but I became aware of a buzz of conversation that was different from the normal background noise of chatter that is typical of the Legions when they are standing idle like we were in the camp. One's ear becomes attuned to these minute changes, especially as a Centurion or Optio, because more often than not it spells trouble. Turning from watching our cavalry, I saw that a large number of men had clustered together and were engaged in an animated debate of some kind. I looked around for one of my Centurions, but since Celer was the only one nearby and I did not trust him, I decided to go see what the commotion was on my own. Before I could descend the parapet, three of the men left the group and headed in the direction of the Primus Pilus, who was standing farther down the parapet. Wanting to hear, I changed direction and walked to join the Primus Pilus, arriving at the same time as the delegation.

"Primus Pilus." I guessed that this man, an Optio from the First Cohort as I recall, was elected as spokesman to approach the command group with whatever these men had in mind. "We want you to go to Caesar for us."

That was certainly guaranteed to get all of our attention, and the Primus Pilus looked nonplussed.

"For what?" he demanded.

"To convince him to send us across the ford now, so we can end this once and for all."

There was a sudden silence. Even the buzzing group of men stopped their talking to hear this exchange. I looked at the Primus Pilus, a man named Torquatus, and while his face was expressionless, I was close enough to see the slightest twitch at the corner of his mouth. I knew that they had approached the right man. However, he was not about to give in immediately; that just is not how things work in the Legions.

"And why would I want to do that? Are you so anxious to die?" He gestured in the direction of the ford. "The last I heard, the water was neck deep, and the current was still strong. A midget like you would be swept away like a turd in the sewer."

There was an eruption of laughter, and the Optio flushed, but his tone was calm. "That may be, Primus Pilus. But we're all going to die anyway. I'd rather do it trying to end this war than to wait a few more days."

That stilled the laughter immediately and I could see that he had struck a chord that, in all honesty, resonated with me just as much as with the rest of the men.

Primus Pilus Torquatus did not answer immediately, staring down at the men now gathered in front of us with narrowed eyes. Finally, he gave a curt nod, and said, "Fair enough. I'll speak with him. Pullus," he surprised me because I had not even been sure that he had seen me, "come with me."

Off we went, to talk to Caesar, with the men wishing us luck on our quest.

~ ~ ~ ~

In fairness, it did not take much persuasion to get Caesar to agree. The one concession that he demanded was that we choose men who we thought were strong enough to cross through the current without being swept away. We also agreed to leave all baggage behind. Hurrying back, I gave the necessary orders while the Primus Pilus went to tell the other Primi Pili of the other Legions what we were about. Immediately, the camp was thrown into the flurry of activity that to an outsider would look like utter chaos, but which is, in fact, a well-practiced dance that most of us had performed hundreds and thousands of times, save for the raw Legions.

I let my Centurions do their job; one of the hardest things to learn for a senior Centurion is to rely on your subordinates and give them the freedom to do their jobs the best way they see fit, without constantly interfering. Having command of veterans like the 10th made everyone's jobs easier, since every man knew exactly what he was supposed to do at any given moment, and it was this experience that saw us formed up and ready to march a little more than a third of a watch after the command. During the time we were preparing, our cavalry continued with the harassment, but Afranius' army had managed to march a couple of miles across the plain, heading for slightly rougher country, broken with a seemingly unending series of low hills and gullies choked with brush. About five miles further began a small mountain range, with terrain so undulating that if the Pompeians could make it that far, it would be practically impossible for us to bring them to battle, thereby allowing them to escape. That made it of the utmost importance that we bring them to heel before that point, and with that in mind, we trotted in formation to the ford. Caesar ordered about a hundred of the cavalry to come back to the ford to assist with the crossing, using the same method we had used to such good effect in Gaul. About half of them entered the river above the ford, standing their horses side by side to lessen the flow of the current, with the other half forming up below the ford, ready to catch any man who lost his footing. It was in this way that, despite a few men being swept off their feet by the current, almost the entire army crossed without the loss of a single man. Still, despite the relative speed of our movements, it took more than two parts of a watch to get the whole army across, and it was a soggy, tired lot that was given the order to move out after Afranius, who used that time to continue his march south, getting a couple miles closer to the mountains. Despite how waterlogged we were, we still marched much faster than the Pompeians, who might have been dry but were still encumbered with all of their baggage and supplies.

Toward the end of the day, we came within sight of the rearguard, still being harassed by our cavalry. The Pompeians were fighting a running battle, with our forces lasting the better part of four watches now. With the sun beginning to sink, they marched to a group of small hills to occupy the high ground. While two of their Legions stood in formation on the slopes and watched, the rest began to build camp. For our part, we were still sodden and tired ourselves, but since we left our baggage behind, the best we could do was to occupy a hill a short distance away, making a cold camp without walls or ditch. We settled down the best we could, shivering in our cold clothes, the men continually grumbling about the water setting in and ruining their gear. Since we had no real way to dry and oil our armor and weapons, they worried about having to replace it, knowing it would come out of their pay. I began using handfuls of the sandy soil to scour my own equipment and the rest of the men quickly followed suit, but I knew that we would have to have a cleaning party at the first opportunity, if only to stop the complaining.

Meanwhile, our scouts were ranging ahead along the Pompeians' line of march, surveying the country, and they came back to tell Caesar what they found. Once past the small range of hills that we were occupying, the land was fairly open and only gently rolling for four or five miles, until it reached a series of sharply defined ridges that generally blocked passage to the Iber. However, a narrow defile was there that was apparently a dry watercourse feeding into the Iber. Whoever got to that defile first could block passage to the boat bridge. As they were hurrying back with this report, the scouts captured a detachment of Pompeians sent to get water. Under interrogation, we learned that Afranius was planning on a night march, and was at that moment preparing to try and slip away. Immediately, Caesar ordered the *bucina* to sound the order to make ready to march, in turn issuing the corresponding commands. Between the horn and the bellowing of the Centurions, the sound rolled across the space between the hills, alerting Afranius that we had discovered his plans. He then countermanded his own marching orders, and after a lot of bustling about, things settled down again for the rest of the night.

Shortly before dawn, I was summoned along with the other Centurions to a meeting of the command group. We were standing together as the sun rose, and with the light turning the sky first gray, then the coppery blue that promised another hot day, we discussed our options. From the spot in camp where we were talking, we could see a small knot of men in the Pompeian camp and I smiled grimly to myself, thinking that their conversation was undoubtedly an exact copy of our own; what was the other side thinking? What were they going to do next? As it turned out, they did nothing for the whole day, and neither did we, other than sitting and watching each other. Since we had marched out with only the normal three-day's rations and had not brought any of our baggage, the wagering in camp was that the Pompeians would be content to sit on that hill to starve us out. They would force us to withdraw back to the main camp for supplies, or to have a convoy sent to us, thereby providing enough of a distraction for them to slip away. Nevertheless, as proud as we were of Caesar's skill and fortune, the Pompeians were equally wary of it. Consequently, they determined that they could not just sit and wait for something to happen. That next day passed uneventfully, but during the night, shortly before dawn, we could hear the horns sounding the orders to break camp. Almost at the same moment, Caesar gave his own orders and since we had less to break down, we were ready to move well before the Pompeians. Dawn found us moving off the hill, but this time seemingly back in the direction from which we had come, the cries of joy and the jeers of our foes carrying across the small valley to us. Normally, such calls of cowardice would have been bitter as gall to us, but now we all looked at each other, grinning from ear to ear, thankful that we were too far away for the enemy to see our faces. Once again, Caesar had pulled one over on his enemies.

~ ~ ~ ~

We were not withdrawing, although it looked like we were. Caesar's scouts had surveyed the ground well, determining that there was a route that would allow us to swing us past the Pompeian camp, thereby putting us directly between them and the defile, through which ran the only passage to the boat bridge. The problem with that route was that it was over extremely difficult ground, littered with small ravines and crumbling fingers of land that oftentimes forced us to clamber hand over hand, with our comrades helping us up the steep sides. Fairly quickly, the Pompeians realized their error, and despite the distance, we could hear the cries of alarm echoing over the hills as they scrambled to cut us off. There began a race of sorts, with Afranius leaving his own baggage behind in camp, with some Cohorts to guard it, beginning a parallel march, creating a plume of dust that contrasted with our own, marking our respective progress. Both sides put everything into the pursuit but Afranius had the added disadvantage of being harried by our cavalry, whereas his own was of such poor quality that he did not even bother sending it at us. Despite the rough terrain, we drew ahead of the Pompeians, arriving at the mouth of the defile gasping for breath and barely able to stand erect, but nonetheless we made ready for Afranius to attack.

~ ~ ~ ~

Afranius obviously knew the folly of trying to force his way through the mouth of the defile, because he halted his men some distance away. For almost a third of a watch, neither side moved, which we were thankful for since it allowed us to catch our breath. Afranius' problem was that as narrow as the defile was, he could not bring his entire force to bear in an assault, instead being forced to feed his Legions in piecemeal even as they were chewed up. Also in our favor was the fact that so steep were the sides of this narrow canyon that we did not have to worry about anyone trying to swing around to come down on either flank. For that reason, the Pompeian commanders retreated to a nearby small hill to stop and consider their options, which were precious few. Off to their right and to our left was the highest peak in the area, off the shoulder of which ran a ridgeline that, if they could gain that peak, they could then follow all the way down to the confluence of Sicoris and Ibis. From there, it was a short distance to the boat bridge. Accordingly, Afranius ordered about four Cohorts to strip down to just their weapons, in order to give them every possible advantage of speed, sending them in a dash towards the base of the mountain. Now, for a short distance, a man can actually outrun a horse because they start much more quickly. Unfortunately for these men, the distance they had to cover was more than a mile, and even with a head start, they were doomed from the beginning. The moment it became clear what they were about, Caesar sent the cavalry in pursuit. Swinging wide of the main Pompeian force, they fell upon the running Cohorts more than a quarter mile short of the slopes of the hill. The slaughter was quick, and it was complete; not one man escaped, the cries of despair and curses of the Pompeian forces carrying clearly to us across the distance. Despite the fact that these men were the enemy, none of us felt like cheering the sight of brave Romans being cut down, especially when we all knew that there might be childhood friends or kinsmen among them.

~ ~ ~ ~

Once more, we were at a stalemate; our army commanded the ground through which the Pompeians must pass, and now *they* were cut off from their supplies. The only thing in their favor was the fact that they had chosen a hill with steep sides, meaning that assaulting it would be difficult but not impossible. Despite the challenges, the senior Centurions went to Caesar in a group, urging him to allow us to assault the hill, thereby stopping this war once and for all. Caesar listened politely, but he refused to give in to our pleading, saying simply that he believed he could win this war without losing another drop of blood, either from his own men or from those of the enemy. For the first time since I had marched under the eagle, and marched with Caesar, men openly disagreed with him, and while I do not remember exactly who said it, I do remember hearing something that shocked me to my very core.

"Caesar, remember this moment," the voice rang out. "The next time you call on us to fight for you, you may find that we're not as willing as we are today."

I was stunned, but what was even more shocking to me were the mumbles of agreement from a large number of the other Centurions. While I might have expected such sentiments from the rankers, I was completely taken aback that the most senior members of Caesar's army would dare to say something so brazen, or to openly agree with it. Almost immediately after the words were spoken, the very air seemed to change, the import of what was said immediately hitting all of us, and you could almost hear the intake of breath sucking the air out from around us, the grumbling immediately ceasing as all eyes turned to Caesar. Whether or not that was how some of us felt, we also knew that to openly disagree in such a manner was an invitation to the harshest punishment available to a commander, and Caesar would have been well justified to order the Centurion who made this threat seized and executed on the spot. However, Caesar did not appear to be in the least perturbed, instead saying gently, "I understand your frustration, comrades, but these are my orders, and I know that you won't let your personal feelings interfere with your duties. As far as the next time, and whether you choose to take up arms at my command," he finished dryly, "I'll have to cross that bridge when I come to it. I've already crossed the Rubicon, so one more won't make much difference."

His words had the desired effect; despite the tension, his attempt at humor was met with appreciative chuckles, and in that instant, the situation was defused. Returning to our areas in small groups, I chose to walk alone. I was extremely troubled by what I had just heard, on a number of levels. It had not even occurred to me to question Caesar's judgment, but it obviously had to several of my comrades, men that I respected a great deal. Was my loyalty to Caesar blinding me? I could see the sense of what the others wanted him to do; what better way to end this war but to march up that hill and end it the best way we knew? Nevertheless, I had such faith in Caesar's judgment that I never stopped to question whether he might be wrong. That was something that my comrades obviously had done, and it worried me. Would they really carry out their threat the next time he called for us to come to arms?

~ ~ ~ ~

We spent another entire day waiting for the situation to develop and thanks to our cavalry, who had gone back to our original camp to escort our supply train back, we were not in the same predicament that the Pompeians were, stuck on their hill, and cut off from their own supply base. The other problem for the Pompeians was water, more accurately the lack of it, and they began sending out Century sized detachments out to try finding the precious liquid. We were in the part of the country that is exceedingly dry in the summer months, and almost all of the streams that fed into the nearby Sicoris were completely dry. The natives used man made reservoirs to catch rainwater, and the Pompeians located one such reservoir some distance from their camp on the hill. Rather than risk continual capture of their detachments, they made the decision that it was ultimately safer and more secure to dig a ditch and throw up a rampart leading all the way from their camp to the nearest reservoir, a reservoir that we ourselves were using. This ditch traveled more than a mile in length to the reservoir, terminating on the opposite side, but our camp was situated in such a manner that the water was a distance of just a few paces from the gates of the camp. Therefore, we were on one side of the reservoir and the Pompeians on another, yet it was a matter of not much time before some of the men began talking to each other. As we had known all along, acquaintances and kin were discovered in each other's ranks. What happened next marks the tragedy of civil war more than any other event that I saw or heard about during that period, at least in my mind.

Some of our men invited their friends on the other side to come into camp, under their protection. Normally, a Roman Legionary would never accept such an offer, but these were not normal times, and besides, the Pompeians still had fresh in their memory Caesar's refusal to send us in an assault on their hill the day before. I was sitting in my tent, which had arrived with the relief column, when Zeno announced that Vibius requested entrance into my tent. I gave my assent, and he came in with a grin from ear to ear. Looking up, I saw there was a man behind him and I swallowed my irritation; I did not feel like having a party in my quarters at that moment because I was swimming in paperwork that needed to be caught up.

However, my displeasure did not last long, as Vibius announced, "Pilus Prior Pullus, I have a surprise for you."

He stepped aside, and I saw as I rose that it was indeed a surprise, and a great one. Dressed as I was, in the uniform of a Centurion, stood none other than Cyclops, my former brother-in-law, and the instructor of our youth. I was speechless. He had disappeared since my sister, Livia, with whom he had been very happy in marriage, had died in childbirth. Nobody around Astigi had any idea of his whereabouts. I assumed he had either died or gone off to some far land, except here he stood in the flesh, a little older and grayer at the temple, but otherwise unchanged, his one good eye staring at me, with the other still the puckered hole surrounded by scar tissue.

"Well, it's good to see that you're still no good at small talk," he said by way of greeting.

In truth, I did not trust myself to speak, instead stepping forward, ignoring his outstretched hand to grab him in a bear hug, and for once I was not ashamed of my tears. Neither, I suspect, was Cyclops.

~ ~ ~ ~

We sat at my table and caught up. Cyclops told us that once my sister had died, his desire to be a farmer had died with her.

"The only reason I was content to stay on the farm was because of her," he said quietly, both Vibius and I staring into our cups.

I was lost in memories of my sister and how happy she was with Cyclops; I know not what Vibius was thinking, but I suspect that Juno was involved in some way. Cyclops spoke with the tone of a man whose pain has dulled to the ache of an old wound that will never truly heal, yet is no longer fresh and raw.

"So I went back to the only home I knew, outside of the farm and Livia, and here I am."

I suspected that there was much more to his tale, but Cyclops was as miserly with his words as my father with his money. Both Vibius and I exchanged amused glances, knowing that no amount of prodding would get much more out of him than that.

Changing the subject, he said, "So, can your man Caesar be trusted?"

Before I could speak up, I was surprised when Vibius answered, "Absolutely. Caesar may be a lot of things, but he's an honorable man. You and the rest of the men who came into our camp are safe, that I can promise you. Right, Titus?"

By rights, I should have been the only one giving such assurances, but I did not begrudge the breach of protocol, so surprised was I that Vibius would defend Caesar. My feelings were obvious, since I saw the color rise to Vibius' cheeks.

Before we could get into an argument, I simply said, "What Vibius says is true, Cyclops. You and the rest of your comrades will come to no harm."

He nodded with some relief at our words. "Good, I thought as much. I'll be honest, I don't know about you boys, but none of us are really all that eager to keep on fighting." He looked at us to gauge our reaction, yet neither of us spoke, so he continued. "It's just that we look across the field at you, and we don't see the enemy, we see men just like us. Men that we know, and are related to, both by blood and marriage."

Despite my attempts to remain impassive, I was touched that Cyclops still thought of me as kin, since in reality his bond with me had died with Livia.

With that knowledge, I lowered my defenses, and agreed. "We feel the same way, Cyclops. Although I will say that yesterday, there was some sentiment among the senior Centurions that we should go ahead, assault the hill, and get it over with. I can't help but wonder now if they still feel the same way."

"Why's that?" Cyclops asked, looking at me in a speculative manner.

"Because I assume that there are reunions of this sort happening in a lot of tents in this camp," I said honestly. "And it's one thing to want to end the war with one final battle when we look across the distance at your camp. But now that you've come, you're flesh and blood, you're all too real, and I think that there are going to be some men who see things differently in the morning."

"I hope you're right, Titus," Cyclops said, raising his cup in a toast, which we joined.

~ ~ ~ ~

I was more right than I knew. The very same men who had been openly questioning Caesar's decision not to attack were now singing his praises and commending him on his vision. Still, I did not hear many of them taking themselves to task so much as they were praising Caesar, but I did not push the point. There were reunions going on all over the camp and before long, men were going in both directions; our men went into the Pompeian camp under the supposed protection of Afranius, many of them carrying loaves of bread in search of hungry friends and kinsmen who had not come into our camp. Meanwhile, some of the senior Centurions in Afranius' army had gathered, asking to approach Caesar to request of him that he promise the same sort of leniency to their generals and officers that he was showing to the rankers, to which he readily agreed. As he had told us the day before, there was nothing to be gained by further bloodshed of men who were the same as us. His attitude was a great relief to the Pompeians, some of whom agreed to join our standards, so great was their admiration of Caesar. It was a festive atmosphere in the camp to be sure, and soon any attempts at maintaining some sort of discipline about who went over to the Pompeian camp to visit fell apart. In my own Cohort, some 20 men were given permission to visit, and I suspected there were at least as many who had simply just slipped away to go with their friends.

I asked the Primus Pilus what was to be done, and he just shrugged with a wry grin and said, "Just hope they get back in one piece. I don't want to have to flog half the Legion."

Looking back, I realize that it never occurred to either one of us that we could not trust the Pompeian generals; after all, what did they have to gain by harming our men? That is a question I am still asking.

~ ~ ~ ~

Piecing the events together, after the proverbial dust had settled, this was what we learned happened in the Pompeian camp, leading to one of the darkest episodes of the civil war. While Afranius had acquiesced to the actions taken by his men in reaching out to Caesar, and indeed, according to some prisoners who worked in the headquarters, had actually instigated the delegation of Centurions who went to Caesar, the other general Petreius harbored no such feelings. Completely ignoring the safe conduct offered by Afranius, he armed his personal slaves while summoning about a Cohort's worth of his lackeys, those men who fawn all over a general in order to gain his favor. He deputed these men to do his dirty work. I was alerted to the change in the situation by alarmed yells, followed by the screams of our men who were caught, the first few of them completely unaware that they were betrayed. Most of the men were mingling in the area of the reservoir, but a fair number of our men had actually gone all the way into the Pompeian camp. These men were the first to fall, butchered where they were found, some of them dragged out of the tents of the friends and kinsmen whom they were visiting. Once the alarm was raised, a large number of our men rallied together, forming a makeshift *orbis*, using their *sagum* as makeshift shields wrapped around their left arms. They had gone into camp bearing only their swords and daggers, as regulations prescribed, but they presented enough of a defense that they were able to move slowly towards our camp. Our guard Cohorts were summoned and had sallied forth out the nearest gate, where they absorbed the refugees into their midst before retreating into the camp. There was complete pandemonium inside our camp as everyone tried to determine exactly what had happened. Cyclops was standing with us outside my tent as men came running up, shouting that we had been betrayed by the Pompeians and that every man of ours in the camp, except for the group who had formed up, were slaughtered. Despite not knowing if that were indeed true, it certainly seemed possible, and I looked at Cyclops, his face gone gray with shock.

"Who did this?" I demanded coldly of him, for such was my anger that I would have struck my old mentor and friend down right there had Vibius not put a restraining hand on my arm.

The moment passed; I realized that there was no way he could have known this was going to happen, and if he did, he would have warned us because of the type of man that he was. Still, I was wary and looked at him with new eyes. All he could do was shake his head, and it took him a moment before he composed himself enough to speak.

"I don't know," he admitted. "This doesn't strike me as something Afranius would do; he's more politician than soldier, and he wouldn't want to create this kind of bad blood. It has to be Petreius, but I don't see how he could be so foolhardy. He's no great shakes as a general, and he's not fit to stand in your man's shadow, but I didn't think even he would be this stupid."

"Well, someone is," I shot back, then turned and trotted over to the Primus Pilus' tent to find out what I could.

An assembly was called to determine who was still missing, and the numbers were sobering. Of my Cohort, I still had 12 men missing, and the identity of one of those men worried me most. Scribonius, as was his norm, had been scrupulous about asking permission to go visit a cousin, which I granted, but he had not returned in the group. The only positive note at that point was that none of the escapees recalled seeing him struck down. Four of my other men were not so lucky, however; I received reports from multiple eyewitnesses that they were hacked to pieces. There was still daylight left, and we could see across the way in the Pompeian camp that they were calling their own assembly. What we learned later was that Petreius had countermanded the order of Afranius for safe conduct, but after the initial slaughter, went from Cohort to Cohort, begging his men to remain true to Pompey, blubbering big baby tears. Not satisfied with this, he then called an assembly to make every man in camp swear an oath of loyalty to Pompey, and further, demanded that any remaining men of ours that they were hiding now be turned in for summary execution. Fortunately, while most of the Pompeians were willing enough to swear loyalty, they were loath to fulfill the second part of this requirement, although a few of the craven bastards did what they were asked, causing several more of our men to be put to death in the forum in front of the assembled Pompeian army. We could hear their cries for mercy drift across to us, while we stood in helpless anger on the ramparts watching them put to death. At the distance they were at, I could not distinguish individuals, so I was unable to tell if Scribonius or any of the other of my men were the unfortunates.

Now there was a choice to make, although I do not believe any of us thought that it would turn out any differently, about the fate of the Pompeians now stranded in our camp. I will not lie; there was a good bit of sentiment among all the ranks that we return the treatment of our men in kind to the Pompeians, but I do not believe any of us really thought that Caesar would take that action. And he did not. In contrast, he allowed any man desiring freedom to return to his own camp, free of any retribution and under armed escort to our gates. Despite a good number of men doing just that, there was about an equal number who, disgusted by the actions of their general, swore allegiance to Caesar, abjuring any oaths of loyalty to a man who would do such a thing as Petreius. Neither Vibius nor I were particularly surprised when Cyclops was one of those men. We saw in his face the contempt and horror at what transpired, and I was happy to speak for him, this being the only requirement that Caesar made of the men staying behind, that someone vouch for them. Cyclops was sent to the 14th, having lost their Primus Pilus in the assault on the mound, along with a couple other Centurions, whereupon he took command of the Seventh of the 14th. I will admit that it was quite a relief to have him safely on our side, since that was one less friend we had to worry about having to face in battle. But by the time night fell, I still did not know the fate of Scribonius or the other seven men still in the Pompeian camp.

~ ~ ~ ~

As it turned out, most of the men in my Cohort did return, having been hidden by their friends and kinsmen despite the oath they were forced to take. Of the eight whose fate I did not know as the sun set that day, six of them returned, including Scribonius, escorted under cover of darkness out of the Pompeian camp by the men who hid them. The sentiment was such that none of the sentries on the Pompeian side raised any alarm at what turned out to be almost a hundred men crossing back to our lines, and there was much relief as one by one, the missing men reported to their respective Centurions. However, that feeling of relief was tempered by sadness and anger, once it was determined that not all of them were coming back. I was luckier than some of the other Cohorts in the army. I ended up losing a total of six men: four in the initial attack and two who were betrayed, not by the friends or kinsmen of the men who invited them to come over, but by the tentmates of those men, although we did not learn this until much later. I remember wondering how much damage their actions did to the trust and bond that normally mark men of the same tent section, thinking that at some point in the future there would probably be a reckoning between them. I sat with Scribonius as he gulped down unwatered wine, still breathless from the dash he made once outside the Pompeian gates.

"I thought for sure I was a goner," he gasped. "My cousin hid me under his bunk and piled all of his gear around me, but they had provosts come into each tent and they poked and prodded the beds and the gear. The provost assigned to search my tent stuck his sword right down into the middle of the pile, and the blade passed not more than an inch from my throat. If he had moved it around at all, I'd be dead."

We looked at each other in mute anger and disbelief. Finally, Vibius broke the silence. "Well, this changes things," he declared. "I don't think Caesar is going to be so quick to forgive now, and I can't say that I blame him."

Again, I was surprised; this was twice in one day that Vibius had spoken up for Caesar, more than in the past five years.

Before I could respond, Scribonius shook his head. "I don't think so, Vibius. I think he knows that it was the act of one man, and that man is going to be the one to ultimately pay."

"True, but he wasn't the one who did the actual killing," Vibius protested, and there was truth in what he said. "I think every one of the friends of the men who were butchered today is going to want to exact vengeance on the man holding the sword, as well as the man who ordered it."

"You might be right," conceded Scribonius, "but I also think that they were just following orders, the way they, and we," he motioned in a circle at all of us gathered about the fire, "have been trained to do, without question. That's why I don't think this will change things for the likes of us all that much. I know I'm no more anxious to kill my cousin and his friends than I was before."

"We'll see," grumbled Vibius, but I could see that Scribonius had scored points with the rest of the men gathered about.

Scribonius and the other escapees became minor celebrities in the camp, and they were plied with wine as they were asked to recount their tales of escape. With Scribonius continuing to answer questions, I walked off to check on the rest of the men who the gods had smiled on this day, while at the same time wondering what was to happen with the bodies of our slain and if they would be allowed at least to rest in dignity and peace.

~ ~ ~ ~

The sun rose to the pall of smoke hanging above the Pompeian camp and we learned that at least our comrades had been cared for in the proper manner. Under banner of truce, a Tribune was sent to assure us that their remains would be sent to their kin, with all proper honors and rights, and while we doubted their word, we had no choice but to believe them. In the meantime, their command group held another council, apparently deciding that their position on this hill, even with water, was untenable. Just as both command groups were conferring, a new development changed the balance further in our favor in one way, but caused us more hardship in another. The auxiliary force of the Pompeians, like all auxiliaries, were neither as well equipped nor as well supplied as the Legions, meaning their supply situation was even worse than the rest of the Pompeian army. Not seeing any relief coming from any source, they began to desert to us, first in small numbers, then in a veritable flood of men who came streaming to our camp, begging us to give them shelter and food in exchange for their service. Again, Caesar ordered clemency and we took all of them in, even with the extra strain it put on our own supply situation.

Despite these desertions relieving some of the pressure from the Pompeians, it still was not enough, and they made the decision to march back to Ilerda to their supply base. This time the Pompeians marched in a double column, except that they prepared to defend against our cavalry by having their rearguard march without their packs, putting them on mules to give them the best possible mobility against our horsemen. Again, the terrain proved to be a challenge, but for both sides this time. With the Pompeian column marching up one of the hills, the rearguard was then protected by their comrades on the higher slopes, who could fling their javelins down at our cavalry. However, once they reached the crest of the hill to start down the opposite side, the rearguard no longer had the protection of their comrades, thereby immediately coming under assault from our cavalry, who charged in to fling their own missiles, inflicting several casualties. After this was repeated a couple of times, the Pompeians adjusted by sending their rearguard in a headlong charge at our cavalry, while the main body would hurry across the level ground to the next slope. The rearguard would then turn and run to join their comrades in the time it took our cavalry to regroup. In this manner, they made a slow but steady progress, covering about four miles before halting on a hill, fortifying the slope that faced us, although they left their baggage packed on their mules. We did likewise, making camp, except that we did unpack our mules, pitching our tents and going about the business of digging the ditches and throwing up the walls.

Although from outward appearances we had taken the bait, once again, Caesar was a step ahead, having passed the word that we were to be ready to drop everything to resume our pursuit at his order. Several Cohorts were ordered to remain behind to pack the camp up should the Pompeians make a break for it, and we did not have long to wait; perhaps a third of a watch had passed when the alarm was raised that they were again on the move. Springing into action, we fell back into marching formation and were in pursuit no more than a sixth part of a watch later, with our cavalry soon back harrying the Pompeian rearguard. This time, our cavalry attacks inflicted heavy casualties on the rearguard; whether it was due to more vigor on the part of our men, or fatigue on the part of the Pompeians we could not tell, but the ground was soon littered with bodies as the bulk of the enemy still struggled towards Ilerda. The Pompeians had gotten back into the open ground surrounding the town, no longer even having the cover and protection of the small hills and rocky terrain, and it was not much longer before their commanders called another halt. Since our baggage had not been retrieved yet, we did what we could to make ourselves comfortable and secure, watching the Pompeians working feverishly to improve on their position.

Once more, the Pompeians were in desperate straits because they had halted a distance away from one of the reservoirs, while Caesar had halted us much closer to it so we did not have the same problem. As they had previously, the Pompeians began extending their fortifications towards the reservoir in an attempt to secure a supply of water, working the rest of the day and through the night. Now, however, their problem was twofold; not only did they have to get to the water, the reservoir itself was smaller than most of the others in the area, our own needs draining it almost dry by the time their ditch and wall got close. The sun rose to a desperate plight for the Pompeians when they were greeted by a sight that had caused despair in countless other enemies of Caesar; he had put us at work building a contravallation. Our baggage had caught up with us in the night, whereupon we were put immediately to work, save for a number of Cohorts left on guard. The enemy started slaughtering their remaining cattle and even killed their mules, sparing only the cavalry horses, which were sent, along with every spare man, out to find water. We were too occupied in throwing up our fortifications to spend any time pursuing the Pompeians, who went scrambling about the countryside looking for water, besides the fact that our own cavalry had already scoured the region and if there was a drop of water or a kernel of grain, it was in our possession. We spent the entire day digging, chopping, and sweating, the Pompeians only able to watch in frustration and I suspect not a small amount of fear as what was effectively a noose neared completion. Finally stopping at sunset, the men were exhausted, filthy, and barely able to pick at their evening meal. Conversation was desultory; the almost nonexistent grumbling was a sure sign of their fatigue, it simply took too much energy.

While the men rested, I was called to a meeting of the senior Centurions of the army with Caesar, who praised the work that the men had accomplished before telling us his plans for the following day. We would be finished with the contravallation by the end of the next day, and Caesar believed that the Pompeians would be forced to make a move before that happened. Accordingly, he ordered that we not commit all of our men to the work, instead having them work in shifts so that they might spare their energy. Despite knowing this would slow the work somewhat, he believed that the Pompeians would not be willing to wait and would make a move the next day. And as usual, he was right, although it was not quite the battle that we thought it would be.

~ ~ ~ ~

We began working the next morning at dawn in the manner prescribed by Caesar, and there was a sense of anticipation running through the men, a sense that the Centurions shared. Once an army is forced to slaughter its pack animals, that is a sure sign that the end is near because they are sacrificing their mobility; they must either stand and fight, or in turn be slaughtered themselves. The progress of our work slowed because of the reduced labor force, but it was still significant. Finally, in the afternoon, there was a stirring in the Pompeian camp. Since our camps were not more than a few hundred paces apart, we could clearly hear the sounds of the *cornu* and *bucina* that were sending the Pompeians into a frenzy of activity. Not long after, Caesar issued his own orders, so our horns added to the din, calling the men working on the contravallation to stop and make their way back to camp, while the men in camp who were resting now hurried to gather their weapons and fall into formation. I walked around my Cohort area, while Longus and Crispus brought back our men out working on the contravallation, and I made sure the rest of the men were moving as quickly as I thought they should be, helped by an occasional prod from my *vitus*.

Before the end of the watch, the Pompeians left their camp to form up in an *acies triplex* facing ours, and there they stood waiting for us. It was another third of a watch before all of our men had returned from their work, whereupon we in turn left our camp to face the enemy. Despite also forming up in an *acies triplex*, Caesar modified it from our usual practice by placing the archers that had arrived with the Gallic column, along with a contingent of slingers with us from the beginning, in the center of the formation. He then deployed our cavalry in two wings, one on either side of the formation. The 10<sup>th</sup> took what we considered our rightful place on the right wing, making ready for whatever was to come. Because of the relatively narrow space between the two camps, by the time both armies arrayed themselves, there was little more than 200 paces between the two armies, putting us close enough to recognize some of the men facing us. I believe to this day that it was that recognition of friends and kin that stopped the battle, since the sun crept through the sky and no orders were issued by either side. There was a constant buzz of excited muttering, as men recognized each other.

"By the gods, Glabius, isn't that that bastard Serenus over there? I haven't seen him since the three of us . . ."

"Pluto's thorny cock, I didn't know Fuscus was still under the standard! I thought he was dead!"

"Quiet down, you bastards," I roared. "You act like you've never been on a battlefield before."

"Not on one where I'm staring at my cousin," came a voice from the ranks.

I whirled around, knowing that I should find the man who said that, but truly, my heart was not in it because I knew how he felt. Meeting up with Cyclops had brought home to me what it meant to these men to be standing here, facing friends and relatives. Oh, we had gone through multiple skirmishes, but our cavalry had done the bulk of the fighting; they were Germans and had no connection with the men standing across from us. Even after the incident in the Pompeian camp, we still largely held no animosity towards the rank and file of the Pompeian army, knowing that the slaughter of our men was the doing of Petreius and, to a lesser extent, Afranius, who had not stopped Petreius. Consequently, we stood there, waiting for a command that I do not believe any of us wanted to follow, but one that I knew we would if it indeed came.

Fortunately, Caesar was no more eager for this battle than we were. Obviously, neither were Afranius and Petreius, because the sun dipped to the edge of the horizon before the horns sounded the recall, first on the Pompeian side, then on ours, and we all filed back inside our respective camps, wondering if we would be doing the same thing the next day.

~ ~ ~ ~

The next morning found us resuming the work on the contravallation, while Petreius and Afranius took one last desperate roll of the dice by sending groups of their cavalry out to find possible fords across the Sicoris, now only a couple of miles distant. Caesar countered the move by sending detachments of our own cavalry, beating the

Pompeians to the river and setting up a chain of outposts at every likely crossing point, thereby defeating the Pompeian attempt before it even started. The end had come for the Pompeians. They had been out of forage for their remaining stock for four days, had run out of food for the men the day before, and were now out of water. Shortly before midday, a party of Pompeians approached the camp under a flag of truce, asking for an audience with Caesar, which he granted. The representative asked Caesar that he grant the request of Afranius that the discussion take place out of our sight, which Caesar denied, indicating that the negotiations should take place in the open between the two camps. Afranius had no choice but to agree and sent his son over to us as a hostage, waiting for Caesar roughly halfway between our two camps. Our ramparts were packed with men watching the exchange between our two generals and I am not ashamed to say that I had one of the best seats in the theater, by virtue of my size and reputation as much as by my rank. We could not hear what was said, meaning we had to try to translate the body language and gestures of the two men in order to try to make some sense of what was taking place. As usual, there was always some wit who provided his own version of the dialogue; while I do not remember who it was on this occasion, it brought to mind the painful recollection that in the past it had been Calienus who kept us almost doubled over in laughter as he played the part of some Gallic chieftain begging Caesar for mercy.

"Oooooh, great Caesar, I am here to beg you not to kill us, and I'll do anything you ask." This was spoken in a high falsetto voice by someone a short distance down the rampart, causing some snickers.

"Really? What do you mean by 'anything'?"

Although the part of Caesar was spoken in a deeper voice, it obviously came from the same man.

"Why, I'll get on my knees and suck your cock, right here in front of everyone," the falsetto replied, and the snickers quickly became guffaws of laughter.

"Well, that's certainly a tempting offer. I haven't had my cock sucked in, oh, well since this morning . . ."

I could not hear what he said after that, since it was drowned out by laughter. I knew that either myself or one of the other Centurions should be shutting the unknown comedian up, but I glanced over at Primus Pilus Torquatus and he was grinning from ear to ear, clearly enjoying himself as much as the rest of the men. And so was I, so I laughed along with everyone else.

"But I'm afraid that my men would need to have their cocks sucked as well. It's been much longer for most of them."

"Welllll," the falsetto tried to convey a sense of doubt, "it would take me a while, but I suppose..."

At this point, our laughter must have reached the ears of Caesar, because he turned around to glare back at us, and there is no way to describe how quickly the mirth died away. Each of us felt sure that he was looking directly at us, even we Centurions felt a flip-flopping in our stomachs. Caesar was a fair and even-tempered commander, but we had all seen him lose it and none of us wanted to bear the brunt of his anger. Turning to snap an order to be quiet, I instantly saw that there was no need; you could have heard a gnat fart in the silence.

The conference continued, and we clearly saw Caesar shake his head, the gesture met by a look of dismay on the face of Afranius. However, Caesar continued speaking and we could see Afranius' expression change, his face assuming a look of unmistakable relief. Whatever was said could obviously be heard by the Pompeian Legions standing on their own rampart, because a huge roar of joy came rolling across the ground, assaulting our ears in waves of exultation.

The Primus Pilus turned to me, and with a grin said, "Well, I guess we won."

~ ~ ~ ~

Won we had, and then some. With a minimum of bloodshed, Caesar had achieved the disbandment of Pompey's entire army, in a manner that left the Pompeians neither embittered nor destitute. Caesar promised that he would restore to the men of the Pompeian army the property they had lost when their camp was overrun, although that was not one of his more popular decisions, I can tell you. Further, Caesar ordered that the three Spanish Legions of Pompey's army, the 4th, 5th, and 6th, whose discharges were due, were to be disbanded, paid their final amounts and be allowed to go home. Not surprisingly, at least to some of us, this also did not sit well with some of our own men, particularly with the 7th, 8th, and the 9th because their time was up as well, enlisting at the same time as the Pompeian Legions. The sentiment was that, since their discharges were up as well and they were on the winning side, the right thing for Caesar to do was to grant them their own discharges. The 10th, on the other hand, still had some time left on our enlistments, meaning it was not an issue for us, but the 9th, in particular, was the most vocal in their grumbling. Caesar chose to send back the Valeria and 3rd Legion to their home territory in Cisalpine Gaul, He decided to send the 7th and 9th with them as an escort, promising the Pompeians that they would be discharged and paid off once they were back in their home territory. The 7th and 9th were ordered to continue marching back to Italia, to report to Marcus Antonius and await Caesar's orders. Despite this being an unpopular command, at least with the two Legions involved, it was nothing compared to the reaction to his final order, the release and parole of Afranius and Petreius. This act was met with outrage by the army, and I confess that I was just as angry as any man, having lost a number of good men at their hands, not by honorable battle but by treachery. Still, Caesar's will was to be obeyed in all things, and accordingly we stood in formation and in stony silence watching the two generals and their staffs given their paroles and allowed to leave. It was only a small comfort to us to see the look of fear and apprehension on the faces of both Afranius and Petreius as they rode through our ranks out of the camp. Then it was over, at least this part of it, but only part of the province was ours. There was still the west to subdue, and Caesar now turned his attention to it.

~ ~ ~ ~

Remaining with Caesar was us, the 14th, the 21st and 30th. He took the 21st and 30th with him, along with 600 of his cavalry to confront the remainder of Pompey's army in Hispania, the 2nd and Indigena. Sending the two Legions one route under the command of Quintus Cassius Longinus, brother of the traitor Gaius Cassius Longinus, Caesar took the cavalry on a separate route, along the way sending word to the towns in the territory to throw out their Pompeian garrisons and surrender to him without any fear of retribution. He ordered an assembly of province officials to meet at Corduba, where the Pompeian commander Varro had decided to make his defense, and to where Varro was now hurrying himself. It became a race to see who would occupy the town first. As usual, Caesar was too quick for Varro, aided by the citizens of the town, who expelled the Pompeian garrison and sent word to Varro that the gates would be shut to him in the event that he arrived before Caesar. The Indigena promptly came over to Caesar, forcing Varro to surrender the 2nd, despite the Legion remaining loyal to Pompey. However, Varro recognized the futility of his plight, and the resistance to Caesar in the rest of the province collapsed without any bloodshed. Caesar acted with his usual liberality in order to assure the loyalty of a region that heretofore had been staunchly for Pompey. He granted citizenship to the native tribes who were not yet invested with such, remitting all the money appropriated by Varro, and returning all of the valuables that Varro had taken for "safekeeping" to the temple of Hercules at Gades. Leaving Longinus behind as governor, with Varro's two former Legions to garrison the province, Caesar was now free to turn his attention to other more pressing matters. Not everything was to go Caesar's way, however. We in the army felt vindicated when we learned that Afranius and Petreius had remained true to their oaths only long enough to get out of sight before showing their true colors and throwing back in with Pompey, but not before convincing the men of the 4th and 6th to join them in their flight to join Pompey in Greece.

~ ~ ~ ~

Now that Hispania was pacified, it was time for Caesar to turn his attention back to Massilia. Despite the defeat of the Pompeian fleet, the city itself still held out, so we were given the order to pack up and, leaving the 14th behind, we accompanied Caesar back to the east. Before we left, however, Caesar issued one of his most unpopular orders, recalling the men whose enlistments had expired and been allowed to go home by Fabius, those veterans that had salted our ranks when the 10$^{th}$ Legion had been first formed. This news was met with a huge uproar in the army, because it cast doubt on the status of the men promoted into the empty spots when the original men left the army. The fact that I was not one of them, promoted before the discharges as I was, did not blind me to the plight of the men in that situation. While it was hard for me to share their anger, I did sympathize. On the other hand, I looked forward to seeing Gaius Crastinus return to the Legion, although I was not sure what frame of mind he would be in, or any of the men for that matter. Despite the furor it caused, Caesar would not budge, but he did do his best to see that men were given the opportunity to make a lateral move into other Legions where there were vacancies at the same rank and title that they were forced to relinquish to the returning men. Not everyone could be accommodated, so that men like Cyclops found themselves being in effect demoted because of Caesar's orders. As men were shuffled from slots in the 10th over to the 14$^{th}$ and the other Legions to make room for Crastinus and the others, Cyclops found himself moved all the way down to the Sixth Century of the Tenth Cohort of the 14th.

In the 10th, the biggest change came with the return of Crastinus as Primus Pilus, but it was with some trepidation that I answered his summons for a meeting of the senior Centurions of the Legion, since I did not know what frame of mind he would be in. For all I knew, the months he had spent in retirement were the happiest of his life, and I could think of all kinds of possible outcomes if that was the case, none of them good. Being Primus Pilus, Crastinus held absolute control over all of us, and if he was angry at his recall, he could in turn make all of our lives miserable. Entering his tent, my heart sank at the sight of his scowling face, with its livid scar along the jawline, courtesy of a Nervii sword. He gave no sign of recognition, save for a curt nod as I entered to join the other Centurions who had already arrived. Luckily I was not the last to arrive, sparing me the scathing tongue-lashing with which Crastinus skewered the unfortunates, obviously having spent some of his time in retirement coming up with more inventive terms to describe their mothers, using curses I had never heard before from his lips. I also took notice of the fact that the customary cups of wine were nowhere in sight, further increasing my suspicions that our Primus Pilus was not particularly happy to be back with us.

Once we had settled in, he began speaking. "All right, there's no need to go over why I'm here. Caesar commanded it and that's that. All I have to say about it is..."

He paused, and I found myself holding my breath, waiting for him to unleash some sort of invective aimed at Caesar and the army. But as usual, Crastinus was a man of surprises.

"Thank the gods," he shouted, his battered face creasing into a smile. "I was bored out of my fucking mind! I was almost ready to show up at the next *dilectus* and start over as a *tiro*! Farming is the worst job in the world, and I hope I never see another plow as long as I live!"

There was an explosion of air as I realized I was not the only one holding my breath, and we laughed uproariously, as much from the release of tension as at Crastinus' wit. Amid the laughter, Crastinus reached down from behind his campaign desk where he had hidden an amphora of Falernian wine and enough cups for all of us. Within moments, we were toasting his return and laughing at his tales of woe as yet another failed farmer. We passed the evening drinking to his failure as a farmer, and everything else we could think of, and I vaguely remember weaving my way back to my own tent, aglow with a happiness that was fueled as much by the relief I felt that Crastinus was happy to be back as it was by Bacchus. The next morning was a slightly different story, and I am afraid the Cohort suffered from my hangover as much as I did. Such are the privileges of rank.

## Chapter 2- Greece

We did not stay in Massilia long, and I will not spend time recounting the siege and conquest of the city, mainly because we played no real part in it. Once the city was occupied, with Caesar acting with his usual clemency, a policy that was growing increasingly unpopular with the army, he issued orders for us to begin the long march back to Italia, all the way down the peninsula to the heel and the port city of Brundisium. This was going to be the port of embarkation for the invasion of Greece, where Pompey was gathering his own army, building fortifications at strategic points along the coast in preparation for our crossing. This was the longest march we had ever undertaken at this point, but Vibius and I were excited to finally see Italy; despite the fact we were not going to enter Rome, we would be passing nearby, and we talked about the sights we would see. We would also be passing through Campania, and depending on our exact route, I thought I might stop in the town where my father came from to meet the kin I had never seen before. Despite the anticipation of seeing the home province for the first time, none of us was looking forward to being on the march for more than a month. Even with the roads that are the best in the known world, day after day of marching in formation wears a man down, no matter how fit he is. My job as Pilus Prior meant that I had to be constantly on the alert for men falling out on the march, either because of exhaustion or because some comely wench caught their eye. The farther east we marched, the more settled and prosperous the land, and it was somewhat unsettling to realize just how dingy and poverty-ridden the regions we had originally come from were when compared to the peninsula. Crossing the Rubicon, I know that I for one was struck by the moment. After all, this river had ultimately launched the civil war. I must say that I was not impressed, expecting something more substantial than the muddy stream that we waded across without having to lift our shields above our heads. It didn't seem to be much of a barrier, or much of a symbol to use, as the line over which no general could march his troops. Now, I know this has caused some confusion. Indeed, I spent the equivalent of many watches trying to explain it to Gisela because I will admit that it is puzzling. Her question was simple; if no general could cross the Rubicon with an army, how did that explain when a general was given the honor of a triumph in Rome, and he could march at the head of his army through the streets of the capital? I had wondered about this myself, finally working up the nerve to ask one of the older men, who laughed and said that he had asked the same question. It is a matter of form more than anything else. A general is not allowed to lead an army over the Rubicon. However, if he crosses first and enters the capital, then summons his army, that is acceptable. But to ride at the head of an army is expressly forbidden, since it signals evil intentions against the Republic. When I had explained this to Gisela, she snorted in her usual contempt for some of our finer points of custom and tradition.

"So he can ride ahead, lull your stupid fat Senators into believing that he has only good intentions, then summon his army to descend on Rome?"

When I grudgingly agreed that this was one way to look at it, she simply shook her head in wonderment. "How you lot managed to conquer most of the known world is beyond me."

I knew better than to argue the point with her, and in truth, sometimes I wondered myself.

~ ~ ~ ~

Such was the tone of my thoughts wading across the muddy river. I had left Gisela and the baby behind, and it was at moments like these when I thought of times spent with her that the ache of loneliness was the worst. While the rankers brought their women along with them wherever they went, it was not seemly for a Centurion of my rank to do the same, meaning Gisela and my child were far away, safe enough, but I longed for their company at night when the army bedded down. However, these were not thoughts I could express to anyone, not even Vibius, so I would sit in my tent at night, brooding over the daily reports and ration requests. It was a mark of my frame of mind that I insisted on doing these myself, rather than let Zeno do them like I normally did, but I needed something to keep my mind busy and away from thoughts of my family. I would make the rounds of the fires at night, trying to present a normal front to the men, but there are no secrets in the army, and I could tell they knew something was bothering me. Still, I was not willing to talk about it with anyone, except that Vibius was unwilling to accept that and persisted in showing up at my tent every evening, demanding to know what was bothering me. Finally, a couple of days after we crossed the Rubicon, I broke down and told him, more out of exasperation than anything else. We were sitting in my tent, and he looked across my desk at me somberly, his wine cup in his hand. I am not sure what I was expecting, yet he did not mock or tease me, the normal reaction any man got when he displayed any type of emotion or behavior that his comrades considered soft.

Instead, he nodded and said simply, "I thought so." He suddenly stood and turned away so that I could not see his face as he continued, "Titus, I know how you feel, trust me in that. Remember how I felt about Juno?"

This was the first time I had heard her mention her name since that awful time back in Hispania, and I took it as a sign that the wound was no longer raw and open, but had begun to scab over.

"I remember," I said quietly, and I thank the gods that I caught myself from adding that it was different, because I know that would have wounded Vibius deeply.

"I wish I could say that it gets easier, but it doesn't." He drank deeply, then turned to me, shrugging with a sad smile on his face.

"Well, if you're trying to cheer me up, you're doing a piss-poor job of it," I said, only half-jokingly, but he laughed anyway.

Then he turned serious again and said simply, "I just wanted you to know that I know how you feel."

"Thank you, Vibius. It does help, a little."

There was a silence, then Vibius cleared his throat and awkwardly set the cup down on the desk. "Yes, well. I'll be off then, Centurion."

"Thank you again, Vibius. It's good to know I still have a friend."

"Always," he replied simply, then turned and left the tent.

Oh, how I wish those words had held true.

~ ~ ~ ~

One of the small benefits of marching in Italia was that we no longer had to construct the standard "marching camp in the face of the enemy" as it is called in the manuals, meaning that we would be settled down earlier in the day than usual for us. While this was a boon for the men, for the Centurions it was a never-ending source of headaches because idle time is our worst enemy since it gives the rankers more time to get into some sort of mischief, and the number of men on charges was getting to be a serious matter. I called for my Optio, glad at least that I finally had someone in the position that I knew I could rely on totally, my old comrade Scribonius. When I had first been made Pilus Prior, I was forced to name a man named Albinus as my Optio, for reasons that I no longer even remember. He had been almost useless; a weak, indecisive man who showed little initiative and even less enthusiasm for his job, thinking of it as a benefit rather than a responsibility. Unfortunately, his performance was not substandard enough for me to relieve him without a major headache, but the gods smiled on me by striking him down with the bloody flux, and he had the good grace to die shortly before we left Massilia. This time I was not going to make the same mistake, immediately approaching Scribonius, who had turned out to be one of the best choices I could have made, not only because he was one of the most popular men in the Century, but in the whole Cohort as well. His courage was unquestioned, but most importantly he was respected for his fairness and his ability to use reason instead of brute force. That did not mean he was soft; he could crack skulls with the best of us, yet he did not use force as his first resort, like some of the other officers. Now, he stood before me and I was sure my expression mirrored his, one of exasperation and a wry amusement at the ingenuity of the men. One of my saltiest veterans, Figulus, had gone missing, despite the best attempts of both Scribonius and I to keep the men too busy to think up ways to sneak out of camp. Figulus had been a close companion of the late Atilius, but possessed a shred more common sense, usually knowing when to rein in his wilder impulses. He had also been one of the men Caesar recalled and like Crastinus, had expressed his joy at being back in the army, civilian life proving not to be to his taste. But now, the fat countryside with the pleasant towns and pretty girls were proving too much of a temptation and he had managed to slip out of camp to go sample the local wares.

"The best I can tell, he managed to hide himself in the supply wagon that came this afternoon," Scribonius reported. I considered this, stepping outside to look at the sun to calculate the time. There were still a couple of watches of daylight, but we were scheduled for an evening formation, the Primus Pilus deciding to hold it as a deterrent for just such behavior, and the penalty for missing formation is a flogging. Knowing that, I was fairly sure that Figulus had every intention of returning before evening formation.

"Very well. We'll hold the report until the last possible minute. As long as he makes it back before formation, then we won't have to write him up."

"Yes, sir. But we can't just let him get away with sneaking off like that."

"Don't worry," I said grimly. "He won't. I'll see to that myself."

~ ~ ~ ~

As it turned out, I was right; Figulus magically reappeared, getting past the sentries on the gate about a sixth of a watch before evening formation. I saw him striding back to his tent, looking immensely pleased with himself, and I smiled, but it was not a friendly smile.

"Figulus!" I barked his name, pleased to see the expression on his face change instantly as he froze in mid-stride. "Get over here, now!"

He immediately turned and ran to me, stopping and coming to *intente*, eyes riveted to a point above my head. "Gregarius Figulus reporting as ordered, Pilus Prior," he rapped out the standard response.

To someone who did not know Legionaries in general and Figulus in particular, all would have appeared normal, but I could detect the hint of worry in his voice.

"How are you, Figulus?" I asked with a tone of concern, a senior Centurion checking on the welfare of his men, deepening Figulus' confusion.

"Sir?" His tone and manner was one of uncertainty, appearing confused by my solicitous tone, precisely the effect I was intending.

"I just haven't had a chance to talk to you lately, and you're one of the veterans that were part of our *dilectus* and came from Pompey's Legions. You were there when Vinicius bought it, weren't you?"

The mention of our old Optio's name brought a shadow of sadness across the older man's face, and I instantly regretted bringing up the unpleasant memories associated with his name. We had watched him incinerated in front of our very eyes, during our very first campaign in Hispania under a then little-known Praetor named Gaius Julius Caesar. It was to Vinicius I owed my first position as weapons instructor; he had taught me almost as much as Cyclops had about how to fight.

"Yes, sir," he said quietly, and while his face remained expressionless, I could see his eyes soften at the memory.

"There are just so few old-timers left that I try to keep an eye out for all of you, and we haven't had a chance to talk lately. So, is everything all right? Your old bones holding up to the long march?" I asked this in a slightly teasing tone, trying to lighten the mood.

I saw his chest puff out, indignant at the implication that his age was catching up with him.

"Pilus Prior, I'll march any man's cock into the dirt!" he exclaimed, and I laughed.

"I know you would, Figulus. I just wanted to make sure all was well."

"Right as rain, Pilus Prior," he had adopted the same bantering tone that I had, an old veteran wise in the ways of flattering his superiors and giving them exactly what they wanted to hear.

"Good, I'm very glad to hear it. Very well, carry on Figulus. Remember we have evening formation in a few moments."

He saluted. "Yes, sir. Haven't missed a formation yet, sir."

When he turned to march away, I could see the relief and joy at having gotten away with his misdeed written all over him.

"You didn't really think you would get away with it, did you?" I said softly, gratified to see his body go rigid with shock as he came to an abrupt halt.

After a moment's hesitation, to compose himself I was sure, he executed an about-face, his face a mask. "Sir? I'm not sure I understand the Pilus Prior's question."

The friendly face I had been wearing was gone, instead I stared at him with all the cold fury I could muster, and I found to my own small surprise that not all of it was feigned. I was actually angry with Figulus, although he had not done anything more egregious than a half-dozen other men in my command over the last several days, or any man in the Legion for that matter. Still, I could not let Figulus' deed go unpunished, but I also did not have any desire to have him flogged, because truth be told, I did have a soft spot in my heart for the men who had marched with me all these years.

"Oh, you fucking understand it well enough. You actually thought that I didn't know you hitched a ride on the supply wagon?"

That last was a total guess, but I was gratified to see that Scribonius had surmised correctly, because the look of surprise and guilt on Figulus' face would have been clear to a blind man.

"P-Pilus Prior, I . . ."

"You what?" I snapped. "Were you about to say what a piece of *cac* you were? If so, I wholeheartedly agree."

I stepped close to Figulus, confident that the combination of my size and my authority would be enough to cow him, and I was happy to see him visibly shrink back. "Oh, you're right to be scared," I said in the same quiet voice. I saw his fear immediately turn to panic, and I recognized that I needed to offer him some small hope. "But you're not going to be flogged." The look of relief on his face actually made me angrier. "But I promise you this; you're going to wish you had been. See me after the formation. Dismissed."

And with that, he marched away to ponder what was waiting for him.

~ ~ ~ ~

I beat Figulus worse than I had beaten anyone in my life up to that point, but I was careful not to break any bones to keep him from having to appear on the sick list. Besides, I wanted him fit enough to march because I knew his misery would be compounded, and he would be on display for the rest of the Century and Cohort to see. I did not do what I did to Figulus lightly, but I knew that if I did not take some drastic action, the men would continue taking advantage of what they saw as my weakness in enforcing discipline. Soon we would be at a point where a formation was missed, or even worse, a Legionary missed the morning formation before we began the march. Such a case is considered desertion and there is only one punishment for that, inflicted by his own tentmates, who are ordered to break every bone in his body before he dies. After talking it over with Scribonius, I knew that this was the only option open to me that the men would understand. Most importantly, the fact that it happened to a veteran like Figulus, and a man from my own Century at that, sent a message through the entire Cohort. It also had the added benefit of inspiring caution in men like Celer, who could plainly see the consequences of crossing me. Consequently, it was a much more obedient Cohort that marched its way down the peninsula; we had no more incidents of anyone sneaking out of camp, but we were getting closer to

Rome, and I knew that even the deterrent of a beating or a flogging might not be enough. What made it doubly difficult was that I did not blame the men in the slightest, since I was dying to see Rome myself.

~ ~ ~ ~

In the larger world, outside the confines of the 10th, things were not going smoothly for Caesar since Massilia had fallen. There was the matter of the 9th, having marched ahead of us but who were now in open revolt in their camp at Placentia, along with the 7th, demanding their discharges. Also, young Curio, the Tribune of the Plebs that Caesar had purchased some time before in an attempt to forestall this civil war, had been given an independent command by Caesar to invade Africa to face the Pompeian general Varus and the Numidian king Juba, and there had been no word. Caesar left the army to go on to Rome to attend to the political situation, getting himself appointed dictator, which under Roman law gave him absolute power over the Republic. Needless to say, this did not sit well with Catonians like Vibius, meaning I had to endure dark mutterings whenever I got close to the fire of my old tent section, or what was left of it.

As quickly as Caesar gained the upper hand in Hispania, the fortunes seemingly swung back to favor Pompey and the Senate, again making me wonder about the fickle nature of the gods themselves. Did they truly favor one side over another, or did they just enjoy watching us struggle with the events they put in front of us? Caesar had to leave Rome to go to Placentia to put down the rebellions of the 7th and 9th, while we continued marching to Brundisium. The only excitement came when we got within a half-day's march of Rome, whereupon we started coming into contact with some of the traffic that poured into and streamed out of the capital city. Traders, merchants, caravans of exotic animals from all the corners of the known world were forced to step aside as we marched by, the Legions always having the right of way on the roads. There was a constant buzzing of excited talk among the ranks as we were assailed by new sights on an almost momentary basis. At one point on the Via Appia, we crested a hill, giving us a view down a valley towards the city, and we could see a dark smudge on the horizon that one of the people we passed heading away from the city swore was the smoke from the fires of the city of Rome. I found myself standing with Vibius, gazing in that direction, straining our eyes to try to pick out any detail possible.

"It's hard to believe we're this close but we can't go into the city," Vibius said with a longing that surprised me. He had never expressed all that much interest in visiting Rome, and I glanced at him with a quizzical expression.

"What?" he asked defensively, then shrugged his shoulders. "It just seems a shame to be this close and not be able to see it."

R.W. Peake

I slapped him on the back and said, "Don't worry, we will. I promise."

"I should live that long," he said sourly, then fell back in.

"All right ladies," I roared. "Get back on the road. We still have miles to go before we can take a break and we're not going to get there if you stand here grabbing ass."

I was gratified to see the men obey me with some alacrity, Figulus' blackened eyes and limping gait doing more to instill discipline than any flogging.

~ ~ ~ ~

We were almost to Brundisium and in camp one night when Zeno announced that Celer was requesting entrance to my tent. Knowing how much he loathed having to take such action, I realized that it must be of some importance, either as it pertained to the Cohort or because of our personal feud, but I still decided to let him wait for a bit. I told Zeno that I would see him after I finished the very important paperwork I was doing, which in fact was a letter to Gisela, and while it did give me a twinge to see the discomfort on Zeno's face at the prospect of telling a Centurion to wait, it was not enough to stop me. I wish I could say I was above such petty revenge, but I was still relatively young and despite now having been Pilus Prior for some time, I still experienced moments of insecurity, most of them caused, at least in my mind, by Celer. Therefore, any regret I felt at forcing Zeno to have to tell Celer to wait was outweighed by the satisfaction I felt at exerting my authority. Finishing the letter, although to be fair I did wrap it up fairly quickly, I called for Zeno to bring Celer into my office.

A Centurion's tent is actually composed of two parts, the parts created by a partition provided by a leather panel that basically cuts the tent into two pieces. The front half of the tent serves as the Century or Cohort office, where Zeno worked, and the second half is a combination of my personal office and private quarters. I knew some Centurions who had ordered the creation of wooden floors for their personal quarters, but I disdained such luxuries. It was partially because I thought it useless frippery, but mostly because I was still not secure enough in my position that it did not worry me, except that was something I would never share with others. I sat at my desk, seeing by Celer's body posture that he was extremely angry, so I congratulated myself on making him wait. Any victory over Celer was one to be celebrated, at least in my mind.

"Yes, Celer?" I asked pleasantly, leaning back in my chair, enjoying the sight of his clenched jaw grinding his teeth at the insult I had offered him by making him wait.

"Pilus Prior, I bring some news I thought you might be interested in," he began, albeit through clenched teeth.

48

I affected an air of disinterested nonchalance, but my mind was instantly alert, knowing that Celer would never share something with me that was not momentous, such was our mutual hatred.

"And what news is that, Centurion?" which was something of a further insult, since I did not refer to him by his proper rank as Pilus Posterior, and for an instant I worried that I had gone too far, but to his credit, he overlooked it and continued.

"I have a cousin in the 9th, and he sent me word of what happened when Caesar faced the Legion to answer their demands for a discharge."

I dropped my feet from the desk and sat forward; this was indeed something in which I was interested. The talk in the Legions had been rife with speculation about how Caesar would handle the mutiny of the 9th, so I was definitely attentive. Now, Celer held something of the upper hand, and I swallowed my irritation at his smug expression. Reaching for the amphora of Falernian, one of the last ones willed to me by Pulcher, I offered him a cup, and it had the desired effect. He took a deep draught, smacking his lips in appreciation before silently holding the cup out for a refill. Now it was my turn to grit my teeth, but I decided it was a small price to pay for what he had to tell me, and I poured some more.

"So, what did you hear?" I asked, and I was rewarded with Celer's tale of what had happened in Placentia.

~ ~ ~ ~

Even now, all these years later, it still amazes me how often men of all stripes continually underestimated Caesar, and in the case of the mutiny of the men of the 9th, they committed a serious error. I am sure they were sincere in their belief that Caesar would cave into their demands, particularly since Marcus Antonius had made a bad situation worse. As Celer told it, his source was a cousin who was a Centurion in the Fifth Cohort, and he had relayed to Celer that a delegation of men of first the 9th, and then the 7th, had attempted to seek an audience with Antonius to air their grievances, only to be continually rebuffed. As far as the men were concerned, their mutiny was justified because they were not given their due process under army regulations, a sentiment with which I had to agree. Antonius then sent a desperate message to Caesar, who already had his hands full pacifying Rome while proving that he was not a blood-drenched dictator in the mold of Sulla, begging him to come pull his fat from the fire, as it were. The men of the 9th were sure that once Caesar was told of Antonius' refusal to give them a hearing, he would want to address their grievances to make up for Antonius' blunder. They were wrong. Calling an assembly of the Legions, Caesar responded to the demands of the men of the 9th, whose chief complaint was the non-payment of a bonus promised by Caesar, plus their discharges. Caesar, in turn, reminded the men that they had agreed to follow him for the entire campaign, not for part of it, and if anyone was to blame, it was our common enemy for refusing to acknowledge that their cause was doomed and for running away rather than fighting. Caesar pointed out that he was not known for the slowness of his movements, that this was evidence that he was doing everything in his power to end this war. He went on to say that he was disheartened and surprised at the discontent of the men of the 7th and 9th, but more so with the 9th since they were clearly playing a leading role. What he said next was as shocking as it was drastic; blaming the 9th, he ordered its decimation. The decimation of a Legion, as its name implies, is the ritual execution of a tenth of its strength, but what makes it even more brutal is that the rest of the Legion is responsible for carrying out the execution. Unlike the punishment for desertion, which requires the condemned man to run a gauntlet between his tent mates who are armed with axe handles and staves, the condemned men are stoned to death by their comrades, who surround them in a circle. Usually the punishment is reserved for a Legion that has shamed itself by running from battle or exhibiting cowardice in some other manner, and it is the worst humiliation a Legion can suffer, which is precisely why Caesar chose it.

According to Celer's cousin, there was an uproar as the men realized that they had pushed Caesar too far, and it was only through the intercession of some of the Tribunes that Caesar relented. In the end, Caesar decreed that the 9th would be spared the punishment provided the men volunteered to give up the identities of the ringleaders of the mutiny. The men of the 9th obeyed with alacrity, with 120 names offered up, including several Centurions. Those 120 men were then ordered to draw lots, and 12 of them were sentenced to death. In a further twist, it was discovered that one of the condemned men whose name was submitted by his Centurion had proof that he was not even in camp at the time, having been granted leave to visit family nearby. Instead, the Centurion who submitted his name was substituted in his place as punishment for his perfidy in trying to even an old score. While Celer was loath to admit it, I persisted in questioning him and found out that his cousin was one of the ringleaders but had avoided drawing the short straw. That told me something, at least as far as I was concerned; duplicity and betrayal ran in the Celer family tree, and I resolved to remember that. Where the fate of the 9th was concerned, once the executions were carried out, the mutiny was a thing of the past. Caesar informed them that they and the 7th would be part of the invasion force, and were ordered to Brundisium. They were still closer to Brundisium than we were at that point, arriving at the depot before us. In fact, we were the last Legion to arrive, marching into the city in late autumn, just days before the end of the campaigning season.

~ ~ ~ ~

I had never seen a camp as large as the one at Brundisium; in fact, nobody in the army had because this was the largest gathering of Legions in anyone's memory, if not in our history. The depot stretched as far as the eye could see, with a stout wooden wall, much more substantial than our normal marching camps. We had just marched more than half the entire breadth of the Republic. All of us were thankful that it was the end of the season, meaning we would not be expected to embark immediately for Greece, since we were in no shape for any kind of combat operations. Our boots were falling apart, and I had almost 20 men down with some sort of foot problems, each of them deemed injured enough to be given a spot on the Legion wagons. I am not sure that this was better for them, given the amount of complaining I heard about how rough the ride was. Still, as bad as we were, I was proud that my Cohort had the lowest number on the sick list in the Legion. It was incredibly important to me that our Cohort be seen as the absolute best in the Legion. If the low numbers of sick and injured was due as much to their fear of being administered the kind of justice that Figulus had received, as the level of care I demanded my Centurions give to the men. I did not really care. By this time, my habit of forcing the men to bathe more often and cook their meat more thoroughly had been completely accepted within the Cohort, even by Celer. Regardless, we were a travel-worn bunch that marched down the Via Principalis past the throngs of men from the other Legions, calling to friends and relatives in our midst, renewing acquaintances and issuing good-natured jeers and catcalls. In other words, the normal activities when the Legions gathered. I knew that this meant extra vigilance on my part and the rest of the Centurions; once the initial good humor of our reunion passed, there would be the inevitable brawls and even worse fights between the men. It is the nature of the beast, so to speak. We were warriors, our job to fight, and when there was no fighting with our enemies, we turned on our comrades. In truth, the rivalry between the Legions was such that some of the men held almost as many hard feelings towards fellow Legionaries as they did whatever enemy we were fighting. I was just thankful that it would be a couple of days before the men sufficiently recovered their strength and energy and that became a real issue. Even I was exhausted, although I could not betray that to the men, and once we settled into our quarters, which at least were constructed already, I struggled to stay awake while going over the daily reports with Zeno. The first order of business was to replace our worn and unserviceable gear. Naturally, a form had to be filled out for every pair of boots, and almost every man needed a new pair. I remember thinking that this was one of those times when I questioned if I was truly following the right path.

My second order of business was of a personal nature, sending for Gisela and young Vibius to come to Brundisium, where I had arranged for quarters for them. I was forced to pay dearly, space being at a premium, and I refused to do what many of my comrades had done, trusting my family to one of the new insulae thrown together to meet the demand. I had heard too many stories from the men who lived in Rome of what happened when the chance for profit was such that builders cut corners, with greedy landlords cramming too many people into a poorly constructed building. If my comrades were to be believed, buildings like the ones that now lined the streets immediately outside the gates of the depot collapsed on an almost daily basis in the capital, so I dug deeply into my purse, finding a set of rooms on the second floor of a cloth merchant, complete with a cooking area and two rooms. I was taking a bit of a gamble, I knew, but I was as close to certain as I could be that we would not be shipping to Greece for several months, given the series of events that had transpired.

Shortly after we arrived at the depot, we learned of the disaster in Africa and the loss of two Legions, the 17th and 18th as I recall, but the biggest blow to Caesar's plans for invading Greece came with the news of Gaius Antonius' misadventure. The younger brother of Marcus Antonius had, on his own authority, launched a punitive expedition across the Inland Sea to Greece, where he was promptly surrounded and forced to surrender. Not only did Pompey gain two Legions from his folly, but more importantly, Caesar lost more than 40 of the desperately needed transport ships to ferry the huge army across the sea. Finally, Caesar still had his hands full in Rome, working to secure his power base and beginning the push for his legislative reforms, so we were all confident that we were not going anywhere for some time.

~ ~ ~ ~

The winter we spent in Brundisium was one of the dreariest, most trying of my career to that point, brightened only by the arrival of my small family. Just in the months we were separated, Vibius had begun toddling about and was forming his first words. I am afraid I frightened him half to death when we were reunited, and looking back, I can see how fearsome I must have been, rushing to the apartment straight from duty when Gisela sent word that they had arrived, not bothering to change out of my uniform. The combination of my size and the sight of me in my full regalia was more than enough to send him running to his mother's arms, and I must say that it hurt quite a bit that my own child was scared of me. Happily, once I doffed my helmet and my armor, his curiosity soon overcame his fear and he came toddling over to me, helped along, I suspect, as much by the candied plum and carved toy Legionary I had brought, as by me. But I was not going to quibble and it was not long before he was settled on my lap and things were right as rain between us. Gisela looked lovelier than ever; she still took my breath away whenever I laid eyes on her, and she blessed me with a smile of such happiness that I did not think that life could possibly be better than that moment when we were reunited. Sitting there, snug in the apartment still filled with crates, bags, and boxes containing our household goods that she brought with her, with a cold, drizzling rain beating against the shutters and the fire blazing merrily away, I suddenly let out a laugh of sheer joy. Because I did so in the middle of Gisela's description of the horrible journey, I was rewarded with an arched eyebrow as she pursed her lips, a clear sign of irritation that I was not listening.

"And what," she demanded, "could be so funny about hearing how your son and I had to suffer staying in a flea-infested inn, being groped by some drunk?"

I held up my hand in a placating gesture. "*Pax*, my darling." I did not often use endearments, but I judged this was strategically a good time to do so, and was rewarded with a slight softening around the corners of her mouth. "It's just that I was struck by the thought of what the men would say if they could see me now." I drew her to me, my arm around her waist, and she came willingly, a smile beginning to form. "They're sure that I sprang up from dragon's teeth; I even overheard a couple of the men arguing over whether I actually had a mother."

Although we both laughed, I felt the pang of an old ache that I thought had long passed, because in truth I did not have a mother, at least in the sense that most people know, but it was at odd moments like this where I felt the loss most keenly. I shook those thoughts from my head, adding, "In truth, it surprises me as much as it would them."

"What, that you're happy to see your family?" Gisela pulled away and put her hands on her hips, a severe expression on her face but I could tell that she was being playful.

"That I even have a family," I said quietly, and I think it was at that moment I came closest to accepting the idea that I might leave the Legions when my enlistment was up.

I had indeed mellowed with age, although I laugh now at the thought that I considered myself old at the age of 28, which I would be my next birthday. To be fair, I had experienced more in the last 12 years than most people did in their lifetime and indeed, thanks to Caesar, had seen more action than most Legionaries did their entire career. Still, I was young, especially compared to now, and life was full of possibilities.

I settled into a routine balancing my family and duty, not all that hard given the level of inactivity in the depot as the winter passed. Most of my time was spent working with the senior Centurions of the other

Cohorts and Legions in keeping our men from killing each other. In the spirit of honesty, however, I must confess that it was not only the rankers chafing at the idleness and there were a fair number of brawls involving Centurions, which I somehow managed to avoid, although I do not know how or why. I began spending more time with Priscus, who I had come to appreciate as the best of the Centurions under my command. Celer and I were in what can only be described as an uneasy truce. I believe that he had resigned himself to the idea that I was not going anywhere, and since every scheme to undermine me had gone awry, he was beginning to grudgingly accept his lot. Niger was still his toady, the two seldom apart, so I guess it was only natural that I teamed up with another Centurion.

My friendship with Vibius was still intact, more or less, but the differences in our rank made fraternization difficult, along with our differences concerning Caesar. Vibius was growing increasingly isolated in his resistance to Caesar's charms, our general being elected Consul, then promptly pushing through legislation that was exceedingly popular with the people of our class. Additionally, he continued to act with restraint against his enemies, refusing to use his powers to exact revenge. In short, Caesar was becoming increasingly harder to hate, and whereas before when Vibius had held forth at the fire about his grievances against Caesar there had been some heads nodding in agreement, even that silent support had dried up. I cannot say that I was not secretly amused at seeing Vibius' surprise and subsequent irritation the first time he began one of his diatribes against Caesar and tongues previously always still were now roused to Caesar's defense. It only took a few times for Vibius to realize the futility of arguing, so he would sit fuming by the fire, unable to give vent to his frustration. I had long since given up the idea that Vibius would eventually come around on the subject of Caesar; while I did not, and still do not truly understand the nature of his dislike, I did recognize that he would hold his opinion of Caesar until one of them was dead. Not that I imagine Caesar lost much sleep over the idea that Sergeant Vibius Domitius did not approve of his actions. Vibius' disapproval notwithstanding, the overwhelming majority of the rankers, along with the civilians of the lower classes did approve of the actions that Caesar was taking, and Pompey's support had ebbed away to nothing, at least publicly. Even so, what the people wanted more than anything was the two combatants to make peace without further bloodshed, but that did not look likely.

~ ~ ~ ~

Pompey had indeed been busy, using his contacts and influence on the eastern fringes of the Republic to summon troops and supplies from all the various petty kings, satraps, and other puppets of the region, along with building extensive fortifications along the coast in preparation for our landing. Then, Caesar decided to prove me wrong in my judgment that we would not be mounting an assault for a few months by relinquishing the dictatorship and leaving Rome, arriving in Brundisium in mid-December. He immediately issued orders to begin preparations for embarkation, despite the dearth of reliable transports. Deciding that rather than waiting, he would launch the invasion in three waves, we were summoned to headquarters one frosty morning a couple days after Caesar had arrived. An excited bunch made their way from our Legion area across the sprawling base to the designated building. All of us were animated at the idea of action, save for one, and that one was me. I had honestly believed that we would spend the winter on this side of the sea that separates Italia from Greece, and I did not relish the idea of telling Gisela that I would be leaving shortly. She knew, like everyone in the area did, that Caesar had arrived, but she had taken my assurances that it was just an inspection, meaning nothing. Unfortunately, now I was going to have to tell her differently. We had been together barely a month, and if the rumor mill were to be believed, we would be embarking just as quickly as the ships could be loaded. When the ten of us arrived at the headquarters building, we were shown into Caesar's presence immediately, another sign that things were moving rapidly. I was shocked when I saw him; he looked like he had aged overnight, his face deeply lined, with the deep grooves etched in his forehead that some call "worry lines." He had dark circles under his eyes, and his skin was even paler than it normally was, since he had the kind of complexion that did not darken in the sun as much as men who had skin tones such as mine. Despite all these signs of woe, he displayed the same energy, and after greeting some of us warmly by name and making the obligatory joke about my size, he got down to business.

"Gentlemen, we are about to embark on the last phase of this operation, one that should culminate in the end of this unfortunate and unhappy war." We stood silently at *intente*, watching him gather his thoughts for what he would say next. Looking down at some papers on his desk for a moment before resuming, he continued, "I intend to launch an amphibious operation, an operation in which the 10th will be accorded the signal honor of accompanying me in the first wave." So far, nothing was a surprise, the rumor mill being extremely accurate to this point. Caesar noted our lack of expression, and his face darkened for a moment before he expelled his breath with a harsh chuckle. "And I'm not telling you anything you don't know already, am I? I should remember that there are no secrets in the army." Pursing his lips, he let out a sigh. "Very well, that's the gist of it anyway. I will also be taking the 11th, 12th, 25th, 26th, and 27th, along with the Cohorts of the 28th that held faith with me instead of going over to Pompey like the rest of that lot."

While our role was not a surprise, the identities of the other Legions were, and I exchanged a sidelong glance with Crastinus, who raised an eyebrow, which did not escape Caesar's attention.

"Is there anything you care to say, Primus Pilus Crastinus?" Caesar asked mildly.

Crastinus reverted back to the age-old soldier's trick of going rigid and staring off into space. "No, sir, nothing at all, sir."

Caesar picked up a stylus, tapping it thoughtfully against his chin, then replied, "I would prefer it if you spoke your mind, Gaius Crastinus. You know I value the opinions of my Centurions."

Crastinus was now off the hook; he had just been ordered to speak his mind, no matter how politely it was phrased, and he did not waste the opportunity.

"It's just that, given everything we've heard from the intelligence reports, that bunch over there has had a lot of time and put in a lot of effort in fortifying the possible landing spots." Caesar nodded his agreement with that statement, and Crastinus continued, "Given that, sir, it just seems a bit . . . chancy to include green Legions like the 25th and the rest in the first wave. I mean," he added hastily, "we're happy that the 11th and 12th are with us as well, but wouldn't it be good to have the boys from Gaul in the first wave?"

When Crastinus finished, Caesar looked to the rest of us to see if we had anything to add, but we did not. Not only was Crastinus our senior and therefore our spokesman, he had summed up exactly what constituted our fears. More than half the army would be untested troops; granted they had been in the army for more than a year, but they had not seen any action.

Seeing us remain silent, Caesar nodded, heaving a sigh that seemed to contain all the weariness of the world in it. "Ideally, you would be correct, Primus Pilus. It would indeed be better to put all my veterans together in the first wave to ensure the highest probability of success. But I'm sure I'm not telling you anything that you don't know when I say that the men of the 7th, 8th and 9th and I had a bit of a . . . falling out." Despite the seriousness of the topic, a ghost of a smile played about his face at the understatement, eliciting a couple of chuckles from us. He grew serious again, and continued, "Given that, I'm not sure how far I can trust the men of those Legions, and until I am sure again, I'm not willing to risk the consequences if they should decide to switch their allegiance."

Although we understood and accepted his reasoning, it was still sobering to hear our general voice his fears about the loyalty of part of his army aloud, and I think he read in our faces our consternation.

"I do not make this decision lightly, because I know that some might see it as an insult." His voice hardened, the memories of Placentia evidently coming back. "But it's no more of an insult than was given me by their attempted mut . . ." he clamped his mouth shut, biting off the last word before it could be uttered fully. Such is the specter of dishonor associated with that word that our general did not even want to speak it aloud. Instead, he substituted the word "misunderstanding," which I thought was a bit generous. If only I knew what lay ahead of us, I am not sure how I would have felt.

~ ~ ~ ~

We departed headquarters a few moments later, Caesar telling us that written orders would be coming our way shortly, but we now had a lot of work to do, and a short amount of time in which to do it. Caesar also informed us that he would be addressing the entire army later that day to announce his plans, so we hurried back to get the men ready for the formation. Delegating the task to my Optio, Scribonius, and confident that the other Centurions would get their own Centuries ready, I plodded across the depot for the main gate, and headed to our apartment to break the news to Gisela. I had learned, to my own peril, the folly of delaying bad news where Gisela was concerned and I prided myself, as I do to this day, on not making the same mistake twice. That does not mean I was looking forward to it in any way, and I remember thinking wryly that I had to remember to put in an order for more crockery, because I suspected there was going to be some breakage in the very near future. I did pause for a moment outside the door to gather myself and was struck by the thought that this was becoming a habit, but unlike other times, I was aware for the first time that there was an alternative, that I did not always have to do this to Gisela and my family. Vibi, as we called him, was too young to know this time, but if I stayed in the army there would be a time when he would be just as hurt as his mother. I shook my head angrily; these were unwelcome thoughts, particularly at this moment, except the idea that I might have a life outside the army had taken root and would not seem to die. Forcing this from my mind, I entered the apartment by way of a stairwell on the outside of the building so I did not have to go through the cloth merchant's establishment. Gisela was feeding Vibi, who appeared like most of his meal had somehow missed his mouth, and he beamed up at me with outstretched arms, giving me a gummy smile sprinkled with a few white, even teeth. Despite the mess, I welcomed the distraction, swooping him up into the air as he laughed with delight.

"And what brings you home in the middle of the day, Centurion?" Gisela had almost as much food splattered on her as Vibi, but she still looked desirable to me, and she must have sensed it because she added, "Are you here for a quick romp? Can't you wait until tonight?"

Despite her words, she was smiling up at me, and I knew that if I wanted, I could have had her right then, making me feel even worse. I am not good at hiding my feelings and just as quickly as it had appeared, her smile fled as she searched my eyes. Before I could speak, she took a staggering step and sat back down on the chair from which she had been feeding Vibi.

"You're leaving again, aren't you?"

All I could do was nod, bracing myself for the explosion of her temper, automatically checking for breakable or dangerous objects within her reach. But what happened was far worse; instead of anger, I got tears, and lots of them. Gisela threw herself down on the table, covering her head with her arms, and I could see her body wracked by huge sobs. Seeing his mother in such obvious distress, Vibi started wailing in my arms, pushing away from me, and reaching for his mother. I felt horrible; I had not even said anything yet and my family was falling to pieces. I let Vibi down and he toddled over to his mother, grabbing at her thigh, then trying to crawl into her lap. Gisela sat up and pulled him up to her, and began to hug him fiercely, which seemed to do both of them good, their tears gradually subsiding. Poor Vibi got more than he had bargained for, however, and I suspected Gisela was clutching him more tightly than normal, because he began to squirm as he struggled to escape from her grasp. Now his tears of fear turned to tears of outrage, his face turning bright red from his struggles to escape his mother's grasp, but she was not relinquishing it. She was now staring fixedly at me, her eyes still brimming with tears, but I could see by the set of the mouth and the tilt of her head that the anger was coming too. Perversely, I welcomed that more because I was more familiar with her anger than her sadness.

"When are you leaving us?" she asked bitterly, and all I could do was shrug.

"We don't know for sure yet, but it's a matter of days, no more."

She flinched like I had struck her, then took a breath and said, "And how long will you be gone?"

Again, all I could do was shrug, and I thought that perhaps it had not been such a good idea to rush back and tell her. Maybe it would have been best to wait until I knew more, but then she would have heard from the other wives, or through the traders, or from talk in the street, and I would have been done for either way.

"Caesar's holding an assembly later today; I should have more of an idea after that."

She shrugged. "I don't suppose it really matters when I'll be all alone again."

"No you won't." I tried to keep the impatience from my voice but it was hard, "you have Vibi."

The look she gave me could have burned the hair off my face if I had any. "That's very nice. I was referring to my husband and having adult conversation."

I did not know how to respond because I honestly had never thought about it like that before. I realized it had to be hard for her to be all alone with just Vibi; the couple I hired to serve her in Narbo had refused to come with her to Brundisium, and there had not been time to find someone suitable here. All I could do was shrug helplessly, and she refused to kiss me when I bade her goodbye to return to the base.

~ ~ ~ ~

Never before had so many Legions been assembled in one spot, and as big as the forum of the depot was, we still had to crush together in much tighter formation than was normal to accommodate everyone. The cramped conditions did not make anyone more cheerful. A number of squabbles broke out while we waited for Caesar to mount the rostra. Finally, the *bucina* sounded the signal for a general officer approaching and the army was called to *intente*. While I had a spot close enough to hear with no problem, Caesar's words had to be relayed back by designated Centurions so that everyone could hear. He stepped up to the rostra, clad in his gilt armor and *paludamentum*, and began in his customary style.

"Comrades," he began, "I stand here before you, ready to take one final step to end this horrible war with our misguided brothers, led by evil men who have no interest in the welfare of the Republic, but only in their own enrichment."

He paused while this was relayed back to the rest of the men, and then he continued. "We are nearing the end of our toil and struggle. There is one last barrier to be overcome, one last battle to be won. With your help, we can bring peace to our great Republic. I ask you now, will you follow me? Will you help me accomplish this last task before we can rest and enjoy the fruits of peace?"

There was considerable chaos the next few moments, with the men who were able to hear Caesar roaring their affirmation, while the Centurions in charge of relaying Caesar's words were drowned out by the noise. We had to issue commands to shut everyone up so that the men in back could have their opportunity to respond. Honestly, it was all rather anticlimactic by the time it was finished, and I could see the color rise to Caesar's face. I remember thinking that even Caesar slipped up from time to time. Once things settled down, he picked up where he had left off.

"As you all know, we do not have as great a number of ships as I would desire for this operation." I noticed that he did not mention the reason why we did not have the ships. "Therefore, I would ask of you that you leave all unnecessary baggage behind so that we can transport as many men in the first wave as possible. In any event," he said with a theatrical smile and flourish, "there will be no need for baggage since we will not be campaigning long. And you do not want to already be loaded down when it's time to divide the spoils of this last battle."

As usual, Caesar knew his audience and played them with skill. Another roar issued from the throats of thousands of men at the thought of untold riches that waited across the sea, and by approbation, the army gave its full-voiced approval to Caesar's plan. We were dismissed to begin preparations, the tentative date for the invasion to be the end of December, just a week away. Even with leaving the baggage and servants behind, there was a lot of work to do to ensure weapons were in good order, all stores and equipment were up to proper levels, and rations were drawn for the appropriate time period. We also took the time to perform a couple of forced marches with full gear in order to shake off some of the rust from our idle times, and it was in this manner that the next few days flew by.

~ ~ ~ ~

Before we embarked, I arranged to recall two of my slaves, which I was leasing to a business in town, bringing them to the house for Gisela's use. They were both Gauls, and in the past, Gisela had been extremely resistant to having them serve her. She would not say why, but I assumed that it made her uncomfortable to have some of her own people as slaves, even if they were of a different tribe. By this time, whatever reluctance she had was outweighed by her loneliness and need for help around the house, so she gave her consent to the plan, albeit grudgingly. I made sure to pick a female for her, and the male I selected was a big, burly sort who was not very smart but was biddable and docile, yet presented a pretty fierce countenance that I was confident would discourage anyone with a mind towards mischief. Despite my attempts to make her more comfortable, I was given the cold shoulder every evening when I went home, with Vibi picking up on the tension and therefore was also fussy, compounding all of our misery. Finally, the date for sailing was set for the 4th of Januarius, and it was only then, on the day before we sailed, that there was a thawing between us. Since the embarkation was going to start at dawn, I could not stay the whole night, and when I left, Gisela sobbed hysterically, clinging to me as she clutched the baby. It was all I could do to extricate myself, and in truth, I felt horrible leaving them standing in the doorway of the apartment. The picture of my wife and child, framed by the light from the apartment, is burned into my memory.

~ ~ ~ ~

The loading of the army took the whole day, and as luck would have it, the 10th was one of the first to embark, meaning that we bobbed about in the harbor, waiting for the rest of the army. Because of the time of year, the water in these parts was excessively choppy, so it was not long before men were draped over the side, spewing their guts out. Fortunately, I managed to avoid the embarrassment of joining the men on the side, but only just. We spent almost two full watches dipping about like a cork while the transports were loaded up, and it was full dark before the fleet formed up, turning to the east to begin the crossing. It was a miserable trip; the last time we were onboard ships was when we invaded Britannia, and I for one had forgotten just how horrible an experience it was, being doused with icy spray and trying not to fall over on the pitching deck. At least I was lucky enough, by virtue of my rank, to be above deck instead of crammed into the hold like the rankers, who were shivering and puking as the ships bucked against the waves. We were perhaps halfway across when the wind changed, blowing from the north, pushing the fleet away from the intended landing site at a spot near Palaeste, which Caesar chose for its good landing beach and relative seclusion. Now we were being forced southward down the coast, bad news because it pushed us closer to the last known location of Pompey's fleet. As if that was not bad enough, once we were pushed a few miles off course, the wind then died down completely, leaving us motionless in the water. Despite the fact that was good for the men's seasickness, it was dangerous because it left us vulnerable to being spotted and attacked by the enemy, whose warships were almost exclusively powered by oar, the same as ours, while the transports were sail-driven craft. Standing tensely on the deck, we strained our eyes in the direction of land, where we could see lights of a village that the sailors told us housed the base of the Pompeian fleet. We watched to see if any of the lights began moving, signaling that they were on the warships of the Pompeians and were headed for us. There was no talking; even if we were so inclined, we had been ordered to maintain complete silence, sounds carrying great distances over water. A very tense third of a watch passed as we sat motionless, the only sound the lapping of the waves against the side of the boat, but as usual Caesar's luck held and none of the lights at the Pompeian base detached themselves to head our way. Finally, a murmur of relief started at the rear of the vessel. Turning to see what the commotion was, I felt the breeze on my cheek, coming from the southwest now, and soon we were underway again, heading back to our original landing site.

~ ~ ~ ~

The sky was beginning to lighten when the lookout whispered down that he had spotted land, causing us to strain our eyes in the direction that he was pointing in the gloom. I imagined more than saw the dark bulk of the hills that rise almost immediately from the edge of the coast in that part of the world, and I exchanged a glance with Crispus, wondering if he was thinking the same thing. There just did not appear to be much of a beach for us to land on, but my hopes were that because of the darkness I was missing something, that there was in fact a sufficient beaching area for us. The chop had picked back up along with the wind so that men were back to retching again, but I kept my eyes focused in the direction we were heading, straining to pick up any details of the landing area. While I did, I called quietly to my Centurions arrayed about the deck, and began relaying instructions to them to rouse the men and get them ready to disembark. The plan was to land on line, with each transport holding a Cohort, with the First, ourselves, Third, Fourth, and Fifth scheduled to be first, depending on the condition and width of the beach.

In the darkness, I could see a blur of white foam off to the right, the hiss of the surf pounding the rocks carrying on the wind to our ears. I felt my throat tighten at the thought of those rocks, waiting to tear the bottom out of the ship, and I automatically walked over to the hold to peer down at my men huddled below. Gazing down at them sitting miserably in the fetid darkness, I sensed someone's eyes on me and I turned to see Vibius staring balefully up at me. Despite myself, I grinned at him, and he mouthed an obscenity, causing me to realize that it was almost full light if I could read his lips. Blowing him a kiss, I walked back to my spot at the bow of the boat, staring landward. I was able to begin making out more detail, finally seeing the beach we were heading for and I bit back a curse. Essentially, the beach was lodged between two promontories of rock that jutted out into the sea, and it was plain to see why the beach was undefended, since it appeared to be suicide to try guiding any number of ships between the teeth of those rocks. Not for the first time, I wondered at Caesar's confidence and questioned if it indeed was hubris, although I could also see why he chose the beach, because it presented a wide enough front for almost the entire Legion to land at once, provided every ship managed to steer past the rocks. I stood motionless as our own boat slid past the rocks to the right, no more than a hundred paces away, and it was not until we were safely past that I realized I had been holding my breath. Once it was clear we were safe, I turned my attention to preparing for the landing, watching as the men stood and gathered their gear up, making themselves ready. Since the decks were packed, the men in the hold were forced to wait for the men topside to go over the side before they ascended the ladder. This was the reason why I had ordered that the Centurions, Optios, and *signifer* of each Century be the first over the side, so they could stake out a spot for their units to assemble. The beach was deserted, and I thanked the gods for the small blessing that there would be no opposition, calling the news down to the men in the hold.

"At least it won't be like that fucking beach in Britannia then," a voice called out.

"You're right about that," said another man. "I almost fucking drowned that day, and had to worry about one of those Brit bastards taking my head off."

"That's because you're such a short-ass that was the only thing showing above the water," the first man shot back, and there was a rumble of laughter.

By rights, I should have told them to shut up, but I had learned that at times like these, humor went a long way to easing the pressure of what was about to take place, so I let it pass. It was only a couple moments later that I felt the crunching of the bottom of the boat, followed by a lurch as it slowed to a halt. Instantly, I moved to the side and swung my legs over, since I would be the first of my Cohort to hit the beach. Looking over my shoulder I roared, "All right you bastards, over the side! We're not paid by the watch! Centurions, get your parties formed up on the beach. Make sure there's enough room for your sections! I don't want anyone standing in the water because you didn't count your paces correctly!"

Then I leaped down, gasping despite myself when the shock of the water hit me. There was a flurry of men slipping over the side and I heard the splashing behind me, followed by the inevitable curses as the cold water hit men in their most sensitive bits, but I was already wading ashore. Looking to the side, I bit back my own curse as Crastinus grinned and waved at me; we had a wager about who would be the first on the beach, and he had beaten me by several feet. That did not help my mood, and I cursed at what I thought was the ragged performance of my Cohort as they came streaming onto the beach, looking for their Centurions and Optios, each of them bawling out their Century number. The men spilled off the boats, dripping water and squeezing out the hems of their tunics as they shuffled into their spots in formation. It did not take us long to get formed up, partially because of our experience, but also because there were so few of us left. At times like this when I could graphically see the toll the years of fighting had taken, I was struck by a wave of sadness, thinking of all the comrades that were not there to take their places. Compounding the problem was that an outbreak of the bloody flux had swept through camp in the weeks before we had arrived, so despite the 10th being spared, the other Legions were hit hard. The average strength per Legion was barely 2,400 men; we were just a little better with 2,800 men. My Cohort could field 305 men, and the First Century, my original unit, was down to 47 men standing on that beach. It was a sobering sight, but I would not have traded one of these men for ten new *tirones*. What we lacked in numbers, we more than made up for in experience; years of campaigning had weeded out the weak, the slow, and the unlucky. What was left was the fighting core of the Legion, the men who had always borne most of the burden, even when we were at full strength, so it was with the utmost confidence that I took my place at the head of my Cohort and waited for the command to step off.

~ ~ ~ ~

Our first mission was to take Oricum, which lay about 25 miles to the northwest, at the base of a deep inlet that provided a sheltered harbor for the Pompeians. The only way to approach was by a roundabout route that followed a dry riverbed through steep mountains, actually heading east before gradually turning in the direction of the town. As we set off, Caesar ordered the fleet, commanded by a general named Calenus to go back to get the next wave. The 10th was the vanguard, and it was not long before we were huffing and puffing because of the steep climb up from the beach. Taking a look back, in the growing light I could see the rest of the army hundreds of feet below, looking like a group of well-organized ants waiting their turn to begin the climb up the trail. The path we were following was little better than a sheep track, forcing us to move single file for large stretches of time, making the going very slow. By the time we descended from the hills onto the plain that surrounds the landward side of Oricum, the sun was high in the sky. We had to halt to wait for the rest of the army making its way over the track to join us, so we took advantage of the delay by eating a quick meal and resting a bit, stretching out, and using our gear as a pillow. With the men resting as we waited, I walked with Crastinus and some of the other Centurions to take a look at the fort that was situated in the western corner of the inlet, with the water to the north and a steep ridge to the west. The water of the bay was a striking deep blue, and there were a number of ships of all types anchored there. As was usual in such cases, there was a town hard by the walls of the fort, although I do not know which came first. Even from where we stood, we could see that the walls of the town were lined with people watching us, although we could not tell if they were soldiers or civilians.

"That's going to be a tough nut to crack," commented Crastinus. He pointed to the possible approaches. "To get to the fort, we're going to have to cross in front of the walls of the town, which will expose us to fire." Shifting his attention, he indicated the town. "But if we take the town first, we're not only going to have to worry about fighting in the streets, we'll have to keep at least one Legion and more likely two in reserve to watch for any sortie from the fort."

"Unless they commit their forces to defending the town and abandon the fort," I suggested. "Then we'll have to commit everything to the assault on the town or it's likely we won't even get over the wall."

"What we don't know is what quality of troops are in the garrison." This came from a swarthy Centurion from the First Cohort named Plinius, another of the men who had been recalled by Caesar.

"We have to assume they're some of Pompey's veterans," Crastinus replied grimly.

Our scouting trip had been sobering and when we returned to the army, the last of the first wave was descending from the track, falling into their designated spots. Crastinus went to report to Caesar what we had seen while the rest of us returned to our respective Cohorts, kicking them awake and on their feet. Shortly after we landed, Caesar freed a prisoner that he had brought with us, a patrician named Rufus who had been a Legate of one of Pompey's Legions, with instructions to go find Pompey, making one last offer of a peace settlement. There was considerable wagering about the outcome of his mission, most of the money being placed on the mission failing. Meanwhile, after receiving Crastinus' report, Caesar gathered his staff and all his panoply together, including the lictors he was entitled to by virtue of his Proconsular authority, and approached the walls of the town to parley. As we stood watching, he rode with grave and stately *dignitas* towards the walls, which had grown even more packed with people, waiting to see what their fate would be.

~ ~ ~ ~

The parley lasted less than a third of a watch. At the end of it, the gates of the town were thrown open, surrendering without a fight. Simply put, the citizens of the town were not willing to wage war against a Consul of Rome and the garrison commander, Torquatus was his name, was forced to capitulate. With the fate of the town and fort settled, we were given orders to make camp outside the walls, and access to the town was put off-limits. For once, the grumbling was muted; we were all tired from the rough march through the hills and thankful for the rest. The next morning we set out, marching north along the bay, leaving the 27th behind to man the fort and town in the event that any of Pompey's fleet decided to show up. Our next goal was Apollonia, taking two days of hard marching to reach, but when we did, the result was the same; the townspeople refused to resist a Consul of Rome and the commander of the town was forced to surrender. In quick succession, the towns of Bylis and Amantia followed suit, and we began to think that perhaps this war could be won without any bloodshed after all. The next objective was the site of Pompey's main supply depot at Dyrrhachium, some 70 miles away, and we made haste to reach it before Pompey did.

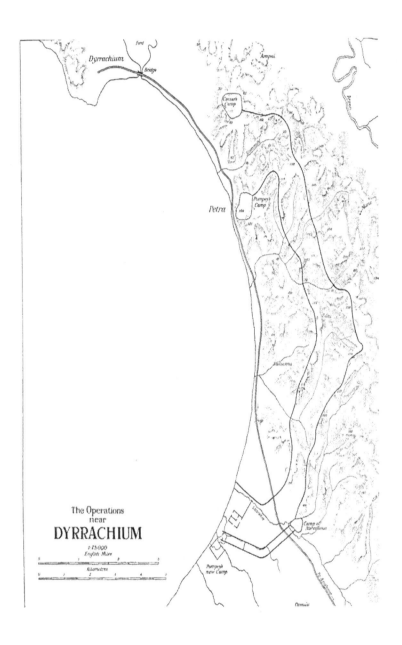

The Operations
near
**DYRRACHIUM**
1:75,000
*English Miles*

*Kilometres*

## Chapter 3- Dyrrhachium

There were three rivers that we had to cross, although once we were past the mountain ranges ringing Oricum, the terrain was almost flat. Unfortunately, along with the offer of a truce, that bastard Rufus also brought a warning to Pompey that we were approaching. Learning that Apollonia was lost, Pompey turned his army to Dyrrhachium, giving orders for a forced march. In his advantage was the fact that they were marching on the Via Egnatia, while we had to cross open ground, thereby taking longer, even when the terrain was flat. The rivers also delayed us, since we had to scout for fords rather than stop long enough to build bridges. That also would have taken too long because of the lack of timber in the area. Consequently, Pompey's army beat us to Dyrrhachium and we were greeted by the sight of the tail end of his army reaching the walls of the city while all we could do was watch in frustration. The only heartening sight was the obvious disorganization and seeming panic in the movements of Pompey's army; as we would learn later, the green troops that comprised a large part of his army had taken fright at the sight of us, turning the march to Dyrrhachium into a wholesale flight to the safety of the city. Pompey ordered his army to set up camp outside the walls, while Caesar actually withdrew us some distance away to set up our own camp on the south side of the Apsus River that runs east and west to the sea. Now that the race was over and Pompey had won, Caesar gave orders that we would remain here for the winter and we would be joined by the rest of the army as soon as it was ferried over. To that end, we began building a fortified winter camp. With some of us working on the camp, others went foraging, since we had not brought much in the way of food. The news that we would be spending the winter was met with some grumbling, because this was in direct contradiction to what Caesar had told the army when he asked them to leave their excess baggage. I was not happy because Zeno had been left behind, meaning that all the paperwork fell on my and Scribonius' shoulders, and one does not realize how much someone else does until they are not around to do it. But we had our orders, and we worked diligently to prepare for a lengthy stay.

~ ~ ~ ~

The days passed with no sign of the rest of the army, before Caesar was finally forced to send someone back to Italia to find out what had happened to them. I did not envy their mission, or what it would take to get it done. In order to avoid detection and capture by the Pompeian fleet, the unlucky bastard selected for the job had to cross the rough winter water in as small a vessel as possible. I am sure that is part of the reason that Caesar sent more than one man, spread over a number of days. It was not a suicide mission, but it was as close to one as you could get, and it was one job I was more than happy to have someone else do. As it turned out, it was a smart move since out of the five men Caesar sent, only one returned and the news he brought was about as bad as it could be. The fleet that carried us across the sea had been intercepted by the Pompeian commander of the fleet, a man named Bibulus who was a great hater of Caesar, and a large number of transports were captured. The ships that escaped were now bottled up in Brundisium, and when they made one attempt at crossing, a combination of bad weather and pressure from the Pompeian fleet had forced them to turn back. During that endeavor, one more transport was captured, with all the men onboard executed, Bibulus' hatred of Caesar and his cause serving as his excuse.

Now Antony was sitting waiting for the winds to turn favorable, or so he claimed, but that did not set well with those of us who were facing a force twice our size. Nevertheless, we had no choice; first the days, then the weeks passed, waiting for Antony to arrive, and just like what happened in Hispania, it proved to be impossible to keep the two armies from fraternizing. The meeting spot was the river, serving as the water source for both armies, with acquaintances once again renewed and kinships rediscovered among the Spaniards of Pompey and Caesar's Legions. Before long, the highlight of our day would be the gathering of the men down by the river. There was almost a festival atmosphere, with much wine flowing, bones being thrown and money changing hands as the wagering and gaming ran rampant. Of course, such good spirits and amicable exchanges could not go unnoticed by the generals, but while Caesar and Pompey were disposed to let it continue, that motherless cocksucker Labienus would not let it lie.

One day, after a series of speeches by men on both sides about the need for peace, two Tribunes, one from each side, made a mutual agreement to go to the general of the other side to make a plea for a settlement. This was met by much cheering and joy from the men on both sides. I do not know if Labienus was warned about what was happening, or his suspicions were aroused by all the commotion, but he came charging down to the river with a bodyguard and furiously berated the Pompeian troops for showing such faithlessness in their cause. He threatened to kill any man of Caesar's who set foot on his side of the river, no matter what their mission was, then made an oath to Jupiter Optimus Maximus that the only way to end the war was with Caesar's head on a spike. He was soundly jeered and in truth, he was lucky that by common consent nobody came to the river fully armed, because he would have looked like a porcupine if we were. That did not stop men from picking up rocks and hurling them at the traitor, forcing him to withdraw, but the Pompeians, with an obvious show of reluctance, left with him.

That put an end to the good times down by the river, and in my mind, ruined the last chance of ending the war peacefully.

~ ~ ~ ~

Caesar kept up the pressure on Antonius to make the crossing, but the excuses kept coming and finally Caesar resolved to go himself to Antony, disguising himself as a slave and hiring a small fishing boat to make the crossing. His officers argued vehemently with him about the folly of this, but he would not be swayed, and he left the camp one evening in his disguise. I happened to be commanding the guard Cohort that evening, and warned the men to make absolutely no sign that they knew the identity of the roughly-dressed man who rode out of the camp in a wagon sent to fetch firewood. Still, it was hard not to stare at Caesar, and I for one thought his disguise was useless; he did not have the bearing of a slave, no matter how hard he tried. However, I supposed that as long as he was viewed only from a distance, he would escape detection. What was more worrying were the dark clouds towering over the nearby sea, and we clearly saw the flashes of lightning streaking through them, the sky a leaden gray from the rain sweeping down. The evening turned into night, the storm moving onto land, and we were soon soaked by the deluge, the wind whipping my sagum as I walked the palisade checking on the men. It was shortly after dawn that the wagon returned, light enough to see Caesar's anger and frustration, sitting next to a very nervous driver. We learned that the captain of the fishing boat was a brave soul indeed, because his fear of drowning was greater than his fear of Caesar, and after about two parts of a watch at sea, he insisted that they turn back, claiming that he was not willing to commit suicide for his passenger, no matter who he was. Luckily for him, Caesar did not have the same temperament or cruelty of a man like Labienus, who probably would have had the man scourged or crucified, no matter how sound his judgment. Fortunately, shortly after this, word arrived that Antonius had at last decided that the winds and conditions were favorable and was embarking the rest of the army, with the goal of landing somewhere on the coast to the south of us.

However, the gods were not through tormenting us by switching their favor back and forth between the two sides, meaning that it was now our turn to be the butt of the gods' joke. To be fair to Antonius, he had his hands full with a raid by a Pompeian named Libo, who rowed right into the harbor at Brundisium to burn several transports. Antonius should have been better prepared to handle such a thrust, but Libo was not much better; after Libo's initial success, Antonius capitalized on his overconfidence. With a force composed of nothing but some rowboats, Antonius managed to lure several of Libo's larger ships back into the Brundisium harbor, where they were set upon and destroyed. This put the enemy on their heel, and having seized the initiative, Antonius decided to take advantage of the favorable winds that had begun to spring up from the south now that the winter was almost over, launching his ships. He carried the rest of the Spanish Legions, the 7th, 9th, and 11th, along with a green Legion and a force of cavalry. However, yet another fleet of Pompey's spotted our fleet and gave chase, forcing Antonius to run before the wind, thereby ending up landing far to the north of where he was supposed to be. In fact, he landed at Lissus, many miles north of Pompey's position, and despite being greeted not as a conqueror but as a savior by the people, we now had the army on the right side of the water, except that it was split in two, with Pompey in between.

~ ~ ~ ~

Because Antonius landed closer to Pompey than Caesar, Pompey was the first to learn of the landing, and wasted no time in sounding the assembly. While the sentries on the ramparts of our camp reported the activity, we had no idea why they were on the move until much later, when a courier sent by Antonius finally reached our camp, having to take a circuitous route that swung inland in order to avoid detection by Pompey. Moments after delivering his message, the *bucina* sounded the call for all Centurions to report to the *Praetorium*, where we were informed of Antonius' landing and given orders to get our respective Cohorts prepared to march the next morning, because the courier had not arrived until close to nightfall and it was too late to march that day. Setting out the next morning, we left five Cohorts of one of the new Legions behind to guard the camp, and it was now a race to see if we could link up with Antonius before Pompey could fall on him, despite Pompey's significant head start in time and distance. Regardless of Pompey's advantage, we were Caesar's men, used to moving quickly and the next morning by dawn we were assembled, ready to march. However, we had the added burden of having to skirt Pompey's camp, where it appeared he had left at least a full Legion behind, along with a substantial force of auxiliaries. Fortunately, some of the Greeks living in the area that were friendly to us raced ahead of Pompey's army to warn Antonius, who had built a fortified camp while he waited for us to join him. Pompey did his best to surprise Antonius; for example, when they stopped for the night, Pompey ordered that no fires be lit to avoid detection, but it did not matter, since Antonius would not budge. We put in a hard march, only stopping for less than a watch to rest, so that soon enough Pompey was in the difficult spot; stuck between two armies, forcing him to withdraw to the southeast. He could not make it back to Dyrrhachium because we blocked his way; consequently, he marched his army to where the Via Egnatia forked with the road down to Apollonia, stopping at the town of Asparagium. Strategically, it gave him the ability to use either road to move quickly, thereby blocking us should Caesar decide to swoop south and attempt to take Dyrrhachium, while also keeping an eye on us in the event Caesar had something else in mind. Despite the fact Caesar now had all of his army together, we were still not out of danger, with further events putting us in even more peril.

~ ~ ~ ~

Word came that Pompey's father-in-law, Scipio, was marching to Pompey with the Syrian Legions, choosing to take the long march overland rather than attempt moving his troops by sea and risk losing them to our warships or foul weather. To keep them from joining Pompey, Caesar sent the 11th, 12th, and a force of 500 cavalry to intercept them. Additionally, he sent the 27th into Thessalia because a delegation had come from there, asking Caesar for his protection. Finally, we needed grain and it had to be foraged, prompting Caesar to take five Cohorts from the tribune Acilius, left behind at Oricum. Oricum was also where part of our fleet was now based, and because he was now shorthanded, Acilius took further precautions to safeguard the fleet by sinking a couple of derelicts in the harbor mouth. Although we recognized the need to provide men for the tasks that Caesar had set for them, none of us liked the idea of whittling down the size of the army. As it was, we were essentially stranded in territory that had been Pompeian for many months before we arrived, and despite being greeted like conquering heroes by the people of the towns we had entered so far, none of us put much faith in the steadfast nature of the Greeks. We would not have been a bit surprised if the towns that opened their gates to us just as quickly closed them if they thought that Pompey held the upper hand. What happened at Oricum did not help that feeling, when Pompey's son Gnaeus in a single raid managed to overcome the obstacles Acilius had put in place, destroying the part of our fleet harbored there. Not content with that, Gnaeus then hurried north to Lissus where Antony's fleet was moored, burning most of the ships there to the waterline. We were well and truly fucked, stuck in Greece even if we wanted to leave and our supply situation just became even more critical now that we had no way of bringing supplies from Italia. I think it was because of these events that Caesar decided to make a move that he hoped would end the war.

~ ~ ~ ~

Within a couple of watches of receiving word of the fleet at Lissus being burned, Caesar ordered us on the march, leading us to a spot just on the other side of the Genusis (Seman) River from where Pompey was camped at Asparagium. Caesar was determined to goad Pompey into doing battle, ordering us into battle formation, where we stood for the better part of a day, but Pompey refused to take the bait. That night,

Caesar called a conference, announcing that his next move was to march on Dyrrhachium.

"My hope is that by moving swiftly, Pompey will be forced either to hurry to Dyrrhachium, where we will face him, or he will abandon it, and give up his supply base. Of the two, I frankly prefer the second option because not only will it deprive Pompey of his supply base, it will solve our own dilemma."

We all saw the sense of what he said. Having received our orders, we dispersed to our respective Legions and Cohorts to get them ready to move in the morning. Because Asparagium was between us and Dyrrhachium, we could not make a direct march, instead first marching westward in the opposite direction of what would be considered the shortest distance, before turning north once we put a range of hills between us and Pompey. Quite naturally, Pompey assumed that the reason we were marching away was because of our supply situation. Consequently, he made no move to follow us, nor did he return to Dyrrhachium for almost half a day. When we turned north, Pompey realized what we were about, whereupon our scouts reported his breaking camp and beginning to move towards Dyrrhachium. We only stopped for perhaps a full watch to rest, not even bothering to make camp but just laying on our gear before resuming the march in the night. Reaching the Arzen River, we turned west to follow it downstream until reaching a ridgeline that pointed towards the coast before following that until the road to Dyrrhachium was visible, with Dyrrhachium to our north. Less than a third of a watch later, we saw Pompey's advance guard approaching from the south; we had beaten them and cut them off from Dyrrhachium.

~ ~ ~ ~

Now, both sides were in difficulty, although we were still in greater peril. Our army was cut off from our supply base across the water, but now Pompey's army was cut off from Dyrrhachium. However, Pompey's problem was more easily solved because he still had control of the sea, and it was a short cruise from Dyrrhachium to his current camp for the ferrying of supplies. Between the two armies was a rushing stream, and with this barrier forestalling an attack, we began fortifying our respective camps. Despite the immediately surrounding area being extremely hilly, there were numerous hill farms where grain was being grown and we knew that there would be a sharp struggle for the food growing there. The only way to have any chance of success in foraging was to keep Pompey's troops at bay, giving us free access to what grain there was available. To accomplish that, once again we began to dig. As we had done at Alesia, Caesar ordered the building of a contravallation, although this would not be as elaborate as at Alesia because we had some help, courtesy of the terrain, there being places where there were hills with such steep escarpments that we could use them as part of the defenses to keep Pompey's army penned in. In effect, what we were to do was to build a series of forts on the tops of these hills, then link the hills with a line of double entrenchments. Although we set immediately to work, Pompey divined what we were about, consequently beginning his own counter-works, with the intent of claiming as much open-grazing land along the coast as he could, since he possessed many times our number of animals, both for use as cavalry and for transport, as well as for food. Thus began a race, with both sides working southward; our goal was to extend the line past Pompey's, curving west to the coast and cutting him off. His goal, of course, was to keep us from doing that. It was grim, hard work, done in shifts through all watches, but after a few days, the shifts stopped. Every man from then on expected to work to his utmost before staggering off to snatch perhaps a watch's worth of sleep before returning.

While I and the other officers did not do much actual digging, we were expected to be present whenever any of our men were working, along with attending the briefings that were held every morning, meaning that sleep was in even shorter supply for us. Nevertheless, I had to set an example for the men, making the idea of acting like I was tired simply out of the question. I made sure I shaved every morning, a task I had long since stopped performing myself, having Zeno do it, one of the few luxuries of rank in which I indulged. The first couple of days before I got used to the onerous job again, I looked like I had been in a skirmish after each shave, coming out the worse for it with nicks and cuts all over my cheeks and jaw. The men thought this hilarious, and while normally I would have smacked them for their impudence, I saw that it helped morale, so I took the ribbing with as much grace as I could muster. Day by day, foot by foot, the work continued on the double line, although not without some excitement, with Pompey sending out sorties on a regular basis to try disrupting our work. Of course we did the same, and finally the time came when my Cohort was selected to go raiding the Pompeian lines. It was an opportunity we welcomed, although not for the reason one might suspect. It was less about the chance at glory and finally doing battle than it was a break from the monotony of digging, at least where the men were concerned, making for an added element to the normally charged atmosphere in our Cohort area the evening before the raid as the men made their preparations. It was almost like we were going on parade; I found myself quite at a loss because the men turned to making their equipment ready with such zeal that I essentially had nothing to do. Seeing almost immediately there was no need for the *vitus*, instead I strode down the lines of our tents; to a man, they were all bent over their armor, scrubbing furiously, restoring the shine and getting the last specks of rust off of them. Or they were honing their swords; the men from the Century long ago designated as armorers bent over a pile of blades, working each one of them before handing them to their owner, who would then go through their own ritual of sharpening the blade, usually just before the call to assemble to go into battle. The shields were being attended to as well; bosses polished, paint touched up on the Legion emblem, the finished ones standing in a line in front of each tent, ready for my inspection. I do not think I could have been any prouder of my Cohort than I was at that moment. Here were true professionals, men who did not need the *vitus* across their backs, knowing what needed to be done because they knew that part of the battle was in the details being attended to at that moment. It may sound simple, perhaps even silly, to think that shining armor or a polished helmet would make a difference in battle, but it does. It makes a great deal of difference because it shows not just the enemy but their fellow Legionaries that they are proud of the job they do, making them fight harder because they do not want to let their comrades down, and knowing all the hard work that went into preparing for that moment of battle. This is one of the secrets that made us, the armies of Rome, so formidable and impossible to defeat, at least on a regular basis. Of course, this time I could not banish the thought from my mind that across the open ground between the two lines were men doing the exact same thing. Maybe not at that moment, and probably not directly across from us; the odds of both commanders picking the exact same spot to send men across in a raid at the exact same time were too high to waste time contemplating. Nevertheless, I knew that whether or not they were actually performing the same ritual that we were at that moment, the instant they saw my Cohort marching across the open ground, they would understand why we looked like we were standing for inspection.

The sound of a throat clearing interrupted my thoughts, and I turned to see Celer standing at *intente*.

"Yes?"

"Pilus Prior, I was wondering if you wanted the men to wear their plumes?"

I thought for a moment, then nodded. "Yes, why not? If we're going to get prettied up, there's no need in doing it halfway. We'll let Pompey see what real Legionaries look like, right?" Celer nodded, like he was expressing his approval of my decision and I swallowed my irritation, trying to keep my voice even. "Give the order, Celer."

"Very good, sir."

He saluted and marched off. I knew that he would make sure the men got the impression that it was his idea, but I shrugged it off. I could only worry about so much, and by this time I was feeling fairly comfortable in my command of the Cohort. Turning back to my examination of the ground over which we would be marching in the morning, I looked for any obstacles, mentally plotting the best course over which to cross. Straining to see if I could spot the telltale bulk of artillery dotting the palisade of the hillfort that was our objective, I could not see anything suspicious, not that it meant anything at this distance. Well, I thought, we will find out one way or another in the morning.

~ ~ ~ ~

I was up before dawn, grumbling to myself about having to don my own gear and feed myself for the fiftieth time since we had landed. Pullus, I thought wryly, you have gone soft. Here you are bitching like a patrician about having to shave, dress, and feed yourself. By the light of the oil lamp in my tent, I went through my own pre-battle ritual, doing things in the exact same way that I had done them since the morning of the first battle back in Hispania those 13 years before. We soldiers are a superstitious lot, and despite being less so than most, I still was not willing to tempt the fates by altering what had worked so many times previously. Consequently, I pulled on my boots, left foot first, wrapping the thongs with the left over the right, opposite of the way most men I knew did it, but that first morning in Hispania, in my haste I had reversed the order and therefore had stuck to doing it that way ever since. Taking my armor off the stand, I dropped it over my head, the weight of it feeling like a comforting hand draped over my shoulders as I strapped on my belt, again doing things exactly the same way as always, then attached my sword, nestled in my scabbard, to the belt. I drew the Gallic blade, having spent an entire third of a watch sharpening it the night before like I always did, carefully inspecting it, despite my head knowing that nothing could have happened to it in the scant time I was asleep. Still, it was what I always did, so I did it again. Finally, I picked up my helmet, critically eying the transverse crest, making sure that it was spotless. I would not don that until I stepped out of the tent, mainly because with my height the top of the crest would brush the roof of the tent and get dirty from all the soot that collected on the roof. Picking up my *vitus*, I stood for a moment, letting my thoughts settle and my mind focus on what lay ahead, ignoring the churning in my stomach. Actually, that is not true; I did not ignore it, I welcomed it as an old friend, because it told me that my body was readying itself for battle. I remember wondering to myself if there would ever be a day where I did not have that feeling, and if I did, whether it would be a good thing or a bad thing. You think too much, I chided myself, stepping out and taking a deep breath of the cool air, tasting the salty tang carried by the breeze from the sea just a couple miles away.

The call to start the day had not sounded and most of the army was asleep, so I was gratified to see there was already a lot of activity in the Cohort, the men going through their own last-moment preparations. Our orders were to be in place and ready to begin the assault immediately before sunrise, with the goal of reaching the hillfort just when the sun was topping the hills behind us. This would put the sun in the eyes of the Pompeians, giving us an advantage as we made the assault. That was the hope anyway, but a part of me was aware that it would also mean that we would be sharply outlined, just like targets at the javelin range. Nothing to be done about it, I thought, filling my lungs to roar out the command to assemble. We would not be using the *bucina* or even the *cornu*, since the sounds of horns would carry too far. Before I actually bellowed out the order, I stopped myself. Most of my life I have been chided for having a voice that could be heard for miles; when I was a child Gaia was always scolding me about yelling too loudly indoors and how the neighbors could hear, something I thought was quite funny since they were a couple of miles away. Having a voice that could break rock had served me well in the army, but now I thought better of using it. While it was not likely that my voice would carry the more than a mile to the enemy lines, it was still very quiet and it did not make sense to take the risk. Instead, I walked down the line, calling in what I considered my quiet voice for the Centurions of the Cohort. Once they had all arrived, I was pleased to see that they were already dressed and ready to go, with one exception, and that exception was Celer. He was still wearing just his tunic, and I tried to hide my glee at having caught him out.

"Well, Celer," I said in what I hoped was the right combination of joviality and mocking condescension, "I do apologize for rousing you from your beauty rest." I paused, relishing the laughter of the others. Even in the gloom, I could see the flush rising from the neck of his tunic. "However, if you don't mind, I was wondering if I could impose on you gentlemen to quietly get your men formed up. It looks like the boys are already spoiling to go, with one exception, of course."

I looked at Celer and was about to add a comment that perhaps he was not ready because he was not as keen as his men to get after the enemy, but quickly realized that this would be too far over the line, and bit it back. Instead, I waited for them to give their acknowledgment of my orders, gratified to see Celer absolutely sprinting back to his tent to don his gear. I could not help feeling a bit smug at catching him unprepared. That will show you, I thought, smiling to myself as I walked to report to Crastinus that we were forming up. All was right with the world.

~ ~ ~ ~

The men assembled quickly, and I understood that while I did not need to, my failure to go through with an inspection would be taken as an insult. They had spent time that they could have been sleeping or otherwise enjoying themselves making sure that they were turned out in a manner that would bring credit to their Pilus Prior, so for me not to acknowledge that would be as close to giving each of them a slap in the face as I could get. Therefore, despite my impatience to get us marching, I walked through each Century, spending a moment here to point out some imaginary speck of dust, a moment there to share a joke with one of the men. While I believe in discipline as much as any Centurion, I also believe that there are times when it pays to lighten the mood a bit, and I always found that the proper time for that was just before men were about to go off and possibly die. I wanted men to fight for me because they wanted to, not because they feared the consequences, although if forced to, I would use fear, like I had to with Figulus. Speaking of Figulus, that day, when I stood in front of him and inspected him, I praised his efforts, commending him for having gone above and beyond with his gear, loudly proclaiming that he was by far the most outstanding of the men I had inspected to that point. In truth, he was no better or worse than any of the other men, but I wanted to reinforce that what I did to him those months ago was not personal, that I had not been out to get him, and I was rewarded by the look of surprise and pleasure on his face as I stepped away. Almost a third of a watch had passed, the sky beginning to glow pink over the eastern hills when I stepped to the front of the Cohort. Suddenly, I was struck by the thought that the inspection should have taken much longer, but did not because I ran out of men to inspect. I currently had seven men on the sick list, and despite it still being the lowest in the Legion, that meant that there were barely 290 effectives, and that number would probably be lower in just a short while. It saddened me to think about that but I pushed it from my mind, giving the order to move out.

Marching out of the gate of the camp, we crossed the portable bridge that was thrown across the ditch for sorties like ours, with the men from the other Cohorts standing to the side and wishing us luck. They knew the score as well as we all did; they were aware that some of their friends would not be coming back whole, or at all. Still, the men were in good spirits by the way they marched, shoulders back, their chins up, ready to get after the men who hopefully did not know we were coming....yet. But they would soon enough.

~ ~ ~ ~

The ground we marched over was fairly level but was broken and choppy, making maintaining a parade ground precision as we marched next to impossible. Moving along, I could see my shadow grow more and more defined, stretching out before me, making me look like I was 20 feet tall. We were at a point in the line where our works had bulged outward in order to be aligned with the hills, so despite the distance between our works at most points being about a half mile, we had almost a mile to cover. Our mission was to attack the hillfort that at this position was anchoring the southernmost end of Pompey's works, since he was still trying to extend his own line of entrenchments. His progress was such that he had extended his entrenchments from the hillfort we were assaulting only a couple of hundred feet. Therefore, our plan was to circle around the end of the entrenchments to hit the hillfort from the side, gambling that the fortifications would not be as formidable as from the direct front. Besides inflicting casualties on the Pompeian workforce, our other goal was to destroy the engineering equipment that would undoubtedly be housed in the fort, along with any artillery we found. It was the artillery I was worried about the most, particularly if they had ballistae, since just a few missiles flying through our ranks could tear us apart. That was another reason we were circling around, because it was highly unlikely that if there was artillery it would be deployed on the flanks of the fort. It also meant that speed was of the essence; the faster we covered the ground once we were in range, the less time under fire, and I cursed at the unevenness of the ground. The bad footing really was going to hamper our assault once we picked up the pace. Not only would it slow us down, it was already wreaking havoc with our cohesion, and I continually scanned the bulk of the fort, trying to spot the telltale shape of artillery. Although my mind knew we were closing the distance, my eyes were telling me that we seemed to be marching in place, the fort not seeming to get appreciably closer, and I was thankful at least that the sun was now directly behind us, making it almost impossible for their sentries to spot our advance. Even as that thought passed through my mind, I saw something that made my heart freeze; my shadow was growing dimmer! Risking a glance back, my stomach now joined in the tumult at seeing a large bank of clouds sliding inexorably across the sun.

~ ~ ~ ~

Almost instantly, I heard the thin cry of alarm from the sentry on the wall of the fort, followed immediately by the blaring of their *bucina*, the detached part of my brain struck by the irony that they used the same calls that we did to sound the alarm. Taking another look back, I saw the grim faces of the men of the First Century, my eyes meeting those of Vibius, marching in the last rank on the outside of the First Century, the first in the formation. Giving me a grimace, he shrugged his shoulders as if to say, we're in the *cac* now, what can we do about it? He was right of course; this was how the dice had come up, now all we could do was let them ride and see who Fortuna favored.

Turning back to the fort, I saw a flurry of movement as a number of men clustered together, and now that we were close enough, I could tell that they were huddled around something. Recognizing the shape, I let out a string of curses; it was a ballista. Scanning the rest of the rampart, I was thankful that it appeared that there was only one, although one was bad enough. We were still marching in column; my plan was to keep us this way for as long as possible, since it allowed us to cover ground more quickly. I was counting on the experience of the men, so that when I finally gave the command, the pause in our forward progress when we deployed into line would be minimal. With that moment rapidly approaching, I needed to make a number of decisions. If they had slingers, then the manual called for the formation of *testudo* by Centuries, since even lead shot is not strong enough to penetrate our shields. The problem was that with a ballista present, forming a *testudo* was suicide; the heavy iron bolt would not only penetrate through shields, it would pierce several men, and having the men huddled together meant that any hit by the catapult would result in multiple casualties. However, if I dispersed the men into an open formation, despite the fact that it would minimize the casualties from any hit by the iron bolts, it also meant that the men would more or less be on their own, defending themselves from the slings. They would not have the protection of the man to their right whose shield covered his vulnerable side, forcing them to keep their eyes open and prepared to try dodging the slingshot. Although no slingers had appeared as of that moment, Pompey's army was well known for its extensive use of the sling, a weapon that we in Caesar's army were not particularly fond of, just as we hated archers. I thought it was a safe bet that before long there would be men standing on the ramparts of the hillfort, whirling their leather slings over their heads. We were not yet in sling range, but I could see the ballista being prepared to fire, making the decision for me. Giving the commands to move from column to line, followed by the one to open ranks, there was no missing the looks of surprise on the faces of the men, but they reacted instantly, spreading out, with the other Centuries wheeling into place. Starting out, I ordered that we advance in a line of five Centuries, with the Sixth in reserve, and because of their respective placement, the maneuver went smoothly. We advanced just a few more paces when the thwack of the ballista firing its first bolt sounded clearly in the morning air. The Pompeians aimed directly at me, and I did not even have time to react as the bolt shot by me no more than a full arm's length away. It felt like an invisible hand slapped my face as it flashed by, making a whirring sound, and before I could even flinch I heard a sickening thud, followed by a sharp cry as the bolt meant for me hit another man instead. I turned to see that it was Figulus, the bolt going through his right arm just above the elbow, practically severing it, the limb hanging by little more than a shred of muscle. He stood staring down at his useless arm, blood spurting out in a spray that pulsed rhythmically with every beat of his heart. I knew that if someone did not tie the arm off immediately he would bleed to death, but I could not worry about Figulus; there were another 292 men still whole and marching forward. And in truth, it might be a mercy if Figulus did bleed to death. His time in the Legions was now done, finished in the amount of time it took for that bolt to leave the catapult, and now he would receive only a pittance of his pension, although like all of us he had gotten rich in Gaul. If, that was, he had not gambled, drank and whored it all away, which was fairly likely. Turning away, I shouted to Scribonius to attend to Figulus, then fall back in. Luckily, the bolt that passed through Figulus had not hit anyone else, and I thanked the gods for that small favor. Continuing forward, the Centurions and Optios were roaring at men ranging too far ahead of their line, or falling too far back. Meanwhile, I saw a line of men arraying themselves along the palisade of the hillfort. Approaching sling range, I called out the warning to my Century, the other Centurions doing the same for theirs. This was where it would get interesting, I thought, but there was nothing to be done about it now. We were marching directly at the hillfort, coming to the point where I was going to order a shift to an oblique angle, aiming for the spot where the Pompeians had left off the entrenching work the previous day. Once we made the turn, I would have to give the order to increase speed to double time, because it would then become clear what our intentions were. From that point, it would be a race to see if we could get behind the trench to attack the fort from its vulnerable side. On the parapet, the arms of the men began to whirl around, building up the momentum needed to launch their slings.

"Watch out, boys," I heard someone cry out, and I snapped at them to shut their mouths, cursing myself for giving in to the pressure I was feeling.

The near miss with the bolt had badly unnerved me; while it was not the first time we in Caesar's army had faced our own artillery, it was the first time the Second Cohort was exposed to it, and not surprisingly, I liked it not at all. The first volley of slingshot was released, a blur of movement coming streaking towards us, slow enough that our eyes tracked the movement, but too fast for us to do anything about it. The air around me was split with what sounded like thousands of angry bees, and I held the shield I had drawn from stores over as much of my body as I could, cursing my large size. There was a loud cracking sound and I felt a tremendous impact on the upper portion of my shield as one of the shot hit it. The force was akin to someone hitting my shield with a hammer and I felt my arm go a bit numb. Behind me were similar sounds, punctuated by the different thudding sound of some of the shot striking flesh, followed immediately by screams of pain and calls for help from comrades who could not stop for them. It was always this way during an assault like this, and we all knew that once hit, we were essentially on our own until the slaves and clerks who worked as stretcher bearers, or the *medici* themselves came up behind the Legion. Yet for some reason, that never stopped men from calling out for help, sometimes prompting a man to risk violating orders to stop and help a particularly close friend. Looking back to make a quick check, I saw we had been lucky that first volley, with only a couple of men down. When I scanned down the line to see how the other Centuries fared, it appeared to be about the same. We were at the extreme range of the slings, meaning the next volley would undoubtedly do more damage. Still, we had to endure at least one more volley because we needed to get closer before giving the command to change direction, and I clenched my teeth as I saw the slingers begin to wind up for their next barrage. Again, we were lashed by shot, this time with my shield hit twice, followed by more cries of pain and fear around me as more men were hit. Regardless, we kept marching forward, reaching the point where I issued the command to turn to the left a half-turn, followed immediately by the command to double time. The catapult fired twice more, but I could not tell what the damage was, just thankful that they had shifted their aim and were not shooting at me. Making the turn as quickly as I had hoped, we began to trot, and across the remaining distance, I heard the cries of alarm as the Pompeians saw what we were about to do. Now the race was on.

~ ~ ~ ~

We closed the distance quickly, but it also meant that the range for the slingers was shortening as well, although it was not all good news for them, since now that we were running, we were harder to hit. Our faster step also meant that we could not use our shields as effectively as when marching at our normal pace either, yet speed was now vital, so we would have to take whatever losses came our way. The Pompeian Centurions were now shouting orders and we were close enough to hear them calling for the men on the parapet facing us to shift to the threatened side. The Pompeians obeyed, stopping their onslaught with the slings. Running at the head of my Century, I had placed us on the left to put us closest to the gap, and now when we went from column to line, the other Centuries were required to run across the face of the fort to follow us. That meant the cessation of the sling fire was a good piece of luck, because the trailing Centuries' flanks were now exposed. Turning to give the order to close ranks back up, as I did so I saw that there were a number of bodies marking our progress, and I bit back a curse. The men closed together on the run just as, in the lead, I reached the leading edge of the ditch, turning parallel to run the hundred feet or so to where the ditch ended. We had not been running long, but I was already feeling winded and I worried at the state of the men, since it is no easy thing to conduct an assault when you are huffing and puffing. Reaching the end of the ditch, I turned past it, and it was only then that I stopped for a moment, directing the men as they moved past me to form back into a more cohesive line. We would have to pause, but it could not be long enough to allow the enemy time to shift enough men to the weak side of the fort, at least so I hoped. Some of my men carried poles with iron hooks attached that they would use to pull down a section of the palisade in order to make our breach there. I was pleased to see that as I suspected, the Pompeians expended most of their time and energy on fortifying the side of the fort that faced directly across from our lines; on this side, it was nothing but a turf wall and palisade, with the ditch only deep enough to construct a spoil of perhaps four feet high. There were men on this part of the wall, and I could see that it would not be nearly enough to stop us, but only if we hurried. Thinking rapidly, I made a decision; I would not wait for the rest of the Cohort, and the men would have to go in without a chance to rest.

"First Century, advance!"

I almost smiled at the startled expressions, but I was proud to see that there was no hesitation, and no grumbling. I think they understood that our best chance was to strike quickly, and they immediately began marching forward. The men with the hooks were ordered to pass them forward, but we had gone only a few paces when I heard a command that chilled my bones.

"Prepare javelins!"

We were about to experience what all the tribes of Gaul had come to fear, and my mind raced. Then I roared out my own command.

"*Porro!*"

There was no sense in waiting for the volley to land, and the faster we crossed the distance the less chance they would have to throw a second volley. Nonetheless, the sky became streaked with black lines and in the instant before the javelins landed, I had time to thank the gods that there were still just a handful of men throwing them. Still, I heard the thud from a few shields being struck, but thankfully, there were no cries of men being hit, just curses of men forced to drop their shield. Running full speed now, we began roaring out our general's name as we came pounding up to the wall. Immediately, the hooks were passed to the front, and men began yanking at the palisade stakes, while the men on the rampart tried desperately to stop them. Now it was time for a taste of their own medicine, as I ordered the rear two ranks to launch their own javelins, and I was heartened to hear the cries of men being struck down.

"That's it, boys," I roared. "Kill the bastards!"

My cry was met with the roar of the men, their blood now up, as we were committed to killing or being killed.

~ ~ ~ ~

The Pompeians on the parapet fought desperately, stabbing down at my men who were furiously yanking at the palisade stakes with their hooks, but not enough Pompeians had arrived to stop our assault and in a matter of moments, a number of stakes were pulled up. Our men then turned their attention to the turf wall, using the hooks to grab at the squares of sod stacked up. This was more difficult, with the Pompeians standing on the sod, and it quickly became clear that we were not going to be able to bring down the rest of the wall before more of Pompey's men arrived. I knew what had to be done, and before I could talk myself out of it, I drew my Gallic sword as I ran to the breach, pushing my men out of the way.

Pausing just long enough to look over my shoulder, I waved my blade and shouted, "Follow me, you bastards! Do you want to live forever?"

"*Yes!*"

Several men shouted this at me but I still did not wait, climbing up onto the parapet, thankful that it was not higher. Even so, I was forced to scramble up the wall, using my shield for leverage, but just before I got to the top, my foot caught on something and I found myself sprawling headlong into one of the Pompeians, saving my life. Since I was so tangled up with the Pompeian Legionary, a thin older man whose breath was one of the rankest smells I had ever encountered, it stayed the hands of his comrades, who did not want to strike him down by accident. Rolling around in a heap, he was snarling curses in my ear as I struggled with him, his left hand clamping down powerfully on my right wrist, preventing me from using my blade. Utilizing my greater weight, I muscled him off me, but before he could bring his own sword up, I smashed his face in with the boss of my shield. Hearing the bones in his face crunch as he let out a gurgling cry, I rolled off him, scrambling to my feet, making ready to defend myself. Immediately my arm shivered with the shock of a blow that I blocked with my shield, another man similar in age and stature to my first opponent lunging forward in his place. He too was clearly a veteran because he did not overextend his thrust, instead recovering quickly from his blow, ready for a counterstroke. Immediately, he was joined by another Legionary at his side and now I was in trouble, unless help arrived. Moving to put the palisade to my back, I still had to watch to my left side. The two men were approaching from my right, yet I did not sense anyone else out of my peripheral vision coming from the opposite side. Regardless, these men were very good, as the instant they saw my eyes flicker to my flank, one of them lunged immediately, his blade snaking inside my shield to strike me a glancing blow in the ribs, my armor doing its job of preventing it from penetrating. The wind rushed from my lungs, accompanied by a searing pain that took my breath away even further, whereupon it was the second man's turn to make a thrust that I barely parried with my own blade. As good as I was, and the gods know I am not boasting when I say I was very, very good, I still could not last forever against two such skilled opponents, and the thought flitted through my mind that perhaps my time had come. This idea filled me with a desperate rage, and bellowing a roar, I lashed out, relying on my superior strength to muscle both men off me to give me some room to operate. They reeled back, but both of them recovered quickly, my momentary advantage disappearing as quickly as it had come. Working as a team, they now lunged forward, both of their blades flashing like the tongues of a serpent, flicking at my defenses, looking for a weak spot. Desperately, I used both shield and blade to defend myself, but I knew my life was measured in a few heartbeats. Then, as I peered over the edge of the shield during a momentary pause, I saw the eyes of one of the men widen in shock, blood suddenly gushing from his mouth before he collapsed to the ground, the figure of Scribonius appearing behind him. His partner's head whipped around to locate the new threat, giving me all the opening I needed for my blade to punch through his throat and out the back of his neck. I would have thanked Scribonius for saving me, but there was no time, and had the situation been opposite, he knew I would do the same for him. Only a matter of a moment had passed, but there were still only two of us yet on the parapet and I turned my attention back to the larger situation, now that I was out of immediate danger. More Pompeians were running along the parapet at the front of the fort, making their way over to our side.

Needing more of our men up here, I called out, "Vibius, where in Hades are you? Get your short ass up here and give me a hand!"

Before the words were completely out of my mouth, I had to turn back to face one of the Pompeians, giving a start when I realized that I was facing a fellow Centurion. He was a short, squat fellow, with a lined face that reminded me of Crastinus and again I was struck at the tragedy in which we were involved. If my adversary felt any hesitation as I did, he did not show it as he unleashed a lightning attack, lashing out at me with his own shield. Landing a grazing blow, it still carried enough force behind it to stagger me, but I managed to strike out with my own blade, seeing that I scored a hit as he hissed in pain, a red line appearing just beneath the edge of his armor on his upper arm. It was not a deep cut, but it would make him more cautious, and he took a step back as he looked for an opening. Out of the corner of my eye, I could see more of my men clambering up onto the parapet, with the sound of fighting growing louder, but I was still occupied with my personal battle. Seeing one of the recent arrivals on the parapet start moving towards the Centurion, I shouted at them to stop.

"Leave him be; he's all mine."

I heard a curse, the voice familiar, but I gave it no more thought as I lunged towards the Pompeian, who whipped his shield around to block my thrust, exactly what I had hoped for, my thrust a feint without my full force behind it. For an instant, his shield was out of position, and my feint aimed low, as he dropped it just a fraction to block, leaving a gap where his throat was exposed. Whipping the blade up, as it thrust home, our eyes met and I saw the despair in them, along with the knowledge that he was bested. Usually I felt a fierce exultation when I killed a man in combat, but I felt nothing but sadness at ending the Centurion's life. He toppled off the parapet, leaving me to stand there motionless for a moment, absorbed in sorrow that matters had come to this. If any of the Pompeians had their wits about them, they could have ended me right then, but the death of their Centurion shook them as much as it had me, and like me, they remained motionless staring at him for a moment before I heard my name called.

"Titus, you better pull your head out of your ass," I looked up sharply at those words that could have earned a man a flogging to see Vibius standing there, looking uncertainly at me. Shaking my head, I shoved him with an elbow and quietly said, "Thanks," then pushed past him.

We had made a breach, but we were not done by a long shot.

~ ~ ~ ~

The Pompeians had lost control of the parapet on this side, yet we still had to clear the side where the ballista was located, and I saw the Pompeians desperately trying to pull up the stakes that stabilized the piece so that they could turn it on us. The Second Century had arrived at the breach, but I saw that our opening was too narrow to feed the rest of the Cohort in with any speed. Once the Second poured through the gap, where I directed them to head for the catapult, I stopped the Third Century, pointing to another spot in the palisade.

"Open a breach there," I directed, then indicated another spot, ordering the Fourth Century to attack that.

Finally, I turned to the *bucinator* and ordered him to sound the call for the Sixth Century to come to join us. I still planned to keep them in reserve, but I wanted them closer. Returning my attention back to the fight, I saw that the Pompeians were themselves busy; in the small forum of the fort, they were gathering quickly, men either coming from other parts of the wall or disengaging from the fight if they were able to trot back to where their Centurions were calling for them. Scanning the inside of the redoubt, I estimated that they had perhaps half a Cohort, seeing only two Centurions, the third lying dead at my feet. The only problem was that it appeared that they were close to full strength, meaning that they had almost as many men as we did. Despite killing or wounding quite a few, there were still a lot of them left, and we could not allow them to get organized.

"Niger, hurry your men up, we don't have all day for you to avoid getting dirty. Tear those stakes down now!"

His face flushed with anger, but he simply nodded, turning to his men and snapping at them to hurry. I had to get as many of my men into the fort as quickly as possible and I strode further down the parapet to where the Third was doing the same, although they were making better progress, those men beginning to stream through the breach they created. The remaining Pompeians were almost formed up by this point, and I needed to have a force ready to meet them. Yelling to Longus and Priscus, most of their Centuries making it inside the fort, I ordered them to form up at the base of the parapet and prepare to face the counterattack of the Pompeians. The Second was engaged around the ballista, and it appeared that they were gaining the upper hand. I turned my attention to the group of men that were now tramping towards us, their shields thrust out in front of them as they approached. Staying on the parapet to see better, I recognized that there were times where I best served the Cohort when I did not lead from the front and this was one of those times. This was still something I was learning, but it was extremely hard to do. Even by that point in time, I was still nagged by a sense of insecurity, fueled by men like Celer that I was not up to the job of leading a Cohort. At moments like this, when I had to make the choice not to lead from the front did not help, but I had to do what was best for the Cohort. This was one of those times, so instead I stood and directed the men in front of me.

"Priscus," I called out, pointing to the Pompeians. "Stop them," I shouted. "Cut those bastards to pieces!"

He nodded, throwing a salute before he turned back to his men. "You heard the Pilus Prior, boys," he roared. "Let's get 'em!"

With a shout, the men of the Second Cohort ran headlong towards the Pompeians, who began their own countercharge. Even from where I stood, I felt the force of the collision as the two groups smashed into each other. Each man went at the one across from them, and for a moment, I could almost imagine that this was nothing more than a training exercise, when we would engage in mock battles against each other, so familiar was the sight of Roman on Roman. Soon enough, however, I saw men fall horribly wounded or dead, and I could not fool myself any longer. The best course for my Cohort was to get this fight over as quickly as possible, with as much overwhelming force as I could bring to bear, prompting me to turn to where Crispus was standing with the Sixth Century, ordering them to enter the fray. Niger's Century had finally made their way through their breach. I beckoned to him and he walked towards me, his body stiff with anger.

Ignoring his attitude, I pointed towards the rear of the fort, the side facing the sea and ordered him, "Take your Century around along the back of the fort and circle around and hit those bastards down there from behind. When you're in position, have your *cornu* give a blast. Then wait for my return signal."

He nodded that he understood and saluted, turning to trot back to his Century. I hoped that my rebuke was enough to ensure that he did not take his time getting his Century into position, since every moment that passed meant that more of our men were getting hurt, or worse. Turning back to the fight, I bit back a curse, not wanting to betray any sense of anxiety to the *cornicen* and runner standing next to me, but we were not making any headway. The fight was at a stalemate, neither side inflicting any more casualties or giving ground, despite Priscus being prominent in the front rank, cursing at the enemy and his men. Even with the addition of Crispus' Century, the enemy was holding their own. It seemed the only way to break the deadlock was through Niger, and now we had to wait for him to get into position. Glancing over to where Celer and his Century were mopping up the last resistance on the front parapet, it looked like he was just about through with his part of the job. The parapet was littered with bodies, but from the distance I was standing, it was impossible to tell friend from foe, all of us being dressed alike, so I had no idea what his casualties were.

Turning to the runner, I said, "My compliments to Pilus Posterior Celer. Tell him that if his Century is still able to fight, I want him to circle around the opposite side of where Niger is." I pointed to the standard that we could just see bobbing over the line of tents that blocked the men from our view. "When he gets in the same position as Niger on his side, tell him to sound the signal that he's ready. Then he's to wait for my signal. Understand?"

As is our custom, the runner repeated the orders back to me word for word before running across the parapet to relay the orders to Celer. We still had some equipment to destroy, but first we had to get rid of the men defending the fort. Hopefully, we would be done in the next few moments.

~ ~ ~ ~

Recognizing that I had done all I could do at this point, now I was forced to wait for Celer and Niger to get into place, while I could only watch the rest of my men fighting it out below. There were now four Centuries committed to the fight in the fort, but the Pompeians had their own reinforcements, when survivors of the fight for the parapet, realizing their cause was lost, broke away and went streaming towards the mass of men in the forum, joining the fight on the other side. Consequently, things were still close to evenly matched, with neither side able to gain the upper hand. The sounds of the battle were dying down at a rate equal to the gradual loss of energy. The men were now content to push against each other, snarling and cursing their opponents' ancestors, mothers, and anything else they could think of before making a token thrust at each other that held little of the force behind it that was present just a few moments earlier. In short, the men were nearing exhaustion and this interlude would end only when one side caught their second wind, or something else happened to break the stalemate. It was then that I heard the blast of the *cornu,* coming from the side of the camp where I had sent Niger, and I could just see the standard dip to signal that they waited for the response from me. However, I was not ready to unleash them yet, because I wanted Celer to be in position as well, so I held the *cornicen* in check while we waited. The blast of the horn caused the Pompeians in the rear rank to start looking back anxiously, but from their position on the floor of the fort, they could not see our men approaching, so they reluctantly turned back to the front, although I could see some of them continually peering over their shoulders. Scanning the area where I thought Celer's Century should be, I searched for the sight of his standard. It took me some time to spot it bobbing along, and seeing it nowhere near the spot I hoped they had reached by that point, for the thousandth time that morning alone, I cursed. It was taking them much too long, and even as that thought crossed my mind, I heard another blast of the *cornu* from Niger's Century. Now there was no doubt that the Pompeians had a force behind them, and the back two ranks whirled around to face the new threat. Snapping at my *cornicen* to sound the charge, not willing to wait for Celer any longer, I also told the player to sound the charge a second time, the moment Celer signaled he was in position, then pulled my blade and leaped down from the parapet. I could not take standing there any longer, and now the die was cast. It was time for me to get back in the fight.

~ ~ ~ ~

The sound of Niger's Century's roar as they charged, energized, the men already engaged, on both sides, all of them knowing that the end was near, one way or another. With renewed vitality, we began laying into the Pompeians, who responded with equal vigor, realizing that they were effectively surrounded. Striding to the front of the melee, I pushed men out of the way, and just before I reached the front, I heard the blast from Celer, followed immediately by the signal to charge from my player. Thrusting myself into the front rank, I began laying into the man in front of me and he fell to my blade in a few strokes. Celer and Niger's men were howling at the top of their lungs, but the men surrounding me were mostly silent, not wanting to waste any excess energy, as were the Pompeians. The only sound in our part of the fight was the clashing of metal and the thudding of blades striking the wood of the shields, punctuated by grunts, gasps, and moans when men were struck down.

This was nothing like our battles with the Gauls, with the howling madness and the raging fury that their race displays. This was a brutal fight between professionals; two highly trained units who waged war because it was our jobs. I found it quite unnerving to fight in almost total silence, but it did not stop me from killing whoever stood in my way. Because of my rank and my size, I drew more than my share of attention and I had my hands full, but I was well protected by the men around me, covering my sword arm as I thrust, parried, recovered, all while doing the same for the man on my left. The Pompeians were now being squeezed from two sides, and I could see that our line was starting to overlap the ends of the Pompeian lines. Shouting a quick order to Priscus to swing a couple of sections down onto one flank of the Pompeians, I then ordered Longus to do the same on the other.

In immediate response, the lone surviving Centurion of the Pompeians bellowed out, "Form *orbis!*"

This is the formation of last resort for a Roman Legion, and it told me that the end was near if we could keep up the pressure. However, it also meant that they planned to fight to the last man, a prospect that I did not relish, for my men and for the Pompeians. I had no desire to slaughter such brave men, nor to lose the men it would take to do so, so I made a quick decision, signaling for my runner.

~ ~ ~ ~

The *cornu* sounded the order to suspend the attack, but it took a couple of blasts before all the fighting stopped. Once our men disengaged, they took wary steps backwards, their shields still held in position, blades ready to resume the attack, but the Pompeians did not press, understanding what the call of the *cornu* meant and seemingly content for a breather.

I turned to the man next to me, "Do you have anything white? A bandage maybe?"

He looked at me as if I had grown a third eye, but nervously shook his head. Irritated, I turned around, shouting for someone to produce something to be used as a flag of truce, and it was a moment before I saw something passed through the ranks and handed to me. I looked at it in disgust; it would be extremely charitable to refer to the soiled bandage in my hands as white, but it would have to do.

Picking up a spent javelin, I stuck it on the end, holding it up and stepping into the space between our two forces, calling out, "I propose a truce and I request to speak to the commanding officer."

It was relatively easy to spot who that was, there being only one man left standing wearing the transverse crest of the Centurion, and the Pompeian men immediately looked to him. Reluctantly, he stepped forward, pushing through his men to stand facing me a few feet away. I was surprised to see that he was somewhere around my age. I had become accustomed to being one of the youngest Centurions in Caesar's army, making it rare to see someone like me in the uniform of a Centurion. He was clearly a man who had seen fighting, having a long, vividly red scar running up the length of his sword arm. Standing stiffly, he waited for me to speak, and I cleared my throat, knowing that what I had to say was as much for his men as for himself.

"I am Secundus Pilus Prior Titus Pullus, of the Tenth Legion," I said clearly, hoping that my voice did not hold the tremor that I felt. A lot was riding on my ability to convince this man that it was useless to keep fighting. "Who am I addressing?"

He did not speak for a moment, then grudgingly answered, "I am Decimus Princeps Prior Quintus Albinus, of Pompey's First Legion."

Raising an eyebrow, I turned back to my men, saying with a smile, "Funny, I thought that the Legions belonged to Rome, not one man."

This was met with chuckles from my men, but Albinus apparently did not find it humorous.

"Pompey Magnus is Rome," he snapped. "And you are traitors to the Republic."

There was a low growl behind me, and I knew that if I did not do something quickly, my attempts at avoiding further bloodshed would be for naught.

Stepping closer to Albinus, I said so that only he could hear, "Quiet, you idiot! I'm trying to save your life!"

"Don't worry about my life," he shot back. "I'm happy to die today if I can take more of you bastards with me!"

I looked him in the eye, saying quietly, "Do they feel the same way?" With a jerk of my head, I indicated the men behind them. Before he could answer, I continued. "And don't you have a duty to your men as much as you do to Pompey?"

I saw the doubt in his eyes, and I was about to say more before deciding that silence was the best approach.

We stood looking at each other for a moment, then finally, his shoulders slumped and he nodded sadly. "You're right, Pullus. I do owe them their lives. They fought well today."

"That they did," I agreed, being totally honest. "And we would treat you with honor; all we ask is that you surrender your weapons, and swear a solemn oath to leave the fort and fight no more."

"You know I can't do that," he protested. "We can't very well go back and tell Pompey that we won't fight again."

I knew he was right. I shrugged and said, "Honestly, I don't care what you do once you leave the fort, as long as you don't try stopping me and my men from what we're supposed to do. Once you go back to your camp, you can rearm yourselves and we'll fight another day." I grinned at him. "And who knows, maybe next time things will be different, and you'll return the favor."

I could tell he did not want to, but he smiled back, saying with heavy humor, "Don't bet on it. You don't know our officers. If they're involved, we won't have any choice."

"Oh, I know them all right. Labienus was our commander, remember. In fact, you tell him that Titus Pullus sends his regards and if I see him on the battlefield, I'm going to cut his balls off and feed them to him for what he did."

He gave a startled laugh, then saw that I was perfectly serious, and he swallowed hard before answering, "Well, I'll give him the first part of the message at least."

"No, you tell him the whole thing," I said firmly. "And tell him if I don't, one of my boys will. Now," I said, turning back to the business at hand, "I've given you my terms. What is your answer?"

He stood there, looking at the ground for what seemed like several moments, then finally nodded and responded faintly, "I accept your terms. But only for my men, you understand?"

I nodded, for I truly did and I said so. "Who else but a fellow Centurion could help but understand? You're doing the right thing, for your men. I salute you Quintus Albinus."

Then I offered him my hand and for a moment, I thought he would refuse, but he grasped it and I could hear the collective sigh of relief from both sides flow around us.

~ ~ ~ ~

Making arrangements for the Pompeians to stack arms and with my Centurions supervising, Albinus and I stood to one side. At first, there was a strained silence, but before long, we were talking like we had known each other for years. His story was similar to mine; he was from Gades, and he had been in his first enlistment when he was promoted to the Centurionate. He had seen action against the pirates and in the East, and against the Parthians. We carefully avoided any topic that could prove contentious, such as the war currently going on, but it was there between us. He was a good sort and I would have enjoyed sitting with him, sharing a jug of wine and swapping stories, but we both knew that it was impossible under the current circumstances. Once the surrender of the weapons finished up, I cleared my throat and asked Albinus, "What would you like to do with your dead? Your wounded will be cared for by our *medici*, and I think you know that Caesar will treat them as his own."

He nodded and replied grudgingly, "Traitor he may be, but I will say that we've been impressed with his clemency."

"He's only a traitor if he loses," I reminded him, and he shot me an angry look, then shrugged.

"We'll see."

He turned to gaze at the bodies strewn around us, then said sadly, "How do we tell which is ours?"

His words struck at my heart like a dagger; he was right. It would take much too long to try to separate our dead. The wounded would be easier, at least those who were still lucid. "Albinus, I swear to you by any god you care to choose that I'll see that your men are accorded the proper funeral rites, and we'll treat them as if they were our own dead."

"Very well, Pullus. And.....thank you," he said, offering his hand again. With that, he and his men marched out of the fort. Now we had to do what we came for, destroying every piece of engineering equipment and artillery.

~ ~ ~ ~

It took us the better part of a third of a watch to pile all the tools into a pile, drag the catapult down off the parapet and wreck the fort. We could not spare the time to pull up all the stakes to add to the pyre, but we removed a number of them at strategic points around the fort, putting them on the pile. A Century was kept on the parapets to keep an eye on the Pompeians, since I was expecting some sort of sortie from the next fort along the line, a little more than a mile away. It took the released Pompeians almost half that time to reach the fort, and I calculated that it would take them a few moments to organize and get marching back towards us, but they would undoubtedly cover the ground more quickly than Albinus. That gave us less than another third of a watch to finish up, and I detailed the Sixth Century to go fill in as much of the ditch as they could in the time we had left before we left. The *medici* had already gathered up the wounded from both sides, while I detailed men to help carry the dead back to our lines, using scraps of wood as makeshift stretchers. The numbers were dismaying, but there was nothing I could do about it except make sure as many men made it back as possible. I cursed myself for making the promise to Albinus that I had, but I was not about to go back on my word now. The flames began licking at the wood and other flammable material, then in moments, a column of smoke was billowing up into the air. If there was any doubt about what had happened it was gone now, I thought, giving the command to form up and march out of the fort.

Just as we were leaving the burning ruin, one of the men I had detailed to act as a scout shouted a warning, and I looked to see that the relief column of the Pompeians had broken into a trot in a desperate attempt to cut us off. Well, two could play that game and I gave my own command to pick up the pace. We easily outstripped the pursuit, making it back to our own camp. The Pompeians quickly realized that they were not going to catch us, having to settle for shouting their frustration and contempt, jeering at us as we called back to them, pointing to the burning fort and ruined defenses. Our mission was a success, but it had been a costly victory, and I could not help wondering what was accomplished, exactly? We did not stop Pompey's construction of his defenses, we had only slowed it down, and I had lost a lot of men in doing so. Was it worth it?

~ ~ ~ ~

The final butcher's bill was 17 dead, 30 wounded, five of them, including Figulus, so severely that they would be dismissed from the Legions as invalids. Although the rest would recover, for some it would take weeks before they would be fit for duty. In effect, I had lost almost ten percent of what was left of my Cohort, and the mood among our tent lines was somber, with every man in the Cohort losing a friend. Our numbers were shrinking and our supply situation was not going to help the wounded regain their strength. The foraging parties kept returning with less and less grain, forcing Caesar first to put us on three-quarters rations, then after a few days, half rations. Our sortie resulted in no more than two or three days delay for the Pompeians, and that did not help morale either. There was a lot of muttering about the waste of good men for nothing more significant than a couple of days, although it was muted and the men stopped whenever I was nearby. One result of our raid was that Caesar forbade the further use of Legionaries in any sorties against Pompey's works, realizing that he could not afford the losses of such experienced men, and from then on, the auxiliaries carried out these operations. Still, it was dangerous for us because of the large number of Pompeian slingers and archers that targeted every man wearing a Legionary uniform, with special attention paid to Centurions.

That was how Longus died, one ordinary day when he got careless during his Century's guard shift, turning his back on the Pompeians, who had sent out a small group of men in the night to hide and wait for just such a moment. They were of course cut down, but the damage was done; Longus and one of his men died, another was wounded. Now there was a vacancy in my Cohort and it did not take long for Celer to try putting forward one of his toadies, his Optio, a man named Scrofa. Scrofa was not a bad Legionary, but there was no way that I was going to allow him to be promoted if I could help it. My choice was Scribonius, but despite my choice carrying some weight, it was not a done deal by any stretch, because he was junior to Scrofa. The only thing Celer and I agreed on was that Longus' Optio, a wormy little man named Postumus, was completely unacceptable. He was promoted by Longus on the basis of loyalty alone and had been Longus' confederate in his shakedown schemes. Despite being successful in somewhat curtailing Longus' habit of disciplining his men excessively as a means of enriching himself, I was unable to stop it completely, something that I was not happy with to say the least. In fact, I suspected that all I did was make Longus and Postumus more creative in their schemes, another reason I was not grief stricken at Longus' death. Nevertheless, it also created a problem between Celer and me, since we had competing interests. I would be less than honest if I denied that our goals were not the same; we each wanted a man that would be loyal to us, but in my mind, I held the greater right being the Pilus Prior, making it my Cohort, and I still believe that to this day.

~ ~ ~ ~

I went to the Primus Pilus, my old commander Gaius Crastinus, making my case for Scribonius, arguing that his record spoke for itself despite his lack of seniority over Scrofa, while Celer argued that Scrofa, being the most senior of the Optios in the Cohort, was the natural choice. Ultimately, it cost me a pretty sum to convince Crastinus to select Scribonius over Scrofa, something that I have never uttered until now, yet I considered it an investment in not just my future, but in the future of Scribonius. Once Scribonius was promoted to take Longus' position, over his vigorous protests I made Vibius my Optio, a promotion that I did not have to justify to anyone at this point. The added benefit of Scribonius' promotion was that it made Celer apoplectic with rage. Meanwhile, our larger situation remained desperate, as it became more and more difficult for our foragers to obtain any supplies whatsoever, while Pompey still controlled the seas. The only success we had was in cutting off the forage for his livestock, but his men still ate well, whereas we began a diet of barley bread, something normally reserved for men on punishment. Our contravallation reached a point where it made sense to begin to turn westward, at a place where it would cut Pompey off from one of his best sources of water. The problem for us was that making that turn took us from the protection of the ridgeline that ran north and south, and was across open ground. With the only geographical feature a hill that stood all by itself, it quickly became the focal point of contention between the two armies, as Pompey occupied a smaller mound nearby. The men of the 9th were charged with fortifying this hill but Pompey, also recognizing its importance, committed a large force of slingers and archers to rain continuous death down on our men. The 9th was commanded by Antonius, and the Pompeians made it impossible for them to both defend themselves and to fortify the hill, forcing Caesar to give the command to vacate the position. When the Pompeians saw our men withdrawing, they tried to press the advantage, sending out auxiliaries while bringing up artillery within range to inflict as much damage on the 9th during their retreat as possible. Now Caesar was forced to intervene personally, sending a scratch force of engineers out to throw up a series of hurdles, wicker baskets filled with dirt and buttressed with poles, placing them on the slopes of the hill in an attempt to provide some protection as the 9th gathered their gear and made their withdrawal. Additionally, Caesar ordered the digging of a ditch behind the hurdles to impede the Pompeians in their pursuit, but this backfired, the Pompeians simply using the hurdles to fill in the ditch by pushing them into it. Caesar was forced to stop the 9th in its withdrawal, turn them around and order a countercharge to throw the Pompeians back long enough for the 9th to make good its retreat, with a loss of only about five men. While in the grand scheme of the campaign this qualified as little more than a skirmish, it was the first time since we had landed where Pompey had inflicted what could be called a defeat on Caesar, and the Pompeians celebrated it like the whole war was won. Of course, this was not the case, but it did put even more of a damper on the army, since we now could not use the hill as the pivot point to finish the contravallation. Instead, we had to continue digging to the south to the next hill, a couple miles further along, and in our weakened state because of our supply situation this was a heavy blow indeed. At this point, we were digging up a root that the locals claimed was nutritious and tasted good when ground into a flour then baked into a loaf of what they claimed was bread. I will say that it was better than eating dirt, but just barely. Although we in the Spanish Legions did not have a problem, the new Legions were now faced with deserters at an alarming rate, and apparently, one of those deserters carried one of the loaves to show to Pompey as evidence that we were in desperate straits. Somewhat surprisingly, it actually had the opposite result intended, alarming Pompey that although we were reduced to such measures, we did not show any sign of giving in.

~ ~ ~ ~

All was not going Pompey's way, however. As he had foreseen, Pompey's men were eating well but his livestock was suffering from lack of forage and were beginning to die off. Additionally, Caesar now ordered work to begin on damming off the rivers flowing to the coast that supplied Pompey with his fresh water, using one of the new Legions and some auxiliary as labor. It took a few weeks, but once it was completed, it forced Pompey to evacuate his livestock, including most importantly his cavalry, by sea back to Dyrrhachium, relieving some of the pressure on our foragers who no longer had to worry about Pompey's cavalry patrols. Not that it mattered all that much; we had picked the country clean of just about every grain of wheat, every chicken, in fact everything that a hungry Legionary could eat. It was now getting close to summer; we had crossed over from Brundisium more than five months before, meaning the fields of grain that we had protected with our lives were just beginning to ripen, and we knew that shortly our hunger would be a thing of the past. For those of us who were at Avaricum, Alesia, and Ilerda, this was nothing new and nothing that we could not cope with, but it did not stop the Pompeians from using their artillery to fling loaves of bread at us, with taunts about how they were just throwing the leftovers that they did not want at us. Despite our hunger, it made me proud to see that not one man in my Cohort deigned to pick up a loaf, despite it laying there for all to see. I heard that the boys in the new Legions were not so quick to turn their noses up, gobbling up the loaves that the Pompeians flung at them, making me happy that I did not have to worry about disciplining any men for showing such weakness. During the time all of this was taking place, an event happened that, when one reads Caesar's account of the civil war, is missing and I do not know of any other account. I want to caution you, gentle reader, that this is not a firsthand account, but is what I heard from members of Caesar's staff who were present, and I trust that what I was told is as close to accurate as it is possible to make it. What I am about to relate is how close Caesar came to being killed and is an example of how, at least in those days, the gods truly did smile on him.

~ ~ ~ ~

During the time that Caesar was busy extending the contravallation and cutting off Pompey's water, he was approached by a delegation from the city of Dyrrhachium. Claiming that it was clear that Caesar was going to win the war, they wanted to show that they recognized this fact, making an offer to show Caesar in a tangible way that they supported him. What they offered was nothing less than the surrender of the city. In one stroke, Caesar's supply problems would be solved, and Pompey would be gutted, effectively ending the civil war. It was too good an offer to pass up for Caesar, so he agreed to meet the townspeople, who told him that they would open one of the gates to the city near the temple of Artemis that very night. Like almost every city of any size in the Republic, it had long since outgrown the original town walls, meaning that Caesar would have to approach the gate down a street lined with buildings. Accompanied by Antonius, Caesar took with him only his German bodyguard, along with a single Cohort of auxiliaries to enter the gate, at midnight that night, as arranged. However, it was a trap; Pompey had men waiting for Caesar, hiding in the buildings along the road approaching the gate and Caesar was forced to fight his way out of the extremely difficult situation. At the same time, Pompey launched three separate assaults at various points along our lines, the most dangerous being against a Cohort of the 8th commanded by a Tribune named Minucius, with Pompey throwing an entire Legion against them. In order to prevent us from sending reinforcements to Minucius, Pompey also launched an assault on another of the redoubts, this one in Legion strength but composed of auxiliaries, along with a cavalry assault led by none other than the traitor Labienus on yet another point in our lines. The *bucinae* were sounding at every one of the 24 forts that had so far been constructed, each one further down the line picking up the alarm. The Second responded immediately, manning the ramparts and straining our eyes in the night, trying to determine what was happening. While we searched in vain for an attack on our position, Caesar was fighting for his life in the streets of Dyrrhachium, conducting a fighting withdrawal now that he realized he had been betrayed. Since Antonius was with Caesar, the next in command was Publius Sulla, the nephew of none other than the bloody dictator, but fortunately he acted with alacrity and prudence, leading a force to relieve the men of the 8th, hard pressed by a force many times its size. Rallying the rest of the 8th, along with one of the new Legions, Sulla marched to relieve the Cohort. Meanwhile, Caesar was still conducting his fighting withdrawal through the streets, and it was only through the bravery of his German bodyguards, buying Caesar and Antonius enough time to escape with the sacrifice of their lives, that they escaped the trap. By dawn, the fighting was almost over, although there was some mopping up being done by the relieving Legions. Nothing was officially said about what happened, yet there are no secrets in the army, and long before the sun was high in the sky, the word of what happened had whipped from one fort to the next. Men went running to the makeshift temples that each Legion has as part of their headquarters to give thanks that our general had not fallen, or worse, been captured, and I admit that I was one of those men. Losing Caesar would have been a catastrophe, and none of the officers had any illusions about what our fate would be if the unthinkable had happened. We were in a life and death struggle, and the only way to see it through alive was by winning.

~ ~ ~ ~

Despite these setbacks to our cause, Pompey was feeling the pressure at least as much as we were, if not more so. Their supply of fresh water was substantially reduced, while we had all the water we could drink. We had finally begun the turn towards the sea to finish the enclosure of Pompey's forces, but there was still treachery afoot, this time coming from within our own forces. There were two traitors, commanders of the Gallic cavalry, faithless bastards named Roucillus and Egus. Their father was the chief of the Allobroges, and they had been with the army since early in the Gallic campaign, making their treachery all the more infuriating. The word was that they were caught shaking their men down, similar to what Longus was doing, but on a much larger scale since they commanded several thousand men. Learning that they were discovered, the pair deserted one night, going over to Pompey. In exchange for safe entry into enemy lines, they offered Pompey information about a weakness in our defenses. Despite having almost completed the contravallation, we had not yet linked the inner and outer trenches. There was a distance of about 300 paces between the two trenches and while the trenches themselves were complete, a transverse ditch linking the two had yet to be built, and it was this fact that the two traitors relayed to Pompey. To his credit, Pompey understood that this was his chance to break the blockade by launching a simultaneous attack. Pompey knew that the men in the nearer trench could not be relieved by reinforcements from the outer trench. He was further armed not only with the knowledge supplied by the traitors, but how we operated, and he launched an assault at the precise moment that the 9th was in the process of relieving the guard at the farthermost point in our lines, closest to the sea. The nearest reinforcements were almost two miles further up the line and inland, where the rest of the 9th was placed after they were forced to abandon the hill. Pompey sent more than 60 Cohorts, composed of equal parts Legionaries and auxiliaries across the flat plain from within his own lines. At roughly the same time, he landed a force in between the two trenches, consisting of a large number of archers and slingers, along with a force of auxiliary and Legionaries, and finally a force of equal size to the south of the outer trench. Consequently, the men of the 9th were caught completely by surprise, while Pompey did everything he could to give his men an edge, including equipping his men with special wicker faceguards to protect them from any slingshot. As it happened, the precaution was unnecessary, since the relief had not brought their slings with them, and as a substitute were forced to resort to picking up rocks and throwing them at the Pompeians, with the effect you might imagine. The two Cohorts of the 9th were quickly overwhelmed, but not before the alarm was raised, the other eight Cohorts of the Legion immediately running to the aid of their comrades. This was exactly what Pompey was counting on.

~ ~ ~ ~

It is easy to say, looking back, that Caesar made a mistake when he placed the men of the 9th in the most vulnerable point in our defenses. They were, after all, still unhappy about their overdue discharges, a fact that the two traitors clearly communicated to Pompey, making it a question of whether they would fight hard. Coupled with the nature of the attack, coming at dawn when one Cohort was relieving the other guarding the westernmost redoubt, the two Cohorts were quickly surrounded. However, they were only acting as the bait for the rest of the Legion. Their Legate, a patrician named Marcellinus, was a sick man and confined to bed at the time of the attack, but he roused himself to assemble the rest of the Legion, save for two Centuries left behind to guard the camp. This was precisely what Pompey wanted, since even with these reinforcements he outnumbered our men by ten to one at the point of the assault.

Dawn found us running to the ramparts at the alarm being passed from fort to fort. The 10th was several redoubts away, about midway in the line of defenses, so we knew it was unlikely that we would be called on, but Crastinus still gave the order for the men to make ready and assemble in the forum of the fort. I could not tell what was happening, but we knew something big was taking place, with mounted couriers seen galloping over the ground between the two trenches, carrying word to Caesar of the attack. In the growing light, I could just make out the sails of the transports that carried the Pompeian assault force, but truthfully, I was not overly concerned. I could see that Pompey had committed a large number of men, who at this distance looked like a swarm of ants pouring into the interior trench, yet I did not think that they would pose a threat to our whole position. The Pompeians would have to fight up both trenches, and despite it appearing that they were getting the best of the 9th, they still had a number of redoubts manned with Caesar's veterans before they got close to us. To say they were getting the better of the 9th would be an understatement; in the First Cohort, one of the Cohorts performing the relief, five out of the six Centurions were killed, including their Primus Pilus, who died protecting the eagle of the Legion. When the two Cohorts were pushed back, they ran into the first of the Cohorts rushing to relieve them, creating a panic, since by this point the men who bore the initial onslaught were only concerned with getting away from their attackers, running across the open ground between the two trenches to do so. Of course, this was the most direct route to the rear, meaning that the reinforcements were blocking their way and the resulting confusion as the two forces collided made things even easier for the Pompeians. Nevertheless, the men of the 9th managed to delay Pompey long enough for Antonius to assemble a mixed force of about 12 Cohorts of the 7th and 8th, and they hurried to reach Marcellinus' camp before the Pompeians.

~ ~ ~ ~

The Pompeians began the assault on Marcellinus' camp itself just as Antonius and his force arrived, and despite Antonius being unable to prevent the Pompeians from taking the camp, he was able to stop the Pompeian advance from going any further. Caesar had assembled his own force consisting of another 12 or 13 Cohorts, but again we were not involved, instead being ordered to remain at our station to keep an eye out for any other tricks that Pompey had planned for us. And Pompey did indeed have some more in his bag; even while we watched, he set part of his force to the task of building a camp on the outside of our lines, which would effectively end our blockade. At the same time, yet another force of Legion size marched in our general direction, taking position on the hill that the 9th had been forced to vacate. In one stroke, Pompey ended the blockade, and if this position on the hill remained, he would have a force effectively in our rear, able to strike us and disrupt our supply. Even more than the new camp near the sea to the south of our lines, this position was exceptionally dangerous to our campaign, a fact that Caesar recognized immediately. Now that the attack on the southern end of our lines was contained, he took the men of the 7th, and 8th, along with the survivors of the 9$^{th}$, marching them through the trench to a point near the hill, leaving behind two Cohorts to keep those Pompeians occupied. The Pompeians on the hill turned out to be the bastards of the 24th who defected to Pompey when Antonius' brother had botched his operation in Illyria. Despite it being a green Legion, they possessed an advantage in that the 9th had done a fair amount of work in fortifying the hill before they were repulsed, so dislodging them was not a given under the circumstances. There was no choice in the matter; the Pompeians could not be allowed to remain on that hill, therefore Caesar sent everything he had in an assault. Dividing his force into two columns, he sent one swinging around to the eastern side of the camp, and the other marching past it to come down from the northern side. I cannot help think that things might have been different if Caesar had called on the 10th instead of using the boys in the other Spanish Legions, who not only had already done some hard fighting, but had taken some casualties and were ill-used. However, that is just an old man and his pride talking, and it does not really matter. Caesar led the left column that attacked from the east, assaulting the gate and forcing entry into the camp. Unfortunately, the right column got confused by a trench that the Pompeians had added when they first took the camp, designed to give them access to the nearby river, thinking that it was the rampart of the camp. Following the dirt wall to look for the gate to the camp, they only realized their mistake when they reached the stream itself. Deciding to cross the trench at that point rather than backtrack, they tore down the wall, filling in the trench with it before crossing over. The second column was now well north of the camp by several hundred paces, and began to march towards it.

Pompey was warned of the attack on the camp on the hill and in consequence, he immediately suspended work on the camp to the south of our lines in order to lead a force of five Legions along with a strong contingent of cavalry to relieve the defenders. The cavalry moved quickly, sweeping north parallel to the sea before turning to the east to strike down on the right column, which itself had a small contingent of cavalry to act as a screen. The Pompeian cavalrymen made short work of our own cavalry screen, all of whom turned and ran like rabbits, making for the narrow breach where the 9$^{th}$ men had filled in the ditch. Naturally, there was not enough room for so many men and horses at the same time, with chaos ensuing as men abandoned their horses to jump into the ditch in their haste to escape. Panic infected the Legionaries of the right column as well, now more mindful of the cavalry threatening their rear than their duty, and they began running after our cavalry, compounding the problem at the ditch. Horses were milling about, some riderless and some still with their riders aboard trying desperately to make good their own escape. Once the Legionaries arrived on the scene, they began pushing into the already packed mass of man and horse, many of them trampled to death by their own comrades coming up from behind.

Meanwhile, in the camp, Caesar had pushed the Pompeians all the way to the rear gate, where the Pompeians were preparing to make their last stand, knowing that because of their treachery they would not be given any quarter. It was at this point they saw the five Legions coming to their rescue, giving them heart to continue the fight. Launching a spirited attack, the combination of this Pompeian counterattack and the sight of their own comrades fleeing the field took what little fight our men had left, and they immediately began to turn and run for the gate through which they had entered. Running like that was shameful enough, but when Caesar tried to stop them, taking hold of one of the standards in an attempt to rally them, the *signifer* holding the standard tried to stab Caesar with it, so panic-stricken was he that he would have struck down his own general. Only Caesar's German bodyguards saved him, cutting the *signifer* down then forming a barrier around Caesar as the men ran for their lives past him. In one stroke, Pompey had put himself in a position to end this war, along with ending Caesar's life and career right then. Fortunately, the gods were still looking out for our general.

~ ~ ~ ~

To my dying day, I will never understand why Pompey did not finish Caesar off at that point, but I have thanked the gods many times, sacrificing a small herd of goats and lambs in offerings to them for stopping Pompey. Caesar's force was completely routed, running for their lives and unwilling or unable to offer any resistance to even a half-hearted effort by Pompey to overwhelm and take Caesar, dead or alive. Yet as unprepared as Caesar may have been for defeat, Pompey was at least as unprepared for victory. Seeing the men of Caesar's army running for their lives, Pompey refused to believe that it was anything but a ruse on the part of Caesar. Accordingly, he stayed put, not ordering any kind of pursuit of Caesar or his Legions as they fled for their lives. Instead, his men stopped the chase to begin celebrating their victory, hailing Pompey as Imperator and offering him a grass crown, which he refused to accept because his victory was against other Romans. That did not stop him from sending word back to Rome that he had crushed Caesar and that the war was all but over. For our part, while we were far from defeated, the mood was somber to say the least, especially once the final butcher's bill was presented. The toll was grim; 32 Centurions, 960 Gregarii, and 200 cavalry were either killed, badly wounded and could no longer serve, or captured. The fate of the captured was especially bitter because they fell into the hands of Labienus, who showed them no mercy, having every one executed, but not until he paraded them in front of the jeering Pompeians and scorned them for running away. Even more bitter was the loss of 32 standards, even though no eagles were lost, but now Caesar was faced with the ruin of all his plans unless he did something, and as usual he did not wait long to make a decision. That very night a courier arrived at our redoubt, relaying orders for us to assemble near the former camp of Marcellinus, now occupied by the enemy, at daybreak the next morning. Leaving behind a Century to guard the redoubt, we marched to the designated point, discovering that the entire army was assembled to hear Caesar's plans for us. It did not take long for us to settle down, since we were all anxious to hear what our immediate future held. As always, the wagering was fierce and even I, who rarely gambled, threw a few denarii down, and now we would all find out whether we had bet the right way. The 10th was in its normal place of honor, putting us near the makeshift rostrum made of a bunch of crates thrown together, and from my vantage point, I could clearly see the wear on Caesar's face, looking drawn, tired, and even paler than normal. However, he still moved with the same sense of confidence and authority that he always displayed as he stepped up onto the rostrum, waiting a moment for us to fall silent. Then, raising his hands in the classic orator's gesture, he began speaking, his tone pitched high, voice carrying clearly across the distance, though he still had to pause, waiting for the Centurions farther back to relay his words.

"Comrades," he began in his customary style, but his next words felt like a lash. "Why do you stand here looking so downcast? Why are you acting as if we are defeated? Is this the army that I have led these many years to victory after victory, that they would let one minor defeat take their courage?"

I could feel the ripple of surprise and dismay pass through the ranks, along with some muttered exclamations.

"*Silete!*"

I could see that Primus Pilus Crastinus was genuinely angry, not just putting on a show like he normally did. "The next man to utter a word I'll flay the skin off myself, damn you!"

His words had the desired effect, and I was thankful that Caesar acted as if he had not heard anything and was merely waiting for his words to be repeated. Then, he continued.

"We have conquered Gaul; we have conquered Hispania; we have conquered Italia, and we crossed through stormy seas to land here without losing one man, yet you still doubt that I am unable to overcome even such a slight setback? I have done all that a general can do to ensure our success."

He paused, and I sensed that there was more to it than just waiting for his words to be relayed, and the moment he began speaking again, I knew I was right because his voice became harsh.

"It was not me who turned and ran; it was not me who turned on his general and threatened his very life!"

This was the first I had heard of what took place the day before, and I shot a glance at Crastinus, who looked as puzzled as I did, but there were men who obviously knew what he was talking about, because the character of the murmuring was different. To my ears, they sounded ashamed and Caesar glared over my head in the direction of where the men of the 8th and 9th were assembled. For several seconds after the Centurions relayed his last words, Caesar said nothing, instead just maintaining his scowl and glaring at the men who had turned on him. Finally, his expression softened, and his tone became, if not conciliatory, at least softer.

"But what is past cannot be undone, and as you and my enemies know, I am not one to bear a grudge. And the service you have rendered me in the past outweighs this one lapse in your duty to me. In truth, it matters not whether this setback was due to a lack of fortitude on your part, or if it is simply a matter that the gods did not favor us this day. What does matter is that I, your general, will not allow this to stop us from achieving our goal."

There was an audible sigh of relief while we waited for his next words, but as quickly as it came, the sense of having escaped further punishment blew away like smoke before a strong wind. "However, while I can forgive your lapse in your duty, I cannot forgive the loss of so many standards. Therefore, I now call on the *signifer* for each Century and Cohort that surrendered their standards to the enemy to step forward and receive punishment."

There was another commotion as the men Caesar had named made their way to the front of the formation. Some of them came, if not willingly, at least on their own power. Others among them had to be shoved forward by their comrades, and I felt my lips curl in contempt at the naked fear shown by some of the men. These were veterans, acting like they were raw *tirones*, quaking in fear as they stood at some semblance of *intente* in front of Caesar. Is this what happens when a man finally loses his nerve, I wondered, and I was troubled by a fleeting thought that if it happened to men charged with carrying the standard, it could happen to anyone. Immediately, I dismissed the idea from my mind and turned my attention back to the rostrum, where Caesar stared down at the miserable specimens in front of him.

"You have failed in your duty, not just to your general, but to them."
He swept his arm over the rest of the army. "Your comrades, men you
have marched with for many years. And it is your failure to them that I
must punish, not your failure to your general. I hereby reduce you all to
Gregarius, and sentence you to 60 days on barley and water. I further
order that each of you be given ten lashes, which I will suspend for the
time being until such time as I deem appropriate. You are dismissed."

The humiliated men turned stiffly about, marching on unsteady legs
back to their respective Centuries to take their place in the ranks. After
they had resumed their spots, Caesar turned his attention back to the
matter at hand.

"Now, my comrades, we must move on to the next phase of this
campaign. This position is no longer tenable, and I have decided that we
must move to a new position . . ."

"Noooooooooooo!"

"Caesar, do not shame us this way! Let us stay and fight!"

The roar of protest swelled as Caesar stood, listening impassively to
the men shouting at him to let them fight. He listened for a moment, then
lifted his hand, but it took the Centurions a moment to quiet the men down
before he continued.

"I understand your feelings, my comrades. Believe me, I do. We are
leaving many of our friends behind; their blood has soaked this ground.
But my responsibility is to put this army in the best position to win, and
that is what I must do now by moving the army to a better location. I ask
you to show the same zeal that you are displaying now in preparing to
move. And I swear to you on Jupiter's Stone that you will have the
opportunity to avenge your fallen comrades!"

The last words of Caesar were drowned out by the roar of the army,
and he let us carry on for several moments before he silenced us with
another wave.

"Centurions, you will receive your orders by the end of the day.
Prepare your men to move out. That is all."

And with that, he stepped off the rostrum in a flurry of his
*paludamentum* to stride away, followed by his bevy of staff officers,
moving in his wake like a gaggle of ducklings following their mama.

~ ~ ~ ~

Breaking down the camp began immediately after we came back.
The men needed little prodding to move quickly. True to his word, near
the end of the day, a courier arrived carrying the orders to the Tribune,
who in turn relayed them to Crastinus, who passed them to us. We were
ordered to vacate the camp and form up for the march at sunset, the
assembly point being the same spot where Caesar had held his formation.
Caesar had already ordered the wagons carrying the wounded to head for

our destination, Apollonia on the coast. His decision to take the wounded with him was one that the army appreciated, because in circumstances like this it would have not been unheard of for him to leave them behind. However, I suspect that he knew that we needed as much of a morale boost as we could get, and nothing is worse than leaving a helpless comrade behind to the mercy of the enemy. Not only morale was at stake; given the fate of the captured men at the hands of Labienus, we would have been condemning them to death ourselves, for all intents and purposes, and many of these men would recover to fight again. The wagons rumbled off into the dusk while the rest of the army began to form up, which would take about two parts of a watch. My Cohort was assigned to be flank security on the march, prompting us to move out a short distance from the rest of the army, whereupon I set out pickets facing the Pompeian lines to give a warning in the event that Pompey roused himself and tried to prevent our leaving. However, Pompey was content to bask in the glory of his victory, not even sending out his cavalry to harass us, thereby allowing us to slip away unnoticed. Shortly before dawn, our turn came to march, following the rest of the army to Apollonia, where we would regroup and wait for Caesar's next move.

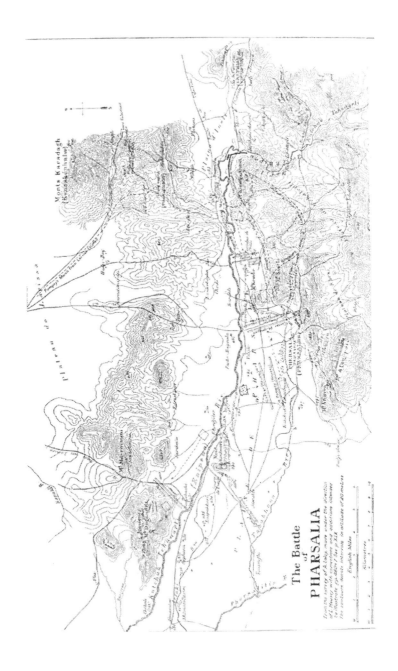

The Battle
of
PHARSALIA

# Chapter 4- Pharsalus

Our withdrawal to Apollonia was not without incident. Despite somehow managing to give Pompey's scouts the slip during our initial march, it was impossible to hide the fact that a whole army had disappeared. Nevertheless, our absence was not noticed until the 10th, acting as rearguard, had already reached the banks of the Genusis River. The banks of the river ford we were using were very steep, rising more than 30 feet above the riverbed, requiring the men to scramble up the opposite bank, thereby slowing our progress. Naturally, the men coming down the near side practically tumbled down the slope to the river, creating a massive jam while they waited for the men on the far bank to clamber to the top. This was the state we were in when Pompey's cavalry found us, the *cornu* immediately sounding the alarm at the sight of enemy horsemen. I had already crossed and was standing on the top of the opposite bank with my Cohort, with the men yelling to their friends down in the riverbed of the approaching danger. Immediately, Caesar sent a squadron of cavalry back and they went pounding down the slope and across the river, scattering the men in their path as they rushed to meet the Pompeians. The Primus Pilus acted as quickly, shaking a Cohort out in skirmish formation, armed with not only their own javelins but extras taken from the other men. This Cohort began showering the Pompeians with the javelins, and we heard the screams of men and horse as the iron heads punched into flesh and bone. For perhaps the hundredth or thousandth time, I reflected on how much I pitied the poor horses more than the men; after all, the men had a choice but the poor beasts did not. We made short work of the Pompeians, forcing them to retire with heavy losses, then finished crossing the river and marched to join the rest of the army, who were already stopped for the day at the site of our old camp near Asparagium.

Because of the circumstances of our last visit, although we burned the gates and towers, we had not filled in the ditches. This made it a matter of short work to throw the stakes back up on top of the wall, and then rebuild the gates and towers before settling in for the night, giving us about a watch for extra rest that we normally spent making camp. As we were settling down, we finally saw the leading elements of Pompey's army come hurrying after us, their commanders ordering them to hurry ahead of their baggage train in order to catch up with us. Like us, they settled in their own old camp, it being in the same shape as ours, yet unlike us, this proved their undoing. Sitting in their camp without their luxuries, many of the men decided to go back to the baggage train to retrieve their belongings in order to make their stay more comfortable.

Since we had crossed over to Greece without any of our baggage, we did not have to worry about such things, and in their laxity, Caesar saw his opportunity to steal a march. With a large part of Pompey's army out of the camp, the orders were given to us to pull up our stakes, pack what little we had, and get back on the march. Pompey could only watch in frustration as we marched out of camp, being neither desperate nor crazy enough to try to pursue us with only part of his force. He was forced to wait for the rest of his men to return, then wait even longer for them to repack their baggage on the train, and only then did he begin the pursuit. By that time, we had gained more than eight miles on Pompey, an advantage that we would keep for the next four days it took us to reach Apollonia. We maintained it by never fully unloading the baggage train when we made camp, then sent it ahead long before daybreak, giving it a head start. It was in this manner we were able to prevent Pompey from closing the gap. Pompey finally gave up the pursuit and took up position along the Via Egnatia, waiting for us to make our next move.

~ ~ ~ ~

Now that we were back on the coast and safe within the fortified walls of Apollonia, it was time for Caesar to ponder his next move. Meanwhile, we spent the time resting and refitting as much as our supply situation allowed, although as usual with Caesar that was precious little time. The most important thing that we did was to deposit our wounded within the walls, of which there were two or three thousand, most of them from all the Spanish Legions, thereby enabling us to move quickly. We were at Apollonia only a couple of days when Crastinus summoned us to his quarters to inform us that we would be moving the next day. Caesar had decided to march to join Calvinus, who had taken the 11th and 12th after they landed with Antonius to forage and put pressure on Scipio, who was commanding an independent Pompeian force of two Legions in Thessalia, getting there by marching overland from Syria. By joining forces with Calvinus, we had a chance to crush Scipio before Pompey could move to his aid. Almost as important, even if Pompey reached Scipio in time, it would draw him farther from his own base of supply, and Caesar was counting on the fact that we had been dealing with deprivation and short rations, whereas it would be new to Pompey's men, giving the advantage to us. Accordingly, we marched out of Apollonia, leaving behind four Cohorts in the city, along with those already in Oricum, heading east to meet up with Calvinus and his two Legions. Calvinus was waging a campaign of attrition against Scipio, with limited success and in doing so had managed to turn a good number of the natives against Caesar and his cause. The news of Pompey's victory did not help either, and as we marched through the countryside, we found towns closing their gates to us, not wanting to incite Pompey against them. In fact, Calvinus learned of Pompey's victory through friends of the two Gallic traitors who were now scouting for Pompey, looking for Scipio but finding Calvinus instead. Calvinus also learned in this way that Caesar was nearby, since the couriers that Caesar sent out were obviously intercepted, and consequently sent out his own scouts looking for us, which is how we linked up. Now it was time to turn on Scipio, although there was also the matter of our supply situation and the issue of these towns that had turned their back on us. One such was the town of Gomphi, and it was to there that we marched, much to their misery and misfortune.

~ ~ ~ ~

Arriving at the walls of the town around midday, after a quick reconnaissance, Caesar determined that we could take the town by assault, rather than to try to reduce it by siege. He ordered us to knock together assault ladders and make bundles of sticks to throw into the ditch at the base of the walls. We did so in plain sight of the townspeople lining the low wall and we heard their cries of despair, but they were lost on us. They had supplies that we desperately needed, and while I know that they would have gladly surrendered them once they saw we were about to take them by force, it was too late for that. I think Caesar had a number of reasons for ordering the assault, not least of which was to restore some of the morale we had lost by allowing us to exact a measure of revenge. It was just the people of Gomphi's misfortune that their leaders chose to change sides upon hearing of Pompey's victory at Dyrrhachium. It did not take us long to build the ladders and gather the bundles together, and the 10th was one of the Legions selected for the assault, but because of the casualties my Cohort took during our assault on the fort we were put in reserve. The men were not happy, the rumor being that Caesar was going to give the town over to us, meaning that they would not get first pickings of loot and women, although we would still do better than the men who were not taking part in the assault at all. No matter how hard the provosts tried, despite the fact that the town was supposed to be divided up, with a section of the town designated for each Legion, the first men over the walls always managed to slip into areas in which they were not supposed to be. They nabbed choice bits of loot before the men actually assigned to the area got there. However, it is when the men stop grumbling that the Centurions have to worry, so I was not concerned about my men and their complaints. The assault started about a full watch before dusk, yet it took barely a third of a watch for the walls to be taken, and not much more than another third of a watch later for the last defender to be slaughtered. By dusk, we had rounded up the civilians that were not well hidden, and on Caesar's orders, put them to the sword. Normally, we would not have been happy about this since we all profited from the sale of slaves, but our desire for revenge outweighed our greed in this case, and it was just the bad luck of the townspeople that they were the objects of our wrath. The rest of the night was spent stripping the town of everything of any value, the men drinking anything that held the remotest possibility of getting them drunk, except this time it was with Caesar's blessing. He understood that the men needed something to cheer them up; I suppose it seems odd to say that the rape and pillage of a peaceful town would be considered sport, yet that is the nature of the Legionary. It is a harsh life we lead, and there is no place for finer notions like sensitivity, which is viewed as a weakness, and indeed in many ways it is. One cannot be mooning about thinking about whether or not what you are doing is the right thing when thrusting a sword into a man's guts, not unless you want to be the one stretched out on a funeral pyre. Still, there are men who participate with less gusto than others, and there are those like Didius who lived for moments when they were allowed to run wild.

I walked the streets of the town, listening to the screams of the women who had not been killed yet, making sure that my men did not stray into areas designated for other Cohorts, or worse, other Legions. In the beginning, it would be fairly easy to keep order, but once the supplies of wine were uncovered and consumed, it would be harder and harder to maintain discipline. Consequently, I had ordered my Centurions to keep a tight rein on the men. With every sacking of a town there is always one Cohort that goes farther than any other; it was almost a given that there would be punishments forthcoming, and it was not unheard of that the crimes committed by men inflamed by wine, lust, and greed were sufficiently serious enough to warrant execution. I was determined that my Cohort would not be the one to be made an example of, and I was worried about Scribonius, since this would be his first big test of command of his Century. I knew the men liked him well enough; but did they fear him, because that is what it took at times like this. Once men are robbed of their senses by drink and debauchery, the only thing that they understand is fear, fear of a beating at the hands of their Centurion or Optio. Whereas my reputation was already made, and in truth, I had no reason not to allow Vibius to handle any disciplinary issues in the First Century, Scribonius would have to handle any problems himself this time. Later it would not be necessary, but because this was his first such challenge, it was crucial that he be the one to keep his men in line.

With that in mind, I held a briefing with my Centurions, stressing the importance of keeping a lid on the men. Now we were patrolling the streets, watching for trouble. What we feared occurred about two thirds of a watch after midnight, over on the next street from where I was standing talking to Vibius. It was normal by this point in the sacking of the town that the air was filled with the yells and curses of the men, but above that came first the noise of men shouting at each other, followed by what sounded like amphorae being smashed against the stone walls of the houses. In short, what we were hearing was different from the normal sounds of a town being ravaged, and we instantly understood that it meant trouble. Celer, Niger, Crispus, and I were standing together, along with Vibius and a couple other Optios. We did not hesitate, turning and running down the street to round the corner and head up the street where the sound was originating. I was in the lead, so I saw immediately that what was happening was the worst possible scenario; the men of Scribonius' Century were involved in an altercation with some men I did not immediately recognize, which could only mean they were from another Legion. Despite the time of night, the flames from the piles of furniture and other odds and ends that the men had dumped in the middle of the street then set alight made the scene clear, like it was almost high noon. Scanning the faces of the small knot of men standing angrily facing ours, my heart sank as my worst fears were confirmed. None of the men were from the 10th, and I vaguely recognized one of the men, thinking he was one of the 9th, which, if true, helped to at least partially explain what the problem was. Ever since their mutiny, we had not thought very well of the 9th, then after the debacle at Dyrrhachium, our opinion sank even lower, believing that they brought shame onto the army and to Caesar. The men were arrayed facing each other, and despite no weapons being drawn, a number of men on each side had picked up lengths of wood from the pile by the fire to use as clubs, and were brandishing them at each other, shouting vile threats as they did so. I saw that Scribonius was standing in between them, but it did not look like he held more than a tenuous hold on the situation, with both sides looking poised to throw themselves at each other. Striding through the middle of my men, I pushed them roughly aside, their faces showing first angry surprise, then fear when they recognized me, and I made my way to Scribonius.

"What in the name of Pluto's thorny cock is going on here?" I demanded, my voice pitched to the level I used when issuing commands.

Scribonius saluted, then responded calmly, "Pilus Prior, these men," he indicated the men of the 9th, "have strayed outside of their assigned area and mistakenly started clearing the houses on this street."

"That's a lie," spat one of the men on the other side who did not wear any insignia of rank but seemed to be in charge. One thing I was sure of was that he did not outrank Scribonius, or he would have immediately taken charge and used his authority to send our men packing empty-handed, whether it was right or not.

"And who the fuck are you?" I stepped towards him, my suspicions immediately confirmed when he shrank back and instinctively drew himself to *intente*.

"Optio Lucius Vetruvius, First Century, Fifth Cohort, 9th Legion, Pilus Prior."

I paused, looking him up and down, making sure that the sneer on my face was easily seen by everyone. "So Vetruvius, you're saying my Centurion is a liar, neh?"

Once I repeated it back to him, the full import of his words hit him, and he licked his lips nervously before replying, "I . . . I . . . didn't say that exactly, Pilus Prior . . ."

Before he could finish, I cut in, "That's exactly what you said, Optio. You said that Secundus Hastatus Prior Scribonius," I deliberately used his full rank, "is a liar. That's a very serious charge, Optio. Do you have any proof to substantiate that charge?"

As I expected, he began to splutter, his face turning bright red. "I . . . I . . . apologize Hastatus Prior. I didn't mean any offense. Forgive my rudeness; it's the wine talking." He tried a grin, but it was met with stony silence, both of us staring at him impassively, and he gulped as he struggled to find words. "I simply meant to say that there was a misunderstanding. We've been assigned this street by the provosts, and by rights, this street is ours. Right, boys?"

He turned over his shoulder, and the murmured assent of his comrades seemed to stiffen his backbone a bit. He turned to me with a defiant expression on his face.

"Really?" I asked as if I were actually interested in what he had to say, because I had already seen what I needed, and he nodded his head.

"Yes, sir. It's just that your boys seem to have gotten here by mistake, but there's no harm done. All we ask is that we be allowed to finish the street. Right, boys?" he repeated, and I was not surprised that his men thought this a grand idea.

I pursed my lips as I pretended to think about it. "Well, that certainly seems fair," I began, and I saw Vetruvius' face light up, Scribonius' correspondingly flushing at the idea that I was going to side with the enemy, as it were.

The men of the 9th began clapping each other on the back and smacking their lips in anticipation of what lay in wait behind the closed doors of the houses lining the street. It was in what was obviously the wealthy section of the city, Caesar rewarding the 10th with the choicest areas to loot, and I could see the gleam in the men's eyes as they silently congratulated each other. Suppressing a smile, I remember thinking to myself, Titus you are not a very nice man.

Then I spoke. "But . . ."

The change of expression on their faces would have done Mercury proud, so swift was the transformation, their looks going from quiet exultation to wary suspicion.

Seeing that I held their undivided attention, I continued, "There are one or two problems with that. If you would notice," I pointed back over the head of the Optio, so that he and the rest of his men craned their necks to follow my finger, "as you can clearly see, the provosts marked this street for the exclusive use of the Fifth Century, Second Cohort of the 10th Legion. You know," I couldn't resist adding, "Caesar's favorites."

And just as I had seen it, chalked high up on the side of the house that resided at the corner of the street, was the number of the Century, Cohort, and Legion that the provosts had designated for the exclusive use of Scribonius' Century. I must confess I took rather too much pleasure in the crestfallen looks of the boys of the 9th, and I could have let it go there, but I could not resist, such was my desire absolutely to crush anyone who resisted me back in those days.

"So you can see, Optio, you're the ones who are mistaken. But if the mark of the provosts isn't enough for you, then there's this." I leaned forward, lowering my voice, but I knew that every man could hear me. "You're of the 9th, the Legion who turned on Caesar. Do you *really* think that you deserve such ripe pickings as these?" I gestured with my *vitus* at the surrounding houses. "And if your treachery wasn't bad enough, you're the bastards who turned tail and ran like rabbits at Dyrrhachium and forced us to abandon several months' worth of work."

I saw that my words had scored a direct hit, wounding Vetruvius, along with his comrades to the very core. His face turned bright red, his eyes narrowing as he clenched his fists.

I looked down at them and sneered, "Oh, so you do have some backbone after all? That's good to see. Too bad you only turn it on your comrades and not the enemy."

As quickly as it had come, the fight fled from him and he visibly sagged. His body communicated a defeat that his pride could not allow him to utter. The men around him all watched, ready to follow his lead, but he slowly raised his head, his eyes dull, and I saw in them the pain, making me feel a sharp twinge of regret. I did not realize how true my words must have sounded to him, and when I saw his hurt, I suddenly took no joy in vanquishing this man, on this night, but it would have been unthinkable for me to make an apology in any form, especially in front of the men. Therefore, I merely pointed them back to the end of the street, and with a curt command, Vetruvius and his men trooped away, leaving us the victors. Vetruvius lingered long enough to make sure that none of his men stayed behind to cause any trouble, and seeing him standing separate, I stepped away from the rest of my own men to walk a way down the street before calling his name. At first, I did not think he heard, or if he did, he would not obey, but the habits of a lifetime of obedience are hard to break, and with obvious reluctance he came to stand before me, stopping to stand at *intente*, his back to me as he stood rigidly, waiting to hear what I had to say.

I leaned closer to him and said quietly, so that only he could hear, "Vetruvius, you know you were in the wrong, don't you?"

He did not reply for a moment, then said in the tone that I recognized all of us use when addressing a superior that we loathe, "As you say, Pilus Prior."

"But you think I went too far casting slurs on the 9th, don't you?"

The silence was longer this time, and I could almost see the wheels turning in his head as he struggled to think through the fog induced by too much wine, searching for the right answer.

Finally, he chose honesty over discretion and looked directly at me when he said, "Yes, Pilus Prior."

Our eyes met for a moment, and I saw not only defiance, but the pain in his eyes, before he looked away.

"You're right," I said so that only he could hear, "I did go too far and for that I apologize, Optio Vetruvius."

I do not know who was more surprised at my words, he or I, because I had not planned on saying any such thing, but I suppose I saw in him something of myself, despite the undeniable fact that he was a few years older than me.

Before he could say anything, I continued, "You're a good leader of men, Vetruvius, I can see that in the way the men look to you. But you need to learn to pick your battles, understand? In this case, you picked the wrong battle, with the wrong Centurion. But that doesn't mean you're not a good leader, Vetruvius." He stood for a moment, not saying a word, only nodding thoughtfully. Finally, I stepped away, then snapped in my parade ground voice, "Very well. Dismissed. And make sure you pay attention to the provosts' markings in the future, Optio."

"Yes, Pilus Prior," he said, giving me a salute, which I like to think was more than just a bare formality.

Just as he turned to walk away, we exchanged a look and once again, he nodded to me, then scurried away, following his men. I turned back to Scribonius, who was clearly angry with me, and I sighed, walking over to him.

Before I could say a word, he said, angry as I had ever seen him, "Forgive me, Pilus Prior, but I had the situation under control. Your intervention wasn't needed . . . nor was it wanted."

While I knew that he would not be happy that I had stepped in, I was a bit surprised at his last words, despite knowing now that I should not have been. I struggled to keep from making a sharp retort, both because I did not want to quarrel in front of the men, but also because I truly valued Scribonius as a friend. In a number of ways, he had supplanted Vibius as my dearest friend; because of his rank, I could be more open with him than Vibius, and I had always admired his quiet intelligence and dry wit. Vibius would always have a special place in my heart and esteem, yet Scribonius was as valued to me in his own way, so I bit back the sharp reply that came to mind, saying with what I hoped was the right tone of patience and good humor, "Oh, why's that, Scribonius? I can understand why you think you had the situation under control, but at least now I'm the bad one, not you."

He shook his head impatiently, and responded, "Nobody had to be the bad one, Titus. I was just about to point out to the Optio that the provosts had marked this for us, but you couldn't wait."

I shook my head, biting back my irritation. "From where I was standing, he didn't look disposed to reason, Scribonius."

"How would you know?" he shot back. "You didn't give me a chance to talk."

I sighed. He was right, but I was equally sure that he would not have been able to stop Vetruvius, yet I did not want to say that outright.

Instead, I simply replied, "I didn't want things to get out of hand, Scribonius. I'm sure that you could have handled the situation, but when I showed up, it looked like the men were ready to throw themselves at each other."

Not deterred by this response in the least, Scribonius retorted, "Well, we'll never know now, will we? I still think I had things in hand when you showed up."

I put my hands out, "*Pax*, Scribonius. It wasn't my intent to undermine you in front of your men. I was just worried and didn't want things to get out of hand."

He pursed his lips, then nodded. "Very well, Titus. I understand what you were doing."

He turned to watch his men swarming over the row of houses on the opposite side of the street, whooping and hollering and acting like it was their birthday, and I let the matter drop as we both stood there while the men of the Legions sacked the city.

~ ~ ~ ~

Quite understandably, they were less than enthusiastic when roused the next morning, the chorus of groans and curses clearly heard all across the camp, the Centurions and Optios doing their own share of cursing as they kicked and poked the men into life, the rhythm of the army reasserting itself. We were ordered to make ready to march, Caesar thankfully ignoring the fact that it took us a bit longer than normal before we were formed up and ready to start. Continuing our march south, we reached the next city, Metropolis, two days after the sack of Gomphi. Unlike Gomphi, however, Caesar deemed that he had made his point and gave strict orders that Metropolis was to be spared the same fate. It still took some persuasion by Caesar to convince the citizens of Metropolis to open their gates to us, but he was true to his word and no harm was done to the citizens or the city. We stayed at Metropolis for just a couple of days before marching east towards the vast plain of Thessaly, where fields of ripening wheat awaited our sickles. The army was now marching with a light spirit, knowing that soon our hunger would be over, and it was in this mood we came to a spot along the Enipeus (Enipeas) River, about six miles to the north of the town of Pharsalus.

~ ~ ~ ~

Our scouts alerted us that Pompey was coming, so that our chance at harvesting what little wheat had already ripened was limited. It also meant that our attempt to crush Scipio's army alone before linking up with Pompey failed. As Pompey approached, he met up with Scipio at Larisa and their combined forces continued south until their scouts came in sight of our camp. My Cohort had the watch when one of my men sounded the alarm, pointing out the thin trail of dust rising in the sky to our north to Vibius, who happened to be on the rampart at that moment. Vibius came running to me to report what the sentry saw. While I trusted not only Vibius and the Gregarius who sounded the alarm implicitly, I knew Caesar well enough to know that the question would come up if I had seen this sign of the approaching enemy myself, having learned his lesson from the affair with Considius against the Helvetii years before. Consequently, I followed Vibius to where the Gregarius was standing, pointing with his javelin in the manner we were trained. My eyes followed the length of the shaft to the point, seeing for myself the first signs of Pompey approaching, before hurrying off to the *Praetorium* to make my report. Striding along, my mind raced with all the things that needed to be done to make the Cohort ready for battle, because despite no such orders being passed, I was convinced that this time we would not be running. We were going to fight Pompey here and now, I was sure of it. The view of Pompey's army was blocked by the range of low hills to the north, but I had seen enough to tell me that this was his whole army; nothing other than that would make a dust cloud of the size I had witnessed from the ramparts. Giving my report to the duty Tribune, who deemed it important enough to disturb Caesar at whatever he was doing, I quickly found myself hurrying with my general back to the ramparts so that he could see for himself. Even though I had been in Caesar's presence hundreds of times by this point, it was still hard not to feel a little nervous, because I never really knew what to say to him outside of my official duties. Fortunately, Caesar was never at a loss for words and usually would initiate conversations on topics that I could easily follow along with, without feeling like I was stepping over some line between us.

"So Pullus," Caesar spoke in a conversational tone, but I still felt a thrill of fear shoot up my backbone, "what do you think? Is it time that we get this over with?"

I considered the question carefully; unlike most men of his station, I knew that when Caesar asked a question of this nature, he was actually soliciting opinions and not just making conversation.

"Well, General," I said carefully, "the question is what do we benefit by delaying and going on the march again?" Before he could answer, I continued, "And while you know we in the 10th will follow you wherever you take us, Caesar, we're getting tired of breaking down camp and marching. So I say let's face Pompey here and now. Let's end this once and for all."

He nodded, but did not say anything. Instead, he turned to favor me with a smile and I marveled that even now, after all these years, my heart still leapt at the sight. Mounting the steps to the parapet, where Vibius had been joined by Celer and Crispus, we surrounded the poor Gregarius who originally sighted the army. I managed to suppress a smile at his expression; I knew that he would rather have been cleaning out latrines than to be standing in front of Caesar at this moment.

"Are you the Gregarius who raised the alarm?" Caesar asked, and even from where I stood, I could see the man's throat working as he tried not to stammer.

"Yes, sir."

"Good job. Who's your Centurion?"

"Scribonius, sir."

Caesar turned to Scribonius, saying loudly so that all the men nearby could hear. "Your man is to be commended, Scribonius. Make sure that he has a ration of unwatered wine tonight as my thanks."

This elicited a cheer and the sentry beamed with happiness at the thought of the wine, probably thinking how much food he could get with it in barter, since this was one of those few times when bread was more important than wine. Meanwhile, Caesar stared thoughtfully at the dust plume; in the time it took me to go get Caesar, the vanguard of Pompey's army had crested the hill, and we watched them spilling down the slope in a glittering display of winking silver and red. Caesar said nothing for several moments as he watched, then abruptly turned and descended the ladder to the ground, striding back to the *Praetorium* with a string of aides in his wake. Caesar waited until he was out of earshot before he turned to one of his scribes and began dictating orders, but I was reasonably sure that we were not going to be going anywhere, that we were going to fight.

~ ~ ~ ~

Pompey elected to erect his own camp on the hill to the north, and we watched them go about their business. This campaign had gone on now for more than six months and Caesar's admonition to us not to bring our personal baggage with us from Brundisium had become something of a running joke, albeit with an edge of bitterness. Whatever the case, we were all more than ready to end this here and now, and the men were not shy about voicing their feelings whenever there was an opportunity. Accordingly, the day after Pompey arrived, the army was ordered out to stand in formation on the plain between the two camps, where we took our place on the right as usual, with Caesar offering Pompey battle. There was no more subterfuge, no more strategic gambits; Pompey could plainly see our entire force and know that he outnumbered us substantially, giving him no reason to delay further. Despite this, we stood there the better part of the day under the hot summer sun, waiting for Pompey, who did nothing. As we would learn later, Pompey and his cronies were busy arguing over the division of the spoils that would come after their inevitable victory, the dispute becoming so heated that the army would not move until matters were settled. All we knew at the time was that Pompey refused to meet us on the field, and we marched back into our camp frustrated and angry. This became the pattern for the next few days, the only change being that each day Caesar would march us closer to the slopes of Pompey's hill, about three miles distant from our own camp. Still, Pompey did nothing, although after the third day he began sending out part of his cavalry to harass us, prompting some minor skirmishes between our forces. The only event of note was that during one of those skirmishes, one of the Allobrogian traitors who caused us so much trouble at Dyrrhachium was killed by our troopers, although I do not remember which one. It appeared as if Pompey had no intention of budging from that hill, and it also became apparent that his goal was to starve us again. The wheat was not yet fully ripe, but even if it was, now that Pompey and his army were present, harvesting it was not going to be easy. The granaries at Pharsalus were rapidly being sucked dry, so Caesar called a council of war, where he announced to us that despite our desire to stay put and fight it out, we were to prepare the men to break camp. This announcement was met with much dismay, and while nobody spoke openly against his plans, Caesar could easily see that we were not happy. Holding his hand up to quiet the muttering, he spoke in a reasonable tone, without any obvious anger.

"Comrades I know how you feel, but consider this. I do not take this decision lightly, but I believe with all my heart that this army is much better suited to deal with the deprivation of hard marching on short rations than Pompey's fat youngsters." This brought a chuckle, and he continued, "Since it's clear that Pompey wants to weaken us by having us stay put, while he can continue receiving almost unlimited supplies from his rear, it only makes sense that we try to even the odds. And the best way to do that is to put them on the road chasing us."

Despite our desire to fight, it was hard to fault his logic, and I looked around to see heads nodding as the rest of the Centurions accepted the idea.

"Very well. We'll break camp day after tomorrow. Let the men rest tomorrow; we won't be making a demonstration. That is all, gentlemen."

With that, we were dismissed to go pass the word to our men and walking back, I thought about all the complaints that would be forthcoming at the news that we were moving out.

~ ~ ~ ~

The day of the move came, and as was usual on such days I was up about a full watch before dawn. In truth, the Centurions and Optios had more reason to hate marching days than the rankers, since we had to be up and ready before any of the men. Yet it would have been unseemly to complain about it, at least in front of the rankers, so I contented myself with grumbling in my tent as I packed up my gear. Stepping outside, I sniffed the air, sensing no hint of rain or other sign that it would be anything but hot once the sun rose. There was no mist at night to cool the air in this part of the world, something that I did miss about Gaul. I went to Vibius' tent, but he was already up, so we talked quietly as he finished his own packing, while the rest of the Centurions and Optios made their way to us, following the sound of our voices. By the light cast from the torch carried by the sentry, I could see that the others felt much the same way that I did about this move, but there was nothing to be gained by sulking about it.

"All right, let's get 'em up," I commanded, the others immediately marching over to their respective Century areas, the air soon split by the sound of Centurions and Optios rousing their men.

"Good morning, ladies, time to rise and shine," Vibius bellowed, answered immediately by a chorus of groans and curses, and I could not help smiling.

After all these years, the men still acted like children roused from slumber to do their chores, which I suppose in a sense they still were. Every decision was made for them; where to go, when to eat, when to sleep, so it made sense that they acted like children most of the time. This was the nature of my thoughts as I made sure that I stayed out of the way of the men breaking down their tents, followed by loading the mules. It did not take long for us to pack, and once finished, we marched to the Via Praetoria to take our assigned spot in the marching column, designated by a series of stakes, each engraved with the number of the Cohort that would occupy that spot in the column and painted a certain color denoting each Legion. I was happy to see that we were one of the first Cohorts in place, but I also knew that this meant we would be standing and waiting for the rest of the army to finish packing and fall in. As usual, I thought sourly, those youngsters in the new Legions are the ones holding us up, and it did not take long for my thoughts to be echoed by the men, who first began grumbling, then wagering on which Legion would be the last one to show up. Finally, just as the sun rose above the hills to the east, the *bucina* sounded, prompting a mixed chorus of groans and shouts of delight when the identity of the last Legion to make its way to its spot in the column was known.

"None of you bastards better be betting your rations again," I called out, and I was rewarded by a couple of guilty looks.

I made a mental note to find something particularly odious for them to do the next time we stopped. All in all, it was just a normal day on the march, signaled by the second, then third, and final call of the *bucina* that was the command to march. Stepping out, the vanguard began the movement, and since we were near the front of the column this day, it was only a few moments before it was our turn. Immediately ahead of us, across the plain, I saw Pompey's army arrayed on the slopes of the hill. This was not unusual in itself; in fact, it was almost a custom for one army to stand to watch the other as it marched away, just in case there was some trickery planned. As we moved towards the road leading further south, I strained my eyes, thinking that there was something different this time, but I could not tell exactly what. Finally stepping to the side, I stopped, staring at the lines of men across the valley floor, finally recognizing what was different. Instead of standing still as they watched us move, Pompey's army was actually marching down the hill towards us! I turned my head, looking for signs that someone else had noticed what was happening, and I saw that Caesar was sitting his horse, one hand shielding his eyes, looking over at Pompey and his army. In the next instant, he snapped an order to one of his aides, sending him galloping off down the column, then turned to his personal *cornicen* who immediately sounded the call to halt the army. Instantly, orders were relayed, the horns sounding twice more, and we ground to a halt. There was an excited buzz of conversation as the men relayed what they thought was happening, and after a moment I bellowed at the men near me to shut their mouths, telling them they would know soon enough. Meanwhile, the aide came galloping back, accompanied by the Legates of the Legions, the feathers on the crests of their helmet streaming in the wind like a flock of crows taking wing.

I walked over and found Primus Pilus Crastinus, who looked at me and grinned. "Well Pullus, looks like ol' Pompey has finally pulled his head out of his ass and wants to fight, neh?"

I nodded. "It looks that way, Primus Pilus. Maybe this'll be the last battle."

Crastinus looked at me, a shocked expression on his weathered face. "By the gods, I hope not! I'm no good at peace, Pullus. If we don't have any more battles to fight, I'll go mad."

I laughed. "I meant the last battle of this war, Primus Pilus. There are always other enemies to fight, like Parthia."

His lips pulled back in a sneer at the mention of one of Rome's bitterest enemies. "I would love to get stuck into those pricks." He spat on the ground to emphasize his point. Then he grinned again. "Besides, I hear they're richer than we are, that their warriors' armor is inlaid with gold, not just the officers mind you, but the rankers as well."

Of course, I had heard the same tales, but I was not as sure that I believed them as Crastinus did. Nevertheless, I was not about to disagree with my Primus Pilus, and I simply said that I had heard the same thing and would not mind finding out. As we were finishing our conversation, the call sounded for the Primi Pili to go to Caesar's standard, and Crastinus clapped me on the shoulder and said, "Well, let me go find out what we're going to be doing."

"A thousand denarii that we're on the right," I called out to him, but he just laughed and waved off the bet, knowing that it was as close to a sure thing as could be found in the army. As he moved away, I turned and went back to the Cohort, calling for the rest of my Centurions and Optios, who came trotting up.

"We're going to be getting orders in a minute, and I'm guessing that we're going to be shaking out over there." I pointed out what I thought was the likely spot Caesar would want us to occupy, given the direction that Pompey appeared to be marching. Now that he had moved most of the way down the slope, Pompey ordered his army to execute a wheel maneuver that pivoted his lines so that they were perpendicular to his original line of march, putting the river on his far right. A few moments later, Crastinus came striding back, shouting for all first grades to attend to him, and I trotted over along with the other Pili Priores to receive our orders.

"Good thing I didn't take that bet, Pullus." Crastinus grinned at me, pointing out where we were to form up before detailing who would be to our left.

Once we received our orders, we returned to our Cohorts, moving them into their positions a few hundred paces away, but not before having them ground their gear where they were standing. The Second would be in our normal spot on the front line next to the First Cohort, but because of our depleted numbers, in order to present the proper width along the front, we had to reduce the depth of the formation to only four men deep. While doing this, Caesar ordered parts of the turf wall of the camp pulled down to enable the rest of the army still inside the camp to move into position more quickly, rather than trying to squeeze through the front gate. The air was filled with the shouted commands of Centurions hurrying their men into their designated spots. Since we were one of the first to form up, we were left with nothing to do but wait, the hardest thing to do before battle, especially when one is alone with their thoughts. I passed the time trying to count up the number of battles this made for me, but soon gave up the attempt. Glancing at my men, I was filled with pride at seeing them stand quietly, with almost bored expressions, professionals simply waiting to go do their job. Oh, when you looked closely, you could see a telltale tapping of fingers on a shield, or a man would be yawning excessively, but those were the only signs of any nerves among them. I turned and headed toward the front rank; Vibius spotted me and turned to call the men to *intente* but I waved him off. Moving among them, I began tugging on straps, checking buckles, and testing the edges of their blades, even as I knew I would not find anything to complain about. I exchanged jokes, slapped men on the shoulder and teased them about one thing or another; the good times that make life in the army bearable, the funny times that help pass the long watches of monotony. Then I stepped in front of my old nemesis from back when we were *tirones*, none other than Achilles himself, Spurius Didius.

"Well, Didius, here we are again," I said, pulling on his straps.

He grinned at me. "Yes, Pilus Prior. A lot of miles, neh?"

"And a lot of fights." I laughed, and he laughed too, knowing that I was not talking about the battles we fought against Gauls, Spaniards, and Romans, but our own private wars over the years. I looked him in the eyes and said quietly, "Good luck today, Didius."

Then I offered him my hand, which he took, his eyes glinting with unshed tears. "Same to you, Pilus Prior," then withdrew his hand, came to *intente* and saluted me, a salute I was happy to return.

~ ~ ~ ~

By the time I was finished inspecting the Cohort, the army had formed up in the standard *acies triplex*, mirroring the formation that Pompey was presenting. Commanding the right wing was Publius Sulla, and while not of the same quality of general as his father the Dictator, he was competent. Once Caesar was satisfied with the disposition of the army, he trotted over on Toes, stopping in front of us to look us over for a moment before speaking.

"Comrades," he cried, "you all know that I have done everything in my power to avoid this moment. Did I not send envoys to Pompey on several occasions in an attempt to end this peacefully? At every opportunity, I have tried to find some sort of accommodation that would leave both of us with our *dignitas* intact and preserve peace for the Republic, but Pompey has steadfastly refused these overtures."

He paused for a moment, scanning the faces looking up at him, resplendent in his gilt armor and scarlet *paludamentum*. Caesar was still bareheaded, it being his habit to wait to don his helmet until the last moment, and it hung by its strap from his saddle.

"I have also done everything I can to preserve this army, to avoid shedding your blood whenever possible. You are all as sons to me, and when one of you falls, I weep. But now we have no choice. Those men," he swept his arm in the direction of where Pompey's command group was gathered behind their formation, "leave us no choice but to fight. Will you fight for me?"

Immediately, he was answered with a roar from every throat as the men raised their javelins, thrusting them into the air before beginning to beat them against the rim of their shields. Caesar sat impassively, listening to this demonstration for a moment before lifting his hand, and we fell silent again.

Turning Toes, he walked him to a spot just in front of Gaius Crastinus and called to him, "What say you, Gaius Crastinus? What are our hopes for victory?"

Crastinus stiffened his back, replying in his parade ground voice, "Victory will be yours Caesar." Saluting, he finished, "You will conquer gloriously today."

We cheered again, and while we did so, I saw Caesar lean down to say something to Crastinus, who listened intently. The Primus Pilus nodded, then saluted as Caesar turned Toes, galloping down the line to the left, where he would undoubtedly repeat his speech to the rest of the army. While he did so, Crastinus called some men by name from the First Cohort and had them assemble in front, then trotted over to me.

"Caesar has given me a special assignment," he said, "and I need at least ten of your best men for the task. But they have to be rankers; we can't spare taking you or your Optio."

I thought for a moment, then turned to call out the names of nine men. As they made their way forward, I hesitated for a moment before adding another name.

"Didius!" The surprise on his face was clear, but he came without hesitation. When they were assembled, I told them, "Go join the men from the First over there. Primus Pilus Crastinus has a special assignment from Caesar and we need our best men for it."

Crastinus had moved onto the next Cohort, and in a few moments, he had a force of about 120 men formed up in front of our line. We could follow Caesar's progress down the line by the roaring of the men as he exhorted them to give him their best, the sound growing fainter the farther away he went. The far left was commanded by Antonius, where the 8th and 9th, because of their losses at Dyrrhachium, were combined to make one under-strength Legion. The middle was commanded by Domitius, with the youngsters placed in a spot where they could do the least damage. The 11th and 12th were to our left, forming the rest of the right wing. Waiting for Caesar to finish, we saw the enemy cavalry move into position on their far left, to our right, and I immediately saw that we were in trouble. The enemy cavalry force was huge, many times the number of our own, and where they were lining up meant that they intended to swing out before coming down on our right flank in an attempt to roll us up. As Caesar came trotting back, he saw the same thing and stopped at his command group, issuing some orders that sent his aides galloping off to the rear of the formation. I turned to see what was happening, watching as the aides selected roughly every other Cohort in the rear line, then pulling them back into a fourth line. While I was not sure what was planned, I was comforted to know that Caesar saw and understood the danger and I held every confidence that whatever it was he had in mind, it would take care of the problem. Besides, there was nothing I could do about it, so I turned back forward and waited for the command to move out.

~ ~ ~ ~

Despite Sulla being in nominal command of the right wing, Caesar chose to position himself on the right as well, knowing that this was where the biggest danger was, so once more he came trotting back, stopping in front of Crastinus and his hand-picked men.

Crastinus saluted Caesar, then the Primus Pilus turned to the men. "Boys," he began, "you've been my comrades and followed me for a long time. Give Caesar the loyal service you've shown me for all these years now. There's one last battle, and when it's over, he'll recover his *dignitas* . . . and we'll be free to get drunk and chase whores!" Turning back to Caesar, he gave a final salute and said, "Today, General, I'll give you a reason to thank me, whether I'm dead or alive."

Caesar returned the salute before trotting through the lines to take his place at the rear of the formation. Once he took his position, the command was given to march and we stepped out to close the distance so that we could charge without having to run too far. Pompey's army had continued marching towards us, but seeing us close the distance, they came to a halt to dress their lines. Meanwhile, we continued forward a few moments longer, waiting for the command to begin the charge, which would be given the instant Pompey's army began its own. However, even as we closed the distance, no such command was given by Pompey. His army just stood there, waiting for us to charge, seemingly determined not to launch their own countercharge. Finally, the order was given to halt in order for us to redress our lines and to catch our breath, since we would now be covering more distance than we originally thought. We were close enough now to see exactly whom we were facing, and as we were catching our breath, I walked over to Vibius and pointed.

"That's Pompey's 1st, and isn't that the 15th next to them?"

Vibius peered at the enemy lines for a moment, then nodded. "I wonder how the 15th feels about facing us, after all the miles we marched together in Gaul?"

That was the question in my own mind, but since there was no real way of knowing the answer, I just shrugged.

Vibius looked over at the massed cavalry standing motionless except for the horses pawing at the ground, creating a veil of dust that made it hard to distinguish individuals, but managing to make out at least one, he pointed and exclaimed, "Isn't that that prick Labienus over there?"

I squinted, then after a moment I could make out a figure sitting a horse in a familiar manner, and I nodded. "The gods know I saw him enough to know how he sits a horse. That's definitely him," I said.

"We better win then, because that bastard will show us no mercy." Vibius smiled grimly.

"And if I get the chance, I have a promise to fulfill," I replied, thinking about my conversation with Albinus.

~ ~ ~ ~

For several moments, the two armies just stood there, looking at each other, and there was a pervasive silence that I have never witnessed before or since. It was so unnerving that the Pompeians became clearly agitated, moving around and even as we watched, their cohesion began to fall apart. Their Centurions started snapping orders at their men to keep still, but we watched the carefully ordered lines simply begin to fall apart. Even as this was happening, Pompey issued the orders for his cavalry to charge, the ground starting to shake when more than 6,000 horses began thundering towards us. Instantly, Caesar ordered our own cavalry to countercharge, despite there being barely 1,000 of them, and now both groups of infantry stood watching them crash together with a horrific sound. Almost immediately, the dust churned up by thousands of pounding hooves obscured most of the action, with only glimpses of what was taking place coming when some freak of the wind cleared the dust away for a moment. In those moments, I spotted Labienus swinging his *spatha*, the long cavalry sword, above his head as he shouted out commands to his troopers. Through the dust, I saw men falling, and at first, I took heart because it appeared that it was more Pompeians than our own men on the ground, but deep down I knew that with a disparity of more than six to one it could not last. With the cavalry battling on the plain to our right, Pompey ordered his force of archers and slingers, positioned just behind the cavalry, forward into the space just vacated by them, whereupon they began launching volleys of slingshot and arrows at us.

Now, above the sound of the cavalry battle, came the whirring sound of slingshot zipping by, and I yelled out to my men, "Shields up! If any of you bastards gets hit by any of these piddling missiles, you're on a charge!"

As I expected, this brought a laugh, and not for the first time I had the fleeting wish that I was back in the ranks, safe behind a shield, rather than standing out front with nothing but my *vitus* to wave at the slings and arrows headed my way. While it is considered bad form for a Centurion to hop and dance about, trying to dodge things headed his way, it is acceptable for us to take a step in one direction or another. The next few moments found me taking such steps back and forth, convinced that the entire Pompeian force had decided to aim right at me. I was so busy trying not to be skewered or smacked in the face with a lead shot that I did not see Labienus split off part of his force, disengage them from our cavalry, and begin to gallop around our right flank.

~ ~ ~ ~

I honestly do not remember hearing the signal, but it must have been given because as a single unit, the army stepped forward, beginning the advance again, at the quick step. We closed the distance rapidly, then the *cornu* gave the signal to ready the javelins.

"Prepare, Javelins!"

Behind me, I heard the indrawn breaths of thousands of men readying themselves to hurl their javelin at the enemy, who in turn hunched behind their shields, waiting for the volley to come their way.

"Release!"

The air was filled with the whistling sound of thousands of shafts arcing through the air and despite myself I winced at seeing the slender slivers of wood turn downward to pick up speed. Enemies or not, I could not help feeling sorry for anyone forced to endure a volley of javelins. The sound of the metal heads punching into the wood of the Pompeian shields made a thunderous racket, overlying which were the high-pitched screams of men not fast or lucky enough to block one of the missiles coming at them with their shields.

Immediately after we discharged our volley, I heard a familiar voice roar out, "Follow me boys, it's time to earn our pay!"

And with that, Crastinus and his handpicked group of men let out a roar before charging headlong into the men of Pompey's 1st Legion. Just heartbeats later, the rest of us followed, slamming into the stationary line of the Pompeians. Once more, I found myself staring at men just like myself, looking over the rims of their shields at me as I ran forward, dropping my *vitus*. Reaching out, I made as if to grab the upper edge of a

126

man's shield who reacted instantly, sweeping his blade along the edge in an attempt to cut off my fingers, but that was exactly what I wanted him to do. Instead, I whipped my hand down, grabbing the left edge of his shield and giving a tremendous yank. If he had relinquished his grip on his shield, he would have lived, at least for a bit longer, but instead he held on for dear life, the combination of my size and strength serving to pull him bodily out from his own line, stripping him of the protection of the man to his left. Instantly, I saw the silver of a blade flicker out as one of my men saw the opening, his sword punching through under the man's elbow and into his ribcage. The man crumpled to the ground and I immediately grabbed his shield to use as my own. Before we could exploit the hole made by his loss, however, the man behind him stepped into his place, lashing out with his shield to knock me a step backwards. All along the line, men were bashing at each other, and like our raid on the hillfort, I was struck by the thought if bodies were not falling and blood flowing, this could be nothing more than a training exercise. Because we were so familiar with each other's tactics, it was impossible for one side to gain an advantage over the other, yet we stood there bashing at each other, trying nonetheless. Now that we were engaged, I had no idea what was happening to our right flank; I just had to trust that Caesar had the situation under control. Besides, turning my attention away from the matter at hand would be a deadly mistake with men as experienced as we were facing, so I concentrated on the action immediately around me. The second line was ordered forward earlier than usual, but even the added weight pushing those of us in the front line, we were unable to budge the Pompeians. After the initial clash, where we had unleashed our battle cry as we slammed into the enemy, there was very little sound issuing from the men, aside from the grunts, gasps and groans of someone being struck down. I had never been involved in a battle where there was so little sound coming from the combatants, even more so than the fight at the hillfort, and it was a little unnerving, to put it mildly. I am convinced that because of this silence, I was able to hear a cry that chilled my heart.

"Crastinus is dead! They've killed the Primus Pilus!"

Immediately after that call, there was a roar of triumph from the Pompeians to my right, followed by an answering roar of rage by my comrades in Crastinus' volunteers. Turning and looking over my shoulder, I saw the same look of shock on the men's faces that I felt; Gaius Crastinus was invincible. If he fell, what hope did any of us have? I think for the first time in my life in the Legions, I felt the icy grip of doubt threaten to take hold of me. Oh, I always knew that there was a possibility that I would fall whenever we lined up in battle, but I never truly believed it might happen, until this moment. Gaius Crastinus was my first commander, and I was proud to watch his rise through the Legion, just as

I knew he was proud to watch mine. The idea that he could be dead brought home the fact that if he could die, I could just as easily die, and I know that's exactly what every man behind me was thinking. Well, Titus, if today is the day you fall, I thought to myself, then you will be in good company and you may as well go out covering your name in glory. You have to give these men an example to follow, like Crastinus did.

"All right boys," I roared, waving my Gallic blade above my head, "I'm going to go join Crastinus. We're going to share the same rowboat over to Charon. Who's with me?"

And without waiting for an answer, I waded into the Pompeians in front of me.

~ ~ ~ ~

Over the years, I have been asked by many civilians about the famous battles I have been in, and there is none better known throughout the Republic, now called the Empire, than the Battle of Pharsalus. However, it is a funny thing, because when one is actually standing in the line, fighting as a lowly Gregarius or even as an Optio or Centurion, your perspective is usually drastically different than that of the general or Tribunes who ultimately end up being the men that the historians listen to when they are writing their version of events. That is one reason I have taken on this endeavor, because I have read some of the accounts of our time in Gaul and the civil war and my hope is that my feeble attempt to convey what those of us who actually did the fighting were feeling will be appreciated by you, gentle reader. And on that hot, dusty day on the plains of Pharsalus, I have never been so sure that we were defeated as I was then. Despite managing to push the Pompeian line back a few paces, nowhere along our front did we have the kind of breakthrough that could be exploited by the men of the third line, standing ready for such an occasion. The best it could be called was a standoff, where whatever gains we made were simply not sufficient to carry the day, but where the enemy could not do any better, except that on this day a draw was the same as a defeat for Caesar and the army, and we all knew it. Even with my best attempts to create a breach, I never got farther than a few paces deep into the Pompeians, with my men pushing right behind me, yet it was not enough. All I could tell about the larger battle was from the calls of the *cornu*, so I heard the signal for the Cohorts of the fourth line that Caesar had created to move forward. Regardless, I did not have the time to give it any thought as to whether or not his stratagem worked. However, it did and it worked very well indeed. The men of the fourth line were ordered to lie down in the tall grass that was a feature of the plain, and as our own cavalry fell back under the onslaught of the Pompeian cavalry, the dust raised by the horses' hooves further shielded them from view of the enemy.

When Caesar ordered the attack of the fourth line, they were barely a hundred paces away from the Pompeian cavalry, and over such a short distance, a running man can close with a mounted man, especially against such a tightly packed mass of man and horseflesh as the Pompeian cavalry presented, and that is what happened. Once they closed with the Pompeian cavalry, rather than throw their javelin, they used them as lances to stab upward at the faces of the cavalrymen, inflicting horrific damage, maiming and blinding whoever was in their path. In a matter of moments, the Pompeian cavalry charge disintegrated, the horsemen wheeling about, intent only on saving themselves, thereby leaving the slingers and archers completely unprotected. Consequently, their slaughter was total, the remainder of our cavalry force now turning back about and running the missile troops down. With both the Pompeian cavalry and missile force disposed of, the men of the fourth line now turned to fall on the left flank of the 1st and 15th, rolling them up like a carpet. From what I was able to reconstruct after talking to some of the men in the fourth line, their charge into the cavalry happened just moments before Crastinus fell, and I have been left wondering if he was not so reckless if he would be alive today. Not that it matters; such thoughts are meaningless, doing nothing but haunting an old man's sleep. Indeed, at the time, he was doing his duty by setting an example of bravery to give his men courage by leaping onto the wall of shields in an attempt to create a breach, much as had been done during the fight against Ariovistus. Just as he leapt against the Pompeian line, he was struck on the side of the head, knocking his helmet askew and causing him to fall to his knees, as close to a certain death in battle as one can come. Only losing your footing in close combat leaves you incredibly vulnerable, but the blow to his head further robbed him of his awareness so that he kneeled on the ground, weaving about, making no attempt to defend himself, and the inevitable happened. The shield of the man in front of him moved six inches to the side, a flash of silver darted out, the blade of the sword entered his open mouth and punched through the back of his head. Just that quickly, Primus Pilus Gaius Crastinus, hero of the 10th Legion and one of the most respected Centurions in the army, was dead. It was not more than a dozen heartbeats later that the men of the fourth line slammed into the side and rear of the Pompeian left, forcing the Pompeians to start yielding ground. Where I was at, we were only alerted that something had happened by a change in the sounds of battle when our fourth line slammed into them. Additionally, it was at this moment that Caesar also ordered our third line forward. At first, the Pompeian line did not waver, but the unrelenting pressure on two sides became too much and we heard the *cornu* call that signaled a fighting withdrawal. Immediately, the Pompeian front line lashed out with their shields, pushing us back a step to give them the freedom to take their own step backwards, but we immediately moved back in to engage them again. Now their Centurions were calling out the count that we use to pace the formation as they slowly, grudgingly gave ground, even as the added weight of our third line exerted even more pressure.

Inch by inch, then foot by foot, we pushed the Pompeians backward, bashing and smashing, their progress backward marked by bodies of both their fallen and ours, but still they held formation, refusing to break. The sun was now high in the sky, causing both sides to suffer from thirst and exhaustion, but we could not stop putting on the pressure, while they could not stop resisting our advance. Fortunately, while our battle on the right wing was still at something of an impasse, the raw recruits of Pompey's Legions holding the center were not made of the same stuff as the veterans on the wings, and shortly after the third line engaged with them, their cohesion shattered as they simply turned to run for their lives. The 15th was to our left, next to the Pompeian center, but once they lost the support of the Legions on their right, they too finally broke and fled. Now that the third line was engaged, those of us in the first two lines moved to the rear to catch our breath and I immediately called to my Centurions to give me a tally of casualties. Since we had dropped all of our gear back by the camp, we had also left our water behind, so I ordered some men to go through the bodies of the Pompeians to see if anything could be scavenged. The dust cloud was the most oppressive and obscuring that I had ever seen in battle, making it almost impossible to tell what was going on. However, I could see that the Legions to our immediate left were pushing forward in pursuit of the fleeing Pompeians. If I strained my eyes, I could make out the far left wing where the 8th and 9th was engaged, but could only see that they were roughly in the same position that we were, so it appeared that only the center and the 15th had given way. At that point, that was my total knowledge of the situation, so without thinking, I began to move over to where Crastinus would be with his volunteers to see what his orders were before stopping short. Crastinus was dead; that meant that the Primus Princeps was now in command, a short, squatty little man named Torquatus who had been the Primus Pilus briefly before Crastinus returned, so I went looking for him instead. The men were breathing easier by this point, but I could see that they were close to the edge of exhaustion, yet I knew that we were not through, and I cursed myself for not thinking to make the men bring along their water at the very least. Just before I reached where Torquatus was standing with the rest of his Centurions from the First, through the veil of dust I saw Caesar himself coming, his face covered in dust, except for where rivulets of sweat had streamed down his cheeks. My immediate thought was that he looked like a Narbo whore with her makeup ruined after a hard night's work, the thought forcing me to bite back a laugh since I did not want my general to ask what was so funny at a time like this.

Stopping where Torquatus was standing, Caesar asked, "Where is the Primus Pilus?"

There was a pause as Torquatus exchanged glances with the other men around him, then said quietly, "Primus Pilus Crastinus is dead, sir. He made good his promise to bring you glory dead or alive."

Caesar did not respond for a moment; his head bowed, he closed his eyes, and I saw his lips move in what I presumed to be a silent prayer for Crastinus. Then, commander once again, he looked up and said, "Very well. We'll mourn him later, but as of now you're the Primus Pilus and I need you and your men to make one last effort." He pointed in the direction of Pompey's camp, and continued, "We have them on the run, except for the 1st here, but the third line has them engaged. I want you to take the remaining Cohorts, circle around, and cut them off, but I don't think you'll have to engage them. Once they see they're completely isolated, they'll break and run like the rest of them, I'm sure of it. Instead, I need you to push on to the camp. If we stop here, we've won a battle. If we take the camp, we've won the war. Do you understand, Primus Pilus?"

Torquatus came to *intente*, saluted, and said crisply, "Perfectly, General. We won't let you down."

Caesar favored Torquatus and the rest of the men standing there with one of his most dazzling smiles and said, "I know you won't, Torquatus."

Then he wheeled Toes around and galloped off towards the center, a string of aides hurrying after him, making the dust cloud even worse for a moment, causing me to cough and spit out a glob of mud, cursing this dusty country as I did.

Walking to Torquatus, I saluted, and he said, "Well, you heard the man. Get the men up and ready to move on my command, quickly!"

Trotting back to where my men were waiting, I gave the order to make ready to move again. I could see how tired they were when there was not one word of complaint, instead men just staggering to their feet and picking up their shields.

~ ~ ~ ~

We moved around the 1st Legion, but for once Caesar had misjudged the caliber of his enemy, because they did not panic at the sight of us in their rear. I do not doubt that we could have broken them if we had attacked, but those were not our orders, and it was a suicidally brave or stupid man who disobeyed an order of Gaius Julius Caesar. Torquatus was neither, therefore we continued past the 1st, headed to the camp. The ground along the way was littered with discarded bits of equipment, dead or dying horses, and bodies of men lying sprawled in attitudes that told a tale of headlong flight. Normally in situations like this, while we marched along we would finish off any wounded men we came across, but on this day, we did not do so because these were our countrymen. In the heat of battle we would do our very best to slaughter each other, yet none of us had it in them to slaughter a helpless Roman who under different circumstances could be a comrade with whom we shared the same marching camp. I did have men stop and search for any water that might be lying about, as did the other Cohort commanders, but otherwise we marched steadily towards the Pompeian camp, where a fierce fight seemed to be taking place. On our approach, we saw what appeared to be forces composed of at least two Legions detach itself from the melee at the walls of the Pompeian camp, then begin to march away towards the hills to the northwest of the camp, clearly intent on escape. Even as they did so, we joined the other Cohorts that had made it to the walls of the camp and without waiting for orders we began to shower the men lining the walls with javelins that we picked up on the march, making short work of scouring the walls clear of the enemy.

Immediately thereafter, we assaulted the gates of the camp itself, these actually being made of timber rather than dirt, and without the use of any equipment other than just brute force, we managed to bring the gate crashing down by sheer weight of numbers. Pouring through the gate, we were met by a scratch force of Pompeians, and without hesitation, we threw ourselves at the enemy. My lungs were burning, my legs ached and my arm felt like it was made of lead, but I was a Centurion in Caesar's army, and I had to give my men an example to follow, so I was one of the first to go crashing into the wall of shields.

~ ~ ~ ~

The fight for the camp was furious, yet it was over quickly; I think the heart had gone out of the Pompeians by this point, and once it was clear that our superior numbers made the outcome inevitable, they quickly threw down their weapons to surrender. I did not come out unscathed; sometime during the fight I received a fair-sized gash on my left arm just below the shoulder, due to a moment of carelessness when I dropped my shield too low blocking a thrust. I like to think that it was due to my fatigue and not that the man I was facing bested me, although I exacted my revenge on him with a thrust through his gut. With the main resistance ended, all that was left was to mop up, hunting down survivors and small groups of men who decided to make a stand. Making our way through the camp, it was only then that I got my first inkling of how complete was our victory. The camp had been hurriedly sacked, that much was clear, but since we were the first of Caesar's men into the camp, the only people that could have been responsible were Pompey's own men. Before we had a chance to investigate further, the *cornu* sounded the recall at the main gate, so I rounded up the men, then we all half-trotted, half-stumbled back to find out what was happening. Falling back in once we got back to the gate, it became clear how our numbers had shrunk just since the beginning of the day, but taking a quick head count, I was pleased to see that I had not lost any more men at the fight at the camp. So far, I had 20 dead, twice as many wounded, with roughly the same amount unaccounted for, making the strength of my Cohort less than 200 men. The other Cohorts were in much the same shape, but our work was still not finished.

"One final effort, comrades, one final effort is all that's needed," Caesar's voice was almost throbbing with intensity, trying to convey to us the urgency and importance of what he was saying. "We can't stop and plunder the camp right now. The remainder of Pompey's army has taken position up on that hill over there." He pointed to the spot where we could plainly see the Pompeians frantically entrenching around the crest of the hill that loomed above the walls of the camp to the northwest. "If we can get around the base of the hill, our scouts have reported that we'll cut them off from the only source of water, but we must hurry before they can dig a ditch down the hill to protect it. I have ordered that every entrenching tool that can be found in this camp be brought to us, but first we must hurry to get into position. One more effort, my comrades. Just one more!"

The fact that we cheered his words at all should be considered a tribute to the leadership of Caesar, because in truth I was not sure the men had the energy for what he was ordering, but I knew that we would die trying.

~ ~ ~ ~

Despite our almost overwhelming fatigue, we marched quickly, although it was more of a stumbling half-run than a march, out of the camp to the base of the hill about six miles from the rear gate by the route we took, swinging around to the north. By this time, the sun was close to setting, meaning we would be working well past dark, and Caesar quickly made his dispositions, placing us in a circle around the hill before ordering us to dig. At first there were not enough spades and picks to go around, something of a blessing in disguise for the men, since it allowed them to work in shifts and get a small amount of rest. Nevertheless, once we began, I sent the men who were not working to fetch water, using their helmet as makeshift buckets. Beginning the job, we had to use our bare hands, but finally men came with mules loaded down with entrenching tools. Once all the men had tools, the work progressed rapidly, despite it being done in the dark. This was the advantage gained from all the digging we had done all over Gaul, Hispania and now Greece, enabling us to work just as quickly in total darkness as if the sun was shining high in the sky. The Pompeians could not see us, but there was no doubt that they could hear us digging, and I am sure it was that sound that compelled a deputation from the Pompeians to come down the hill under a flag of truce, asking Caesar for terms. His reply was that he would only take their unconditional surrender, whereupon the deputation marched back up the hill to discuss the matter. It was a short discussion, and at daybreak the day after the battle started, the remainder of Pompey's army threw their weapons down, falling to their knees and begging Caesar for mercy. And of course, Caesar showed them mercy, in the same manner he had been doing the whole civil war, ordering us not to molest our prisoners in any way and to respect their property. This did not set well with the men, who felt that they were being cheated of their just reward for all that they had done, especially since the contents of the camp traditionally went to them. Ultimately, I believe that this was the final straw for the men and was a direct cause of what happened next. For it was on this day of Caesar's greatest victory that came not only the greatest challenge to his leadership, but to mine as well, along with the death of the friendship between Vibius and myself.

~ ~ ~ ~

The details of accepting the surrender of such a large force of men took at least a couple of watches, making it mid-morning before things settled down sufficiently to allow our own men the chance to rest. Once given permission, they finally just dropped to the ground in their normal spot in formation, with adjustments made for our losses. With the men sitting on the ground talking quietly among themselves, I called my Centurions to my side, or more accurately, the Centurions who were still standing. Niger had fallen, victim of a slingshot to the eye that penetrated his brain, killing him instantly. Crispus was down with a serious wound to the thigh, but he would probably recover if the wound remained clean. In their places were their Optios; Niger's was Gaius Vatinius, a man who was part of my *dilectus* and in fact had lived not very far away from me and Vibius. In Crispus' place was Vibius Flaccus, also one of our *dilectus*, but I do not remember where he came from. We went looking for Torquatus, finding him standing grim-faced with the remaining Centurions of the First Cohort. I could tell by the postures of the men surrounding him that something was amiss, and we soon found out the cause.

"Caesar wants us to be ready to march in two parts of a watch," Torquatus said grimly, and despite myself, I gasped with shock, the only saving grace being that I was not alone in my reaction.

"Why?" Celer blurted out, and I was still in too much shock to admonish him for speaking out of turn. Truthfully, he only asked the same question I would have asked.

Torquatus smiled, but it was not a happy look on his face as he said, "Because as many big fish as we may have bagged, the biggest one got away. Pompey was spotted heading for Larisa and Caesar wants to hunt him down. He's ordering the Spanish Legions to march with him."

"How many men does Pompey have?" I asked, but the answer was only a shrug as Torquatus looked away, clearly not wanting to answer the question.

Again, I was not alone, evidenced by one of his own Centurions asking him again.

Finally, Torquatus let out a sigh and said, "Perhaps 30 mounted men, and less than a Century of infantry."

"And he wants to chase that with four Legions?" someone asked in astonishment; I do not remember who.

Now Torquatus' face started to suffuse with red and he snapped, "I don't remember hearing that the Legions have become a debating society. Caesar has ordered it, and that's that. Make your men ready."

As quickly as it had come, his anger passed. He could only look at us and shrug helplessly, "I know that it stinks, but those are our orders."

"The men are really not going to like this."

All heads turned to the one of us with the courage to utter aloud what we were all thinking, and it was with equal parts pride and irritation that I saw that Scribonius had opened his mouth. His tone was less of an admonishment than it was thoughtful, and looking at him, I saw an expression that I had come to learn meant that he was thinking things through.

Torquatus, however, was in no mood for indulging Scribonius' mental exercise, and he said angrily, "You think I don't know that? Well, I do, but I also know that they're going to do what they're fucking told, or I'll flay every last one who so much as whispers a word against my orders."

"Primus Pilus, with all respect, I'd be careful what you say, because I think that you'll have to carry it out on almost every man of the Legion, and not just in the ranks."

I cannot convey the quality of shock that immediately descended on the group when these words were uttered, not just from the words themselves but who had uttered them. Quintus Balbus was the Primus Princeps, the Centurion in charge of the Third Century of the First Cohort, and outside of Gaius Crastinus himself, was one of the most respected Centurions of the Legion. He was a large, muscular man, although not as large as I was, and his arms were covered with scars, as was his face, where a Gaulish axe had sliced off one ear and left the right side of his face a knotted mass of scar tissue. Balbus was well regarded enough that if he were to be permanently appointed Primus Pilus over Torquatus, none of us would be particularly surprised, nor displeased. Except Torquatus, of course. Balbus did not talk much, but when he did, he usually said something that needed to be said, and apparently, he believed that this was one of those times.

Despite there being no love lost between Torquatus and Balbus, the acting Primus Pilus could not afford to ignore such dire words from a man like Balbus, and his face clouded with doubt as he asked warily, "What do you mean Balbus? Spit it out, man! Don't talk in riddles."

However, Balbus was not one to be cowed, even by his superior, and he did not speak for a moment as he gathered his thoughts.

Finally, he spoke in a lower tone of voice to keep his words from carrying far. "Simply this, Primus Pilus. The men are as exhausted as any of us have ever seen them. Would anyone disagree with that?" We all shook our heads, and Balbus continued. "Add to that the men weren't allowed to plunder the camp, nor were they allowed to take the Pompeian baggage as spoils of war."

"But you know why Caesar did that," Torquatus protested, but Balbus held up his hand in a placating gesture.

"I'm not saying I disagree, Torquatus. What I am saying is, put yourself in the men's boots for a moment and see it how they see it. I'm not saying they're right; in fact, I think they're in the wrong, but right now I don't think right or wrong much matters." Grudgingly, Torquatus nodded his head, indicating that Balbus should continue. "We all know that there's already been trouble with the men, although thankfully it hasn't been with the 10th . . . yet." He looked meaningfully at each of us, then finished, "I think that the men are at the end of their tether physically, and they feel like they've been wronged. What I'm afraid of is that if those bastards in the 9th refuse to march, and I think that's exactly what they're going to do when they get the order, that our boys are going to follow suit."

We stood for a moment, digesting what Balbus said.

Finally, Scribonius spoke, his face creased in a thoughtful frown. "But the men of the 9th have at the least a legitimate complaint because of their discharge situation. None of the 10th is due for a discharge for some time yet. So what do you think they'll use as their excuse?"

No sooner had the words left Scribonius' mouth than I was hit with a sickening certainty, making me feel like I had been punched in the stomach.

Slowly, I said, "I think I know what it'll be."

Almost like it was on command, all heads turned, the eyes of every Centurion fastening on mine. By this time, our small group was joined by most of the rest of the Centurions of the 10th, and before I spoke, there was a whispered account of what had been said to that point. Seeing the mixture of expressions sweep across the face of the other Centurions as they digested what had transpired, my sick feeling increased when I saw that surprise was not one of them.

Finally, I spoke again. "I know that the men have been muttering for several days about the bonus that Caesar promised them."

Despite myself, I glanced at Scribonius, and saw that he knew exactly where my thoughts were, because one of the loudest complainers was my very own Optio. I had hoped that promoting Vibius to Optio would at the very least modify his feelings about Caesar, because now that he was an officer, albeit a junior one, he could no longer engage in the kind of talk that pervades the ranks about their senior officers. Also, I hoped that by more exposure to Caesar and his decisions, he would come to see the man for what he truly was and not what Vibius had made him out to be in his mind, just another patrician who used the plebs to further his own ends without any regard for the greater good. However, nothing of the sort had happened; if anything, Vibius' animosity towards Caesar had increased. And I was guilty of turning a deaf ear to his talk around the campfire, except in truth, I was not ignoring his talk any more than I did over the last several years, but that was, and is, a shabby excuse. Being my Optio, I should have called him to account long before and made him shut his mouth, no matter how it had to be done, but I had not. And now, I was sure that if Balbus was right, and there was a mutiny, the men of the 10th would use the bonus as their justification for joining their comrades.

Now that I had spoken my suspicions, I saw several heads nodding, and someone said, "I think Pullus is right. I know that my boys have been moaning about it for a couple weeks now."

"I can't say that I blame them," said a voice.

I whipped my head around to see who had uttered such nonsense, but was shocked to the core when I heard many voices add their agreement, and I looked over at Torquatus, who looked as surprised as I did. But significantly, or at least so I thought, Balbus did not look surprised at all, and wondered what that meant.

"So what do we do about it?" someone else asked, stopping the muttered conversations as we all looked at Torquatus, who rubbed his face wearily as he thought. I remember thinking then that perhaps the cost of ambition and my goal of rising to Primus Pilus bore a price that ultimately was too high for me to pay, yet I quickly shrugged it off, thinking that somehow I would never find myself in this position.

Waiting for several moments as Torquatus stared at the ground, he finally spoke. "Nothing. There's nothing we can do until it happens." He glanced up to see how his decision was being received, and encouraged, he continued, "We can't very well start dragging men out for punishment because they've been the loudest complainers about this bonus. Especially when it's clear that a number of their Centurions agree with them." He glared around as he said the last bit, and was rewarded by a few heads bowing, some of the Centurions suddenly finding something about their boots incredibly interesting at that moment. Torquatus then gave a tired shrug. "I think we just have to wait and see what happens, and whether Balbus is right. And then," he looked meaningfully around at the Centurions of the 10th, "we'll see who stands where, won't we?"

And with that, we were dismissed to go pass the word to our men to make ready to move out. Or to mutiny, we weren't sure which.

~ ~ ~ ~

As matters turned out, Balbus was about as right as he could have been. When the order was given to make ready to march the men of the 9th, led by their Centurions, simply refused to budge. They were followed quickly by the 8th, then the 7th, and thanks to the warning that Balbus had raised, the only person shocked when the 10th followed suit was Caesar himself. Stepping in front of the Cohort, despite my belief that I had prepared myself, I was still a bit shaken when Vibius was not standing there ready to receive my orders. Instead, he was standing in his former spot in the formation, and I think I was trying to postpone the inevitable because I did not order him to me.

Instead I acted like everything was normal, turning to the *cornicen* to sound the call for the men to pick up their gear, who actually hesitated for a moment, opening his mouth as if to say something before I said to him quietly, "Don't. Just carry out the order, and whatever happens will happen. Don't compound your crime by refusing a direct order."

His face darkened, but he obeyed and blew the call, whereupon the men of the Cohort followed the lead of the rest of the army. Instead of picking up their gear, almost in unison, they sat down on the ground next to it. Even knowing it was coming, actually watching it happen was a blow almost physical in nature. I stood for a moment, not sure what to do at this point, looking over at the First Cohort to see if Torquatus had any ideas, but he just looked at me and shrugged helplessly. Finally, I walked towards Vibius, who sat calmly watching me approach, but did not come to his feet.

The anger that was building inside me at being put in this situation flared up through my chest, and I spoke sharply, "Get on your feet when your superior approaches, Optio."

For a moment, he did not move, then slowly got to his feet, coming to *intente*. For moments that seemed to last forever, we stood staring at each other, neither knowing what to say. Finally, I shook my head.

"Why, Vibius?"

He looked at me as if I had gone mad. "Why," he said incredulously, "why? You know very well why, Titus. He lied to us, Titus. Surely you can see that?"

I shook my head. "First, I don't believe that just because he hasn't given us our bonus it's a case that he's lying to us. If you haven't noticed," my voice was heavy with sarcasm, "he's been a little busy the last few weeks."

"I know exactly how busy he's been because it's been thanks to our sweat and blood," he shot back, and this I could not argue.

For a moment, we stood there, neither of us speaking and I could almost pretend that we were just two friends standing in comfortable silence, but we both knew it was just that, a pretense.

Finally, Vibius placed a hand on my arm and said, "Titus, you know that I'm right. You know that he owes us, and he owes us more than just some bonus."

Now, all these years later, I will finally confess that at that moment, Vibius had almost convinced me. The surprise of that realization almost undid me, because I nearly opened my mouth. I had not realized until that moment that I had some resentment built up inside me that I was unaware of, some *numen* that inhabited my soul, feeding a flame of bitterness and anger that I did not even know was there until that moment. And standing there thinking on it, I also realized that I did not really know why I felt this way. After all, Caesar had favored me, not as much as some other men, but more than most; however, I was also tired. I was tired of all the marching, and I was tired of watching my men bleed and die. When all was said and done, was it not really for the reasons that Vibius had been arguing about all these years, that we were just pieces on the board of some great game being played by Gaius Julius Caesar? That all of his high-flown rhetoric about preserving the Republic and stopping tyranny were just empty words, that this was about little more than one patrician trying to gain ascendancy over another? These thoughts rushed through my mind staring down at Vibius' hand resting on my forearm, and through all of the confusion and emotions running through my body, I remembered how Vibius and I had met, and how much we had seen together. When I first saw that hand, I thought, it was so much smaller and white. Now, it was as brown as a piece of leather, the knuckles scarred from hard work and fights. So was the forearm it rested on, his hand partially covering the long scar that ran down my arm, and I frowned, trying to remember where I had gotten it. What battle had it been, I wondered? Then I remembered; it was from the Gallaeci all those years ago, and one thing I knew was that Vibius had been by my side.

"Join us, Titus. Caesar will listen if you're with us."

And there it was; all I had to do was say yes, and my friendship with Vibius would be preserved. Besides, was there not something to what he was saying? Perhaps the way the men were going about it was not the right way, but surely they had just cause, and ultimately, did Caesar not owe us what he had promised? I do not know how long I stood there, looking down at that hand resting on my arm, but then I shook my head. Looking up, I saw Vibius frowning at me, and I was suddenly filled with a sadness that I had never felt before, because I knew that this time, our friendship could not survive.

"No, Vibius. I won't join you. You're rising in mutiny against our general. And I can't justify that, no matter what the cause."

Vibius jerked his hand away as if I had suddenly become red-hot. His face turned bright red, something I had seen so many times over the years, telling me that he was not just angry; he was enraged.

"Mutiny," he hissed between clenched teeth, his jaw muscles bulging. "This is no mutiny! This is a just act by Roman citizens who are simply demanding their rights. The men of the 7th, 8th, and 9th have been wronged . . ."

I cut him off with a harsh laugh. "Spare me, Vibius. You could give a fart in a *testudo* for those faithless bastards. You hate them as much as I do, so please refrain from acting with such righteous indignation about their rights."

For a moment, Vibius said nothing, his jaws working as he chewed on his rage. "Fine," he spat, "you're right. This has nothing to do with them. It has everything to do with what Caesar owes us. And while we're being honest," he continued hotly, "let's not pretend that the reason you won't join us has anything to do with what's right or what's wrong. It has everything to do with wanting to be in good with Caesar. You'll do anything to be his lapdog!"

Before I had conscious thought, my hand gripped my sword, whipping the blade out but not bringing it up, pointing it at the ground instead. Vibius' eyes widened, but he stood his ground, his own hand reaching down.

"You'd be dead before you got it out, Vibius," I said calmly. "It's been a long, long time since you could best me."

He said nothing, but his hand dropped from the pommel of his sword. That is how things were for dozens of heartbeats as we stood staring at each other.

His mouth opened and closed several times before he finally said in a croaking whisper, "You would strike me down? Your best and longest friend? It's come to that?"

All I could do was nod my head; then there was nothing left to say about it, and I saw the death of my longest and dearest friendship pass through the eyes of Vibius Domitius.

Finally, he nodded, his voice becoming cold and formal. "Very well, Pilus Prior. But if that's what the gods will, then so be it, but I'm not marching. And," he turned and indicated the men, "neither are any of the men of the Second Cohort. We took a vote and it's been decided."

"You took a vote?"

I do not know why, but I found that the most astonishing thing; the men had voted behind my back, and I did not know it had taken place. Of course, it could very well have been that Vibius was lying about a vote, yet it certainly seemed creditable at the time, and since we never spoke about that day after this, I never did find out the truth.

~ ~ ~ ~

For the first time ever, Caesar was flummoxed and he did not seem to know what to do. First, he approached the other Spanish Legions, who steadfastly refused to budge, demanding their discharges.

Then he came to the 10th, standing before us for several moments in silence, before he finally spoke. "Comrades, I know that of all my Legions, I can rely on the 10th to follow its general and hunt Pompey down. What say you?"

For an instant, just a brief instant, there was not a sound and I dared to think that when it came down to it, standing here facing their general, the men could not go through with their threat, but then one man, quickly followed by other voices, called out.

"No, Caesar! We won't follow you until you pay us the bonus you've promised!"

Immediately, the air was rent by the cries and calls of the men. Despite not being given leave to move, I whirled around, glaring at the men of the Second Cohort, but none of them except Vibius met my gaze. He was the only man with the courage to stare directly in my eyes as his voice was raised in refusal to his general, and despite my anger at him, I felt a grudging respect that he was at least a man among mice.

Turning back to Caesar, I saw he had gone white with shock seeing his most favored and to this moment most loyal Legion refuse his orders to march. I watched his face transform, the color rushing to his cheeks and I could see that he was growing terribly angry.

Finally, he roared louder than I had ever heard him. "***Silete!***"

And the men immediately shut up, faster than they ever had before, stirring in me a flicker of hope. It was clear that Caesar still possessed some sort of hold over the men, and I held my breath waiting for what was to happen next.

That silence hung in the air for several moments, before Caesar said coldly, "Before I say anything more, I first want to know who among the Centurions and Optios feel the same way as the men?"

What happened next staggered Caesar, as it staggered me. For a moment, there was no movement, then I sensed something out of the corner of my eye and looked over to where it originated in the First

Cohort, and despite myself, I let out a gasp. Balbus had stepped forward, his back straight, his chest thrust out as he stared at Caesar calmly. A second later, two more Centurions of the First stepped forward, and I thought that Torquatus would have some sort of stroke at the sight. However, I quickly realized that if the Centurions of the First felt this way, then it was almost a certainty that my Centurions would betray me as well, and I whirled around to see who the vipers at my back were. I cannot say I was particularly surprised when Celer stepped forward, nor when Vibius did the same, but I was surprised when the only other Optios to step forward were Celer's toady and Vatinius, who I guess would be more accurately described as acting Centurion in Niger's place. Scribonius and Priscus, along with their Optios remained standing, stone-faced and watching their comrades step forward in defiance of Caesar. And of course, at Vibius Domitius, who for the first time at least did not look quite as sure of himself when he stepped forward to join the others. Looking down the formation, the only solace I could take was that my Cohort had less of its officers' side with the men than any other, but it was small comfort. And Caesar clearly did not take any comfort in anything that was happening, standing there watching the Legion he had favored above all others betray him. There was a silence for several moments, with both sides staring at each other before Caesar finally spoke, and what he said next chilled me to my very marrow.

"Very well, you have made your choice, and now you leave me with none." Turning to one of his aides, I do not remember who it was, he said something quietly and even from where I stood I could see the aide's face turn ashen but he merely nodded then began writing with a stylus on the wax tablet that they carried with them everywhere. Caesar then turned back to announce in a voice that carried to the other Legions as well as ours, "Since you have chosen to disobey a lawful order from your general, I hereby order that the 10th Legion be decimated!"

The gasp of shock and dismay carried to a place where I was sure that the gods would hear, and it did not come just from the men of the 10th, but the entire army that was within hearing distance. And the moment his words were relayed to the rear ranks, the gasps became a roar of outrage that seized the entire army. From where I stood, I could see that Caesar was dealt yet another shock, and there was a moment where I got very angry at Caesar as I thought, what the fuck did you expect? That the army would just simply stand by as you decimated your favorite Legion? Do you not understand why the army would reject such a notion? If you would decimate your favorite, then what hope did any of the others have of escaping your wrath? My faith in Caesar was never tested more than it was at that moment in time, seeing him for the first time as a man who was very much like us, a man who made serious errors in judgment.

Because I was, and am convinced that Caesar was very much in the wrong in this matter, and while I would remain loyal, I could never view him in quite the same light as I had before. The army was now in full cry, with the howls of protest at Caesar's judgment raining down on him from all quarters, and I could tell that if his generals did not feel the same way, they at least understood that matters hung on the edge of a sword at this instant. Depending on the next few moments, they could have a full-scale revolt on their hands, something that went well beyond mutiny. One of them, I do not remember who it was, whispered something urgently in Caesar's ear, the general clearly reluctant, shaking his head. Finally, Caesar held up his hand, but the gesture was not immediately obeyed like it normally was, a further sign that Caesar barely had control of the army.

Finally, the men quieted down enough for him to speak. "I can clearly see your discontent, and I do not want to act with undue haste. I will further deliberate on this matter and render my decision in the morning. Until then, all men will stay in their areas of the camp, and any violation of this order will be meant with the harshest measures. That is all."

And without saying anything more, he stepped down and strode away, leaving a very angry and confused army in his wake.

~ ~ ~ ~

The men went to their respective tents, and there is no way that I can accurately describe the feeling of tension that hung over the camp. Walking back to my own tent, with only Scribonius following me, I took one of the stools as I started to take my gear off, then thought better of it. I have to wear my armor in my own camp, I thought with dismay.

For several moments, nothing was said before Scribonius finally broke the silence. "So what happens next?"

I sat and thought, then shrugged. "Your guess is as good as mine, Scribonius. I just hope that Caesar relents on the decimation, because I really don't know what'll happen if he tries to go through with it."

"I do," Scribonius said glumly. "We'll have a revolt of the whole army, sure as I'm sitting here."

I knew he was right, yet for some reason I still had trouble fully believing it. It was like it was too big a thing for my mind to get around, and it was not a feeling with which I was comfortable. I have always been accused of thinking too much, and there had been other moments like this when my train of thought took me places that seemed to overwhelm my mind, but never before had it encompassed something so terrible but so real. Hence we sat there, listening to the sounds of the camp, our ears alert for the first sign of trouble, except it was deathly quiet, more quiet than I had ever heard before. Men were gathered about their fires like they normally did, yet their conversations were held in little more than whispers as they talked about the events of the day. The provosts were patrolling in force, making sure that Caesar's orders were followed to the letter. Normally this task would fall to the Centurions and Optios, but after so many of us had sided with the men, Caesar was not willing to trust us with the job. Instead we sat, Scribonius and I, drinking the some of my Falernian, wondering what the next day would bring.

~ ~ ~ ~

Morning dawned with Scribonius and I sitting in much the same spots we had occupied when we first entered my tent, and despite the wine we consumed, neither of us had felt the effects, neither drunkenness nor hangover. I suppose we were too consumed with what was happening around us for it to have its normal power over us. The camp had remained quiet all night, and that morning when the *bucina* sounded the morning assembly, we did not know what to expect when we emerged from the tent. Still, the men assembled readily enough, sullenly silent, but they stood there, waiting for Caesar's final decision. I refused even to look at Vibius, taking my place in the formation without so much as a glance in his direction, hoping that my face did not betray the tightening knot in my stomach. We stood in formation for almost a third of a watch, and while this normally would have brought about a spate of fidgeting and mumbling in the ranks that the officers would have to stop with threats or worse, this day there was not a whisper. Finally, Caesar appeared from the direction of the *Praetorium*, followed by his entire command staff. Looking neither left nor right, he strode to the rostra at the front of the forum and mounted it. There he stood, his body motionless, only his head turning to scan the army assembled before him, not saying a word. As much as I usually admired Caesar's flair for the theatrical, I wished this time that he had simply gotten to the point and announced his decision. I still wonder if he truly understood just how much peril his command of the army was in at that moment, or if it was something beyond his comprehension. Given the way his life ended, I cannot help thinking that ultimately this was Caesar's fatal weakness, his inability to see the world through anything other than his own eyes. Finally, he spoke, and I was immediately struck by how hoarse his voice sounded, not its usual clear, carrying tone, and I wondered how much yelling must have taken place in his quarters the night before.

"After thinking it over, I have decided that I will not have the punishment carried out that I ordered yesterday, despite the fact that I am within my rights under Roman military law and custom to do so."

There was a great whoosh of air as thousands of lungs expelled the breath they were holding, and I felt my knees sag in relief.

Ignoring our obvious display, Caesar continued, his voice cold and formal. "I, however, will continue my pursuit of Pompey with troops that

I can rely on. I hereby command the army to be dismissed from the current campaign, and it will return to Italy under the command of Marcus Antonius." This elicited a buzzing of comment from the ranks, which Caesar ignored, finishing with, "Only after I have completely defeated Pompey will I address the issues of your discharges and your bonuses that you have raised. That is all."

And without another word, he turned to stalk off the rostra, leaving a relieved but bemused army behind him. If he was sending the whole army back, who exactly was he going to be marching with? I was thinking about this as I turned to begin the necessary work to make ready to march when I heard my name called. Turning, my heart skipped a beat seeing that the person calling me was none other than one of Caesar's private secretaries, although I do not remember his name. Standing next to him was Marcus Antonius, his face registering no emotion whatsoever, no hint of what was on his, or by extension, Caesar's mind.

"Pilus Prior Pullus," Antonius called to me, "Caesar requires your presence in the *Praetorium* immediately."

This cannot be good, I thought, hurrying over to the headquarters tent, and I barely heard the secretary calling out another man's name as I made my way to meet Caesar.

~ ~ ~ ~

Entering the tent, I gave my name to the junior Tribune who acted as the watchdog to Caesar's private office, waiting for only a few heartbeats before he returned and with a curt nod, indicated that I should enter. This only increased my anxiety, because it was normal to keep us waiting for a few moments just, I suspected, to remind us of our places. Entering the office, I marched over to Caesar, who was standing over a table looking at a map, and saluted. For a moment, Caesar continued his study of the map before looking up and returning the salute.

"*Salve*, Titus Pullus."

Before I could return the greeting, he turned and said loudly enough for all to hear. "Gentlemen, I need to talk to Pilus Prior Pullus alone. Please give us this room. I'll send for you when we're through talking."

One could have heard a gnat fart in the thunderstruck silence that filled the room, I suppose because it was currently full of all the fine young men, not to mention the likes of Antonius, Sulla, and the rest of the Legates. Still, not even men as high-ranking as they were wanted to draw Caesar's wrath at this time, so they filed out, not without some of them shooting poisonous glances at me over their shoulders. Once the room cleared and it was just Caesar and I, it made me realize that this was the first time I had ever been alone with my general, which did not help my stomach any. Since there was no way I was going to break the silence, I waited for Caesar to speak, and it seemed like he had the same thought because we stood there saying nothing for a moment before he finally laughed, but it was not a happy sound.

"Interesting day, neh, Pullus?"

I could not help laughing myself, but I was careful in my reply. "That's certainly one way to put it, Caesar."

Pursing his lips, he seemed to be thinking about the best way to begin. Finally, "What happened with the 10th has . . . disturbed me, to say the least. Of all my Legions, I didn't think that the 10th would turn on me."

I might have imagined it, but I thought I detected a tone that indicated that he was hurt by what had happened and not just surprised or angered.

Be careful, Titus, I thought as I answered him. "I can't say that I was surprised when it actually happened, Caesar."

He looked at me sharply, his lips turning into a thin white line as he clearly tried to suppress his anger. "What do you mean, Pullus? Why weren't you surprised?"

My heart started hammering in my chest, and I was as thoroughly scared as I had ever been. Although Caesar did not have a reputation of taking his anger out on his subordinates, neither had he been in this position before, and I had said something that angered him, perhaps leading him to believe that I had not alerted him to the danger.

Realizing that my career and perhaps my life hung on the next words out of my mouth, I chose them carefully. "What I meant, Caesar, was that in a conference of the Centurions, one of them brought up the men's dissatisfaction with the bonus situation, and thought that it was possible that it would be the bonus that served as the spark that lit the fire, as it were."

I went on to relay the entire conversation as I remembered it.

"When did this happen?" His tone was sharp, but I sensed that his anger was easing.

"Less than a watch before you gave the order to march."

"And you didn't think it sufficiently important to come to me with this piece of news?"

His tone was not accusatory, seemingly more curious than angry, but now I found was getting annoyed; the position Caesar was putting me in was patently unfair.

"With all due respect, General, it wasn't my place to do so. That kind of information should have been passed to you by the Primus Pilus, not from any of the Pili Priores. That would have been outside the chain of command."

He nodded thoughtfully, then said, "And if Crastinus were still alive, I have no doubt he would have come and told me. Torquatus . . . ?"

He shrugged and did not finish the sentence, but I could tell by the expression on his face and his body language that Torquatus was not likely to be in the slot of Primus Pilus very long. A sudden thought struck me, and again I felt weak in the knees but for an entirely different reason. Could it be, I wondered, that Caesar plans on making me Primus Pilus? When I was promoted to Pilus Prior, it had been a surprise then, so why not now? I did my best to contain my excitement as I waited to hear what Caesar had on his mind, but it was clear that Caesar was not finished going over the events of the last two days yet, and he turned back to it.

"I understand that your Optio, Domitius isn't it, was one of the officers who sided with the men?"

I was not sure where this was going, but I would not lie to him, so I answered him that Caesar had the rights of it.

"And if I remember correctly, you and he have been friends since childhood, true?" I could not hide my look of astonishment that he would know this, but he laughed and said, "What? You don't think that I know the backgrounds of the men I appoint to the Centurionate? Besides," he finished, "you two were hard to miss. You were an unlikely pair, at least from appearances sake, you being so large and he being so . . ."

He did not finish for there was no need since I knew exactly what he spoke about. Vibius and I had taken a lot of abuse over the years because of our physical mismatch, so it was no surprise when Caesar mentioned it.

His face turned serious as he continued questioning me. "I also understand that you drew your blade on him when he made his feelings known. Is that true as well?"

When it was put like that, I experienced a sense of shame, but it was nothing more than the truth, and I said as much. Caesar said nothing for a moment, looking thoughtfully at the map laid before him on the table, yet I do not think he was looking at it.

Finally, he looked up and directly into my eyes. "Would you have struck him down if the circumstances had warranted it?"

"Yes."

I said it before I thought the question through, and it felt like I was punched in the gut when the word came out, because I knew it was the truth. I would have struck down the best friend I had ever had, a companion since childhood, and I did not, nor do I now know what that says about me.

Caesar's reaction was to stare into my eyes for a moment before giving a simple nod. "Very well. Thank you for your honesty, Pullus. I know that that couldn't have been easy for you." Turning, he began pacing about the room and continued, "So now we come to the matter which I wanted to speak with you about. There was a reason I asked about you and Domitius, which I will explain in a moment. Suffice it to say that I'm somewhat wary about who I can trust out of my Centurions, and who I cannot. I've made a vow to continue my pursuit of Pompey, and I will not be deterred by anyone or anything. However, the refusal of the army to march has put me on the horns of a dilemma in a manner of speaking. While we have either killed or accepted the surrender of a large part of Pompey's army, by our intelligence estimates, he still has about three Legions' worth of men, composed mainly of men from the 1st, 4th, and 6th, along with about 5,000 auxiliaries, although as you saw on the field their quality is very low, and about a thousand cavalry."

He turned to see if I had digested this information, and I nodded for him to continue.

"Now, I know that Pompey actually left camp with only four, perhaps five men, and shortly afterward was joined by about 30 cavalry and perhaps a Century of men as he fled to Larisa. And that's one reason, albeit a minor one, why the army refuses to march. Why should I force several thousand exhausted men to tap further into what reserves of energy they have left to chase down less than a hundred men? It is a fair question."

He put the elbow of one arm in a cupped hand to tap his lips with his index finger, as if he was giving the matter serious thought, but I knew it was just a show. He had already thought this through, except Caesar was at heart a performer, among other things, and he could not help himself at times like this.

"But herein lays my dilemma. As a general, I can't operate on the assumption that those three Legions won't march to join Pompey. In fact, they may be doing just that even as we speak. The same goes for the auxiliaries; even with their poor quality, there is something to be said for their numbers. Therefore, it wouldn't be prudent of me to go chasing after Pompey with just my bodyguard and whatever scraps I could muster up. I need good hard men, veterans who know their business. That was why I ordered the army to march, because I thought I could count on them. That was where I went wrong, obviously."

He finished this statement through clenched teeth, and I could see his anger was beginning to come back as he touched on the sore in his mind that was what had happened. It took him a moment to compose himself, then sighed and in that sound I could hear all the weariness and turmoil that came with being Gaius Julius Caesar.

"So now I must choose between breaking my vow, or finding another group of men who I can count on to march with me, and I believe that I have found them. And that's where you come in."

He looked at me to gauge my reaction, but in truth, I had no idea how I was supposed to react. The only thing I was sure of now was that this was not about making me Primus Pilus of the 10th, because he had already given the order for the 10th to return to Italy, and up until moments before I thought I was going with them. So I just waited for him to continue, which seemed to irritate him a bit.

"Do you know about the two Cohorts of the 6th who have sworn their allegiance to me?"

I nodded; it was common knowledge that during the battle, the 4th and all but two Cohorts of the 6th had managed to cross the river and escape. These two Cohorts were completely surrounded and prepared to fight to the last man, but the men of the 8th and 9th were looking at fellow Spaniards, and began calling to Antonius to offer them the chance to surrender honorably, which Antonius offered and the men of the 6th took. Then Caesar offered them clemency in exchange for their agreement to fight for him, which they agreed to do, under the condition that once the war was over they would be allowed to take their discharges, just like the 7th 8th and 9th, all of whom were part of the same *dilectus*. Caesar agreed to these terms, although I would be lying if I said that it had not crossed my mind that the men of the 6th were essentially running the same risk of having what happened to the $7^{th}$, 8th, and 9th happen to them. Regardless, desperate men could not be choosy men, and that apparently worked for both parties, because Caesar was as desperate in his own way as the men of the 6th.

"They're who I will take in pursuit of Pompey."

My mind began working rapidly, and I asked, "And what's their strength, Caesar?"

"Since they're the 7th and 10th Cohort, they're actually close to full strength. Combined, about 900 men, give or take a few."

"And you're going to take 900 men and chase after three Legions' worth, of which a number of them are their comrades from the same Legion?"

Despite knowing it was not wise, I made no attempt to hide my skepticism, but Caesar was, as ever, a man of surprises.

Instead of getting angry, he threw his head back and laughed, a true laugh, not forced in any way. "Why, Pullus, that is exactly what I am proposing." He turned serious, and continued, "Which is why I need someone I can absolutely trust in a position of authority, and I believe, no I know, that man is you. You proved your loyalty to me by your actions against your closest friend. Pullus, I have watched your career closely, and you've proven time and again that not only are you loyal, you are resourceful and your courage in battle is almost unmatched. You probably don't know this, but one of your biggest supporters was Gaius Crastinus. He told me on more than one occasion that he saw in you a Primus Pilus worthy of Dentatus."

That was high praise indeed, and my heart soared at the words that Caesar was speaking. Then, in my mind I heard a little voice speaking quietly, telling me to be careful in accepting Caesar's words at face value. I do not know why that voice chose to speak; perhaps all the carping and complaining that Vibius had been doing about Caesar all these years had more of an effect on me than I was aware. Whatever the cause, my elation at hearing Caesar's flattery was short-lived, because all his honeyed words still did not answer the question that was at the heart of this matter.

"So what is it you wish me to do, Caesar?"

He nodded, clearly pleased that I had accepted his praise. "I would like you to come with us, and I'm appointing you as *de facto* Primus Pilus. The two Cohorts will retain their senior Centurions, but they will report directly to you. You'll command the entire force, answerable to me, of course," he finished, in my mind unnecessarily, as if I was not clear that he would still be in overall command.

So there it was, and now I had to make a decision. It was not the decision you might be thinking, gentle reader; there was no real question whether I would go, at least if I did not want my career to die in front of my eyes. After all that Caesar had been through in the last two days because of the army, my refusal to accompany him would finally give him something, or someone, tangible to punish and on whom he could take out his frustrations. As much as I have talked about Caesar's mercy, and the clemency he showed his enemies, there was the other Caesar, the Caesar of Uxellodonum, where a pile of bones of the hands of the defenders still moldered. There was the Caesar who gave us Gomphi just to make a point, and I had little illusion that he would make an example of me should I refuse him, so I was going. However, he was making a request of me, and I was well within my rights to demand something appropriate in return, but the question was what? I turned it over in my mind; aware of Caesar's eyes on me, I finally spoke.

"Caesar, I'm deeply honored by your words, and by your request, and I hope you know that I would follow you across Charon if you asked it of me," I said as sincerely as I could, thinking to myself that there were two of us in the room who could lay it on thick. "But I'm concerned about my Cohort. Who did you plan on appointing as the Pilus Prior? And what happens when you're done with the 6th? What happens to me then?"

He smiled at me like I was a prized pupil, and perhaps at that moment I was. "Do you have something in mind, Pullus?"

In truth, I had not really thought things through at that point, and I suppressed a flash of irritation at Caesar, whose mind always worked more quickly than almost anyone else's in the world, and who assumed that others were able to marshal their thoughts with the same speed that he did. I did not answer immediately, then decided to turn the tables on him somewhat.

"Before I answer, Caesar, perhaps you tell me what you've been thinking along those lines?"

His smile broadened, and he sat on the table with his arms folded, looking at me. "Pullus, I think I may have underestimated you," he said equably. Without waiting for a reply, he pressed on, "As I see it, given what's transpired, getting you away from your Cohort for a time might actually be to your benefit. While every Cohort has been split apart by a number of Centurions and Optios, none have been as . . . dramatic as the split between Domitius and yourself. You were the only one of my Centurions who demonstrated a willingness to take physical action, and while I applaud and thank you for that display, I can't help but think that the men of your Cohort won't view things the same way."

I had never thought about things in the manner that Caesar was describing. In fact, I had not been thinking about the situation much at all. The reality was that I had been trying to avoid thinking about it, which is why I had tried to get drunk with Scribonius the night before. However, I could see that I should have been thinking along the lines of Caesar, realizing instantly that he was right. If I was willing to strike Vibius down, how sure could I be that Vibius did not feel the same way and would not take action? That was when the full import of our rift hit me; I was now thinking of Vibius as a possible threat to my life, the force of what it all meant hitting me almost like a physical blow. I felt my knees start to shake as my stomach, which had settled down since my initial entry, now threatened to rise in revolt. I was assaulted by such a swirl of conflicting emotions; anger at the very idea that Vibius might pose a threat to me. Later I was forced to acknowledge, if only to myself, how hypocritical it was of me to be angry with Vibius for such a possibility, when I had stated openly to my general that I would have done the same thing I was angry about. I felt indignation at the idea that the men I had led for these years might actually side with Vibius against me. Underlying it all though, was an incredible sadness, and it was this feeling that was the hardest to suppress, and horrified, I felt the beginnings of tears start to form in my eyes. Nothing would be as humiliating or unforgivable as crying like a woman in front of my general and it was only through a huge force of will that I managed to keep the tears from spilling down my cheeks.

"I know this is hard for you, Pullus," Caesar said gently. "It always is when someone is as a brother to you, and then something happens to destroy that bond. But you know I speak the truth. Right now, getting you away from your Cohort is the best possible solution, which is another reason why I chose you for this endeavor."

Forcing my mind back to the topic, I repeated my question to Caesar.

"Well, it would be customary for the Pilus Posterior to take your slot, but given Celer chose to side with the men, that is quite out of the question, as is Domitius of course."

"And he doesn't want the job," I said instantly; despite myself I was still thinking of Vibius and what he really wanted. Old habits die hard.

"So did you have someone in mind?"

"Scribonius," I again responded instantly, and I saw that I had caught Caesar by surprise.

"Scribonius," he said doubtfully, then shook his head. "He hasn't been Hastatus Prior very long."

"No, only a matter of months," I agreed, but an idea was forming in my mind, and in that moment I decided that this would be my price. "But the men respect him immensely. In fact, I would go so far as to say that he's the most respected, outside of me. At least until the other day," I amended, feeling another twinge of emotion. Caesar said nothing, so I plunged on. "He's smarter than I am, and he's almost as good a fighter. Well, perhaps not that good." There were limits to how far I could bend, I realized. Finishing, I spoke plainly, "That's my price, Caesar. The only man I trust to run the Cohort effectively is Scribonius."

"Well, you don't ask for much," he replied dryly, re-crossing his arms as he leaned backward on the desk. His brow furrowed as he thought about it, then finally he shrugged, "Very well, I'll make it happen." His eyes suddenly narrowed. "Are you sure that Scribonius will go along with this?"

"Yes, I'm sure of it."

Truthfully, I had no idea, I realized. If he was unwilling I would just have to convince him somehow, but I had a feeling that I would not have to. Although we had never talked about it, I sensed that Scribonius had his own ambitions. I would just have to find out.

"What about when I come back to the 10th? What position will I occupy?"

His brow furrowed as he thought about it, then he said, "I can't honestly say at this point, Pullus. But what I can tell you is that when you return, there will be a promotion, and I'll also make sure that your status as Primus Pilus of the 6th is made official." He grinned. "Although at this moment, I have no idea how, but I'll think of something. I always do."

I could not argue that, recognizing that this was the best I could do under the circumstances.

With that business settled, I asked Caesar the next most pressing questions. "When do I meet the men? And when do we leave?"

Caesar looked surprised. "Why, we leave immediately, of course. You can meet the men when we form up for the march. I'll say something brief, and we'll get on with it."

I was struck by another thought. "Do the men of the 6th know about this yet?"

To my relief, he nodded. "Yes, those were part of the terms I discussed with them. They're not happy about it, but they will obey."

During the course of this extraordinary interview, I had spoken more freely with Caesar than at any point in my career, and I decided that there was no point stopping now.

"What makes you so sure that they'll obey?"

Caesar favored me with a smile, and responded simply, "Because I have every confidence in your ability to make them obey, Pullus."

And with that, Caesar ushered me out of the room and the fine young men came trooping back in, shooting me glances, again some curious, some poisonous. And for once, I did not particularly care; I had too much on my mind to take much notice.

~ ~ ~ ~

As it turned out, the men of the 6th were not quite as ready to march as Caesar hoped. During their surrender, they gave up all their weapons and armor, then in the resulting confusion nobody had catalogued it and checked it in, meaning that now the men had to draw from stores. There were some problems finding all the proper bits, keeping the army quartermaster Quintus Cornuficius quite busy. It also turned out that the deal Caesar made with the 6th was a bit more complex than he made it out to be. The men had recognized that in all reality they held the advantage in the negotiations, and accordingly made several demands that Caesar acceded to, since he had no real choice in the matter. These men had lost their entire fortunes and all their possessions when Pompey's camp was sacked. There was no question of trying to retrieve either the money or the possessions, especially since it had been done by their own comrades, who fled. Therefore, the men of the 6th had submitted a list to Caesar that they claimed itemized the monetary value of these possessions. There is little doubt that the amounts were highly inflated, but Caesar was in no position to dispute the figures, and both parties knew it. Also, the men stipulated that they would not take arms against their comrades of the 6th which, while it did not surprise me when I learned of it, it did tell me that Caesar had not been totally forthcoming with me during our talk. I also learned that they were refusing to allow any men to be added to their numbers from outside the 6th, even if they were part of Pompey's army and drawn from the prisoners we took. I was the only exception, and while I was never told I surmised that I was a concession in exchange for Caesar's granting of the amounts submitted by them without argument. What I did not know at the time was what this meant in the grand scheme of things, but I did recognize that I would have to watch my back whenever we finally did fight someone. Because of the delay in setting out, I had the time to meet the men I was to lead while still in camp, and a formation was called for the occasion, the difficulty compounded by the fact that Caesar himself had pushed on after Pompey already, leaving me to face my new command alone. Using one of the few surviving captured slaves who was an attendant for one of Pompey's Tribunes and knew what needed to be done, I had him make me look more than presentable. Wearing all of my decorations, my hope was that between all of them and my size, the men would be sufficiently wary of me not to start testing me immediately. I was experienced enough to know that the moment would inevitably come where someone in the ranks would try something to see what I would allow them to get away with, but it was important that it not start immediately. My confidence in myself was such that I was sure that given a few weeks under my command that the men would adjust to their new reality, but first I had to have that period of time before any of them tried to test me. What I was counting on was using the dark pillar that is one of the two foundations of respect, and that was fear. Before their regard for me could grow, they had to fear me, although I knew that it could not just be fear of me, and me alone; it had to be a combination of fear of me personally, along with the regulations and customs of the Legions. They had to be afraid of not only the unofficial, but the official consequences of disobedience and treachery, yet I also knew that the most immediate dread they needed to have was of me personally. Such were my thoughts striding through the forum, using an old trick of coming up from behind the men rather than in front of them. This trick had been taught to me by Crastinus, the idea being that nothing made the men quite as nervous as the idea of a superior lurking somewhere they could not see them, knowing that they were under the scrutiny of a Centurion. This made them extremely reluctant to risk whispering to each other as they gave their opinion on whatever matter was at hand. It also carried the added benefit of not putting me in the position of feeling like I was being judged, since all eyes would be watching me if I approached from the front. Moving quietly, I approaching the rear ranks, and from several feet away I could hear the buzzing of muted conversation as they waited for me.

"So this is the way he introduces himself, keeping us waiting?"

"Just trying to keep us on our toes, I guess."

"On our toes? Who does that prick think he is? We're the 6th, not some bunch of *tirones*! If anything, he should be waiting for us!"

I spotted the two men speaking and aimed for the man who spoke last. They were in the next to rear rank of the formation, members of the 7th Cohort and I pushed past the men in the rearmost rank, who started to mouth their protest but quickly shut up when they saw who it was pushing them aside. Stopping silently behind the two men, I studied them for a moment. They had to be brothers, I thought, because they looked like two peas from the same pod. Both were short, brown, scrawny things, with twigs for arms and sticks for legs, yet those appendages also bore their share of scars. They were Spanish Legionaries all right, I thought to myself; not an ounce of fat, just meat and gristle and tough as old boot leather.

I smiled grimly, then leaned forward and said quietly in the second man's ear, "Prick, am I?"

I was gratified to see both their bodies go absolutely rigid, and there was a moment where neither of them said anything.

Finally, the man who had uttered the insult said in a voice that did not waver, "Yes, sir. That's what I said. No disrespect intended. In fact, we Spaniards use it as a term of affection sometimes sir. Not sure what your custom is, sir."

I had to suppress a chuckle; at least the man could think on his feet, and he did not immediately fall to the ground quaking. Well, we will see how long that lasts, I thought, stepping around and turning to face him, looking down where his face was gazing straight into my chest. I was pleased to see that suddenly he did not seem so sure of himself, sure that I detected a hint of a quiver run through his body, but if it was there he quickly got it under control. Then I leaned towards him, another favorite trick of mine, and despite himself, he in turn leaned back, trying to maintain some distance between us. I smiled, but it was not a nice smile as I looked him up and down, curling my lip in the same manner that Crastinus had all those years ago, and I was struck by a sudden urge to laugh. Apparently, the *numen* that had once waved the invisible turd under Crastinus' nose back when I was a *tiro* had transferred itself to me now that he was gone.

Finally, I spoke again. "You're a short-ass little piece of *cac*, aren't you?" He did not say anything, and I snapped, "I believe I asked you a question, Gregarius!"

"Yes, sir," he barked. "I'm a short-ass piece of *cac!*"

I nodded. "I thought as much. But it's good that you see yourself for what you are. The path to true happiness lies in knowing your shortcomings. And you want to be happy, don't you, Gregarius?"

A look of confusion flitted across his face, but he knew the game well enough to know that no matter where this was going, he was going to lose. It is one of the secrets to being as close to happy as one can be in the army; knowing that your superiors are playing with loaded dice that will come up Venus for them on every roll. Once one accepts that, it makes life for everyone go much easier, and by this point in time, every man who thought he could beat the system had long since died or deserted.

"Yes, sir. I want to be happy, sir."

"Do you know what another brick in the road to true happiness is, Gregarius?"

"No, sir, but I hope that the Centurion will instruct me. Sir."

Despite myself, I was enjoying this exchange and I suspect that the Gregarius was as well. It is all just a big farce really, and we each have a role to play.

Now I bent my knees so that I was looking directly into his eyes, saying slowly and distinctly, "Do. Not. Fuck. With. Me. Or I will beat you to death with my bare hands. Do you doubt that, Gregarius? That I could do just that?"

Role it may have been, but I was also deadly serious, and looking into his eyes before he looked away, I saw with satisfaction that he knew it as well.

"No, sir. I don't doubt it at all. Sir."

His tone was clipped, but his voice held no emotion, his eyes now back to looking at a point above my head.

I nodded again. "What's your name and rank, Gregarius?"

"Gregarius *Immunes* Gaius Tetarfenus, sir."

I turned to the first man, asking him the same, and my suspicions were confirmed.

"Sergeant Quintus Tetarfenus. Sir."

I raised an eyebrow as I turned to the Sergeant. "You're a Sergeant? And you're talking in the ranks like a washerwoman?" I gave a loud, theatrical sigh then shook my head. "I am surprised." I raised my voice so that more of the men could hear. "When I was told that I'd be leading the men of the 6th Legion, I thought to myself, here's a group of men worthy of my leadership at least. Men that I, Primus Pilus Titus Pullus," I savored the taste of my new title on my tongue, "would be honored to lead wherever Caesar deems it necessary to send us, whether it's to Hades or to the top of Olympus to fight the gods themselves!" Pausing, I looked at the men around me out of the corner of my eye, and I could see them straining to hear my words. I let out another huge sigh. "But what's my first impression? My first impression, courtesy of the Tetarfenus brothers, is that they gossip like camp whores, and they have no respect for their superior officers!"

My voice was like a lash by the time I finished, and I was pleased to see that the reaction of the men seemed to be equal parts anger and shame. I had little doubt that some of the anger was directed at me, but the majority would now be aimed at the brothers Tetarfenus and when I turned to walk towards the front of the formation, I saw by their ashen expressions that they indeed felt that way. Taking my place at the front of the formation, I executed an about turn to face my new command. Staring back at me were men almost identical to the men of the Second Cohort of the 10th. Oh, the faces were different, but the men were exactly the same. Some larger than others, none as large as me, although there were a couple who came close, all browned by countless days in the sun, without an ounce of spare fat on their frames, and there were scars and decorations in abundance.

"As you just heard, my name is Primus Pilus Titus Pullus, recently promoted to this grade by Caesar himself from my post as Secundus Pilus Prior of the 10th."

I am not completely sure what I was expecting, but the reaction I got at mention of the 10th was not it. Instead of respect, or at the least regard for what we had accomplished, I saw lips lifted in sneers, clear signs of contempt. I was bewildered; I know now that at the very least it was naïve of me to think that men who just days ago were on the other side of the battlefield would automatically accord the 10th the kind of respect that we were accorded by the rest of the army. At that moment, however, I honestly could not understand what was behind the reactions I was seeing, and the subsequent wave of anger that flowed through me was something white-hot, literally making my blood feel like it had suddenly turned molten. My legs began to shake with rage, and I could tell that this beast was about to burst out of my chest, just like when the madness took hold of me in much the same way it had that first time on that hill in Lusitania all those years ago. This killing rage prompted me to do something that as far as I know, had never been done before and likely has not been done since. As if my hands had a mind of their own my left hand unclenched, dropping my *vitus* to the ground, then I untied the straps to my helmet, laying it down on top of the *vitus*. I could see that I held the men's undivided attention, but I was not finished. Unstrapping my harness next, and laying my weapons next to the helmet, I then very carefully removed my phalarae, torqs, and other decorations before pulling off my armor, laying it on the ground as well. All this was done in total, and shocked silence, but the quiet was about to be broken, by me. Now I was only in my tunic, the standard army issue tunic that in my case stretched tightly across my chest and shoulders, the sleeves barely covering my shoulders, leaving the bulging muscles of my arms exposed. Stepping away from my gear, I suddenly filled my lungs and roared more loudly than I had ever done before in my life.

"I am Titus Pullus! I am the son of Mars and Bellona! I am of the 10th Legion, and I challenge any one of you motherless *cunni* to step forward and face me! I spit on your ancestors, dogs and whores that they were! I am not a Centurion, I am not the Primus Pilus at this moment! I am Titus Pullus! Do any of you have the courage to challenge me?"

I could feel the cords of my neck straining as I shouted these words, the blood suffusing my face as I clenched my fists, stalking up and down in front of the assembled men, glaring at each of them, none of whom met my gaze.

I gave a harsh, mocking laugh. "So these are the men of the vaunted 6th Legion? None of them even dare to look me in the eye, so I know that there's not a man among them who dares to challenge me." My lips curled in a sneer. "Do I need to make it any plainer? I'm not standing here as your Primus Pilus, or as a Centurion. I give you my word that there will be no official punishment for any man who bests me. In fact, I offer a reward of a thousand sesterces if you do beat me, and I'll exempt the man from any fatigue duties for a month!"

I was in fact offering much more than that, and the men and I knew it. If their champion bested me, my ability to command these men was over before it started. The word of my defeat would spread through the army like a wildfire, and my career would effectively be over. I was risking everything I held dear on one throw of the dice and I was struck by the thought that perhaps during my time marching with Caesar some of his habits were rubbing off. While what I was doing was not unheard of, particularly during the early days when a Legion was first formed, as I said before, I had never heard of anyone doing it in the manner that I was doing it now. The most common form was after watch, behind the latrines, in an unofficial manner. Doing what I was doing in the forum, in front of not only a formation of Legionaries, but any other member of the army who happened to be walking by that could witness what was happening is what made my actions so unusual, but I was beyond caring. It was like all the anger and hurt from the sense of betrayal that I felt about what happened between Vibius and me, and the 10th as a whole, had been bottled up and was now bursting forth, and I wanted someone to pay. The men still stood there, but they were uneasily glancing about, making me think for a moment that none of them would answer my challenge, so that I had indeed turned back towards my piled gear, when there was a stir from where the men of the 10th Cohort stood. From the rear ranks came a man, a whispered name preceding him, whipping through the ranks, and it took me a moment to understand what they were saying.

"Publius!"

While the man Publius was not as tall as I was, he clearly weighed at least as much as I did, if not more, and none of it was fat. He walked with a rolling gait, but there was a litheness about his movements that told me that he was quick on his feet. His face was scarred, but they were not the marks of battle, at least the kind of battle like what just took place on the plains of Pharsalus. His scars were the kind picked up in the wine shops outside camp, and he clearly had a reputation among his comrades, their faces splitting in wide smiles at the sight of him. His broad, flat face bore little emotion and I recognized in this Publius a man that perhaps even more than me was born for nothing but combat.

He walked up to me and said flatly, "I accept your challenge."

~ ~ ~ ~

Even now, all these years later, years that have served to rub the edges off of some of my hubris and have seen me humbled on more than one occasion, I still can say with utmost honesty and clarity that the beating I gave Publius was as thorough, and more importantly, as quick as any I had administered, even to poor Figulus. The fact that he barely laid a hand on me only made my victory more meaningful, at least as far as the men of the 6th were concerned. With Publius lying unconscious at my feet, I walked back to put all of my gear back on, taking the time to carefully reattach my decorations. Picking up my *vitus,* I turned back to the men, taking great satisfaction in the looks of shock and dismay written on their faces as they stared at the hulk at my feet, his head now lying in a pool of his own blood. Slowly looking the men over, I finally spoke, making sure that I controlled my breathing so that they could see I was not exerted in the least, my tone sounding like none of what had just happened ever took place.

"I look forward to leading all of you to great glory, wherever it may be. I know that I can count on you to obey me in all things, and acquit yourself as professionals in the army of Rome." Pausing again, my gaze traveled over the assembled men, who were looking at me in a manner very different than a few moments before. Turning as if to go, I paused as if I had just thought of something, and said, "Oh, and just so you know. I'm from Hispania myself; Astigi to be exact. And I know that Spaniards don't use the word 'prick' in an affectionate manner. Greeks might, but not Spaniards. Dismissed."

As I walked away, I was rewarded with a few chuckles at my last remark, but only a few.

## Chapter 5- Alexandria

Pompey made good his escape, taking ship for Mytilene, among other stops, where he continued to try to rally support, while the 1st, 4th, and the rest of the 6th was gathered up by Cato to be shipped off to Africa. They were joined there by the rest of the traitors who escaped from the battle; Afranius, Petreius, and the worst of the lot, Labienus. Meanwhile, the rest of the 6th set out for Macedonia, following in Caesar's wake as he in turn trailed Pompey, and I marched at their head. Despite the fact I had not won the second pillar of respect, I was confident that they feared me, since Publius was still confined to being carried by one of the Legion wagons, unable to walk. The added benefit to my thorough beating of Publius was that, just like my defeat would have, word of what I did flashed through the rest of the army before we left. I took some satisfaction that Vibius knew what I could have done to him if I had so chosen.

Finally catching up with Caesar in Asia at Pergamum, where he was lingering to deal with a number of matters pertaining to the running of the province, we were ordered to make a camp outside the walls to wait while he finished attending to his business. Additionally, we were waiting for five Cohorts of the 28th, one of the newer Legions that had not participated in the revolt in camp. I looked at this time as an opportunity to start establishing firmer control of the 6th; to that point we had not spent two nights in a row in the same place, save for almost a week waiting for shipping to take us to Caesar, and that was not an appropriate time or place for what I had in mind. In Pergamum, I would have the time, and my approach was basic, focusing on what had been my first step up the ladder of promotion, with weapons training. I was going to give every man willing to try a chance at besting me in mock combat. How cocksure I was in those days, how convinced of my own strength and skill! I must laugh at myself now, not so much for having those thoughts, but at how unbearably earnest I was in my belief in myself. I also must laugh at myself because after several weeks in which to think of the best solution to my problem, this was the best I could do, simply resorting to my physical skills instead of using my brain. Elegant it was not, but it was effective, although I did not escape entirely unscathed. When all was said and done, I faced just short of 40 men willing to test themselves against me, and despite besting all of them, it was not without a supreme effort and quite a few cuts and bruises on my part. I also demanded that the men adopt the grip of the sword first taught to me by Vinicius, and while they resisted at first, after the first few bouts when I knocked the wooden sword from my opponents' hands, they became convinced.

At this point, I think it is appropriate to mention the Centurions who served under me; some of them would go on to become good friends, some not. The Septimus Pilus Prior was a man named Gaius Valerius Valens, a Spaniard just a couple years older than I was. Of medium height and build, he was a competent officer, respected but not loved by his men. The Pilus Posterior was Quintus Annius, a greasy little speck of nothing who held aspirations of reaching the first grade rank, except that he did not have enough of what it took to get there. He was clever but not smart, unable to think past the immediate benefit or downfall of whatever scheme he was cooking up, and would prove to be a rock in my boot. The Princeps Prior was Gaius Sido, an older man on his second enlistment. Sido had risen about as far as he was ever going to go, but he was competent enough to do his job. In command of the Fourth Century was Princeps Posterior Lucius Serenus, a companion of Annius with about the same level of competence but not nearly as wily as Annius, and who looked at Annius as being much smarter than he was, which should tell one all they need to know about him. The Fifth was under the command of Marcus Junius Felix, who reminded me of Scribonius in many ways, both in his physical appearance and in his outlook. It was perhaps because of that resemblance that I would grow closer to Felix than perhaps any of the other men. Finally, the Hastatus Posterior was Publius Clemens, and there was nothing merciful about him. He was a fighter, one of those men like Publius who lived for battle, although he was smarter than Publius, which is why he was a Centurion. Clemens was well liked, even loved by his men and he loved them back. His weakness was the same as with so many men: Bacchus and the grape. Regardless, he was still one of my best.

The Tenth Cohort's Decimus Pilus Prior was Gaius Fuscus, originally from Etruria, and he ran the Cohort in name only. The real muscle running the Tenth was a brute named Gaius Cornuficius, the Pilus Posterior. A combination of guile and enormous strength, Cornuficius was reputedly a fearsome fighter, but he was not one of the men who challenged me during my weapons training, which I would learn later was a sign that he was actually quite smart. Interestingly, he had the appearance of being dull, looking at the world through blank, bovine eyes, but it was all a sham, as I would learn the hard way. The Princeps Prior was Lucius Salvius, more or less a non-entity who did the bare minimum needed to run his Century, relying on his Optio, a man named Porcinus who, just on ability, should have been in that slot. Princeps Posterior was Marcus Favonius, and he was Cornuficius' toady, much in the same way that Niger was to Celer. Of all the men under me, I think Favonius was the most tragic, because he had a great deal of potential to be a real leader, if he had not been polluted by Cornuficius. The Fifth's Centurion was

Quintus Sertorius, and based solely on ability he should have been the man running the Cohort. Like Clemens, he was well loved by his men, but unlike Clemens, he did not have any obvious weakness. Finally, was Marcus Considius, commander of the Sixth Century, and there is not much I can say about the man one way or another. I believe that he was promoted to the Centurionate because of connections and not ability, something that sometimes happened, although thankfully not in any Legion Caesar commanded. However, Pompey's army had apparently been run differently and I was stuck with Considius until I could think of other alternatives.

~ ~ ~ ~

Being *de facto* Primus Pilus, I was not only given a raise in pay, I was also accorded the other benefits that come with the position. Namely, I had a larger tent, and I was eligible for two clerks and a personal body slave. Because I was only running two Cohorts, I chose not to take advantage of the second clerk, although I did take on the body slave, choosing the slave who helped me prepare for my first meeting with the 6th. He was a miserable looking, short-ass little thing, scrawny even for a Greek, and it was not until several weeks into his service with me that I even bothered to learn his name. He said it was Diocles. Yes, gentle reader, the very same man hurriedly scribbling away as I speak, I first met many, many years ago in a dusty army camp. I am smiling now at the memory, and am pleased to see that he is smiling back. He was barely out of his teens, ten years younger than me, and when I first took him into my service, it was only as an attendant to my physical needs. At the time, I was unaware, and truthfully did not particularly care about Diocles' many other talents of a more cerebral nature; that would be a pleasant surprise, but down the road after many, many miles and battles.

*(Since I am the topic of this part of my master and friend's narrative, I am inserting my own recollection of the event of our meeting, because it was much more momentous for me than it was for him. As he mentioned, I had indeed been in the service of a member of Pompey's staff and had managed to survive what was a horrific experience when first Pompey's very own men sacked the camp, followed by members of Caesar's army. I hid myself under a pile of bodies dispatched by Pompey's men, servants and retainers of Pompey's staff, along with clerks and the like who tried to stop our own troops from looting their officers and comrades' valuables, but I have never seen such a madness come over men as I saw that day. I burrowed into a pile of corpses, and when Caesar's men came into the camp, they more or less picked up where Pompey's men had left off, taking whatever was left, and killing whoever they found. It was not until Caesar came and took control of the camp, and even then I waited a full watch for nightfall, before I felt safe enough to climb from my*

*gruesome refuge. I surrendered myself to the provosts, who herded me into a large holding area, separate from the combatant prisoners, where I stayed with others like myself who through some combination of luck and guile had managed to survive the madness. We were well treated, considering our status and our station, and it was from this state that I was plucked by none other than Titus Pullus. I first laid eyes on him when he came to our enclosure, calling for anyone with experience as a body slave. As he now knows, I had absolutely no practical experience in such matters, although I had seen it done more times than I could count, having been my former master's personal secretary. Even now, these many years later, I do not know why I chose to step forward and raise my hand, despite giving the matter much thought over the years. But that is exactly what I did, entering the life of Titus Pullus, as he entered mine. Neither of us at the time had any idea that we would be together so many years; at that moment I just made the determination that what Titus Pullus was offering was better than what my immediate future seemed to have in the offing. He has described me (accurately I might add, as much as it pains me to admit it), but here is what I saw when I first laid eyes on him. While my master and friend may not be shy about proclaiming the greatness of his deeds, he does not exaggerate in his descriptions. When he says he was a large man, if anything it is an understatement; in truth I had never seen a man as large and powerful as Titus Pullus up to that moment. He was not in uniform, but he carried his* vitus, *so I knew that he was a Centurion, and if I had contented myself with just taking in his physical appearance, I would have dismissed him as a typical Roman, his size notwithstanding. But as we stood in those few moments studying each other, I thought I detected something in his brown eyes that indicated that there was something there that was more than a professional soldier of Rome's army. I hesitate to call it intelligence, because to say as much would give the Centurions of Rome's army short shrift; most of them are intelligent, strictly speaking, but there is more to a man than how quickly he can think through a problem. Perhaps what I saw was a certain sensitivity (which will undoubtedly cause my master to spew a mouthful of wine all over when he reads this), or a spark of what might be described as imagination. But no, that is not it, and as I write this I think I may have touched on the quality I saw in his eyes, and that was curiosity. As boastful as my master may be about his physical deeds, he is the exact opposite when it comes to his other qualities, and one thing that I have noticed missing in his description of himself is his absolute curiosity and willingness to learn more about the world around him. He says that he only became interested in learning to read better because of his promotions, but that is not a complete truth. In fact, one of the duties that kept me the busiest, then and now, was laying my hands on reading material for him. He was and is a voracious reader, and now in the twilight of his life his library rivals that of any patrician or equites of Rome. I know why he did not speak of his habits while he was on active service; soldiers view literacy with suspicion, for a number of reasons. To men in the ranks, and even to other officers, it speaks of a dissatisfaction with one's station in life, since education is one of the most vital components for a New Man to rise in Roman society. They also view it as a sign of cleverness, and to a Roman that is not a compliment. Lastly, a literate man is more likely to know the rules and regulation of the army and can use those to enrich himself, at the expense of others.*

*My master has made no secret in his narrative that his primary goal when he decided to join the Legions and make the army his career was to better himself and his descendants, but such ambition must never be spoken of openly in Roman society when one is of the lower classes. It is funny; even after almost an entire life spent in one of the pillars of Roman society in the army, I still view myself as an outsider, looking in on the workings of the society and culture that I believe will enter the annals of history as the greatest of all time. I say this with some pain; I am a Greek by birth, and slave or not, I am as proud of my heritage as any Roman citizen, but while the Romans may lack culture and refinement, they make up for that lack in many other qualities, not all of them martial. What has made the Romans great is not in their ability to just conquer, but in to hold what they have conquered by offering the subdued both tangible and intangible benefits that far surpass the benefits that the conquered society offered its citizens before Rome showed up. And one of the things that Rome offers is the ability to improve one's circumstances. But make no mistake, it is rigidly controlled and is not an easy course to pursue. Equal to the suspicion of the lower ranks when a man displays too much interest in literacy (and I shudder when I say that to Romans there is such a thing as too much) is both the suspicion and the resistance to such a man from the upper ranks of Roman society. While the lower ranks and their attitude towards a man bettering himself is a barrier, the resistance of the patrician class to such a man can be downright dangerous, and not just to a man's status, but to his life. The countryside of the Republic is littered with the bones of men who some patrician deemed to be getting above himself. So I understand and at the time, I approved of my master's reluctance to display his literacy to anyone other than those few he trusted completely, but those days are long past. His status is secure here towards the end of his life and career, so I am somewhat puzzled why even in this account of his life he is reluctant to speak of this aspect of his character. Perhaps it is as he has said himself; old habits die hard. So that is what I saw in the eyes of Titus Pullus on that day those many years ago. In that moment, our fates intertwined, and I have enjoyed the experience immensely.)*

~ ~ ~ ~

I was called to the villa of a Roman citizen living in Pergamum, a merchant I believe, where Caesar made his headquarters. I was ushered in immediately and I saw that Caesar was amidst his usual whirlwind of activity, dictating to a number of different scribes on a number of different topics. Waving me closer, he stopped his dictation, whereupon almost every one of his clerks immediately went scurrying off to either relieve themselves or get something to eat. Service with Caesar at any level or function was not easy, but I believe that his clerks had the absolute worst of it.

Looking at me, Caesar grinned. "How's Publius?"

I know I should not have been surprised, but I was, which I think was half the reason Caesar said such things, just to keep people around him off balance.

"He's almost recovered, Caesar."

"Good." As quickly as it came, his smile disappeared, and he looked at me coldly. "Because if he had died, I would have had no choice but to have you executed."

I was determined that he would not keep me off balance, so I merely replied, "I know. But he's not dead and will make a full recovery."

He gave me a speculative look. "Pullus, while I understand what you did, I must ask if there wasn't some less . . . dramatic and violent a demonstration that you could have made?"

In truth, I had never thought about it, but when he said it, I realized that I probably could have done something else, and I felt a sense of shame wash over me. Damn the man, I thought! Can he always find something to make me feel like I am inadequate for the job he has given me? But I had undergone more exposure to Caesar in the last few weeks than I had experienced in my whole time in the army previously. What I learned during that time was that he was always testing the people around him, that every exchange with him held more meaning than met the eye, and I was determined that I would not be flustered by his questioning.

So I just shrugged. "Perhaps, Caesar, but rankers aren't as appreciative of subtlety as other types of people. I could have tried something else, I suppose, but I'm fairly certain that it would have been as successful as trying to teach a pig how to speak our tongue."

He threw back his head and laughed, and I was pleased with myself for amusing him.

"Well put, Pullus. Well put. And I take your point." That done, he became all business. "The reason I called you is to tell you to prepare the men. We're leaving."

"Where to, Caesar?"

"Alexandria. I've received reliable reports that Pompey has decided to head there with the goal of trying to convince their young king that his cause isn't doomed. I want to get there as quickly as possible and end this nonsense once and for all."

Although that sounded good to me, I had my doubts about whether it would in fact end, and obviously, the reservation showed, because Caesar read my face and gave a sigh.

"You have your doubts, neh, Pullus?"

I nodded. "Yes, Caesar, I have my doubts."

Crossing his arms, he sat on a table, regarding me steadily, then asked, "And why is that?"

"Cato."

I am not sure what reaction I expected, but he pursed his lips and considered me with narrowed eyes. "And why do you fear Cato?"

Before I could stop myself, I retorted, "I don't fear Cato, Caesar. There's not a man born that I fear, and I certainly don't fear a . . ."

I stopped myself before I made what could have been a huge error. No matter what Caesar may have thought of Cato, Cato was of his own class and the upper classes of Rome are incredibly touchy about any slurs or even criticism leveled at men of their own station, particularly by one as lowly born as me, Centurion or not. But I need not have worried, for Caesar finished for me.

"You don't fear a . . . prick like Cato?" His eyebrow arched as he asked, and I laughed.

"Actually I was going to call him a '*cunnus*,' Caesar. But 'prick' will do just fine."

"So why do you think Cato poses a threat?"

It was then that I explained to Caesar the longstanding argument between me and Vibius about Cato, how I had sat by more fires than I could count as Vibius recounted all that he thought Cato represented. He said nothing as I relived our endless arguments, but finally held up his hand.

"Pullus, as much as I appreciate hearing about Domitius' feelings about Cato, it still doesn't answer the question."

I felt the heat rising through my neck to my face, mainly because I realized he was right. I was not touching on the heart of the matter.

Thinking for a moment, I finally said, "I worry about Cato because he hates you, and is fanatical in that hatred. I think the reason he hates you so much is because you represent change, and despite all of Cato's talk about preserving traditions, at his heart, he's just a small man who hates change. And small men hate great men with a passion that never dies." I finished by saying, "Pompey may not agree with you, but he doesn't hate you. Cato does, and he'll never stop. And he has three Legions."

Caesar leaned back, arms still crossed as he regarded me thoughtfully. "Pullus, I said once I may have underestimated you. Now I know that I have." Then he shrugged. "I have no doubt you're right, Pullus. But it makes no difference; as soon as I finish with Pompey, we'll go and meet Cato. And defeat him."

With that, the interview ended. I was given my written orders by one of the harried clerks, and returned back to the camp, nodding to the Primus Pilus of the 28th who had been summoned as well, absurdly pleased that I was summoned first.

~ ~ ~ ~

Reading my orders, Caesar very specifically stated that I was not to mention our destination to anyone, and thereby unwittingly, or so I like to think, created the first big challenge to my command of the 6th. Once I returned to camp, I called a meeting of the other officers in my tent, regretting that since this was the first big occasion I had run out of the Falernian, it forced me to make do with whatever was available. Despite being indifferent to such things, I knew that many men thought highly of what type of wine they were served by a superior, viewing it somehow as a reflection of the regard or lack thereof in which they were held. However, there was nothing I could do about it, although looking back at how things transpired, perhaps if I had paid more attention to such things, my life would probably have been easier. I sent Diocles out to inform the command group to meet at my tent, and at the appointed time, I was pleased to see that they were all there, seated on stools and attentive to what I had to say. First having Diocles serve them, I waited the obligatory time for them to take a few sips of their wine, getting my first inkling of trouble from the sidelong glances some of them gave each other as they swallowed.

I resolved to head things off, and started by saying, "First I'd like to apologize for the mediocre quality of the refreshments. Unfortunately, this was the best I could procure." My heart sank a bit, seeing the patent doubt on some of the faces, but I pressed on. "I've been given orders by Caesar. We're to prepare to move by ship. We embark day after tomorrow."

"Where to?" This was posed by Annius, and it was an innocent enough question, but I could not help hesitating, unfortunately instantly alerting the men, and I cursed myself.

"My orders are very specific about that. I can't say."

If any of them had only been paying partial attention, this served to bring them around, and almost to a man, they straightened up on their stools, instantly alert. As I would learn, it was no surprise that Cornuficius raised his hand, yet that was a lesson for later. Nodding for him to speak, his seemingly blank eyes regarded me for a long moment before he did so, very slowly.

"And why's that, Primus Pilus? Why do you suppose Caesar has chosen to keep that from us?"

I opened my mouth to answer, but thank the gods I stopped myself, because I might have made things even worse. The answer, to me at least, was obvious; the loyalty of the 6th was still very much an open question. They had been Pompey's men, enlisted by Pompey, and most importantly paid by Pompey. If they were alerted that we were going after Pompey himself, it was very much a wager as to whether or not they would have somehow alerted Pompey that we were coming, and I know which way I would have bet. However, to say that openly would cast doubt on their honor, and there are few things that Legionaries are touchier about than their honor, even when there is good reason to question it.

Finally, I just shrugged. "I have no idea, Cornuficius."

Even as I said it, I realized how weak it sounded. Nobody answered immediately, and it was during this silence, watching the men closely, that I first saw that Cornuficius held sway, and not just over the 10th Cohort either.

He sat, sipping his wine, eyes staring off at something none of us could see. Setting the cup down, he said calmly, "We must be going after Pompey."

My heart began thudding heavily, and I could hear the indrawn breath of the men, having a flash of insight that either Cornuficius was smarter than he appeared, or the others were not very smart; only time would bear that out. Of course, we were going after Pompey! What else would we be doing? Suddenly the quiet dissolved, the men speaking at once, and I held my hand up for silence. To their credit, they obeyed instantly, although I think it had more to do with wanting to hear my response than out of any respect.

"Cornuficius, that's speculation on your part, but it's only speculation."

He regarded me blandly, scratching an elbow. "Do you know where we're going, Primus Pilus?"

I had just been outmaneuvered, and I knew it. If I chose, I could simply lie, saying I had no idea, but that posed its own problems. First, it meant that I was not fully trusted by Caesar either, and part of my hold over the men at this point came from their view that I was favored by Caesar, so that any disobedience of me meant drawing his wrath as well as mine. Second, if I chose to lie, and the lie was discovered at some point later on, then whatever trust I had built by that point would blow away like sand in the wind.

I took a deep breath. "Yes, I know where we're going."

Now they regarded me with close to open hostility, and Cornuficius pressed his advantage. "So neither you nor Caesar trusts us."

The situation hung on the edge of a sword; whatever hold I had gained over these men could crumble with what I said next, and I felt a flare of anger, letting it show in my voice.

"First, I was given an order, and I follow orders. To the letter. Second," I was struck by a sudden thought, "what would you do in my position, Cornuficius? Are you saying that you would not only violate your orders, but the trust placed in you by your commanding officer by telling what you knew despite very specific orders to the contrary?"

I was pleased to see a look of discomfort pass through those cow eyes, but it was only a flash.

"Well, Primus Pilus, the fact is I'm not in your position. But if I were, I guess what I would have to determine is wherein lies the greatest threat to myself, betraying my general, and worrying about him finding out about it, or having men at my back who do not trust me and what might happen because of their distrust."

I was flabbergasted and shocked into speechlessness, which was something of a blessing, because it gave me a moment to observe the reactions of the other men. A couple of them, Annius being most prominent, had a look on his face similar to what I had seen on the faces of men watching the games when a kill was about to be made. But there were others, Felix, Clemens, and Sertorius being most prominent, who looked at the very least uncomfortable.

I forced my voice to remain calm. "Well, that's certainly one way to look at it, Cornuficius. And if I were a suspicious man, I might think that you were actually making a threat, and as you know, as Primus Pilus, I would be well within my rights to have you arrested and executed, without trial."

Oh, he was a cool customer; I will give him that, because he did not even blink. He merely nodded and replied, "As you say, Primus Pilus. That would be within your rights. However, I don't think that it would endear you to the men of the 6th, and in turn, your command of them would be doomed to failure. Which in turn would mean that you failed your general and patron, Caesar."

"That would be a risk I'd have to take," I replied evenly, "but you'd still be dead, neh? And I'd be alive, and where there's life there's always hope. Not so much hope when you're dead."

"So we're at an impasse then." He sipped his wine again.

Nobody spoke for several moments, each of us deep in our own thoughts.

Finally, I shook my head and said, "Not really. Ultimately, it's not just Caesar and by extension, me, you have to worry about. If things were to play out as you've described, do you really think that all the rest of Caesar's army wouldn't have their revenge? Especially my comrades in the 10th," I saw no need to reveal the true state of the relationship with some of the men of the 10th and me, "who I have no doubt whatsoever would take their revenge."

I could see that I was making an impact, and I pressed on. "Oh, it would never be anything official, you know that. A brawl outside camp, where suddenly the men of the 6th found themselves surrounded and outnumbered by the men of the 10th. Just a typical soldier's brawl, although it'd be a bit bloodier than normal. A death here, a death there. Never more than one or two at a time, but they'll add up over time, until the 7th and 10th Cohort of the 6th no longer exists, and the clerks at headquarters are left scratching their head trying to figure out what happened."

This had them thinking all right, and they did not like the direction this was taking, but I was determined to hammer home the point I was making.

"So it's not really an impasse. If I can't convince you to accept and obey your orders, exactly as they're relayed, because of the sacred oaths you all have taken at the lustration ceremonies, then you'll just have to content yourself with the knowledge that my comrades would exterminate each and every one of you. Unofficially, of course."

All eyes turned on Cornuficius, and again there was deadly silence. Finally, someone cleared his throat.

I turned to see Felix stand, and it was in the expression on his face that I first saw Scribonius, frowning while forming his thoughts. "Primus Pilus, I want to make sure you understand that Cornuficius is only voicing the concerns we all feel."

Everyone's head nodded, with the exception of Cornuficius, I noticed, whose bovine eyes narrowed, watching Felix, and I remember thinking, there is no love between these two, something I would do well to remember.

"However, I want to assure you that you can rely on me and the men of the Fifth of the Seventh to do their duty to Rome." He put emphasis on the last word, looking directly at Cornuficius as he said it, then continued, "Because ultimately that's who we all serve. Not an individual, but Rome."

I do not know whether he meant that as a rebuke to me just as much as to Cornuficius, but I chose to take what he said at face value, and I nodded my agreement. "Thank you, Felix, that's well put. And I absolutely agree. We all serve Rome, and right now the orders of our general are that we're going to leave day after tomorrow, and I'm not at liberty to say where. Does anyone else have anything to say?"

Predictably, nobody did. Dismissing them to go make their preparations, I stopped Cornuficius, motioning him to sit back down. He did so willingly enough, and I poured him another cup of wine and more for myself. We sat for a moment, sipping our wine while I tried to decide the best way to begin.

As usual, I opted for the frontal assault. "So, Gaius Cornuficius. Am I going to have to kill you?"

Of course, I had waited until he had started to take another sip of his wine, but instead of choking on it, he actually chuckled, lifting his cup to me in mock salute.

"You're welcome to try, Primus Pilus. Many have, but none have succeeded."

"None of them were me," I said calmly, and now his expression changed.

For just the briefest of moments his mask slipped and I saw a blaze of hatred and anger flare, but it was gone as quickly as it had come.

"That's what some of the others said."

I leaned forward, my elbows on my knees so that I could look directly into his eyes. "Was my demonstration with Publius not enough? Or the fact that I faced more than 40 of the men and bested every one of them?"

He gave a short laugh. "Publius is a profoundly stupid man, Primus Pilus. I wouldn't set a lot of store in besting him. But I'll admit that I'm not your equal with a sword; in truth, I don't think I've seen anyone as good in all my time in the Legions."

My eyes narrowed as I tried to determine if he was playing to my vanity, but his face was expressionless, giving me no clue.

Continuing, he said, "But there are many ways in which men do battle, Primus Pilus." Sitting back, he rolled the cup in his hands, looking into its depths. Evidently coming to some decision, he said, "But to answer your original question, the answer is no, you won't have to attempt to kill me, Primus Pilus, at least right now. I'll do my duty in a manner that you'll find no fault with. As Felix said," as he spoke, he gave a small smile, just to make sure I knew that he thought no such thing, "we're all doing our duty for Rome, and not one man." He looked at me, I at him, and I knew in that moment that I had an enemy who I would have to watch very carefully indeed. "Will that be all, Primus Pilus? If so, I must go get the men ready to move out."

I stood, indicating that the audience was over, watching him depart as I thought about all that had taken place. Calling Diocles, I told him that I wanted to speak with Felix, then sat down heavily, pulling the wine to me.

~ ~ ~ ~

Felix was announced, and I bade him enter. Clearly ill at ease, he stood at *intente*. Even after I gave him leave to sit, he relaxed only marginally and remained standing.

I decided to jump right in. "I just wanted to thank you for what you said, Felix. Your words eased the tension quite a bit."

His eyes narrowed, and I could see he was trying to determine if there was anything hidden in my words that he needed to worry about. I laughed at the sight, thinking that he looked very much the way I felt whenever I was around Caesar, and I told him as much.

Shrugging, he said, "I just told the truth, Primus Pilus."

"Yes, but sometimes speaking the truth, especially under such circumstances, can be extremely difficult, especially in front of your comrades. I just wanted you to know your courage was appreciated."

"Thank you, Primus Pilus."

He was still standing stiffly; finally, I had to order him to sit down. Offering him wine, he accepted a cup, but did not drink. Sighing, I realized that this was going to take more work than I had thought.

"Look, Felix, I'm not very good at this kind of thing."

"Neither am I, Primus Pilus."

I do not know why, but I found this funny and burst out laughing. At first, he looked offended, then in a moment, he began chuckling himself. Before long, we were both roaring with laughter.

Finally, I caught my breath. "Tell me about yourself, Felix. I just realized I haven't sat down with any of you to find out more about each of you."

"I know, Primus Pilus." He said this without obvious thought, and just as quickly, I realized the error that I had made.

I had been so consumed with proving to the men that I was a physical force to be reckoned with and ensuring respect out of fear that I had not taken one of the most basic steps to guaranteeing that men obey because they want to, and that was to get to know them as men.

"Really? What else have I done wrong?" The instant I said this, I realized that it had not come out the way I meant it, and I could see as much by Felix's change, his posture becoming tense and defensive. Before he could reply, I held my hand up. "*Pax*, Felix. The instant I said that, I realized how it sounded, but I'm being completely sincere. I truly want to know if there is anything else that you think would help with making things run more smoothly."

Normally, I would never have asked this of a subordinate, at least not one I barely knew. Unfortunately, none of us, men, officers, nor I had ever been in a situation like this, and it was because of the straits we were in that I decided to throw the dice, hoping they came up Venus. I was taking a huge gamble that Felix would not simply tell me what he thought

I wanted to hear before running back to the rest of the Centurions to relay how insecure I was truly feeling in my command. However, I felt that I had picked the right man for such a question, and the more I have thought about it, I have to believe that the similarities between Felix and Scribonius played a huge role in my choice. And my luck held; I had chosen the right man, who proceeded to help me more than I think even he knew.

~ ~ ~ ~

Boarding ship two days later, the men were sullen and quiet, angry that they had not been informed of their destination, something I chose to ignore. The Centurions were in a similar frame of mind, but were too professional to let it show openly, treating me with an icy professional courtesy, even Felix. At first I was puzzled by his demeanor, yet after thinking about it, I realized that while I thought we had made progress towards establishing a rapport two nights before, it was still too early for him to declare his allegiance openly. Fortunately, the worries that always accompany an ocean voyage soon took precedence in the minds of the men. Their problems with me and where they were going took second place to the fear of drowning. The fact that Caesar chose the most direct route from Pergamum to Alexandria did not help matters, because it meant a voyage across the open sea out of sight of land, something that did not make me any happier than anyone else onboard. Just as it was for the rest of the men, this was my first time on a ship where we spent more than a matter of a couple of watches without land in view, and the only thing I could be thankful for was that I had lost my tendency to get seasick. A number of the men were not so lucky, spending the majority of their time draped over the side of the ship. Luckily, the weather held, the sea never particularly choppy, with the winds blowing steadily. Even so, we spent three full days out of sight of land before the flagship sent the signal that land was sighted. There was a mad scramble as men roused themselves from their misery to run to the sides of the vessel, and I stifled a laugh at the sight. Despite having only gotten a glimpse of the maps of this region, I knew where we were headed and off what quarter of the ship the men should be looking for their first sight of land, but such was their disorientation that the betting was fairly evenly spread around all points of the ship. Watching the frenzy of wagering, I became aware of the sensation of being observed, turning to see Cornuficius standing with his Optio, a man named Furius, his bovine eyes studying me. Even as I turned, I saw Cornuficius speak a quiet word to Furius and hand him a coin purse, whereupon the Optio scurried off, presumably to make a wager. I frowned; it was a bad idea on a number of levels for Centurions to engage in any of the wagering that the men did, although in fact, it rarely stopped many of them. It quickly became clear that Cornuficius was one of the men who saw nothing wrong with it. I walked across the rolling deck and approached him, returning his salute.

"Taking part in the betting action, Cornuficius?"

He nodded.

I regarded him for a moment, then said, "I don't like my Centurions engaging in betting with the men. With other Centurions and even Optios, it's fine, but not with the rankers."

Cornuficius gave a small smile, like there was some private joke he was reliving, and I felt my anger stir, but there was nothing I could fault in his tone.

"As you wish, Primus Pilus, I'll refrain from such activities in the future. And just so you know, it's not something I do regularly." He paused, as if trying to decide if he should continue, then gave another small smile. "It's just that I seldom have an opportunity where I'm so sure of the outcome, I just couldn't resist."

"So you think you know where to look for land, Cornuficius?"

He nodded again. "Absolutely, Primus Pilus."

"And how can you be so sure?"

Now the smile that had been playing at the edges of his mouth finally won the battle, quickly turning into a laugh. "Because you told me, Primus Pilus."

And with that, he asked to be excused, which I granted, wanting a moment to myself. What had he meant by that? Thinking about it, I realized that he must have been watching me when the announcement was first made that land had been spotted and seen me look off the port side of the ship. That in itself was not a huge thing, but thinking on it more deeply, I was struck first by a question, then just as quickly by the answer, and the conclusion I drew was deeply unsettling. How could he have known to look at me when the signal came that land was sighted? The answer was that there was no way he could have known, which could only mean that he had been watching me already, and the chance to enrich himself was just, at least as far as he was concerned, a happy accident. It also explained why he thought it so amusing; he was having a laugh at my expense. I think what I found most disturbing was that up until the last moment, I had been unaware that he was spying on me, meaning that he was very, very good at being unobtrusive. My respect for Cornuficius raised a notch, but so did my dislike and distrust. I felt my jaw muscles tighten, determined that he would not best me again, at anything.

~ ~ ~ ~

Our first sight of Alexandria came courtesy of a blinding light that appeared out of the darkness. I am of course referring to the light coming from the great lighthouse of Alexandria, and since it was dark by the time we slid up the Egyptian coast towards Alexandria, this was indeed our first sight of the great city. The sight of such a light, appearing out of nowhere so to speak, caused a near panic among the men, and it was then I was forced to reveal to them our destination, some of the men becoming so frightened of what they thought was some ghostly apparition that they threatened to throw themselves overboard. Calling a hasty formation on the deck, I announced that what the men were seeing was no *numen*, it was the light from the great lighthouse. Instantly the cries of panics turned to a combination of shouts of delight from the winners and groans of despair from the losers, and in the darkness, I could hear the clinking of coins changing hands. Peering through the gloom and by the dim glow from the light reflected from the lighthouse, I could just make out the bulk of the ship carrying the other Cohort, wondering how Valens was faring with the men of the Seventh. I had little doubt that there was much the same scene being played out on the decks of his ship, although he did not have the advantage of knowing where we were going. It turned out the panic onboard was stopped from what I thought an unlikely source, the Princeps Prior Gaius Sido. As I mentioned, he was an older man on his second enlistment, and had actually served with Gabinius when he invaded Egypt. Therefore, he had seen the lighthouse before and knew it for what it was, none of which I found out until we landed. Now that the men knew where they were going and were not about to be consumed by some great sea monster that had a light on its head that it used to lure ships and men to their doom, the chatter focused on what pleasures awaited them in Alexandria. Like every Legionary serving Rome who has not actually been there, Alexandria was legendary for the supposedly limitless opportunities for debauchery available and was a topic of conversation around every fire I had ever sat around at least once a week since I had been in the army. It generally started with something like, "My cousin served with Pompey when he fought the Parthians, and on the way back they stopped in Alexandria. He said that you could find a woman who . . ." Whereupon the man with the cousin would describe the most lascivious, lewd act that he could think of, some of which I do not think were anatomically possible. Alexandria had fired more men's imaginations, along with their nether parts, than any other location that men talked about, even Rome. Hearing the excited murmurs of men gleefully planning to sink to depths that they had only previously dreamed of, I felt a stirring of pity. These men had not marched with Caesar for long; even when they had served with us in Gaul for those two years, they had done very little but garrison duty, guarding of the baggage or had been under the command of one Caesar's Legates or Tribunes and not the great man himself. Consequently, they were blissfully unaware that it was highly unlikely that we would be idle long enough to fulfill any of their fantasies. For a moment, I debated the idea of breaking it to them, but decided against it, knowing that they would not hold me in any gratitude for shattering their illusions. So I turned away, shaking my head and going to look for Diocles to make sure we were ready to disembark.

~ ~ ~ ~

Waiting outside the harbor until it was daylight, we got our first good look at what is rightly one of the wonders of the world. It was one of the few times that the men were struck into silence, so awe-inspiring was the sight of the huge white tower looming above us as our ships slid by. Craning my neck upwards, I was struck by a wave of dizziness as I imagined what it would be like to stand on top, looking down. The statue of Zeus that stands astride the top of the tower by itself would have been massive and intimidating; the fact that it stood on top of a tower that was more than 400 feet high made my jaw drop, and I was not alone. The tower consisted of what almost looked like huge children's building blocks, in three basic shapes. The bottom of the tower is square, built of whitewashed stones and more than 200 feet high. Sitting atop the square is an octagon, but I could not tell with what material it was constructed, and it is not as tall as the square. Finally, there is a cylindrical tower upon which is a cupola where the light burns in front of a huge polished metal mirror. I would learn later that during the day, fire was not used; instead, the sun is bounced off the mirror to send a signal. Around the base of the lighthouse is a high wall, which I was told served to protect the base of the lighthouse from the raging waves caused by storms. Spiraling around the entire tower is a stairway leading to the top, and I did not envy the men whose job it was to ascend that stairway, between the height and the exertion it would require. Sliding by, I could also see that the construction of such a massive structure was not just a matter of vanity; Alexandria is a well-protected harbor, and I instantly understood why it has the reputation of being the most secure anchorage in the world, because the entrance is narrow and the approach is surrounded by rocky shore. The lighthouse is actually on an island called Pharos Island that serves as a barrier, with a huge man-made causeway built out from the mainland that not only links the island but also bisects the harbor, dividing it into a section called The Great Harbor, which is where we were sailing, and the Harbor of Eunostus. The lighthouse was built on a spur of land extending from the eastern end of the island, jutting into the harbor and serving as the upper of what could be called two jaws. The lower jaw is provided by a spur of land that protrudes out north from the mainland, so that the only way to approach the Great Harbor is heading from the northeast; I learned later that it is called Cape Lochias. Between the two jaws are clumps of jagged rocks, further narrowing the entrance.

Taking this all in with the fleet making its way into the anchorage, I was also struck by the sight of so many ships, of all shapes and sizes. I had never seen numbers like it, even when we were in Brundisium, and I was not alone in my wonderment. The men lined the sides of not just my ship, but every transport, pointing at first this sight then the next, talking excitedly about what they were seeing. And we were under just as much scrutiny; I could see men stopping in their work to watch our fleet pass by, some men actually dropping whatever they were doing to dash off down whatever pier they were working on. I would learn that the man-made causeway, lined with docks and being where we were headed, is called the Heptastadion, Greek for Seven Furlongs, which is its actual length. At each end of the causeway is an arched bridge that allows smaller boats to pass from one harbor to another. Caesar's flagship moored first, followed by my transports then the others containing the 7th Cohort, with the next third of a watch occupied in securing the ships and making ready to disembark. Once all was prepared, I was given orders to secure the dock and the immediate area in preparation for Caesar disembarking. The pier was now swarming with curious people, and although I would not describe their posture as welcoming, I did not see anything that I considered threatening. The gangplank was lowered and I walked down the ramp, followed by the men of three Centuries of the Tenth Cohort. Giving the order to set up a defensive perimeter, I told Fuscus, Sertorius, and Favonius to handle the civilians gently, since I did not know the Egyptian temperament at that time, or how they would react to being manhandled. We were able to clear the area without incident, and I remember thinking to myself that perhaps things would go smoothly the rest of the time we were there. The way events unfolded, I only had a matter of a few moments before the first problem arose.

~ ~ ~ ~

When I gave my report to General Pollio, one of Caesar's staff and the commander of the cavalry, I informed him that the area had been secured without incident, and he in turn strode back up the gangplank of the flagship to let Caesar know. After several moments, there was a commotion and I turned to see that Caesar had decided to make an entrance worthy of his status. Down the ramp marched his 12 lictors, their bundles adorned with the ivy, as was Caesar's right, having been hailed as Imperator on the field. Following the lictors were a number of Caesar's other attendants, with the great man himself walking behind, clad in his gilt armor and with his *paludamentum* flowing behind him. He had barely set foot on the quay when there was a hue and cry from the people standing on the outside of the perimeter formed by the men. Because I could not understand a word that was being said, I had to rely on what I saw, and surrounding us was a very angry mob, shaking their fists, hurling what I have to believe were obscenities down on us. Despite none of them doing anything overtly offensive or violent, it was clear that it would not be long before someone in the crowd reached down to pick up a brick or a stave and then things could get ugly. They began chanting something in their language, shaking their fists in rhythm to what they were saying. I saw that it was beginning to affect some of the men, who stood with their shields raised in the first position, as they started to shift their feet or glance over their shoulder back at their Centurions, waiting for us to tell them what to do. Turning about, I saw that Caesar was as surprised as any of us at the sudden turn of events, and I marveled that he seemed unsure of himself. He beckoned Pollio and another general, Tiberius Nero, to his side and they talked quickly. As they were doing so, Sertorius called to me from his spot immediately behind the men who were the farthest away. Saying something that I could not hear over the racket being made by the Egyptians, he pointed and I spotted what had alerted him. From beyond the fringes of the crowd ran a fairly large group of men that, while not exactly heavily armed, were attired in uniform and appeared to have some official capacity. They were pushing their way through the crowd who, once they saw who was pushing, readily gave way. Leading the way were two men; one was wearing the same uniform as the others and was clearly the commanding officer. He was also the darkest man I had ever seen. The second had lighter, honey-colored skin, but that was not what made him so remarkable, because he wore makeup heavier than I had ever seen on a woman, let alone a man. His eyes were outlined in black, with lines drawn outwards from the edge of his eyes, I guessed in an attempt to make them look larger and slanted, although why anyone would want to do that I could not fathom. His attire was of the finest material, richly brocaded with gold, while around his neck he wore what I took to be some sort of symbol of his office. The uniformed men shoved the people out of his way more roughly than I had allowed the men to handle them, but they made no protest, instead immediately shrinking away when they saw the official. The man's bearing bespoke of a haughtiness that comes from being accustomed to being obeyed and feared, but he was respectful enough as he approached.

I walked to meet him, whereupon he held up a hand in greeting, which I returned cautiously, then he spoke, but since he spoke in Greek and the only Greek I knew at that point was not likely to help smooth diplomatic relations, I shrugged and said, "I'm sorry, sir. I don't speak Greek."

A look of what could be considered distaste flashed in his eyes, except he covered it so quickly that I might have imagined it, immediately switching to Latin.

He spoke our tongue flawlessly, although something in the tone of his voice that I found disquieting, but I knew not why at the time. "*Salve,* Centurion. I am Paulinus Eupator. I am one of the city's magistrates, and I hurried here as soon as I heard you and your general landed. What is his name, if I may ask?"

"Gaius Julius Caesar, Consul of Rome and commander of the Eastern Army."

This last bit I made up on the fly; we had no official name, but this he did not know. The reaction to Caesar's name was gratifying, his eyes immediately widening and in some sort of reflex, his hand went up to touch the amulet he wore around his neck.

He recovered nicely, however. "We are most honored to receive a personage as great as Caesar; his fame is well known, and deservedly so, throughout the civilized world." He cleared his throat. "And what is the purpose of such a great man who visits our humble city?"

I shrugged. "That I can't tell you, Paulinus. You'll have to ask Caesar. I do know that right now he intends on marching to the royal palace to pay his respects to your sovereign."

Now there was no hiding his discomfort and he pursed his lips, making me notice for the first time that his lips were painted along with his eyes. And there was that voice, I thought.

Almost like a woman's voice, not just in pitch but in inflection as well. "I regret to say that there is a difficulty with his request, Centurion."

Despite myself, I barked out a laugh. "Request? It's not a request. Caesar is coming to pay his respects." Then my brain registered what he had said. "And what do you mean by 'difficulty'?"

Oh, he was very uncomfortable now, and I saw a bead of sweat pop out on his forehead. "It's just that our laws are very specific, Centurion. The men who precede Caesar who carry those bundles of rods and axes? As I understand it, they represent Caesar's power to punish men if he deems it necessary, correct?"

"Not just Caesar. Any Roman who's served in a type of office, both currently and if he's held this office in the past, is entitled to his lictors. The number depends on the office. What of it?" I asked impatiently, aware that while the noise had died down, now there was an air of anticipation hanging over us, and it was not just coming from the Egyptians. Caesar was not renowned for his patience.

"No person in Egypt other than Pharaoh has the right to take a man's life, Centurion, even a Consul of Rome."

"It's a symbol of office," I argued. "I haven't seen or even heard of a lictor administering punishment in my lifetime. It's simply a mark of the status of Caesar and men like him to have lictors."

"I understand that, Centurion, truly I do." He indicated the crowd behind him with a minute nod of his head. "But they do not. I must respectfully request that Caesar not be preceded by his lictors as he makes his way through our city."

I stood there for a moment, although I knew delaying was not going to make things any easier. "Very well," I said tersely, "I'll relay what you've said to Caesar. Wait here."

Whereupon I turned and walked back to Caesar, fighting the urge to break into a run because it would not be dignified. Caesar had been standing there for a few dozen heartbeats, and for a man like Caesar that is a lifetime, so his impatience and irritation was clear to see even as I approached him.

"Well?" he snapped as I saluted him, which he did return, despite his obvious impatience.

I relayed what Paulinus had said, and I saw the same puzzlement in his eyes that I had felt.

"But it's a ceremonial office," he said in exasperation.

"I told him that, Caesar, but he says that although he understands that, those folks over there," like Paulinus, I used my head to point, "they don't know that."

"Well, that's too bad for them. I'm a Consul of Rome, and they would do well to remember that. Tell the emissary that I won't be dismissing my lictors, and I will make my way to the palace."

"Yes, sir."

And with that, I turned to walk back to Paulinus, informing him of Caesar's decision.

His chin quivered, and for a moment, I thought he might actually cry, but he took a breath then said slowly, "Very well. I will inform the City Guard that you and your party are to be escorted as they are currently formed. Do not worry, Centurion. The City Guard will ensure your safety."

I threw my head back and laughed, which he did not care for in the slightest. "Thank you Paulinus, but," I indicated my own men, "these are Legionaries of Rome. I think we'll be safe enough."

"Fine, Centurion. As you wish," he snapped.

Again, I was struck by how womanish he sounded. Paulinus turned away, walking over to the commander of the City Guard to say something. I saw the man's body stiffen in anger, then he looked over Paulinus' shoulder at me, and if looks could kill, I would have dropped stone dead. I merely winked at him, then turned to my men and ordered them to form up to march. And that is how we entered Alexandria.

~ ~ ~ ~

Despite Paulinus' warning, we marched to the royal palace without major incident, save for a couple of rotten vegetables thrown our way, thankfully not at Caesar because we would have had to punish them, and one thing I was learning, tramping through the streets, was that there were a *lot* of Egyptians. Normally, Caesar would have led the way with his retinue, but given the tensions, he ordered me to send a Century ahead, and I chose Felix's, marching with him as we cleared the way for Caesar. I had never seen so much humanity crammed into one place in my life, and I wondered if perhaps it was a case of every citizen choosing to be out in the streets to watch our approach. They gave way easily enough, yet were clearly not happy with our presence. I am just happy that none of us knew the local language because I am sure someone in the crowd said something that guaranteed their head leaving their shoulders prematurely, and that would have been bad. Another thing I noticed was the layout of the city itself, never seeing anything like it before. The streets for the most part are perfectly straight and intersect each other at right angles. As we marched, I studied the layout, trying to think why it was so foreign but so familiar at the same time. Finally, I made mention of it to Felix.

"That's because it's laid out like a Roman army camp."

I started; he was right. That was why it had seemed so familiar, but was also so strange, because none of our towns or cities is laid out in a similar fashion.

"So these bastards stole our design," I said smugly, but was surprised when Felix laughed.

"No, Primus Pilus, it's the other way around. We stole the design from them."

"*Gerrae*," I replied indignantly, "how's that possible?"

"Well, you know who Alexandria is named for, don't you?"

"Of course, I'm not that uneducated," I shot back indignantly, nettled at his presumption of ignorance on my part.

"Well, Alexander lived more than 200 years ago, and we've only been making our camps this way for about 150 years. So I think it's safe to say that we copied Alexander. Not," he added hastily, apparently worried that he had offended me, "that Alexander is a bad person to copy from."

I regarded what he said, then asked, "And how did you know this, Felix?"

Now he looked uncomfortable.

Finally, he shrugged and looked away as he mumbled, "I like to read a bit. I just picked it up from somewhere, I guess."

I looked over my shoulder to make sure Felix's Optio and men were out of earshot, then told him quietly, "So do I. I read quite a bit."

He looked so surprised that I am sure a strong wind could have blown him over. I recognized that here was the opening I was looking for, in my attempt to make him an ally.

"In fact, I've built up quite a little library over the last few years," I said, hoping my voice sounded casual. "If you ever have the urge, please feel free to borrow anything that strikes your fancy."

Through the cautious expression, I saw the blaze of interest at my words, and recognized that look, for I suspect there were times when my own face was a reflection of his. Once I finally started reading for reasons other than reports and tallies, a whole world had opened up to me, and now rarely a night went by that I did not spend some time reading whatever I could get my hands on. I knew that look because I knew that feeling, and I hoped that this would be enough. Following the Street of the Soma, one of the principal north-south thoroughfares, we passed by the great Library, interesting the men not at all, but Felix and me greatly, and we exchanged a secret smile, knowing what the other was thinking.

"I could get lost in there for months," he said wistfully as we marched by

"More like years," I replied, my tone matching his.

~ ~ ~ ~

Upon reaching the Canopic Way, which is the primary east-west road, we turned left, and I marveled at how the roads not only ran straight, but how wide and well maintained they were. The streets were made of carefully fitted stone, much like our military highways, with curbs and gutters. Now the gutters were lined with people standing shoulder to shoulder and several people deep, and gazing down the length of the avenue, I realized that I could see almost a mile down the thoroughfare without my view being obstructed. And as I looked down the road, my heart sank; every step of the way was lined with people, a great brown, heaving mass, none of whom looked happy to see us.

"How many people you think live here?" Felix's question mirrored my own thoughts, but I could only shrug.

"More than I've ever seen in one place is all I can say," I answered.

"It has to be bigger than Rome."

I looked at Felix in surprise. "You've been to Rome?"

He nodded. "Several times."

"How does this compare?" I asked him.

He gave a short laugh. "This place is much, much cleaner."

"So are the streets laid out this way?"

Another laugh. "Not even close. I don't think there's a street in Rome that runs straight for more than a few paces."

That did not make sense to me and I said so. "But if we make our camps like this, and we copied from Alexander, and Alexander laid his cities out like this, then why don't we?"

He shrugged. "I think it may be because it's too late. The only way to make Rome look like this is to tear everything down and start over. And I don't think that's happening anytime soon."

I was struck by a thought. "Don't be so sure," I replied. "I have a feeling Caesar is going to be changing a lot of things about Rome. If he

looks at Alexandria and thinks it's a good idea for Rome, he'll do it. He'll
tear everything down and start all over again, and nobody will stop him."

He looked at me for a moment, saying nothing. Then, "You have
that much faith in him?"

"Yes." I was about to continue, but decided against it.

"Well, that's understandable. You're his client, he's your patron."

I felt a surge of anger well within me, but I pushed it aside, forcing
myself to think about it from someone else's perspective. I recognized that
it was a logical conclusion for one to draw, and in fact could be true, but I
just had not realized it.

"I understand why you think so, Felix," I said carefully, trying to
decide how far to go. "But it's not that simple. Caesar's my general; in
fact, he's the only general I've ever followed for any length of time,
except for that bastard Labienus. I was part of his *dilectus* when he raised
the 10th. And say what you want, nobody can argue with what we did
under Caesar because it's never been done in the history of Rome. We
conquered more territory and people in Rome's name than any other time
in our history. Through all that time, I've come to one conclusion. Caesar
is blessed by the gods; he is truly their favorite. I'm not a particularly
religious man, but there are things that even I can't ignore, and all the
signs are that Caesar will go down in the history of Rome as its greatest
man." I turned to look him in the eye. "Greater even than Pompey." I
could tell that he did not like my words about Pompey, but he said
nothing. Turning my head back forward, I continued, "The simple truth is
that I've never seen Caesar fail, and over the years I've simply come to
the conclusion that it's wiser to be on his side than against him. As you
and the rest of the men should well know."

He liked that even less than my remark about Pompey, but I was
speaking nothing but the truth, and I saw that he understood that. He did
not like it, but he accepted it.

There was a silence between us for some time before he shrugged.
"That makes sense, Primus Pilus. I understand what you're saying. It's
just . . ."

He looked away, and I could tell he was torn about what he wanted
to say next. "Go ahead, Felix, speak your mind."

"It's just that while I may understand what you say about Pompey
and Caesar, I don't think the men are ready yet to accept that reality. Just
like you, they were part of Pompey's *dilectus* and view him as the father
of the Legion."

I nodded, and I replied, "And I understand what *you* are saying,
Felix, and I'll bear it in mind. Thank you."

By the time our conversation ended, we had reached the gates of the
palace enclosure, home of the boy king Ptolemy. We halted, waiting for

Caesar to make his way to the front of the formation so that he could be the one to ask for entrance, and I had to suppress a smile when he was preceded by his lictors. He strode up to the very nervous looking Nubian guards, big brutes of my size with skin so black it looked very much like a ripe plum, but before he could say anything, one of them turned to open a small door inset into the huge gate, disappearing from sight, drawing a chuckle from us. A moment later, the door opened and a creature that could have been the twin of Paulinus stepped out, although if anything he was more richly attired, wearing an elaborate wig, black as night. His face was made up in the same style of Paulinus, and when he spoke, I was shocked because it was as if this thing and Paulinus shared the same voice. His name, he said, was Pothinus, and after listening to his oily blandishments for a moment, I felt in desperate need of a bath. However, Caesar behaved with impeccable courtesy, showing none of the impatience he had displayed at the dock. After a brief exchange that I could not clearly hear, Pothinus turned to the guards, who in turn put their weapons down to begin straining against the gates. Ponderously, and with much shrieking protest from hinges that did not seem to have been oiled in my lifetime, the gates opened up, giving us a glimpse into what would turn out to be our home for the next several months.

~ ~ ~ ~

We marched into the enclosure, and thank the gods that the palace compound was so large, given what would take place. There was still not enough room for everyone to assemble in formation, so I was ordered by Pollio to send one Cohort back to the docks, accompanied by Nero, who was going to arrange billeting for the men. Choosing the Seventh to remain in the palace complex, there immediately arose another complication, with Pothinus haughtily informing Caesar that we were not allowed to remain under arms while inside the palace compound.

There was much back and forth over this, but Caesar ended the impasse by saying simply, "If you think your men can take their weapons, Pothinus, by all means order them to do so."

We kept our weapons, although Caesar did have us stack our arms and allowed us to take seats on the ground while he entered the palace proper. He also ordered that his two Primi Pili, meaning me, and the Primus Pilus of the 28th, a man named Gnaeus Cartufenus, to accompany him and his senior officers into the palace. Gnaeus Cartufenus was about ten years my senior, but he had spent most of his career in garrison or frontier postings and did not have a fraction of the combat experience that I had,. Thankfully, Cartufenus recognized his lack of experience and despite being technically senior, he usually deferred to me over questions concerning tactics. That was how Cartufenus and I were present for what happened next. Caesar formed us up, with Cartufenus and I naturally

R.W. Peake

bringing up the rear, then marched into the palace. It was hard not to gawk and I was relieved that at least Cartufenus had the same problem. We had never seen anything so ornate; it seemed that everything was covered in gold, with even the most common objects made of precious metals and encrusted in jewels. That, however, was not the strange part. All around us were statues of the most bizarre creatures I had ever seen before, or since for that matter. A man's body with the head of what looked like a dog was just one example, and as I looked more closely, I felt my skin crawling. If that was indeed a statue, it was made out of a substance I had never seen before, making me queasy as I wondered if what I was seeing was a real man. There were several stuffed crocodiles, their eyes replaced by gems like emeralds and rubies. We were marching down a very long passageway, and if I squinted, I could just make out what appeared to be a throne at the far end, and I recognized that this was all for the effect of overawing visitors like us. Lining the walls were dozens of men and women, most of the men dressed in the same style as Pothinus and Paulinus, while the women were wearing almost nothing at all, most of them lounging on couches. They all had their faces painted in what I was quickly learning was their fashion, and they were engaged in a variety of activities. Some of them were puffing on what I took to be some sort of pipe, although it was more elaborate than anything I had ever seen before. Meanwhile, others seemed to be engaged in some sort of sexual activity, and only the discipline of many years, along with a healthy fear of drawing Caesar's displeasure, kept me from openly staring. Cartufenus was not quite so successful, and I had to nudge him a time or two. Now that we were closer, I saw that the throne was empty, but arrayed before it stood Pothinus and a number of other creatures like him. Caesar ordered us to halt as he stood a few feet away from Pothinus, and I saw that one of the creatures next to Pothinus held a small wicker basket.

Caesar spoke, "Greetings to the House of Ptolemy. I am Gaius Julius Caesar of the Julii, direct descendant of the goddess Venus, Consul of Rome and I hold the imperium granted me by Rome, which gives me the authority to engage in treaties and adjudicate disputes. I am here to see Ptolemy XIV and pay my respects."

Pothinus' heavily made up face was a mask, making it almost impossible to read his expression, which, as I would come to learn, was one of the main reasons they did as much.

He bowed when Caesar was finished, and said, "Alas Caesar, I am desolate."

Caesar raised an eyebrow. "And why, may I ask, Pothinus are you made desolate by my visit?"

Pothinus held his hands out and while his voice throbbed with emotion, it was disconcerting to see the completely blank expression as he said, "It is not your visit that is so distressing Caesar. It is that our glorious Pharaoh Ptolemy, Lord of the Two Ladies Upper and Lower Egypt, Master of Sedge and Bee, Child of Amun-Ra, Isis and Ptah is not here."

For the second time in a day, Caesar was nonplussed "Not here? You mean not in the palace?"

Pothinus shook his head. "No, great Caesar. I mean that he is not in Alexandria. He is with his army, a few days' march away from here."

"Very well, then I will see his wife. Or his sister, however which you wish to style her."

Now I was confused; it was not until a day or so later that I learned the custom of the Ptolemaic dynasty that brother and sister also be man and wife, which I find despicable. But Pothinus knew exactly what he meant and for the first time I thought I detected a crack in his mask, matched by a tone of uncertainty when he answered Caesar.

"Alas, Caesar, that is not possible either."

"Ah, so she is with her husband then?"

I had been with Caesar long enough to recognize his tone; he was asking a question to which he already knew the answer. Since this was undoubtedly one of his many tests that he subjected people to, I felt a glimmer of sympathy for Pothinus, but it passed. Now Pothinus began fidgeting with his hands, and despite his face still looking serene, there was no mistaking the distress when he answered, "No, not exactly, Caesar. It would appear that our beloved queen Cleopatra has fallen prey to listening to evil counsel. She has raised an army in rebellion against her husband."

"Ah," Caesar repeated, then said gently, "that's not very good, is it?"

Pothinus shook his head vigorously, agreeing with Caesar that it indeed was not very good.

Caesar spoke again, his voice becoming brisk. "Rome cannot afford to have strife in this region since it will impact our grain supply. Therefore, I will adjudicate this dispute between the two and come to a decision about how to resolve it. You will send for Ptolemy at once, and I will send for Cleopatra and have her escorted here safely."

Pothinus' body went rigid, whether it was from anger or fear I do not know which, but his voice was controlled. "I will send word immediately, Caesar, but that is all I can do. Ptolemy is sovereign and this is his kingdom. I do not think he will take kindly to being summoned."

"If he knows what is best for his people, he will come," Caesar was curt. He turned to us, indicating that we were leaving. Turning back, he said, "I will of course be your guest here at the palace while we wait. I assume that meets with your approval?"

Pothinus bowed, and I marveled at his self-control as he said smoothly, "I would have it no other way, Caesar. We would be most honored if you availed yourself of these quarters, humble as they may be."

I fought back an urge to laugh, but only just and I could see I was not alone. Before we turned to leave, Pothinus asked us to wait. "While I am sorry that we could not accommodate everything you requested at this moment, Caesar, I do have a gift that I think will help put us in a more favorable light."

Caesar turned back, eyebrow lifted. "Oh, and what would this precious gift be?"

Turning to the creature next to him, Pothinus took the basket from his hands, holding it out to Caesar. Caesar took a step forward and at Pothinus' signal, the creature next to him lifted the lid of the basket with one hand, and with the other raised the object inside so it could be viewed by all. Caesar recoiled in horror, although it took me a moment for what I was seeing to register, before shooting a quick glance at Cartufenus, who was standing, mouth agape, as dumbfounded as I was. For as you probably know, gentle reader, that precious gift was the head of Gnaeus Pompeius Magnus, preserved in some sort of oil.

Caesar quickly gathered his composure, his face becoming a mask very much like that worn by Pothinus, but one did not have to know Caesar well to hear the barely controlled rage in his voice when he spoke.

"Put his . . . him back in the basket," he spoke through clenched teeth, whereupon the creature dropped Pompey's head back in with a thud, almost causing Pothinus to lose his grip. "This act brings great shame on the house of Ptolemy. Shame! Do you understand me?"

Pothinus was clearly taken aback, along with all the other creatures, their expressions mirroring ours from a moment before as they looked at each other in shock and confusion.

"But he was your enemy," Pothinus protested, "I thought you would be pleased!"

"He was a Consul of Rome," Caesar roared more loudly than I had ever heard him. He shook his head, his voice suddenly sounding tired and I saw his shoulders slump. "You had no right or cause to meddle in internal Roman matters. You have shamed not just yourselves, but you have shamed me." He took a deep breath before regaining control of himself. "This changes nothing," he declared. "You know what you must do. And I know what I must do."

With that, he turned away, but before I faced about to wait for him to pass, I am sure that I saw a glimmer of tears in his eyes.

The news of Pompey's death angered the men greatly. Fortunately, their anger was not aimed at Caesar but at the Egyptians because of their treachery. It also told Caesar that he had to watch himself while in their midst; if they would murder Pompey, it was not out of the realm of possibility that they would try to murder Caesar. Now that Pompey was dead, there was really no need to linger where we were so clearly not wanted, at least as far as the men were concerned, but we were staying put while Caesar waited for Ptolemy to answer his summons. However, Caesar was not idle; he commanded his admiral Cassius to set sail as quickly as possible with orders to retrieve the 27th Legion, along with two new Legions he had ordered to be formed out of Pompey's veterans, numbered 36th and 37th. Meanwhile, we set up our quarters inside the compound in a series of buildings near the royal theater, and I was ordered to bring the rest of the 6th within the enclosure, with the 28th setting up camp on the quay. Our presence was still a festering sore to the Egyptians, and they had taken to making daily demonstrations expressing their displeasure. At first, they contented themselves with gathering in a crowd to hurl insults and an occasional rotten vegetable or small dead animal. Then a couple boys from the 28th wandered too far from their Cohort area, evidently in search of some of the fleshly delights they had heard so much about, winding up with their throats cut and dumped in an alley. Their Centurion took his Century out in search of them; while they found the two men, they also found themselves surrounded very quickly by a mob, and this lot was not content just to throw fruit and whatnot. According to the Centurion, it started out in the usual manner, but then out of the crowd came one of the bricks that the Egyptians use to pave their streets, striking a man in the chest and knocking him down. An instant later, the air was filled with bricks, stones, and whatever else the crowd could get their hands on, with several men struck and injured, a couple of them seriously. That in turn ignited the rage of the men, who were already eager to lash out because of their two dead comrades, and without receiving any orders, they rushed the crowd, striking a few dozen down before the crowd ran for its collective life, whereupon the Century marched back to the camp carrying their dead and wounded. That was the beginning of daily riots before Caesar finally ordered first Century-sized, then Cohort-sized sorties out to disperse the crowds, with orders to stop just short of deadly force. However, this merely served to escalate the violence, and soon there were pitched battles going on between our men and the Egyptians. It was not until Caesar finally allowed us to unsheathe our weapons that a semblance of order was restored. I do not know how many Egyptians were killed, but it was in the hundreds, although we did not survive unscathed. Since both of my Cohorts were now at the enclosure, we were not involved in any of these actions, but I suspected that if we stayed much longer, we would see more than enough action, and it appeared that Caesar had every intention of staying. The question was, what was he staying for?

~ ~ ~ ~

I know that there has been much speculation about the true reason for Caesar's time in Alexandria; some men who claimed to have inside knowledge have even said that it was for love. These men are at best fools, and at worst liars. I know why Caesar chose to stay and wait for Ptolemy to answer his summons, although I also know firsthand that he was very well aware that when Ptolemy finally did come, it might be at the head of an army that outnumbered us by more than ten to one. While I cannot claim that Caesar told this to me directly, we had enough conversations where the subject came up and he made some sort of comment that now leads me to be as sure as I can be that I know the real reason that we stayed in Alexandria, and love was not it. However, before I impart what I know, I cannot deny that there might be a partial grain of truth that Caesar had feelings for young Cleopatra, although I can say with certainty that she was not the driving force behind his decision. No, it was more mundane and as a result more pressing reason than love; Caesar needed money. I have already detailed the agreement Caesar struck with the men of the 6th, yet the 6th was just the tip of the javelin. Caesar had made similar promises to his Spanish Legions to quell their revolt, and had just formed new Legions from the Pompeian survivors who chose to fight for him. As a result, he knew that to renege on these promises would bring on his destruction more surely and more quickly than Pompey or his minions ever could. The amounts we are talking about were massive, and that was just for the troops; Caesar also had to rebuild a Republic torn apart by civil war. Although his Gallic conquests would go a long way towards providing the kind of income he needed, the cash that he had accrued through the sale of hundreds of thousands of slaves was long since expended and it would be years before the new provinces started providing the kind of revenue needed. The wealth of Egypt was well known, even by people as lowly born and uneducated as me, and it was this that Caesar planned on using to keep his enterprise going. What I do not know was whether he planned to take the contents of Egypt's treasury outright, or if his goal was more subtle, by placing Cleopatra on the throne, knowing that she would be a pliant ally. First though, he had to settle the question of the squabble between brother-husband and sister-wife, but before that could begin, he had to find Cleopatra. Especially now that, after several days of waiting, we received word that young Ptolemy was returning to the capital.

~ ~ ~ ~

Surprisingly, the young king chose to leave his army behind, bringing only his immediate entourage. His retinue included Pothinus, whom I have already mentioned, and was left behind to manage matters in his absence, along with an old toad by the name of Theodotus, who was a tutor of some kind. I thought it the height of irony, and not a little amusing that Ptolemy had to come to his own palace seeking an audience with Caesar, despite Caesar taking pains to avoid the appearance of Ptolemy being a supplicant. I was not present at the meeting, but Caesar's secretary Appolonius was friends with Diocles, so I heard of what took place in a matter of a watch. During the time Caesar waited for Ptolemy to arrive, he had Appolonius and the rest of the staff turn the palace upside down looking for a document, which in a palace the size of Ptolemy's, crammed full of a few hundred years' worth of documents was no small feat. But they did find it, and Caesar had this document in front of him when the young Ptolemy finally made his appearance.

"He's a spindly, weak-looking thing," sniffed Appolonius, sipping the wine Diocles had poured.

He was sitting in my quarters, but in the front room that served as the Legion office where Diocles spent most of his time. I was in my private quarters, but the walls were thin, the door open, and I suspect that he knew full well that I was listening. Something that I was learning from Diocles was that much could be learned, and one's life could be made much easier, if one treated their slaves and servants well. As quick as slaves are to swap tales of woe about cruel masters with each other, they are just as quick to speak well of kind ones, and when all is said and done, slaves run Rome and the Republic. Also, when one has a reputation for kindness to his own slaves, he finds that the slaves of others are much more willing to do small favors for him, though I do not really know why, so I know that what Appolonius was saying was as much for my ears as it was just two slaves gossiping.

"Of course, it's hard to tell what he really looks like with all that horrid makeup; he even had a beard made of wool on his face," he exclaimed. Taking another sip, he laughed at the memory. "Oh, he tried his best to be regal and very solemn, but it was clear from the first moment that he's little more than a puppet and it's Pothinus and that other one, Theodotus, that are pulling his strings. You should have seen their faces when Caesar produced the will of Ptolemy XIII; even through the makeup you could see their faces go white as bone."

"What does the will say?" asked Diocles, I knew for my benefit.

"That the Senate and People of Rome should help ensure that Ptolemy XIII's last wishes were carried out, and that Caesar was the duly appointed representative to arbitrate the dispute."

"And what were his wishes?"

"That Ptolemy XIV and Cleopatra share the throne of Egypt equally, as co-regents."

"That seems fair enough," Diocles commented, and I thought so as well.

"Oh, it's fair. But it became clear very quickly that the real source of conflict is less between Ptolemy and Cleopatra than it is between his advisers and their queen. I think that they're worried that she'll have more influence over her little brother-husband than they will. And from what I gather, she's quite intelligent and sees those two for what they are. I have a feeling that they're also worried that their respective heads may not stay on their respective shoulders if she returns."

"Does anyone know where she is?"

"We don't know exactly; all we know is that she's hiding somewhere along the coast. And certainly Pothinus and Theodotus don't know or she'd be dead."

Of course, when dealing with the Egyptians, as we were to learn, nothing is ever that straightforward. After seeing that Caesar found the will and heard his decision, Ptolemy and his toadies asked for a day to discuss matters, which in itself was not unfair. But one day stretched to two, then three, then four before Caesar finally had enough, ordering an audience, this time making no pretense that he was not the one in control. It was at this meeting that the farce that young Ptolemy was in charge finally became exposed for what it was, when Pothinus and Caesar engaged in a shouting match. Appolonius' hands were still shaking, this time gulping the wine Diocles offered instead of taking his usual sips.

"Well, that went to *cac*," he gasped, shaking his head. "It started out with the normal 'how do you do's,' then Caesar informed them that he was calling in the loan taken out by Ptolemy XIII, which they were none too happy about, but when they asked how much the amount was and Caesar told them, Pothinus hit the roof!"

"How much was the loan?" Diocles asked.

"Seventy million sesterces."

Diocles' gasp was audible through the wall, and I was thankful for it because it covered the sound of my own. It was fairly easy to understand why the Egyptians were so put out, I thought.

"What did Ptolemy say?"

Appolonius scoffed, "Say? He didn't say a word. He just sat there like a lump. It was Pothinus who did all the talking from then on."

There was a pause as Appolonius took a drink, but it soon became clear that he was enjoying building the suspense.

Finally, Diocles burst out, "Well? What did he say? Or are you just going to sit there swilling wine?"

Appolonius laughed, clearly enjoying tormenting Diocles, and I smiled at the thought as I sat working on ration requests at my desk.

"Well, I would say that I'd rather just sit here and drink your wine, but I know that you wouldn't just let me be, so I guess I'll have to. Where was I? Oh, yes, so Caesar tells them the amount, and Pothinus jumps out of his seat and suddenly gets all haughty and says, 'I suggest that you go and attend to your other affairs, Caesar. You won't be getting any money from us now; we'll pay you at some other time.'"

The astonishment in Diocles' voice was clear. "And how did that go over?"

Appolonius gave a shaky laugh. "How do you think it went over? Caesar jumped up and said, 'When I need an Egyptian woman to be my counselor, I will keep you in mind, Pothinus. Until then you should hold your tongue!' You would have thought Caesar had struck him he was so shocked. Then Caesar threw the lot of them out of the room."

"So now what?"

Appolonius did not answer, so I assumed he just shrugged. Finally, he said, "I have no idea."

Appolonius may not have had any idea but thank the gods Caesar did. It was time for him to introduce the third actor in the drama that was playing out, and she was more than eager to be used by him for whatever he had planned, while I would have a minor role in his production.

~ ~ ~ ~

I was summoned to headquarters in the palace without being told why, and I hurried over from my quarters. It was shortly before midnight, but I had not retired yet, making it only a moment to throw on my uniform and get there. Sertorius was the Centurion of the guard, and when I arrived, he was standing with a man wrapped in a nondescript cloak, his head covered by a cloth wound round it, with one end pulled down to partially obscure his face. I had seen many Egyptians wear this style of clothing, but for some reason I did not get the impression that the man with Sertorius wore these clothes naturally. His bearing was haughty, and when he pulled the veil from his face as I approached, I could see that his demeanor matched his posture. At his feet was what looked like either a large carpet or bedding rolled up, but I gave it only a passing glance.

Sertorius spoke to me, indicating the man, "Primus Pilus, this man claims that he bears a gift for Caesar and is seeking an audience. I thought I better inform you."

I turned to the man, who spoke in flawless Latin. "My name is Apollodorus. I am an adviser to Queen Cleopatra, and I come bearing a gift for Caesar from my liege."

I looked at him, then down at the bundle, and I remember thinking that it seemed like a paltry gift from a queen whose skin needed saving. Nevertheless, I indicated that he should pick it up and follow me. I probably should have been suspicious when he did not protest at being told he had to carry the gift on his own, since palace types like Apollodorus are about as pampered a lot as you will find, but knowing now what the true nature of the gift was, I can see why he did not protest. Leading him into the palace complex, I guided him towards the wing that served as a combination of Caesar's private quarters and headquarters, alerting Appolonius to fetch his master. Hirtius and Nero were already there, sensing that something was afoot, and the room used as the headquarters suddenly filled up with the rest of Caesar's staff. Caesar entered the room, and I had Apollodorus wait at the entrance while making my report. He had set the bundle down again at his feet, but otherwise did not make any move as he stood waiting. Giving my report to Caesar, he told me to allow Apollodorus to enter, indicating that I should wait nearby in the event that there was some treachery afoot. I returned to tell Apollodorus that Caesar would see him, and he bent down to pick up the bundle, then approached Caesar while I waited by the door. Apollodorus spoke, his voice pitched so that all in the room could hear, his tone that of a herald announcing the presence of some important personage, which as it turned out was exactly what he was doing.

"Oh great Caesar, I bring you greetings from Queen Cleopatra, Pharaoh, Lord of the Two Ladies Upper and Lower Egypt, Mistress of Sedge and Bee, Child of Amun-Ra, Isis and Ptah. My mistress has asked that I, Apollodorus, her loyal servant, present you with this humble gift as a token of her esteem and appreciation."

With that, he untied the ends of the bundle then unrolled it, while all the men in the room crowded around, blocking my view of what was contained in it, but gasps of astonishment and surprise brought me running as I pulled my blade. I was the only man of Centurion rank there, meaning I was the only one fully armed, and I ran to the group of men surrounding what appeared to be a very small person. Getting nearer, I saw that it was indeed a person, and that person was a woman, a very tiny woman, the sight causing me to sheathe my weapon sheepishly. A very tiny, very ugly woman, with a great big nose and hardly any chin at all, although her eyes were large and expressive, even through all the makeup. On her head was a huge wig, and while she wore a gown that I heard described as diaphanous, I do not know what that means. All I know is that you could see through it, and what I saw was not much to my taste. She had curves in the right places, but she was not very well endowed, having almost a boyish figure. Yet Caesar stared down at her in frank admiration and appreciation, and I was struck by an unwelcome thought that perhaps all that talk about he and King Nicomedes was not just malicious gossip. Then I heard her laugh at something he said and even as I watched, her face transformed, and while I cannot say that I suddenly saw her as beautiful, I could see how some men might find her attractive.

It has been my experience that high-born men tend to like their women on the frail, pasty side, except I have to think that there might be a link between their women's physical frailty and the fact that more high-born women seem to die in childbirth than those of the lower classes. Caesar, spotting me, waved me over and I marched to him, rendering a salute.

He returned it as he said, "Pullus, may I present Queen Cleopatra. Your Highness, this is Primus Pilus Titus Pullus of the 6th Legion. As of this moment, you are under my protection, and it will be the Primus Pilus and his men who provide that protection."

She turned her large brown eyes up to me, smiling at me. This caused me to go weak in the knees, as I realized I had no idea the proper way to behave, never having met a queen before, so all I could think was to bow and mumble, "Highness. It is a great honor."

"Thank you, Centurion. I know that I am in good hands just by looking at you!"

I felt the heat rising to my face and I honestly do not remember much of the rest of the exchange, such as it was. Quickly enough I was dismissed back to my place by the door while Cleopatra and Caesar talked, with his generals sitting nearby and listening. They talked for at least two thirds of a watch, before Caesar stood and beckoned me.

"You are to escort Cleopatra and her servant back to her quarters. She's going to take up residence in her wing of the palace, since that will be where she'll be most comfortable, among her own things. You will post a guard; use however many men you see fit, but I think it should be at least two sections per entrance. Nobody is to be allowed in, except for me, or one of my secretaries. No exceptions, do you understand, Pullus?"

I saluted, saying that I did. I had sent for some men to come to headquarters when I brought Apollodorus so that I would not have to reduce the guard in the event I needed them, and they were waiting outside for us. Forming them around Cleopatra and her servant, I was about to give the order to march when I realized that I had no idea exactly where we were going, since I did not know where her quarters were.

Embarrassed, I turned to her and mumbled, "Er, Highness? If you would be so kind and point the way to your quarters, we'll get under way."

She laughed, and pointed the direction. "It's down this way. Follow me."

And without waiting, she marched away, leaving us running after her as I cursed under my breath.

~ ~ ~ ~

Cleopatra was installed in her wing without incident, and after examining the layout of the building, I realized that in order to secure it to the standard that Caesar required would take almost a whole Century per shift. Cleopatra's quarters were actually a wing of the palace in name only; it was, for all intents and purposes, a separate building, consisting of two sections separated by a central passageway that served as an audience chamber. One wing was for Cleopatra's private use, with perhaps a total of 40 or 50 rooms. The other wing was split into two stories, with the lower floor dominated by a huge formal dining room, the upper story containing the living quarters of the servants belonging to Cleopatra. There were two staircases leading to the upper floors on the outside, one on each side, with a covered veranda running the length of the upper floor, again on each side. There were entrances at each end of the building, but what made it difficult to control were the half dozen small, secret doors scattered all over the building, each of which had to be covered by at least a section. We used the standard watch length, with a Century taking each watch and their Centurion the commander of the watch, who reported to me at the end of each shift, or sent for me in the event of an emergency. The only event of any note was the fact that Caesar came to Cleopatra's quarters that first night, his appearance being reported to me with a leer by Annius. His departure shortly before dawn was also reported to me, this time by Cornuficius, his face carefully expressionless, but there was no mistaking the amusement in his eyes, and I was forced to swallow my irritation. It was in this manner that the next several days passed; Caesar did not miss spending a single night with Cleopatra, so she must have had something going for her that was not readily apparent to the eye.

"Maybe there's something to be said about all those tricks Egyptian women supposedly know," I mused to Felix one night as we shared some wine.

He laughed, then shrugged. "I'd like to find out, though not with her. She's really not much to look at it, is she?"

I shook my head. "No, she's not. But I overheard her talking with Caesar when they went for a walk around the grounds the other day. She's got a pretty good sense of humor, and she doesn't miss a thing. She said a couple things that caught me by surprise, I can tell you that."

"Oh, what was that?"

I looked at him, suddenly embarrassed, realizing that I had said too much. As curious as I may have been about what he saw in her, I was also reluctant to be seen as gossiping about my general, so I just shrugged and mumbled, "I don't recall exactly. It was just interesting."

Fortunately, he did not press, and we continued sipping our wine in companionable silence.

~ ~ ~ ~

The day after Cleopatra arrived, Caesar called a meeting of brother and sister, ordering both Cohorts to be present, so we formed up, lining up against the walls of the main palace to watch the fun. We were there to remind Ptolemy, and more importantly Pothinus and Theodotus, who held the whip, and to discourage them from doing anything as silly as trying to argue. At the assembly, Caesar announced that Ptolemy had thought things over and decided that Egypt would be best served by the restoration of Cleopatra to her throne, and that they would once again co-rule their kingdom in peace and harmony. It was very hard not to burst out laughing, looking at the faces of Ptolemy and his toadies as Caesar spoke, but they were smart enough not to argue the point. That night Caesar ordered a banquet held, with Ptolemy, Cleopatra and their retinues as the guests of honor. I was ordered to keep a Century standing by outside the palace, but within hailing distance, taking command myself. During the banquet, the Egyptians drank themselves silly, exactly as Caesar had planned, counting on the loosening effect on their tongues to provide him with useful information. And it worked; during the festivities one of Caesar's staff, the barber as it turned out, one of the faceless, nameless masses that upper classes and palace types think of as part of the furniture, managed to overhear of a plot by Pothinus and the general of the Egyptian army still at Pelusium, a man named Achillas, to kill Caesar. I was called to Caesar, who informed me of the plot and ordered me to surreptitiously bring some men in and scatter them about the palace, ready to spring to his defense should it be more than just drunken talk. Caesar stayed up the entire night, which of course meant that we stayed up as well, but nothing happened, at least that night.

~ ~ ~ ~

It was only a day or two later when word arrived that Achillas was now bringing the Egyptian army from Pelusium. Even with leaving a garrison force behind, Achillas was marching with 20,000 infantry and 2,000 cavalry, which we could meet with not even two full Legion's worth of troops, and only two Cohorts of those hardened veterans. The men of the 28th, while not *tirones*, were certainly not what I considered seasoned veterans, so I honestly was not sure exactly how they would react. One of the difficulties facing us, besides overwhelming numbers, was the fact that our command was essentially split, with the 28th securing the docks and the 6th securing the palace. Cartufenus, and sometimes his other Centurions, came in for staff briefings, yet for the most part, we ran our commands separately, having little contact with the other. Now we were about to see what we were all made of, but as usual, Caesar was not content to wait. Caesar summoned me to headquarters to brief me on what he had planned and I had to suppress a smile when I walked out, not wanting the Egyptians always hanging around to get a whiff that something might be up. Later that night, I marched out with the Century that was relieving the one on guard. Fortunately, I had done this often enough that it was not cause for any suspicion on the part of the

Egyptian guards in the towers and on the walls, although when I did it before it was more to keep my own men on their toes than any attempt to lull the Egyptians. Approaching the guard Century, I was challenged by Considius, giving him the watchword, then went about the process of changing the guard, with only one slight variation. Instead of the relieved Century now marching back to their quarters, they stayed put and we immediately began to move, knowing that we only had a matter of moments before the Egyptians noticed that a Century of Romans was not marching back down the street. They did start off like they were doing so, but very quickly they veered across the Canopic Way to Ptolemy's wing, where I dispatched a section to rush the two guards standing at the entrance we had chosen, catching them completely by surprise. We did not kill them; Caesar had been very explicit that we were not to shed blood unless absolutely necessary, but speed was essential and when the men went through the door, I had every other section go to the left, the rest in the opposite direction. Taking a section with me, we headed down a long hallway towards where we were told Ptolemy's private bedroom was located, running almost full-out, trying to beat anyone sounding the alarm. There were a few sharp cries, but there was not enough of a commotion to fully alert people who were, for the most part, sound asleep. Finally taking a left down another long hallway, at the end of it we could see two Nubians, armed with axes.

Immediately ordering the men to stop running, I slowed to a walk myself and as I approached, I said in my most commanding voice, "Caesar needs to see Ptolemy immediately!"

Of course, neither of them spoke my tongue, and I did not speak theirs, but I knew they would recognize Caesar and Ptolemy's names, and I hoped that would be enough to allow me to get close. Turning to the men with me, I told them to stand there as I approached more closely, then repeated myself. They were both looking at each other and grasping their axes, clearly unsure of what to do, and then I smiled and shrugged.

"Upper classes, neh? Never know what they're up to, right boys?"

While it did not put them completely at ease, I could see them relax somewhat, but they were both still too alert for me to try anything on both of them without running the risk of getting myself hurt or killed. Shaking my head again, I paused like I was catching my breath, unstrapping my helmet, and making a show of pulling up my neckerchief to mop my brow.

"I had to run all the way here," I explained, knowing that they had no idea what I was saying but I just kept chattering like this were nothing but routine.

Finally, I saw them relax, and that is when I struck. Using the helmet as a weapon, I lashed out with it, catching one of the guards flush in the face, dropping him like a stone. Before the other man could react, I swung my left fist, catching him in the face as well, except he did not go down, instead staggering back a step before he swung his axe at me, barely missing me as I leaned back, feeling the blade whistle past my ear. In the instant that it took him to recover, I leaped on him but he was by far one of the strongest men I had ever fought, so that in a moment we were rolling on the floor, grabbing at each other's throats.

For a moment I thought he had me, his hands closing around my windpipe until I started seeing stars, as I barely managed to croak out, "What are you bastards waiting for?"

Suddenly, the weight lifted off me, his hands finally jerked from my throat as the men pulled him off me, knocking him cold.

Staggering to my feet, I glared at the others, all of them looking ashamed, and one of them said, "Sorry, Primus Pilus, we thought you had him."

"I'll sort you out later," I growled, then kicked the door open, stepping quickly inside.

There was a startled squeal that I thought was from a woman, but it turned out to be one of those creatures like Pothinus who slept at the foot of Ptolemy's bed. Ptolemy was just sitting up, and without any of that ludicrous makeup he looked exactly what he was, a teenage boy. I could see the resemblance between him and his sister, once more striking me with revulsion at the thought that Cleopatra was more than his sibling. He was blinking the sleep away as I strode to his bed, saying exactly what I had been instructed to say.

"Your Highness, there are matters of utmost urgency that Caesar has deemed requires your presence for consultations with him. I am to escort you to headquarters immediately."

He looked up at me, clearly confused. "Can't this wait until morning?"

"No, Your Highness," I said firmly. "In fact, we are already running late. Please rouse yourself and come with me."

"Without getting dressed?"

Now he was getting indignant as his mind started working. I had been warned by Caesar not to be swayed by his youth.

"Ptolemy has been raised on court politics and intrigue. You've seen yourself how treacherous these people are, so don't let him have time to start thinking," Caesar told me, and I had this in mind as I watched Ptolemy frowning.

Before he could say anything, I spoke in a commanding tone. "We don't have time for that Your Highness. I'll make sure that men bring proper attire but we need to leave . . . now."

I do not think he had ever been talked to like that. His jaw dropped as he looked at me in astonishment, but then I saw his face color and I could see he was getting angry. I took a step towards the bed, causing him to call for the guards.

"They're not coming, Highness," I told him calmly. "They've been . . . detained."

"How dare you," he hissed, and now he was getting really angry, though he did rouse himself from the bed.

I remember thinking that even his nightclothes probably cost more than every stitch of clothing I owned, yet they did nothing to enhance his royal dignity. That did not stop him from drawing himself up to his full height, such as it was, as he looked up at me.

"I am Pharaoh! I am lord of the Two Kingdoms and I will not be spoken to as if I were a vassal!"

"I mean no disrespect, Highness," I replied, "but I have my orders, and they are specific. You're to accompany me right now. Now," I turned and indicated my men, "we can do this one of two ways, and I think we would both prefer that you come with us under your own power."

That took all the wind out of his sails, his shoulders suddenly slumping, and he came with us, giving no further trouble except when we first stepped through the door and he saw the inert bodies of his guards.

"You're going to kill me," he shrilled, making a move to try and run, forcing me to grab a handful of his nightclothes, picking him up off the ground so his feet could not get traction, though that did not stop his feet from moving like he was, a comical sight, I can assure you.

"That's not true, Highness. These men aren't dead; they're simply knocked unconscious. Look." I nudged one of them with my toe, eliciting a low moan. "See? They're just out cold. They'll wake up with a headache and nothing more."

That settled his nerves, but just a bit, although he did not give us any more problems and we brought him to Caesar as ordered. The other sections had also collected his younger siblings, a girl named Arsinoe and another Ptolemy who was a few years younger than the king. Cleopatra had also been brought to Caesar, albeit more gently than her other siblings, but nonetheless the entire Egyptian royal family was now located at Caesar's headquarters. I was standing in a corner of the room when Caesar appeared to face the confused and angry youngsters. I do not know if Ptolemy XIV appointed himself the spokesman for his siblings or just took it upon himself, but he angrily confronted Caesar.

"What is the meaning of this?"

By this point, he was almost apoplectic with rage. Whatever timidity he felt when I roused him from his bed had been washed away with anger, but Caesar did not seem put out in the slightest.

"Your Highness, I have received reports that your general Achillas has decided to move his army against my forces. This is merely to ensure your and your family's safety."

"Our safety? We have nothing to fear from Achillas! You're the only one who has anything to fear!"

"That remains to be seen," Caesar said coolly. "But regardless, the situation is very dangerous and I'm doing this for your safety."

"You are doing no such thing," Ptolemy scoffed. "We're nothing but hostages!"

I do not know if I was the only one who saw the corner of Caesar's mouth twitch as he suppressed a smile.

"I can certainly see how you might see it that way, but nothing could be further from the truth, Your Highness, I assure you. I have only your welfare and the welfare of your family as my goal. We will do everything we can to make your stay as comfortable as possible, but I'm afraid that space is at a premium and your accommodations may be more cramped than you're accustomed to."

Ptolemy was clearly unhappy, but was intelligent enough to know that there was nothing he could do about it. With the royal family secure, my men and I were dismissed for the time being to return to our quarters. I went looking for Diocles to talk over all that had transpired and to find out what he knew of the situation from Appolonius. Meanwhile, Caesar had a use for Ptolemy, and he put the next phase of his plan into operation.

~ ~ ~ ~

Caesar ordered the boy king to summon two of his advisers, named Serapion and Dioscorides, giving them instructions to go find Achillas and order him to turn around in the king's name. Not only did Achillas not listen, he tried to kill both of them, succeeding with Serapion while seriously wounding Dioscorides, who barely managed to escape. He made his way back to Alexandria, carried in a litter by his servants, only being allowed back into the city gates because of his status as Ptolemy's ambassador. The City Guard had learned of Caesar's taking of the royal family, but they were too poorly organized, trained, and led to do anything other than shut the city gates and wait for Achillas' army. I was summoned shortly after Dioscorides came back to find that all of Caesar's staff was already present, all of them looking grim.

"What's going on?" I whispered to Apollonius.

"I'm not sure, but I don't think it's good news."

"I can pretty much tell that, thank you," I snapped, moving off towards Caesar and his generals. Caesar saw me, indicating to take a seat, which I did.

"Cartufenus should be arriving shortly," he announced, "so we'll wait for him before we begin."

He arrived a few moments later, taking his own seat.

Without waiting any longer, Caesar began. "As you all know, Achillas approaches with his army. That's no surprise. However, what poor Dioscorides has informed me about that *is* a surprise is the composition of the army of Achillas. Do you remember how it was something of a mystery what happened to the bulk of Gabinius' army?"

The generals nodded their heads, but I was only vaguely aware of the story of Gabinius and his trials for extortion and corruption, nevertheless, I nodded along with the rest of them.

"Well, it appears that a good number of his former men joined the army of Ptolemy, and have been acting as cadre for the rest of the army. They've been training the Egyptians in our tactics, although I do not know to what extent. What I do know is that they're battle-hardened veterans."

"Any idea of their numbers?" This came from Pollio, I believe.

"Approximately four thousand."

Someone let out a low whistle.

"That's almost a quarter of their total numbers."

"Thank you for that lesson in figuring sums," Caesar snapped, somewhat peevishly. "The question at hand is how we handle this information."

"Bribe them," Hirtius said immediately. "They're Roman, after all. It shouldn't be too hard to bring them back to our side."

"That may have been true at one time, but there are a couple of factors that I think would make that impossible. First, these men have been here for many, many years. From what Dioscorides said, most of them have gone native, taking wives and raising families. Besides that is the fact that they were originally raised by Pompey. I don't think they would be well disposed to serving the man who brought their original patron down."

"The men of the 6th did, as well as the ones who formed the 36th and 37th," pointed out Nero, and despite the truth of what he said, I felt a flash of irritation at his smug tone.

"The men of the 6th were at the point of a sword, and the rest of them had just been defeated. These men haven't tasted defeat yet, and they're not likely to be well disposed towards the man who conquered their patron." Caesar repeated, looking around at us. Seeing that we accepted this, he continued, "So we must determine whether or not we leave the walls and meet them in open battle, or if we wait for them to come to us."

Pollio spoke immediately. "If you have any hope of employing my cavalry, we'll have to meet them on open ground. We'll be practically useless inside the walls of the city."

"But if we move to meet them on open ground, they can bring their numbers to bear on us," protested Hirtius, and I for one agreed with this assessment. "We need to find a way to negate their numbers, especially now that we know that they have Roman veterans in their ranks."

"We don't have enough men to man the walls of a city this size," Pollio pointed out, and this also was true. This was the nature of the argument back and forth for some moments, during which time Caesar only listened. Finally, he lifted a hand to silence the others, looking to Cartufenus and me.

"Cartufenus, what do you think?"

All eyes turned towards Cartufenus, who shifted uncomfortably, shooting me a sidelong glance before clearing his throat. "Well, Caesar. I don't think we can face such a large host in open battle, especially with my boys." The men around him gave him sharp looks, and he hurriedly continued, "I'm not saying they're not good men, but you all know that they're not the most seasoned troops. So I think anything we can do to give them every advantage, we must do if we're to have a chance."

Caesar turned to me. "Pullus?"

"I agree with Cartufenus, but I'd take it even further. I think we need to choose one point in the city to defend and pull all of the men in to give us the best chance."

"The only problem with that is that if we do that, we give up access to the docks," Nero spoke up, and I had to admit he was right.

"We can't abandon the palace and concentrate on the docks," Caesar decided. "So we'll compromise and defend both points. The palace complex is too large to defend completely, so we'll form a perimeter around the buildings south of the Canopic Way. I have already sent Mithradates in one of the thirty's to get help in the form of more naval vessels, and he's bearing messages for the provinces to supply troops and supplies. Since I haven't heard from Cassius, I have to assume that he didn't make it through for some reason, so now we must rely on Mithradates."

We discussed a few more details before we were dismissed to make preparations, and I had a lot to do before Achillas showed up.

~ ~ ~ ~

We learned very quickly that Achillas was a competent general, not overawed in the slightest by facing Caesar. I believe that the destruction of Curio and his Legions a couple years before had shown him that we could be beaten, and he did not dawdle on his march, arriving at the city gates barely a day after our meeting. Caesar had hoped that Achillas' actions against the two envoys would show that he was acting against the wishes of Ptolemy, causing the people to rise up against Achillas and his army, but no such thing happened. In fact, Achillas was greeted as the savior of the city, the eastern gate where he approached thrown open to him without any resistance. Immediately after entering the city, Achillas divided his force into two, sending one column to the docks, while taking the other to our position at the palace. We were alerted to their approach, first by the cheers of the people crowding the streets, then by our own pickets running back to warn us. A series of barricades had been erected, made of wagons turned on their sides then loaded down with anything we could get our hands on that weighed a good deal and was not flammable, so that even in the event they fired the wagons, the contents would still provide protection. Another part of our preparations consisted of knocking down the interior walls in the buildings fronting the street, allowing for men to pass from one end of a building to another without being exposed to fire. Our scorpions were positioned on the flat roofs of the part of the palace that we were defending, and I was thankful that we did not need to worry about fire, since the buildings of Alexandria are almost completely composed of stone, with very little if any wood being used in their construction. The Egyptians made the focus of their first assault the breastworks at the junction of the Canopic Way and the street that ran north to the harbor along the eastern edge of the palace compound. They marched several men abreast, forming a solid wall of men, completely filling the avenue. I was standing with the Fifth and Sixth Centuries of the 7th, next to Felix and Clemens, watching as the enemy stopped to dress their lines in preparation for their attack. I selected these two Centuries because I had the most confidence in them, although it was confidence based on nothing more than a feeling in my gut, since we had not done any fighting to this point. Felix stood calmly, calling to one man or another, giving them last-minute orders and encouragement, while Clemens was bouncing up and down on the balls of his feet, but I could tell that it was from eagerness and not from a lack of courage or resolve.

Felix turned to me, indicating the front rank of the enemy. "They don't look all that formidable. I thought you said that they were veterans."

I looked over the edge of the barricade, and Felix was right. The men in the front ranks were lightly armored and wearing the traditional garb of the Egyptians, though some of the men wore a helmet of a sort.

I frowned as I thought about it, then a notion struck me. "I think that's because Achillas isn't convinced that he can dislodge us and he doesn't want to waste his best troops yet. Or," as another thought came to me, "he's using his best men somewhere else. Like down at the docks."

Once I said it, I became more certain that this latter idea was indeed the case, but there was nothing I could do about it, because the Egyptians finally launched their attack. They came pounding down the avenue, their voices in full cry and waving their weapons above their heads. We had brought extra javelins so that the men could throw at least three and maybe four volleys, and I told Felix to give the order to loose the first one. The air filled with missiles, slamming into the packed mass of men, knocking a dozen in the front rank down. Immediately, the momentum of the attack stalled, with the men in the rear ranks stumbling over the bodies of their comrades. Most of these men carried shields, except they were much smaller than ours, appearing to be made of wicker like our training versions, and the men who were not struck bodily by the volley had them knocked from their hands. The enemy milled about as they tried to reorganize, providing a stationary target for the second barrage. This time they were a bit better prepared, but a number of the men in the front who managed to dodge the first volley by sacrificing their shields were not so lucky the second time. All we could do was delay them, however, and it was a credit to their officers that they reorganized and resumed the charge so quickly, preventing us from hurling the extra javelins that we brought at them.

"Draw swords!"

Even over the roars of the charging men, I heard the rasping sound of the blades of two Centuries being drawn then our own men added to the din with their cries of defiance as the front ranks of the Egyptians threw themselves at the barricade. Dust flew from the loaded wagons from thousands of pounds of angry men slamming into them, briefly obscuring the action. Egyptians began throwing themselves at the wagons, clawing at the sides, trying to pull themselves up to where my men were standing, ready to thrust down at them. The enemy possessed no missile troops to try scouring us from the makeshift parapet, making it short work of chopping men down as they clambered up. It took the enemy a couple of moments to realize that they had no chance of dislodging our men from their position, and by the time they withdrew, the area immediately around the breastworks was covered with the bodies of their dead and wounded, the latter being finished off as my men jeered at the retreating Egyptians. They re-formed down the avenue, out of range of the javelins, and we waited as their commander tried to decide what to do. During the respite, Clemens walked down the avenue to the next street that gave an unobstructed view down towards the harbor. Hearing him cursing, I trotted over to him, and when he pointed to the north, and I followed his finger, I began cursing as well. Huge clouds of black smoke were billowing up from the direction of the harbor, the sounds of fighting carrying to us on the wind, blowing from the north at that time of year. Because of the buildings in between it was impossible to see exactly what was taking place, but the signs were not encouraging, since our men were defending the docks and the structures around it. I assumed that anything set alight had to be done by the enemy, incorrectly as it turned out, but there was no way of knowing that then. All I knew for sure was that was where Caesar had chosen to go and assume command, meaning I had to trust that he had things well in hand, despite the signs to the contrary. Also, there was nothing I could do about it anyway, so I turned my attention back to the immediate situation, walking back to see what the enemy had decided to do.

~ ~ ~ ~

The Egyptian commander, who I do not believe was Achillas, ordered his men to turn their attention to a postern gate opening onto an alley running between two of the buildings we were defending, and was used to deliver supplies. They had fashioned a crude battering ram, using what looked like a carved column, to which they had attached a series of ropes to act as handles. When the men carrying the ram moved forward, they were surrounded by comrades carrying their shields high above their heads to protect the ram from our men on the roofs of the buildings. Hurrying over to the new point of attack, using the holes in the walls we had opened, I found Salvius in command, meaning that Porcinus was actually in charge. The Optio had two sections bracing against the gate, their bodies shuddering with every impact of the ram, as splinters flew with each blow.

I waited a moment to see if Salvius would do anything, but after a couple of moments where he seemed content to watch his men desperately struggling to brace the gate, I finally spoke. "Salvius," I snapped. "Don't stand there with your thumb up your ass. Get some of your men to find something to brace the gate. These men can't do it alone. Hurry, damn you!"

You would have thought I poked him in the ass with a red-hot javelin, and he scurried off with several sections of his men looking for something suitable, and I wondered if he would be smart enough to bring something that would be of any value. Ordering another two sections to relieve the men at the gate, the relieved men gasped their thanks as the others took their place. The gate seemed to be holding, but there was no telling how long it would last, because now small chunks of wood were starting to come off with every blow from the ram. It seemed we could either hope the gate held, or we could try to do something about the ram, and with that in mind, I went up onto the roof of one of the buildings. Favonius had his Century on the roof, the men standing away from the edge until they were ready to throw a javelin down onto the heads of the Egyptians. The scorpions were useless because we could not depress the angle enough when they were this close. Although the javelins were causing casualties, we needed a more concerted effort, and something more effective, so I told Favonius to start using the combustibles that we had piled there, small pots filled with pitch stoppered with a rag soaked in oil to set alight. It's a really ugly way to die, but we could not allow the enemy to affect a breach. In a few moments, the men were raining fire down on the heads of the Egyptians, the horrific screams of men set alight and becoming human torches filling the air. It did not take long for the smell of sizzling meat to reach our nostrils, and no matter how many times one smells that odor, it still causes the stomach to turn. Before another few moments passed, the ram was on fire, forcing the Egyptians to drop it and retreat once again, this time leaving scorched, smoking corpses behind. Once they moved back up the avenue, I left the roof, going back down to check the gate, and I was pleased to see that Salvius had managed to find heavy timbers to wedge against it, bracing the timbers with a number of heavy crates. To that point, we had managed to inflict a fair number of losses on the Egyptians and so far had not suffered one man killed, with only a couple of minor wounds. The enemy was forced to regroup again, their commander then apparently deciding a change in tactics was required. Instead of trying to force one point of entry, he sent detachments of a few hundred men ranging around the compound, looking for weak spots in our defensive line. At the sound of a horn, the detachments went rushing at the points they had selected, the air suddenly split by the answering sound of our own *cornicen* from each Century calling the alarm. It was a cacophony of sound, and I was forced to decide very quickly where I was most needed, choosing to go to the southern side of the enclosure to see if there were any problems.

I had put Valens in charge of this sector and found him at the southern gate of the enclosure, where the Egyptians apparently decided on a slightly different approach. Instead of trying to beat down the gate, they constructed about two dozen ladders, and as I trotted up, I saw what looked like Egyptian troops fighting with our men on the parapet. Valens was on the ground directing his men, and I was about to chastise him for not being up on the wall but held my tongue, recognizing that this was one of those times where a Centurion was better off leading from a position where he could more easily see what was going on. The enemy was attempting to scale the wall at several points, and if Valens rushed to one spot that he thought was in trouble, he might not see a more serious breach occur elsewhere. Instead, I told him to continue as he was before, climbing the stairs up to the wall, heading towards a spot where a couple sections of men were trying to stop more of the enemy from adding to a pocket that four or five of them had managed to secure on the parapet. It irritated me that it seemed to be taking my men a long time to dispatch a handful of the enemy, but when I got closer, I saw the cause of the problem. The enemy commander had committed some of those veterans who we had taken to calling 'Gabinians,' to this assault, meaning that we were facing men trained in the same manner as we were.

Their fighting style was the same, but that is about all; pushing my way through the men, I grabbed a shield from one of the boys in the rear as someone yelled, "Make way for the Primus Pilus, boys! He wants a piece of these *cunni*!"

When I got to the front, standing a few feet away from me was a man who at first I would have said was a native Egyptian, judging by the darkness of his skin and style of dress, but he called out to me in perfect Latin, "Primus Pilus, my ass! This boy is barely able to shave!"

It had been a long time since anyone had said that of me, and the flash of anger was immediate. "If you want to try and give me a shave, you prick, come here and see what happens."

He laughed. "You aren't a pimple on the ass of some of the men I've bested," and as he said that, he lunged at me.

He was very quick and I barely blocked his thrust, then he bashed me a good lick with his shield that rocked me, wicker though it may have been. My arm ached from the blow, but I was determined to take the offensive, although I had to be wary not to get too involved with this man and not be alert to his comrades on either side.

Without taking my eyes off the man, I whispered to the Gregarius next to me, Papernus, I believe it was, "When I make my move, you take the man to his left."

I heard him grunt, then made my own move, closing with the man, knocking the breath from him in a great whoosh when I barged into him behind my shield. Sensing Papernus striking immediately after me, I engaged with the man to my undefended side, allowing me to concentrate on my own opponent without worrying about getting stuck, or so I hoped. There was always the possibility that Papernus would be bested by his man but once you start thinking that way, you are already beaten. We pushed against each other and I was grimly pleased to hear him gasping for breath, trying to get the air back into his lungs that I had knocked out. Despite him putting every bit of energy into pushing back against me, my size and strength began to tell, and I felt him start sliding backwards towards the parapet and the ladder. If I could get him all the way back to the parapet, he would be blocking the ladder, thereby keeping any other enemy from ascending. That is the key to defending a wall: not giving your foe enough space where he has any kind of numerical advantage. I looked over the rim and into his eyes. I saw them widen in desperation once his back heel hit the edge. His strength was failing him and in desperation, he made an overhand thrust that almost got me, the point hitting just below my left collarbone but not having enough force behind the thrust to break the links of my mail. It still hurt like the fires of Hades, and I bit my lip to keep from crying out. I quickly let up, pushing against him, and throwing him off balance because he could not compensate for the sudden change quickly enough. He stumbled forward, just a step, but it was enough and we both knew it, my blade immediately flicking out at his exposed throat, the point punching in at the base of his neck, emerging on the other side for an instant before I recovered.

"Not laughing so much now, are we?" I spat as he crumpled to the ground.

His sudden absence immediately exposed the man to his right, who was already being pressed hard, so I ended him quickly. As I had assumed, Papernus had won his own battle, and just that quickly the breach was contained as we pushed the ladder away from the wall, heaving it as hard as we could because there were men on it. They all went tumbling down, the men almost to the top having the worst of it from the combination of the height and falling onto the raised weapons of their own comrades. Turning to look down at Valens, he pointed to another point on the wall where there was a fight, and I ran over to where he directed.

~ ~ ~ ~

That was how the time passed, until the enemy finally had enough and retired, taking their wounded, but leaving their dead behind, to retreat down the avenue one last time. I was too busy to pay any more attention to what was happening down by the docks, but by the time we were done, it was impossible to ignore, since the smoke had now drifted over to cover us in ash, leaving us coughing, with runny eyes and snotty noses. Any exposed skin was covered in soot, the sweat attracting the ash like a moth to a flame, making the men look like Nubians. After making an inspection, I ordered half of them to remain in place while the other half were allowed to get some rest and eat. We dragged the bodies a short distance down the avenue and dumped them, and fortunately, they were gone the next day. Caesar returned at nightfall, and we learned what had taken place at the docks and the immediately surrounding area, which was still burning fiercely. The Egyptian attack on the docks was in fact led by Achillas and had almost been successful, forcing Caesar to take drastic action. In order to avoid the Egyptians capturing, or recapturing as it were, their fleet of more than 70 ships of a number of different classes, he ordered them all fired. Because the wind was blowing stronger than normal from the north, it sent the flames across the water, catching everything flammable on fire. Unfortunately, one of the things that caught was the great library, for which Caesar has been blamed, I suppose with good reason, although it was never his intention to do so. The fire at the library held an unexpected benefit in forcing Achillas to devote a good number of his men to combating the blaze instead of us. Fighting around the docks was fierce, ranging from one street to the next, but from all accounts, the boys of the 28th did a good job, pushing the Egyptians back several blocks from the dock area before they were ordered by Caesar to withdraw with him. When the next day dawned, we now controlled the Royal Quarter of the city, but only from south of the Canopic Way to the southern end of the palace enclosure. Caesar put us to work, creating a series of fortifications linking everything together so that we could move men and supplies from one part to the other. He also ordered us to push our lines out across the road on the southwestern side to give us access to the large marsh that rings the Lake Harbor on that side. The men worked throughout the night, illuminated by the fires that continued to burn, but which also kept the Egyptians occupied so that we were not harassed. The largest building within our position was the royal theater, now designated as our combination hospital and assembly point for our morning briefings. Any building that stood in the way of the fortifications was razed, the stone used for the wall while we extended the work of battering holes in interior walls of buildings so that men could move almost completely under cover from one end of our redoubt to the other. During the battle at the docks, Caesar had ordered a detachment, armed with several artillery pieces, to board a boat that took them to Pharos Island, where they seized the lighthouse. Because of the shoals extending from the lower part of the jaws that guard the harbor entrance, the only clear channel deep enough to allow large ships to enter the harbor passes closer to Pharos Island and the upper part of the jaws. Having artillery emplaced at the lighthouse gave us command over any ships entering the harbor, although I do not know what Caesar was expecting, since we had burned the entire Egyptian fleet. Meanwhile, the Egyptians invested the western side of the city, the eastern side containing a group of people called Jews, who I had only heard mention of before this and who were mainly left alone. As busily as we worked, the Egyptians were just as busy, although they had a great deal more hands to do the work.

~ ~ ~ ~

While we worked through the night, another event occurred that would come to cause us grief. Since Caesar could not spare any of my men to guard the royal family, he used his cavalrymen, dismounted, of course, to watch over them. In the confusion of the night, the princess Arsinoe and her tutor Ganymede managed to escape, making their way to Achillas, where she volunteered to be the symbolic leader and focal point of the resistance, an offer that he gladly accepted. With the major part of the fortifications finished by daybreak, the men collapsed the instant they were given permission to put down their tools. There were minor improvements to be made over the next few days, but the major bulk of the work was done, and walking behind Caesar as he inspected the lines, I could see he was pleased. All in all, it was a good position, but still there were more bad things than good about our situation. Despite extending our works so that the canal carrying fresh water to the city was within our lines, we did not control the source, meaning it was only a matter of time before it was cut off. Because of the rapidity of our work in fortifying our area, the people living in the area were unable to flee, giving us more mouths to feed, thereby exposing the biggest weakness of our position. The only way we could be resupplied was by sea. Although Caesar had removed the threat to our resupply being intercepted before reaching Alexandria by destroying the Egyptian navy, even when it did arrive, we would have to march in force down to the dock area, under fire from the rooftops and the towers that the Egyptians were building surrounding our position. It was not a good situation to be in, and on top of these difficulties, Cartufenus and I now had to deal with the men from two different Legions being thrust into close proximity to each other. One would think that the rankers would have more on their minds than getting into quarrels and fights with each other, but that has never been the case and I suspect it never will be. What made these circumstances slightly different was what the men were fighting about, and it was not the usual of whores or gambling. I first became aware that a problem existed when I was told by Diocles that Cartufenus had come to see me. I went out into the outer office, and could tell immediately by the expression on Cartufenus' face that something had happened.

Indicating my private quarters, he said tersely, "This is better spoken of in private, Pullus."

Once we were settled, he sat looking at his feet for a moment, obviously trying to decide the best way to begin.

Finally, he looked up, his expression strained. "We've got problems, Pullus."

"So I gathered. What happened?"

"Some of your men have beaten one of mine almost to death. The doctors don't think he's going to survive."

This was indeed serious, but the punishment was straightforward and I said as much. In the back of my mind was the belief that because of the circumstances, Caesar could be persuaded to suspend punishment, but I was puzzled by Cartufenus' discomfort.

"It's not quite that simple." He shifted in his seat. "It's why the man was beaten that's the problem."

This got my attention, and I leaned forward, indicating that he should continue.

"Apparently your boys overheard some of my men talking about the situation."

"And? I don't understand. So, some of your men were moaning about our circumstances."

He looked uneasy, but continued, "They were doing more than moaning. The man who was beaten was apparently the ringleader of a group of men who were talking about deserting over to the Egyptians."

That made me sit up, I can tell you. As bad as that was, I sensed that there was more, and I was right.

"They weren't going over empty-handed. They were going to offer the Egyptians information about our defenses in exchange for safe passage, and some money."

"Do you know if they had made contact with the Egyptians yet?"

Cartufenus shook his head. "I don't know. The man that yours beat is unconscious, so I couldn't question him."

"What about the others? You said there were others."

"They scattered to the four winds. Your men didn't get a good enough look at them to identify anyone. I already asked."

"Where are my men now?"

"They're outside the theater under guard."

I sat thinking for a moment. Cartufenus was right; this was a very sticky situation, and was one of those matters better off staying among the ranks and not reaching the ears of Caesar or his generals. I got up and went with Cartufenus to where my men were standing, watched by a section from the 28th. I was about to make a sharp comment to Cartufenus about using his men to guard mine, but I realized that if he had called the provosts there would have been no way to keep this quiet, so instead I quietly thanked him. His only reply was a nod. Even as we walked down the narrow back street towards the theater, the idea formed in my mind about whom I might find under guard, so I cannot say I was very surprised when I saw that two of the men were the brothers Tetarfenus. There were four of them all together. They watched us approach with expressions ranging from apprehension to defiance, and the brothers bore the latter look on their face. Despite myself, I sighed, not wanting any part of this, but knowing that it had to be handled delicately. No matter the reason, the men could not escape punishment for what they had done, yet if I made their penalty too harsh, they had the right to seek an audience with the Legate, and if they were still not satisfied, with Caesar. That, of course, would be the exact opposite result that Cartufenus and I were trying to achieve, making me just as apprehensive as the men, but unlike them, I could not let it show. Sergeant Tetarfenus was the ranking Legionary, and it was to him that I addressed my first question.

"Sergeant, what do you have to say for yourself and these men?"

Tetarfenus was standing at *intente*, along with the other three men, and his tone was emotionless as he gave his report.

"Primus Pilus, we overheard some of the men of the 28th plotting to desert to the Egyptians. In exchange for safe passage, they were offering information about our defenses and dispositions. Oh," he added, "and they wanted money as well."

"I know all that," I said impatiently. "My question is, why did you think it was the right thing to do to take matters into your own hands and beat one of the men half to death without going to your Centurion, or to me?"

He shrugged. "We knew that you and Hastatus Posterior Clemens had other things on your minds."

"Well, thank you very much for your concern, Sergeant," I said, my voice dripping with sarcasm. "But thanks to your little stunt, now it's not just Clemens and I that are involved, but the Primus Pilus of the 28th as well. And you've dumped us in the *cac* up to our necks."

Tetarfenus shifted uncomfortably, and I saw the other three men shooting glances at each other. It was clear that they had talked things over among themselves, but apparently, matters were not going the way they thought they would.

"Er, yes sir. Sorry about that, sir. We just thought . . ."

I cut him off. "And now we come to the kernel of the problem, Sergeant. You've been in the army long enough to know that of all the things a ranker should be doing, thinking isn't one of them. That's what your Centurions and Optios are for. And because you had ideas above your rank, now here we all are with our asses hanging in the air. So, since you decided to think for yourself, what do you think I should do with the four of you? Please, enlighten me."

I crossed my arms, looking down at Tetarfenus, who looked back at me, his expression becoming calculating, though he said nothing. After a moment, I realized that he was unsure how freely he could speak, so I told him that he could speak his mind and I would not hold it against him.

He looked first at Cartufenus, then at me, and finally said, "Well, sir, as I see it, there's not a whole lot you can do. Officially, I mean," he added hastily, seeing my eyes narrow in anger at the suggestion that I was powerless, "but I know that there are . . . other ways that you can punish us. Sir."

I said nothing, just nodded for him to continue. He eyed the others, and I caught an almost imperceptible nod from his brother.

His tone was shrewd as he continued, "But as far as official punishment, I don't think either of you are particularly anxious for the boys and me to tell any of the generals why we beat that prick." I saw Cartufenus' lips thin in anger, but he said nothing. Taking our silence as recognition of the truth in what he was saying, which indeed it was, he went on, "So you're somewhat limited in what you can do to us. But, I also understand that we must be punished in some ways." I saw the faces of his companions turn to him in surprise and not a little anger, but he shook his head, saying firmly, "So, we'll accept whatever punishment you deem fit. The only thing I would add is that I do think that the reason we beat that . . . man should be taken into consideration."

He looked at Cartufenus when he said this last part. The message was unmistakable, and both Cartufenus and I knew it. I could not help admiring Tetarfenus; he had done us both very neatly. If I ignored what he said and punished them harshly, no matter how unofficial it was, the word would get out not just about the punishment but why they were being punished, and my tenuous hold on the 6th would be gone, although it would appease the men of the 28th. Conversely, if Cartufenus pushed for a harsh punishment, there is no doubt that the planned treachery of his men would become common knowledge throughout the army. While his men might appreciate his attempt to exact revenge for their comrade, he would lose Caesar's confidence that he had control of his Legion. Now all that was left was to determine exactly how the men should be punished, but I decided that since we had gone this far, it made sense to continue.

"Very well, Sergeant," I finally replied, my tone as neutral as I could make it. "I understand what you're saying. I'm not saying I agree, but I understand. So if you were me, how would you proceed?"

He suddenly looked uncomfortable; obviously, he had not planned on being forced to come up with a suitable punishment. If it had just been for himself, I doubt it would have been a problem, but now he had to worry about how the other three men, including his brother, would take whatever he proposed. Now, he was in a tight spot, and as he looked at me, I smiled, except it was not a pleasant smile. See how you like it, you little turd, I thought.

He did not speak for a moment, then finally said, "I don't think a flogging or any reduction in rank would be appropriate, nor would any punishment that had to be entered in the Legion diary, like reduction of rations. Besides, unless I miss my guess, we're all going to be on reduced rations before long." He smiled grimly. "I think extra watches for a week, and extra fatigues for the same length of time."

"A month," I responded instantly, and he opened his mouth to protest, yet stopped himself, his mouth reducing into a thin line the only sign that he was angry. The other men did not do as good a job of hiding their displeasure, but I was unmoved. I knew that he would only propose a punishment that the men would laugh about later around their fire because it was so light. And while it may sound trivial, extra watches and extra fatigue duty meant that these four men would be dead on their feet, getting perhaps one watch's worth of sleep a night for the next month. By the last week of their punishment, they would be more dead than alive. Besides, I reasoned, the way things looked, they might very well be dead long before the month was up. The matter settled, the men were dismissed and as they walked back to their quarters, I watched them go, thinking that Sergeant Tetarfenus would bear watching. He had potential as a leader, but he also had a clever streak that might get him into trouble.

~ ~ ~ ~

Just as the doctors had predicted, the man in the 28th died without ever regaining consciousness, creating another problem because of all the paperwork that is involved when a man dies in something other than battle. If he had died just the day before, during the fight for the docks, no questions would be asked. But since there had been no skirmishes taking place anywhere when the man died, we would have to come up with a reason for his demise. Actually, Cartufenus would have to come up with the reason, but since we were more or less bound in this together, I was not surprised when he showed up in my quarters, a stylus and wax tablet in hand, ready to write down what we came up with.

"We can't list him as a fever because it'd be too sudden. Besides, he's beaten from head to toe. If any of the Tribunes or Legates got curious and saw the body, there'd be too many questions."

I nodded, thinking about it. "Why don't we just dump him over the wall? He was going to desert anyway; we can just say that he disappeared."

"I already thought of that," Cartufenus said glumly. "The problem is that the doctor is chummy with our Tribune. He might not say anything, but I can't be sure. If he hadn't been brought to the hospital, that would have worked."

"Who brought him?" I asked, annoyed that some ranker had complicated matters.

Cartufenus shrugged, indicating that he did not know. We sat there disconsolately, not even able to suck down wine because it was being rationed. Finally, we decided to say that he had been found beaten and unconscious, but had no idea of the circumstances. This fiction had the advantage of being partially true, and was completely deniable. Oh, there would be a raised eyebrow, and perhaps even suspicions, except matters like these occurred all the time in the army, and our superior officers were all experienced men who had been under the standard for several years. They knew that there were things that they did not know, and that they did not want to know. I think they may have been surprised about how much they actually were not aware of, even Caesar, although he was better informed than any of the other generals I ever served with. The other thing in our favor was that Caesar and his entire staff had much more pressing problems than the death of a single Gregarius, no matter what the circumstances, meaning that we made our report, then heard nothing more about it.

~ ~ ~ ~

In the larger world, the Egyptians had sent out a call for a *dilectus* of their own, this one going out to the whole kingdom of Egypt. Men began streaming into the city, drawn by the promise of booty, glory, steady meals, or whatever motivated them. Standing on the roofs of the buildings, we watched the Gabinians put the new men through their paces, while the rest of the Egyptian army continued to build towers and walls, constructing them to a height that overlooked our own positions. From prisoners, we learned that Achillas had ordered the conversion of every local smith and metalworker into a military endeavor, where they were churning out weapons and ammunition. Woodworking shops were similarly working on ballistae and scorpions; in short, the entire city had been mobilized to destroy us. With thousands of mouths to feed, along with more than 900 horses, only the horses were eating well, thanks to the marsh grasses that men went out to gather under cover of darkness. The salt grass of the marsh was so rich and plentiful that not only did the horses not suffer from hunger, they actually filled out some, indirectly ending up as a help to the men later. The Egyptians also were focusing their efforts on exacting revenge for the loss of their fleet by attacking ours, moored in the Great Harbor. For their first attempt, they sent small boats loaded with men through the arches from the Inner Harbor, and Caesar's foresight in placing a detachment with artillery on Pharos Island was fulfilled, with every boat destroyed. Undaunted, they tried again, this time sending boats loaded with combustibles that were set afire, except the wind was against them, causing the boats to do more damage to Egyptian shipping than to ours.

It was also about this time that the snake Pothinus was discovered sending secret messages to Achillas, urging him to maintain his pressure on us and not lose heart. He also included what information about our dispositions he had gleaned from his own spies, so it was with a great deal of happiness that the men gathered in the theater to watch Pothinus' head leave his shoulders. True to his nature, he acted like a woman, shaking and crying, having to be dragged onto the stage, where one of Caesar's Germans did the deed. The men cheered lustily at the sight of his bald head rolling across the stage, spraying blood in a trail across the stone floor. His head came to rest not far from where I was standing, and I could plainly see the look of terror and surprise still plastered on his face, his eyes sightlessly staring into the void. I noticed that for once, his face was devoid of that horrid makeup, and remember wondering if he had thought that to be some sort of punishment, not being allowed to paint his face before he died. These Egyptians with their customs are a strange lot, and I have no idea if there is some deeper meaning to all of the paint, but I suspect there is. Unfortunately, but not surprisingly, the death of Pothinus did not deter Achillas in the slightest, the Egyptian general continuing with his training and manufacturing all day and night. He was an implacable foe, with his army gaining strength every week. Consequently, the men grew more worried watching the progress his army made in both their training and their investment of our position. That is why what happened next was further sign of the gods' favor of Gaius Julius Caesar.

~ ~ ~ ~

"Achillas is dead!"

Appolonius came immediately after hearing the news, ostensibly to tell Diocles, but knowing that I would want to hear the news as well. That I did; this time I did not even pretend to be busy in my quarters, coming straight out into the outer office.

"What happened?"

Appolonius looked smug, as only the bearer of news that he knows others wants to hear can, and said, "It appears that our young Arsinoe and her man Ganymede have a bit more ambition than just being a figurehead."

That was indeed interesting, my expression giving him all the encouragement he needed to continue.

"Well, as you know, Arsinoe volunteered to set herself up as the symbol of Egyptian resistance against the Roman oppressors, a role which Achillas was more than happy to give her. But something changed; Caesar thinks that the real string puller is that Ganymede, and that he convinced her that she, or more likely he is just as capable of leading the army as Achillas. So she had Achillas murdered."

Even though we had heard that a rivalry had developed between the two that split the army, we had no idea that it had grown so bitter that one of them would kill the other. From our spies, we were informed that the division in the army was between the Gabinians and the rest of the professional arm of the army, consisting mainly of Cilicians and a few other nationalities, who understandably favored Achillas, against the provincial levies and native Egyptians, who rallied around Arsinoe. Now that Achillas was dead, it was a fair question to ask just how hard the professionals would fight now that the general they favored was gone. The Gabinians in particular had developed a reputation for choosing inopportune times for demanding pay raises, usually by threatening to turn on their masters, so perhaps they would choose this time to do the same to Arsinoe. When word of Achillas' death became known to the men, there was a period of optimism at the idea of facing a 15-year-old girl and her tutor. Unfortunately, that optimism was as short-lived as it was unfounded, because we quickly discovered that while Ganymede may not have possessed the military experience of Achillas, he more than made up for it in other ways.

~ ~ ~ ~

Ganymede began by attacking our most precious resource, our water supply. Despite having done all that we could to secure a supply of fresh water, we were unable to secure the source. Accordingly, Ganymede attacked this source. There were a number of wells in the private residences of the people who were unlucky enough to live in our sector, but the main source of supply was the canal. Blocking the conduits from the canal carrying our water was a simple enough business, except Ganymede was not content with that. Using large capacity pumps that were powered by men turning huge wheels, he began pumping seawater from the Inner Harbor to flood the streets of the city at night. With our redoubt situated in a part of the city a few feet lower than the surrounding area, the water naturally flowed in our direction. It was not long before one morning there was a rap on my door, and I opened it to find the duty Centurion Sido, his face pinched with worry.

"Sorry to disturb you, Primus Pilus, but I think you better have a look at this."

His tone was sufficiently urgent that I did not bother donning my uniform, grabbing only my *vitus* to follow him outside. Standing there was a section of men, each of them carrying two buckets, their expressions a mirror of Sido's.

Indicating the first man, he turned to me and said simply, "Taste the water."

I dipped my hand in, took a sip, then spat it out. It was salty, not completely fouled yet, but close.

I kept my expression neutral, indicating the other buckets. "Are these all from the same well?"

Sido shook his head. "No, Primus Pilus. When we tasted the first bucket, I went to every well that's in the 6th's sector and had a bucket drawn. The results are pretty much the same." He waved his hand at the buckets the other men were holding. "You can check for yourself if you would like, sir, but they're all the same."

I shook my head. "No, that won't be necessary, I trust you. Very well; I'll go to headquarters and see if the 28th is facing the same problem. You're dismissed." As they turned to go, I called out, "Sido!" He turned to stand at *intente*. "Good work. That was good thinking."

His face turned red, but I could tell that he was pleased, opening his mouth, probably to thank me before thinking better of it, then saluted and turned away, following his men. I did not bother telling them to keep this quiet because I knew that there was no way that the men would not find out. Returning to my quarters, I put on my uniform before heading over to headquarters to see if the news was any better.

~ ~ ~ ~

Fortunately, only the water in our sector was contaminated, at least at that point. But while that was good news, it was still going to pose a problem for us, since we now had to draw our water ration from the wells of the men of the 28th, whereupon the *numen* of that dead Gregarius came back to haunt us. Tensions were still high between my men and the 28th. While Cartufenus and I had managed to keep a lid on things, succeeding in avoiding drawing the attention of Caesar or his staff, the fact that we would now have to send detachments into the 28th's sector to take some of their already-rationed water was not going to sit well with them. Compounding the tension was the attitude of my men towards the 28th, who they thought of as a bunch of scared boys. That this was not far from the truth did not help matters for anyone. Cartufenus and I met, agreeing that our water-carrying parties would be escorted not only by a Centurion of the 6th, but of the 28th as well, and we would only do it once a day, in the morning. Calling a meeting of my Centurions to inform them of this agreement, I stressed that there would be no exceptions; we would draw water once a day and that was all. If the men ran out before the next morning, that would be too bad; perhaps it would teach them to ration their water more carefully. However, as it turned out, I need not have worried. These men of the 6th had been part of Pompey's army under Afranius in Hispania when we had cut them off from water, meaning this was not the first time they were thirsty. In fact, they found the whole situation grimly amusing.

"The first time we went thirsty was because of Caesar," I heard one of the men joke to his comrades, "and now this time we're going thirsty because of Caesar. The only difference is that now we're on the same side."

I had to smile; the gods certainly did have a perverse sense of humor.

The 28th's respite from fouled water was short-lived. Barely three days later, I heard another rap on my door, only this time it was Cartufenus who came to bring me the news. When he told me, I was not surprised, but he was not through.

"It gets worse," he said, his face grim. "My men are panicking. There all sorts of wild ideas being thrown around about the cause. Some of the men say that it's one of the Egyptian gods who's favoring Ganymede and his bunch." He saw the look of scorn and disbelief on my face, and waved a hand wearily at me. "Oh, they're very much in the minority. It's the other idea that worries me, and that seems to be what most of the men believe. There's talk that this has to be the work of some of the Egyptians trapped in here with us, that they're working as spies for Ganymede and they're poisoning the water."

"But it's not poisoned," I protested. "It's only salty."

He nodded, but said, "I know that, but I just wish we knew why it's happening." He shrugged. "Maybe they're right. Maybe it IS one or more of the civilians with us."

I should point out that our knowledge of what Ganymede was doing with the pumps and seawater only came after the fact. When this was happening, it was a mystery to everyone, including the officers.

I sat thinking about what Cartufenus had said, then shook my head. "I don't think so. If it were one well, or two, and in the same immediate area, then I might see it. But this is now every well, throughout the entire redoubt. We would have noticed something if any of the civilians had been involved, I'm sure of it."

Cartufenus sighed, then stood up. "I don't know. All I do know is that it's getting ugly with my boys. I need to get back before they do something foolish."

A chill ran down my spine, and I looked at him sharply. "What do you mean, 'do something foolish'? What do you think they'll do?"

He shook his head. I could see the weariness and pain in his eyes, causing a pang of sympathy. The rank of first grade Centurion is what so many of us aspire to, and we work hard to achieve it. But then when we get there, suddenly it does not seem that being a Primus Pilus is as much fun as you thought it would be. That was true if you had a good group of men like the 10th or the 6th. When you got a bunch of scared rabbits like the 28th was turning out to be, it could be a nightmare from which you will never woke up. Without thinking, I walked to Cartufenus to put my hand on his shoulder.

"Don't worry." I spoke with as much confidence as I could muster. "Whatever comes, you're the man to handle it."

He gave a tired smile, but shook his head. "Thanks, Pullus, but I know you're just saying that to help me."

I could not help laughing. "Maybe," I admitted, "but you wouldn't feel so great if I told you that you were fucked, would you?"

He chuckled. "No, I suppose not." He squared his shoulders before turning to leave. "Well, let me go find out what my boys are up to now."

With that, he left me to sit wondering what could go wrong next.

~ ~ ~ ~

What the 28th had in mind was to demand a meeting with Caesar, the whole lot of them. Once that became known, Caesar obliged by ordering a formation that evening at the theater, with all but the guard Centuries in attendance. I sent a runner to Cartufenus asking him a question, and when the runner came back with the answer that I needed, I called a meeting of my Centurions to discuss what I had in mind.

"We're going to hold the men until the last possible moment," I announced.

Nobody said anything at first, yet their faces wore puzzled expressions. At least, all of their faces save one. I looked at Cornuficius, who regarded me steadily, his eyes revealing nothing but I saw a hint of a smile at the corner of his lips. Deciding to confront whatever he had in mind head on, I called on him.

"Cornuficius? Do you have any thoughts on what I just said?"

"Thoughts?" An eyebrow lifted, and I realized that he was considering the question, trying to find some angle that I might be taking of which he had not thought. Finally, he continued, "I don't know that I'd call them thoughts, Primus Pilus. But I think I know why you're doing it."

"Very well. Tell me and I'll let you know if you're right or wrong."

He shrugged, then nodded. As he spoke, he took great pains not to look at me, preferring instead to examine his fingernails, which I could not help noticing were caked with dirt. Well, I thought, we are under water rationing.

"I think you want to keep our men separated from those . . . boys of the 28th who are causing all this commotion, given what's taken place between our two Legions in the recent past. I think that your reasoning is that if we get there early, and spend any time waiting for Caesar to appear, that every moment that goes by increases the likelihood that someone will say something that sparks a riot."

Now he looked at me, his smile clearly evident. You smug bastard, I thought, but I tried to make sure my thoughts were not visible on my face.

"Absolutely correct, Cornuficius. That is my thinking precisely. So, to that end we're going to hold the men on the opposite side of the theater. I've arranged for Apollonius to let my slave know when Caesar departs his quarters, and only then will we march in. Does everyone understand?"

Heads nodded, and I was pleased to see the looks of relief on most of the men. Clearly, they were worried about the same thing as I, taking this as a good sign. Forming the men up as planned, we waited for Diocles to come running to give us the word. Just a short time later, I saw his slight figure running around the corner to give me the signal. I called the men to *intente*. we marched into the theater, where the men of the 28th were standing, and even over the tramping of feet, I heard their mumbling. While I could not hear what was being said, the tone was clearly ugly, and I was struck by a feeling that I have had before and since, of reliving a moment in my past once again, this particular feeling like that day on the plains of Pharsalus all over again. With the noise from our boots subsiding as the men halted, a voice carried from the ranks of the 28th.

"About fucking time they showed up. I guess they think they're too good for us."

Before any of the Centurions could say a word, there emanated from the entire 6th a low, guttural growl, the men too disciplined to speak out, still managing to convey their contempt for their comrades across the floor. That growl was more effective in shutting up the 28th than any threat from a Centurion or Optio and I smiled broadly, though my back was turned to the men so they could not see it. Fortunately, Caesar arrived at that moment and we were called to *intente* as he mounted the stage. Standing there for a moment, looking down at us, it suddenly made me feel old. How many times, I wondered, had I been standing here, looking up at Caesar? The only thing that had changed was my vantage point, since I had started out in the rear ranks. Now I was standing in front, all by myself. But it was always up at Caesar that I was looking, and the question that crossed my mind was, how much more of my life would be spent in this fashion? While I held little doubt that I would be standing here looking up at some general, what intrigued me was the question of whether or not it would ever be anyone other than Caesar. And after Caesar, if there was an after Caesar, would I ever find any general worthy of following again? These were the thoughts crowding through my mind as we waited on the great man to speak.

"Comrades," he began in his customary style, "I have been told by my officers that some of you are discontented. Never let it be said that Caesar does not care for his men, nor listen to their complaints. That's why I am standing here. What do you have to say to me?"

To the men who had been complaining the loudest, that was like a bucket of ice water thrown directly into their face and I fought back the urge to laugh. They were being called out in front of their comrades, and being told to make their complaints public. That is a very daunting task, especially if you are a spineless, gutless *cunnus* to begin with.

For several moments, nothing was said, then Caesar spoke again, "Very well. I have given you the opportunity to speak, but now it seems that nobody has anything to say. Then if there is nothing more, we must return to our duties."

He turned as if to go, causing a panicked buzz in the ranks of the 28th, men whispering fiercely to the man next to them, each of them demanding that the man they were whispering to speak up.

"Why do you refuse to leave this place?"

I do not know who said it, but immediately there was a roar of agreement from the men of the 28th. I turned to look at the ranks of my men, pleased to see that they were standing silently, looking over at the 28th in open contempt.

"We do not leave for a number of reasons," Caesar replied, his hand raised for quiet, "not least of which is that I have never yielded the field to an enemy yet."

Now, that was not exactly true; I vividly recall moving away from Gergovia and Dyrrhachium, but as disgruntled as the men may have been, none of them were crazy enough to bring that up to Caesar, so his statement went unchallenged.

"More importantly, however, is the fact that we can't leave this province in the hands of forces that are hostile to us. Rome relies on the grain grown here; without it, our people, your families and friends would starve. Until we can secure that supply of grain, leaving is not an option. And the only way to secure the supply is to defeat the Egyptians."

They did not care for this, and in the muttering that followed, I heard the name Cleopatra several times.

Then another voice called out, "That's all well and good, Caesar. But how are we supposed to defeat the enemy when we have no water?"

This challenge was met by another roar of agreement, continuing unabated for several moments as men added their own cries of despair to the hue. Caesar stood there, seemingly impervious to the things that were being called out, his face completely expressionless. After a moment, he held both hands up, and finally the men, now little more than a mob, settled down enough so that he could speak. I had looked back again at my men, and while they still had not made any sound, I could see that they were as interested to hear what Caesar had to say next about the water as the rabbits in the 28th.

"So your major concern is the lack of water?"

The men all cried out that this was so, then Caesar held his hands up again.

"If I provide the means to end this problem, so that water isn't a concern, are you willing to stay and fight without further complaint?"

Oh, he had them boxed now, and the quicker ones among them knew it immediately. There were whispered conferences as men argued among themselves. After a couple of moments, the buzzing subsided, followed by a period where nobody spoke. Finally, some men began to mumble their assent, but a blind man could tell that they were not happy about it.

But Caesar was not going to quibble about the quality of their agreement, and he spoke again, "I have your agreement then? Good. Then that is all."

He turned to leave, but stopped at the howls of protest, and now I could definitely see that ghost of a smile playing at his mouth.

"How do we find water, Caesar? You said that you'd provide us with water!"

He affected a look of surprise as he said, "Why, you dig for it, of course."

There was total silence, the men standing in stunned disbelief, and I must confess I was as shocked as the rest of the men. Dig for it? Could it really be that simple? A storm of protest burst forth as the men overcame their shock, their anger at perceiving that they had been tricked by Caesar very real, and very dangerous. However, Caesar was not cowed in the slightest; he merely stood there once again, letting the men spend their fury, waiting for the moment when everyone paused to catch their breath before howling anew.

When it came, he said in his command voice, "Centurions, you will form the men into working parties composed of two sections apiece. Each working party will dig a well, starting in the courtyard of every private residence in our sector. Only the guard Centuries will be relieved of this duty; however, they will stand watch all three night watches while the rest of the men work. No working party will be excused until they have dug a well that produces water. Once they do, they are relieved and can return to their quarters to rest. You have your orders, Centurions. Carry them out."

He turned to leave, but someone shouted after him, "And if we don't find any water?"

As he dismounted the stage, he called over his shoulder. "Then we will leave."

~ ~ ~ ~

At first, the men were not enthused at all about their task, even my men. Walking from one working party to the next, I could hear their bitter complaints about what they viewed as a folly by Caesar.

"He's just making us sweat as punishment for those *cunni* in the 28th calling a meeting," a ranker from the Fifth of the Tenth said, standing waist-deep in a hole and tossing out another shovelful of sandy dirt, his comrades heartily agreeing with him.

This was more or less the tone of every working party as they dug, and these were men of the 6th. I could only imagine what Cartufenus was dealing with from his boys, I thought. I resigned myself to a whole night of complaining, but it was barely a third of a watch into work when I heard a great shout coming a block over from my spot at that moment, where I had sent some men of the 7th to work. Running down the street, I turned the corner to find Valens standing in the middle of the street, but covered in mud from the waist down. He was laughing with some of his men as I ran up, and he managed a salute despite his ear to ear smile.

"We struck water, Primus Pilus. Not more than six feet down."

"And? Is it potable?" I demanded, my heart racing not just from the run over.

"Sweet as any that I've ever tasted."

Despite myself, I let out a whoop of joy, clapping Valens and his men on the back.

"Well, you lucky bastards have the rest of the night off," I said with a smile. "And nobody could deserve it more. Well done."

Even as I hurried to report to Caesar, I heard first one, then another shout as men struck water. Arriving at headquarters, I learned that so far, barely more than a third of a watch into the endeavor, a total of eight wells had struck water. Cartufenus was there, looking immensely relieved; his men had found five so far, and for a moment, I cursed the idea that he and the 28th had beaten the 6th at anything. Deeper into the night, the number kept going up, until by morning more than 60 wells were dug, and it was only because Caesar determined that our water shortage was at an end that he called off the work. In a stroke, not only was our water shortage ended, but Caesar had nipped a mutiny in the bud before it could really get started. Finding water did not solve all of our problems; we were still surrounded and outnumbered, and there was still considerable tension between the 6th and the 28th, yet somehow knowing that you were not going to die of thirst made those problems seem surmountable.

It seemed that luck was once again returning to Caesar, since two days later, a courier managed to slip through the Egyptian defenses to inform Caesar that the 37th Legion, the Legion, which Cassius was charged with finding and sending to us, had arrived and was just a few miles up the coast. They were not without difficulty themselves however; as the courier explained that their own water situation was perilous, having run out the day that the courier left for Alexandria. Caesar decided to go see for himself, but since he could spare none of us from the defenses, took only a galley with its contingent of oarsmen and marines, leaving from the royal docks, commanding the rest of the fleet to follow once it was ready, which it did.

~ ~ ~ ~

I always found it interesting to see what happened when Caesar left others in command. None of his generals seemed willing to make a decision, despite the fact he was not the type of general to second-guess his subordinates. I think it was more a matter of not wanting to disappoint him than any fear they had of his disapproval. The only one who did not seem to worry about that was Antonius; indeed, he made decisions in Caesar's name that caused Caesar untold problems, yet there was some bond between him and Caesar that made Caesar forgive Antonius some of his more outrageous actions, or at least so I thought at the time. Caesar had left very loose instructions when he left, saying only that we do nothing precipitate and maintain our normal routine. The 37th was at a spot called Chersonesus, and when Caesar arrived on the scene, he ordered the marines to go foraging for water, except they went too far inland and were captured by Egyptian cavalry. Under torture, they revealed that Caesar was present on one of the ships, and Ganymede was alerted to this fact. Ganymede threw together a scratch fleet of armed merchant vessels and a couple of thirty's that had been in the Inner Harbor and escaped destruction, then headed after Caesar. Rather, the fleet did; Ganymede was not of the same stripe as Caesar, preferring to pull the strings from afar rather than to get personally involved in the action. Meanwhile, as was his habit, Caesar turned a precarious situation to his advantage. When Caesar arrived on the scene, the men of the 37th and the crews of the Rhodian ships that were carrying them had been without water for two days, meaning in that heat and climate they were in dire straits. Otherwise, everything went Caesar's way once Ganymede's fleet closed with his, temporarily succeeding in isolating one of the Rhodian thirty's that was part of the relief force. However, Caesar turned it to his benefit, inflicting losses on the Egyptians that Ganymede could ill afford. Caesar returned with his fleet, along with the reinforcements, towing the Rhodian ship that was damaged in the fight. And just like that, we were reinforced, our numbers more than doubled.

~ ~ ~ ~

Because of the limited space inside our position, Caesar kept the 37th onboard ship, spreading them around so that every ship of the fleet had at least a Century aboard. Along with what we had brought with us, the ships of the reinforcing fleet, and those that Caesar had captured in his action against Ganymede, our flotilla now consisted of 34 craft of varying size. To protect the more valuable warships, Caesar circled them with the transports, acting as a screen in the event that the Egyptians tried to use their fire boats again. However, Ganymede was not so easily undone. Despite Caesar's success in destroying the entire fleet residing in the harbor at Alexandria, he had not ended the Egyptian maritime threat. There were Egyptian naval vessels patrolling up and down the Nile, and along the coast, while there were a number of larger vessels, quinqueremes most of them, that were in dry-dock because of the expense of upkeep. Now Ganymede brought them out of storage, summoning the patrol vessels to return to Alexandria at the same time, as the shops around the city were immediately set to work refitting the ships. The biggest deficiency the enemy faced was in having enough oars to power so many vessels; therefore, every scrap of wood was ransacked from the public buildings that had the potential of being turned into oars. Working all day and through the night, day after day and night after night, all we could do was watch and wait for the inevitable. One morning, one of the sentries on the roof sounded the alarm, and I went to see what had alerted him. I was dismayed to see no less than five quinqueremes, 22 quadriremes, and four biremes rowing around the Inner Harbor. While we knew that they were working on rebuilding their fleet, until that moment we had no idea of the size, and it was massive. Word of the fleet leapt through the army, meaning that soon every man not on duty was standing on a roof, watching the Egyptians testing the vessels. Our future was passing before us as we watched; if that massive flotilla defeated ours, we were finished, and we all knew it. Even as grim as the prospect was, that did not stop the men from wagering on the outcome, but I was happy to see that most men were betting on us to win.

~ ~ ~ ~

The expected battle played out in full view, with our fleet leaving the Great Harbor, then turning west, heading towards the entrance to the Inner Harbor. Like the entrance to the Great Harbor, there is a line of shoals making entrance to the Inner Harbor treacherous, so the Romans formed up, facing the entrance, while in turn the Egyptians formed up in the Inner Harbor, facing them. One consequence of the coming battle was that both sides that were still in the city temporarily forgot their own fight, climbing to the roofs in their respective sectors to watch. It was almost like a festival atmosphere; all that was missing were the vendors selling meat pies and wine, and the whores plying their trade. Nevertheless, you could cut the tension in the air with a dagger and I found myself tapping my *vitus* against my thigh, while other men chattered incessantly to hide their nervousness, or said nothing at all, their entire attention on the scene in the harbor below them. For the better part of a third of a watch, both fleets remained motionless, and the men began getting restless. Of course, the betting was brisk as they wagered on when the attack would come and who would start it. I was standing with Felix, Clemens, and Diocles, waiting for something to happen and I briefly thought about sending the men down, except what was about to happen was too important and they had a right to know their fate, so I dismissed the idea. Instead, we stood waiting, when finally something happened, with four ships from our fleet suddenly detaching themselves to begin rowing swiftly towards the entrance of the Inner Harbor.

"There they go," someone shouted.

I turned from my conversation with Clemens to watch the first four Roman ships shooting through the gap in single file before quickly maneuvering into a line abreast. Almost as quickly, four Egyptian ships detached themselves from their own formation, then began rowing directly towards our ships, with our vessels turning so their bows were facing the enemy even as they picked up speed. Both sides were picking up momentum and, despite being too far away to hear it, we could tell when the ships struck each other head-on that the impact was tremendous. It reminded me of watching the rams butt each other when I was a child in Hispania, and it seemed to have about as much effect on the ships as it had on the rams back home. Immediately after the initial impact, all the ships reversed their oars, pulling back from their individual adversaries as they maneuvered around each other, looking for another opening. While I am no expert in naval warfare, it was clear to see that whoever it was handling our four ships was highly skilled, moving their vessels to face another attack, this time by four different ships that apparently hoped to catch them engaged with their original adversaries. The Egyptians were unsuccessful, with our ships again meeting this new threat head-on.

"What are they trying to do?" Clemens asked, and we all looked in surprise when Diocles spoke up.

"Their primary goal is to catch our ships broadside and use their ram to hole the vessel."

"I know that," Clemens said impatiently. "But it doesn't look like that's what they're doing."

"If they can't score a hit broadside, then they'll try to shear off the other ship's oars by running alongside and at the last moment shipping their own oars. It appears that our commanders are too skilled for them to get caught broadside, so I think the Egyptians are trying to kill their mobility."

This made what we were watching make sense to us, and I reminded myself to ask Diocles how he knew about naval warfare. Now that our first four were totally engaged, Caesar gave the command to the rest of the fleet, and they rowed quickly through the entrance into the Inner Harbor, using the melee as a screen to keep the rest of the Egyptian fleet from attacking them before they could get into the standard battle formation. Once the rest of our fleet entered the harbor, it appeared as if the surface of the water was completely packed with ships.

"They don't have any room to maneuver," Diocles commented. "That means that it comes down to which side's marines and soldiers can fight onboard ship better. They're going to start grappling each other in a few moments."

And while we watched, that is exactly what happened. Once it started, the battle quickly degenerated into a one-sided affair, with the men of the 37th leaping over onto the ship that their own vessel had grappled with, making quick work of the Egyptians. Our forces captured a quinquereme and a bireme, and sunk three more. The rest, seeing the fate of those ships we came to grips with, quickly rowed to the far western side of the Inner Harbor or towards the Heptastadion, where the Egyptians had artillery emplaced to provide protective fire, driving off any of our ships that got too close in their pursuit. For our part, not a ship was lost, and the casualties among the marines and Legionaries were light. We had won a great battle, but when Caesar returned and called a meeting of his staff and Centurions, his demeanor was not that of a man who had just won a great victory, and we soon knew why he was so downcast.

"We won today, but we didn't really solve anything," he said once we were settled and congratulations were offered. This was certainly not what we were expecting to hear from him. "It's clear that they have vastly superior resources than we do, and at the end of the day, we only neutralized a small portion of their fleet. And it's become clear to me that no matter how many times we bring them to battle, all they have to do if things start to turn against them is to row close to shore and to be covered by their artillery. It would be a war of attrition, and it would be a war that we would lose."

When he finished, there was silence as we all digested this, and it did not take long to realize that he was absolutely right. As much of a boost to morale as the victory was, in the grand strategic sense, it was almost as bad as a loss.

I believe it was Hirtius who said, "I doubt that you would have brought up such cheerful news if you hadn't already thought of a solution."

Caesar smiled at him. "And you'd be right, Hirtius. As we made our way back to the royal enclosure, we had to pass the island, and I examined it thoroughly. Ganymede hasn't invested the place properly. It can be assaulted, and that's what I intend to do."

Men looked at each other; generals looking at generals, Tribunes looking at Tribunes and Centurions looking at Centurions. Even at moments like these, hierarchy is important to us Romans.

Caesar either did not notice or chose to ignore the reaction of his staff, and went on talking. "By taking the island, we can do the same thing to the Inner Harbor that we've done to the Great Harbor. Emplacing artillery on the western mole will bottle up the Egyptian fleet. If we do that, it won't be necessary to destroy the fleet. I also plan on capturing the Heptastadion, which will deprive them of the whole eastern side of the harbor."

Nero objected. "But don't we want to destroy their fleet anyway?"

Caesar shook his head. "No, we have to think about the days after this is over. If we completely destroy their fleet, Egypt will be vulnerable to depredation by pirates, and their neighbors might be tempted to take advantage of their weakness. Then we'd find ourselves back here fighting all over again. No," he repeated, "what's necessary here is to neutralize the fleet, not destroy it."

Even if anyone was disposed to do so, there was really no argument to be made, mainly because what Caesar said made perfect sense. Seeing our acceptance, Caesar turned his attention to his plan for taking the island.

"Pullus," he said without warning, catching me by surprise. "I'll need you and your men. Can I count on you?"

I snapped to *intente.* "Absolutely, sir."

~ ~ ~ ~

The plan, such as it was, called for ten Cohorts, of which the 7th would be one of them and that I would lead. This meant that we would have to make a run from our positions through the streets of Alexandria to join the assault force, a prospect that the men were none too keen on doing. Additionally, we had to do it quickly, when the moment came, and without making any preparations that might alert the Egyptians what we were about, thereby compounding the difficulty. Once at the harbor, we would board a number of open boats that would row us to the island. The rest of the Cohorts were composed of the 37th, along with one Cohort from the 28th, which also did not sit well with the men. The 28th was considered suspect by the men of the 6th, and not a few of Caesar's staff, if the gossip was any indication. Augmenting the force were a couple Cohorts worth of missile troops that were part of the relief force, along with about a hundred of Caesar's cavalry that he thought were best suited to fight as infantry for this sortie. The day for the assault was set for three days after the naval battle, and since it only took a few thirds of a watch for the men to make themselves ready, this ultimately meant that we sat and waited. This was incredibly wearing on everyone, because there is nothing quite as maddening as knowing that in some short period of time, one is going to be facing death, yet having nothing to do to occupy the mind during the waiting period. It is also a trial of the patience of the Centurions and Optios, since the men are determined to cram as much debauchery and high living as possible into those days, meaning that we were running from one building to another in the sector that housed our quarters as the inevitable quarrels and fights broke out. Very quickly, I determined that trying to stop the men completely from drinking and whoring for the entire three days would result in exhausted officers, along with half the Cohort up on a charge, so I instructed the Centurions to turn a blind eye towards a certain level of debauchery and carousing while we waited. Of course, if you give a Gregarius an obol, he wants a sesterce; if you give him a slice of bread, he wants the whole loaf. It is their nature, and even relaxing the rules a bit, there are always men who will try to push to get away with more, both with their Centurions and Optios, and their comrades. The only saving grace was that with men as veteran as these, when compared to a Legion composed of younger men, the problems they caused were not of sufficient scale to draw the attention of the senior officers. Still, by the night before the attack, the Centurions and Optios, myself included, had dispensed bathhouse justice on a number of men and I was extremely tired. I hope that it does not surprise you, gentle reader, when I mention that the men were doing as much whoring as drinking and gambling, perhaps more so because of the relative scarcity of wine. As I have mentioned, when we cordoned off our area, we did it so quickly that a large number of civilians were given no opportunity to flee. If I were not a suspicious man, I would simply ascribe the relatively high number of women who made their living on their back to a happy accident, and that we had somehow managed to select the quarter of the city where the whores congregated. But, since we were around the royal enclosure, the resulting neighborhood that sprang up around it was composed of the homes of wealthy government officials and merchants who did business with Pharaoh. In other words, there were no businesses catering to the fleshly desires in this quarter of the city, at least of which I was aware. Somehow, however, a force of a couple hundred whores managed to get themselves trapped inside our redoubt, and in fact one back street had become their own headquarters area, so to speak. The citizens of Alexandria that remained in our area had decided to turn a blind eye to the steady stream of Gregarii who headed for the street the moment they were secured from duty. The only reason that no wine shops had opened on the street, since whores and drinking go hand in hand, was due only to a lack of supply and not any finer distinction. Consequently, it was to this street that the Centurions and Optios found themselves running when some word of a problem reached them, although more than one of them managed to wander over there under their own power a time or two, if my meaning is clear. Another complicating factor was that while the street was actually located in the 28th's area, there was no way that my men would have sat still if I made the area off-limits to them, meaning that there was ample opportunity for trouble when the men of the two Legions mingled. All in all, it was a touchy situation, and the three-day wait for my men did not make things any easier. By the night before the attack, I was so tired that I slept more soundly than I ever had the night before a battle, and I suspect that the rest of the officers felt the same.

~ ~ ~ ~

The day dawned bright and clear, without a cloud in the sky, promising a day of heat and humidity. In other words, a normal day in Alexandria. By the time of this operation, we had been in Alexandria several months, and by rights, it was getting close to winter, except there are no real seasons there, even more so than my home in Baetica. Fortunately, the men were tough, mostly Spaniards who had lived most of their lives in a climate that was not terribly dissimilar, if not a bit more extreme here in Alexandria, and we no longer had to ration our water so closely, so the heat was not a terrible worry. What was a concern was what we were about to do, as we used the cover provided by our internal passageways to move through the buildings to the point where we were going to leave our lines. By this point in the siege, we had improved our defenses to the degree that we had constructed a number of gates of varying sizes, which of course the Egyptians countered by building towers and strong points immediately opposite, the size of their defenses commensurate with how strategically important they considered the gate. It was with this in mind that we selected one of the smaller gates, in the hope that Ganymede's men at that point would not be of high quality, or particularly alert. We also decided to launch our sortie in the third of a watch before the Egyptian watch changed, having long since learned each other's habits and knowing exactly when it would occur. Moving the men as much as it was possible inside the buildings, we crammed the entire Cohort into the building directly opposite the gate, located on the other side of a minor street. While I was given very explicit orders about when we would make our break, the location from where we would leave was left to me. One precaution I took was that we left from a gate that was controlled by the 6th, although it meant that we would actually have a few blocks farther to go to the harbor. This was the level of distrust that I held for the 28th, a feeling that I knew was completely shared by my men, and this frame of mind led to the first time that I openly disagreed with Caesar. The original plan called for both my Cohort and the Cohort of the 28th to leave together, moving as one unit down to the docks, but I had flatly refused. The silence, as it is said, was deafening, the members of Caesar's staff looking at me in absolute shock. To be completely fair, it was not so much that I had objected. Men regularly argued with Caesar when he gave an order, and he would invariably listen. I was present on more than one occasion where he had modified his decision because someone made a compelling argument. What I believe surprised the staff was that this was the first time that it was me who actually disagreed. And perhaps it was the fact that I did not try to couch my refusal in the form of a question or some other gentler declaration as well.

"No, Caesar."

To his credit, he was the only who did not seem to be totally shocked, or irritated for that matter. He simply sat back, crossed his arms in a pose with which I had now become very familiar, and only asked, "And why is that, Pullus?"

For what was probably the hundredth time in my life I had said the first thing that popped into my head without thinking things through beforehand, but never before had things been so potentially explosive. My mind raced; this was not the time or the place to bring up the animosity and distrust that the men of the 6th held for the men of the 28th, for a number of reasons, not least of which was that Cartufenus was sitting there watching me. It was easy to see by the expression on his face that he knew exactly why I was objecting, and I felt a pang of sympathy. I had come to like Cartufenus a great deal, and while it might not have been his intent, he taught me a lot. For example, it was from Cartufenus that I learned that sometimes pure leadership is not enough, that a healthy dose of luck is almost as important in certain circumstances, and it was Cartufenus' circumstances that showed me how lucky I had been in my career at that point. In that moment, standing before Caesar, I had no desire to do any further damage to Cartufenus, since his career was, for all intents and purposes, finished the moment that the 28th had almost mutinied, unless some sort of miracle occurred. I was struck by a sudden flash of what I hoped was inspiration.

"Caesar, if we combine our forces and leave by the same gate, we'll be moving almost 900 men in one group."

"Yes, Pullus. That is the point," he said mildly, and I could hear the snickers of a couple of the men.

I tried to ignore the heat rising to my face as I continued, "That would mean running almost a mile with a force several hundred yards long, which would make a fat target. Even if we catch them by surprise, it's likely that the last Centuries won't be clear by the time the Egyptians recover and start hurling the gods know what down on our heads."

"Then have the men march in *testudo*," interjected Nero, and I tried not to give him a look that conveyed my contempt at the idea.

While Nero was not completely useless, I considered him to be the weakest of Caesar's generals.

"Yes, sir." I kept my tone neutral. "And that would be a very wise maneuver, if we weren't expected to go into battle just a few moments after marching such a distance. I realize, sir, that you've never had occasion to actually be part of a *testudo*, but I can assure you that even for men superbly fit, marching in *testudo* for more than a hundred yards can be exhausting."

Even though I addressed Nero, I was trying to judge Caesar's reaction out of the corner of my eye and I was relieved to see that upturned lip that I had come to know. Some of the other men, the generals Hirtius and Pollio in particular, were not so circumspect and were grinning broadly; Nero was not taking my retort with as much good grace, making me happy to see that now I was not the only one with a red face.

Having disposed of that question, I turned back to Caesar. "As I understand the plan, sir, we'll have to load into a number of different boats, which will require even more exertion, as you well know. Then, it will probably take no more than a tenth part of a watch to row from the enclosure to the island, where we're going to have climb the rocks, probably under fire. Caesar, if we do as General Nero suggests, which I would agree if we were to march with our forces combined would be the right tactic." I was not completely politically inept, so I threw this bone to

Nero. "The men won't be sufficiently recovered by the time we're expected to assault the island." I could see that I had gotten Caesar's full attention, and I pressed the advantage. "The other benefit of splitting the force and having them come from different points in our position is that it will spread the enemy a bit more thinly. We can compound the surprise if we leave at exactly the same time, on a prearranged signal."

Caesar considered this, then gave a nod. "Very well. You'll lead the 6th, and Cartufenus will lead the 28th, and you'll leave our position at different points, but at the same time."

And with that, he turned his attention to other matters. I had escaped Caesar's wrath.

As Cartufenus and I left headquarters, he said quietly enough so that only I could hear, "Thanks, Pullus."

I was somewhat surprised, and I looked at him with a question in my eyes.

"I know why you really don't want to combine our forces," he said quietly, then sighed. "And I can't say that I blame you, or your men."

I looked at him in sympathy, clapping him on the shoulder. "No worries, Cartufenus. You'd do it for me."

He gave me a speculative look at this and shrugged. "I hope so, Pullus. I hope so."

~ ~ ~ ~

Now, we stood waiting for the sound of the *bucina* that would signal that it was time for us to leave. While the building in which we were hiding was large, it was still crammed full of men, the smell of sweat and fear hanging rank in the air in the close quarters. I glanced at Valens, who gave a grimace.

"It stinks in here," he said, and I laughed.

Suddenly, the *bucina* sounded. Without hesitation, I threw open the door, roaring as loudly as I could to Fuscus, who I had ordered to be present to ensure there would be no mistakes, to open the gates. Running across the street, I heard the men clattering behind me as they followed. Fuscus bellowed at the men standing at the gates, who grabbed the attached ropes to begin pulling them open. Fuscus had timed it perfectly, and we did not need to slow down as we ran through the open gates, whereupon I took a left turn, heading for the nearest corner leading to the north-south thoroughfare. Even with the clatter of the men pounding behind me, I could hear the cries of alarm from the Egyptian sentries, though they did not start yelling until we had already covered a couple hundred paces. I just hoped that it would be enough of a head start to avoid taking many casualties, because even if a man was wounded, if he could not keep up he would be left behind, and everyone knew what that meant. It was inevitable that we would lose men running this gauntlet; I just hoped that it would not be too many. Keeping my head turning, I looked not just at the rooftops, but also when we approached an intersection, although the biggest threat to us was from missiles thrown down at us. We were more than halfway before the first resistance was met, the men above us starting to hurl stones or whatever else was at hand down at us, though they did little damage. It was not until we could actually see the harbor that the first volley of proper missiles rained down at us, and I heard a couple of men shout in a manner that told me they were hit, but we nevertheless continued running. Bursting out of the relatively confined space of the city streets, we ran the rest of the way down to the enclosure, where Caesar had assembled a few score of small boats that would act as our landing craft. The guards at the gate to the enclosure threw them open and we ran down to the docks, where most of the other men of the 37th were already loaded in the boats. A provost directed us to the boats designated for our use, and we immediately began loading the men into them. Each boat carried a contingent of oarsmen, the boats themselves all open-topped with no decks, which was a mixed blessing. It made loading and unloading easier, yet it also meant that the only cover from artillery and missile fire would be what we could provide ourselves with our shields. The 28th arrived shortly after we did, but it appeared that they suffered slightly heavier casualties than we had. For our part, we had three men wounded to the point that they could not keep up, with another half dozen slightly injured. I pushed the thoughts of the three men out of my mind, knowing that we could not do anything for them. The loading operation was finished in a matter of moments, then the signal was given for the men at the benches to begin rowing, and we set off for the island.

~ ~ ~ ~

Caesar had sent some of his heavier ships out of the harbor around to the north side of the island, where they were laying down a barrage with the artillery that the ships carried in order to draw the defenders away from the south side of the island. Pulling closer to the island, I could see that if it was successful at all, it was only partially so, the rooftops of the buildings closest to the shore lined with men.

"Uh-oh."

I looked over at Valens, the one who uttered the warning, then followed his gaze. Coming towards us from the Inner Harbor were five warships, along with a number of smaller craft, heading for the northern drawbridge of the Heptastadion. Their intent was obvious; they wanted to head us off and keep us from landing. The island had originally only been home to the lighthouse, but in the intervening years, what was in effect a suburb of Alexandria grew up around it, so that now almost the entire island was covered with buildings and streets. The houses were mean; it was clear that the island was home to the lower classes, probably seafaring men, shipbuilders, and their families. Now those houses appeared to be filled with soldiers of the Egyptian army, and once we approached within missile range, the first bolts from their scorpions and rocks from their ballistae began hurtling our way. Nothing struck our boat, though I was soaked to the skin by a near miss, causing some amusement among the men.

Now within a hundred paces, I scanned the shore, feeling a tightening in my throat. We knew the shore was rocky, but viewing it from a rooftop a mile away and then seeing it up close were two different things. It was clear that we would have to climb more than ten feet over rocks, all while the Egyptians were firing down at us. The first of the boats was pulling up to the shore, men beginning to leap out into the water and wade ashore, trying to grab a foothold while keeping their shields above their heads. Almost immediately men were hit, most lucky enough to fall onto the rocks, but a small number of men fell backwards into the water, their armor dragging them under before any crewmember on the nearest boat could offer them an oar and pull them to safety. It quickly became obvious that there were only one or two suitable spots where the water was shallow enough for men to jump out without drowning, and our boat headed for where the first boat had landed, pausing long enough for it to move away. Our craft scraped the bottom several feet from the shore. Without waiting, I jumped over the side, landing in water slightly above my waist, Valens right behind me. Naturally, we drew the most fire by virtue of our transverse crests and the fact we were not carrying shields so we had to dodge everything coming our way while trying to keep our footing. I made it to shore, beginning the climb over the rocks, Valens and the men of his Century close behind. We made it across the rocks, joining the other men who were looking for their standards to form up.

"Seventh of the 6th, on me," I bellowed, grabbing Valens' *signifer*, pointing to a spot that gave us room to form up. With men streaming ashore, I noticed that the missile fire was slackening. I looked up to see that for some reason, the Egyptians were leaving their position on the roofs, not that I was complaining since it gave us a respite from the constant harassing fire. If they wanted to give up a strong position, I was not going to argue. The other benefit was that it gave us time to form up. Once we did so, we began marching along the length of the island on the gravel path serving as the ring road around the outside of the buildings, looking for an entrance into the village. While we marched, the reason for the disappearance of the Egyptians became apparent when they appeared from around the corner of a side street, coming face to face with us, arrayed in their own formation. For a moment, both sides stopped to stare at each other. During the pause, I took a look around to see that two of my

Centuries were leading the assault force, aligned side by side. Without waiting, I gave the command to move forward in assault positions, and we began closing the distance. Making a quick decision, I ordered the men to drop their javelins to go immediately to the sword. Raising my arm, I held it aloft for a split second, then let out a roar.

"*Porro!*"

The men leaped forward, sounding their battle cry, closing the distance quickly to slam into the Egyptians, and I had just enough time to see the look of shock and fear on their brown faces as we cut them down. It was only a matter of moments before they broke and ran for their lives. Our men slaughtered them, running after them and killing as many as possible before they could escape. The panic of the soldiers infected the civilians who had remained behind, the narrow streets of the village quickly becoming choked with fleeing people. At times like this, it is hard to restrain men whose bloodlust has been set afire from putting anyone with whom they come into contact to the sword, so a large number of civilians were killed in the rout, and it took several moments to get the men under control. We had penetrated several blocks into the village, but we were still short of the Heptastadion, and Caesar sent orders from his flagship to stop the advance and wait for the rest of the landing force. Since there were only a couple suitable sites, the landing was taking longer than expected and Caesar deemed that it was better to wait than press the assault with only a part of our force.

Unfortunately, Ganymede was not waiting. Once he saw what we were doing, he ordered a scratch force assembled from the contingents of marines on the ships in the harbor, sending them to land on the southwestern end of the island, which had better landing sites than where we came ashore. Egyptians began streaming off the rocky beach and heading into the depths of the village to join the others already there. Looking over my shoulder, I cursed that we were still not disembarked, though it appeared that there were only three or four boats left. Calculating that it would be another few moments before they were finished, followed by the time it took to finish forming up, I knew that gave the enemy ample time to land a few thousand men and have them take up positions in the village that could make them difficult to dislodge. I could only hope that they would make the same mistake twice in not taking advantage of the high ground. While we waited, I called a conference of my Centurions.

"Have any of you or the men had any experience fighting house to house?"

They glanced at one another, but they all shook their heads.

"Have you, Primus Pilus?"

I thought back 14 years to the first town in Lusitania that we had assaulted when I had first drawn, and shed, blood. Looking at the square stone buildings that stood before us and comparing them to my memories of that town, and all the other towns and cities of Gaul we had assaulted, I shook my head.

"Not anything like this. In Gaul, most of the houses are made of mud and sticks. They're solid enough, but only the main halls and barracks were made like even the smallest house here. No, I don't."

We regarded each other and I just shrugged. There was nothing to be done about it now; we would just have to do our best.

~ ~ ~ ~

Once the rest of the assault force joined up, we arrayed our lines along the first north-south street, shaking out into Century formation, three Centuries for each street running east and west, one following the other. Once the men got into position, we waited for a moment, and then Caesar, who had come ashore, dipped his standard as the *cornu* sounded the advance. The men began to march, moving only a few blocks when we ran into the first line of resistance and I saw that we would not be so lucky this time. The Egyptian marines had climbed back onto the roofs originally abandoned by the militia, arraying themselves on a north and south axis, where they began flinging their javelins at us. The windows and doors on the ground floor were full of men as well, some of them armed with bows, with the rest flinging rocks at us. The missiles started flying thick and furious, forcing me to give the command for the front Century to form a *testudo*. The racket of javelin, arrow, and rock striking the shields of the men of Clemens' Century, who I had given the lead, was horrific, and I could barely make myself heard. The air seemed like every inch of it was filled with some sort of missile. I heard men crying out and cursing as they were hit or scared by a near miss, but I knew that either there would come a moment where the enemy would stop, even if no signal were given, because their supply of missiles ran low or they had to grab a breath. This was the moment I was waiting for. It is a tricky business going from *testudo* to wedge formation under any circumstances and normally I would not have tried it, but I had confidence in these men, trusting that they would understand what I was doing and would perform the maneuver as quickly as it needed to be done. The order to charge would immediately follow the call to wedge, and I was going to aim the wedge directly for the door of the nearest building containing the enemy. Turning to yell to Felix, whose Century was following Clemens, I told him to form his own wedge, pointing towards the next building over as his target. I did not know what Valens was doing; he was one street over, but I could only be in one place at a time and I would have to trust him to do the right thing. The moment I was waiting for came, the sound of the missiles striking whatever was in their path subsiding, much in the same way when rain suddenly lets up, almost ceasing altogether, and I gave the command. I was pleased with how quickly the men moved, smoothly lowering their shields while shuffling into their assigned spots in the wedge.

Addressing the men in the rear ranks of the wedge, I commanded, "When we get halfway across the intersection, I want you to launch your javelins at those *cunni* on the roof. Keep their heads down while we go in the door." Raising my arm, I yelled as loudly as I could, "Follow me!"

With a roar, we pounded across the intersection, pointing directly for the wide doorway in which a number of Egyptian marines stood waiting, their eyes wide over the rim of their wicker shields. There was a blur of our javelins flying past overhead, followed by a number of sharp screams and cries of alarm. Out of the corner of my eye, I saw a body hurtle to the ground, hitting the stone street with a splatting thud. Clemens was next to me and we smashed into the men in the doorway side by side, knocking three of them off their feet, and staggering a couple more backwards. The blade of my sword quickly became wet as I pushed into the first room, filled with Egyptian marines who were yelling at us and each other in their native tongue. I felt our men pushing in behind Clemens and me, and very quickly, we killed every man who elected to stand and fight us. Stepping over the bodies, I was about to enter the next room, but a hand yanked at my leathers, pulling me back just as an enemy javelin sliced through the air where I had been standing, landing with a wet thud into the body of one of the Egyptians a few feet away.

I looked back and saw Clemens grinning at me. "I want to get promoted, but not like that."

I grinned back, then turned to snap an order to some of the men who still had their javelins. "Throw a few of those in there. We'll see how they like it."

About a half dozen men stepped forward to fling their javelins into the room, leaping into the doorway just long enough to throw before jumping out of the way. Even so, one of the men was not quite quick enough, an enemy javelin striking him in the bicep, the point going out the other side several inches. We pulled him out of the way as he cursed bitterly, trying not to jostle his arm. Immediately after the last man had thrown, Clemens and I burst through the door, him to the left and me to the right, and I ran directly into an Egyptian, my size once again serving me well by knocking him backwards, giving me enough space to gut him. Immediately, I parried a panicked thrust by another man, our blades striking sparks as they clashed, then lashed out with my fist, catching him on the side of the head and knocking him down. I gave him a thrust through the chest; the room was now filled with my men, again making short work of those brave or stupid enough to stand and fight. Within moments, we cleared the ground floor, whereupon I sent three sections to the roof, where they were finished moments later. Going back out the front of the building, I went to check the progress of the rest of the Cohort. Felix's Century was finished clearing their house, so I walked down the block to the next street. Valens was not using the same tactics, preferring instead for his men to stand away, picking off as many men as they could with their javelins before assaulting the house. While it was not how I would have done it, his way seemed to be as effective, because he had cleared his house as well. Annius was another story altogether; his Century was still outside the building assigned to his Century by Valens, the men milling around, some of them scrounging around for more javelins, whether ours or theirs appeared to make no difference, while the others were flinging them whenever an Egyptian presented a target. Naturally, once the Egyptians determined that Annius had no intention of actually entering the building until he first picked off everyone inside from a distance, they scrupulously avoided presenting Annius' men with a target. Every once in a while, a brave soul on the Egyptian side would leap to his feet, and hurl his own missile at Annius' men. In fact, from what I could tell, Annius' Century was getting the worst of it, if the small group of men who was huddled around the corner either nursing their wounds or lying prone on the street was any sign. Enraged, I ran up to Annius, who had positioned himself well to the rear of the front rank of his Century.

"What in the name of Pluto's thorny cock are you doing just standing here?" I roared at him, gratified to see his chin quiver.

He licked his lips, his eyes shifting to his men, who were doing their best to watch without watching, and I saw some of them smile. "Primus Pilus, I'm clearing the building, as you ordered."

"No," I snapped, pointing back in the direction of Valens' Century, whose men were now standing on the roof, flinging javelins across the street at the enemy on the roof across from them, "they're clearing the building. In fact, they've already cleared it, and so have Felix and Clemens. You, on the other hand, are standing here looking very much like you have your head up your ass."

"I'm just making sure that we've killed as many of the bastards as we can before we go in," he protested.

"How about this?" I shot back. "How about actually going into the building, then killing whoever you find in there!" Without waiting for him to answer, I turned, once again shouting, "Follow me!"

To their credit, Annius' men did not hesitate, following hot on my heels as we ran into the building, killing everyone we found. To be fair, there were quite a few Egyptians already dead when we entered, most of them on the roof, so it did not take long for us to clear it. When we were finished, I grabbed Annius by the arm and dragged him outside.

Leaning down, I made my tone as menacing as I could make it. "If I ever see you do something like that again, I'll have you busted back to Gregarius, but not before I flay the skin off your back. Do you understand?"

This time, his chin was clearly quivering, but his voice was firm enough. "Yes, Primus Pilus."

"Centurions in Caesar's army lead from the front, Annius," I continued, in a calmer tone. "It's what makes us so feared, and it's the only real way your men will respect you, if you set an example."

His eyes were locked above my head, his tone flat as he answered that he understood, telling me that I was having no impact on him at all. I sighed and shook my head, dismissing him to go back to his men. Maybe he will do everyone a favor and get killed, I thought.

~ ~ ~ ~

This was the manner in which we secured the island; house by house, floor by floor. Methodical, professional, and completely without mercy, we killed every Egyptian who chose to fight. Finally, after several blocks of buildings fell in this manner, the remaining Egyptians finally lost their nerve, and on some silent signal, most turned to run for their lives. Many of them simply doffed their gear before jumping into the water to begin swimming to safety; some of them even diving from the roofs of a series of buildings built up to the very edge of the harbor. Another portion, about 6,000 in all, chose to surrender, but we did not put these to the sword, being ordered by Caesar that they would be sold as slaves and we would share in the proceeds.

As further reward, we were given a full watch to ransack the village, the men stripping it clean of anything remotely valuable, and even of things that held value only to the man who took it. It always amused me to see what some of the men thought of as worthy of being taken. Usually it is a statue of one of the local gods, which the man who took it would somehow convince himself is incredibly valuable in and of itself, or that it had some magic power that made it so. Sometimes, however, it was little more than an old brass coin or an amulet made of hair or something similar, but the man who took it would consider it his most prized possession and would kill anyone who tried to take it. I saw men kill each other over a comb, or a cloak clasp worth less than a sesterce. Now, we were in a somewhat unusual situation. Normally, there are merchants among the camp followers whose sole business it is to relieve the men of the items that they have looted, giving them cash money in exchange, but none of these merchants had come with us. Additionally, it was doubtful that any of the Alexandrians would be willing to serve in this function, since their neighbors would probably take a dim view of them profiting from fellow Alexandrians' misfortune. Therefore, the men were now stuck with their pile of possessions, and I knew from bitter experience that over the next few days there would be a number of disagreements about combs, amulets, and cloak clasps.

Once we secured the men from their spree, we were ordered to begin tearing down the houses along the southern edge of the island, using the stones from the buildings to build a fort to guard the northern end of the Heptastadion. We also took stones and dumped them in the passageway under the nearer drawbridge to block Egyptian access to the Great Harbor. By the time the fort was finished, it was almost dark and Caesar sent orders that my and Cartufenus' Cohort would return to the redoubt. Loading into the same boats we had come to the island in, we were rowed back to the royal docks. By the time we unloaded, it was now dark, for which I was thankful since it would help us make our dash back to the redoubt. Another factor helping us was the chaos caused by our attack and seizure of the island, so we managed to make it back to the redoubt without a single loss. All told, our losses were almost astonishingly light; a total of five dead, three of whom were wounded on the way to the docks and were never heard from again, with about a dozen wounded, none of them seriously. Before I left, I told Diocles to scour the area to find some wine, and he somehow managed to produce a dozen large amphorae of something that could only be charitably called wine, but I ordered a ration for all the men who participated in the assault. The men passed the night, reliving the battle and bragging to their friends in the other Cohort, waving their spoils and otherwise rubbing it in their faces. In other words, a normal night after a battle.

~ ~ ~ ~

While taking the island was important, it was only a first step; next was seizing the rest of the Heptastadion. The Egyptians held the southern drawbridge, and had built a fort mirroring the one we constructed; an annoying habit of theirs, copying the things that we did. I do not know what was more infuriating, that they copied us, or that they did such a good job of it. Whatever the case, the Egyptians who were manning the fort had to be dislodged, and the day after the island was taken, Caesar gave the order for a total of three Cohorts to make the assault. Two of them would advance up the Heptastadion, while one would make a landing from ships. To provide support, Caesar filled a couple ships with the archers, sending his heavier vessels with their artillery as well. The small flotilla did its job very well, scouring the small fort of defenders, the bulk of whom simply fled back into the city rather than face such a ferocious and sustained barrage, leaving behind a number of dead and wounded. Seeing the defenders flee, the Cohorts from the northern fort left their own defenses, marching down the mole to take the fort without the loss of a single man. The seaborne Cohort landed without incident as well; all of this we were again watching from the rooftops, and Caesar put the men to work immediately tearing up some of the stone docks to use to build a wall and parapet on the western side of the mole, running lengthwise across the bridge.

"What's he having them do that for?" Sertorius asked, clearly puzzled, but I could not help because I had no idea.

"Maybe he's trying to screen the Egyptians from seeing what he has planned," suggested Fuscus.

I bit back a sarcastic reply, chiding myself for letting my personal feelings for Fuscus color my opinion of the validity of his comment. The truth was that what he said was perfectly reasonable, although I did not think it was likely, because I was sure that the Egyptians knew exactly what his intentions were, to fill in the southern passageway the way he had the northern one. Consequently, I chose to remain silent, and we kept on watching as the work continued. One Cohort was given the task of carrying stones from the razed buildings on the island to use to fill in the passageway, earning our sympathy.

"That's got to be a bastard of a job. They have to carry those rocks more than seven furlongs. That's what, about a mile?" This came from Sertorius.

"Near enough," I grunted, trying to disguise the fact that I could not do sums that rapidly in my head.

"In this heat? I'm just glad it's not us," he laughed and I had to agree.

Most of the men carrying the rocks appeared to have teamed up, stacking a number of stones on one of their shields, with each man carrying one end. Some of the men had grabbed the wooden boards that are used as stretchers for casualties, but most of the men appeared to be using the first method. I could not help wondering how long it was going to take for them to block up the southern passageway at this rate. Meanwhile, the Egyptians were not idle either, as Salvius called out, pointing to the western side of the harbor. We watched men begin boarding the ships moored there. In a few moments, the first of the Egyptian craft pushed off from the quay, the oars dipping into the water, glinting like silver when they were pulled out. There is something inherently graceful and beautiful in watching a vessel moving through the water under oar, the hull slicing through the water, leaving a steadily widening V behind it, the oars that power it moving in unison, each one powered by one, two or even more men, individuals acting as one unit. Who else but a Roman could appreciate such precision, such teamwork? The fact that the ship was filled with men who were going to try to kill my comrades was the only thing marring the beauty, and I had to force myself to remember exactly what was going on before us. Another ship pulled away, then in a few moments, the water in the harbor was roiling as more and more vessels made their way across to the mole. Then, something happened, and I do not know if it was part of the plan, or if one of the Egyptian commanders, perhaps Ganymede himself, saw an opportunity to put our men working on the mole into difficulty. Whatever the cause, suddenly a number of ships suddenly veered off their course to the southern end of the mole, instead moving quickly towards the opposite end, towards our northern fort. As is our custom, Caesar would allow only Legionaries to perform the labor for his engineering projects, so in order to keep a presence in the fort, he had ordered the seamen from a number of our ships to land and take up positions there. But seamen, foreign-born seamen at that, are not Legionaries, and now Ganymede or one of his commanders was going to put them to a test. In growing shock and dismay, we watched the Egyptian craft disgorge their passengers, who came swarming up the same rocks that we had been forced to climb the day before, although being more lightly armed they were able to ascend more quickly. We could not hear them, but we could just make out the men waving their weapons over their heads as they charged, and I imagine that they were screaming their heads off. Even if they were not, the effect the sight of the charging Egyptians had on the seamen was immediate and dramatic. As we moaned in disgust, the sailors in the fort simply turned to run without putting up even the pretense of a fight, dashing headlong across the mole to the eastern side, back to the ships from where they had come. Men went scrambling down the sides of the mole since there were no quays this close to the northern drawbridge. Naturally, they were forced to stop at the water's edge and beckon their comrades still aboard ship to come closer so they could climb aboard. No more than a moment later, there was a confused mass of men jammed together at the shoreline, with the pursuing Egyptians beginning to catch the slower of the sailors. Even as all this was happening, the first of the enemy ships heading for the southern end had unloaded their respective contingents at the foot of the newly built rampart, while other ships ranged offshore firing missiles at our men at the wall in much the same way that our archers drove off the original occupants of the fort.

For reasons that I can only guess at, even while all of this chaos was happening, a number of boats from our side pulled up to the mole, with men spilling onto the causeway. However, this group chose to land farther south than where their comrades near the island were being slaughtered, but north of where our Legionaries were battling the Egyptians for the southern drawbridge, landing effectively in between the two battles. It was only later that we were told that this particular group of idiots, having never seen a land battle up close, got the idea into their collective heads that it would be fun to watch the action from close up, and they commandeered a number of small boats to row over to watch the fun. I will say that some of them seemed to get in the spirit of things, as we watched them pick up stones to hurl at the Egyptians onboard the support ships. The sailors at the far northern end had either managed to clamber back onboard their respective ships, or been cut down, although in doing the former they caused a number of the smaller vessels to capsize when trying to climb onboard. Now the enemy on the northern end turned their attention towards this hapless band in the middle, falling down on their completely unprotected rear. For their part, our sailors were so engrossed in watching the battle for the southern drawbridge that they did not become aware that their doom was fast approaching until the enemy was just a matter of a hundred paces or so away. Not surprisingly, another panic ensued with the second group of sailors, their arms waving wildly above their heads in terror, rushing back towards their boats, the Egyptians hot on their heels.

~ ~ ~ ~

Even now, after reading Caesar's account of what happened, I do not know what was in his mind when he chose this same moment to leave the mole and board his flagship. I do not know if he had planned to do so at that moment or if, seeing a fair number of Egyptians pounding down the causeway from an unexpected direction, he decided that it was prudent for him to remove himself. What I do know is that it is from seemingly random events, when they occur in the right order, that the outcome of a battle can turn. Such was the case now, while we stood on the roof watching all of Caesar's plans starting to unravel, started by those Egyptian ships landing on the island to swing down on first our northern fort, then on the idiots, many of whom were now dead, either from wounds or drowning. If things had stopped there, it would have still been a salvageable situation, but now the Legionaries on the far right of the rampart guarding the drawbridge, nearest to the island and the northern fort, first seeing the disaster farther up the mole, then witnessing Caesar remove himself, began to think about their own skins. I must admit that they were subjected to murderous fire from the ships supporting the Egyptian attack on the rampart; we clearly saw a number of bodies lying at the feet of the men still fighting. First, the men on the far right, those closest to the advancing Egyptians coming down the mole, jumped down from the rampart to run across the causeway towards the eastern side, begging the men safe offshore to steer their boats closer so that they could escape to safety. Just like what happened on the opposite end of the causeway, the idiots in the middle had caused several of the boats they tried to board to capsize as well, so that now the harbor was littered with the upside down hulls of what looked like almost a dozen boats of varying size. Floating among them were a fair number of smaller shapes, the bodies of men who were either the cause of a boat capsizing as they tried to pull themselves aboard, or a victim.

"This is a fucking disaster," I muttered, and the shock was such that none of the others could even answer me, only grunting at my words in what I took to be agreement.

What had begun with just a few men on the far right now became a complete collapse, as one by one men peeled away from their position to follow their comrade, usually the man to his right, towards what they hoped was safety. First one, then another ship, their captains either moved by the plight of the men on the mole, or forced to do so by the stranded men's comrades, moved towards the causeway, pulling alongside to throw up their ladders. Perhaps if the men still on the mole had kept their heads, forming a perimeter to keep the Egyptians at bay while their comrades loaded onto the boats in an orderly fashion, disaster could have been averted, but the men were obviously gripped by panic. Just like the seamen earlier, they now pushed and shoved each other, fighting for a spot to descend the ladders of the ships. At first, men were content just to push each other, but it was not long before we saw the flash of a blade as a man struck down one of his own comrades. There was an audible gasp from the men around me, and I suspect from me as well.

"By the gods, is that a Centurion stabbing his own men?" Fuscus exclaimed, pointing down to the second ship, where the scene was more or less identical.

I had been paying attention to the ship closest to us, while Fuscus was pointing at the farthest ship, but when I looked, I saw that he was right. My stomach lurched at the sight of the familiar transverse crest on the head of a man, chopping down his own men. As sickening a sight as that was, I squinted at the ship, and my mouth went dry with fear.

"That's Caesar's ship!"

He had obviously decided to try to rescue some of his men, but they were so consumed with fear that they were now trying to climb over the side of the ship, and we could see it start to lean dangerously, the water just inches from the side.

"They're going to capsize him!" someone said in horror.

It was one of the worst feelings I have ever experienced, watching what appeared to be the inevitable capsizing of our general's ship, but completely helpless to do anything about it. Despite the obvious danger, men continued adding their own weight as they tried to leap down into the ship. The entire side, what little of it was still above water, was now completely obscured by the bodies of men attempting to pull themselves aboard. Then, we saw a number of figures on the opposite side of the ship leap into the water, and for a moment, I could not understand what they were doing. I wondered if the men who dived into the water had simply decided that they would rather drown on their own than be dragged under by men they had thought of as friends. Then my eyes caught something that seemed to be coming from one of the men, and at first, I thought it was blood because it seemed to be a pool of red surrounding his head, the only part of him visible above the surface. Squinting, I saw that the man did not appear to be struggling in the water the way a man who is wounded is likely to, and that pool of blood did not seem right. It did not seem to be growing, despite the man being clearly alive, meaning his heart was still pumping, but it did seem to be changing in size as I watched.

"That's Caesar!" I exclaimed, pointing to the man, "and he's swimming away and taking his *paludamentum* with him!"

~ ~ ~ ~

Indeed it was our general, who chose to abandon the ship, which he recognized was doomed to capsize, and take his chances swimming to safety, dragging his *paludamentum* with him in his teeth so that it would not be captured. Unfortunately, it became so waterlogged that even as strong a swimmer as Caesar could not continue dragging it without running a real risk of drowning, so he discarded it, where it was fished out by the Egyptians the next day and put on display like they had captured Caesar himself. Caesar swam to a small boat that pulled him aboard, then transferred him to one of the thirty's. It was from this ship that Caesar tried to salvage something from the disaster. Directing some of the small boats that had not taken part in the debacle at the mole to go back to the causeway to pull as many men out of the water as they could, Caesar did everything in his power to rescue as many men as possible. These sailors, unlike their counterparts who climbed onto the causeway, behaved with great courage, braving savage missile fire from the Egyptians on the mole, their numbers continuing to swell as men jumped in ships to be rowed to the Heptastadion. Our sailors fished a couple hundred men from the water, some more dead than alive, yet the damage was done, and it was horrific. We continued to hold the island, but we had lost control of the entire length of the Heptastadion. Additionally, the work done in blocking the two passageways was reversed in a matter of a couple thirds of a watch, the enemy clearing the passages of the stone we had dumped there, thereby providing the Egyptians free access to the Great Harbor and giving them the ability to attack our fleet once again. More than 400 Legionaries died, most of them from drowning, although a fair number were cut down by their own comrades, making me wonder how the survivors would find trying to sleep at night with the deaths of friends on their conscience. Only one Century's worth of men actually kept their heads enough to form square, trying to make a stand, led by a Centurion.

Tragically, they were wiped out to the last man. At least as many sailors died as well, if not more, from identical causes as the Legionaries. No amount of honey would sweeten this bitter drink; we were soundly defeated, and had failed in our objectives. The fact that it was the men of the 37th who behaved so shamefully was not lost on any of us, but it was particularly hard on my men, because there were friends and in one or two cases, relatives who died in the mess. The 37th was composed of Pompey's veterans, from a number of different Legions. While I understood why the men had such mixed feelings, what I was not prepared for is how it added to the hostility and hard feelings between us and the 28th. For the men of the 28th, what happened on the mole was something of a blessing sent by the gods, for they no longer were the only Legion in disgrace. What made it worse was that it was Pompey's men who failed so miserably, a fact that the rankers in the 28th were never shy about pointing out to my men. The men of the 6th were in a tough spot; while they understood that the 37th had performed poorly, they still felt compelled out of loyalty to both the memory of Pompey and to their former comrades to offer a defense of their actions. Less than a day passed before I was called on by Serenus, who was the commander of the guard, informing me that there had been a killing down in Hump Alley, which was what the men called the side street where the whores plied their trade. He was accompanied by one of Cartufenus' Centurions who was Serenus' counterpart for the 28th guard shift; his name was Flaccus, as I recall. I sighed, shaking my head, because it was not unexpected, but it was still something that none of us needed.

"What happened?" I asked.

"Well of course there are two different versions," said Serenus.

I saw Flaccus shoot him an angry glance, although I did not know why; the very presence of Flaccus told me that there was a dispute about what happened.

Continuing, Serenus gave his report. "Gregarius Immunes Lucius Verres of the Second of the 10th was off duty and was spending some time in Hump Alley. According to Verres and his witnesses, a man from the 28th started an altercation with Verres."

"He did no such thing," Flaccus interjected, his face flushed with indignation I suppose.

Before he could say anything else, I wearily held a hand up. "You'll have your chance to speak. Until then I expect you to remain silent."

He looked like he was thinking of protesting, his mouth open to say something, but I gave him a look that snapped it shut.

"What was the altercation about?" I asked Serenus.

He shrugged, "It's hard to tell, Primus Pilus. Supposedly it was over a woman that the man from the 28th claimed had been paid for her services during the time that Verres was with her."

Flaccus coughed, opening his mouth, but I shot him a warning look. "Witnesses?"

"Several," Serenus replied. "All of whom said basically the same thing, that the Gregarius from the 28th forced his way into the who . . . the woman's room, where she was with Verres and began shouting at Verres, calling him names, you know, the usual insults. Then the man from the 28th pulled a blade and attacked Verres. Verres defended himself, and in the ensuing fight, killed the man from the 28th."

"He cut his throat from ear to ear," Flaccus burst out, but I did not say anything.

It was clear that Flaccus was upset, more upset than a man who knows his own is in the wrong normally would be, I thought.

Turning back to Serenus, I asked, "Anything else?"

He shook his head. I looked at Flaccus, but before he spoke, I asked him for his full name and rank, so that I would know how to address him. He did not know that I actually knew a bit about him; Cartufenus had spoken of him and thought highly of the Centurion, a tall thin man with what I considered a weak chin. Yet his gaze was direct, and he spoke clearly and firmly, with an accent that told me he was from Etruria.

"I am Tertius Princeps Posterior Gaius Flaccus, Primus Pilus."

I nodded my thanks, indicating he should continue.

He cleared his throat and began, "First, I'd request that we refer to the dead man by his name. He was Gregarius Gnaeus Plautus."

He looked meaningfully at both of us, and I nodded. It was only right that we call the dead man by his name; no matter how he died, we owed him that much, and my respect for Flaccus grew a bit.

"Very well, Princeps Posterior, we shall refer to him by his name. His unit?"

Now Flaccus looked uncomfortable, so I had an inkling that I knew what he was going to say.

"Fourth of the Third."

I was right, and I hoped that my face did not betray my internal groan at the news. This complicates things quite a bit, I thought, because this is Flaccus' man. I have a habit when I am distracted or worried in some way of rubbing my face, and I found that I was doing that very thing.

"So, he's your man then," Serenus said triumphantly, Flaccus shooting him an angry look.

"I assure you, that has nothing to do with my report," he replied angrily, and I made a placating gesture to him.

"Nobody," I looked sternly at Serenus, angry that he had spoken out of turn, forcing me to verbalize this, "is making any suggestion that it will, Princeps Posterior. In fact," I lied, "it means that you may be able to provide even more valuable insight into what happened precisely because you do know the Gregarius . . . I mean, Plautus . . . very well. Please tell us your side."

I took great pains to avoid using the word "version," having learned that when one used that word, others took it that you were inferring that they were not being truthful.

Flaccus nodded and continued, "What Serenus has just described is not what happened." I raised my eyebrows in mock surprise, but he either ignored or did not see my expression. "It's true that Plautus and your man Verres had words, but that is all they were . . . words. Plautus didn't force his way into the woman's room; in fact, it was the exact opposite. According to my witnesses, both men were sitting in the outer room, waiting their turn for their . . . partners. My information is that they were not seeing the same woman. Anyway, what is true is that my man Plautus began talking to Verres, but the subject wasn't which woman they were seeing."

I suspected I knew the answer, but I asked anyway. "What was the topic, Flaccus?"

Now he was looking like he would rather be anywhere but standing in front of Serenus or me, and I felt a pang of sympathy. Serenus was staring at him coldly, waiting for him to speak.

"It concerned . . . the . . . uh . . . the events of yesterday."

I raised an eyebrow, a trick I had learned from Gisela.

"Well, that's certainly understandable," I said reasonably, "since yesterday was an eventful day. Do you know exactly what Plautus was saying?"

Flaccus looked positively miserable, but as much as I may have sympathized, I could not let this question go unanswered, so I repeated the question.

"Plautus was commenting on the . . . performance of the men of the 37th," he could not look at either of us as he finished.

"Let me guess, he wasn't exactly complimentary, was he?"

Flaccus sighed then shook his head. "No Primus Pilus, he wasn't."

"Do you know specifically what he said about the 37th?"

Oh, I am willing to bet my entire fortune that at that moment, Princeps Posterior Flaccus was offering an urgent prayer that the ground beneath his feet would suddenly open to swallow him up.

Closing his eyes tightly, he said something in such a soft whisper that I could not hear, so I had to ask him to repeat himself. "He said . . . he said . . . that the 37th wasn't worth the sweat off his balls, and that they deserved to be decimated."

I had to stifle a laugh at the colorful invective that Plautus had spewed, but it was truly no laughing matter. The last part especially was troubling, because that was about the worst thing one Legionary could say about another Legion, and I said as much.

"But that isn't reason enough to kill him," Flaccus protested, and this I could not argue.

However, Flaccus was not finished; he went on to claim that it was actually the other way around, that Verres had followed Plautus into the room his whore occupied, where he stabbed him to death.

When Flaccus was finished, I sat thinking for a moment. "Flaccus, I'm curious about one thing. You're the commander of the guard for the 28th in your sector, correct?"

"Yes, Primus Pilus."

"Isn't it customary that the commander of the guard and the Century on watch be from the same Century?"

He nodded, and I asked, "So why was Plautus not on duty?"

"Because I was doing a favor for a friend of mine who commands the Sixth Century, and I took his shift."

I had suspected as much; Centurions swapped guard shifts all the time, despite there being regulations against it, which are almost universally ignored. There was no way that this matter was going to be handled quickly, or quietly, for that matter. I would have to talk to the witnesses for both men. Biting back a curse as I stood up, I grabbed my helmet and *vitus*.

~ ~ ~ ~

I was not surprised that the men were no help, on either side. They were uniformly as solemn and sincere as Vestal Virgins, each of them swearing to their household gods that they were being completely truthful and not embellishing a thing. However, I did not really need to hear what they had to say, because I was as close to convinced as I could be that I knew the real story, and unfortunately, it was closer to Flaccus' version than Serenus'. I think that this Plautus saw a golden opportunity to pay those uppity bastards from the 6th back for all the *cac* they had been making the 28th eat. What he did not count on was one fact in particular; Verres' older brother was a Centurion in the 37th, although he had survived the disaster, and I could not help wondering if Verres' brother was the Centurion we saw cutting his own men down. However, there was no way I could ask Verres that, or that Verres would have known, even if his brother had confessed, since the 37th was still down on the ships. Still, knowing the truth, and proving it were two different things, which was only part of the problem. The bigger issue, at least in my own mind, was that by choosing to believe that the version Flaccus gave was closer to the truth than what Serenus, Verres and his friends had provided, I would be siding with the 28th against my own men. The fact that I was as close to convinced as I could be that Verres had killed Plautus simply for what he said just made things more difficult. In the larger picture, this was a no-win situation; if I sided with Verres, the men of the 28th would be even more embittered towards us, while siding with Plautus would make the 6th not only angry at the 28th, but at me as well for siding with them. The fact that I would simply be acting in the interests of justice and the truth had nothing to do with it, because rankers only care about what is fair when it somehow benefits them. If they see the right thing as somehow taking something from them, you can forget them wanting to do the right thing. On the surface, it appeared that the decision, while not easy, was at least clear. The lesser of two evils was to accept Verres' version of events. I did not think it could make relations between the 6th and 28th any worse, and indeed, Verres escaping punishment might at least encourage the 28th to keep their mouths shut about what happened to the 37th. I also had to consider the fact that while in command of the 6th for several months now, the men still had not fully accepted me. The assault on the island had helped a great deal to solidify my hold over the men, but I knew there were still doubters, and some of them were Centurions and Optios. I could easily see Cornuficius turning this to his advantage; as I was learning, he was much cleverer than Celer, and more devious. I resolved that I would sleep on it, but I got precious little of it, tossing and turning instead, and it slowly dawned on me that the cause of my distress was . . . anger. The realization struck me suddenly, shortly before dawn, when I sat upright, my mind racing. This had less to do with what was true than with the idea that I felt that I was being manipulated by not only my men, but Cornuficius as well, since Verres was his man, and all the witnesses were not only in the same Century, they were Verres' very own tent mates, a fact I thought was very odd. There was little doubt that they had gotten together and worked out their story, probably rehearsing it. In truth, this was not unusual at all, having done it myself many times when I was a ranker. Except, somehow I convinced myself that this was different, that the men thought that they were getting one over on me, so by the time I was through thinking about it, I envisioned them sitting around the fire laughing uproariously at their gullible Primus Pilus and how easy it was to fool him. By the time the sun rose, I was in a cold fury, and the fate of Verres was sealed.

~ ~ ~ ~

"You're sure about this?"

I looked at Cartufenus, sitting across from me but this time at his desk, in his quarters and not mine. I nodded.

"May I ask why?" His tone was very polite, but I would have answered him regardless.

"Because I don't believe Verres, or his tent mates," I said simply.

He regarded me with an even gaze, his eyes giving away nothing, then he replied, "While I'm sure that my men will appreciate your sense of justice and will think more kindly of you, I somehow don't think your men will feel the same."

"I couldn't give a flying fuck what the men think about me," I snapped, instantly regretting it. Cartufenus' face flushed, clearly angry, and I made haste to apologize. "I'm sorry, Cartufenus. This has just put my nerves on edge. I meant no disrespect to you."

He inclined his head, signaling that he accepted my apology.

Folding his arms, he looked thoughtfully down at his desk. "And you plan on taking this matter to Caesar? And to recommend the maximum punishment?"

"Yes."

For that was the decision that I had reached the night before, and although my anger had cooled, my determination to see this through had not.

"Aren't you worried that the whole story of our . . . difficulties will come to light?"

This was the crux of the matter, at least as far as I was concerned. By making this official, and bringing it to the attention of Caesar, there would undoubtedly be questions asked that would expose the months-old rift between our two Legions.

Indeed, I was very worried about it, but to Cartufenus I just shrugged. "I've been thinking about it, and maybe we didn't do the best thing in keeping this quiet after all." He was not convinced, so I continued talking. "It's only a matter of time before there's a really ugly incident, and not one involving just one or two men. There's going to be a riot, and there'll be no way to hide that. Then where will we be? No, I think it's better to get it out in the open now while it's still relatively minor and something that we can handle."

He did not like it, but I could see that he accepted the sense of what I was saying. His expression sharpened; he had a pair of very bushy, thick eyebrows that when he frowned merged to form one single line of hair, so despite the gravity of the subject, I had to keep from laughing when I saw what looked like two caterpillars crawling towards each other on his forehead.

"Caesar's no fool; he'll know that there's more to the story, and that this just didn't suddenly flare up."

The urge to laugh fled from me with his words, the way those sailors had on the Heptastadion .

"I know," I said soberly. "I'll just have to deal with that if it happens."

"Oh, it'll happen. I may not know Caesar as well as you do, but I know him well enough. He doesn't miss a thing."

With that, our conversation was over and I left to go deal with what was coming next.

~ ~ ~ ~

"You're going to do what?"

Not surprisingly, the reaction I got from my own Centurions was more vehement than Cartufenus', with a babble of voices as all the men tried to talk at once. My nerves were already very raw, so I was in no mood to indulge my Centurions in what I considered useless chatter.

"*Tacete!*"

Even I could feel the walls vibrate from the sound of my voice, and the men instantly obeyed. I waited for a moment, observing the men's sullen silence, the hostility and anger written plainly on almost every face. Felix looked less angry than puzzled, while Considius looked like he had no idea what we were talking about.

Calmly, I repeated what I had originally said that caused all the excitement. "I said that after investigating the matter, I've determined that Gregarius Immunes Verres stabbed Gregarius Plautus to death without sufficient provocation. While I don't doubt that Plautus said something offensive, I don't think that it warranted the reaction that he got. I therefore intend to take the matter to Caesar and recommend that Verres be punished."

"But Verres has witnesses that saw the whole thing and corroborated his story," protested Severus, with several of the others loudly voicing their agreement.

"Yes, and I believe Verres' tent mates were showing commendable loyalty, but I simply don't believe them. Don't any of you find it somewhat odd that every witness on Verres' behalf was from his section? I know men usually spend most of their time with their tent mates; remember, I was in the ranks myself." As I said this, I thought back to all those nights around the fire with Vibius, Scribonius, Romulus, and Remus.

Seemingly out of nowhere, I felt my chest tighten as my eyes began to burn, forcing me to blink rapidly to keep from shaming myself. Fortunately, the others were too absorbed in their own thoughts to notice.

"But it's very, very rare that every single man in Verres' tent section just happened to be present, in the exact same whorehouse, at the exact same time."

There was not much that anyone could say about this, for they knew what I was saying was true. I suppose it is possible that every single member of a tent section got along with each other so well that they were all good friends and went everywhere, even whoring together, but I had never seen it happen. It certainly had not worked out that way in my tent section, and I thought of Didius, wondering if anyone had caught him cheating and beaten him to death yet.

"Perhaps it was a special occasion."

All eyes turned towards Favonius, the one who uttered these words. I felt my jaw clench, knowing that whatever he was up to, it was highly unlikely that I would like it.

"Oh?" I laughed, making no attempt to hide my sarcasm. "And what momentous event could prompt something that we all know never happens? Somebody's birthday, perhaps?"

While my words were meant to unsettle Favonius, they did not seem to have any effect at all.

He merely shrugged and replied quietly, "I don't know, but I think it might be a good idea to find out."

I could not tell what he was playing at, which made me nervous, particularly since his idea had merit, at least in the sense of tying up any possible loose ends, but I decided not to press the matter at that time.

"Primus Pilus, with all due respect, I have to say that I vigorously protest your decision and I resent the implication that somehow my men are lying to cover up for one of their comrades." For the first time I could recall in our short relationship, I seemed to have Cornuficius rattled, his normally blank face clearly angry.

In reply, I feigned surprise as I responded, "I'm not censuring your men in the slightest, Cornuficius. They showed admirable loyalty in trying to protect their tent mate, however misguided that loyalty may have been. And neither am I saying that Plautus was completely blameless, but what I *am* saying is that while Verres may have had just cause to be angry, he overreacted. He acted in the heat of the moment, which is something I intend to stress to Caesar. It's very likely that Caesar will show clemency; he's famous for his mercy. You all should know that better than most."

That was a calculated slap in their collective faces, but I was gambling that the fact that it was true would keep the men from speaking up. I was relieved to see that I was right.

"That's all I have to say on the matter. I'll be making my report to Caesar later today. In the meantime, Verres is confined to quarters; I don't see much point in keeping him in close confinement. As bad as things may be for him inside, I'm fairly sure that the Egyptians will have something much more unpleasant in store for him if he decides to go over the wall."

I stood, as did the men, and I dismissed them. Cornuficius lingered, so I hardened myself for whatever was to come, but he was ever one for surprises. He did not argue, or make any kind of threats, veiled or otherwise. He just stood there, looking at me in what I was learning was his speculative manner.

Then he spoke suddenly. "You're pinning your hopes that Caesar won't have him executed, aren't you?"

That was exactly what I was hoping for, but I was not about to admit that to Cornuficius, so I responded with a question of my own.

"What makes you think that?"

He considered my question carefully, but I sensed that he was being as honest as he was capable of being when he answered. "Because you're in a tight spot. Let's say that you're right. I'm not saying that you are, but suppose the men did get together and concoct this story and that things happened as you say they did, that this Plautus character mouthed off and Verres overreacted. From your point of view, I can see how it would anger you that the men are conspiring against you, and the way you see it, they're making a fool of you."

He seemed to be enjoying talking about me being a fool a bit too much for my taste, but I said nothing and continued to listen.

"That can't go unpunished, at least from where you're sitting. I understand that. But what if that isn't the reason? What if Verres is truly so well liked that what the men are doing has less to do with getting away with something and more to do with saving a man they truly respect and admire?"

As he spoke, I felt my stomach tighten, because he was absolutely right about one thing; I had never even considered the possibility that Verres' tent mates were doing anything other than what I suspected them of, which was trying to put something over on me. What if everything was as Cornuficius said, that Verres was a good man who made one terrible mistake and his tent mates were only concerned with keeping a good man from suffering a terrible punishment?

"Do you know Verres' brother? The one who's a Centurion in the 37th?" I asked, more out of idle curiosity than anything.

Cornuficius looked startled, just for the briefest of an instant. However, it was enough for me to notice, and I felt an intense and grim satisfaction. Oh, he was a slippery one all right, and very, very smooth. He almost had me convinced that this man was almost as much of a victim of circumstance as Plautus was. Cornuficius recovered quickly, but I had seen enough.

"Only by sight, when we were together in Pompey's army. He came to visit Verres a time or two, but we never spoke."

He was lying, I was sure of it. "How much did he pay you?" I asked quietly.

Cornuficius stiffened for a moment, his mouth in a thin line. Then the tension left his body and he did something that I was not expecting; he laughed, and I could tell it was a real laugh, not forced.

"A pretty tidy sum," he admitted. Then, shrugging, he continued, "Something for me and for Verres' tent mates. He hoped that you'd stop with the tent mates; I was the backup plan. He loves his little brother dearly."

"And you know him more than just by sight, don't you?"

Again he laughed. "I guess you could say that." He paused, seeming to make a decision. "I was his Optio in the Third a few years ago."

Things were starting to fall into place, but I certainly was not prepared for his next bit of information.

"Oh," he added as if it were an afterthought, "he's also my cousin."

I stared at him, sure that this time he was trying to put one over on me, though I could not for the life of me think why he would want to do that, but I saw that he was deadly serious.

"Which means Verres is your cousin as well." I tried, but I could not keep the bewilderment out of my voice.

"That's usually how it works," he agreed.

Normally I would have taken offense, except my head was spinning too much for me to take much notice.

A thought struck me. "So why hasn't he come to see me personally?"

Cornuficius looked at me levelly, his face back to its bovine, blank look. "Oh don't worry, Primus Pilus. He will."

~ ~ ~ ~

He would have to come that night, since I had announced that I would seek an audience with Caesar in the morning. He waited until third watch; I imagine he hoped to catch me unprepared, but I was still in full uniform, sitting at my desk when Diocles knocked on my door. When he entered to announce that Quintus Pilus Prior Sextus Verres Rufus wished to see me, while I cannot say that he looked scared, he did look concerned. Before I sent Diocles to fetch him, I drew my dagger, lying it on the desk and covering it with a scroll, then I picked up my harness from its normal place on the stand at the foot of my bed to drape it over the back of the chair, as if I had just dropped it there. Satisfied, I nodded to Diocles, who turned and went back into the outer office. I heard Diocles' voice, then the slapping sound of hobnails striking the stone floor, and in walked Verres Rufus. Instantly, I felt my body tense, although he did nothing overtly menacing, and I realized that what I was reacting to was the sight of the man himself. He was of medium height, but he was almost square, so thickly built through the chest and shoulders that his arms did not seem able to hang straight down at his sides, instead sticking out at an angle. His face was broad, carrying many scars, mostly over his eyes with one prominent one on his left cheek. His nose had been broken several times, while his lips were thick, seemingly formed into a permanent sneer, and when he smiled there were a couple of gaps in his teeth. I call it a smile, but there was nothing pleasant about it. This was a man who was comfortable knocking heads together and probably preferred it to actually trying to use his brain. The fact that he was a Centurion would have impressed me more a few months before than it did now; I am afraid exposure to the Centurions in Pompey's former army had left a negative impression on me. As he marched to the desk, I was struck by the odd feeling that he looked familiar, but I did not know how that was possible, so I dismissed the idea.

"Quintus Pilus Prior Gnaeus Verres Rufus, requesting permission to speak to Primus Pilus Pullus, sir."

I could not fault his delivery of the obligatory greeting, although his voice sounded like a cup full of gravel being shaken. I stood and offered my hand, and for a moment, I thought he was going to refuse to take it, but then grudgingly accepted it. As I expected, he proceeded to try to crush my forearm in his grasp. He did have quite a grip, yet I responded in kind before we both released and stood back. He was a bruiser, except I thought I detected a kind of cunning intelligence in his hooded eyes, which were almost covered over by scar tissue. I motioned for him to sit, and he did so, leaning forward in his chair.

"So what is it you wish to see me about, Pilus Prior?"

"I think you know," he growled. "You're going to Caesar tomorrow about my brother, despite the fact that he has witnesses who've sworn that he was attacked by that *cunnus*."

"That's no way to speak of the dead," I said mildly.

"I piss on the man, and his whole family," he spat, shifting in his chair.

"Whether you piss on him or not is beside the point." I struggled to keep my temper, sensing that this was exactly what he wanted, for me to lose control. "And the next time you try to buy your brother out of trouble, try not to bribe every single one of his tent mates to say that they were all together at the same place at the same time. The only time that ever happens is in formations. But I can tell that thinking isn't your strong suit, is it?"

Now he was the one getting angry, his face turning bright red, giving me a clue where his cognomen came from, and I watched as a vein in his forehead started throbbing. I could literally hear the wood of the arms of the chair creaking under the strain as he gripped them tightly.

"Do you know who I am?" This came out in a choked whisper. "I am Gnaeus Verres Rufus, the boxing and wrestling champion, not just of the 3rd Legion, but of Gnaeus Pompey Magnus' whole army!"

"Do you mean the same army that a few half-strength Legions from Caesar's army ground into the dust at Pharsalus? And isn't Pompey dead now?"

He leaped to his feet, his fists balled up and I thought for a moment that he would lose control of his senses and actually attack me. I had kept my right hand draped over the back of my chair as I sat in it in an offhand manner, but the hilt of my sword was just inches from my grasp.

"It would be a shame if the Verres line ceased to exist in the space of a couple of days," I said calmly. "Unless, of course, there's another brother I don't know about."

He gasped like he was dashed with a bucket of cold water. Then he sat down abruptly, his mouth working, except no sound came out. I eyed him coldly while he collected himself.

A man of even moderate intelligence would have at this point changed his approach, seeing that his blustering had not worked, but Verres Rufus was clearly a horse that knew only one trick, so he began again. "You're making a big mistake if you go to Caesar. I could break you in half if I wanted. I don't care how big you are."

"And I could have you scourged then crucified for threatening a superior officer."

Some of his bluster was coming back, because he gave me his version of a smile. "There's just the two of us in here. Who's to say what was said?"

"I'm to say, and that'd be enough. Don't tell me that your cousin, Cornuficius," I was pleased to see his eyes widen in surprise, "didn't warn you that I'm one of Caesar's favorites. After all, he did pick me to be the Primus Pilus of the 6th."

The wheels turned in his head, but, oh, they moved slowly indeed. I could see him struggling to try to think of something to counter what I had just said.

The best he could do was, "I have friends too, and they'll be more than happy to help me stop you from hurting my brother. I've broken many a man who got in my way, and I'll break you too."

That's when the nagging feeling that I had seen him somewhere before made something click in my brain, and I asked suddenly, "Were you involved in the fight on the causeway the other day?"

Clearly startled, his eyes darted about as he tried to think through what I was up to.

Finally, he answered suspiciously, "Yes, why?"

I did not say anything, just stared at him, looking into his eyes, and ever so slowly, I could see the realization dawn in his eyes.

The silence hung between us, until I finally spoke. "I saw you. I saw you cut down your own men just to save your own skin."

This time his face went utterly white, his mouth sagging open for a moment before he struggled to regain control. "I don't know what you're talking about." His voice was hoarse, yet even as I was staring into his eyes, he could not keep his gaze locked with mine and he looked away. "Besides, there's no way you can prove what you're saying."

He looked back at me defiantly, as if daring me to argue the point.

"You're right," I conceded. He looked at me triumphantly, but it was short-lived, "I can't, but some of your men saw what you did. You didn't cut all of them down."

His laugh sounded like a dog barking. "They won't say a word. They know better. They know what would happen to them if they opened their mouths."

I had heard of Centurions who ruled only by brute force, but I had never run into one. Even men like Longus who viewed their Centuries as means of making money knew that there were times where something other than a good beating would accomplish what they wanted done. If your only means of enforcing obedience is by beating a man, sooner or later you put him in a position where he has nothing to lose. Either way, all he can expect is a beating, so he might as well make it worth his while. But sitting here before me was a Centurion who ruled by terror, and I thought for a moment of trying to goad him into actually attacking me. I had no intention of fighting him with my bare hands; it had been several years since I last entered the Legion games, and I was sure that even if I beat him at his own game, it could not be done without him inflicting a fair amount of damage to me. What I thought about was somehow prodding him into doing something where I would be justified in pulling my sword, but I quickly dismissed the idea. There were too many things that could go wrong, although the idea that he could best me with a blade never occurred to me. What I was most worried about were the questions that would be raised; even if I got away with it, there would be a black mark hanging over me the rest of my career. I would just have to trust that the gods would arrange an appropriately horrible end for a man who would kill his own.

Finally, I just shrugged. "Well, now we know where each other stands. But I'm still seeing Caesar tomorrow about your brother. If you want to try stopping me, by all means go ahead, and I'll gut you and put you on a spit." I pointed to the door. "Now that's settled, get out of my office."

He was shaking with rage as he stood up, but he turned to walk out the door. As he exited, he said savagely, "This isn't over, Pullus. I swear that it's not."

"As you say," I replied then pretended to read a report on my desk.

~ ~ ~ ~

The next morning came without incident; nobody came to my quarters to try anything, and once I disposed of my morning business, I made my way to headquarters for the morning briefing. Once we were through, I caught Appolonius to tell him that I needed to see Caesar on an important matter. Normally, it was not an easy thing to secure an audience with Caesar, but there were two factors working in my favor. The first was that of all the people who wanted Caesar's time, he gave the highest priority to his Centurions, even over his generals. The second was that I very rarely requested an audience with Caesar, so Appolonius knew that it had to be important. Moments after the briefing was over, I was ushered into Caesar's office, where he was dictating to several scribes, each occupied with a different subject. As I came to *intente*, Caesar looked up at me. One glance at my face must have told him something, because he immediately dismissed the scribes from the room.

After they left, he looked at me gravely, and said, "I don't know why you're here, Pullus, but from the look on your face, it can't be good news."

"No, sir. It's not."

He sighed, then gave a rueful laugh. "Well, I was hoping anyway. So, what is it?"

As briefly as I could, I described the events that led to the death of Plautus, my investigation and my conclusion that the version of events that I was given by Verres and his witnesses was not what had happened. I went on to say that while Plautus certainly held some culpability, he had not done anything that warranted being killed for, at least in my view. I did not expand on what had actually been said, holding out a very faint hope that Caesar would not ask, since this would be the thread that would unravel everything. A hope that lasted all of a heartbeat.

"So what exactly was it that Plautus said that caused all this to happen?"

I took a deep breath then relayed the exchange that led to the killing. Caesar's mouth twitched a little at the colorful terms Plautus used, but it only lasted for a moment. After I finished, he stayed silent for a moment, his brow furrowed as he thought about what I had told him.

Finally, he said, "It seems very straightforward. While I appreciate you keeping me informed, this appears to be a routine matter, which I'm sure you'll handle in the proper way." His expression changed, and he eyed me with that shrewd look that made me feel like he was staring right through me. "But I suspect that there's a bit more to this situation than meets the eye, or you wouldn't be standing here looking like you would rather be facing the Egyptians naked."

"Yes, sir. There is. The problem isn't between Verres and Plautus. There's been a long-running feud between my men and the 28th that Cartufenus and I have been trying to keep a lid on for months now; the business with the water just made things worse. What happened with the 37th on the Heptastadion apparently gave the 28th the idea that their *cac* doesn't stink, pardon the expression, sir, but it's not the 37th that the 28th hates, it's my boys. And," I admitted ruefully, "it's not without cause. The 6th has been giving the 28th the business pretty good, especially after they tried to mutiny. What Plautus said about the 37th was just an excuse for Verres to strike a blow in this feud."

While I was speaking, Caesar did not interrupt, instead just sat on the edge of his desk, giving me a look that I could not interpret, only serving to increase my own tension.

When I finished, his only reaction at first was to purse his lips as he thought. "And why am I just now being informed of these problems between your men and the 28th?"

There it was; the question that I had been dreading was now in the open. My career and all that I had achieved and hoped to achieve flashed before me, yet I knew that evading the question or trying to tell Caesar what I thought he wanted to hear would make things worse. So I plunged in and opened my mouth to tell the truth, but before I could get started he interrupted.

"Before you say anything, let me take a stab at what's been happening."

I was not likely to argue, so I merely nodded for him to continue, as if he needed my consent.

"You and Cartufenus, perhaps with the agreement from the other Centurions, decided that it was best, given our situation here and all that you see me dealing with, to try and keep this…feud as you call it, contained to a level that it didn't come to my attention, or that of my generals. Do I have that part right?" I said that he did, and he continued, "But things haven't calmed down, they're getting steadily worse and now you're faced with a situation where, depending on my decision, I may be facing a full-scale riot between my troops."

His tone was calm, but I could clearly hear the icy anger underlying it. Despite myself, I felt my legs start to tremble.

Trying to keep my voice calm and steady as I answered him, I hated the fact that there was really only one answer. "Yes, sir."

"Pullus, did it ever occur to you that if you had come to me sooner, at the first signs of trouble, that this could have been nipped in the bud?"

He turned to rummage around on his desk, then found what he was looking for and waved a scroll in front of me. "As with any situation like this, the best way to contain it is to stop it early, and there are always a few key players, the malcontents whose words and actions fire up the rest of the men to do things that they wouldn't normally have the inclination, the energy, or the brains to do on their own. If you had come to me earlier, I could have arranged it so that the few men listed on this scroll could have been removed over the period of a few days. The crisis would have been averted, with only the loss of a few men who weren't very good Gregarii anyway, which would have helped the 28th in the long run. It would be a case of addition by subtraction, if you will. But now, tensions are too high; the men are too much on edge, and this murder has everyone paying attention, waiting for what happens next. If these men were to disappear now, it would guarantee the thing that you're rightly afraid of will happen."

As Caesar explained the full extent of my error, I was assailed by a number of thoughts, some of them conflicting. What I remember most vividly is the shock at Caesar's matter of fact tone as he basically admitted to using murder for his own purposes, although I do not know why I felt that way. I had been marching with Caesar for a long time, and I remember other times when men, singly or in very small groups, just disappeared from around the fires. When that happened, we all shot sidelong glances at each other, touching the side of our noses and winking, since the men who disappeared had always been involved in some unrest at the time of their disappearance. However, suspecting a thing and having the architect of such events openly discuss it are two different things. Now, here he was calmly telling me that our suspicions about these men who disappeared were correct, and that he was behind them. Still, his logic could not be faulted, and I knew that he was right. I had made a grave error in judgment. The only thing that remained to be seen was whether my career would suffer irreparable damage because of it.

"Now my options are limited, Pullus. If I accept your judgment, and I must say that I think you're right, and I punish Verres in the manner called for, both by regulation and by custom, I alienate the 6th, not to mention putting you in extremely difficult circumstances. And, because you were my choice as Primus Pilus for the 6th, it would be a blow to my own *dignitas*."

Now he seemed to be heading in the direction that I had hoped for when I came to see him, and I waited for him to make the decision to suspend punishment of Verres, but that was not where he was headed. "But, if I do what I think you want me to do, and not punish Verres, then I have a problem with not just the 28th, but the 37th, because the story of what this Plautus said has undoubtedly spread throughout the army." He shook his head, clearly frustrated. "The only way that I might be able to retrieve something from this disaster rests on a question, but I'm afraid I already know the answer. Pullus," he stared at me closely, "who did you tell that you were coming to me on this matter?" My face gave him the answer that he needed, and he gave a bitter laugh. "Of course, you told everyone involved, didn't you? In fact, you probably threw it in their face, as a challenge. The great Titus Pullus couldn't appear to be afraid, could he?" The sarcasm in his tone lacerated my soul, made worse by the truth of his words. "There's also the matter of Verres' brother and the fact that he's undoubtedly bribed Verres' tent mates," my look of astonishment finally evoked a smile from Caesar, albeit a sour one. "Pullus, I'm surprised at you. Surely you know by now that I'm intimately familiar with every Centurion in my army and their backgrounds. I know a great deal about Verres Rufus." He looked directly into my eyes, conveying to me in that moment that he was aware of what Rufus had done on the causeway. "And I know that while punishing Verres might be the right thing to do, it will undoubtedly make Verres Rufus very angry, and in his position he can cause a great deal of harm. But, neither am I willing to let Verres Rufus think that I'm acting in a way because of whatever threat he may pose to the stability of the army. Here's what I'm going to do." He turned away from me so I could not read his expression. "After hearing your report, I'm sentencing Legionary Verres to be executed."

I experienced a shiver of dread, even though this was exactly what I was hoping for, but as Caesar spoke, I had been thinking. Was I pushing for Verres to be executed because I honestly believed that he was guilty of murdering Plautus? Or was I just reacting to the pressure and threats from Verres Rufus by showing that I did not fear him or any man? A few years before, I would never even have considered the question, but I had gotten to an age where I was able to view myself in a more critical light. Now that Caesar had confirmed the sentence that I expected, I was awash in doubt. Still, there was a second part to my plan, and I waited for Caesar to make further comment.

After a moment, I realized that he was finished, and he said as much. "Was there anything else, Pullus?"

I swallowed, feeling a huge lump in my throat, knowing that I should speak but was unable to do so. Instead, I dumbly shook my head, then saluted. I turned about, marching to the door.

Just as I was reaching for the latch, he called to me. "Are you so anxious to die, Pullus?"

That caught me by surprise, I can tell you.

I turned to look at him, curious and disturbed at the same time. "No, Caesar, I'm not anxious to die. Why do you ask such a question?"

"Surely you have to know that as soon as Verres is put to death, your men are going to feel that you betrayed them. We have some hard fighting yet to do, and it's highly likely that someone in your Cohorts will see an opportunity to take their vengeance. Not to mention you'll have earned the undying hatred of Verres Rufus."

I wondered if he ever got tired of being right, but I did not say anything that would betray my thoughts.

"It had occurred to me," I spoke carefully, but said nothing more.

"And what was your plan to stay alive?"

Caesar being sardonic was not a dish I cared for much.

"To be honest, I hadn't given it much thought."

"Perhaps an offering to Nemesis to stay the hand of your assassin might be a good idea." His tone was so neutral I could not tell if he was being sarcastic. After all, he had once been *flamen dialis,* so perhaps he was being serious.

"I prefer to rely on this." I tapped the hilt of my sword.

Caesar gave a great sigh, then replied, "Even you can be bested, Pullus. You don't have eyes in the back of your head, and you don't have the same bond with these men that you did with the men of the 10th. Is there anyone you trust sufficiently to stand at your back among the men of the 6th?"

I considered, then shook my head. Despite developing a friendship with Felix, I was not confident that it was strong enough that I would trust my life to him, at least in these circumstances. In the face of the enemy, without a doubt I would trust him, but against his own comrades, men he had marched with for many years longer than we had known each other, I could not be so sure.

"As difficult a circumstance as you've put me in, I can't afford to lose you, Pullus. I need you where you are, especially now. For that reason, I'm going to do nothing about Verres, and neither are you."

I opened my mouth to protest, but the words died in my mouth, such was the look he gave me.

Another thought occurred to me, and I asked, "But what about Verres Rufus? As you said, you can't have him thinking that you're sparing his brother because of his threats."

In all reality, I cared less about the damage to Caesar's prestige than to mine, but I could not very well say that to him.

At the mention of Verres Rufus, his lips compressed into a thin line, his blue eyes glittering with anger. "Don't worry about Verres Rufus," he said tightly. "I'll deal with him, in my own way."

"What am I supposed to do now?" I asked. "I'm going to go back to the 6th and maybe I won't have to watch my back, but now the men are going to think that I'm nothing but talk."

"That's your problem," he replied, looking at me the way a parent looks at a wayward child. "Think of it as your punishment for not coming to me before now. You'll just have to figure something out."

With that, the audience ended and I left headquarters, deciding to take the long way back to our sector as I tried to decide how I was going to handle the gift that Caesar had given me.

~ ~ ~ ~

We were still in a precarious position, particularly after the defeat on the Heptastadion. All the men knew it, and it was their preoccupation with our overall situation that I credit for making my announcement that Verres would not be held accountable for the murder of Plautus somewhat anticlimactic. Oh, there was a certain amount of gloating to be sure, which I endured with gritted teeth, although I was surprised that Cornuficius was not one of them. When I made the announcement to the assembled Centurions and Optios, most of the men looked relieved while a couple of them smirked triumphantly, happy to see me humbled. However, Cornuficius just regarded me thoughtfully. In fact, I may have been mistaken, but my impression was that he was not altogether pleased that Verres was not going to be punished, though I could not figure out why. Regardless, I was not in a position to question such a gift from the gods, and after a day or two, the larger events of our situation seemed to erase any difficulties that I would have encountered otherwise.

After the defeat at the Heptastadion, there was a period where things lulled into an uneasy truce between the Egyptians and the Roman forces. I cannot help thinking that if Achillas had still been alive, he would have seen this as the opportunity to continue pressing and we may have been wiped out. Ganymede was clever enough, but his inexperience in military matters was evident in a number of ways, including his lack of activity immediately after our defeat. I am thankful that he was as green as he was, because even without taking advantage of our defeat, he caused us innumerable problems. One of them became evident a few days after our defeat when Caesar was approached by a delegation of Egyptians, supposedly to talk about peace between the two forces. We never learned what prompted this move by the Egyptians. Given what happened, it is likely that Ptolemy's advisors were in contact with Ganymede and they concocted the whole thing between them. Whatever the case, the delegation claimed that they had endured enough of Ganymede and Arsinoe, and asked that Ptolemy be released and restored to his throne, making the argument that he would then promptly order his army to lay down arms to submit to Caesar. I was not present at the meeting that Caesar held with his generals to discuss the Egyptian proposal, but through Appolonius, I learned that his generals were unanimously against the idea. Caesar even admitted that he knew that the Egyptians were deceitful, untrustworthy people, yet he said that it would be politic to accede to their request. Subsequently, Caesar called Ptolemy to his presence, where from all accounts, the young king put on a performance worthy of the greatest Greek actor. He cried, tearing his fancy robes, swearing to all of his gods that he would rather die than leave Caesar's side. He claimed that Caesar had become like a father to him, and he could not bear the thought of being forced to part from his father. This display of emotion apparently moved Caesar a great deal, and he embraced the young king, promising him that they would be reunited the moment Ptolemy returned to his people and convinced them to give up making war on us. Ptolemy swore that he would do that very thing, so Caesar released him, along with Theodotus and Dioscorides, the latter having survived having his throat cut by Achillas and was now fully recovered. I do not believe a full day passed before we learned that Ptolemy, true to the faithless nature of all Egyptians, had assumed command of his army and instead of ordering them to lay down their arms, exhorted them to complete our destruction. His troops needed no prodding, and before that night fell, we were under assault at a number of different points along our lines. Not content with pressing the attack on land, Ptolemy ordered the Egyptian fleet out of the Inner Harbor and out to sea. We did not know for sure why he did so, but the most logical explanation was that he had gotten word that more relief was headed our way across the water. It also could have been a trick, which to us in the ranks seemed likely, given that we felt that Caesar had already been tricked once. Nevertheless, Caesar could not afford to take the risk that it was a ruse, immediately giving orders for our own fleet to sail in pursuit of the Egyptian fleet. I cannot fault Caesar for making this decision, but I do find fault with sending Nero as commander, instead of Hirtius or Pollio. At the very least, Caesar should have given Nero explicit instructions that he was in command in name only, allowing Euphranor, the Rhodian, who had led the four ships in the previous naval battle, to actually control the tactics of the fleet, but that was not Caesar's way with members of his own class. This meant that when our fleet closed with the Egyptians and Euphranor engaged with the enemy, he did so unsupported, because Nero did not follow Euphranor into the battle. Euphranor rammed and sunk one Egyptian vessel, yet without any support from the rest of the fleet was quickly surrounded then rammed himself, going down with the ship. The only positive was that it stopped the Egyptian fleet, which turned around and came back to Alexandria. Actually, that is not completely true; while the fleet was out, a courier ship caught up with them to let us know what the Egyptians had learned and why they had sailed. Help was on the way.

~ ~ ~ ~

Mithradates, the son of the great king Mithridates who had been an enemy of Rome for many years, was the man marching to our relief. He was bringing the 27th Legion, marching overland to the port of Ascalon, a few hundred miles east of Egypt, the 27th being ordered to march from Asia by General Domitius. Mithradates had raised a force of archers himself, with the Nabataeans sending a contingent of cavalry, but Mithradates did not believe that this force was sizable enough to complete a march through enemy territory, since he would have to reduce a number of garrisons on the way. This caused Mithradates to pause in Ascalon for several weeks, but finally he began his march again, and with this message, the courier ship was dispatched. By this time, the new year had begun; the Consuls for that year were Quintus Fufius Calenus and Publius Vatinius, Caesar's men, of course. We had been in Alexandria for almost seven months, and much had happened, not least of which being that young Cleopatra was now pregnant with Caesar's child. That kept the tongues around the fires wagging, I can tell you!

Coming with Mithradates was Antipater, a king of the Jews, or whatever they call their leader, bringing 3,000 Jewish soldiers with him. This force now made its way west, heading to our relief, composed of about 12,000 men total. Between them and us was the city and fortress of Pelusium, sitting at the eastern border of Egypt. While Mithradates could have bypassed the fort, it would have put a force in his rear; therefore, he halted his army, encircled the city, and reduced it in a day. Leaving behind a garrison to hold the city and guard the prisoners taken, Mithradates continued marching. News of his approach reached both Roman and Egyptian ears, with equally emotional but violently opposing sentiments. Immediately upon hearing this, Ptolemy ordered a scratch force of regulars composed of the remaining Gabinians and militia to march east to confront and destroy Mithradates. By this time, Mithradates had entered the Nile Delta, and while there, he was approached by a delegation of Jewish and Egyptian citizens of Memphis, the traditional home of the Pharaohs of Egypt before Alexander came and changed everything. They offered Mithradates free entrance to the city, with the sizable Jewish population also providing Antipater a large number of soldiers to bolster his forces, bringing the numbers of the Jewish contingent to about five thousand. With these reinforcements, Mithradates began marching down the Nile towards Alexandria, which ironically meant that he was marching north instead of the normal south, with the river to his left. Marching to meet him, the Egyptian commander, our old friend Dioscorides, was informed by Ptolemy that defeat of Mithradates was not crucial to success; delaying his force would be enough, because our supply situation had become extremely critical. Ptolemy's reasoning was that there was no need to waste men on an assault when starvation and the resulting weakness that came with it would do the work for him. All in all, it was not a bad plan, and one that came very close to working.

~ ~ ~ ~

I was summoned to headquarters in the afternoon one day, where I learned that there had been a battle between Mithradates and Dioscorides. Despite the Egyptians being repulsed, the defeat was not decisive enough to move the Egyptian army out of Mithradates' path. The enemy had encamped, directly blocking the line of march for our reinforcements, and now the two sides were staring at each other from behind their respective ramparts. Both Mithradates and Dioscorides sent dispatches to their respective commanding generals apprising them of the situation and it was this message that was the cause for my summons.

"Prepare your men for march, Primus Pilus."

Appolonius handed me the wax tablet with my written orders.

As I read them, Appolonius continued, "We're embarking on ships, and we're going to head east towards the Delta, but once it grows dark, we're going to turn back west to sail past Alexandria and land to the west of the city. Then we're going to march overland to link up with Mithradates. Our goal is to meet up with Mithradates without a fight. Be prepared to board in one watch."

I ran back to our area, my mind racing with all the things that needed to be done. Thankfully, the years spent with Caesar had taught me to keep the men prepared to move at a moment's notice, but it was still a daunting task. I called a quick meeting of the Centurions, giving them their orders and listening to the inevitable groans of dismay and claims that what Caesar was asking was impossible, before they ran off to their respective Centuries to get them moving. Three Cohorts of the 28th, plus the auxiliaries that came with the 37th were going to be left behind to man the defenses, but this was not going to be a surreptitious move; Caesar wanted the Egyptians to be well aware that we were leaving. The enemy had their own agenda, their courier arriving at roughly the same time as ours, bearing the same news. This meant that both sides were absorbed in the task of preparing to move out, easing the burden of maintaining vigilance against any sortie by either side. We would be marching with our full kit, including entrenching tools. Despite the short preparation time, I could see that the men were excited. After being ground down by the mind-numbing routine of what was essentially garrison duty, even with the added danger of the almost daily attacks against our lines by the Egyptians and the stress of short rations, the idea of going on the march again actually filled the men with enthusiasm. Normally they would have been complaining about the idea of a forced march, but it was a sign of their boredom that they were extremely cheerful, going about their tasks with gusto. The added incentive was the belief on the part of the men that we were nearing the end of this ordeal; with the reinforcements provided by Mithradates, we were all confident that we would crush the Egyptians, and be free to go home. Consequently, the men were finished packing and forming up almost a sixth part of a watch early, whereupon we marched down to the docks without any problem, the Egyptians being busy with their own preparations. The sun was setting, so Caesar ordered large fires built to enable the Egyptians clearly to see what we were doing. Filing on board, I was thankful that either Caesar or Appolonius had the foresight to segregate us from the 28th, since nothing good could have come of my and Cartufenus' men being crammed together in the hold of a transport for any period of time. It was dark by the time we were all fully loaded and departed the Great Harbor, heading east with every lantern on every ship blazing forth, ensuring that the Egyptians could clearly see where we were headed. Hugging the coast, the fleet headed east for perhaps two parts of a watch before the order was given to douse the lanterns and we turned about to head west, swinging out of sight of the coast when we passed Alexandria. Naturally, this made the men nervous, but the seas were calm and we made it past the city without incident, landing several miles to the west at Chersonesus shortly after dawn.

Disembarking as quickly as possible under the circumstances, we began marching immediately, with the months of relative inactivity and the heat, even now in early March making the problem of men straggling something that the Centurions had to be especially vigilant about. The knowledge that any man who dropped out would be left to the tender mercies of the Egyptians and the desert was enough to keep men from dropping out altogether. The farthest any man dropped out was the rear of the column, where there was a Nabataean cavalry contingent marching drag. Caesar set his usual cracking pace, and we covered the flat ground quickly, choking through the thick dust that soon covered us from head to foot, the sounds of the men coughing and spitting out mouthfuls of sand ranging up and down the column. My eyes were burning, the grit under my eyelids making the continuous blinking I had to do to clear my eyes an agony, and my nose was clogged, no matter how often I tried to blow it clean, yet there was no slackening of the pace. Caesar chose to forego the standard break every third of a watch, marching us for a full watch before pausing for perhaps a sixth part. The men collapsed where they halted, grabbing for their canteens to wash their mouths out, while trying to snatch a few moments of sleep. Like most veterans, they fell asleep immediately, using their packs as a pillow, the air soon filled with the sound of snoring and mumbled conversations between the few men who could not sleep. I wished that I could do the same, but I had to get a head count and find the stragglers wherever they had stopped in the column to boot them in the ass to make them catch back up. Knowing as I did that the men who fell out would simply fall out again shortly after we resumed marching with those who were recovering from wounds or had been on the sick list, I was not as strict about making them spend some of the rest break rejoining their comrades. However, there were men who were as healthy as the rest of their comrades who simply were lazy. After all these years, these men were the best of the malingerers, the smartest of that portion of a Legion composed of men whose sole purpose in life is to do as little as possible and not get caught. Their slower, dumber, and less crafty counterparts had long since been winnowed out; by either being too slow in battle or deserting, or in some cases, being caught in a serious enough crime to be executed. What was left were the cream of the crop of the do-nothings; the shirkers and tricksters who could conjure their way onto a sick list, or mysteriously disappear when a work party was called. These were the men that I went looking for, kicking them to their feet, shoving them up the column. Resuming the march, we plodded across the barren terrain, the lake that rings the southern side of Alexandria barely visible on the horizon to our left. Once night fell, we made camp in the usual manner, although cutting turf blocks in the sandy soil was quite a challenge, while the men barely had the energy to chew what little rations we brought with us before retiring in their tents, not spending any time around their fire. I was as exhausted as the men, as were the rest of the Centurions, and it was times like these that I was thankful to lead such a veteran group of men, for they made my job much easier.

Morning came and Caesar had us only pull up our stakes, not tearing the rampart down or filling in the ditch, as is standard practice, preferring to spend the time marching instead. Before we had been marching a third of a watch, we were back to choking and spitting. Thankfully, it was relatively short-lived once we came into the Nile valley. It is a valley in name only; it is more like a magic line seemingly drawn by the gods, where we crested a very low rise, seeing spread before us lush green fields, laid out in geometric patterns. The stalks of wheat were just beginning to shoot up, and there were men in the fields, pulling weeds or spreading manure, doing the things that farmers have been doing since only the gods know when. I remember thinking as we marched past the farmers who were standing to watch us: how many different fields and how many different men had I marched by, following Caesar? The men were different, at least from the Gauls, although they were similarly dark like some of the Lusitani and Gallaeci farmers, yet the jobs are essentially the same. If I had stayed on the farm, I would have been doing much the same thing as these men, growing old before my time from the back-breaking work, the worry about rain, insects, floods and droughts, all of it wearing me down until I was bent and broken, praying to the gods to take me away. I shuddered as we passed; just thinking about what could have been my fate made me shiver, and I offered a prayer to Fortuna in thanks for blessing me with the idea of being in the Legions. As hard a life as it could be, and as boring and dangerous, there was still no other life I would have chosen for myself.

~ ~ ~ ~

Continuing our march upriver, we stayed about a mile from the banks, expecting to see Ptolemy's fleet once we got nearer to Mithradates. The camp of Dioscorides was on the other side of the river, according to our intelligence reports, along with the camp of Mithradates, although it was approximately eight or nine miles further south. We were sure that Ptolemy would beat us, since he was coming by ship, which would move day and night. Yet with the day wearing on, we saw no sight of his fleet anywhere. Finally, a halt was called and we made camp, all of us knowing that the next day would bring us to Mithradates, and to what we hoped was a decisive battle within the next day or two. I held a surprise inspection, pleased to see that the men's gear was as ready as could be expected under the circumstances. Despite leaving the sand behind, it seemed like a great deal of it had come with us, getting into everything and being extremely hard to clean out. The worst was with our armor, the grains of sand sticking to the light coating of oil that we apply to keep the links free of rust and as supple as we can make it. Another problem that had to be given attention were our scabbards, the mouth getting clogged with sand, making it hard to withdraw the blade. As you can imagine, this is not a good thing. However, the men had attended to these matters, and I was pleased, though of course, I did not show it, but they knew. The night passed uneventfully, and we had no trouble rousing the men the next morning, the anticipation of the coming day ensuring that they were awake well before the *bucina* sounded. Shortly after dawn, we were on the march again. Barely a third of a watch into the march, we began running into enemy pickets, our cavalry running them down before they could give the alarm. There was no way to hide our presence for long, but every moment counted, so Caesar put us into the formation we used when enemy contact was expected, with an *ala* of cavalry out front and Centuries marching on either flank a half-mile away from the main column. Shortly before midday, a mounted scout watching the river came galloping to Caesar. The word immediately was passed that we had spotted the enemy camp, yet somehow we marched past it without incident. By this point, we were only a full watch's march away from the camp of Mithradates and we ran into his scouts at roughly the same time that we were marching past the Egyptian camp. One puzzling thing was the absence of the Egyptian fleet and Ptolemy, along with his reinforcements. They had left at roughly the same time that we had and did not have as far to go. Coming by ship, they should have been there before us, but they were not.

~ ~ ~ ~

There was a reunion of sorts, at least that was the feeling when we joined with Mithradates. It was somewhat understandable with the men of the 28th who had marched with us, seeing the 27th, since they were sister Legions and the men came from the same region. I found the Jews an interesting lot; their arms and armor a motley collection, no two men seeming to wear the same thing, some with little better than a leather jerkin. However, their weapons seemed to be well cared for, and they had a tough look about them that marked them as good fighting men. They certainly were talkative, which I did not understand because they kept jabbering at us in their tongue as if we would suddenly learn to speak it. No matter, it was still good to see friendly faces, even if they spoke gibberish. Mithradates was a sight to behold; I had never seen an Eastern satrap, I believe they are called. His hair was black as a crow's wing, arranged in curled ringlets that had so much of an oily substance applied to it that his hair gleamed in the sun like polished ebony. He had a black beard, neatly trimmed and treated with the same substance as his hair, while his eyes were lined with kohl, not in as dramatic a fashion as the Egyptians, but the effect was striking nonetheless. He was well built, not as tall as I was, but taller than most of the men around him, the richly brocaded gown he wore not hiding the width of his shoulders. Mithradates had the kind of commanding presence that comes with being born into a royal family, and I could not help noticing the similarities in mannerisms between him and Caesar. I suppose that our patrician class is as close to royalty as we Romans will allow, although we would never utter such ideas aloud, if we do not want to be torn apart by an angry mob.

The camp that Mithradates had erected was almost identical to a Roman camp, so it did not take us long to find the appropriate section to erect our tents and to get settled in, while Caesar and Mithradates conferred. In a matter of a watch, I was summoned to the *Praetorium* to attend a briefing, where we received our orders. It took a bit longer than normal, since some of the commanders of the various contingents did not speak our tongue and someone had to translate. Looking around, I began to worry a bit; never before had Caesar commanded such a varied assortment of men. There were easily a half-dozen different tongues being spoken inside the large tent, and I could not help wondering what would happen in the heat of battle, when orders had to be instantly given and instantly obeyed, without the slightest hesitation.

"Quite a scene, isn't it?"

I was startled from my reverie, so absorbed in my own thoughts that I was unaware of the man approaching to stand next to me. I looked over to see that it was one of the Jews, a man of average height and build, with a bushy beard of ginger-colored hair and piercing brown eyes that regarded me with open amusement. He was clad in a leather jerkin that had metal plates sown on, each one overlapping the other, while on his head he wore a simple leather cap, not dissimilar to our helmet liner. His Latin was heavily accented but understandable and his manner was friendly.

"It is that. I was just wondering how this was all going to work when it's time to face the Egyptians."

"I was wondering the same thing myself. I guess we will just have to see." He offered his hand in the Roman manner, saying, "Joseph ben-Judah. I am the commander of the forces from Memphis. We joined Mithradates and Antipater a few days ago."

"Titus Pullus, Primus Pilus of the 6th Legion. Or," I amended, "the two Cohorts that are with Caesar."

We shook hands, then stood in silence for a moment, watching the scene as men argued back and forth, trying to translate their individual orders being given by one of Caesar's staff into their own language. Hands were waving about, and, as inevitably happens when people are having a hard time understanding each other, voices started to raise in volume as frustration grew.

"How long do you think this will take?" Joseph broke the silence between us. I shrugged.

"Who knows? I just hope that everything is straightened out here and there's no confusion when we meet the Egyptians. I mean, any more than normal," I added.

"Well, I know what we are supposed to do. We are on the left wing as part of the allied forces. I suppose you are on the right?"

I nodded, only partly engaged in the conversation. The more I was watching, the more disturbed I was feeling about the upcoming battle. Realizing that standing here I could not do anything to help improve communications, I turned to Joseph and wished him well.

"If I do not see you before we fight, may your gods protect you," I said, and I was both surprised and slightly irritated to see his mouth lift at the corner in obvious amusement.

"There is only one god, Roman," he laughed. "But I thank you and I return your wishes back to you."

I left the tent completely bemused by both what I had seen and what Joseph had just said to me. One god? What did he mean by that? I wondered, and I resolved that I would find out more about these Jews whenever I had some spare time. In the meantime, I had to get my men prepared for what hopefully would be the last battle with the forces of Ptolemy.

Marching out of the camp at dawn, we headed south towards Ptolemy, leaving behind perhaps a Cohort-sized guard contingent. Caesar put us in the vanguard, with a cavalry screen of course, the men moving out in good spirits, all signs of fatigue gone from their stride. The sun made our highly polished helmets appear as if they were on fire, and soon enough our heads felt like they were when the heat started to broil our brains. In accordance with his normal practice, Caesar had ordered us to wear full parade gear, with all plumes and decorations, making for an impressive sight as we tramped along. We marched perhaps a third of a watch before we came across our first obstacle, a substantial one at that. A tributary of the Nile was cutting directly across our path, running roughly east and west. Not particularly wide, it was deep; the scouts reported that their horses could not touch bottom, and the sides were unusually steep. That meant we would have to construct a bridge, already difficult enough because of a scarcity of timber, but compounding the problem was that Dioscorides beat us to the spot. Arrayed on the far bank was a sizable force of cavalry, along with what looked like skirmishers. Faced with this obstacle, we stopped, remaining out of range while waiting for Caesar to make his way to us, and during the pause, I sent two Centuries out to look for trees of a suitable size to use for bridging material. Caesar arrived, and I gave my report. Surveying the situation, he called for his Germans to range farther east to look for a ford, giving them orders to cross if they found one then immediately attack the enemy's left flank. After about two parts of a watch, during which the Centuries returned with the location of an orchard that held trees of sufficient size to be used to construct a bridge, our cavalry came thundering down onto the enemy's flank, making short work of them and scattering the men to the four winds. Immediately setting to work, the Germans stayed on the other side of the river to keep the Egyptians away from us while we built the bridge. It was finished quickly, but the heat took a toll, and when we started out again, it was not with the same spring in the step as when we had started.

Marching for another two parts of a watch, our scouts once more came galloping back to report that the enemy camp was close, and further it was announced that finally Ptolemy and his fleet were present. Consequently, we halted again to wait for Caesar to decide what we were to do. Deeming it unwise to march to the attack after all the work we had done, we were ordered to make camp, giving us time to rest and to scout the enemy works. Ptolemy, or more likely one of his Gabinian commanders, had chosen the site for their camp well, locating it close to the river, on a small rise, with the northern approach blocked by a steep bluff with an area of swampy ground to the south. There was a village perhaps a half mile from the camp that the Egyptians linked to the camp by a wall that covered access from within. The only practicable approach was from the east, where the ground gently sloped up to the walls of the Egyptian camp. Additionally, the village was situated in such a place that it would need to be reduced first before we assaulted the camp, or we would have an enemy force in our rear. Accordingly, these were the orders that we received that put us immediately to work building assault ladders and checking the artillery to make sure it had not been damaged during the march. We would form up for the assault at first light, Caesar making it clear that he intended to end this once and for all tomorrow. The mood around the fires that night was one of grim determination, the men talking in low tones about what they planned on doing to the Egyptians the next day. To a man, we had our fill of these people and this place, considering the Egyptians to be one of the most faithless, devious, and scheming people we had ever met. Perhaps not surprisingly, it was accepted as fact that the only reason we were unable to break out of Alexandria to crush the Egyptians was due to a combination of numbers and their refusal to fight in a manner that we considered worthy.

After making the rounds, I retired to my tent to go through my own pre-battle ritual, sharpening the blades of my sword and dagger, running through all the things I needed to remember. No matter how many times we lined up for battle, I always worried that I would forget my duties in the heat of the fight, therefore I would go through the battle and how it would begin over and over in my mind. Once the *cornu* sounded the first call, all the written orders and the briefings disappeared like smoke before a strong wind, but there was much to do and remember in those moments before that happened, so I had found it useful to think about things as if I were on the battlefield at that moment. I do not know why, but I also found it relaxing to do so; perhaps it was the familiarity of the routine, or because it was one of the few things that I had any control over. Either way I found it comforting and it helped pass the time before I laid down to try to get some sleep.

~ ~ ~ ~

The next morning we were up well before dawn, and as I expected, during the morning briefing Caesar told me that the 6th would be the lead assault element attacking the village. Depending on how things went, we would continue our attack on the camp in the lead as well, unless we took heavy casualties, something that I did not want to think about. Caesar gave his usual pre-battle speech, firing the men's enthusiasm, though it needed little enough stoking, then we marched out of camp, dispensing with shaking out into a *triplex acies*, using a double column three Centuries across, with the 7th Cohort on the left and the 10th Cohort on the right. The sky was just beginning to lighten as we marched closer to the village, the silhouettes of the men lining the ramparts barely visible. When we were just out of missile range, I gave the order to form *testudo*, the men moving smoothly, with no wasted motion. Moving to the side of one of the leading Centuries as they performed the maneuver, I watched the ramparts for the first volley of arrows and slingshot, cursing the sun that seemed to be taking its time in peeking over the horizon. Because the only practical approach was from the east, we would have the advantage of the sun shining in the eyes of the enemy, but the sun still had not fully risen, meaning I had to strain my eyes to watch for movement on the wall. We only had a second of warning as I saw men suddenly point their bows skyward, the movement of their arms drawing the bowstring giving me the sign that they were about to fire.

"Jupiter Optimus Maximus, protect this Legion, soldiers all."

Someone shouted this, a lot of the men mumbling their own prayers, just as the air filled with streaking black slivers, going up, up, up before turning point down to begin falling towards us. Instinctively I hunched my shoulders, something I always did, though I do not know why, since it would be of no help if I was indeed struck. There was a whistling sound, followed immediately by a sound like a number of carpenters striking a blow against a block of wood at about the same time. Unfortunately, some of the arrows did not strike only shields, and I heard a few muffled screams and groans, where a man had gotten careless, moving his shield too far to one side or another, or had dropped it a bit too much to relieve the ache in his arm. Now they, or even worse, one of their comrades had paid the price for their carelessness. I stopped briefly as the men continued marching forward, looking behind the lead *testudo*s to assess the damage, relieved to see only four or five men wounded badly enough that they could not continue, with none of them looking mortally wounded. Trotting back to the lead Century just as another volley was fired at us, an arrow narrowly missed me, the wind softly slapping my cheek as it passed. I was pleased to see that after the first arrows had been fired that the men were more alert, nobody falling to the ground. More enemy on the walls were moving, their arms whipping above their heads, now clearly visible, the sun finally making its appearance. While the eye can somewhat track an arrow, slingshot is much harder to spot and I felt particularly vulnerable, cursing myself for forgetting to grab one of the wounded men's shields. The air was filled with what sounded like very angry bees buzzing, the sound reminding me how much I hated slingers. Shot slammed into shields, making a similar but slightly different sound than the arrows, a sharper crack than a thud, and it quickly drowned out all other noise, but still, we continued forward. Stopping to check the casualty situation once again, I was heartened to see that our losses were still light. There was one dead man from the Third Century, a neat round hole in his forehead from where he had evidently decided to drop his shield to risk a peek, and it was his that I took since he no longer needed it. Closing the distance and getting into javelin range, I ordered the formation opened, timing the command so that most of the enemy had just released their arrows or slings in order to give us a moment where the men could drop their shields and move without being skewered. The slight pause was all we needed, the men in the rear ranks who did not carry ladders drawing their arms back, javelins in hand, waiting for a target. Without being told, the men carrying the ladders moved forward, one man sitting with his back to the wall to brace it with the other men lifting it into place. Each Century had four ladders and I pushed my way to the nearest one, watching the other Centuries to make sure that all ladders were in place. Now the men in the rear were flinging their javelins as a number of Egyptians risked exposing themselves in order to try to push the ladder nearest them back down. I heard screams at the top of the wall of men being hit, a couple of them tumbling down to land at the feet of our men, who quickly finished those that were not dead already. Turning to the *cornicen,* I gave the order to sound the advance, then drew my sword and mounted the ladder, saying something to the men behind me, though I do not remember what it was. Then I began ascending the ladder, shield above my head. I was the first over the walls of the town, and for that honor, I was decorated by Caesar, earning the *corona muralis*, but that was in a future I had no thought for at that moment.

~ ~ ~ ~

It took a matter of just a few moments to clear the wall, and not much longer to sweep through the village, killing everyone we found. Truthfully, the Egyptians did not put up that much of a fight, I suppose because they knew they had a fallback position in the camp. Over the rear wall of the village and through the rear gate most of the defenders of the village now went, streaming back towards the camp. Wanting to keep up the pressure, we ran after the Egyptians, thrusting our blades into the backs of those who were too slow. Compounding the confusion were the villagers themselves. They panicked at the sight of Romans sacking their village, and they joined the soldiers who tried to get into their camp. Despite allowing in the first few hundred Egyptian soldiers , the men at the gates saw us in hot pursuit and shut them quickly, leaving the villagers to look out for themselves. The assault had reached a point where the men's bloodlust was fully aroused, meaning that I and the rest of the Centurions would have had our hands full trying to keep them from putting the civilians to the sword, but the truth is I was not disposed to stop them. The slaughter was total, the only thing stopping us being the men on the walls of the camp who hurled their javelins down at those of us who got carried away in their pursuit and got too close. I lost a couple of men before I ordered the recall sounded, setting the *signifer* at a spot out of range of the enemy javelins. The detachments of men I sent back to retrieve the ladders had yet to join us, and I could see that Caesar was getting impatient.

Now that we had secured the village, we could approach the camp from all four sides, prompting Caesar to give an order that, when I heard it made me look at him carefully. He ordered three Centuries of the 37th to circle around to the side of the camp that paralleled the river, there being a narrow strip of land between the wall and the riverbank. The reason I was caught by surprise was twofold; there was a large contingent of archers and slingers that had remained onboard the ships of the Egyptian fleet, meaning there would be a threat to the rear of the men of the 37th when they assaulted the camp. The other surprise was that Caesar had picked the Century of Verres Rufus to be one of them, and I wondered if this was an accident, but even if I were so inclined, I would never bring it up with Caesar. There was nothing in Caesar's demeanor that would lead me to believe that this was anything other than a simple command decision, yet somehow I knew there was more to it. However, it was not something I could dwell on, since I had my own orders. Finally, the ladders arrived so I ordered the men forward, again forming *testudo* with them carried inside. Ptolemy's best men were facing us on this wall and it appeared that he had deployed more than half his force on just this side of the enemy camp. Among them were archers and javelineers, so that again we were assailed by missiles flying thick and fast, creating an unholy racket. Fairly quickly, the lead *testudo* looked like a porcupine, the shafts of arrows and javelins protruding in almost every man's shield. More than a dozen arrows and a couple of javelins struck my own shield, and it quickly became clear that we could not mount an assault unless we did something about the missile troops. Once we got within range, I gave the command to launch javelins again, having rotated the Centuries so the men who had supported the attack on the village were now the assault element. A shower of our own javelins streaked upwards, some of them striking the wooden stakes of the rampart but many of them burying themselves in flesh. It was still not enough; the volume of fire diminished, just not enough for us to place the ladders, so I ordered another volley, waiting for a lull in the enemy fire. A second round of javelins, and the men of the leading Centuries were now out, but the enemy fire was still too heavy.

Now I was faced with a choice, since it was clear that we were at a standoff with the men on the wall, and neither alternative was palatable. In order to break the stalemate, either we could march back out of range, or we could press hard up against the wall of the camp, making it extremely difficult for them to fire down at us without exposing themselves. The problem with the second choice was that our men were basically out of javelins, so we had no missiles of our own to stop the Egyptians when they poked their heads out to fire at us. As far as I could see, we had no choice but to withdraw. There was a fair amount of cursing when I gave the order, but the men began marching backward, those in the ranks closest to the camp completely relying on their comrades to warn them of any obstacles in their path, meaning the bodies of both friend and foe. Moving backwards as well, my shield was held high while I tried to avoid tripping as the missiles flew about me and the rest of the men. An arrow, shot at a slightly flatter angle, hit the ground a few feet in front of me but instead of sticking into the earth, the missile bounced off of it, hitting me a glancing blow in the calf, the point of the arrow gouging a chunk of flesh out. Despite myself, I let out a roaring curse, although at first it did not hurt. Yet when I took the next step, my leg buckled and I felt myself falling backwards, so I tried to tuck as much of my body behind my shield as I could before I hit the ground, the impact knocking the wind out of me. For a moment I could not move, during which time I felt the impact of what seemed to be a dozen arrows thudding into my shield, the points poking through an inch or more as I held it up. If I did not get up, I was a dead man, except my leg had started to throb and I could feel the wetness of the blood running down my leg, already sticking out from under the edge of my shield as it was. Unlike most of the men, I could not curl myself up into a small enough of a shape for the shield to cover my entire body, and I could feel arrows striking the ground around my feet. If I took a direct hit in the leg, I would not be getting back up at all, so despite the pain I forced myself to climb back on my feet, remembering to keep my shield held up in front of me, pulling myself first to my knees before staggering upright. The *testudo* I was next to had continued moving backwards so I was now all alone, a tempting target for every archer on the wall. The hammering sound of missiles striking my shield was almost continuous, yet I managed to stay on my feet to keep limping backwards. Once I finally got out of range, I was panting with exertion and feeling lightheaded from the wound, which I bound up with my neckerchief. The rest of the men were not much better; the *testudo* is one of the most exhausting formations to perform properly, and we had just marched up to the walls and back again. They stood there, collectively trembling like a dog trying to pass a large bone, some with hands on knees and gasping for air, others shaking their arms, trying to get the circulation back in them.

Caesar was standing nearby, his disappointment plainly written on his face. For a moment, I considered ordering the men to form back up and try again. However, I was ambitious, but not sufficiently so to march men who were already exhausted back into that maelstrom of missile fire. Fortunately, Caesar did not order me to do so, instead calling for Cartufenus to come to him. He issued Cartufenus an order, the Primus

Pilus immediately running off to execute whatever he had been told to do. I could not tell what was happening on the far side of the camp against the river, but I assumed since none of the men manning the front wall appeared to be leaving the parapet, no breach had been executed. Standing there waiting, the Egyptians on the front wall jeered at us, greatly angering the men, who called back to them with their own insults, most of them having to do with the Egyptians' mothers. I saw Cartufenus leading three of his Cohorts towards the far side of the camp, the side where the bluff overlooked the wall. This was the most protected side of the Egyptian position, and normally would not have been the choice for an assault, but we were not making any progress on the front wall, nor obviously on the back wall either. The auxiliary troops had joined us, the Jews standing in what could only charitably be called a formation, where they stood banging on their shields, calling for Caesar to release them to try their luck on the wall. I could tell Caesar refused them by the animated way that the commander of the Jewish forces waved his arms about as he stood before Caesar, and I marveled at the impunity of the man to behave in such a manner, yet Caesar did not seem to mind.

Turning my attention back to my own men, I called for the Centurions to make a head count so I could get a proper butcher's bill. To pass the time while I waited, I counted the number of arrows and javelins protruding from my shield, which had been rendered useless. I stopped counting at 30, when I was given the tally. Our losses were heavy; thankfully there were few dead so far, although I did not know the condition of the wounded, but my experience told me that as much as a tenth of the wounded would go on to die of their wounds, or to be so badly injured they would be dismissed from the Legion. The ground in front of the camps was covered with bodies, most of them Egyptian, either soldier or civilian, but there were many Romans lying there as well. Most of the wounded had been pulled off the field, except for the men who fell too close to the walls, and they were still there, most of them pulling their bodies under their shield like I had while they waited for rescue. I knew that for some of them it might be too late, if they were unable to stop the bleeding or if the missile pierced a vital organ. It all depended on something happening, and happening soon. As I looked at the men, it was clear they had physically recovered from their exertions earlier; what I did not know was how deeply they had tapped into their reserves. I pondered whether I should approach Caesar to volunteer the 6th to try again, but thankfully, I did not need to, hearing a great shout come from the walls, and they were clearly cries of alarm.

~ ~ ~ ~

Cartufenus and his three Cohorts had scaled the bluff overlooking the rear of the camp. Then, by tying ladders together, they created a number of bridges from the bluff to the wall. If the wall had been defended, they would have had no chance, yet the gods were with us. Most of the men posted on that wall deserted their posts to go join the fighting on the river side or the front wall. Cartufenus led his men across the makeshift bridges, quickly overwhelming the few men who had remained at their posts before descending into the camp, killing everyone they found. The resulting chaos triggered the cries of alarm that we had heard and Caesar did not hesitate. Turning to the Jewish commander, he gave the orders that he had been pleading for a few moments earlier, and they wasted no time either. With a great roar, the Jews rushed towards the wall, carrying their own ladders, while Caesar turned to his *cornicen*, ordering him to sound the advance for the Romans.

"All right, let's not let those Jewish bastards have all the fun," I yelled, giving the command to move at the double time, with the men immediately responding to go running after the Jews, who had already reached the wall and were flinging ladders up.

The volume of fire from the enemy on the wall had dropped drastically, only a few arrows and javelins slicing into our allied troops. Men fell, but not enough to stop the tide of Jews swarming up the ladders. However, I could not spend any more time paying attention to them, having reached the wall ourselves. This time the ladders went up with no problems and I began climbing, carrying a fresh shield that was not riddled with holes, not even noticing my leg at that moment. Vaulting over onto the parapet, I was ready to strike, but there was nobody left in our area, and I looked down into the camp to see that the defenders in our sector had decided to flee, heading for the opposite side, towards the gate that led to the river and the fleet anchored there. Of course, there was a force of Romans between them and the safety of the ships, but I suppose that panic had set in and they were not thinking clearly. The Jews were not so lucky; the Egyptians in their section of the wall were still putting up a fierce fight, though the Jews were getting the better of it and I saw that the wall would be cleared in short order. Sending Clemens' Century down the parapet to slam into the side of the Egyptians fighting the Jews, I also sent Felix to follow the parapet around to the side opposite the bluff to cut off the retreat of as many of the enemy as we could. I was not about to let men escape that we could catch and kill; I was as sick of this war as anyone, wanting to go home just as much. By this point, my leg started throbbing, but I could not tell if it was from the wound or from the makeshift bandage being too tight, so I had to descend the ladder carefully. Some of the more aggressive of the men leapt down into the camp and were now running down the streets in pursuit of the Egyptians, while others began looting the nearest tents, something that I had to stop immediately.

"There'll be enough time for that later!"

I roared this at the top of my lungs as I hobbled about, grabbing men to push them towards their standards, wanting the rest of the men formed up to sweep the camp and to push the enemy into where I hoped Clemens would be waiting. Unfortunately, it took longer than it should have, so I was in a foul mood by the time we got started. It took several moments to get the men formed on their standards, which may not seem like much, but it was giving too many Egyptians the opportunity to escape. I heard someone shout my name and turned to see Felix and his Century come pounding towards us. The wall was cleared, and the Jews now swarmed into their section of the camp. Shouts and screams of men fighting and dying filled the air, making it hard to be heard, but somehow we began marching down the streets. Each Centurion issued orders for a section of men to do a quick search of every tent that we passed to make sure we left nobody in our rear, and a number of the enemy were killed in this manner, hiding underneath their bunks. I smelled smoke, cursing the fool who had indulged in that particular passion. It should not surprise you to know that just like there are men who live for the time when they are allowed to rape with impunity, there are some men whose passion is to see things go up in flames, and they are always quick to fire whatever is at hand and is flammable. Now we had to worry about the fire getting out of control, but more of a worry was the smoke, because if it got bad enough it could obscure our vision. The streets were littered with bodies as the men marched through, where we would come upon small pockets of men who for whatever reason decided to quit running to make a stand, these holdouts being cut down as quickly as we could do it. By listening to the sounds of battle, we could tell us that there was a real fight going on in the middle of the camp, close to the gate leading to the river. Accordingly, I had Fuscus take his Cohort heading in that direction, with the 7th continuing to push forward to the rear corner of the camp. My plan was to herd as many of the enemy as we could into the corner of the camp, where there was no gate, in the area where the swamp would bog down any men who leaped from the walls. Block by block we continued forward, while I struggled to keep up, let alone lead from the front. I realized that I could no longer feel my foot; I had indeed bound my neckerchief too tightly, but I was afraid that if I loosened it the bleeding would start again, so I limped along, wondering if I was doing permanent damage to my foot. The smoke was getting thicker, coming from the area where the Jews were clearing the camp, and I could finally see flames rising up as a number of tents caught fire.

"Stupid bastards, I bet they didn't bother to clean those tents out before they set them on fire. Probably a pretty bit of loot going up in smoke."

I do not know who said it, but I heard a chorus of agreement, the men looking regretfully at the sight.

"Never mind what they're doing, we have our own job to do," Valens snapped, shoving one of the men who had stopped to gawk back into formation.

Now just two blocks away from the corner of the camp, the Egyptians we had pursued were jamming together, clawing and knocking each other down in their panic. A few, a very few turned to fight, and these we ground into the dust, their bodies piling up in bloody heaps. I did not participate in the carnage since I was barely able to walk, but the men needed no leadership in this most basic task of slaughtering a virtually helpless enemy. After the few who put up a fight were cut down, their comrades began throwing themselves at our feet, begging for mercy, but there was none to be had for the next several moments, the men continuing to hack and thrust their way through the mass of packed bodies. I should have called them off, but too much had happened; we had suffered too much at the hands of these people, so I let them kill every last man who stood or groveled before us. Once they were through, my men stood, shaking with exhaustion, most of them almost up to their knees in bodies, some still twitching. After the cacophony of battle, with men shouting their battle cries or screaming with pain from a mortal wound, all punctuated by the sound of metal clashing on metal, the aftermath is always almost eerily quiet, the only sound now the panting of the victors and the moans of the dying. Ordering a couple sections of men to finish off any Egyptians still living, they walked around the piles, pulling bodies to one side to get to men who still showed signs of life. With them going about that business, I hobbled over to the wall to look back toward the center of the camp to see what was happening. The Jews had advanced through, but had obviously run into stiffer opposition, as what looked like Ptolemy's royal guard formed square around the rear gate. They were being assailed on two sides, by the Jews from the front and the 28th on their left flank, all while behind them a mob of men were pushing their way through the rear gate itself, intent on trying to escape. There was no sign of Fuscus and the 10th, so I decided to put more pressure on the Egyptians, ordering the 7th to reform facing the right flank of the enemy, then marched them to within a few paces before giving the order to charge. The leading Centuries slammed into the Nubians, whose formation buckled under the added strain, triggering what had been a mob on the edge of panic into full-blown hysteria, with men abandoning their attempts to push through the gate and instead beginning to claw their way up the wall, intent on nothing but escape. In an instant the wall was swarming with men, the first of them jumping over the parapet and down onto the other side, where presumably the three Centuries of the 37th were waiting. Even so, when the men still on the ground saw their comrades were successful, at least in escaping the immediate danger, they followed suit. Immediately, the wall disappeared from view, covered in scrambling, desperate men. Meanwhile, the Nubians were fighting with the desperate courage of men who are doomed and want nothing more than to take as many of their enemy with them as they can, making them oblivious to what was happening behind them. When the wall collapsed, it happened abruptly, the piled turf suddenly tumbling outwards in a huge cloud of dirt and debris. The Nubians, no matter how disciplined they were, could not avoid being distracted by the commotion behind them, and almost to a man they turned to see what had happened, spelling their own destruction.

~ ~ ~ ~

With that last disaster, it was over; all that was left to do was to turn the men loose to looting the camp, except we had to send men to fight the fire that the Jews had started first. Fortunately, it did not take long to put out, being confined to a relatively small section of the camp. Soon after, the men were busy grabbing everything they thought held any value, whether it really did or not, and I finally took the opportunity to sit down, grabbing a stool from a tent, dragging it out into the street to keep a partial eye on things. Only then did I dare to loosen the bandage and as I feared, the bleeding started again, not to mention the excruciating pain, once feeling returned to my foot. I summoned a *medici*, telling him to bandage it properly, but he took one look at it then informed me that the best he could do was a temporary bandage and that I needed to have it stitched up. Every few moments there would be a commotion in one part of the camp or another when men found an Egyptian who had escaped the first cursory search and was summarily dispatched. Once my leg was bound back up, I stood, intent on finding Caesar and the command group to receive orders, but I only went a few steps before I realized that I could not go much farther without some sort of help. Hopping over to a tent, I yanked down one of the tent poles, cut some leather to make some binding material, and with another short piece of wood, fashioned a crutch that allowed me to move more easily. I was not happy about the idea of hobbling up to Caesar, but it could not be helped, and I navigated my way to the Porta Decumana, looking for his standard. The carnage around the back gate was massive, the ruins of the wall studded with body parts protruding from it where men were crushed. Finally, spotting Caesar's standard outside the gate, I made my way towards it, almost tripping and falling several times. Passing through the ruins of the gateway, I got my first glimpse of what turned out to be the end chapter not only of the Alexandrian war, but of Ptolemy XIII himself. A number of the ships in the river were capsized and there were hundreds, if not thousands, of bodies floating in the water. One of the capsized craft was larger than the rest, but at the time, I gave it no more than a passing glance as I hobbled up to Caesar, who looked at me in surprise and with not a little concern.

"*Salve,* Pullus. What happened to you? Are you all right?"

I grimaced. "A lucky shot, Caesar, it took a chunk of meat out of my calf, but I'm fine."

He laughed. "You don't look fine, but I'll take your word for it."

"What are your orders, Caesar?" I did not want to appear rude, but neither did I want him to think I was weak.

He shook his head. "None for now. Let the men enjoy themselves tearing the camp apart."

"Will we be going after Ptolemy?"

He looked at me in some surprise before pointing out to the large ship I had barely noticed before. "There's no need, Pullus. Ptolemy was on that barge and the men fleeing from the camp swam out and in their panic pulled the barge over. Ptolemy is at the bottom of the river. At least, that's what it appears at this moment and we've fished everyone out of the river that was still alive and none of them are Ptolemy. And some of the survivors reported that they saw him go under." He gave a tight smile, but there was a hint of sadness. "Apparently his ceremonial armor wasn't conducive to floating."

I said nothing for a moment, taking in what he said, trying to understand that it was indeed all over. A thought struck me and once again, I blurted it out without thinking, except this time I will blame the blood loss for loosening my tongue.

"Appropriate, I guess."

Caesar looked at me sharply, then asked, "Appropriate? How so?"

"What happened to Ptolemy is the same thing that happened to us at the Heptastadion. I guess Nemesis decided to balance the scales."

The instant I said it, I realized I should not have. Caesar's face flushed, his lips tightening into a thin line, the sign that he was trying to control his temper.

Then he took a breath, exhaled it, and nodded. "Yes, perhaps you're right," he said slowly. He looked me in the eye as he said, "But that's not something I would have you repeating, Pullus."

I knew a warning when I heard it, so I emphatically agreed that such words would never pass my lips again. And they did not, until I uttered them to Diocles just now. Caesar dismissed me, telling me that there would be a meeting of the command group at the beginning of second watch, which is shortly after sundown. I hobbled off, wishing that I could lie down, but knowing that I had to keep a tight rein on the men to ensure they stayed in their assigned area. Of course, Ptolemy's tent was marked for Caesar, but Ptolemy had a lot of retainers who traveled with him, meaning there were rich pickings in the camp to be had by the men, of which I got a cut, of course. The responsibilities of a Centurion in Caesar's army were many and never-ending, yet I cannot lie and say that there were not many benefits. Reaching the Centurionate meant that if I did not gamble or drink my money away, I would retire a wealthy man, provided I managed to live long enough. Few of us did, but that was something I refused to think about very often, preferring to take each day as it came, much like I put one foot in front of the other on a long, difficult march. If I had stopped to think about the number of Centurions who died before they managed to reach retirement age, I might as well have fallen on my sword right then. Limping back to the stool that I had been sitting on, I dropped heavily upon it, sending a runner to find Fuscus, whose Cohort I had still not seen nor had any report from about what had happened. Men were dragging larger pieces of loot into the street, marking them with their initials, or their particular mark if they could not make their letters, with the Centurions and Optios marking down a description of the piece and who it belonged to on a wax tablet. In other words, it was the normal scene after the taking of a camp or town by the Legions of Rome. Finally, I heard my name called, looking up to see Fuscus approaching me, and I could tell by his posture and his expression that he was feeling guilty. Watching him march to me, I said nothing, instead waiting for Fuscus to give me a salute, which I returned. I waited for him to finish before I spoke, wanting to see if there was anything he wanted to say, but he stood there looking over my head, something I immediately recognized as a bad sign.

"Decimus Pilus Prior Fuscus," I made sure to use his full rank, "what is your report? I expected to see you pushing through the center of the camp and fall onto the right flank of the enemy, but instead I had to order the 7th to do so, after they had already fought their way to the corner of the camp. What happened?"

He stood for several heartbeats, saying nothing and I could see by his face that he was struggling to form the words.

Finally, he said, "We saw that the Jews had matters well in hand. They were pushing the enemy back easily, so the men began searching the tents."

I felt my face begin to flush. Seeing my expression, he hastened to add, "To make sure that nobody could surprise us by falling on our rear after we passed."

"Really?" I said in mock surprise. "That's interesting. We did the same thing, but the 7th managed to carry out their orders without delay."

His face colored, and he protested, but I could see that it was half-hearted.

I held up my hand, cutting him off. "Tell me what really happened, Fuscus," I said quietly so only he could hear.

His head dropped and I could see his jaw clenching as he tried to decide what to do.

He looked up then said one word; a name actually. "Cornuficius."

Even when you expect something, sometimes it is still a shock when it actually happens. I had suspected that somehow, Cornuficius was involved in the disappearance of the 10th, but until I heard it from the lips of Fuscus, it was only a suspicion. Waiting for Fuscus to continue, I could see the shame he felt at being forced to admit what I had known for some time; Cornuficius was the one who really ran the 10th.

"I gave the order to advance, but the men just ignored me. Cornuficius said that the Jews had everything in hand and that since we were near the center of the camp and Ptolemy's tent, the pickings would be richer than the men could imagine. He said it so that everyone could hear, and before I could say anything the men had scattered to the four winds."

"What did you do?"

"I ordered Cornuficius to summon his Century from what they were doing and get back into the fighting, but he just laughed like I was joking."

I looked at him incredulously. "And you didn't smash his face in?"

Fuscus shrugged helplessly, but said nothing.

"What did the other Centurions do?" I demanded.

"Nothing. I suspect that they were looking to me to do something. And I failed."

The bitterness in his tone was plain to hear, causing my contempt for him to lessen a little; it was clear that he had more than enough for himself to serve the both of us. I sighed, looking past him at the men, some of whom, as was their habit, had found the stores of wine and were beginning to stagger about.

"I expect that you'll be relieving me, Primus Pilus."

I shook my head. "And give the Cohort to Cornuficius? That's exactly what he wants. He counted on your weakness, and he knows that if I were to go by regulations, I would relieve you."

"But he was insubordinate," Fuscus protested. "That would be more than enough cause to not only pass him over, but to bust him back to the ranks."

"True," I agreed. "But there would have to be another witness of Centurion rank in order to make the charge stick. Who else was present? Let me guess." I knew the answer already and saw the realization hit him. "Salvius? Considius?"

He nodded.

"Not Sertorius though, correct?"

He shook his head, not saying anything, but I saw that I had made my point. There would be no witnesses that would back up Fuscus and we both knew it.

~ ~ ~ ~

The evening briefing was held in Ptolemy's headquarters, which of course had been stripped of anything valuable by Caesar's bodyguards. Caesar arrived, the assembled officers hailing him as Imperator, which he acknowledged with a wave and a smile. He gave fulsome praise to the leaders of the Jewish contingent, and it was at this point that I learned their names were Hyrcanus, who was a priest of some sort, and Antipater, who was their king. I was pleased to see that Joseph ben-Judah had survived the battle without much more than a scratch or two, for which I teased him.

"You're just jealous because I'm faster on my feet than you are," he laughed, a charge I could hardly deny given my condition.

As we waited, I scanned the faces, looking for one in particular, which I did not find. After the briefing was over, when Caesar was making his way towards the exit, I managed to get his attention, not that hard since I towered over the rest of the men. Waiting for me to hop to him, while I paused until the men around him turned their attention away to other matters, I asked him a question once we were relatively alone. His face revealed nothing as he gave me the answer and I did not make any further comment, then he clapped me on the shoulder and I returned to where Valens and Fuscus were standing.

"What was that about?" asked Valens, and I told him.

"I asked about the casualties among the Centurions."

Valens stared for a moment, then gave a short laugh. "Why? You're already Primus Pilus of the 6th. Where else would you rather be?"

"I asked about one in particular."

His laugh was cut short. He and Fuscus exchanged a knowing glance. "Verres Rufus?"

I nodded.

"And?"

"He was killed in the attack on the river side of the camp."

"Well, that was to be expected," Valens said carefully. "They were attacking with those missile troops in their rear."

"True," I admitted. "But the funny thing is, he was the only Centurion killed."

~ ~ ~ ~

Caesar left shortly after the evening briefing, ordering the infantry to stay behind, clean things up, tend to our wounded, and bury our dead. Taking the cavalry, he rode straight for Alexandria, his purpose being to stop Ganymede from rallying the remaining garrison to continue resistance, but he had no cause for worry. Word of Ptolemy's death took any thought of further opposition from the people, and we heard that they gathered in great crowds along the wide avenues, coming to Caesar as suppliants to beg for his mercy. I think that this was entirely calculated on their part, since by this time Caesar's mercy and clemency was widely known and the Egyptians were simply doing what so many of Caesar's enemies had done. Caesar would not disappoint them either. The only action he took was to have Arsinoe removed from the city, along with Ganymede, while the younger Ptolemy was installed as co-regent with the very pregnant Cleopatra, but he was just a puppet and I suspect he knew it. Of course, Cleopatra was not much more than a puppet, yet for reasons I never fully understood, Caesar trusted her, letting her rule as she saw fit for the most part. Nonetheless, I heard from Appolonius, through Diocles of course, that he had to forbid her from killing her sister. Ganymede he was less gentle with; he was clapped in irons for leading young Arsinoe astray, but from everything I saw and heard when I was in her presence in the royal compound, she needed no encouragement. The whole family was a nest of vipers as far as we were concerned, though we could not verbalize that sentiment.

Before he left for Alexandria, Caesar did give us a task to perform, and although it was a bloody one, it was done with enthusiasm. Our job was the execution of the surviving Gabinians. These men were Romans who had turned on their own kind to serve the Egyptians, and nothing could have saved them, even if they had not caused us so much trouble. The other matters that had to be attended to were promotions because of losses. The 6th had not lost any Centurions, although Clemens and Sertorius had been wounded, but we had lost three Optios out of the 20 dead, and one of the men I promoted was Sergeant Tetarfenus, who I had kept an eye on, thinking that he had the makings of a good leader. I still found it somewhat strange to be in a position where I was judging the merits of men older than I was, although they were not that much older in most cases. After a few days, Caesar returned, but he was not alone, coming with Cleopatra, along with the entire Egyptian fleet. We were about to spend the next few weeks doing things that most Legionaries dream about their whole career but never get to do, and that was absolutely nothing.

~ ~ ~ ~

I think that Caesar must have decided that he deserved a respite from all the trials and travails of the last seven months. I cannot say that I blame him, particularly since we were the recipients of this leisure time. To be more accurate, I should say that it was the 6th who were the beneficiaries; the other two Legions were sent back to Alexandria to help clean the city up, much to their dismay and our delight. When I said that

Caesar brought the Egyptian fleet, I am not exaggerating. There were at least 300 ships of varying types, and it is testament to the massive size of the Nile River that the entire fleet could sail on the river without running into each other. The royal barge was the most massive vessel I have ever seen, literally a floating palace, with a dining room, throne room, and gods know how many private chambers. It was powered by sail and oar, and I did not envy the men chained below decks who had to move that massive craft. My men and their Centurions were spread out so that we were not nearly as cramped as we were on any of our other voyages. In most cases, each Century was given their own ship and the men scarcely knew what to do with such luxury. I was given accommodations aboard a trireme, with the captain's cabin as my private quarters, something that he was not particularly happy about. When Appolonius and I met so he could discuss our arrangements, I asked him what was going on.

In his maddeningly typical Greek way, he answered my question with a question. "What does it matter? You're going to be living like a king, and so are the men."

"Can you swim?" I asked this in a pleasant enough tone, but he did not mistake my meaning.

He put his hands out in a placating gesture. "*Pax,* Pullus. By the gods, you're touchy as a Vestal about the flanks."

I grimaced at the comparison, but he was right. "I apologize. It's just my damn leg hurts like I don't know what. You'd think that this was the first time I had been wounded."

"I know why it pains you so much," he replied, and I was in so much discomfort that I did not notice the gleam in his eye as he said this.

"Why then? Come on, out with it you miserable Greek cocksucker!"

"It happens to every man. When they get older, it takes them longer to heal. You're getting old, that's all."

He was a quick one all right, and not just with his tongue, dodging out of the way when I took a swing at him.

"Old? I'm not even 30 yet!"

The moment I said it, I knew I had made a mistake, though he did not seem to notice. While I was not particularly worried any longer about the lie that had gotten me into the Legions a year early, it was still not something I wanted known, but Appolonius simply laughed. I pushed the conversation back to the original topic, repeating my question about what Caesar had planned.

He shrugged. "Nothing. Cleopatra has been at him for months to let her show him Egypt and all that it has to offer, and now that things are back in order, he's agreed."

"So we're on a holiday?"

"Something like that. Oh, I suppose that you'll be called on for ceremonial duties whenever Caesar wants to give the natives a show that impresses upon them the might of Rome. And there's to be a Century on guard on the barge at all times. Otherwise, you're free of any duties. And Caesar has ordered that the wine ration is doubled for all men."

Now, this might seem like wonderful news, and in some ways it was, but mostly it was a boon for the men. For the Centurions, it was as close to disaster as we could get. Something that every Centurion knows from the first day they pick up the *vitus* is that idle men mean trouble in one form or another. Keeping them busy, any kind of busy, is the key to keeping them, and yourself out of trouble. The fact that they would be in close proximity onboard ships was something else to worry about, while the double wine ration just compounded matters. I sighed, knowing that this was not going to be a holiday for anyone wearing the transverse crest.

~ ~ ~ ~

We began our procession up the Nile, and that is exactly what it was, a royal procession with all the panoply and pomp that only royalty can produce. The men lined the rails to watch whenever we stopped at some village or small town, where the locals would turn out, the elders wearing their finest, dropping into the dust at Cleopatra and Caesar's feet. All the wailing, beating of breasts and tearing of clothes when the royal couple departed was a sight to behold, at least the first two or three times we witnessed it, though it got old very quickly. What we found infinitely more interesting were the creatures that lined the banks of the river. While we had seen some of the crocodiles that the Egyptians kept as pets, we had never seen any as large as what we saw sunning themselves on the bank. I was just glad that we had been warned about entering the water when we were close to shore, but that did not stop some of the men from goading each other into leaping off the boat and swimming back before being devoured. Fortunately, not many of the men knew how to swim, so this was relatively isolated. Huge herds of large cow-like creatures with wide, sweeping horns would come to the edge of the river to drink twice a day, in the thirds of a watch just after dawn and just before sunset, and we soon learned that this was when the crocodiles would go hunting. Very quickly, this became one of the favorite pastimes of the men, lining the rails and wagering with each other on when the crocodiles would strike and which animal it would take. The roars of laughter and howls of delight or despair as the crocodiles would suddenly rear out of the water to snatch some unlucky beast rolled across the river. I must say that I participated with equal enjoyment and enthusiasm. Although I appreciated having a ship more or less to myself with only Diocles as my companion, it soon got old, so it was only a day or two into our journey that I summoned some of the other Centurions to take the small boats each ship carried to row to my vessel. Usually it was Felix, Clemens, Sertorius, and Valens, but I knew that at some point I had to deal with Cornuficius and Fuscus. However, I was not ready, because I was not yet sure what I should do about it. On the second night after we set out, Apollonius rowed over to my ship to inform me that there was going to be a victory banquet that night, with all the Centurions invited. The banquet was on Cleopatra's barge, with over a hundred guests, which should give an idea of the massive size of the vessel. Calling a meeting for the Centurions onboard my ship, I pressed Appolonius into duty as teacher on the proper way to behave. Needless to say I was very nervous; while I had dined with Caesar in the officers' mess more times than I could count, this was the first formal affair that I had been invited to attend. With royalty in attendance, it was even more nerve-wracking. Having to worry about 12 other men, some of whom I did not trust at all made it even more so, but Apollonius did his best to soothe my nerves.

"You'll be dining on couches, in the normal manner," was how Apollonius started out, prompting a chuckle from some of us.

"It may be normal for you, Greek," called out Clemens, "but there's not usually a couch by the fire of an army camp."

Apollonius looked slightly embarrassed, but he continued. "You'll be seated according to rank. Caesar has asked that Primus Pilus Pullus sit with his group, on the *Lectus Summus*. Caesar is doing you a great honor, Primus Pilus Pullus."

If he had hoped that telling me this would somehow soothe me, he was gravely mistaken, but given the nature of our relationship, I think Apollonius was taking perverse pleasure by exacting revenge for all the insults I hurled his way on a daily basis.

"Of course, you'll be sitting in the third position, but it's still a great honor."

That it was; once I got over the shock my immediate thought was for my sisters, and I hoped that wherever Livia was in the afterlife, she could see her baby brother and how far he had come. I wish I could say that my first thought was for Gisela and Vibi, but sadly, I had not given them much thought since I left her weeping in the apartment in Brundisium. I had received a letter from her; not from her personally, she paid a scribe to write what she dictated, and the letter had arrived with the reinforcements. It was then I learned that she was pregnant again and was hoping for a daughter. Things had not been right between us before I left, but we obviously had moments where we got along, one of them resulting in the news that I was expecting another child. Now here I was, more miles away than I could count, about to have Caesar sitting, or more accurately, lying across from me, but truthfully, I was more worried about Cleopatra than I was about Caesar.

~ ~ ~ ~

Apollonius finished his class about the proper way to behave, leaving us to prepare ourselves, making sure that our decorations and plumes were in good repair and properly polished. Which meant, of course, that there were sweating Gregarii in every Century who performed the actual work of making us presentable. At the appointed third of a watch, we were rowed to the barge, where a combination bodyguard of Nubians and our own men were waiting to help us aboard the barge. One of the perfumed creatures of Cleopatra's court was awaiting us as well, trying not to wrinkle his heavily made up nose in distaste at the sight of us, causing us to snicker as we followed him. As ornate as the palace of the Pharaohs had been, the barge was at least as much so, if not more heavily bedecked in gold leaf and silver trimming. The columns had every appearance of being made of real marble, with gold capitals wrapped in ivy, and I had to wonder how stable this vessel really was. We marched through the throne room, where we could not help stopping to gape at the throne of the Pharaohs, made of what I was sure was solid gold, with ebony and ivory carvings in the form of twisting serpents wrapped around the legs. Rising up from the back of the throne was what looked like the head of a dog of some sort, again made of solid gold by all appearances, with eyes made of inlaid lapis lazuli, by the look of it. I would have liked to spend more time examining it, but our escort was getting impatient so we continued into the dining hall. There were a series of low, Roman-style tables, around each of which were three couches, with an attendant at each one, armed with wax tablets with the names of the occupants of their particular table. The rest of my party were led to the far end of the dining room, while I was shown to my spot on the couch, the farthest point on the couch opposite Caesar's spot, with Cleopatra in the place of honor to his left. Neither of them had arrived, but most of the other guests had, and I was distinctly uncomfortable to find myself next to a member of Cleopatra's court on the couch to my immediate left, though I cannot remember the creature's name or title. I was just aware that he was of the same nature as the late Pothinus, one of those men called a eunuch, smelling of perfume and oils, and I did not like the way he looked at me. The only relief was that on the opposite side was General Hirtius, who for the most part was a good sort, for a patrician snob anyway, and was at the very least a Roman. Once we sat down, servants appeared to start pouring wine, served unwatered. I immediately signaled for a servant to add water to mine, ignoring the warning hiss and shake of the head I got from Hirtius. I was determined to keep a clear head, and had ordered my Centurions to do likewise, though I had my doubts whether some of them would obey. After we were seated for several moments, long enough for many of the guests to down more than one cup of wine, there was the sound of horns, all of us rising at this signal. Cleopatra and Caesar made their entrance, and I imagine it would have been more impressive if Cleopatra had not been so pregnant and forced to waddle more than walk to their places. To her credit, she did not seem in the least embarrassed by her condition, and while she was very plain as I have said, I must say that the pregnancy gave her something of a glow that made her more attractive. Still, I would not have given her a poke with my stick, if you take my meaning. Nevertheless, Caesar was so obviously taken with her, making no attempt to hide it, something that some men scoffed at but for which I admired him. I was becoming more aware of how important the opinion of others was to me, so I envied his self-assurance and whatever quality it is that allows a man to do as he pleases while not worrying about what others think of him, and this quality Caesar had in abundance. The couple took their seats, our signal to do the same, and immediately the first course was brought out. Normally I am indifferent to food, but I vividly remember most of what was served that evening, especially the first course, which were crocodile eggs. But these were not eggs that I, or any Roman for that matter was accustomed to, for the eggs had been fertilized so that when the shell was broken, half-formed baby crocodiles awaited our consumption. I felt my stomach lurch, taking a quick glance around at the other Roman guests and was pleased to see that they looked as disconcerted as I was. Wise enough to know that a refusal to partake of what the Egyptians obviously considered a delicacy would be a mortal insult I hardened my heart, and stomach, then popped one into my mouth, swallowing it quickly, with a minimum of chewing. Surprisingly, what little I tasted was not that bad, though I decided against chewing the next one more thoroughly. My Egyptian counterpart had no such hesitation; he chewed and smacked away, and I caught a glimpse of a tiny tail protruding from his oily lips before it disappeared with a slurping sound. I leaned back to shoot a glance over to General Hirtius, who caught my eye, rolling his while giving me a sympathetic smile.

"So, Primus Pilus, what do you think of our cuisine so far?"

It took a moment for it to register that I was being addressed, slightly longer to make the connection that it was a woman's voice, and that Cleopatra was the only woman at our couch. By the time I realized what was happening, every other set of eyes, including Caesar's, were staring at me and I could feel the heat shooting up from my toes.

"It's . . . it's very . . . interesting, Highness," I stammered, then I saw Caesar's eyes narrow ever so slightly, making me even more uncomfortable, but Cleopatra laughed, and it was a very pleasant sound.

"Put like a diplomat, Primus Pilus." Her eyes became mischievous, and she pressed, "But what exactly does that mean, interesting? Is that good or bad?"

I gulped, trying to choke the mouthful of baby crocodile past the lump in my throat. "Well, Highness. The taste isn't so bad. I guess I'm just not accustomed to the idea of eating something that normally would be eating me."

I cannot describe the relief and pride I felt at the whoops of laughter this evoked, and Caesar rewarded me with a brilliant smile and a mouthed "well done."

~ ~ ~ ~

The rest of the evening flew by, as we were treated to what had to have been every animal and bird that inhabited Egypt. I must say that once I got over my initial nervousness, I enjoyed myself immensely. Evening turned to night, then night to day, the conversation and entertainment never seeming to end. There were jugglers, acrobats, dancers, mimes, the latter being the most popular with the Romans, and wrestling matches among huge Nubian champions. Even with watering the wine, I felt myself getting more and more inebriated, but after a few thirds of a watch, I did not worry so much about making a fool of myself, for which I give Cleopatra the credit. She was astonishing, so much so that by the time the banquet was ended in the morning of the next day, I no longer wondered what Caesar saw in her. She had a wit that was both cutting and charming at the same time, while she told some jokes that would have made the saltiest Gregarius on his third enlistment blush, which made them no less funny. In fact, I think that it came from such a tiny, pregnant girl made them even funnier, so that even men like Hirtius, who was not normally susceptible to her charms, was doubled over with laughter, his face turning redder than I had ever seen. I do not believe I have ever eaten as much at one time before or since, and I am known for my prodigious appetite. The men behaved themselves perfectly and we wobbled out of the hall to where our boats waited to take us back to our respective ships, arms around each other as we sang marching songs, reliving all that we had just seen. I needed help being hauled aboard my ship, but it was not due to my leg, which at least for that day was not bothering me at all. Diocles staggered under my weight as he helped me to my quarters, where I collapsed on the bunk and fell asleep immediately, not waking up until sunset later that day.

~ ~ ~ ~

This was the manner in which we passed the days, but while there was a banquet on the royal barge almost every night, all of us were only invited that one time. I was invited back, just myself, twice more but never at Caesar's table again, which was fine with me, since it meant I could relax more. Cartufenus and I usually sat together, also fine with me because we enjoyed each other's company and had more fun. Every so often, the fleet would stop sailing to allow Caesar and Cleopatra to disembark, with the queen wanting to show Caesar one of the local sights, usually a temple or monument. They were always accompanied by one Century at least, depending on how far they were going, along of course with Caesar's personal bodyguard, while I usually went along. It was during one of these trips that I saw with my very eyes one of the most amazing and awe-inspiring sights in the known world. I am of course referring to those massive structures called the Pyramids, and there are no words to describe them adequately. They are as tall as small mountains, built of huge blocks of stone. Cleopatra was quite knowledgeable in their construction, and of course, Caesar, being the engineering genius that he was, asked innumerable questions and was keenly interested. What I found most astonishing was that as large as these structures are, ultimately they are to hold the remains of one man, even if they were Pharaoh. The other thing that struck me was how old they were; Cleopatra claimed that they were more than a thousand years old, something I still find hard to believe, but it was clear that they are very, very old indeed. Regardless of how old they are, they still remain as the most impressive sight these old eyes have ever seen, even more impressive than Rome itself and all that it has to offer.

~ ~ ~ ~

Caesar and Cleopatra may have been enjoying themselves, but the men were getting bored. After the first few days of watching crocodiles eating cattle, and the huge creatures we called river horses that live in the Nile, even with the double wine ration, the men were running out of diversions. Before a full week had passed, my morning report contained details of fights between the men, or with the crew of the ship they were on. One evening, after our trip to the Pyramids, Felix rowed over to my boat, his face grim. He had barely sipped his wine before he started giving me the bad news.

"Primus Pilus, I don't really know how to put this," he began, and I waved him silent.

"Then just say it and don't worry about how I'll take it. I promise I won't hold it against you."

I had hoped this would put him at ease, except it did not have the effect I intended. Instead, he did not reply, looking into his wine cup as he seemed to be considering something. I was about to say something but I bit it back, sure that I would make things worse.

"It's just that what I'm about to tell you is.....awkward," he said carefully. "It's awkward because it concerns one of my fellow Centurions, and as much as I've come to admire and respect you, I've still served with these men longer than I have with you."

He looked at me to gauge my reaction, but I still said nothing, deciding to wait for him to continue. Very briefly, I thought about reminding him of his duty, that he owed his first allegiance to his commanding officer and to the 6th Legion, except I knew things were not always that simple, so I remained silent.

Seeing that I was not going to speak, he sighed. "Very well, you're not going to make this easy are you? It concerns Cornuficius. He's been working on the men, convincing them that they need to put pressure on Caesar to end this . . . whatever you want to call it, and go home so we can finish this business once and for all."

I shook my head, taking a deep drink from my own wine cup. It was always Cornuficius; he was turning out to be more of a pain than Celer ever thought about being.

Felix looked at me, waiting for me to speak. "That would be a huge mistake. You were there when the Spanish Legions threatened to mutiny. In fact that's why you're here and they're not, and I can tell you this." I leaned forward, pointing my finger at him, something he did not deserve, but I was angry. "The Spanish Legions and the 10th in particular did more for Caesar than the 6th ever has or ever will, and he still sent them home in disgrace. Trying to pressure Caesar is absolutely the worst thing the men could try."

"I know." Felix held his hands up in protest, "and I told Cornuficius that, but he won't listen. Ever since that business with Fuscus, he knows he runs the Cohort. That's why I came to you."

"What do you know about what happened with Fuscus?" I asked sharply.

"No more than what everyone knows, that Fuscus ordered the Cohort to leave the tents alone and Cornuficius ignored him. And once he did, the rest of the Centurions followed Cornuficius' lead. They're all afraid of him, except Sertorius, but he had been wounded by that point and wasn't there."

"The 10th isn't your Cohort," I pointed out. "So why are you the one to tell me this?"

"It doesn't matter. They're part of the 6th, and this is just as much my Legion as it is Cornuficius' or anyone else. And you're right; I was there in camp and I saw what Caesar did. I also heard that he ordered the 9th to be decimated before that, and I know that if he would do that to a Legion who marched with him in Gaul, he wouldn't hesitate to do the same thing to us."

I rubbed my face, trying to think of what to do. For a moment, I thought about going to Caesar, telling him what Cornuficius was up to, and suggesting that the same thing happen to Cornuficius that happened to Verres Rufus. Almost immediately, I rejected the idea, for a number of reasons, not least of which was giving Caesar any indication that I was unable to handle the problem. That meant I would have to handle this on my own, so I sat with Felix, making small talk while I worked on a solution. Cornuficius had to be stopped, one way or another, and I was beginning to come up with an idea on how to make it happen.

~ ~ ~ ~

Fortunately, not only the men of the 6th wanted to go home; Caesar's generals were anxious to leave as well, they finally prevailed upon Caesar to end his holiday. Turning about two days before my 30th birthday in April, our progress back down the river was much swifter than it had been in the opposite direction, since we were going downstream and we did not stop at every village, town, temple, and monument on the way. Entering the open water, we sailed to Alexandria, bringing Cleopatra and her entire retinue back home, while the men began preparing for what they thought would be a voyage back to Italy, especially once word got out of what was going on back home. Antonius had been making a mess of things, appointing men to posts based on nothing more than his whim at the moment, or how much money they paid him, of course. Payoffs for offices have been part of the system for the gods know how long, but usually there is some minor consideration given to the ability of the men vying for office, yet apparently, this was something that Antonius was not paying any attention to at all. One man in particular, Dolabella, was running rampant and causing much trouble. Also waiting for me personally was word that Gisela had indeed given birth to a baby girl, and she was asking what name should be given to her. After thinking about it, I wrote that I wanted the child called Livia to honor my dead sister. The situation with the Legions was not much better than the political situation in Rome; the men had been sitting in camp on the Campus Martius for the last several months waiting for Caesar to return to make good on his promises, and there was increasing unrest. All in all, there were numerous reasons that Caesar needed to return to Rome. Perhaps that is why he chose to do nothing of the sort and attend to a completely different matter.

~ ~ ~ ~

Caesar had appointed Domitius Calvinus governor of Asia, and he had sent the 37th to Caesar while retaining the 36th, despite Caesar calling for both Legions to join us in Alexandria. To be fair to Domitius, he had good reason not to send the 36th; another son of Mithridates, Pharnaces was his name, was raising havoc in the region, invading Cappadocia and Armenia with a large host. Deiotarus was the king of Galatia, the invaded regions part of his domains, so he went to Domitius, begging for help. The fact that he had originally sided with Pompey meant that he could not come to Domitius empty-handed, so he was forced to promise a substantial sum to help defray the costs of the war we were fighting in Alexandria, to which Domitius promptly agreed. Domitius then marched with the 36th along with Galatian Legions trained in the Roman manner and a force of auxiliaries to confront Pharnaces. In the ensuing battle, Domitius was soundly defeated a few miles from the city of Nicopolis. This was the matter that Caesar was now determined to address, judging that it posed a greater threat to the security of the region than the events in Rome. Consequently, I was summoned to headquarters and ordered to make ready to march overland to the province of Syria. I must say that I was not happy to receive these orders, knowing how the men would react at being told that instead of boarding ships for home, they would be marching to fight yet again. Most worryingly, I had to think about Cornuficius and what emotions he would arouse with this news, wondering which Centurions would side with him. Although I had begun to form an idea on how to neutralize him, it was still not the right time for me to implement my plan, and I worried that this news would render what I had come up with so far useless. These thoughts were at the forefront of my mind when I returned to our quarters to tell Diocles to summon the Centurions. When they arrived, they were in a boisterous, happy mood, sure that I was about to tell them what they had been expecting since we returned to Alexandria.

"We're marching day after tomorrow."

The Centurions' first reaction was to cheer. After a moment, I could see that my words were sinking in, their expressions rapidly changing. Not surprisingly, Cornuficius raised his hand.

"When you say 'march,' do you mean down to the docks?"

I did not see any point in delaying the inevitable reaction. "No."

I might have to deal with their displeasure, I thought, but I do not have to make it any easier on them than they would on me.

"Then march where?"

"Wherever Caesar orders us to," I replied sharply, immediately regretting it. Because Cornuficius was my enemy did not mean I should punish the other men. "We're marching to Syria," I relented.

There was a moment of shocked silence, then the air was filled with protests, and Cornuficius shot me a triumphant look.

"*Silete!*"

I did not mean to be so loud, but it had the desired effect, the men immediately shutting their mouths, their expressions sullen.

I decided that I needed to make an attempt to give details on why Caesar made this decision. "We received word that General Domitius suffered a defeat at Nicopolis at the hands of Pharnaces," I explained. "Deiotarus has asked for our help to expel the Pontics from the territory they've seized. That's what Domitius was trying to do when he was beaten. Caesar has decided that affairs in this part of the world take precedence over what is going on back in Rome."

"That's fine for Caesar, but I don't see what it has to do with us," Cornuficius replied. "Our agreement with Caesar was very specific. We would march for him until the civil war is over. What happens in Armenia or fuck-knows-where doesn't concern us."

I saw that there were men nodding their head in agreement, something that I expected, but what worried me was that some of those expressions were worn by men who were not normally aligned with Cornuficius. I knew I had to tread very carefully, and I made a vow right then to Dis that I would make Cornuficius pay for all that he was putting me through.

"What happens in Armenia very much is our concern, and it has everything to do with the civil war. Caesar can't return to Italy with the situation in Asia so unstable. Not to mention that the whole reason that Pharnaces felt confident enough to try to invade was because of the civil war and our situation here. That makes it very much our concern."

It was thin; oh, it was very thin but I remained silent, waiting for the others to digest this. I was heartened to see that the men who were not allies of Cornuficius seemed to accept my argument.

Of course, Cornuficius was unmoved. "So you say, Primus Pilus, but that's your opinion. . ."

Before he could say anything more, I cut him off. "No, that's what Caesar has ordered, and that's what's going to be done. Are you refusing a direct order, Decimus Pilus Posterior Cornuficius?"

The silence that followed hung like a wet *sagum* over the room as I waited for his reply. I was gratified to see that he did not look quite as smug or comfortable now, his eyes darting around to the others, looking for support. However, men like Cornuficius only surrounded themselves with people weaker than they were, meaning that men like Considius and Favonius were not likely to stick their necks out at a moment like this. Quickly seeing he was alone, he licked his lips nervously, obviously calculating what his odds were of facing me down. Making his decision, there was no mistaking the bitterness in his tone when he spoke.

"No, Primus Pilus, I'm doing no such thing. I'm simply voicing the concerns that I know many of the men have about our situation."

"Your concern is duly noted, Pilus Posterior, and you're to be commended for your genuine concern for the welfare of your men; it's an inspiration to us all, I'm sure."

I made no attempt to hide the sarcasm in my voice and it made me happy to see that my words scored a direct hit, his normally placid features becoming flushed and his lips tightening in anger. He opened his mouth to say something, and for a moment, I thought I had him, but he regained his self-control, instead saying nothing.

Looking around at the rest of the group, I finished, "If there's nothing else to be said, then we have work to do and it won't get done sitting here."

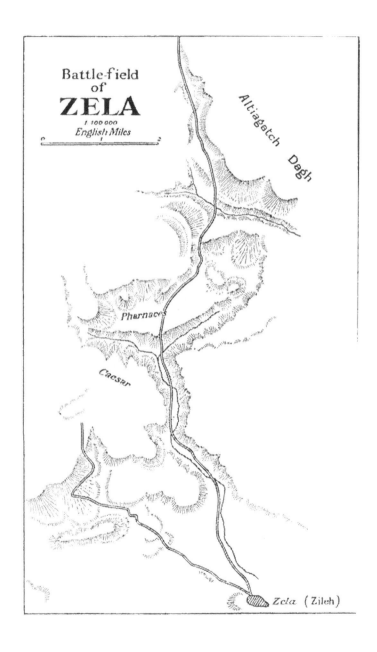

## Chapter 6- Veni Vidi Vici

Two days later, we left Alexandria, just the men of the 6th, the Jewish contingent and other allied forces, and the cavalry. The men were not in the best of moods, but they marched at the pace Caesar set with no problems, and I was thankful that at the end of the day they were generally too tired to do much complaining. I watched Cornuficius the way a buzzard eyes a dying animal, waiting for him to do anything that I could use to finish him, for that is the conclusion I had come to, that his career in the Legions must end. It was not a decision I came to lightly; even during my problems with Celer, I had never considered taking such a drastic action like what I was contemplating now, but I had seen enough of Cornuficius to know that he was a detriment to the Legions. Even now, after all these years when my passions have cooled, I am comfortable with my decision. I just had to wait for him to make a mistake, one that I could use to achieve my aims. However, he was cautious, knowing that I was watching him, so it became something of a grim game. I would suddenly stop by his Century area whenever he was sitting at a fire with some of the men, hoping to catch him saying something that would put him where I wanted him. Unfortunately, I am hard to miss and he would always be chatting innocently away.

With this private battle playing out, we continued marching, entering the province of Syria, traveling along the coast so that our resupply came from the sea, before turning inland and heading for Ace Ptolemais. At this point, we crossed over a series of mountain ranges, making the going slow and the days long, but it kept the men sufficiently tired so that trouble was kept to a minimum, for which I was thankful. Reaching Ace Ptolemais in early Junius, we made camp outside the city walls, whereupon Caesar took up where he left off in Alexandria, that is to say putting things back in order. During the years of civil war, the running of Roman provinces had not been a high priority of the ruling class, and the civil administration suffered as a result, something that Caesar was determined to put to rights. During our last days in Alexandria, he had disbanded the Egyptian army, establishing the two Legions he left behind, the 28th and 37th as permanent garrisons. Here in Ace Ptolemais, he filled several administrative posts, appointing a number of minor officials to offices that were vacant, along with hearing petitioners, all of which took time. The days passed as he went about his business and we quickly settled into a routine where the men would go into town when they were off duty, unerringly finding the part of town that caters to fleshly desires. Following just as inevitably was trouble, particularly now that there was no fighting going on to keep the men occupied and their bloodlust sated, forcing me to begin making my trips into town with my purse full of coin once again. Trouble with the civilian population was nothing unusual and in reality was to be expected. What was not expected, at least on my part, was an incident that gave me exactly what I needed to destroy Cornuficius, because it happened with our allies, the Jews.

~ ~ ~ ~

"Caesar summons you to attend to him immediately."

Apollonius looked grave, but try as I might I could not pry a word from his lips as to what it was about, so I was in an agitated state of mind when I arrived. Caesar looked every bit as grim as Apollonius and he was not alone. With him was none other than ben-Judah and Antipater, their moods matching Caesar's.

I saluted, then Caesar jumped right into the matter. "Pullus, we have a serious problem. Are you aware of a disappearance of one of Antipater's officers?"

I shook my head. "No, Caesar, this is the first I've heard of it."

Caesar turned to ben-Judah and said, "Perhaps you should tell him since you're more familiar with the details."

"Yes, Caesar."

Ben-Judah turned to me and there was nothing friendly in his eyes as he spoke. "As Caesar said, one of my officers, a man by the name of Joseph of Gaza has disappeared under suspicious circumstances."

"What makes it suspicious?"

I thought it was a reasonable question, but ben-Judah was clearly irritated. "I was getting to that," he snapped. Now I was growing angry and seeing this, he softened his tone. "I am sorry, Pullus, I did not mean to speak harshly. It's just that Joseph was a good friend of mine. Anyway, he was off duty and he was drinking at one of the shops near the forum that's become a popular place for both your men and mine. While he was there, he got into a game of dice with one of your men and I suspect that is the cause of the trouble."

"How much did he lose?"

Ben-Judah shook his head. "He didn't lose. He won, and apparently, won quite a bit."

I bit back a curse, sure that I knew where this was going, but I was wrong. "So you think he was robbed by one of my men?"

"I wish it were that simple. No, he wasn't robbed because he didn't have any money on his person."

Now I was completely confused and I said as much.

Ben-Judah glanced at Antipater and Caesar, and Caesar signaled that he should continue. "He wasn't gambling with a man from the ranks. He was gambling with a Centurion. The Centurion gave him a marker to cover his debt, and that's the only thing of any value that Joseph had with him, besides a few coins of his own."

I went cold, now understanding why the others were so grave.

"Do you know who it was?"

Ben-Judah hesitated. "While I can't be positive, from the description given to me by some of my men who were there, it is in all likelihood your Centurion, Cornuficius."

I kept my face composed, but it was difficult, I can tell you. Here was the opportunity I had been waiting for, or so I hoped. That was not something that I wanted Caesar, or the Jews for that matter to know, so I made a show of skepticism.

"I don't know," I said slowly, "that doesn't seem like Cornuficius. Not that he'd gamble and lose," I said hastily, seeing that I had angered ben-Judah, "but it's just not his style to do something so risky. He's usually cleverer than that."

"It was supposedly quite a lot of money," countered ben-Judah and I asked how much.

"We don't know for sure of course, but from what my men overheard, it was in the neighborhood of 5,000 sesterces."

I was flabbergasted; that was a small fortune, and while Cornuficius could certainly afford to lose that much, that did not mean he would part with it willingly.

I forced my mind to move to another part of the problem. "What were the circumstances of his disappearance? When was he first noticed missing?"

"He didn't leave the wine shop immediately. According to our witnesses, your man Cornuficius left before Joseph, after Joseph refused to continue playing. Cornuficius naturally wanted to win his money back, but that is what he had been trying to do for the last third of a watch that they played, and Joseph finally said 'enough.' When Cornuficius left, he was very angry."

"I can imagine," I said dryly.

"Joseph left some time after Cornuficius did, and was seen heading towards the Jewish Quarter; he had friends living in the city. They are friends of mine as well, so when he went missing, I immediately went and asked these people. They said he never showed up."

"And when did you realize he was missing?"

"He was scheduled to be commander of the watch for the second watch for our part of the camp. He never showed up, so we went looking for him. That is when we heard what happened."

I rubbed my face, forgetting that Caesar was standing there as I thought through what I had heard. I had no doubt about what happened, knowing Cornuficius as I did, but I could not voice that in front of Caesar because it would raise questions I did not wish to answer. I had to appear to have Cornuficius' well-being in mind, at least at this point, meaning I had to ask a question that I knew would anger ben-Judah and probably Antipater as well. I was not sure how Caesar would react.

"Is it possible that he went to another place to celebrate, drank too much, and is sleeping it off right now?"

"Joseph drinks very sparingly; I have known him for more than ten years and never once seen him drunk. Nor has he ever missed duty before," ben-Judah said coldly.

"I'm sorry, ben-Judah, but I had to ask. This is one of my Centurions we're talking about."

I looked over at Caesar, asking him silently for direction. "Pullus, I need you to investigate this, but it needs to be done discreetly." He turned to Antipater and ben-Judah. "I'm looking to you two to continue your search to try and find your man while Pullus asks some questions. If matters are as you fear, at the very least we need to find a body before we can proceed with any kind of disciplinary action."

The Jews nodded their understanding. When Caesar asked them to leave so that he could speak to me privately, they did so.

Once they left, Caesar turned back to me and without preface asked me, "I don't know Cornuficius well; he's not been serving me that long and I've been extremely busy the last few months." He smiled thinly. "So you're in a better position to know. Do you think he did this?"

I was about to just blurt out that of course I thought he did it, but managed to stop myself.

Pretending to consider this, I answered, "I honestly don't know, Caesar. But I'll find out."

Putting his hand on my arm, Caesar looked up at me, his eyes boring into mine. "Pullus, I hope I don't have to tell you how incredibly sensitive this is. If this were a civilian, or even a Gregarius, we could do whatever was necessary to make it go away, but of all the allies for this to happen to, the Jews would have been my last choice. They're as touchy about their honor as we are, and they take any crime perpetrated against them by a non-Jew almost as an insult to the whole group." He shook his head. "I truly don't understand them, but what I do know about them makes me believe that if things aren't handled properly we'll have no end of trouble. And not just with the army. Do you understand?"

I did not, really, but Caesar saying it was important made it so for me and I told him what he wanted to hear.

Caesar dismissed me, but before I left he told me, "Time is critical here, Pullus. This needs to be resolved as quickly as possible. That means that I'm authorizing you to use whatever means you deem necessary to extract evidence from the men you suspect being involved in this."

I had just been given permission to torture Cornuficius, and despite how much I loathed the man, it chilled me to think about it.

~ ~ ~ ~

I did not know with whom I could trust this matter among my Centurions, and I wished that I could talk to Cartufenus, but he was back in Alexandria. One thing that I was fairly sure about was that Cornuficius had not done anything to Joseph personally; he was too clever for that. He would have had some of his toadies in his Century do what needed to be done then dispose of the body, but the question was who they would be. Another thing to consider was how to go about asking questions without alerting Cornuficius and alarming him to the point where he ran for his life. I realized that it was extremely important to Caesar and the Jews that Cornuficius be brought to justice, formally and with due process and there was no way to do that if he escaped. I wish I could say that was my motivation as well, but in plain truth I did not just want him gone, I wanted him dead. Summoning Diocles, who I had grown to trust implicitly by this point, I confided in him the situation I was facing, asking him for ideas. It was he who came up with using himself to begin the preliminary questioning, talking to the slaves of the other Centurions along with some of the men with whom he had contact. Being my personal slave and clerk, Diocles was one of the most popular men in the Legion, the Gregarii bribing him for information about duties and such, something that I am sure he did not think I knew, judging by the look of surprise on his face as I dictate this fact. However, it was something I turned a blind eye to because I knew that he would not betray any truly important or sensitive information, therefore it was Diocles who began asking questions.

Somewhat to my surprise, he returned in about two parts of a watch, his manner one of suppressed excitement. "Publius was one of them," he announced.

Now, there were a number of men named Publius in the Legion, but I knew exactly who he meant; it was my old friend Publius, who I had met the day I was introduced to the Legion. What I did not know at the time was that he was one of Cornuficius' men, in more ways than one. In fact, Cornuficius had put Publius up to challenging me that day. Publius was Cornuficius' muscle for keeping the other men in line and for his other schemes, extortion mostly, along with collection of money owed to Cornuficius for gambling debts. To be more accurate, the debts owed to the men Cornuficius used as his fronts for his gambling operations, since it is against regulations for Centurions to gamble with the men. Cornuficius was certainly not the only Centurion who skirted regulations, but every other Centurion I knew only did so occasionally, usually on things like crocodile feedings or something similar, and they did it honestly, winning or losing fair and square. But Cornuficius was not content to trust to Fortuna, preferring instead to rely on men he had trained with loaded dice. I had known, or more correctly suspected, what Cornuficius was up to for some time, yet I had been unable to prove it and frankly, I was more concerned with other matters like keeping as many of my men alive as I could. I supposed that Cornuficius felt comfortable gambling with Joseph because he was a fellow officer, but what puzzled me was how a sharp operator like Cornuficius had managed to lose to someone like Joseph. However, that was not my major concern, and now Diocles had given me a place to start, except I could not just go to Publius, grab him up, then drag him back to my tent; instead I would have to rely on someone I trusted. Thinking about Felix, I decided against it, not because I did not trust him but I did not want to put him in an awkward position with the other Centurions when this came to light. Then an idea struck me, and I told Diocles to go fetch someone.

This was the first time that Gaius Tetarfenus had an occasion to be called into my presence and he was understandably nervous. I was struck by an unexpected pang of sympathy, remembering what it felt like to be a ranker called into the presence of the Primus Pilus. I immediately set out to put him at ease by offering him a seat, which was unusual and in fact had the opposite effect intended, making him even more nervous than when he first walked in. Consequently, I had Diocles bring some wine, offering him a cup, and I could clearly see his hand shaking as he took what Diocles offered.

"Tetarfenus, you're not in any trouble. In fact, I need your help."

This seemed to help his nerves, but now he looked at me suspiciously; it is not often that a Primus Pilus asks a lowly Gregarius for anything other than sweat, blood, or both, sometimes at the same time.

"There's a matter that I'm charged with investigating, and it involves Publius from Cornuficius' Century."

I decided to be at least partially truthful with him, plus I was counting on a piece of information that I had been aware of for some time and I was gratified to see Tetarfenus' lip curl at the mention of Publius' name.

"What has that piece of *cac* done now, sir?"

I suppressed a smile at Tetarfenus' open contempt, happy that I had guessed correctly and chosen a man whose hatred of Publius was so virulent, for that was the information I had received some time before, that there was much bad blood between Publius and the brothers Tetarfenus, though I did not know why.

"That's something you don't need to worry about. But I need him brought here so I can question him, except it needs to be done discreetly."

He looked confused, so I rephrased my words. "Nobody should know that you bring him here. Particularly his Optio or Centurion."

I heard the sudden intake of breath as he looked at me sharply, suddenly wary. "May I ask why, sir?"

"You can ask, but I'm not going to tell you, for a couple of reasons, which you don't need to know either. You need to trust me."

He did not reply, but finally nodded his head.

His eyes narrowed in thought, then he said, "I'll need some help; he's a big bastard. I can rely on my tent mates to give me a hand."

"And they'll keep their mouths shut?"

He gave me a cold look, and while his words were polite, there was no mistaking the anger in his voice. "I'd trust them with my life Primus Pilus. I have been trusting them with my life for more than 16 years."

"Fair enough. I meant no offense. It's just that, as I said, this must be kept quiet."

"I swear on Jupiter's stone that we'll get him here without anyone knowing."

"How do you plan on doing it?"

He grinned at me. "Primus Pilus, you don't really need to know that."

I laughed, then sent him on his way, but my stomach was in knots.

~ ~ ~ ~

Tetarfenus was as good as his word. Shortly after midnight, when the camp was silent and dark, the men sleeping soundly, I heard a commotion outside my tent, whispered curses, and the sound of something being dragged. I was lying on my cot fully dressed, so I leaped to my feet, walking quickly into the front part of my tent just as Diocles was opening the front flap. Tetarfenus and three other men struggled past Diocles, dragging an inert form, dropping him at my feet. It was Publius, who was out cold, but when I examined him, I did not see any marks on him to indicate that he had been knocked out.

I gave Tetarfenus a questioning look and he grinned at me. "Not a mark on him, Primus Pilus. We invited him to our tent to have a drink. We drugged his wine."

"But you hate him. He doesn't know that?"

Tetarfenus and the other men laughed, and he gave a shrug. "Nobody ever accused Publius of being smart. All he heard was free wine and he came running."

"Well, I can't question him here. I have a wagon out back. Drag him to it and throw him in. Then you're dismissed."

They dragged Publius, who was snoring so loudly that I was sure that the sentries on the walking posts would hear him and come to investigate, dumping him into the back of the wagon. Before they left, I handed Tetarfenus a bag of coin, telling him to split it with his friends as he saw fit. His teeth gleamed in the moonlight as he saluted me before walking off, keeping to the shadows of the tents as he and his tent mates made their way back to their area. Jumping onto the bench, with Diocles beside me, we drove the wagon out of the camp. Nobody stopped to challenge me; I was the Primus Pilus of the 6$^{th}$, my coming and going answerable only to the Legates and to Caesar himself. Driving to the building Caesar had selected as his *praetorium*, I dragged Publius out of the wagon and hoisted him over my shoulder, staggering under his weight. With Diocles leading the way, we headed for the basement. The building Caesar occupied was the provincial administrative offices, and there were cells in the basement where prisoners were held awaiting trial, along with a bare room that served as an interrogation chamber, and was where we headed. The headquarter guard that night were members of Caesar's own bodyguard, replacing the men who were scheduled to stand guard, men from the 6th, since I did not want them seeing me dragging Publius off to gods know where, and they let us pass, not even giving us a second glance. It struck me that this had to be a common enough occurrence for these men that it did not warrant any extra attention, then shrugged the thought off. Publius was heavy and unconscious he was dead weight, making my legs shake from the strain, but I staggered down the stairs, following Diocles, who was carrying the lantern. We fumbled our way past the cells, which fortunately were empty, entering the chamber. There was a single chair, with arms that had ropes attached to them, along with leg irons chained to the feet of the chair. The two men from the torture detachment were standing there waiting for us, hard-faced men who looked almost bored. With their help, I dumped Publius into the chair, bound him with rope and chain, then we sat waiting for him to wake up.

~ ~ ~ ~

Publius came to consciousness slowly, his eyes blinking as his scarred head lifted and he began looking around, clearly confused. He tried to stand, but the ropes and chains held him in place, causing him to fall back heavily, and he stared dumbly at his bindings as his brain, not the fastest part of him under best of circumstances, tried to make sense of his surroundings. I waited for his mind to register that he was not alone before stepping into the circle of light thrown by the single lantern that Diocles had lit. Debating with myself about wearing a mask or otherwise disguising myself, I quickly decided that besides being pointless, I could use it to my advantage. Not only was I Primus Pilus, I was one of the few men who had beaten Publius in his life, and I had done it fairly efficiently and easily. Once you do that to a man, you own a piece of his soul for the rest of his life, which was what I was counting on. So I stepped into the light, watching his face transform as he struggled to focus on me, the realization written plainly on his face when he recognized me that he was in deep trouble.

"Gregarius Publius, I'm going to ask you some questions. You're going to answer the questions truthfully and you're going to tell me everything I want to know. Do you understand?"

"Why am I tied down? I haven't done anything!"

"That's not what I've been told. What I heard is that you're involved in something that has drawn the attention of Caesar himself. That's why you're here."

His face turned white at the mention of Caesar's name, as it should have. For a ranker, to have his name mentioned in the same breath as Caesar's meant either great things, or truly terrifying things, and Publius was smart enough to know that if Caesar was aware of his existence it was not for anything good.

"I didn't do anything, I swear by all the gods!"

He began pulling at his bonds, and for a moment, I worried that he might break free, because Publius was nothing if not exceptionally strong.

However, they held, so I waited for his struggles to subside before I spoke again. "Publius, I won't lie to you. Your fate is sealed. The only thing that is at question is the manner in which you die. It can be a quick, clean death, or you can spend your last watches in a torment of agony that you can't imagine."

Like all bullies, Publius' strength was a sham, something superficial that was easily cracked under the first sign of pressure, and I was putting pressure on him now.

"But why?" he whined. "I told you, I've done nothing!"

"I need to know what happened to Joseph of Gaza."

His reaction was one of genuine puzzlement, so that for the briefest of moments I was struck by doubt. Then, I added, "The Jew that Cornuficius lost all that money to."

The words were barely out of my mouth when I saw his face change, a look of guilt flashing across his battered features, instantly banishing any doubts that I had.

"I can see you know exactly what I'm talking about. You're going to tell me everything I need to know."

"What do you need to know?"

I sighed in exasperation. "I need to know what happened to him, Publius. I need to know what you did."

"I . . . I don't know what you're talking about, Primus Pilus. There must be some mistake."

"The mistake is that you chose to follow Cornuficius' orders."

I could see the wheels of his mind turning, but they turned very slowly indeed. "Orders from Cornuficius? I'm sorry, Primus Pilus, I don't know what you mean."

I hit him with my open hand, the smack of the blow sounding loud against the stone walls. Before he could react, I hit him several times, all with my open hand but it was a hand hardened by many watches of training with a sword, and I put all of my weight behind it. Once I had finished, there was a thin trail of blood trickling from his nose and he was shaking his head, trying to clear it.

"Perhaps this will jog your memory," I said.

Turning to the men from the torture detachment, I signaled for them to begin.

~ ~ ~ ~

I will not go into the details of the next couple of watches. Eventually, Publius confessed everything. He and two other men were summoned by Cornuficius, told to follow Joseph, with orders to kill him quietly, then dispose of the body. Publius gave a detailed description of where they dumped the corpse, or at least most of it; they had decapitated him, then fed his head to some pigs so that it would be harder to identify the corpse. They took Cornuficius' marker for the debt, nothing more than a scrap of parchment to give back to Cornuficius, who was waiting in his tent for the deed to be done. What neither I nor Publius knew was that the Jews considered the pig an unclean creature, so apparently feeding Joseph's head to such a beast made the crime that much more horrific, further enraging them. Once I had Publius' full confession, I had Diocles summon Fuscus and Sertorius, the latter being the one man I trusted in the 10th Cohort, summoning the former because he was the Pilus Prior, and whom I suspected would not mind being part of Cornuficius' downfall. Diocles led them down to the basement where I was waiting outside the interrogation room, both of them still trying to shake the sleep off, obviously bewildered.

"I need you two as witnesses and to accompany me when I arrest Cornuficius."

Clearly shocked, they looked at each other before Fuscus asked why, and I told him. I had expected at least Fuscus to be, while not happy, at least relieved that we were about to remove the man who was undermining his authority with the Cohort, but he was visibly shaken and seemed skeptical.

"Forgive me, Primus Pilus, but I don't think that Cornuficius can be arrested without evidence."

Sertorius had remained silent, regarding me steadily, but he nodded his head in agreement. I had not planned on this and I felt the anger welling up within me, yet somehow I swallowed it down, forcing myself to acknowledge that Fuscus was acting correctly. Reluctantly, I opened the door to the interrogation chamber then waved them in, where Publius sat slumped in the chair, the men from the torture detachment sitting on the floor against the wall, resting from their exertions. At least, it was what remained of Publius, who was more dead than alive and had been begging me to kill him. I was glad that I had not done so yet, though it was not because I had any pity for him. The two Centurions both recoiled in shock at the sight of him, Sertorius giving me a look that I will never forget, an expression of mingled respect and disgust at what I had done to one of my own men. Ignoring him, I walked to Publius to shake him, and he almost tipped the chair over as he tried to avoid my touch, whimpering in fear.

"I'm not going to hurt you again, Publius," I said gently, and his pathetic expression of gratitude was like a javelin in my gut.

Unlike many men, I took no pleasure in inflicting pain; it was a tool to get what I wanted, nothing more. Perhaps this is what Diocles calls a rationalization but it makes it no less true.

"I need you to tell the Centurions what you told me, that's all."

Publius the man had long since disappeared. All that was left was a creature eager to please me, so he repeated everything he had told me. He was somewhat hard to understand, between his swollen lips and the rest of the teeth he had managed to keep now missing, but he was clear enough that there was no doubt that Fuscus and Sertorius understood him. Once he was finished, his head dropped to his chest as he passed out from the effort.

I looked at the two men, studying their expressions. "Are you satisfied now?"

Fuscus looked relieved, while Sertorius' expression was harder to read, yet they both answered that they had heard enough.

"Now, I'm going to arrest Cornuficius and I need you both to be there as witnesses, and Fuscus, I'll need you as a witness at his questioning."

They were clearly uncomfortable, but they both agreed to come with me, not that it was an option. Diocles had gone to the provost to arrange for a detachment of men to accompany us, and we met them outside the headquarters building. Marching to the camp, we were passed through the Porta Praetoria, with me leading the small procession directly to Cornuficius' tent. Rousing his startled and very scared slave, I pushed him through the flap separating the Century office from Cornuficius' private quarters and I wish I could say that I was not enjoying the moment immensely. He was asleep, but at the commotion, he reached for his sword immediately, causing me to put my hand on my own, though I cannot fault him for his reaction, because I would have done the same thing.

"Decimus Pilus Posterior Gaius Cornuficius, you are under arrest for the murder of Joseph of Gaza," I announced in my official tone, trying but probably not succeeding to avoid sounding triumphant.

He blinked in confusion, then seeing Fuscus and Sertorius, I saw for the first time the real Cornuficius, his lips curling in contempt at the sight of his Primus Pilus. For a moment, I thought he was going to resist as his fingers curled more tightly around the handle of his sword. However, I think he saw the eagerness in my eyes, so he slowly relaxed his hold.

"I don't know what you're talking about, Primus Pilus, but I'm anxious to get this matter cleared up," he said with a trace of his old smoothness.

"I'm sure you are, Pilus Posterior," I responded. "So let's not delay any further. Please get dressed."

He clearly thought that he was going to be given his privacy to do so, but while I was willing to stand out in the outer office, I ordered two of the provosts to stand watch over him. This clearly made him angry, though I do not know whether it was because of the insult or that he had planned on making a getaway. Either way, he was ready in a few moments, dressed in his full uniform; certainly that was his right, yet it did not make any difference to me. He was being led away under guard no matter what, and I wish I could say that I was not so petty that I was willing to take him quietly. I was not, making enough racket to rouse the dead, or at least the sleeping Gregarii of the 6th Legion. Marching through the camp, men were awakened by the sound of our hobnail boots and to the sight of Cornuficius being marched, clearly under guard, to whatever fate awaited him. What the men did not know was that Cornuficius' future could be measured by watches, and that those watches were going to be filled with more pain than even he could imagine.

~ ~ ~ ~

I had Publius removed from the interrogation room, though I took pains to make sure that the signs of his interrogation were not washed away, the pool of blood around the chair plainly visible. Cornuficius walked into the room, stopping suddenly when he saw the chair and gore around it. The two men from the torture detachment pointed for him to sit down when I shoved him forward. For a moment, I thought he would try to resist, but I think he knew I would welcome it, so he obeyed my order to strip down to just his tunic before walking stiffly to the chair and taking a seat. He watched me intently when I leaned over to tie him down to the chair, but he did not struggle, nor did he speak. Once he was secure, I stepped away then motioned to Diocles, who was standing with a wax tablet and stylus, waiting to dictate.

"I've told you why you've been arrested, Cornuficius. Let me now explain what the evidence is that led us to you, and who gave it."

"I'm most anxious to hear who has lied about me, Primus Pilus."

I have to say that he was remarkably composed.

"Unfortunately for you, Cornuficius, I have no reason to doubt what I've been told so far and I believe that Caesar will find it credible as well." His face remained expressionless and I wondered how long before his composure cracked and if it would take physical means to make it happen. "Gregarius Publius has confessed to killing Joseph of Gaza on your orders, then disposing of his body according to your instructions, including decapitating him and feeding his head to some pigs."

I cannot swear to this, but I believe that I saw a ghost of a smile cross his lips at the mention of the pigs.

"Gregarius Publius is lying," he said calmly.

I nodded; I had expected him to say as much. "And why would he lie about his Centurion?"

He shrugged, or at least made an attempt to do so, despite how tightly bound he was. "Why does any ranker hate his Centurion? I've been riding him hard lately and he's been on the punishment list quite a bit. I'm sure that has something to do with it."

"That's a lie," Fuscus burst out. I looked at him in surprise and not a little irritation. "I haven't seen his name on any list you've submitted one time. Publius clings to you like a fly does to honey; he's your man, bought and paid, and always has been," Fuscus almost shouted.

I chose not to reprimand Fuscus for speaking, curious to see how Cornuficius would react, and he looked at Fuscus with utter contempt, making no attempt to hide it in his voice as he replied scornfully, "As any good Pilus Prior would know, there are two kinds of lists; one that you see and one that only I know about. I'm referring to the unofficial list, but I guess it's too much to expect you would know about that."

What Cornuficius was saying was true, as I well knew. There were matters of discipline that remained completely within a Century, never making it into the Legion diary, because anything that is reported to the Pilus Prior of a Cohort has to be entered into the official record. The reality is that for every entry of punishment that makes it in the Legion diary there are perhaps nine or ten that do not, instead being handled by the Centurion in about any matter that he saw fit. I looked over at Fuscus, whose face was bright red, his body shaking with rage, his fists clenched at his sides as he glared at Cornuficius, who was staring right back. It was clear that the hatred between the two had been there for some time, but it was not something I could concern myself with now.

"I don't think that you're really in a good position to be insolent to your commanding officer, Cornuficius. Apologize to Fuscus for your words and your tone."

Cornuficius looked at me in disbelief then gave a short, harsh laugh. "Or what, Primus Pilus? You're going to beat me?"

"You know how this works, Cornuficius. You're about to be interrogated. That means you're going to get a beating no matter what. What you do have some control over is whether I have these men continue on you after I get what I need from you."

He said nothing for a moment, staring into my eyes. Looking away, he said tonelessly, "I apologize for my words, Pilus Prior. I meant no disrespect. But that doesn't change the fact that Publius is lying."

"Well, then you have nothing to worry about, other than a few bumps and bruises," I said conversationally.

Turning to the men, I told them to make themselves ready, and they began wrapping their hands in fresh linen bandages, arraying the tools of their trade in front of Cornuficius, but I did not give them the order to begin. The truth was that I was stalling, waiting for something that I hoped would speed up Cornuficius' confession because I knew Caesar would awaken soon and be expecting the matter to be resolved.

~ ~ ~ ~

Finally, I was about to signal the men to start, not wanting to delay any longer when there was a commotion outside. Telling them to wait, I signaled for Fuscus, Sertorius, and Diocles to follow me out of the room, where two men stood shaking in fear, surrounded by the provosts. Genusius and Larius were the two men that Publius had admitted going with him to murder Joseph, although I think it did do some credit to Publius that even under torture, he refused to implicate the two in anything more than helping him dispose of the body. I told the provosts to bring the men over to the cell where Publius had been dumped, waiting for execution. He was unconscious but I did not need him awake; I believed just the sight of his battered, broken hulk would loosen their tongues. Faced with that sight, I heard their groans of dismay, then one of them whispered to the other before the provosts led them back to where we were standing. My face was set in stone as I stared at them, pointing back to where Publius lay.

"He's already told us everything. I know what part you both played. What I want to know now is what each of you knows about who told Publius to do this."

The words came tumbling out of their mouths, both of them babbling so hysterically that I was forced to bark at them to shut up. I turned to Genusius first, motioning for him to talk. His mouth worked several times before anything came out and I remember thinking that first I could not get them to shut up, but now I could not get them to speak. Finally, he stammered out what he knew, which was not much more than what Publius had told him, that Cornuficius told Publius to kill Joseph and dispose of the body. Turning to Larius, he reiterated what Genusius said, but then added something that I made him repeat.

"Publius said that Cornuficius had been cheated by this Joseph of Gaza, that he was as sure that the Jew was playing with loaded dice as he was of anything in his life."

I pondered this. While it would not make any difference ultimately, it did make me curious so I ordered the two men to be held in the cell adjacent to Publius.

Motioning to Diocles, when he came to me I asked him, "Did you get all that?"

He nodded, waving the wax tablet as I looked to Sertorius and Fuscus, and while they both nodded that they had heard, their faces looked troubled as they glanced at each other.

"Well?" I snapped, knowing what was bothering them. "What's on your mind?"

Fuscus spoke, and I could see he did so reluctantly. After the initial shock of seeing Cornuficius arrested, I think he had started to like the idea of having him removed, but his hatred of Cornuficius was not enough to stop raising questions in his mind.

"What if it's true?" he asked worriedly. "What if this Jew did cheat Cornuficius?"

Before I answered I looked to Sertorius, who added, "That would make things different, wouldn't it, Primus Pilus?"

I rubbed my face, thinking about it; as much as I hated to admit it, they were right.

Thinking it through, I finally shook my head. "Not really. If Cornuficius was cheated, then he knew the proper channels to go through. And now it's too late, anyway. The Jews won't be satisfied with anything less than his death."

"Who are the Jews to tell us what we do with one of our own?" Sertorius asked angrily. "Especially if what Larius said is true and that Cornuficius was cheated by the bastard?"

Sighing, I shook my head again. "It doesn't matter anymore. But, let's at least go see what Cornuficius has to say."

~ ~ ~ ~

I had Diocles read what he had recorded from Larius and Genusius to Cornuficius, who listened impassively. When Diocles reached the part about Cornuficius being cheated, his face changed, a fleeting look of hope animating his features. One look at me extinguished it almost as quickly as it had come.

"And none of that matters," he said bitterly.

"No, it doesn't," I replied, not seeing any point to lie to him, even if I had been so inclined. "But tell us your version anyway. Perhaps Caesar will be feeling generous."

"Caesar may feel as generous as he likes, but if you speak against me, what chance do I have?"

I regarded him for several moments, neither of us aware of anyone else in the room. I honestly do not know if this moment were to occur now if I would behave the same way. The years have a way of banking the fires of passion and rage in a man so that they barely smolder in the last years of his life. Perhaps it is a way to make the days of one's life longer, for I believe that when the flames in your soul burn bright and hot that it consumes your essence much more quickly; your flame may burn bright in this life, but it extinguishes earlier.

Finally, I spoke, my voice cold. "You have no chance, Cornuficius. None at all. I once asked you if I was going to have to kill you and as I recall, you said 'Not yet,' or something to that effect. Well, I suppose we've arrived at that moment where I must kill you in order to keep the 6th strong and effective. You've been undermining Fuscus for too long. I know all about what happened in the camp on the Nile, that you refused to obey not just his orders, but mine as well, since I was the one who gave them to Fuscus in the first place."

"So you're going to kill me because of his weakness?" Cornuficius sneered.

I could not deny that there was a grain of truth in what he said. Fuscus was indeed a weak man, weaker at least than Cornuficius, but he was still the legally appointed commander of the Cohort.

"No. First, I'm not going to kill you, at least not myself. As much as I may want to, that's not my place. I'm going to see you executed, but not before you confess that you ordered Publius to murder Joseph of Gaza, and that's the real reason you must die, not because of Fuscus."

I glanced at Fuscus as I talked, trying to gauge his reaction to Cornuficius' lacerating scorn. He was indeed shaking with rage, but he said nothing when I was finished.

"So, if I don't confess, then I'll live?"

It was a feeble joke, but I finally saw a hint of desperation in Cornuficius. His eyes kept shooting over to the two men who would be responsible for extracting his confession, standing impassively against the wall, acting like this whole thing was boring. I suppose it was to them; I did not want to think about all the things they had done and seen over the years.

"You will confess, Cornuficius," I replied quietly. "Even if you didn't do it, you'd confess by the time they're through and you know it."

Suddenly, his body slumped, his head dropping to his chest as he closed his eyes tightly, muttering something to himself that I could not make out. At length, he raised his head, and I saw a man for whom all hope was extinguished, who knew that he had come to the end of his road. Despite myself, I felt a twinge of pity.

"He was cheating me." He said it quietly, but it was silent in the room so we heard him clearly.

"How do you know?"

He looked sharply up at me, his mouth twisted in a bitter grimace, then gave a cough that I guessed was a laugh. "How does any cheat know he's being taken? It takes one to know one, I suppose. He was playing with loaded dice."

"Then why didn't you call him on it and expose him?" Fuscus asked.

Cornuficius may have realized he was through, but that did not mean that he had any greater regard for Fuscus, the sneer briefly returning as he gave Fuscus a withering look. "If I could have, don't you think I would have? He was too good, too clever."

His mouth turned down into a grimace that spoke of the bitterness that comes to a man who has always thought he was the cleverest, but discovers that there is always someone better down the road, waiting for you. I knew then that this is a truth that extends to all things, that if I continued in the army, and continued to march for Rome, that one day I would run into that man who was better than I was. On that day, my life would end, but I still had such a belief in myself that I thought that there was a possibility that I was truly the best that lived during my time. Such is the vanity of youth. Now I was watching a man who was being forced to confront the reality that he had been bested at a game that he thought he owned, and I could see it was a bitter drink for Cornuficius indeed.

~ ~ ~ ~

In the end, Cornuficius confessed everything, without being tortured. If he were a slave of course, his confession would not have been valid unless he *was* tortured, something I never saw the sense in, but that has been the law since long before I was born and will be so long after I die. Caesar arrived at headquarters shortly after dawn, as was his normal custom, with Antipater and ben-Judah, along with a small group of other Jews who were not present at our first meeting arriving shortly thereafter. This was when I learned of Jews and their particular obsession about pigs. They had recovered Joseph's remains, or what was left of them and they were clearly enraged. I handed Caesar the wax tablets containing the accounts of Publius, Genusius, and Larius, along with the signed confession of Cornuficius, which he read impassively, not bothering with the others' testimony. He did raise an eyebrow at one point, shooting me a questioning look.

Turning so that the others could not overhear, he asked me, "Do you believe what Cornuficius says? About being cheated?"

As easy as it would have been simply to say "no," I suppose that there is enough of an honest and fair man inside of me that prevented me from doing so.

More importantly, I knew that it would not really matter. "Yes, I do believe him. I think that Joseph was just better at cheating than Cornuficius and that made him angrier than losing the money."

He considered what I had said then nodded, handing me back the tablet as he turned to address the Jews.

"We have a signed confession from Decimus Pilus Posterior Cornuficius admitting to ordering one of his men to murder Joseph of Gaza and dispose of his body. He will be executed immediately, according to the rules and regulations of the Roman army."

I suppose it was too much to ask of the Jews to simply accept Caesar's decision and leave it at that. Still, I was not prepared for the howls of anger and rage from the small group.

"That is not acceptable to us." This did not come from Antipater or ben-Judah, but from another man that I had seen several times yet did not know.

He was dressed differently than the others, not wearing armor or carrying a weapon, wearing a simple but obviously expensive gown and a large conical hat that added almost a foot to his height. I thought he looked slightly ridiculous, but I could see even Antipater treating him with a respect just short of deference. The man continued speaking though his Latin was somewhat hard to understand because of his accent and his tightly clenched jaw.

"He has defiled a high ranking officer of our army, not to mention a well-respected member of our community. We demand justice according to our laws. The criminal needs to be turned over to us immediately so that he can be punished."

Of all the people in the room at that point, I think that I knew better than any of them that this man, whose name I learned was Hyrcanus, had made a grave error. If he had phrased his short speech in the form of a request, I would not have been surprised if Caesar had turned Cornuficius over to them, but he used the word "demand," practically guaranteeing that it would not happen. As great a man as Caesar was, he was still a man with faults and one of those was a stubborn streak that tended to surface at moments like this and I could see by the set of his jaw that Hyrcanus' words had angered him.

"I understand your anger, but what does it matter how he dies? He's going to be executed in the same manner as if he had murdered a Roman citizen."

"It matters a great deal," Hyrcanus countered. "We have our own laws and customs by which these matters are handled and he should be punished according to those laws and customs. Our people demand no less."

"Your people are in no position to make demands. They are subjects of Rome, and no matter what your laws and customs dictate, your people and you," Caesar said pointedly, "are subject to the laws of Rome. And in this matter, the punishment is clear and will be carried out according to our laws, not yours."

To any other people this would have been enough and stopped the argument, but as I was learning, the Jews are not like other people. Instead of accepting Caesar's word, they continued to argue with him, and I could see that he was getting angrier the more they talked. Things were getting out of hand, and I did not know where this was headed, but it was not going to end well for anybody.

"You said that Joseph didn't drink much, is that correct? But what about gambling? How much did he gamble?"

As usual, I had not planned on saying anything, but that *numen* had inhabited me again so the words just came tumbling out, catching everyone by surprise. To my vast relief, Caesar did not seem irritated, a look of understanding crossing between us as he gave me a slight nod to continue. The same cannot be said for the Jews, and I felt a surge of triumph when I saw ben-Judah and Antipater shoot each other a glance, looking very worried indeed.

Ben-Judah spoke, clearly reluctant. "Joseph enjoyed gambling as much as any man," he said cautiously.

"So you're saying that you gambled just as much as he did? Or as much as you?" I pointed to one of the other officers, then swung my finger to another, "Or how about you? Are you saying that he didn't gamble more than any of you?"

Ben-Judah's face flushed, but his tone was even. "Perhaps I misspoke. Joseph did gamble more than most of us. It was his one vice. What of it?"

"Did he ever have any trouble before this concerning his gambling?"

"What do you mean by 'trouble'?" ben-Judah asked hotly, his hand dropping in what I hoped was an involuntary gesture to the hilt of his sword.

"What Pullus is asking is if we were to conduct a deeper investigation, would he find others among your people who perhaps did not share as high an opinion of Joseph as you, particularly when it came to his gambling habits?" Caesar's voice was mild, but there was no mistaking the fact that he was deadly serious.

Ben-Judah and Antipater exchanged a look between each other, then I saw Antipater give the slightest shake of his head before ben-Judah answered Caesar, "When one gambled as often as Joseph did, they are bound to rub some people the wrong way," ben-Judah said carefully.

"Particularly one who won as often as Joseph did?" Caesar asked gently.

Ben-Judah sighed, his shoulders slumping as he closed his eyes, like he did not want to look Caesar in the eyes as he replied, "Especially Joseph."

Antipater exhaled, and as he did so, I realized that I had not been the only man holding his breath.

~ ~ ~ ~

The Jews relented in their demands for Cornuficius, grudgingly agreeing that we would carry out the punishment of him, with them acting as witnesses only.

They filed out of the room and as ben-Judah walked by, he whispered harshly to me, "I hope you're happy now, Roman."

I said nothing, just looked down at him as he passed, keeping my face a mask. After they had left, Caesar let out a great sigh, throwing the tablet on his desk, then sitting next to it while rubbing his brow.

He looked up at me, shaking his head. "This is most inconvenient, Pullus, most inconvenient. Now I'm going to have do something to smooth things over with the Jews before we leave here to go after Pharnaces."

"Like what?"

"I don't know right now, but I'll have to think of something quickly. Now," he turned his mind back to the immediate matter. "I will have Apollonius draw up the necessary paperwork for the execution of Cornuficius. One thing though; we're not going to follow custom and hold a public execution. Your Centurions who already know will be present of course, but outside of that, only my immediate staff and whoever the Jews appoint to attend."

I nodded my understanding, then asked when he wanted it to be carried out.

He frowned as he thought about it. "I want it done today, as soon as the orders can be prepared and the audience assembled. We'll do it downstairs, out of public view. He may have been a murderer and a cheat, but he was a Centurion in my army, and that counts for something."

I saluted, then left the room, heading downstairs, where Fuscus, Sertorius, and Diocles were waiting with Cornuficius. I wasted no time trying to come up with words, just telling Cornuficius that his fate had been decided and what it was. His face went pale, but other than that, he kept his composure, for which I felt a grudging respect. Sertorius looked grim while Fuscus, well Fuscus just looked relieved.

"I don't suppose you could untie me, so I could at least take a piss before I die?" Cornuficius asked, and seeing no harm, I undid his bonds, signaling to two of the provosts to accompany him to the corner of the basement where there was a pit dug for such purposes.

They returned shortly, then I sat Cornuficius back in the chair, but only chained his legs, leaving his hands free. He asked for something to eat, and I saw no point in refusing that either, so I sent Diocles to find some food, while I sent Sertorius to gather the other Centurions, instructing him not to give them the reason why. Finally, I went to see if everything else was ready as far as the written orders. The time for the execution was set for a third of a watch before sundown, and once everything was prepared, there was nothing left to do but wait.

~ ~ ~ ~

I will say that Cornuficius died well. He did not cry or grovel, walking steadily to the spot in the basement that had obviously been used for executions in the past, the stone floor stained more darkly than the rest of the stone surrounding it. The Jews were there, their anger still evident, and as Cornuficius was led past, ben-Judah spat on the floor then said something in his tongue that I can only guess at. Cornuficius did not react at all, staring straight ahead, stripped down to only his tunic. Caesar was present, but he chose Apollonius to read the warrant for execution, saying only what was required of him, that the sentence was to be carried out. Like the men from the torture detachment, there are men trained for executions of condemned men, and one of those men was standing there waiting, armed with a spatha instead of the infantry sword. The blade of the cavalryman, being longer and heavier, makes it a better tool for decapitating a man. Cornuficius knelt, his lips moving in prayer to his household gods I imagine, as the executioner stepped forward, looking to Caesar to give the signal. Caesar waited until Cornuficius was through, then nodded. The blade swung into the air before flashing downward in a brutal arc, slicing through Cornuficius' neck as easily as if it were a loaf of bread, his head falling with a thud that made my stomach lurch. Blood spurted several inches from his neck, the body remaining upright for an instant before toppling sideways to the floor. It was done; one of my bitterest enemies was dead, yet I felt no real triumph, just a sense of relief that I would not have to watch my back anymore. I looked over at the Jews, some of whom looked triumphantly at the corpse, while most of them looked solemn and as if they would rather be somewhere else. Most surprising to me was that one of those was ben-Judah; I had expected him to look, at the least, satisfied at the death of Cornuficius, yet he did not appear to be so.

Despite that, I could not resist saying to him as he walked by, "Are you happy now, Jew?"

A look of real anger flashed in his eyes and he took a step forward, his hand going to the hilt of his sword, but before he could say anything, I nodded down at his hand, saying quietly, "You should be careful of making it a habit of reaching for that whenever you're angry. Someone might think you were going to use it, and that would be bad. For everybody."

He stopped short, but his hand moved away from the hilt, and he let out a breath, nodding slowly. "I suppose you are right. And am I happy?" He considered this, then shook his head. "No, I am not happy. Joseph is still dead. The blood of your man does not change that. But I admit that justice has been done, even if it was not in the manner in which we wanted. I suppose that's the best we can expect . . . being subjects of Rome."

The bitterness in his tone was unmistakable, and I saw in his face the despair that comes from being a people subject to the will of another, more powerful nation. There was nothing more to be said after that, and he left with the rest of the Jews. After they had gone, Publius was brought forth and executed; the Jews were no more interested in him than they were in the sword that had been used on Joseph, knowing that he was just a tool. For his part, he did not die well, sobbing and begging Caesar for mercy, having to be dragged to the spot where Cornuficius had died, his body already removed. Being as large a man as he was, it took three provosts to drag him, kicking and screaming, the spittle flying from his mouth, spraying the others around him. All in all, it was a pathetic scene and we were thankful when it was over. The other two men, Genusius and Larius, were not executed, but they were scourged, again in private and not in the forum as custom dictated. Caesar wanted to keep this affair as quiet as possible, but a Centurion cannot just disappear, therefore I was ordered to call a formation to read the charges, along with the execution warrant at the morning formation. There was also the matter of Cornuficius' replacement, and I promoted Sertorius from the Fifth Century. Additionally, in a somewhat unusual move, I named Salvius' Optio Porcinus, who had impressed me a great deal, into Sertorius' spot. Sertorius' original Optio, a man named Spurius Albus, was not happy about it, but I promised him that the next opening that came up in the 10th, I would promote him to that slot. Into Porcinus' old slot, I promoted Numerius Pupinius, which did not please Salvius in the slightest, but he had been recommended by Porcinus and I trusted his judgment much more than Salvius'. I did this all the evening after Cornuficius' execution, calling a meeting of the Centurions and Optios of the 10th in the headquarters building, ostensibly to inform them of the promotions, not wanting the men to have a chance to find out what had happened to Cornuficius. When I informed the officers of all that had transpired, the only part I left out was the belief that Joseph of Gaza had cheated Cornuficius. Their reaction ranged from shock and disbelief, to what looked almost like panic on the faces of men like Favonius and Cornuficius' Optio, a little worm named Ligus, who had been one of his toadies. Fuscus was no longer trying to hide his look of triumph at the death of his longtime Nemesis, while Sertorius was giving nothing away, looking as impassive as that statue of the Sphinx we had seen on our sightseeing excursion on the Nile. After the announcement, we had the formal promotion ceremony, whereupon I dismissed the men, having Diocles hand the proper warrants to each of the newly promoted men so they could go to the Legion quartermaster to draw the extra gear that came with their new ranks. I returned to the camp, more exhausted than I had been in a long time; it had been a very trying day.

~ ~ ~ ~

While I took care of my own administrative details, Caesar was doing the same, on a much larger scale. As he told me, he had to think of a way to appease the Jews, doing it in his usual thorough and grand way. During our stay in Ace Ptolemais, one of Antipater's rivals, a man named Antigonus had come before Caesar to accuse Antipater and Hyrcanus of trying to poison him, asking Caesar for justice. Antigonus' timing could not have been worse, though he had no way of knowing what had transpired with Joseph of Gaza. In what Apollonius described as a scene worthy to be called theater and to charge people for admission, there was a confrontation between Antigonus and Antipater. Antipater disrobed to show everyone there the scars that he had borne during the battle on the Nile fighting for Caesar. Even if there had not been the Joseph affair hanging over his head, there was no way that Caesar would turn his back on a man who had shed blood for him, meaning Antigonus was sent on his way empty-handed. Both as a reward for his service and as a way to appease the Jews for the murder of Joseph, Caesar told Antipater to pick the office he wanted to hold in Judaea, and Antipater made himself procurator of the province. Antipater promptly appointed his fifteen-year-old son, Phasaelus, governor of Jerusalem, and his other son, Herod, governor of Galilee. Caesar also bestowed Roman citizenship on Antipater, freeing him from taxes for the rest of his life as well. Hyrcanus was confirmed as high priest of the Jews, which Caesar also decreed would be a hereditary post, Hyrcanus' sons and grandsons inheriting the office. With these two acts, the Jews were appeased, enabling Caesar to turn his attention back to the matter of Pharnaces.

~ ~ ~ ~

At the formation the next morning, I informed the men of the fate of Cornuficius, which of course, they already knew. I had to keep myself from shaking my head; I cannot say I was particularly surprised, and I suppose it was a little much to expect that newly promoted men would not draw attention and questions. As I stood there mouthing the words, I looked most intently at the men of the Second Century of the 10th, and was happy to see that, for the most part, the men looked more relieved than anything else. At the very least, they would not have to worry about being extorted, able to keep more of their money for themselves, in order to waste in any manner they saw fit.

Suddenly seeing an opportunity, I began speaking again. "If there's anything to be learned from this, it's that nobody, not even a Centurion, is above the law. No matter what your rank, no matter what your station, the laws of Rome provide protection for each and every one of you. But it also means that there will be retribution against you if you break those laws. Let the example of Cornuficius remind you of that. Nobody is above the law," I repeated. With that done, I turned to other business, informing the men what I had learned in the morning briefing. "We'll be marching very shortly now, perhaps even in the next day. So except for the Centuries on guard duty, you all have passes to go into the city and debauch yourselves to your heart's content after your duties."

The men gave a rousing cheer, but I was not about to let them go without a warning.

Holding my hand up for silence, they obeyed quickly enough that I did not have to yell at them to shut up. "I would hope that the example of Cornuficius and Publius is sufficient warning to keep you out of trouble. But just to be sure, you're all forbidden from going anywhere near the Jewish Quarter. And if you run into any of the Jewish soldiers, you're to avoid trouble with them at all costs, even if that means you leave the premises. Any man who gets into any kind of trouble with the Jews is going to be assumed guilty, no matter what your explanation. And if you get into trouble, you better hope that the Jews kill you, because I will flay you alive. Do I make myself clear?"

The men answered that they did, although I knew that they would agree to anything just to get out of there and get into the city. I just hoped that it would be enough, but had decided to take the risk, knowing that no matter the cause and who had been punished, hearing about a comrade being executed was not good for morale, so I wanted them to have something to take their minds off of it.

~ ~ ~ ~

Just before we left, Caesar was joined by one of his kinsman, Sextus Caesar, who had arrived with a fleet from Italy, bringing dire news of developments back home. According to Sextus, Dolabella had announced that he planned on forgiving all debts and eliminating all rents, which he had the power to do as Tribune of the Plebs. Naturally, despite this being immensely popular with people of my class, it enraged the patricians, who comprised the majority of the landlords in Rome and the whole of the peninsula, along with being the major lenders. Although there was some violence in the Forum, it had been relatively minor so far, but it was not likely to remain that way. Still, as bad as that was, there was even worse news, at least as far as I was concerned, and it was about the 10th and what they had done. As I mentioned earlier, they had been encamped on the Campus Martius now, along with the other Spanish Legions for almost a year, waiting for Caesar, and their patience had finally run out. Despite the fact I did not know the details, I was told by Caesar that at least two Tribunes by the name of Gaius Avienus and Aulus Fonteius, along with several Centurions, had been feeding the flames of the men's discontent, telling them that they indeed held legitimate grievances and deserved all the things that Caesar had promised them. Now, I cannot argue that they were wrong; Caesar had indeed made promises and as loyal as I was to Caesar, I felt strongly that these promises must be kept for a number of reasons. However, the men were running out of patience, and there were a number of incidents of violence against civilians, with tensions rising almost daily, according to Sextus Caesar. When I was told of what was happening, and that Centurions were involved, I knew in my gut that at the very least, Celer was involved. As sure as I was about Celer, I was just as sure that Scribonius and Priscus would not have anything to do with inciting the men. Crispus, I was not so sure about, and Niger's replacement, Vatinius, I did not know well enough to make a judgment either way, but the man I was most worried about was Vibius. Even though he was not a Centurion and had been my and was now Scribonius' Optio, I was sure that his hatred of Caesar, and now of me, would spur him to act in a rash manner. Compounding the problem, at least in my eyes, was the fact that despite not being a Centurion, Vibius held a great deal of influence over the men. As much as I would like to say that it was only because of his relationship with me that would not be the truth; he was as brave as I was, he was well-liked by his comrades and I have no doubt that if he had wanted it as badly as I did, he would have been in the Centurionate. At Pharsalus, I had threatened to strike him down, and meant it, but the habit of a lifetime is very hard to break. No matter how angry I was with Vibius, or how estranged we were, he had been my oldest friend and that was something I could not just shut off, no matter how much I may have wanted. Despite all this bad news, Caesar was still determined to finish what he had started here in the East, both administratively and militarily with Pharnaces, who showed no inclination to vacate the territory he had taken. To that end, we took ship, bound for

Tarsus in Cilicia next, where Caesar did the same thing he had done in Ace Ptolemais, making appointments, hearing cases and putting things in order. For whatever reason, he did not seem to be in any hurry to confront Pharnaces, which I found both puzzling and disturbing, so much so that I grabbed Apollonius one evening when he was sitting talking with Diocles and demanded to know what he thought Caesar was doing.

Having become accustomed to my attempts to bully him, Apollonius was unperturbed. "I imagine that he's giving Pharnaces a chance to reconsider his decision to stay put. Not to mention that he has to give the 36th time to march overland to the place Caesar has designated for us to meet."

He gave me a smug look, raising his cup in a mock salute, giving a girlish squeal when I kicked the chair out from under him.

Meeting Caesar in Tarsus were two men, and I use the term men loosely, none other than Marcus Junius Brutus and Gaius Cassius, both of whom came begging Caesar's forgiveness. More accurately, Brutus had already been forgiven by Caesar, but was now interceding with him on behalf of Cassius, and it should be no surprise that Caesar did indeed forgive Cassius, restoring him to favor. Of course, Cassius went on to repay this kindness with the vilest example of treachery in history. In Tarsus, it took Caesar just a few days to dispose of all outstanding matters, then at dawn one day near the end of Junius, we marched out of the city, heading north through Cappadocia. Stopping in the capital Mazaca for two days, Caesar did more of his administrative work before we pushed on for the Pontus border. Just a day out of Mazaca, shortly before sunset, a large group of horsemen along with a small force of infantry approached the camp, asking for entrance. The leader was none other than Deiotarus, tetrarch of Lesser Armenia, coming not as a head of state but as a supplicant; another bottom feeder throwing himself on Caesar's mercy because he had chosen to support Pompey. I do not know what he said, but I know that Caesar forgave him, except not without a demand for Deiotarus to supply one of his Roman-trained Legions, along with all of his cavalry to augment our force. More accurately, the Legion he ended up supplying was the combined remnants of the two Legions that Domitius had led at Nicopolis, but they were so badly cut up that they had to be combined to make one full Legion. Deiotarus had no choice but to agree, promising that they would be at the same place that Caesar had designated for the 36th to wait for us to arrive, at the appointed time. With this matter settled, we marched across the border into Pontus in late Quintilis, the month now named for Caesar.

~ ~ ~ ~

The 36th, the amalgamated Deiotaran Legion and the Pontic cavalry arrived the day after we reached the spot by a river that Caesar had designated as our meeting place. Rather than go immediately into action, we worked on fortifying our camp, which may sound somewhat strange given the fact that we were there to take offensive action against Pharnaces. However, we had long since learned that the sight of a fortified Roman army camp was one of the most powerful weapons in our arsenal, almost always filling our enemy with fear and dread at the sight of our precision and skill in erecting defenses. It is the same reason why we built a marching camp every single night, almost without exception, because it sent a signal to all who thought to oppose us that there was no stopping us and that we would be relentless foes. I do not believe there has ever been a general in our history who understood the power of warfare against the minds of men better than Caesar; one only has to look at the bridge we built across the Rhenus as an example of that. Therefore, it was into this fortified camp that envoys from Pharnaces came, under a flag of truce, claiming to want peace and that his invasion was nothing more than a big misunderstanding.

I was present at the meeting, along with the other Primi Pili of the 36th, the Deiotaran Legion and the commanders of the auxiliary forces. That is when we learned of some of the outrages that Pharnaces had committed against Roman citizens who lived in the region that he had taken. Aside from the usual rapine and looting, the most outrageous act was the castration of every young Roman teenager that his men could get their hands on, along with acts so despicable that I will not enumerate them here. Yet, despite the horrific nature of these crimes, Pharnaces' envoys stood there, behaving as if these acts were mere trifles, even going so far as saying that he deserved to be praised for not siding with Pompey, unlike Deiotarus. The main spokesman for Pharnaces went even further, saying that if Caesar had pardoned Deiotarus for his siding with Pompey, then it was a case of simple justice for Pharnaces to be pardoned, despite the atrocities committed in his name. They also said that they would be more than happy to return within their own borders and leave Pontus, giving their word that Caesar could trust them to do so, enabling Caesar to return to Rome with his army, confident that Pharnaces would withdraw. Fortunately, Caesar was not buying anything that Pharnaces was selling, telling the envoys that he not only expected them to withdraw immediately, but also to restore all property seized from Roman citizens and to free all those Romans they had taken as slaves. As far as what had been taken from the young men, that could not be restored, but Caesar demanded that each defiled man must be compensated with hard currency, at a rate set by Caesar. To my surprise, the envoys of Pharnaces did not balk at any of this, saying instead that they believed that Pharnaces would agree to these terms, but they had to go to their king to discuss them, which Caesar gave them leave to do. To my eyes at least, it appeared as if we had marched a long way for nothing, but Caesar immediately dispelled that idea.

"They're stalling, nothing more," he said after they had left. "Pharnaces has no intention of withdrawing."

"But why would his envoys say so?" one of the auxiliary commanders asked, and I was pleased that he did, since that was what I wanted to know but was not willing to ask myself.

"Because they have undoubtedly heard of everything that is going on back in Rome, and they're sure that I can't afford to stay here. They'll come back in a day or two and tell me that while Pharnaces has agreed, there will undoubtedly be some condition that prevents him from leaving immediately. I would guess that there will be some sort of horrible illness gripping his army, or perhaps his livestock. Whatever the case, he'll expect me to be unable to wait and that we'll march away. And of course if I do that, he'll never leave Pontus until I return and forcibly expel him."

That is exactly what happened. Two days later, the envoys returned, acting like they brought joyful news, making a great show of announcing that Pharnaces had agreed to Caesar's conditions and that he and his army would be withdrawing, very soon.

"How soon?" Caesar asked as if he was just happy that they had agreed.

The envoy proceeded to explain that it would be very soon. Of course, moving such a large army took time, and regrettably, while Pharnaces' army had been encamped, many of the men were struck down by some mysterious but serious illness, so it would be impossible to move until they were fully recovered. It took quite a bit of willpower for me not to burst out laughing and I could see that I was not alone in my amusement, Caesar included, whose mouth kept twitching, a sure sign that he was secretly amused as well. Once the envoys had finished making their excuses, Caesar gave a great sigh.

"That is unfortunate indeed." He shook his head. "I had hoped to return to Rome, as there are some matters there that I need to attend to, but I'll keep my army right here while we all wait for your stricken soldiers to recover."

The chief envoy began protesting that this was truly not necessary, that he was sure that it was only a matter of a few days before the army would be able to march. There was no need for Caesar to tarry here in that event, he insisted, a look of alarm clearly written on his dark features. Caesar spread his hands and shrugged, as if he were helpless in the matter, and the envoys left once again, this time not nearly has happy as the last. We laughed for several moments after they had gone, then Caesar called us to order to begin planning the battle.

~ ~ ~ ~

Choosing not to wait until the next day, Caesar ordered camp to be broken so that we stole a march, moving through the night until we drew close enough to see the lights from the enemy camp located about three miles north of the town of Zela. Pharnaces had chosen to build his camp on the site of the camp that his father Mithridates had pitched, about a mile from where the old king had defeated a general of Lucullus, one Gaius Triarius when I was about ten years old. At dawn, our presence was discovered and a thoroughly alarmed party, led by the same envoy who had visited us twice previously, hurried to meet us. Caesar did not even dismount from his horse, keeping us on the march while the Bosporans offered Caesar even more than they had previously, anything to get him to stop. Before, on their first visit, they had offered Caesar a gold crown and I must say that it was a very lavish and obviously valuable trinket, but of course, he refused. Now, they were not only offering Caesar the crown, they also offered him Pharnaces' daughter's hand in marriage, which he rejected out of hand. Apollonius told Diocles and me later that Caesar's response was to ask the envoys if they considered it right for a man who caused the death of his father to escape justice. Apollonius gleefully relayed how the Bosporans looked like they had been slapped; such was the sting of Caesar's words, because that is indeed what had happened. There are two versions of the story of how Mithridates had met his end. One was that while Pharnaces did not kill his father outright, he had engineered a takeover of the army, and Mithridates was unable to live with the shame and killed himself. The second version, and the one most widely believed was that Pharnaces engineered his father's death by poisoning, using an extremely rare poison, not one of those that Mithridates had ingested on a daily basis to inure himself to such attempts. When Caesar said this to the Bosporans, it was then that they realized that there would be no negotiated settlement, or any further stalling of Caesar, so they turned around and galloped off to inform their king to make ready for battle. We continued marching until we were about two miles south of Zela and five miles south of Pharnaces' encampment, where we occupied a small hill with fairly steep sides and began constructing our camp. Caesar went scouting while we worked, which progressed quickly despite our fatigue from marching through the night. Once he returned, he immediately called a council to begin issuing orders. When we left Tarsus to march overland, Caesar had drafted a large number of slaves over and above the normal contingent that accompanies an army. While we were meeting, he sent these slaves out into the countryside to find wood of a proper size to use as palisade stakes, ordering them to gather a sufficient amount to fortify another camp of equal size to the one we currently occupied. Caesar told us that he had found a position near Pharnaces' camp that, when occupied, would put

Pharnaces into a situation where he would be forced to fight, because we would be cutting off his access to Zela and his base of supply. Suddenly, for no apparent reason, he began grinning, causing us to exchange puzzled glances.

"It's also a position that's near and dear to Pharnaces' heart," he explained. Seeing that we still did not understand, he continued, "It's the hill on which his father defeated Triarius. When he sees us camped on the hill, I'm fairly sure that he will fight." This was just one more example of how Caesar knew exactly how the mind of his enemy worked, and how he used what he knew about the other general to his advantage. "We'll march at the beginning of fourth watch. As soon as we take the hill, the slaves will then cart over the stakes, while we dig the rampart, which means that we'll be able to build the camp much more quickly than normal. Speed is absolutely essential because the valley that separates the hill we're going to occupy from Pharnaces' camp isn't much more than a mile."

Our orders given, we were dismissed to go prepare our men, and we left the *Praetorium*, talking over what needed to be done.

~ ~ ~ ~

Marching out of camp at the appointed third of a watch, the 6th was in the lead, leaving behind everything but our weapons and our entrenching tools. A Cohort of the amalgamated Legion was also left behind to guard the original camp, while we marched as quickly as possible in the gloom of the night, covering the roughly three miles in a little less than two parts of a watch, giving us barely the same amount of time before dawn. Since we arrived first, we were assigned to guard, moving down the slope in the direction of the enemy camp, the rest of the men beginning to dig the ditch and build the rampart. The sound of a few thousand men digging makes quite a racket, particularly when the soil is rocky like it was there, so I suppose it was inevitable that we would be heard before too much time passed. As soon as we arrived, one of the cavalrymen was sent back to the original camp to give the order for the slaves, who had piled all the stakes in the Legion wagons, to make their way to us. There was considerable wagering going on that the slaves would get lost in the darkness; most of the men considered slaves of the quality that Caesar drafted, the majority untrained labor, to be little smarter than the mules and oxen that pulled the carts, but they arrived safely, if not loudly. Caesar had ordered the wheels of the wagons wrapped in rags to muffle the sound, and for the axles to be freshly greased, but I could not tell an appreciable difference, hearing them long before they actually arrived. Naturally, that meant that the enemy did as well, so that we could also clearly hear the cries of alarm from across the small valley. This spurred us to push the men to work harder and faster to complete the camp now that we were discovered, the air filling with the sounds of Centurions cursing, men gasping for breath as they worked as quickly as they could in the dark, accompanied by the sounds of metal striking rock. I could just barely see the gleam of teeth in the darkness as my own men grinned at each other, ecstatic in the misery of others and in their escape from such intense labor.

"Don't get too happy," I growled at them. "You know how it works; Fortuna will take a dump on us for this."

My words had the desired effect, the little spots of white disappeared all around me, causing me to smile on my own.

~ ~ ~ ~

Cries of alarm then reached my ears; I turned to the source and could barely make out a transverse crest bobbing up and down as one of my Centurions ran towards me. Finally getting close enough for me to recognize that it was Valens, I saw him pointing across the valley.

"Looks like they're up and about, Primus Pilus."

Peering through the darkness, after a moment I could just make out a movement of some sort, followed an instant later by a torch, followed by another, then another. Men holding torches were spreading out, the bright points of light suddenly appearing once they passed through the gate of their camp so that they were no longer shielded by the wall. After a moment, I determined that these men were being sent out to mark the shape of the enemy formation. As we watched, we saw a mass of something darker than the surrounding area moving across the slope parallel to where our own lines were formed. Grabbing my runner, I ordered him to go find Caesar to inform him that the enemy was aware of our presence and was forming up. He ran off, and I heard him trip in the dark, cursing whatever it was that had caught his toe, causing the men nearby to laugh. I did not bother to tell them to shut up; we were about to start fighting and I would rather have men who could laugh at times like this than men scared out of their wits. We could hear the Bosporan army now, the clinking of metal on metal carrying through the air, along with the yells of their officers, though they were just noises, their words not distinguishable. Looking to the east, I saw that the sky was getting light, the silhouette of the low hills in that direction becoming more and more distinct, rimmed in orange. There were no clouds that day, meaning it was going to be light fairly soon and even in the short time since Valens alerted me, I was able to make out more details, the men working on the camp distinguishable to the point where I could tell what each man was doing and not just detect indistinct movements.

"What do you suppose they're going to do?"

I was startled; I had been deep in my own thoughts and forgotten Valens was there. I did not answer, so he asked, "Do you think they'll try and come up the hill and knock us off before we're finished?"

I shook my head. "Your guess is as good as mine, but I think they're going to at least wait until it's fully light before they do anything."

While we stood there watching, the enemy troops continued to stream out of the camp to push their way through the mass of men already standing outside the walls, finding their spot in formation.

"There sure are a lot of them." Valens said this like he was remarking on the weather, but I was struck by the fact that I had been thinking the exact same thing. There did not seem to be any end to them, and now that it was light enough to make out individual men, I began to try making a count, but quickly gave up. "What's our strength, Primus Pilus?" Valens asked.

I thought for a moment, then replied, "We're at 913 effectives. The 36th is just a few more than 3500. The Deiotarian Legion is almost full strength, but that's because it's two under strength Legions combined, so that's about 4,000 men. Then there are about 1,000 cavalry, and a thousand or so Jews. So all told about 10,000 men, give or take a couple hundred."

Valens nodded in the direction of the enemy host, still streaming out of the camp. "I'm not the best at doing sums, Primus Pilus, but I'm pretty sure that there's at least twice that many over there."

He was absolutely right about that.

~ ~ ~ ~

By the time the enemy formed up, the sun was now fully visible above the hills, flooding the valley with the golden-orange light of a new morning, a morning that would be the last for only the gods knew how many men on both sides. I stood facing the enemy, watching them as the last of them moved into place, their officers striding back and forth in front of them, but my gaze was turned inward as it always was at these moments. I was so engrossed in my own thoughts that I did not hear the *bucina* sounding the assembly of officers, and it took Valens tapping me on the shoulder before I became aware of my surroundings. Feeling the heat rise to my face, I turned to trot up the hill to where Caesar was standing.

"How kind of you to join us, Primus Pilus," he said peevishly. "I hope that we're not disturbing anything important.'

"No, sir. Sorry, sir."

That was all I was going to say, but fortunately, he did not press, turning to the business at hand. "Pharnaces certainly didn't waste any time," he began. "But he's just making a demonstration, I'm sure of it. He's trying to force me to deploy the army and stop us from working on the fortifications, but we'll continue."

We were facing Caesar, who in turn was still facing the enemy so our backs were to them. That is when I saw Caesar's eyes narrow as he raised a hand to shield them to squint across the valley, something obviously catching his attention.

Before we could turn to see what it was, he told us, "It seems that Pharnaces has brought his scythed chariots with him. This should be interesting."

As one man, we all whirled around to look for ourselves, and I heard a number of men mutter curses. An even 40 of them came wheeling out of the camp, arraying themselves on the left of the enemy formation, and I felt my heart shudder. Unless I missed my guess, being Caesar's most reliable and veteran troops, we were destined for the right wing, just as the 10th had always been, meaning that we would be facing these chariots. Despite the fact that I had experience with chariots during our time in Britannia, the Bosporan chariots are a different breed altogether than those used by the Britons. Much more heavily constructed, instead of being nothing more than a flat platform with wicker sides, the Bosporan chariot has a semi-circular low wooden wall that serves as a parapet to provide protection to the driver and missile troops onboard. But what makes it a weapon that strikes fear in the hearts of those facing it are the long blades attached to the axle, which act in exactly the same manner as a scythe, except that instead of cutting down grain it is cutting down men. Most Briton chariots were pulled by two horses, although there were some pulled by four and I had even seen a couple pulled by three, but the Bosporan chariot was pulled by four exclusively. It is a nasty weapon, and I did not like the idea of one of those things getting into the midst of my men, let alone forty.

"Well, Pullus, it looks like you and your men will have your hands full."

I nodded; there was not really much to say about it.

Turning back to us, Caesar picked up where he had left off. "As I said, I don't believe that Pharnaces has any intention of actually attacking, so we'll continue to have the 6th standing ready while the rest of the men work. The only change I want to make is to shift the 6th over there," he pointed to a spot that placed us directly across from the chariots, "so that the rest of the army has room to deploy and we're not overlapping their lines on either side."

Suddenly, the sound of enemy horns began blaring across the valley floor. Again, we all turned to see what was happening and we were not disappointed. The Bosporan army was moving, albeit at a slow walk, down their hill towards the valley floor.

"They can't walk in a straight line to save their lives, can they?"

Someone made this comment, bringing a laugh from all of us, including Caesar. They were moving, but we were not concerned, such was our belief and confidence in Caesar's judgment. Turning back to

Caesar, I asked for his leave, explaining that I wanted to get my men redeployed according to his instructions, which he gave. As I trotted towards my men, I saw that they were standing watching the display in front of them, and as I passed by the ranks, I heard the buzz of conversation, the topic being the chariots, and the number of troops facing us. Going to the front of the formation, I turned to face them, yet again struck by the uncomfortable feeling that comes from turning your back to the enemy, no matter how distant they may be. It is a completely irrational response, but I could never fight the nagging suspicion that by turning my back to the enemy that somehow they would manage to suddenly cross whatever distance was remaining between us, in effect all 20,000 of them sneaking up on me. I told you it was irrational, but that feeling never went away.

Using my command voice, I bellowed out a question. "How many of you have faced the scythed chariot before?"

While I suspected I knew the answer, I was still relieved to see that most of the men raised their hands. I knew that the 6th had marched with Pompey when he fought these people before, but I needed to make sure.

"Good," I said, "because I haven't. So you can teach me before the day is out."

It was a feeble joke, but I believe the men appreciated the effort, like I appreciated them making an attempt to laugh. Giving the command to execute a right sidestep, we shuffled into the position that Caesar had designated. Because we were only two Cohorts, we could not deploy into an *acies triplex*, since that would have given us a frontage of only two Centuries per Cohort. That was not wide enough, but I was not comfortable being in single line either, because that gave us no reserve unless I unbalanced the line by pulling a Century out from each Cohort and placed them to the rear. That did not appeal to me either, therefore I ended up having a narrower frontage than I wanted, but at least I would have each Century in the front line supported by a Century behind it. I was so busy shaking the men that I wanted out into the formation, that I was caught completely by surprise when suddenly it sounded like every horn in the Bosporan army started blaring away, followed immediately by a huge roar as 20,000 men filled their lungs to sound their battle cry. Wheeling around, my jaw dropped; Caesar was wrong. This was no demonstration, although in a sense it was an attempt on their part to keep us from finishing or fortifications. The difference was that their apparent method for doing so was to kill every one of us, because they were attacking!

~ ~ ~ ~

The next several moments were eerily similar to the day those many years ago when we were attacked by the Nervii on the Sabis, as our own *cornu* started blasting the call to arms, accompanied by the roaring of the Centurions and Optios trying to push men into their proper position. The Bosporan chariots had lunged forward and were now pounding across the remainder of the valley floor that they had not yet crossed, heading right for the men of the 6th. Offering up a quick prayer of thanks to the gods for being ready, at least more ready than the rest of the army, I snapped a series of orders to my own *cornicen*, who began blowing the proper combination of notes. Immediately the men opened ranks, spreading out in order to present less of a target for the chariots, while simultaneously gripping their javelins in the underhand grip needed to throw the missile. The pounding of the horses' hooves made a drumming sound that made it hard to hear even the *cornu*.

Still, I filled my lungs up to yell as loudly as I could. "Javelins, ready!"

Almost as one, the arms of the men swept back, their leading arm, or shield arm held straight out, angled slightly upward, their rear leg bending at the knee. The ground began to shake as the chariots drew nearer, the vibration traveling all the way up into my thighs.

"Aim for the horses," I bellowed, though I knew that I did not really have to tell them.

"Release!"

The sky was laced with streaking black darts, the tips pointing skyward before they began to slow, then for just a split second, they hovered in mid-air, almost a thousand of them, before whatever force it is that makes all things that go into the air come back down took control, bringing them down, down, down, picking up speed before smashing into the packed mass of horse and human flesh. Immediately the air was rent with the screams of suffering beasts, four-legged and two-legged, followed by the crashing and splintering of wood and metal as the chariots that escaped unscathed went smashing into the bodies of horses struck down, or into another chariot. Men were catapulted into the air when one chariot hit another that came to a stop because one or more of the horses pulling it had gone down. The charge of the chariots slowed, but it did not stop, the drivers in the rear rank maneuvering their way past the wreckage and carnage of those in front.

"Javelins, ready!"

We had one more volley left, but if we could do the same amount of damage that we did with the first, it should be enough, or so I hoped.

"Release!"

The second volley sliced into the remaining chariots, the men concentrating their aim on those that had escaped unscathed so far, and the effect of that volley was as devastating as the first, so that in a matter of a few breaths, the threat posed by the scythed chariots was ended.

Covering the ground in front of us was the wreckage of the chariots, along with their horses, many of them still alive but either pulled down by their harness mates or because of their wounds, their hooves flailing in pain and desperation, making them almost as dangerous as if their chariots were still upright and operational. Horrible sounds, the shrieks of pain of both men and horse, made speaking in normal conversational tones impossible. We remained in place watching the remaining chariots, no more than six or seven, wheel about to flee back to the camp, revealing behind them a formation of men on foot who were still marching towards us. They were trying to stay in formation anyway; forced as they were to pick their way over and around the wreckage of Pharnaces' force of chariots, any attempt at retaining their cohesion was futile. Because we were out of javelins, I gave the order to draw swords, waiting a moment for the men to prepare themselves and to give the enemy's front ranks the chance to clear the wreckage, not wanting my men to go slamming into the Bosporans having to worry about the fallen horses or their footing.

Judging the moment to be right, I yelled the order to charge. "Caesar Victorious!"

With that cry on their lips, the men of the 6th hurtled down the hill, slamming into the front ranks of the Bosporans, the royal guard of Pharnaces as it turned out, though we did not know that at the time. I barely had time to wet my blade before Pharnaces' men followed their chariots, breaking and running for their lives, with us following closely behind, cutting men down as they fled. I considered sounding the halt, as I looked to the center to see that the enemy had not yet broken, although the Deiotaran Legion was pressing them hard, but I decided against it for a number of reasons, not least among them being I doubted the men would heed the call, the walls of the enemy camp being within reach. That meant that just on the other side of the wall lay loot, and my men were not inclined to let the opportunity to be first over the wall slip through their grasp. It was a gamble I was taking, because if the center and left wings did not defeat the Bosporans, we would have a substantial force to our rear, and if that happened it was still possible that these men running for their camp could rally and turn on us. Yet, while I did not know the identity of the force we had just routed at the time, I had seen that they were better equipped and armed than the men fighting in the center, meaning if they had turned and run I was sure that the rest of the Bosporans would be following shortly. Perhaps this is another of Diocles' rationalizations; in hindsight, it is easy to justify my decision because it worked out well, but who knows how things would have turned out if the rest of the Bosporan army had not turned around to run for their lives in the same manner as their comrades facing us? Either way, the men of the 6th ran after the Bosporans, and when they reached the wall, stopped only as long as it took for a few men to scale it, going on to tear the palisade stakes down to allow their comrades through. The only orders I gave were for other Centuries to move along the wall to create a breach, since Legionaries are lazy by nature and would have simply tried to cram through the single hole created by the lead Century if I had let them. It took a few extra moments, but soon enough we had created three more breaches, enabling both Cohorts to make it into the camp, where the force of Bosporans that we routed had managed to regroup and appeared ready to put up more of a fight now they were in the camp than when they were in the valley. Ripping down a number of tents, they gave themselves more room to form up in a position that blocked our access to the center of the camp. The Bosporans favored the long spear, although every man in the group also carried a sword slightly longer than ours, and curved a bit, but it was the spear that we were facing now, a veritable wall of them as the enemy locked shields and stood waiting for us.

~ ~ ~ ~

Pausing only long enough to get formed back up, the men of the 6th charged into the Bosporans, who put up a fierce resistance for a few moments before they broke, but they bought enough time for Pharnaces and a few members of his retinue to escape on horseback out the opposite side of the camp. There was a blast of a horn, an obvious signal to the royal guard that Pharnaces had escaped, then to a man they stopped fighting, throwing their weapons down. Unfortunately, for some of them, it took a moment to get the men to stop cutting them down, despite the Centurions and Optios doing their best to halt the carnage. After they were disarmed, I assigned a Century to guard them before turning the rest of the men loose to loot the camp, which was all they were really concerned with anyway. The rest of the Bosporan force had crumbled by this time as well, so now the camp was filling with the rest of Caesar's army. There was the inevitable confusion and squabbling as we Centurions worked out what part of the camp belonged to which Legion. Naturally I had selected the juiciest bit for my men immediately surrounding Pharnaces' tent, which was being guarded by a couple of sections of my men for Caesar, detailing Felix to command them, knowing I could trust him not to yield to temptation or allow the men to either. Caesar rode into camp, where we hailed him as Imperator three times. He sitting on Toes, smiling down at us and I was struck by a sudden sadness, though to this day I do not know exactly why. Perhaps it was the knowledge that we were through fighting, and that Caesar would be sending the 6th back to Italy, for that is what he had announced as his intention the night before the battle during our final briefing. Oh, I was as anxious as any man to go home; I had a new child and I had not seen my wife in more than a year. While I cannot say that I enjoyed fighting with the same fervor that I did when I was younger and was marching in the ranks, marching to war was what gave my life purpose. I had enough of a taste of peace and garrison duty to know that I did not care for it the way some men did and in fact, found it much more onerous than the hard life of marching camps and campaigning. Gazing up at the man who I had followed for all of my adult life to that point, I felt like something was passing, that there was a change happening that I could not fully grasp, and I was more than a little surprised and mortified to feel my eyes start to fill with tears. I glanced around to see if anyone noticed, thankful that everyone was more occupied with cheering Caesar. He made a short speech, knowing that he needed to say something, but also knowing that he needed to keep it brief, since the men were only half-listening, the rest of their attention focused on the line of tents that they were about to ransack, mentally adding up the loot in their head. Of course, the amount that they imagined and what they would find were rarely in close proximity to each other, but every night around a fire there are tales told of the lucky Legionary who found a king's ransom hidden under a bedroll, or a statue painted over to look ordinary but was really solid gold. The fact that none of the men telling the tales were actually those who experienced such a bounty did not dissuade them from the belief that they were true, and I had long since given up trying to convince any of my comrades who engaged in such fantasy that they were just stories told by bored men. Caesar thanked us for our valor, making special mention of the 6th for our work in smashing the chariot attack, and I could see the men were as pleased as if they had found that statue made of gold. I had to suppress a laugh; here were these hard-bitten men, who had marched for Pompey and had been defeated by the man praising them, yet they looked as proud as if they were the prized pupil being singled out for acclaim by their tutor. Despite themselves, and despite the vows I heard many of them make around the fires at night, they now loved Caesar just as much as the men who had been marching with him as long as I had, and they lived for these moments of praise from him. They had been seduced, just like me, and just like Cleopatra, though in truth I think with her it may have been the other way around. Regardless, the men of the 6th were now Caesar's men. And we would be leaving him to march into an uncertain future.

~ ~ ~ ~

The next day a formation was held, where Caesar made public his plans for the army. I had been sworn to secrecy, meaning the news that the 6th was being sent back to Rome to receive all that they had been promised was a total and wonderful surprise to the men, and they cheered Caesar lustily. We would march overland through Asia all the way to Dyrrhachium, take the short boat trip across to Italy, then march to Rome and we would be escorting the prisoners taken the day before, where they would be sold into slavery. The proceeds of the sale would be evenly divided among the army, but not before they were marched in the triumph Caesar planned when he returned. The 36th and Deiotaran Legions would remain in Pontus for the time being, because Pharnaces had escaped and Caesar did not want to take the risk of him raising another army to try again. For our actions against the chariots, Caesar ordered our standards to be decked in both ivy and oak, and a number of the men were decorated on my recommendation, including Optio Tetarfenus, who was the first over the wall of the enemy camp. The royal treasury of Pharnaces had been captured intact, and while by custom it belonged to Caesar, he announced that the entire sum was also to be evenly divided among the army, which as you can imagine, was wildly popular with the men. Capping it all off, Caesar announced that the next three days were to be spent in thanksgiving, meaning that only the essential duties of guarding the camp and prisoners would be maintained, and that the wine ration was doubled for the entire three days. I do not know which the men cheered the loudest for, the three days off or the wine, but I found myself suppressing a grimace at the thought of the men being idle for three days, with enough wine to get them in trouble. Immediately after the thought struck me, I had to chide myself. Titus, you are in serious danger of becoming an old woman; there was a time when you would have been cheering just as loudly as the rest of the men at the idea of three days with nothing to do. When the men were dismissed, chattering excitedly with each other about the drinking and gambling of their newfound wealth they were going to do, I called a quick meeting of the Centurions and Optios.

"I don't have to tell you that we're going to have to be on our toes," I began, and was happy to see that at least all the heads were nodding in the right direction.

Normally at this point, I could have counted on Cornuficius to make some sort of comment, and immediately after his mouth opened, men like Annius would be echoing him, but with Cornuficius gone, his former toadies did not have the nerve to say anything on their own, for which I was thankful.

"But that doesn't mean that we can't have some fun as well," I continued, and I was rewarded with smiles all around. "I want two Centurions and two Optios from each Cohort on duty at all times, by the normal watches, and make sure that they're all from different Centuries. The rest of you can get as soused as the men, as long as you're sober in time for your turn at duty. Also, I know I'm going to regret this, but tell the men that I'm making my personal supply of wine available to them as well, as my thanks for a job well done."

I bit back a smile as I saw their reactions, which seemed to waver between approval, apprehension, and a little bit of annoyance at the thought that the men were going to get a reward while they were not, but I was not through.

"Of course, I'm not talking about my Falernian, of which I have three amphorae. That's for you and the Optios to share, alone."

I had long since exhausted the original supply of Falernian bequeathed to me by Pulcher all those years ago, but I had learned that the judicious use of a good vintage of wine went a long way towards smoothing the road of relationships with others. Falernian is one of the most prized varieties of wine, so I maintained a decent supply of it at all times, even when it cost me dearly. Suddenly I was a good man again, with my Centurions immediately commending my virtue and impeccable manners. Laughing, I called them "liars," then dismissed them, happy to see that they were now as excited as the men at the thought of taking the next three days in debauching themselves.

~ ~ ~ ~

During that time, the men enjoyed themselves immensely, but I could see that they were ready to march at the end of it, so we wasted no time making preparations to begin the long trek to Dyrrhachium. We would be on the march for almost a month, with the extra burden of watching the prisoners all the way, though I doubted they would try anything rash. It was something I had noticed with people we defeated. Once they were beaten, something seemed to leave their spirit, and they almost always meekly submitted to whatever fate awaited them. These men were no different; they would plod along in chains, with no more than one or two of them making any attempt to escape or even exact vengeance on one of their guards before we cut them down. While I had seen it, I still do not understand it, and it is something that Diocles and I have spent many an evening discussing. Why do some people believe slavery is a better alternative than death? Diocles maintains that my thinking is shaped by the fact that I have never been faced with the choice of death or life as a slave, and he may be right, yet I still cannot imagine that life as a slave would be preferable to an honorable death. In regard to our present situation, the men we were escorting would have their wrists shackled, but their legs would be kept free so that they could march without encumbrance. However, to prevent them from running off, they were all fitted with neck collars with lengths of chain attached, the other end running to the neck collar of another prisoner. In effect, the men were all chained together so that if one tried to run off, every other prisoner would have to do the same thing at the same time. The other problem in moving such a large group of men, who outnumbered us more than five to one, is feeding and watering them. Naturally, they did not receive the same amount of food that we did, but we could not afford to starve them, for a couple of reasons. Most importantly was the fact that we needed them to maintain enough strength so that they could march at a reasonable pace. We did not expect them to be able to match the pace that we could set, but neither did we want to take three months marching, so they had to be strong enough to average at least twenty miles a day, depending on terrain. The second reason was that these men were an investment; the better shape they were in when they arrived at the slave markets, the more we all got paid. This was also the reason why the prisoners were only beaten when absolutely necessary, although along the way we had to make an example of a few of them, executing them for a number of offenses. Meanwhile, Caesar took the cavalry, continuing his tour of Asia, settling affairs, and making appointments to vacant offices. One of the problems of such a long march through the hinterland of the Republic was that we heard nothing in the way of news in the wider world. It was not until we arrived in Dyrrhachium that we learned the news, which had caused Caesar to cut short his work in Asia to return as quickly as he could back to Rome, and also prompted my recall back to the 10th Legion.

~ ~ ~ ~

The men of the 10th had now been simmering in camp for more than a year since Caesar had sent them away from Pharsalus. Despite there being some trouble in the past months, for the most part it had been small-scale and localized to a few men. However, the Tribunes Avienus and Fonteius had continued to agitate the men, telling them that they held legitimate grievances and were owed much by Caesar. This was true as far as it went; Caesar had indeed made promises to the men. Nonetheless, Avienus, Fonteius, and some of the Centurions had convinced them that since Caesar had not produced the promised rewards, they were entitled to take what they wanted. To that end, the men entered the city, going straight to the rich neighborhoods on the Palatine and Janiculum, ransacking houses, and taking everything they could carry off. During their rampage, two former Praetors, men named Cosconius and Galba, were murdered in their homes when they tried to defend their property. Shortly after the men of the 10th began their looting, they were joined by the 8th and 9th, and from all accounts, the city was in terror as the battle-hardened soldiers of Caesar's army ran rampant through the streets. Only the 7th refused to join their comrades, and when Antonius ordered them to cordon off the city, they obeyed his orders. Rather than fight their comrades, the men of the mutinous Legions left the city, heading south to Campania, where the estates of the wealthy lay undefended, ripe for the picking.

This dire news brought Caesar from Asia, moving even faster than his normal speed, so that he arrived in Rome about the same time as the men returning to their camp from Campania, so loaded down with loot that they needed wagons to carry it all. At first, Caesar refused to go to meet the men, sending instead one of his aides, Gaius Sallustius Crispus, who was authorized by Caesar to promise the sum of 4,000 sesterces per man. Unfortunately, when the men demanded that he produce the sum in cash right then and he was unable to do so, Crispus was thrown out of the camp, and I mean that he was physically manhandled when he was ejected. Caesar then was forced to do something that I know had to rub him raw: going to the camp in person to face the mutinous Legions. All of this took place while we were marching, making the first time that I heard of any of it was when a courier came galloping down the Via Egnatia looking for me, carrying orders to make my way to Rome immediately by the fastest possible means. Naturally, this meant by horseback, and accompanying the orders was written authorization from Caesar himself to exchange mounts at government way stations, with the highest priority. The orders did not state why I was so urgently needed, while the courier could only tell me that there had been trouble with the 10th, but could provide no specifics. I did not have time for anything other than a hasty meeting with the Centurions, where I turned over command of the 6th to Valens, who was the senior ranking Centurion, and whose performance over the last few months had erased my earlier low opinion of him and his abilities.

"Will we see you when we get to Rome?" Felix asked.

All I could do was shrug and say that I hoped so, but I did not know. With that, we shook hands before I turned to Diocles, who was standing nearby trying not to look worried, without much success. On his skinny shoulders fell the responsibility of following me with all of my belongings that I could not carry on horseback or the one pack animal I had commandeered, despite not knowing exactly where I was headed beyond Rome. A number of slaves that had come into my possession over the last few years were included in my household, not counting those that were leased out to others, and now Diocles was in charge of all of it. Despite the fact that he had not been in my household for much more than a year, I had come to trust him implicitly, not only in the matter of running my affairs, but in his judgment about all manner of things. However, this was by far the biggest challenge during his time with me, and I could see that he was very concerned, despite doing what I could to assure him that I had complete confidence in him. I would have embraced him, but that would not have been seemly in front of others for a master to show that level of regard for a slave, so instead I shook his hand as an equal, which was probably only marginally better in the eyes of some of those watching. With that, I mounted the courier's horse, grabbed the lead of the animal that had been hurriedly packed with my most necessary belongings, and I left the camp at a trot, heading for Caesar.

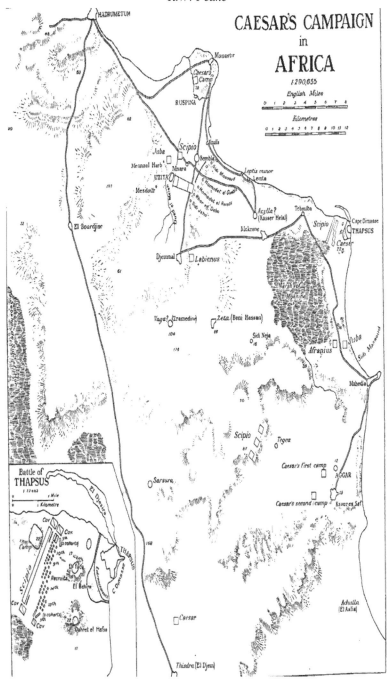

CAESAR'S CAMPAIGN in AFRICA

1:290,655

## Chapter 7- Thapsus

I rode from before dawn until well after dark, stopping only when I was completely exhausted or when the horses were in danger of foundering. Then, I would throw myself down on the ground, wrapping myself in my cloak, trying to get a few thirds of a watch of sleep. In this manner, I covered about 70 miles a day, sometimes more and sometimes, but not often, a little less. Every two or three days, I would run into a courier heading somewhere at Caesar's command, carrying instructions to provincial governors. Through them, in bits and pieces, I learned more details of what had happened with the Spanish Legions in Rome, although it was little enough. The biggest and, I suppose, best piece of news was that somehow things had been worked out to the point that the Spanish Legions were now marching with Caesar down the peninsula. From there, they would take ship for Sicily to prepare for the invasion of Africa, since Africa was where Scipio, Cato, and the rest of the Pompeian generals that had escaped from Pharsalus had fled. It was from these couriers that I learned that if I went to Rome, I would arrive weeks after the Spanish Legions had packed up to begin marching down the peninsula, so I made the decision that I would stop at Brundisium to see Gisela, Vibi, and my new baby daughter. I could not stay long, and in truth, I was not sure it was a good idea, thinking that it might make things worse between us instead of better, but I wanted to see my family. Making it to Dyrrhachium in September, I was forced to wait for two weeks before the winds were right to get a ship to Brundisium, sailing into port shortly before dark.

It is hard for me to describe how nervous I was, walking from the docks to the apartment. I was suddenly worried that Gisela and the children might have moved and I did not know it. Yet when I got to the building, the same people lived on the lower floor, and while they were surprised to see me, they assured me that Gisela still lived on the upper floor. Mounting the steps, yet another thought assailed me, this one much darker and more disturbing. Would she be alone? While I did not think she would be unfaithful, I knew of too many other men who had thought the same thing, only to be wrong, and things had not been exactly harmonious between us when I left. For a moment, I turned to leave. Yet, as much as I dreaded the idea of discovering that she had indeed taken a lover, the need to know was even stronger, so I continued up the steps, making sure that I trod heavily to give her some warning of my coming. Then I found myself standing before the door, knocking once, then twice. Finally, on the third try, I heard a stirring from inside, followed by the sound of the latch being raised. The door opened, and I was face to face with my wife for the first time in almost two years. She was as beautiful as I remembered her, so I drank in the sight of her, eyes wide in shock, tendrils of hair framing her face, the color draining from it at the sight of me. Before I could say a word, she collapsed at my feet in a dead faint.

~ ~ ~ ~

After Gisela fell to the floor, I heard a pair of small feet scurrying from the other room. A little boy burst into view, a look of alarm and fear on his chubby face. He stopped short when he saw me, and we stood staring at each other for a moment before I knelt by Gisela. Then, letting out a howl of rage, he came charging at me, his little fists bunched up, his face contorted in anger.

"You leave my mama alone," he howled.

Before I could react, he was flailing at me with his fists, and I am proud to say that he hit hard.

"Vibi, it's all right." I tried to keep my voice soothing, but I was having a hard time of it since I was trying not to laugh. "It's me, it's Tata."

This had no effect whatsoever, at least the first five or six times I said it, but he began to lose energy and the words I was saying began to sink in. Gradually, he stopped, his little chest heaving, his face bright red as his chin began to quiver. In the time I had been away, he had of course grown, but even more striking was his resemblance to my sisters, Valeria in particular. The fact that Valeria and I favored each other meant that he looked like me as well, yet that was not the first thought that struck me when I looked at him. Gisela had begun to stir, and at her first movement, both Vibi and I looked down at her in time to see her eyes flutter open. She then tried to focus on my face.

Finally, she spoke in a weak voice. "Titus, is it really you?"

"Yes, love. It's really me."

"Tata?" Vibi's voice wavered, all traces of anger gone, and I answered him with a smile.

"Yes, Vibi. It's Tata. I've come home to see my big boy."

Suddenly, he burst into tears. Instead of coming to me, he threw himself into Gisela's arms, while I tried not to show how much it hurt. I had tried to prepare myself for a variety of reactions; after all, I had been gone for most of the boy's life, so I kept telling myself that I should not expect him to remember me, or to throw himself immediately into my arms. Still, it hurt. Gisela had lifted herself onto an elbow, and I bent down, picking her up around the waist then lifting her to her feet, with Vibi clinging to her neck, bawling his eyes out. One of her arms shot out to grab around my neck, squeezing so hard that I started to see stars because she was cutting off my air, and we stood there like that for some time, all of us sobbing. We smothered each other with kisses, then quickly enough, Vibi demanded equal attention from me, transferring himself from Gisela's arms to mine.

"Mama?"

I turned to see the most beautiful child I had ever laid eyes on, a vision of perfection with sleepy eyes and tawny red hair the color of her mother's. Her eyes were green just like Gisela's, but her coloring was more like mine, providing a contrast that was hypnotic. She stood there holding a rag doll, obviously just awakened from the disturbance. Unlike Vibi, her expression was neither of anger nor fear, just curiosity.

"It's Tata," Vibi said with that mixture of disdain and superiority that all older siblings use when they want to show off in front of others. "He's come home."

I almost opened my mouth to correct Vibi that I was not home to stay, then thought better of it. There was no need to ruin this reunion, just moments after it had started. Gisela had composed herself somewhat, and relieved of Vibi, she turned to go and pick up my daughter, bringing her back to me for me to examine. We regarded each other for a moment, then without any prompting from her mother, she reached out for me to take her. I handed Vibi back to his mother, which he did not like at all, and I swept the girl into my arms.

"Titus, meet your daughter, Livia."

Holding her at arm's length, I inspected her closely, as she did the same to me, and I marveled at her. My throat tightened as I glimpsed my dead sister in her features, just a hint in the chin and the set of her mouth.

"She is beautiful," I said hoarsely.

"Yes, I suspect that we are going to have some sleepless nights when she gets older," Gisela said dryly.

I hugged her tightly, reveling in the feel of her tiny arms around my neck and the sweet smell of her scent. At the same time, I was struck by an overwhelming sense of shame, shame that I had not given my family as much thought and attention as they deserved, and at that moment, I thought that perhaps it was time for me to end my time in the Legions.

~ ~ ~ ~

Although the time had grown late, Gisela roused the servants to prepare a meal for me. While we were waiting, I played with my children. I had brought presents of course, things that I bought in Dyrrhachium when I was waiting for the ship to bring me across the sea. For Vibi, I had a set of carved Legionaries; for Livia, a doll and a set of combs made of ivory. Finally, for Gisela, I had a gold brooch with a ruby the size of a robin's egg set in the center of it, though I did not tell her how I had come to possess it, and she knew better than to ask. Women enjoy gifts, but when they come from a dead body, it tends to kill the romance, so to speak. Sitting at the table, I briefly recounted what had transpired over the few months since I had last written, which Gisela did not waste any time in bringing up, I can promise you.

"The only way I knew you weren't dead was that the money kept coming," she said somewhat sharply, regarding me with an angry glare and some well-chosen words in her native tongue, and I resolved to myself to start thinking about what I was going to say before I actually opened my mouth.

It is a promise I have made to myself more times than I can count, and broken almost every time I make it. Naturally, being a woman, Gisela was less interested in hearing my accounts of the battles we had fought, preferring instead to hear about Cleopatra.

"So is she as beautiful as they say she is?"

I laughed. "Gods, no. She's really quite plain. In fact, when I first met her, I was astounded that Caesar would have anything to do with her."

I do not know why, but Gisela looked pleased at this revelation.

Then, as quickly as it had come, her look of happiness disappeared, her eyes suddenly narrowing a bit. "When you first met her you thought that way? But obviously something changed your mind. What was it? Did she suddenly become beautiful in your eyes?"

I knew trouble when I heard it. Gisela had always had a jealous streak in her makeup, which I did not mind all that much, but now I had to steer a very careful course.

"No," I said quickly, perhaps too quickly because her lips thinned out, a sure sign that depending on how I handled things, crockery could be flying. "Nothing like that. It's just that once I spent some time around her, she proved to be quite remarkable in some ways. She has a very quick wit, and she can swap camp stories that would make the saltiest Legionary blush. She has a knack for putting people at ease. That's all, really. She still was as plain as the planks on this table, but her personality made her seem more attractive than she actually was."

I was vastly relieved to see that Gisela accepted this, in fact finding it greatly amusing. Like many beautiful women, Gisela seemed to take a delight in hearing that women who were considered beauties in their own right did not live up to the name for one reason or another. In turn, Gisela caught me up on what she knew of the political situation, which was little enough. It was from her that I learned that Caesar had gone to Sicily, and that the Spanish Legions were marching to meet him.

"Which is where you are going, isn't it?"

It might have been in the form of a question, but it was a statement by Gisela that I only needed to nod my head to verify. When I did, she took it much better than I thought she would, giving a sigh as she bounced Livia on her knee.

"The minute I saw you in the doorway, I knew that was why you had come back to Italy," she said, and there was no mistaking the bitterness in her voice.

I was about to open my mouth, then thought better of it. There was nothing that I could say that would not make things worse, so for once I managed to keep myself from getting in even bigger trouble, concentrating instead on sopping up the last of the stew with a piece of bread, which I split with Vibi. For his part, he munched happily away, oblivious that shortly his world would be turned upside down just as quickly and suddenly as it had when I appeared. Sitting in silence for several moments, things were becoming almost painful before Gisela suddenly stood up from the table, telling Vibi that it was his bedtime, a fact that he had no intention of surrendering to without a fight. Finally, he gave in only when I picked him up, carrying him to his bed, which was across the room from where Gisela and the baby slept. He was very proud of the fact that he slept by himself, and I agreed with him that it indeed meant that he was almost a grown man.

"Soon you'll be standing next to me in a *testudo*," I teased.

"Over my dead body," Gisela said.

I looked up to see if she was smiling when she said it, but she was not. I shot her a dark look, which of course she ignored. Kissing Vibi good night, I was happy to see that he was asleep within moments, one tiny fist tightly clutching one of the toy Legionaries. I stood there looking at him for a moment, with the heavy feeling in my chest stronger than ever as I wondered when the next time I would put him to bed and how old he would be then. Coming home to see my family had certainly made me happy in many ways, but it also raised questions in my mind that I had not experienced in some time. I was not getting any younger, and I was already wealthier than I had dreamed possible, particularly since I had not spent much of my money on drinking, gambling, or whores like most of my comrades. This meant that I could leave the Legions and never work another day in my life unless I wanted to, even if I might not have enough to elevate myself and my family into the equestrian class, but it would not be hard for Vibi to do so when he was old enough to start his own career. All these thoughts and more rushed through my head as I watched my son sleep, and then I felt Gisela at my shoulder. Turning, I saw that Livia was fast asleep, her head lying on Gisela's shoulder as her mother patted her on the back, making me wonder if my mother had done that for my sisters. Gazing at the two of them, with Gisela looking back at me, her eyes glistening with tears, I thought my heart would rend itself at the sight. I moved to her, but she shook her head and stepped away, making my heartache even stronger. Then I saw that I had misunderstood, as she gently laid the baby down on a pallet she had prepared next to the bed.

Once she was satisfied that Livia was comfortably tucked in, only then did she come to me, stepping into my arms, and I remembered all the reasons why I loved her at that moment.

~ ~ ~ ~

"I've been thinking," I tried to sound casual, but I had never been able to fool Gisela. This time was no exception.

"Uh-oh, I don't know if I like the sound of that," she said in a light tone, though her eyes studied my face carefully.

"By rights, my enlistment is up in a little more than a year."

"Yes, I know."

"Maybe I won't re-enlist like I originally planned."

The silence that followed my statement was profound, as Gisela kept looking at me, saying nothing.

"Well?"

She shook her head, her red hair catching the light from the oil lamp so that it looked like sparks were leaping from her. "Maybe? You think maybe you won't re-enlist? What does that mean, Titus?"

As always, I found myself on the defensive with her, yet I was determined that this would not degenerate into an argument this time. "Very well, I will rephrase. I'm thinking that I won't re-enlist when my time is up."

I could still see the doubt in her eyes, and I could not blame her. She, more than anyone, other than Vibius and perhaps Valeria, knew how much being in the Legions meant to me, so it was easy to understand her doubt.

"I have more than enough money to support you and the children in a manner better than either you or I ever knew growing up. Not counting the sale of the Bosporans that we captured at Zela, I have more money than we could spend in a lifetime."

She crossed her arms, her eyes narrowing in thought, recognizing it as the same expression she used when she was haggling at the market or with a merchant. Gisela had an amazing head for figures, much more gifted at doing sums in her head than I was, and she was obviously doing some calculations of her own.

Coming to some conclusion that she was not ready to share with me, she simply asked, "What about buying your way into the equestrian class? Do you have enough for that as well?"

I shook my head doubtfully. "Probably not," I admitted, "but what's more important is whether or not Vibi can when he comes of age, and what we have now can be the foundation for his elevation."

Gisela sat silently, her gaze never wavering from me, and I began to feel the first stirrings of anger born of frustration. I had expected a reaction that, if not outright jubilant, was at least sufficiently thankful that

I did not start having second thoughts. It just shows how much I know women, because her silence was not born of doubt. Suddenly, she bowed her head so that her hair hid her face from me, and I almost bit my lip to keep from shouting at her. Then, when she lifted her head, all the angry thoughts fled from my mind, seeing the tears.

"Titus, I cannot tell you how much it means to me to hear you say this, because I know how much you love the army. Thank you, my love. Thank you, thank you, thank you."

And with that, she leaped into my lap to smother me with kisses, happier than I had ever seen her. I remember thinking that at least this time when I left there would probably not be the anger and recriminations that there had been in the past.

~ ~ ~ ~

It may be true that Gisela did not put up a fuss when I departed the next day, yet the same cannot be said for Vibi, and I got to witness firsthand a full-blown temper tantrum. His face turned as red as my cloak and he threw himself onto the floor, kicking and screaming, using words that I suppose made sense to him, but which I could not hope to understand. His cries were so piercing that I felt like someone was taking an awl and punching it into my eardrums.

"Does he do this often?" I asked Gisela, who laughed.

"Only when he doesn't get what he wants."

"And how often is that?"

"What do you think?" she retorted. "Would you want to listen to that all day?"

I supposed not. Watching his display of temper, I felt a peculiar mixture of irritation and amusement, along with a healthy measure of guilt for being the cause of it all. When I went to kiss him goodbye, he refused to kiss me back, making a show of wiping my kiss from his cheek.

"That he gets from you," I grinned at Gisela, who could not deny it and made no attempt to do so.

Livia was much more affectionate, slobbering on me when her mother thrust her out for me to kiss her goodbye. Gisela was crying, but she was not sobbing uncontrollably like she had the last time we parted. I gave her one last hug and kiss before I walked down the steps, determined not to look back, since I had found this always made things harder on everyone, including me, but this time I was to be thwarted.

"Tata, wait!"

I turned to see Vibi stumbling down the stairs, completely ignoring his mother's pleas not to descend them. While I watched, he tripped on one of the last steps to fall face first into the street. I started to run to him, yet before I could take more than a couple of steps, he was up and running to me on unsteady legs, his face still streaked with tears, snot running from his nose as freely as if it were coming from a pitcher. He threw himself into my legs, wrapping his little arms around them tightly as he looked up at me, cracking my heart like an egg.

"Please don't go, Tata. I am sorry I was a bad boy. Please stay here with me and the baby and Mama."

This was the most painful farewell I had ever experienced. I tried to extricate myself gently from Vibi's embrace, but he clutched to me with all the strength he possessed. I imagine we made quite a sight; there I was, in my soldier's tunic and belt, wearing my sword and dagger, the scars on my arms and legs plainly visible, brown and weather-beaten from countless days exposed to sun, wind and rain, a veteran of Caesar's Legions, brought to a standstill by a little boy who wrapped himself around my leg. I looked at Gisela in supplication, and she descended the stairs with the baby, laughing despite her tears, kneeling beside Vibi. Gently, she pried his arms loose from my leg, saying something to him in her native tongue that seemed to soothe him, whereupon he turned and threw himself into her arms. I leaned down to kiss him again; this time he did not wipe it away, but I could hear him sobbing the length of the street as I walked away. When I left my family standing there in Brundisium, I had made up my mind that I was not going to re-enlist, that I was at the end of my career. Obviously, I did not keep that promise. There are reasons for that, but that is to be told later.

~ ~ ~ ~

Traveling rapidly across the bottom of the peninsula to reach Rhegium, I took a ship for Lilybaeum, the last place I had heard Caesar was located. The harbor was crammed full of shipping, a sure sign that Caesar was nearby, at the least, so when I disembarked I simply followed the other Legionaries until I found the camp outside the city. I gained access to the camp by showing the guards my written orders from Caesar, impressed with his seal. Making my way to the *praetorium*, I was kept outside while the guard took my orders inside. A moment later, Apollonius appeared, smiling at me, to escort me inside. His face turned serious and before he took me to Caesar, he motioned me towards a quiet corner, which was in itself no mean feat, since clerks and aides were scurrying everywhere underfoot. Once we found a spot, I did not wait for him to speak.

"So why am I here? What's going on?"

"You're here because Caesar wants you here," Apollonius said coldly. "And that should be enough."

"It is enough," I snapped. "But if I'm going to be yanked about from one posting to the next, I'd at least like to know why."

Apollonius' expression softened as he placed a hand on my arm.

"It has everything to do with the 10th and what happened at Rome. Caesar wants someone he can trust back with the 10th for the invasion of Africa."

"Surely not every Centurion in the 10th is suspect." I was thinking of Scribonius and Priscus as I said this, not believing that they could have been part of the mutiny.

Apollonius shook his head. "No, not every Centurion, but Caesar hasn't been happy with the Primus Pilus for some time, and he believes that he should have been warned about the seriousness of the mutiny much sooner than he learned of it."

"Torquatus." I said the name, to which Apollonius grunted.

Despite my appreciation of the fact that he had been thrust into the role by the death of Crastinus, such is the fate of every Centurion, to move up when someone more senior than you dies. The fact that Torquatus was unworthy of the job of Primus Pilus was just another example of the gods' sense of humor, since in the short time I was around him, I had heard Torquatus say more than once that he did not ask for the Primus Pilus spot, it had been thrust upon him. Nevertheless, he had obviously not stepped down. While it is relatively rare for a man to abdicate the position, it is not unheard of, and if Torquatus was so desperately unhappy, then he could have, and probably should have, stepped down, but pride is a funny thing. Even when one part of your mind is telling you that you are not suited for something, there is another part that fiercely protects whatever position you have arrived at, warring against the other more rational part of you that knows your shortcomings, and all this merely in order to maintain whatever station you have managed to claw your way up the ladder to obtain. Apollonius regarded me thoughtfully, his brown eyes revealing nothing as he watched me digest the matter at hand.

"What does Caesar want me to do?" I asked finally.

"That is for Caesar to say. Now come on, we've kept him waiting long enough."

With that, he turned to lead me into Caesar's private office. The scene was the usual seeming chaos with men hurrying about carrying wax tablets or papyrus scrolls, whispering to each other importantly about how many buckles needed to be ordered, or how many kernels of grain it takes to feed a soldier. In the middle of it as always was Caesar, dictating to scribes while signing things brought to him, never looking at what he was signing, yet always seeming to know what it was. Seeing me, he dismissed the scribes, waving me over, so I marched over to him, saluting and reporting as he had ordered.

"*Salve,* Pullus. Are you ready to go back to the 10th?"

That was not a simple question to answer and it caused me to hesitate, something that did not appear to please Caesar at all. I was determined that this time I would not just blurt out the first thing that popped into my head, however, so I did my best to ignore his glare while I thought about it. So many thoughts rushed through my head at once and it was very confusing as I tried to sort them out.

Desperate to stall for time, I asked, "In what capacity would I come back?"

"As Primus Pilus, of course," Caesar said impatiently, waving his hand as if the fact that there was a man already in the position was of no consequence.

I felt the beginning of an anger building, surprising me considerably. "What about Torquatus?"

"What about him?"

"Is he still Primus Pilus?"

"Yes, but that can be remedied very quickly."

"How?"

Caesar's eyes narrowed and I could see that his impatience was turning to anger. "What does it matter to you, Pullus? He'll be relieved of his command and you'll take his place. What do the circumstances matter?"

"Because he'll be shamed. His career will be over, and he hasn't done anything to warrant such an action."

"Who are you to tell me whether or not a Centurion in my command is fit for his position?" Caesar's voice was soft but the barely controlled fury was clear to anyone within earshot, and I saw out of the corner of my eye that everyone in my vision had stopped what they were doing, instead suddenly studying whatever they held in their hands very closely as they strained to listen.

How did you get into this mess? I thought to myself. I had taken particular pains to think before I spoke, yet the tiny coal of anger was starting to glow red, and that ember always burned away my best intentions. I think that it stemmed from the resentment of Caesar's station, not his abilities, because that was what was behind the action against Torquatus. Even if I was the beneficiary, I knew that I was just as subject to the whims of Caesar and men like him as Torquatus or any man in the ranks and I did not like it. Often was the time we talked of it around the fires, yet for the most part men just shrugged, saying that this was the way things were. They always had been and always would be. Still, I did not like it. In reality, I had less reason to be upset with Caesar because he was not like the other patricians and high-ranking plebeians, showing up for a campaign before running back to Rome to collect their accolades and honors while bragging to their friends about their tactical brilliance.

Caesar had been in command of the majority of the army for almost my whole career. There was no general that I held in higher regard, then or now but I was still angry about Torquatus and his fate, though I still cannot honestly say why.

Now, I had greatly angered Caesar, and I knew that the politic thing to do was to offer an apology. "Forgive me, Caesar," I said, trying to sound like I meant it. "You're right, of course. I was wrong to question your judgment, and that's not what I was intending. It's just that I know Torquatus and consider him a friend, and I feel badly that any advancement on my part is at his expense."

This was stretching the truth a bit. Torquatus and I had been friendly enough, yet that is not the same thing as friends. I was gambling now that Caesar would respond to my concern for a comrade and I was relieved to see his expression soften a bit as I spoke.

When I had finished, he looked up at me for a moment, his face unreadable. "Very well," he said at last, "I understand and appreciate your concern. I didn't realize that you and Torquatus were particularly close. Instead of having him relieved, I'll order him transferred to one of the new Legions that I'm forming up when I return to Rome. I'll send him back to the city to have him wait for me there. Does that meet with your approval?"

I ignored the heavy sarcasm, pretending instead that it was a sincere question, responding that it did indeed.

With that settled, Caesar turned back to the matter of my assignment, which carried its own challenges, of which I was more than aware, and wondered how to handle. "I need you in command immediately to prepare for our invasion of Africa," Caesar said, beckoning to the scribes to return, telling me that our interview was near an end.

I knew that I had tried his patience, yet I had to ask him a question that I knew ran the risk of making him angry again. "Is there anything I should know? I mean, about the mood of the men and what happened?"

His face darkened, the blood rushing to it, but his tone was even was even as he replied, "Talk to Apollonius. He'll tell you everything you need to know." He took a wax tablet from one of the scribes then offered it to me with one hand while extending the other. "Your post as Primus Pilus of the 6th was *ex officio*, but this is a duly signed warrant for your promotion to the grade of Primus Pilus of the 10th Legion. Congratulations, Primus Pilus Pullus."

I took the warrant and his hand, thanking him for both as I told him that I would not let him down.

"See that you don't, Pullus," he said with a smile that was as much of a warning as it was anything friendly.

~ ~ ~ ~

Finding Apollonius waiting for me at the entrance, I relayed to him that Caesar had instructed me to find out more about the situation with the 10th.

Apollonius sighed, then said, "That will take more time than we have just standing here. Can you meet at my tent in a third of a watch? We'll have some wine. You're going to need it to hear all that I have to tell you."

I agreed to meet him, since I had business with the paymaster, making sure that I was properly entered in the Legion rolls, along with the quartermaster to draw some essential items that I had not brought with me, not knowing how long it would take Diocles to catch up. At the appointed time, Apollonius' body slave showed me into his tent. I had to suppress a laugh at the thought of a slave having a slave, but such was Apollonius' status that I doubt that he would have exchanged his current station for freedom if it meant giving up the luxuries that being a member of Caesar's household afforded him. The tent was richly appointed, with flooring much like Caesar's, which were covered with carpets of the type we had seen in Alexandria. It was one of these that I was studying when Apollonius appeared, making apologies for keeping me waiting.

"Do you like it?" he asked, pointing down to the carpet I had been looking at. "I got it in Alexandria."

That is when it occurred to me, and I snapped my fingers, the memory falling into place. "I knew that I had seen it before. But last time I saw it was in the palace. In Cleopatra's private quarters."

I looked at him with a raised eyebrow and his face flushed, then seeing I meant no malice, he shrugged, giving a guilty laugh. "It's not like she missed it. She had a stack of hundreds of the things that her slaves told me had never seen a floor!"

"So you were actually doing her a favor taking it with you, then."

This time his laugh was genuine and loud. "Exactly! I knew you'd understand, Pullus."

"Enough of carpets. What's going on with the 10th?"

The laughter in the air dissolved immediately, as Apollonius turned to his slave, ordering him to bring some wine, then motioned me to a seat at the table, where he sat opposite from me. Running his hands through his hair, I noticed for the first time strands of silver sprinkled through the black and it made me realize that we were all growing gray serving Caesar. Perhaps it seems strange that as a man of 30, I had such thoughts, but given the life expectancy of a Centurion in the Roman army, I hope that I can be forgiven. Only now, three years removed from my last formation, can I spare a chuckle at myself for thinking like an old man when I was less than half the age I am now.

"Let's begin by you telling me what you know," Apollonius started, "so that I don't repeat things of which you're already aware."

I told him everything I had heard from the number of people who had given me bits and pieces of the story.

When I finished, he said, "That's the bare bones of it. But of course, there's more to it than that."

What I am about to relay through Diocles I do not believe has been recorded anywhere that I am aware of. It is certainly not in Caesar's account of his campaigns, something I can certainly understand. If one of the men like Pollio, Hirtius, or Sallustius has written about it, I have not yet seen that account.

~ ~ ~ ~

After Sallustius Crispus went to the camp to make the offer of 4,000 sesterces per man, the assembly accepted the offer, but demanded that he produce the amount in cash right there on the spot. Naturally, he could not, so he was thrown out of the camp.

"He was lucky to get out of the camp with his life. He needs to thank the gods and his horse for getting him out of there in one piece, literally," Apollonius explained. "That's when Caesar came to the camp himself. The men ran to the forum, but while they got in formation, they didn't stand at attention when he mounted the rostra. Caesar didn't like that, I can tell you!" He took a sip of his wine before he continued, gathering his thoughts. "So Caesar asks them what they want. Now, the men had been clamoring the loudest for the money that Caesar owed them. That's why they broke into the houses on the Palatine, to get valuables that they could convert into the money they believe Caesar owed them."

"He does owe them," I said quietly.

Apollonius' expression darkened, despite my tone. "Not you too!" He threw his hands up in exasperation. "I thought you would understand Caesar's predicament."

"I do understand, but that doesn't mean that Caesar doesn't owe the men what he's promised."

"Which he has every intention of honoring, I can assure you," protested Apollonius. "It's just not possible right now."

I nodded wearily, then indicated he should continue.

"Where was I? Oh, the subject of the bounties. Of course. Well, for whatever reason, the men didn't mention the bounties. Instead, they started calling for their discharges. Now, I believe that the reason they called for their discharges instead of the money is that they knew that Caesar still needed an army for his operations in Africa and figured that in order to keep them in the army, he'd have to give them money." His face creased into a smile, apparently enjoying the memory. "But, as usual, Caesar wasn't willing to act in a manner that the men expected. When they called for their discharges, he gave it to them. He said, 'I discharge you.' That was all. And you could have heard the flap of a butterfly's wings it was so quiet! Caesar went on to tell them that he would give them everything he had promised, but only after he had won the war with other men. Oh, you should have seen the looks on their faces, Pullus!"

As he paused to take a drink, I considered what he had told me so far. I could well imagine the look on their faces, because it would have been the same look on mine: a mixture of amazement and uneasiness at the thought that Caesar could so easily turn away from the men of the Spanish Legions, especially the 10th Legion, men he had enlisted himself, who had marched for him for the better part of 15 years.

"So now, Caesar was silent, and I have to tell you, Pullus, it was one of the most uncomfortable moments I've ever experienced and I obviously wasn't the only one. Hirtius had come with us, along with a couple of the junior military Tribunes. Hirtius begged Caesar to say something more, not to leave men who had served him so well in the past in such a state, no matter what their offenses against him now might be, and he relented. But he didn't do it in the manner that Hirtius was expecting, or the men for that matter. He turned back to the men and began addressing them again. He started by saying one word. 'Citizens,' he said and then didn't say another word for a moment as he let the word sink in. Well, you can imagine the reaction!"

Yes, I could imagine, and I was thankful that I had not been there. Caesar invariably addressed us as "comrades" or "my soldiers," so to be addressed as a "civilian," especially after all that the 10th had been through and the friends they had lost, would have been chilling.

"The men fell to their knees, begging Caesar's forgiveness. They were crying out that they were still soldiers and they still marched for Caesar and nobody else. They cried out to him to punish the men who had led them astray. You should have seen the fingers pointing at those among them who they wanted punished! Caesar said that he wouldn't punish anyone, but he wasn't through yet, oh no, not by a long way. As soon as he said that he wouldn't punish any of the men, he turned and faced the 10th."

Apollonius paused to take another drink. Now I was sure that he was doing it just to torment me.

"He told the 10th that he was particularly pained to see that the 10th had broken faith with him and perpetrated crimes against citizens and their property because he had honored them more than any of his Legions. Because of that, he discharged the 10th and the 10th alone! He also said that they would receive the rewards that he had promised them, but only when he had defeated the Pompeians in Africa and the rest of the army had received their reward first. They would receive the land they had been promised, and it would not be confiscated land, but lands from his own private holdings or free land purchased by him, which as you can imagine was very popular with the men."

It was true. I could easily see why the promise of land that was not confiscated would appeal to the men. In the past, generals had provided their soldiers with the land they were promised by confiscating the estates and farms of their political enemies, who they had arranged to be declared enemies of the state. While this provided for their soldiers, it also saddled them with extra headaches because the men in the ranks were always the ones who were forced to evict the current owners. Also, in the ever-changing political atmosphere of Rome, yesterday's enemy of the state is tomorrow's hero of the Republic, meaning the former soldier's claim on the land could be tenuous. By supplying his soldiers with land that belonged to Caesar that was previously unsettled, the threat that there would be a dispute to the claim on the land would be non-existent, at least from other Roman citizens. The fact that it belonged to Gauls did not bother us overmuch.

"Now the men of the 10th were the ones out in the cold, and they didn't like it a bit, I can tell you. Their Centurions began calling for Caesar to decimate them to atone for their crimes. Caesar stood there listening, but said nothing, which of course made the men clamor even more for them to be punished. Finally, he raised his hand, and I don't believe I've ever seen the army fall so silent so quickly. Then he announced that he wouldn't punish the 10th, and that they too could march with the rest of the army. The cheering was so loud, you couldn't hear yourself think!"

Finished, Apollonius drained his cup then looked at me, an expectant smile on his face, and I knew what he was looking for.

"Caesar is truly a master at playing us like a harp," I said, only half in admiration.

Nobody likes being manipulated like a puppet, and even if I had not been there, I still knew how it felt strongly enough that I could taste the bitter bile of it in my throat.

"How are the men now?"

He shrugged. "Happy enough, I think. They're just relieved that they're back in Caesar's good graces. As they should be."

He obviously could not resist that last jibe but I let it pass. My thoughts were elsewhere by that time anyway, thinking about men like Vibius and how long the relief that Apollonius referred to would actually last. Unless he had changed, I could not imagine Vibius staying happy for long, and I knew he was not alone.

~ ~ ~ ~

After my visit with Apollonius, I went to see Torquatus the evening before I was scheduled to take command of the 10th, not sure what kind of reception I would get. Much to my relief and not a little surprise, Torquatus seemed genuinely pleased to see me, waving me in to his private quarters while offering me wine. At first, we talked about the events in Alexandria and against the Bosporans, and I told him some of the funnier moments that had happened, like when some of the men of the 6th had gotten drunk then tried to ride one of the wild water horses that inhabit the Nile, with the results you can imagine.

Finally, I steered the conversation to the reason I had shown up in the first place. "How are the men, really?"

Torquatus stared into his cup a moment before he answered. I could see how the last year had aged him at least ten just from appearances. "I don't honestly know anymore, Pullus. One day they're like the old days, when we were in Gaul, then the next they're angry and bitter at not just Caesar but all of the Centurions. And some of the Centurions aren't any better."

"Anyone in particular you care to name?"

"Balbus," he spat the name out.

I cannot say I was surprised that he named him, but something about it did not add up to me, so I decided to reserve judgment on Balbus until I could form my own opinion. "And your old friend Celer, though he's just more of a nuisance than anything else. Scribonius has done a good job of neutralizing him."

"How is Scribonius doing?"

He considered my question, then nodded thoughtfully. "He's doing a good job, better than I thought he would just by looking at him."

I laughed. What Torquatus said was true; he was not much to look at, especially when thinking of a Centurion. He had always looked, and in some ways acted more like a tutor of high-born children than a member of Rome's Legions. Yet, I knew better than anyone how deceptive it was.

"And what of Domitius?"

I did not have to identify which Domitius I was referring to; Torquatus knew exactly who I meant.

He rubbed his face before he answered, then let out a long breath. "I wouldn't call Domitius one of the ringleaders of the problems with Caesar, but he certainly is one of the most vocal."

I had to laugh at that, for truer words were never spoken about Vibius, since being quiet had never been one of his strengths. He was always more than willing to speak his mind, no matter who it hurt and while I was not much better, compared to Vibius, I was the soul of discretion.

Torquatus continued, the laughter dying in my throat as he spoke. "The problem is that he has a lot of influence, more than one would think of an Optio, even if he is in the Second Cohort. A lot of men in other

Cohorts look to him for his opinion on things. There are always a lot of people around his fire."

"It's always been that way," I countered.

"Yes, but we never had trouble with Caesar like this before, and now, more than ever, men have to watch what they say."

I stared at him, trying to determine his meaning. It took a moment, except it should have been clear to me immediately, especially after what had happened to Verres Rufus.

Finally, I asked, "Is he in any danger of disappearing?"

Torquatus looked uncomfortable at my open reference to that thing that went on in Caesar's army that we never talked about, his eyes instinctively darting to the darker corners of the tent like there might be someone lurking there writing down all that we said. Seeing his reaction, I almost looked over my shoulder at one point because his eyes fixed on something behind me.

Then he shrugged, saying, "Not that I'm aware of, but I think the more he talks, the higher on the list he'll go. I think I'd have a word with him if I were you."

"I don't know if that's possible. We aren't exactly on good terms."

"I know. I was there, remember?" Torquatus said dryly. "I thought you were going to kill him, I truly did."

"So did I," I said soberly.

For several moments neither of us spoke, each alone with our own thoughts of all that had transpired.

Finally, I broached the subject that had given me the most worry. "Torquatus," I began, knowing I sounded awkward, yet not knowing how to phrase things differently, "I just want you to know that I didn't have anything to do with Caesar's decision to replace you with me as Primus Pilus."

Torquatus waved a hand to reply, "I know that. The truth is I'm happy that you're taking over the 10th. Too much has happened with these men. I'd rather start off with a new bunch of fresh meat that I can mold into what I want. These bastards are too hard-headed now." Suddenly realizing the exact import of his words, Torquatus gave me a look of embarrassment. "Sorry, Pullus, I don't mean to make it sound so grim for you. But the truth is I'm not hard enough for this bunch, and I suspect you are." He leaned forward, staring intently into my eyes. "I know we've never been friends exactly, but know that what I'm about to say isn't meant in any way as an insult to you. All right?"

I nodded that I understood.

"It's just that everyone knows how ambitious you are, and that you'll do whatever needs to be done to advance your career. I think that's why Caesar picked you, because he knows that the 10th needs a firmer hand than I can provide right now. The problem with me is that, between you and me, I agree with the men. I think that we've been given the *cac* end of the sponge by Caesar, and that he owes us and should pay us what he owes us. Now, not tomorrow."

"I agree that Caesar owes the men," I said cautiously, thinking back to my conversation with Apollonius, where I had told him essentially the same thing, if not in quite such blunt terms.

"Yes, but would that stop you from enforcing Caesar's will?"

I shook my head, causing Torquatus to slam his hand down on the table, making me jump. "Exactly! You'd still do whatever Caesar ordered, whether you agreed with it or not. I saw it that day at Pharsalus when you almost cut Domitius in half. I could never have done that, and I know it."

I knew that he was trying to compliment me, yet it certainly did not feel complimentary, when put the way Torquatus had. I did not know what to say, so I just mumbled something about duty and such, then took a long drink of wine.

~ ~ ~ ~

The next morning before formation, I had a case of nerves that was perilously close to those I felt right before battle. I should have felt like I was coming home, but that was not the case, at least not on this morning. Taking extra pains to make sure my awards and decorations were polished to a high gleaming finish, I cursed the absence of Diocles who normally took care of these things for me. Finally, I knew I could delay no longer, and I left my tent to march to the forum, where the 10th, or what remained of them, were waiting, where I saw they were turned out in full uniforms as well. I have to say I was pleased with what I saw, thinking that at least they had made the effort to impress me. Marching to the head of the formation, my eyes traveled over the faces of so many friends, men I had known for half of my life and one that I had known almost all of it. Vibius was standing in his spot as Optio of the First Century of the Second Cohort, his face showing nothing. Scribonius gave me a slight smile and tip of the head, which I returned. I could not see any of the other Centurions of the Second, being lined up behind the First Century as they were, but I would meet with them soon enough. In the ranks, I saw men that I had fought and bled beside, men with whom I had quarreled and men with whom I had spent watch upon watch talking to about all manner of things. In most of their faces I saw what I like to think of as welcome and happiness that one of their own had returned to lead them. Vellusius was positively beaming from ear to ear, while even Didius was looking at me with a grimace that was his version of a smile. The one strange thing about that formation is that I have no recollection of what I said, except in a very general sense, that I was happy to be back and that I expected great things of the 10th that would add more honors to the Legion. I do remember I made no mention of what had happened between Caesar and them, as a message that I did not plan on holding that against them and that we were starting over fresh. Dismissing the men, I then called for a meeting of the Pili Priores to meet in my tent immediately after the formation.

The men arrived, filing into my private quarters where we all shook hands. Each man offered his congratulations, and in some cases, they were sincere. Scribonius, I hugged, kissing him on both cheeks, something I did not normally do, but I was extremely happy to see a friendly face. These men were the best from each Cohort, yet like any group of men, there were those who were stronger than others. What I found comforting was that unlike my introduction with the 6th, I was not walking in cold, because I knew these men. Even if I had not served in the same Cohort with them, men talk about their Centurions, meaning I knew more about each of these men than I had any of the Centurions of the 6th. Of course, there was Scribonius, his command of the Second Cohort solidified and no longer questioned, at least according to Torquatus. The Third Cohort was commanded by Titus Camillus, who had been the Tertius Pilus Prior since before I had been an Optio. He was a good, solid man though he had never expressed any desire to advance to the next grade of Centurion and up into the Second Cohort. The Fourth Cohort was led by Spurius Maecius, who had followed the more traditional route for promotion, climbing from the Tenth to his present position in the Fourth. The Quincus Pilus Prior was Decimus Velinus, a compact, muscular Gadean who was one of the veterans salted into the 10th when we were formed up, making him a bit older than the rest of the other Centurions. The Sixth's Centurion was Lucius Horatius, and of all the Pili Priores he was the one I was most concerned with. He had a reputation for brutality with his men, leading more from fear than from admiration, a trait that I despised. The Seventh Cohort was led by Gnaeus Fabius, another older man, but he was part of the original enlistment, joining at around twenty-four or twenty-five, and was capable, if a bit unimaginative, the kind of leader I would call a plodder. Nonetheless, he was dependable and that counted for much, particularly at this point in time. The Eighth's Pilus Prior was Quintus Falernus, and he was another man I was worried about, but for different reasons than Horatius. He was a sharp dealer, in much the same way as the departed Longus had been, seeing his men as an extra source of income, over and above what was customary and normal for a Centurion. The Ninth was commanded by Publius Sabatinus, and I would say he was from the same mold as Scribonius and in fact, they had become close friends. He was our age, and I had my eye on him as someone who had the abilities to become a Primus Pilus someday. Finally, there was the 10th, led by Vibius Esquilinus, another younger man who was part of our original enlistment and had not been in the Centurionate long, less than two years, but was a solid man and a capable leader. These were the men who I would be relying on and who I also needed to learn more about. Specifically, I needed to find out who had been involved in the business on the Campus Martius, but that would come later. Each of them gave me a brief report on their Cohort; number of men currently on the sick list, on punishment, and total number of effectives. The numbers were disheartening, to say the least, the 10th having been whittled down to less than half strength by this time. Illness had been particularly savage to the men, but that was to be expected from life in camp. I believe I have mentioned that whenever we were in one place for an extended period of time, the rate of illness would go up dramatically, something I have developed my own theories about and had long since enforced in my own command. Now that I was in control of the whole Legion, I was eager to put those measures into effect to see if it would help on a larger scale. The meeting ended with a toast to the health of the Legion, and to success in the coming operation, which I promised to give more details about once I learned them myself. With that, the Pili Priores were dismissed.

~ ~ ~ ~

The next meeting was with the Centurions of the First Cohort, and I held it immediately after the first, sending for the men while scribbling some notes on things that needed to be done based on what I had been told by the Pili Priores. It was quickly becoming obvious that this was going to be a massive job, much more challenging than handling the two Cohorts of the 6th, and that I would be relying on the Pili Priores much more heavily than I had initially thought. The next group of Centurions arrived, requesting entrance, and I waved them in, whereupon we went through the same rituals of greeting and welcome, each of the men formally offering their congratulations on my promotion. Quickly recognizing that if I wanted to get any work done that day, I decided I was going to have to start watering my wine, my head getting a little thick. The Centurions of the First Cohort sat, looking expectantly at me, but before I said anything, I took a quick stock of the men sitting before me. Pilus Posterior was Marcus Glaxus, who had, at some point in the past, been Torquatus' Optio before he was promoted to the Centurionate, and Torquatus spoke highly of the man. Glaxus had a calm, capable demeanor that I hoped boded well for our service together. The Princeps Prior was Balbus, who I have already described, and who sat looking calmly at me, his arms folded as I wondered what was going on behind the mask that was his face. Princeps Posterior Servius Arrianus was a slender piece of chewed leather, his face marred by a scar that ran underneath his mouth, running almost ear to ear, giving him a leering expression. However, he was anything but a jokester, having a reputation as one of the most courageous men in the Legion. Hastatus Prior Servius Metellus, a squat, barrel-chested man originally from Narbonese Gaul, sat looking decidedly nervous, making me wonder if he was one of the men I had to keep an eye on. Finally, the Hastatus Posterior was Gaius Varus, an exceedingly ugly man almost completely covered in dark, coarse black hair, with a thick set of eyebrows that met in the middle of his forehead, making it look like he had one single eyebrow instead of two. He was so singularly unattractive that I had to force myself to keep from staring at him, instead turning my attention back to the wax tablet sitting on my desk, pretending to study it. Finally composed, I began speaking, using the same speech that I had used with the Pili Priores, before asking each of them for a report on their Century. The news was even grimmer for the First Cohort than it had been for the rest of the Legion, since the First Cohort traditionally is one of the first, if not the first into battle, because of its position on the front line. Also, the First is where the Legion eagle is carried, and is always the focal point of an enemy trying to get to it to take it as a prize and as a way to destroy our fighting spirit. Once I received their reports, I answered their questions, all of which had to do with the coming campaign in Africa before dismissing them, while asking Balbus to stay behind. He stood waiting for the others to leave, and I watched carefully as the men filing out shot him glances, trying to see if there were any whispered warnings or conspiratorial looks between them as they left. Balbus remained standing, then once the men had left, I waved him to sit back down, which he did warily, once again his face revealing none of his thoughts.

I swallowed my irritation, forcing to keep my tone light. "So, Balbus, how have things been?"

The instant I spoke the words I almost openly winced, knowing how transparent they sounded.

Balbus' mouth quirked, while he replied, "Things have been eventful, Primus Pilus, but I don't believe that's why you asked me to stay behind."

"No, you're right, Balbus. That is indeed not why I asked you to stay behind. I apologize for phrasing things so awkwardly." I sighed, realizing then I was not really sure why I had asked him to stay behind. Finally, I leaned forward, struck by a sudden urge to be as candid as possible. "The reason I want to talk to you is because I want to tell you that if I were to listen to Torquatus, your time in the Legion would be coming to an end. I'm sure you know that one of the things that Caesar demands is utmost loyalty of his Centurions and after what happened on the Campus Martius, he doesn't know who to trust. All it would take is a word from me that you're one who can't be trusted, and if I were to go by what Torquatus had told me about you, I'd be sending word to Caesar now. But the thing is, I don't really believe Torquatus, though I don't know why. That's why I wanted to talk to you I suppose, to hear what you have to say."

He regarded me levelly, his face still composed and unreadable. "About what, exactly?"

I threw my hands up in exasperation. "About what? About what I've just said."

"I see. So you want to know if I can be trusted?"

When put that way, I realized how ludicrous what I said sounded. If he were involved in the mutiny on the Campus, he was unlikely to tell me, instead telling me what he thought I wanted to hear. I realized that I was dealing with a man of exceptional qualities, with none of the shiftiness of Cornuficius.

Deciding to start over, I began again. "When you put it that way, I can see how ridiculous a question it is, I suppose. No, I don't want to know if you can be trusted, I'm going to decide that for myself. But it's just that I think there's more behind what Torquatus has told me and I want to hear your side of it, that's all. Before I make any judgments, I need to hear as much of the story as I can."

Now for the first time, Balbus looked decidedly less composed, almost uncomfortable, shifting in his chair, then looking down at the ground, the first time he had broken his gaze on me, and I could see that he was struggling with something. I had long since learned that as hard as it may be, the best thing to do in these circumstances is to wait for the other to speak, so I sat fiddling with my stylus.

Finally, he took a deep breath, looked at me, then said, "Very well. I'll tell you why Torquatus hates me so."

~ ~ ~ ~

The affairs of men are such a mess sometimes. I remember Caesar saying that great events result from trivial causes, and that was certainly the case with what had taken place between Torquatus and Balbus. As Balbus told his story, I was also struck by an uncomfortable feeling of my own, like I was hearing a tale that I had heard before. In fact, it was a story that I had lived and after hearing it, it left me sitting up that night, thinking. Torquatus and Balbus were lifelong friends, cousins in fact, their mothers being sisters, and had joined the Legions together. They had been inseparable companions, marching first in Pompey's Legions before volunteering to come over to the 10th in exchange for both being promoted to Sergeants. Of course this meant that they could not be in the same tent like they had been, yet they remained close. They ascended the ranks at roughly the same time, and it was at the end of the campaign in Gaul, when the 10th spent time in garrison and Caesar used the other Legions quelling the various rebellions that the trouble began. Freed of the constant worry of marching, fighting, and all that goes with it, both men decided that it was time to turn to matters of the heart, seeing that it looked very much like we were going to be staying in place for a while, which was true. As nearly as I could figure out, about the same time I took up with Gisela, Balbus and Torquatus fell in love, which is a wonderful thing, except when it is with the same woman. Nonetheless, in all forms of combat, there can only be one victor and in this case, it was Torquatus, or so Torquatus thought. The maid in question became Torquatus' woman, and for several months, things seemed to be all right. Balbus had smarted from the defeat but said that he had gotten over it. Then, Torquatus' father had died, so he had taken leave to go home, whereupon he asked Balbus to watch over his woman, something that Balbus did to such a degree that you can imagine what happened.

As Balbus talked of this, he had the grace to look somewhat guilty, giving a rueful grin. "In all honesty, I had gotten over her at that point, but when she offered herself, what was I supposed to do?" he said.

When put that way, it was a hard point to argue. If it had been just a short-term affair, while Torquatus was gone, that would have been one thing, and it would have been one of those secrets between men and women that many take to the grave with them. However, if there is anything as mysterious and complicated as a woman's heart, I hope never to run into it. According to Balbus, the result of the affair was twofold; the woman decided she had made a mistake in choosing Torquatus, then had gotten herself pregnant. Now, she could not live without Balbus, yet the fact that Balbus no longer had those kinds of feelings for her and told her as much did not seem to deter her from declaring to Torquatus her undying love for Balbus. In this, I had to sympathize with Torquatus, imagining what it would have been like to come back to the Legion, expecting your best friend and woman to be waiting for you, never suspecting either of them of treachery. Perhaps from the woman, for they are fickle creatures, but never that kind of betrayal from a man as close to you as your brother. There I go being naïve again, I suppose. As one can imagine, her revelation put an unbearable strain on the friendship between the two men, a rift that was still unrepaired to that day in my tent as Balbus told me about it.

"I tried everything I could to make amends to Torquatus, but he's never forgiven me," Balbus said morosely.

"What happened to the woman?"

"She died trying to bear my child." Balbus took a deep drink from his wine cup.

Setting it down, he looked at me, and I could see the sadness and pain in his eyes, making me wonder what the main cause of it was, the betrayal of his friend, or the death of a woman who was bearing his child. Both, I suppose.

"So, Primus Pilus, that's the cause of the rift between Torquatus and me, and why he hates me so much. I really can't blame him. I have hopes that being sent to another Legion may make things easier for both of us."

"Don't be so sure." I had not planned on saying anything, but as usual, the *numen* inside me took over. "Although it's from a different cause, your story sounds similar to my own, and the time I was away with the 6th did nothing to make things any easier."

"You're talking about Domitius, I presume?"

I nodded.

"He's a good man," Balbus said quietly.

"As is Torquatus," I replied.

With that, we toasted each other, men who for different reasons had suffered the same result, the loss of their nearest and dearest friend, not to a blade but to affairs of the human heart.

~ ~ ~ ~

I was almost immediately overwhelmed in my new role of Primus Pilus of a full Legion, causing me to begin fretting about the appearance of Diocles, finally recognizing how much I had come to rely on him. During the interval, I appropriated slaves with experience in the daily running of the Legion from the other Centurions. Zeno had died of an illness while the Legion was camped outside Rome, or I would have used him, despite his light-fingered ways. Still, it was not the same as having Diocles with me, so I am afraid that my temper was very much on the raw with not just the slaves, but anyone who happened to be in the wrong place at the wrong time.

The larger situation did not help my mood either. Weather was atrocious, seemingly unending days of unfavorable winds accompanied by fits of rain that made the camp a morass of mud that clung to everything. Despite Caesar's impatience, this weather was still a blessing because it allowed time for all the forces he had sent for to arrive, since some were coming from as far away as Egypt, the 28th in particular. When I heard this news, while I was happy at the thought of seeing Cartufenus again, I was not particularly thrilled with the idea of the 28th being part of the invasion, the memory of their performance in Alexandria still fresh in my mind. The 25th, 26th, and 29th were coming as well, along with the rest of the Spanish Legions, though so far only the 10th had arrived. Other issues facing Caesar were shipping, along with supply, neither situations being sufficient for his plans or ambitions, but that never stopped Caesar and finally, he could take it no longer. The day after Saturnalia, I was ordered to load four Cohorts of the Legion, all that fit on the available shipping, along with Caesar, the cavalry and some auxiliaries, about 3,000 men total. As he had at Brundisium, Caesar ordered all unnecessary baggage to be left behind, along with body slaves, which did not affect me in any way since Diocles had not arrived. We put out to sea, where almost immediately, the choppy conditions we had experienced in the harbor and immediately surrounding waters turned to heaving seas, sending a number of men to the side. I had finally gotten to the point where my stomach was, if not accustomed to sea voyages, at least inured to the point where it took a full-blown storm before it finally rebelled. That is not to say that I was comfortable; I certainly was not, but I was happy that the voyage was fairly short, or at least so I thought. The distance to cover was a little more than a hundred miles by sea, yet it took five full days before we dropped anchor at Hadrumentum, after hugging the coast, only stopping briefly at a number of points while Caesar decided the best place to land.

At Hadrumentum, the gates were closed to us, the garrison commander, one Gaius Considius, having close to two Legions' worth of men manning the walls and gates, so we made camp in sight of the walls of the city, while Caesar went surveying the city defenses. Also, as we were making camp, scouts were sent out into the countryside, and they came back to report that a second force composed of mostly cavalry approached from the direction of Clunea. This was one of the points we had stopped for Caesar to scout and had rejected because it was too heavily defended, so they had obviously been alerted, understanding who we were and what we were about. One of the Tribunes with us, Lucius Plancus, made a suggestion to Caesar that he try to talk Considius over to our side, since Plancus knew him from before the civil war, to which Caesar agreed. Caesar wrote a letter for Plancus to take to Considius under a flag of truce and, with letter in hand, Plancus approached the city walls. He was taken into the presence of Considius, who apparently did not share the same warm memories of their friendship that Plancus had, because as an answer not only did he not bother to open the letter with Caesar's seal but executed Plancus on the spot. This was not made known to us immediately; instead, we spent that night and the better part of the next day waiting for some sort of answer from Considius, while there was much wagering on the fate of Plancus ranging from defection to the Pompeians to losing his head. The other reason Caesar chose to wait was to allow the rest of the army to join us, but there was no sign of the fleet that had supposedly been just one or two days away from Sicily when we left. However, this was not altogether surprising given the weather we experienced ourselves. It was the last day of the year of the Consulship of Calenus and Vatinius, except that was under the old calendar before Caesar reformed it. In other words, it was still October according to the new calendar, but on the first day of the "old" new year, Caesar decided that he could not afford to spend the time investing Hadrumentum now that he had learned of the fate of Plancus, particularly with the large force of cavalry from Clunea less than a day away. The numbers that the scouts had reported of the cavalry force was in excess of 3,000, compared to our 150 mounted troops, with the assumption being that they were the Gauls of Labienus' force that escaped after Pharsalus. Breaking camp, Caesar decided to leave us as a rearguard then set off with only the cavalry, the auxiliaries and the bulk of his staff. Heading in the opposite direction from which the enemy cavalry was coming, Caesar made for the city of Ruspina. They were barely out of sight when the mounted scouts assigned to us reported the cloud of dust that marked the Pompeian cavalry, and who had obviously been warned of our presence because a couple of thirds of a watch later when they came close to our marching formation, they gave us a wide berth. However, they did pass closely enough for us to see that they were not Gauls, their darker skin and lighter armor making that clearly apparent.

"Numidians," Scribonius said, causing me to look at him in surprise as we marched together.

"And how do you know that? When did you ever see a Numidian?"

Suddenly he looked wary, glancing quickly around to make sure that nobody else was in earshot before he answered. "I saw some when I was a child in Rome. They were associated with King Jugurtha in some way, but I don't remember how. They looked and rode their horses the same way as those men do."

Scribonius had become my closest friend, yet this moment reminded me how little I really knew about him. In contrast, between Vibius and me, Scribonius had learned probably more about our childhood and background than he ever wanted to know. Yet, when that moment came around the fire when men talked of home, Scribonius always remained silent, something we had just come to accept, never questioning him about it. I did not press then, since it was not the time or place, indeed, if there was one to begin with. Instead, we watched the cavalry streaming past us, shaking their arms at us while calling out threats in yet one more language we did not understand. Of course, our men replied in turn, marching along while shouting at the enemy what we would do to them if given the chance. I never really understood the point in all of this nonsense, but it was something that seemed to be important to the men even now after doing it for 15 years without influencing one battle. The enemy soon receded out of our sight in pursuit of Caesar and our cavalry, so now all we could do was wait, which is the hardest part of any campaign. Even worse than boredom is when things are happening, but you do not know the outcome of events, having to wait to hear the news that determines whether or not there is cause to celebrate or reason to panic. The numbers of enemy cavalry were certainly daunting, when compared to our own numbers, except at that point we did not know the quality of the Numidians, making it anyone's guess as to what would happen.

While the major part of the fleet that brought us to Africa had been sent back to Sicily to load the hopefully newly arrived reinforcements to bring to us, Caesar's flagship, a quinquereme, along with a small number of other ships were sticking close to shore, following Caesar's progress. If matters became desperate, I was not too worried about Caesar, knowing that he would retreat to the safety of the flagship, the cavalry buying the necessary time with their lives for his escape. As it turned out, this would not be necessary. When the enemy cavalry approached Caesar and our own forces, our paltry band of horsemen turned about, charging into the Numidians and cutting a fair number of them down before the rest scattered to the four winds. Not only did this save Caesar from the embarrassment of having to run for the fleet, it also gave him and the rest of the army a good idea of the measure of the Numidians, at least their cavalry, which was not much. Camp was made that night at Ruspina, which unlike Hadrumentum, had opened their gates to us. Meanwhile, the only sighting of the enemy was their scouts and the Numidians who skulked a short distance away meaning we had no trouble that night, before marching further east the few miles to Leptis the next day, camping outside the town.

Despite arriving early because of the short distance between Ruspina and Leptis, we still spent the best part of the day building the camp, since we had to make it big enough to accommodate the rest of the army, which still had not shown up. By the end of the day, the men were exhausted, yet we still did not have the camp completed because of the size. This meant that we had to mount full Cohort guard through the night to protect the unfinished sides of the camp, something that did not please Caesar in the slightest, though he had to accept it. Fortunately, the fleet carrying the rest of the army showed up early the next day. By midday, the first of the rest of the army from Sicily began jumping over the sides of the transports to wade ashore, cheering my men greatly. We continued working, while I kept an eye out for the rest of our Legion, but as the day passed, I did not see them. Finally, I went to the *Praetorium* to find Apollonius, asking him if he knew where the rest of the 10th was.

"Sallustius said that he couldn't fit everyone into the available shipping and decided to send over the rest of what just arrived."

I did not like this, but there was nothing to be done about it. The Legions that landed were the 25th, 26th, 28th, 29th, and all but two Cohorts of the 5th, which had been in Greece all this time, minus some Cohorts from each of the Legions whose ships had still not landed. I was at least thankful that the men of the arriving Legions were put immediately to work, so that the camp was completed by the end of the day, despite the grumbling of my men. I was also happy to see Cartufenus again, and we spent the evening in my tent catching up.

"It must be good to be back with the 10th." Cartufenus observed me closely as he said this.

Of course, by this time, the news of all that had transpired on the Campus Martius was common knowledge throughout the army, and I thought I could detect a hint of smugness in his tone, for which I guess I cannot fully blame him. I had made my feelings about the 28th's actions in Alexandria fairly clear, and now here was the vaunted 10th doing the same thing, at least as far as Cartufenus was concerned. I thought about pointing out that the 10th had not mutinied while under siege, and there was no real comparison between the length and quality of our service, then decided against it, since he had not really voiced any of the things I thought were running through his head.

Instead, I answered the question he had verbalized. "Yes and no," I admitted.

Cartufenus knew about what had happened between Vibius and me at Pharsalus, having blurted the story out during a wine-filled evening back in Alexandria, so I felt comfortable confiding in him. "It's still early. I've only been Primus Pilus for a few weeks and I haven't had much time with the men. I have my ideas about who I have to keep my eye on as far as Centurions and Optios, but only time will tell if I'm right."

"What will you do if they mutiny again?"

"Whatever I have to," I replied.

He raised his cup. "Hopefully, it will never come to that."

~ ~ ~ ~

As at Ruspina, the gates of Leptis were thrown open to us, and in order to prevent any problems with the men, Caesar ordered a Century to guard each town gate with orders that no man from the army be allowed in, to ensure there was no theft. Caesar was determined to win the populace over to him and these were the kinds of measures he was taking to win their trust. Leptis was to be our supply base, so we built the camp right up to the water's edge to allow for easier unloading. At Leptis, I learned that the missing ships were supposedly heading by mistake for Utica, which was in Pompeian hands, held by none other than Cato, and Caesar was worried that the men and supplies aboard would fall into enemy hands. Because of the danger, he decided that he would go himself in search of the missing vessels and men, along with some of us. I was ordered to load up my Cohorts, along with four Cohorts of the 25th, which we did that night, enduring a miserable night on the water, set to depart before dawn. Our fleet rowed out of the small harbor of Leptis shortly before daybreak, but luckily, we were not a third of a watch gone past sunrise when a lookout shouted down from the mast where he was perched that he had spied a sail, quickly followed by another, then others. At first, we thought it might be the enemy, so there was much commotion as the crew of the ship I was on hurried about making ready to fight. Soon enough, it became apparent that they belonged to us, since each vessel flew Caesar's red standard. Consequently, we turned back, going back to Ruspina instead of Leptis to debark, along with the missing Cohorts of the other Legions, but precious little in the way of supplies. This concerned Caesar most of all, knowing that he could not have a hungry army for what lay ahead. To that end, he dispatched Sallustius to the island of Cercina, where there was supposedly a large supply of grain, and a messenger was sent to Sardinia for the same purpose. Caesar ordered a Cohort from each Legion, including from the 10th, to stay at Leptis under one of the Saserna brothers, though I could never tell them apart, to guard what would be our supply base. I sent Glaxus and his Cohort, confident that he was sufficiently intelligent and resourceful enough to handle an independent command, a judgment that he more than validated during that duty. The rest of the army came to Ruspina from Leptis, and although it was a short distance, there was plenty of grumbling about marching back and forth. Once the disposition of our forces was settled, Caesar gave orders that we were to go about the countryside to procure grain and other foodstuffs so that there would be something to put in our supply base at Leptis. We would leave the next morning to go a few miles south where there were reports of fields of ripened grain supposedly just waiting to be harvested by us.

~ ~ ~ ~

Starting out in the morning, we marched with a force of 30 Cohorts, five from each Legion, with one extra to make up the difference because there were only four Cohorts of the 10th, along with 400 cavalry out of the 3,000 that had arrived, along with 150 archers. Each Legion was represented so they could gather grain for their respective units, every man carrying their wicker basket and sickle, along with their armor and weapons, of course. We headed southwest to where the first of the fields we would harvest were supposedly located, marching in column, with the usual outriders and cavalry screen. Little more than a third of a watch on the march had passed when someone called out, drawing our attention to one of the horsemen who had been out on the flanks but was now galloping back to the command group where Caesar was located. Bare moments later, the *bucina* was sounding the call that enemy was sighted, prompting me to give the order to don helmets, forcing the men to drop their baskets. As we were making ourselves ready, several men shouted that they had spotted the enemy themselves, and I looked to where they were pointing, observing a large cloud of dust. Experience told me that it was either a very large force of infantry, or a smaller cavalry unit, and after observing how quickly it was moving, I knew that it was cavalry. My first reaction was not to be worried, thinking that if it were the Numidians that we had seen days before, we would have no problem repulsing them. That relief was short-lived, as the more sharp-eyed among our number immediately let the rest of us know that it was not Numidians, but Gallic cavalry that was fast approaching. Directly after that news, the *cornu* sounded the call to shake out into single line, open formation, facing the oncoming cavalry. In answer to our move, the enemy likewise deployed into a line, allowing us to determine that the force opposing us was a mixed lot and at least not all Gauls. They had been in the vanguard of the approaching enemy column, initially causing the belief that the entire force was Gallic. However, once they spread out, we could see that there were indeed Numidians, along with a relatively large force of what looked like light infantry, even though they looked more like an armed mob than anything formidable, except in numbers. Our cavalry was split in two, each contingent being sent to our flanks, with the archers arrayed in front of us, and the enemy was doing basically the same thing. However, their numbers, especially in cavalry, were much greater than ours, so that in effect, we were facing a mass of cavalry. We were opposite a force that was not only numerically superior, but was composed in almost exactly opposite proportion between cavalry and infantry than our forces. As we made our final preparations, Caesar sent a man on a fast horse back to Ruspina to summon the rest of our cavalry to help balance the odds a bit, and once we were done shaking out, there was nothing much for us to do but wait. We had been in the lead, meaning we were once again on the far right flank, and despite being glad that it was us, with such a large cavalry force it also meant that we were the most vulnerable to attack from the flank. Surprisingly, for some time the enemy did not seem to be any more anxious to close with us than we were to be attacked, their only action inching closer to just outside the range of our javelins, then standing there, jeering at us. Finally, the move came that most of us were dreading, the enemy formation suddenly wheeling, roughly starting in the center where at an imaginary line bisecting the enemy force, men turned in opposite directions to begin extending their own line outwards in a clear move to envelop us. From behind the horsemen in the center, the Numidian infantry came dashing forward, each man carrying several javelins, smaller and lighter than ours but able to do damage nonetheless. They began flinging their missiles at the men in the center of our formation, who were forced to raise their shields to block the onslaught. When something happens somewhere other than your immediate area, there is a natural tendency for men and officers alike to turn their attention to wherever the excitement is, and I am just as prone to do it as anyone. Fortunately, the movement of the cavalry trotting across our front, heading for our flank, did a wonderful job of focusing my attention on the more immediate threat. My mind raced watching the enemy horsemen flow like water around the edge of our formation, trying to come up with the best solution to the problem.

"Centuries 1, 2, and 3 refuse the right flank." I snapped out the order and the men immediately responded, turning perpendicular to the original line to form a front facing the new threat to our flank, with our own cavalry force blocking the Pompeians from attacking us to allow the Centuries to array themselves.

It was a desperate, stopgap measure since it was a simple matter for the commander of the enemy forces to feed more horsemen to our side of the formation to keep extending their own line, but I had bought us some time. Even as we were dealing with our own threat, the youngsters of the other Legions were getting themselves into trouble, prompted by their Centurions, who gave in to their desire to inflict punishment on the Numidian skirmishers. First one, then another Cohort would suddenly charge forward after sustaining a barrage of missiles, intent on catching the lightly armed enemy to exact vengeance. This was obviously part of the enemy commander's plan, for the moment one of our Cohorts ran forward to try and catch the Numidian foot, they were met by a countercharge of enemy cavalry that pinned our men down, forcing them to quickly form square while holding their javelins out to discourage the horsemen from penetrating the formation. At this point, the enemy light infantry dashed around the pinned Cohort flanks, looking for weak spots at which to fling their own missiles, forcing the Cohort to try marching, still in square, back to their place in line. They would be harassed every step of the way by the enemy, at least until the Pompeians came within range of the Cohorts on either side and their javelins. It would have been bad enough if it happened once, but it happened several times, the Pompeians repeating the tactic because our own men kept running after the Numidian foot soldiers. I could not spare much attention to this, since our cavalry screen that was protecting not only my right flank, but the flank of the entire army, was being hard pressed by the Pompeian cavalry. What I could see was that we had precious little time before we were overwhelmed and the enemy would be able to continue its attempt to get around behind us. I had positioned myself at the junction of the main line and that of the three Centuries and looked desperately back to Caesar and the command group, feeling a small sense of relief that he was looking in our direction while issuing orders to a number of aides. It was about then that we learned the identity of the enemy commander that was giving us such fits.

"It's Labienus!"

The name rippled through the ranks, reaching my ears, and I tore my gaze away from Caesar to see a bareheaded figure wearing the red cloak galloping parallel to our lines, just out of javelin range. As he galloped closer, his face became plainly visible and I recognized the familiar sneer under the great beak of a nose. Following his progress was a roar of noise, men hurling curses and insults, the sound rolling towards me in step with Labienus' mount. Suddenly, Labienus drew up, his horse rearing, though he skillfully controlled the beast. He had always been a superb horseman, even if he was not in the same league as Caesar. Turning to face the men of the Second Cohort, which was next to the First, I heard him call out. I must admit that it was a queer feeling hearing that familiar voice that had issued so many commands through our time in Gaul.

"What are you doing there, *tiro*?" he called out to a man in the line and I craned my neck to see who he was talking to, but I could not immediately tell. I just knew that calling one of us a *tiro* was one of the worst insults one soldier could hurl at another.

Labienus continued his taunting. "You're quite the brave boy," he called in that mocking tone that he used so often that I think it was his normal tone of voice. "Have you been made a fool of by that man over there!" He pointed contemptuously in Caesar's direction. "He's put you in a pretty tight spot, hasn't he? I actually feel badly for you and all your little friends."

"I'm no *tiro*, Labienus," a voice called back. I assumed it was the man Labienus was addressing, but I was still unable to identify him . "I'm a veteran of the 10th. You remember us, don't you? We won you enough victories that you should!"

"The 10th," Labienus sneered. "I don't recognize any 10th Legion. It doesn't exist."

"Let me see if this will jog your memory." There was a sudden motion as the man who had been speaking took several hopping steps forward, his right arm pulled back. I saw the blur of motion as a javelin went streaking skyward.

Even in the heat of the moment, when I saw who it was, I laughed out loud. "That dumbass Labienus picked on Carbo," I called out to the men behind me who could not see his identity.

Gnaeus Carbo was a solid veteran, but his greatest claim to distinction was being the champion of the Legion in the javelin. Before I could finish the sentence, the lance had covered the distance between Carbo and Labienus, the pointed shaft burying itself into the chest of his horse, causing me to wince involuntarily. The horse let out a scream that was almost human, rearing so violently that Labienus was thrown several feet, landing heavily on his back, where he lay motionless.

"Maybe now you'll remember the 10th," Carbo said over his shoulder as he strode back to our lines amidst the roaring cheers of his comrades, myself included.

Several of Labienus' cavalrymen came rushing over, dismounting to render aid to their commander who was just beginning to move, his limbs waving groggily about like an insect knocked over on its back. However, while this was certainly good for morale, it did not change the overall situation at all, and finally one of Caesar's aides came galloping up.

"Caesar orders you to pull all of your Cohorts back and refuse the line with them in the same manner that you did with the Centuries. The center of the line is going to alternate Cohorts and pull to the rear of the formation and the ones that stay in front are going to single Century line to keep the front covered. Move quickly!"

I saluted, then began issuing orders. Naturally we could not just turn about to move into the new position without threatening our rear, so we also alternated, but with Centuries.

"Odd number Century *signiferi* and Centurions on me!" I ordered.

Once they were gathered, I pointed to the line I wanted them to form extending our right line, telling them they had to hurry because our cavalry screen was crumbling even as I watched, falling back closer and closer to where the three Centuries of the First were already waiting. I could only assume that the situation was similar on the left flank and that whoever was giving orders over there was doing the same thing that I had because the enemy was not flooding into our rear from that direction. The dust cloud raised by so many horses and men almost completely obscured the center of our lines, but the sounds of battle clearly conveyed that the fighting was desperate. The men moved quickly into position, yet even as they were doing so, our cavalry screen was pushed back into the ranks of my men, making for a terrible confusion of men and horses as both groups struggled to maintain some semblance of cohesion, the men on foot trying to find their standards, the horsemen trying to stay alive. The Pompeian cavalry took advantage of the chaos, forcing a wedge of horsemen into the churning space, hacking down at my men, who in turn jabbed upwards at them with their javelins. The long swords of the Gallic cavalrymen flashed downward, sparks flying when their blade struck the metal shaft of a javelin or the rim of a shield, a grunt or yell accompanying each strike. Men were calling to each other, both to friend and foe, either offering encouragement or cursing and for several moments, the situation was as confusing and unclear as any battle I had ever taken part in, including Pharsalus. Behind me, the Cohorts pulled out of the center of the line were moving into position, while the Centuries of the Cohorts remaining in the front line that had been in the second rank moved into the spaces vacated by the Cohorts, including mine. The odd-numbered Centuries from the 10th had moved into a semblance of the position that I had designated, but there were still a number of enemy cavalry trying to occupy the same spot. Even as I watched, more enemy cavalrymen appeared out of the dust to add to the pressure my men were already under, so that despite their efforts, I saw the rear ranks of the Centuries start to take a step backwards. The right flank was in immediate danger of collapsing, and with it the possible fate of the army.

~ ~ ~ ~

I could not delay moving the rest of my men into position any longer, so I sent for Scribonius, who came running out of the dust, his face streaked with sweat, the front of his armor caked with blood, causing me to look at him in obvious concern.

Puzzled at first, he followed my gaze then shook his head and grinned. "Not mine. One of those Numidian *cunni* wasn't fast enough jumping out of the way. What are your orders, Primus Pilus?"

I told him quickly that I needed him to take command of the rest of the men and get them into place as rapidly as possible. I had finally divined what Caesar was up to; in effect, he was ordering us to form an *orbis*, albeit on a larger scale than any we had ever been involved with before. Even as I was relaying the orders to Scribonius, I could see more horsemen were flowing around my men, except now they were not trying to engage them, instead trying to skirt past them to get into our rear. The Cohorts ordered to fill out the final piece of the *orbis* to protect our rear were moving into position, but were still more than a hundred paces away from being where they needed to be, and it was going to be a race to see whether the enemy could exploit the gap or our own men could close it. Still, as critical as it was, I could not give any more than a passing glance at it, my own situation with the 10th on the right being desperate. So far, we were managing to retain enough unit cohesion that our casualties had been relatively light from all appearances, but when facing cavalry the moment one man breaks ranks and turns to run, he brings on the possible destruction of his unit and the deaths of most of his friends. I had seen some of the men taking that first step back, so I knew that the next moment or two could determine whether we escaped this day with our lives or not. Scribonius saluted, then ran off to begin moving the rest of the men into position while I, having done all that I could do from a command point of view at this time, pushed my way to the front where the fighting was heaviest. All of these events were happening in much less time than it takes for me to describe; perhaps 200 heartbeats had elapsed since I had received Caesar's orders, and then moved the first of the men into position. I picked out one particularly large Gaul who was slashing down at one of my men with his long sword, which the man on the ground was blocking with his shield. However, I could see my man's legs shaking, the first sign that they were going to buckle, meaning his life was measured in heartbeats but before the Gaul could land the killing blow, I arrived to thrust my blade into the guts of the horse, its entrails dropping out so quickly that they covered my hand in filth and offal. It reared violently before its rear legs collapsed, sending its rider flailing desperately to keep his balance down into the dust. Before he could roll out of the way, the horse landed heavily on his leg, and I could hear the bone snap from where I stood over both man and beast as their screams mingled together. Shaking my arm as free of the horse entrails as I could, I stepped over the horse, its legs still thrashing feebly, to thrust my blade into the Gaul's throat, knocking his weak attempt to parry my blade aside with contemptuous ease.

The immediate threat to his life over, the man I had saved, a ranker named Faculus, I believe, stood grinning at me, pointing to my filth-covered arm. "You're never going to get all that off, Primus Pilus. That stink is going to be with you for weeks."

"True enough," I said pleasantly. "Just like the stink of the latrines is going to be with you for more than the month you're going to be cleaning them out."

The grin fled from his face as he looked intently at me, trying, I am sure, to determine whether I was joking, which I was, though I was not going to let him know that for a while. Turning back to the fighting, I saw it was little better than a brawl between mounted men and those on foot and that despite the efforts of the Centurions, the enemy cavalry was steadily eroding our cohesion.

One of the many threats that cavalry can pose to infantry is by virtue of the amount of space a man on horseback takes up. Therefore, the goal of the cavalryman is to force the body of his horse into the midst of a tightly packed formation, the horse's body acting as a wedge that pushes the men on foot out of position in the formation, thereby allowing another horseman to push himself into the crack to disrupt matters even further. Just like a wedge of iron is used to split wood, that is the nature of the cavalry attack on an infantry formation. Men have a natural fear of any beast larger than they are, making it a natural reaction on the part of any man, no matter how well trained, to get out of the way when something bigger approaches. It takes the iron-hard discipline of the Legions to make that man stand firm instead of move. Whether he stands steady for his comrades, or because he fears the consequences of being charged with cowardice if he turns to flee, provided he survives, matters not. The fact that he stands is what counts. So far, my men were standing but only by the thinnest of threads. Another way a cavalry charge can break a formation is when, as odd as it may sound, the men on the ground successfully defend against the charge by doing what I had just done in attacking the horses. As distasteful as I and a lot of men find attacking essentially innocent creatures, it is the most effective method of nullifying a cavalry charge. The problem is that when you kill or maim a horse, and that horse falls to the ground, it takes up a great deal more space than a fallen man. If the horse and its rider manage to penetrate the first rank of a formation before being struck down and the horse falls where it stands, that is a problem. When it is just one horse it is a manageable problem, but when it is several, the officer in charge often has to make a decision whether to relocate his formation, either in front or more usually behind the pile of dead horses. If he does not do so, then there will be gaps caused by the corpses of horse and rider, which could endanger his unit just as much as if the cavalry wedge is successful, at least if the cavalry is attacking in sufficient numbers. Of course, a commander can also turn the heaps of horseflesh to his advantage by using them as a makeshift parapet, and that is what I did now. During a lull, when the Pompeian cavalry withdrew a few paces to regroup, girding themselves to launch another assault, I had men muscle as many dead horses that we could drag into place in the time allowed, forming a wall of dead animals, using the bodies of a few men as well. This would give my men the space they needed to use their javelins as lances, in the same manner as at Pharsalus, rather than having to rely on their swords while being pressed by animals many times their size. There was a risk that the Pompeian cavalry would simply back away to get a running start, then try jumping the wall to come crashing into us. To counteract this possibility, I had the second rank kneel, with their javelins pointing upwards, ready to thrust them into the bellies of any horse whose rider thought this would be a good idea. By this time, Scribonius had moved the rest of the men into position, and I risked a quick glance around to see that the Cohorts had managed to plug the gap in our rear, but there was still fighting in a number of spots where the enemy was trying to create a breach. However, I had seen enough, so I began to walk about, talking and joking with the men like I did not have a care in the world, acting as if we had already won the battle, which in one way we had. Caesar might not be able to claim this as a victory, but I was now sure that we would survive the day. I called Scribonius, Camillus, and Maecius over to me, and I could see that Scribonius had an expression that was a mixture of puzzlement and worry.

"Primus Pilus, isn't it a little early to be celebrating?" he asked.

I laughed, clapping him on the back as I replied, "No, and you of all people should know that, Scribonius."

He still looked puzzled, shaking his head at my jibe, clearly not understanding.

"Don't you remember back in Spain, when we were *tirones*? That time on the hill?"

"You mean when Didius got hit in the head? And you won your first set of phalarae?"

I nodded. "Don't you remember how upset I was when I heard Calienus and Crastinus laughing about something, when we were surrounded?"

Scribonius laughed, his face changing as the memory came back to him. "I remember Calienus saying something about you being a girl," and I felt my face flush a little, though I had to laugh because that is exactly what he had called me.

"But he also pointed out that the time we should worry is when the enemy concentrated his forces instead of trying to encircle us, remember?"

I indicated our position, turning all the way about as I pointed. "Which is exactly what these idiots have done. Oh, at first they were just trying to get around us and force Caesar to put us into an *orbis,* but now do you see anywhere a concentration of men sufficient enough to break through?"

After looking around, the others agreed that they could not see any spot in our lines where there was an enemy force in sufficient numbers to not only effect but exploit a breach.

"You're right, Primus Pilus. But I remember also that the Lusitani did figure that out later that night, and almost overwhelmed us. Hopefully these men won't, but until they leave and we're back in camp, I'm going to hold off on celebrating."

If this gentle rebuke had come from anyone but Scribonius, I would have been very angry, but he had a way of saying things that made it hard to take offense, because he was invariably right. "True enough, Scribonius. So let's see what happens next."

~ ~ ~ ~

With the army now formed into an *orbis*, albeit more of a rectangle than a true circle, the Pompeians were forced to stand off again to hurl missiles at us. The day was passing, and it was mid-afternoon when the *bucina* called an assembly of senior Centurions to attend to Caesar. Leaving Glaxus in charge of the Cohort, I made my way with Scribonius and the other Pili Priores to Caesar's standard, which was now thrust into the ground roughly in the middle of our large formation, well out of range of even the most ambitious of archers. Caesar was standing bareheaded, as was his custom, even though his hair was now visibly thinning, talking matters over with Hirtius.

Once we were all gathered, he began speaking, his voice hoarse from all the shouted orders he had been giving since the beginning of the battle. "I've decided that we can't stay out here any longer," he announced. "We don't know how long it will take, but we can be sure that Labienus sent for reinforcements, and those reinforcements might be here at any time.

And given that there will probably be Legionary infantry in their numbers, I think it's best that we withdraw back to Ruspina."

I shot a look at Scribonius, who simply shrugged as if to say it mattered not what we thought, this was what we were to do, which was true enough.

"We're going to march in our current formation."

I had to stifle a groan at this. Being on the side of the formation while having to keep an eye outwards for any enemy thrusts was a tricky proposition under any circumstances, but Caesar seemed oblivious to the desire of one of his Centurions for an easier lot in life.

"But before we can begin, we're going to have to do something to get some breathing room. So when you hear the attack signal, I want every Cohort to spring forward and go after the enemy across from you. You will engage the enemy and drive them off as far as you can without risking yourselves from being cut off. If we do it in a coordinated manner, the enemy will be too busy to try and exploit any Cohort that strays too far, but just in case, keep an eye on each other to avoid getting out too far. Are there any questions?"

Caesar answered a couple of minor issues and with that, we went back to our men. As I walked, I tried to ponder how I was going to manage what Caesar had ordered, because I had once more outsmarted myself. By creating the parapet of dead horses, I had created an obstacle that my men would have to negotiate while still trying to catch the enemy enough off their guard that we could close with them. As I have said, for a short distance, especially going from a dead stop, a man can actually outpace a horse, but that advantage only lasts a few heartbeats. Once back with the men, I told Scribonius and the others what I had planned, then had them go pass the orders to their respective Centurions who in turn prepared the men. It was perhaps a tenth part of a watch later when the *cornu* gave the preparatory call to make us ready, followed a moment later by the call to attack. Immediately, the men of the 10th pulled their arms back to launch one of their two javelins, the darts streaking through the air towards the enemy, where most, if not all were going to land short, since the enemy was being careful to stay out of range. Despite knowing that, I was counting on not only man, but most importantly, beast instinctively reacting to the sight of these potentially lethal missiles heading their way. I was rewarded by the sight of lunging horses as men jerked their mounts farther back, the sudden movement of so many animals and men causing inevitable confusion. This was more than enough time for the men as they vaulted over the corpses of the animals and with a roar, launched themselves at the enemy cavalry, now whirling about in their own mass of confusion. We managed to inflict a few casualties before the Pompeians broke contact with us to flee well out of range. Before they could regroup, the recall had sounded and we had trotted back into our spot to begin the march back to Ruspina. But our troubles were not over; in fact, the worst was yet to come.

~ ~ ~ ~

We had marched barely a mile when the scouts came galloping back to Caesar.

"That's probably not good news," one of the men said glumly, causing a ripple of chuckles and comment through the ranks.

"Shut your mouths," Silanus, who was my Optio, shouted. "The next one to say a word is on report!"

I made a mental note to talk to Silanus about being a little freer with the men during desperate times. It had been my experience that letting the men give voice to their fears at these moments, as long as it was kept under control, was not a bad thing. Besides, as it turned out, it was not good news at all. Another mixed enemy force was cutting us off, led by the motherless dog, Petreius, he of the treachery in Hispania that saw a number of our men betrayed and murdered at his hands. The scouts reported a force of about 1,600 men, a mixed force of cavalry and infantry, thankfully not Roman infantry, but more Numidians. While they could not match us in full-on combat face to face, they were definitely proving to be a nuisance, as they moved much more quickly than we did. They also carried several of their light javelins, perhaps a half dozen compared to our two, besides which theirs were not made to bend like ours so they could be reused. I had no doubt that as soon as we marched off, that is exactly what the enemy had done, scampering in to scoop up all the missiles littering the ground to fling at us again. Now we were effectively surrounded again, except by an even larger force, after suffering casualties and fighting for a third of a watch. The 10th's losses to this point had been light; only a half dozen dead and wounded, all but one of the wounded able to march back with us, but the same could not be said about the other Cohorts from the rest of the Legions. The ground we left behind was littered with bodies and a fair amount of them were ours. We never liked leaving men behind, but since we had marched without wagons, it could not be helped. There would be families who never received the funeral urn from this battle. Unfortunately, we had more pressing matters. We were ordered to a halt, this time forming into a more standard *orbis*, although it was still very large, with the command group and our wounded in the middle. The Pompeians picked up where they had left off, darting in on horseback and on foot, flinging their missiles at us, then retreating back out of range of our own javelins. The men had been fighting now for at least two watches, and I could see that the constant barrage of enemy missiles was wearing them down, and despite themselves, their shield arms were dropping lower and lower with each volley. Inevitably, some of the enemy javelins began finding their mark and I heard cries of pain, bodies falling out of their spot in the formation, most of them writhing in pain while more than one lay completely still. I could not imagine that the other Cohorts were faring any better, and probably were doing worse, which as it turned out was absolutely true. The situation was so bad around the center of the formation where Petreius' men, still relatively fresh, were showering the men incessantly with their javelins, that the *aquilifer* of the 29th turned to flee out of range. As he ran past Caesar, completely unheeding of the shame and disgrace he was bringing onto his Legion and the army, our general had to grab him by the arm to point him back in the other direction, telling him that the enemy was that way. Fortunately, at least this time the *aquilifer* in question did not try to stab him with his standard like at Dyrrhachium. The sun was setting like it always did, yet it seemed to be moving more slowly than I could ever remember, probably because we needed it so desperately to get dark, for that was the only way that we were going to escape the predicament in which we found ourselves.

One more time, we were summoned to Caesar by the *bucina* and as we trotted over, Maecius asked me, "Why are you limping, Primus Pilus?"

I looked at him in surprise, not realizing that I had been limping, but when I paid attention, I could feel that he was right and I was favoring my right leg. I frowned in puzzlement; I had not been struck by even a ricochet, despite the enemy's best attempts to strike down a Centurion, yet there was no mistaking it now and I became aware that my calf ached. Finally, I realized that the wound from the battle on the Nile, which had healed well, had left me with a hole in my calf where the hunk of muscle was torn out, and this spot was aching now. I did not stop, but I experienced the queerest feeling of my life up to that point and I suppose it is strange to say but this was the first time in my life where my body had failed me in any way, the feeling of getting older hitting me like a punch in the stomach. All my life, I had been one of the strongest, if not the strongest man in the Legions and now one of my Centurions was looking at me with sympathy as I was struggling to keep up, and I hated that look with all of my heart. Gritting my teeth, I picked up the pace, making sure that I was the first man to reach Caesar from our place in the line, a completely childish thing to do, but one that made me feel better nonetheless.

Once everyone was gathered, Caesar wasted no time. "It seems that our friends Petreius and Labienus have no intention of letting us depart in peace," he said dryly. "So I'm afraid that we must call on the men for one more effort, in the same way as before. This time, however, I'm afraid we can't waste time or the element of surprise by issuing the preparatory call.

You must make your men ready for the first sound of the *cornu* that you hear. Is that understood?"

There were no questions, so we made our way back to our men, where the orders were relayed. I could plainly see the exhaustion etched in the faces of the men of not just my Cohort, but the entire Legion. Yet, they better than any other group of men knew the stakes for which we were playing. The sun was hanging just above the rim of low hills to the west and I calculated that Caesar would wait until the last possible moment, so it was light enough to launch our foray then regroup, but close enough to dark that once we did, we could make our escape in the night. As the moments passed by, the tension increased; the enemy continuing to dash towards us to throw their missiles, which the men continued to try and block. We had already made several rotations of the front line, meaning very few men had shields that were not pierced in several places, the nubs of the javelins sticking out jaggedly from where the shafts were knocked off by our men. A sign of the desperate straits we were in was the complete absence of the normal amount of complaining about the cost that the men would have to incur in drawing another shield from the quartermaster, since the amount for it would be deducted from their pay. I was beginning to think that Caesar either had cut it too fine or even changed his mind when the *cornu* blast finally came. Fighting through the fatigue, the men leaped forward once again, while I was in the lead, determined that I would not be limping along this time.

~ ~ ~ ~

Dispersing the enemy, we sent them flying once again before hurrying back into formation just as the sun plunged behind the hills. In the quickly growing gloom, we prepared ourselves as much as we could to march quietly, wrapping the bits of gear that tended to rub together with strips of cloth from our neckerchiefs or bandages. I personally inspected the First Cohort, instructing the Pili Priores to do the same for theirs, making sure that the men made their preparations correctly, and I was pleased to see that I did not need to make any corrections. This next bit was going to be tricky, because we could not rely on our normal signaling methods of *cornu* call or waving of the standards. Instead, Caesar was relying on mounted couriers, galloping back and forth from one end of the formation to the other, passing instructions. We set out shortly after dark, moving as quietly as we could for a group of armed men of that size, none of us making a sound, not even whispering to each other. Marching quickly under the circumstances, we progressed through the darkness, yet we had no contact with the Pompeians. It was only later that we learned that Petreius had chosen roughly the same time to withdraw back to Thapsus, though I do not know why. We made it back to camp at Ruspina shortly before the beginning of third watch, the men throwing themselves down on their cots, not even bothering to undress, only pulling off their sword belt and armor. Naturally, we Centurions did not have that luxury, having to get a final head count then present the butcher's bill to headquarters. The 10th had lost 15 dead and 30 wounded, while it looked like at least three of the wounded would either die or be so badly crippled they would have to be sent home on a ship returning to Italy as soon as they were able. One of the dead was an Optio in the Third Century, pierced through the eye by a Numidian javelin, so there was the matter of a promotion to attend to at some point as well. When I went to headquarters, my mood was not improved any by the news that first thing in the morning, Caesar had decided that we needed to improve the defenses of the camp.

"We'll construct a ditch linking the camp with the town, so that when supplies come in we can transfer them without being worried that they'll be subject to interception." Caesar was looking at the survey map of the town and the camp that his engineers had drawn for him, his finger tracing the line that would mark where thousands of men would be sweating the next day.

The lines around his mouth were even deeper than normal, while there were dark circles under his eyes, his features drawn and haggard from the ordeal we had just gone through. I am not the only one getting old, I thought to myself as I looked at him, startled at the sudden insight into how much he had aged in just the last year. He still moved with the same vitality, had the same seemingly inexhaustible energy that made younger men like me envious, but the cares and troubles of the civil war could plainly be seen in the contours of his face. Even as I was studying him, he suddenly looked up, catching my eye, seemingly divining my thoughts and giving me an almost imperceptible shrug of his shoulders as if to say, "Here we are. What more can we do?"

I turned back to the map, and when it was my turn to say so, I acknowledged the instructions. I made haste to depart so that I could get at least a couple thirds of a watch of sleep, but not before I walked the tent lines to check on the men on guard, who were the only ones up and about. Finally satisfied, I retired to my tent, cursing yet again the absence of Diocles.

~ ~ ~ ~

Next morning saw the beginning of the work on the defenses that Caesar had outlined, with the men of the 10th assigned to digging the section of the ditch immediately next to camp. The men were not happy about the work, meaning that the Centurions were busy with their *vitus,* making sure that none of them were shirking. Meanwhile, the Legion armorers were put to work creating lead slingshot and javelins, signs that Caesar was going on the defensive.

I was standing with Scribonius, watching his Cohort at work when he motioned to me to walk a few feet away to where the men could not hear. "I think that what happened yesterday shook Caesar up pretty badly," he said, his face turned towards the men so I could not look him in the eye.

If it had been anyone other than Scribonius, I would have rebuked him sharply, but we had been together too long and he was as staunch a supporter of Caesar as I was. For the first time, I heard doubt in his voice and realized that he was looking for some sort of reassurance from me that the situation was in hand, that Caesar was still master of our fates. Unfortunately, at least for Scribonius, I could not disagree with his assessment, because I had seen something in Caesar's face the night before that I had never seen before, real worry and even worse, doubt.

I could do no better for Scribonius than shrug my shoulders, replying, "I can't dispute that Scribonius, I think he was surprised by the number of the enemy and how quickly they showed up." I turned to him and smiled, hoping that it did not look as false as it felt. "But we've been in tighter spots than this and he's always gotten us out on top, hasn't he?"

"I'm not worried about all the times in the past; I'm worried about this time. Everyone's luck runs out and of all the people whose fortune has run longer than normal, Caesar is at the top of the list."

"Just proof how much the gods favor him," I retorted.

"But we both know how fickle the favor of the gods is, and how quickly they can turn their faces away."

I always hated arguing with Scribonius, because he never got upset, nor did he let his emotions rule his tongue. Before he ever opened his mouth on any subject, he thought it through thoroughly, and this time was no different.

Finally, in exasperation, I threw my hands up, signaling that I surrendered. "Scribonius, I'm not sure what you're looking for, but if it's reassurance that everything will be all right, you said it yourself. Everyone's luck runs out and this might be Caesar's time."

"Thanks," he said sourly. "If I wanted to feel bad, I would have kept my thoughts to myself."

His expression was so peeved that I could not help but laugh, and I punched him in the shoulder. "What's the matter? You wanted to live to a ripe old age or something?"

That got a laugh out of him, rueful as it may have been. "The thought had crossed my mind," he admitted.

"Well, let's see if we can survive today and the next couple of days, then we'll worry about that."

"Fair enough," he agreed as we walked back to the men, who had taken the opportunity at our inattention to lean on their shovels and picks.

A couple of whacks with the *vitus* fixed the problem neatly.

~ ~ ~ ~

I suppose at this time it would be appropriate to talk about matters between Vibius and me. He was still Scribonius' Optio, and even I could see that he was very good at his job. Our relationship was strictly professional, and we treated each other with a coldly polite correctness that would lead an outside observer to think that we did not know each other at all, which I suppose at that point was more true than not. I was secretly pleased to learn that he had actually not been one of the ringleaders of the unrest on the Campus Martius, in fact arguing against the idea of looting the homes on the Palatine, but men like Didius had carried that day. This is not to suggest that Didius was in any way a leader of the mutiny. However, he was more than happy to go along with the idea of grabbing as much loot as he could. Still, I was not willing to make peace with Vibius and he evidently felt the same way, for he never approached me, nor I him, and that was how matters stood between us. Poor Scribonius was the one caught in the middle, since he had managed to maintain his friendship with both of us, in fact serving as something of a go-between for the two of us. For instance, when I learned in a letter from Valeria that Juno's husband had died in some sort of accident, I casually mentioned this to Scribonius, knowing that the news would make its way into Vibius' ear. Sure enough, the day after I told Scribonius, Vibius was walking around camp smiling from ear to ear. I almost took a step towards reconciliation that day, because I was not only genuinely happy that Vibius was so clearly pleased by the news, I was also curious to know whether it was because the man who had stolen Juno from him had died, or if she were now free. Perhaps it was a combination of the two, but something kept me from taking that step, so I never asked him. When it came to our official duties, I did not have that much interaction with him, since he reported to Scribonius and Scribonius to me. I think we both liked it that way.

~ ~ ~ ~

In addition to the ditch, Caesar had us add sharpened stakes, along with his favorite lilies, which we no longer thought of as useless after seeing the damage they did at Alesia. We worked hard, making the men wonder if Caesar knew that an attack was imminent, but I assured them that he was simply being prudent. What I did not share with them was the information gathered by a combination of deserters and prisoners, who informed Caesar of the real numbers facing us. Scouts were sent out to confirm what he had been told, and they came galloping back with grim news. Scipio was approaching at the head of an army consisting of eight Legions and about 3,000 cavalry. Adding these numbers to those already in the field under Labienus and Petreius, we were once again significantly outnumbered. Compounding our problems was a continuing lack of supply, since we had been stopped from actually harvesting the grain we marched out to gather. Unfortunately, the enemy had not, so the bounty from those fields was now in their granaries and not ours. Caesar was sending ships to every point he could think of with requisitions, yet to that point, only small amounts had made it to us. To augment our forces, Caesar pulled the rowers and crew of the ships of the fleet, training them as missile troops. Most of the Centurions were doubtful of what use they would be with only a few days of training, though I suppose it was better than nothing. He also pressed some of the locals into the role of skirmisher to work in conjunction with our cavalry in the same manner as the enemy had used against us.

We were also running out of timber, so some of the ships were sent back to Sicily to get wood of sufficient length and quantity to make the number of towers that Caesar had decided we needed. The men worked from dawn until dusk, digging and chopping, so exhausted by the end of the day that they would trudge back to their tents, chew their food listlessly, make only the most desultory of conversation, then fall back into their bunks. The best result for the officers was that the punishment list was non-existent, as the men were too tired to make their normal mischief of sneaking out of camp to go into Ruspina, not that Ruspina was much of an attraction. As we strengthened our position, we passed the next few days in this manner..Scipio arrived, making camp next to the one already occupied by Labienus and Petreius, so of course it was not long before the one thing that Caesar wanted most to keep quiet became known, causing a near panic.

~ ~ ~ ~

"Scipio has elephants!"

I heard the words yelled down the Cohort street and leapt from my cot, cursing whoever it was that had uttered them, both the man who had just yelled out and whoever had told him. I only grabbed my *vitus*, leaving my tent ready to thrash someone. As is normal in these situations, the bringer of the bad news had chosen the evening meal, when all the men were gathered about their fires, so there was the maximum audience. There have always been, and I suspect always will be, men who thrive on being the bearer of bad tidings. The only blessing with a group as veteran as the 10th was that the list of suspects was relatively short and well known to all of the officers by this time. The men were on their feet, a sure sign that they were agitated, given their exhaustion, talking excitedly to their neighbors at the next fire or across their street.

"What the fuck are we supposed to do about elephants?"

"I've never seen one. Are they as big as people say they are?"

"Bigger than anything you can imagine. They step on you and you're dead, no doubt about it."

"It's not their feet you have to worry about. It's those damn tusks. They can spear three men just like chickens on a skewer."

"Quiet!" I roared. I was happy to see the men immediately stop talking and while not coming to attention, at least shut up. "You sound like a bunch of old women! So what? The enemy has elephants. You're the 10th Legion! How many times do we have to go through this, where you act like a bunch of scared *tiros* whenever something new pops up? Have you forgotten all the things we've faced over the years? And we have been and will always be victorious! So shut your mouths and eat your meal and let Caesar decide how to deal with the elephants!"

The men looked suitably ashamed, shuffling and looking at the ground, mumbling that they had gotten the message. With that, I turned to make my way to the next street over to repeat the same speech, knowing that I was going to have a long night before I was done. Being truthful, I was just as worried as the men were. I had never seen an elephant in anything but chains, and that had been relatively recently in Alexandria, the beast being part of the large menagerie of animals belonging to the Ptolemies. It was huge, dwarfing even as large a man as myself, which was a distinctly uncomfortable feeling. I had been told by Apollonius that when used for war, the animals were covered in armor plating, while a miniature fort was strapped atop their backs where several men, usually archers or javelineers were perched. They had a driver as well, but from everything I had been told before, the animals are notoriously hard to control, prone to fits of temper that make them almost as dangerous to their own side as to the enemy, which was why Caesar disdained using them. The biggest effect of elephants is psychological, and that effect was clear to see on the men before they even laid eyes on one, but as bad as it was with the 10th, it was much worse with the youngsters in the other Legions. They were positively beside themselves, as for a day or two it was the only topic of conversation, with the men getting closer and closer to the point of hysteria. Finally, the Primus Pilus of the 5th Legion came to Caesar with a request that they be given the responsibility for combating the elephants, a gesture that the rest of the army simultaneously thanked them for and thought them quite out of their collective minds for doing. Nonetheless, it had the effect of quelling the fears of the army, and while it was never confirmed, I smelled the hand of Caesar in this.

Speaking of Caesar, he was in an increasingly foul temper, spending a good part of the day down at the docks simply standing there looking out to sea for the rest of the army to arrive. We were still waiting for the rest of the 10th to arrive, as well as the other Spanish Legions, while I was waiting in particular for Diocles to show up. I was getting tired of all the paperwork I was being forced to do, though I pushed as much on Silanus as I could. As Caesar kept vigil over the sea, we kept working. The enemy's vast superiority in numbers of cavalry meant that we could not venture outside of the camp, instead having to rely on our supply by sea. This in turn meant that we had to deal with constant and chronic shortages of food and materials, as we were still waiting for the shipments from Cercina, Sardinia and other points. Somewhere in that time came further bad news, when word reached Caesar that King Juba of Numidia himself was coming with the rest of the Numidian army that was not already with Scipio and his bunch. He was supposed to be less than a week's march away when we learned, sending the morale of the army even lower than it had been with news of the elephants. We were even forced to dry out seaweed in a manner similar to what we had done in Alexandria as fodder for the horses, yet unlike the forage from the lake, this had to be rinsed thoroughly of all salt water before it was edible for the animals. The wagering in camp was running very strongly that as soon as Juba joined the Pompeians, they would not waste any time in attacking. I was reminded more and more with each passing day of the conversation I had with Scribonius, and I was beginning to think that perhaps this time the gods had turned away from Caesar for good. Just as suddenly, the gods turned back and, if not smiling at Caesar, at least they were favoring him with their gaze. Finally, Caesar's forays down to the docks finally paid off, a fleet of ships finally sighted, making their way for Ruspina. The ships carried the 13th and 14th Legions, along with another 800 Gallic cavalry and 1,000 archers. A second convoy arrived at roughly the same time, this one carrying the grain from Cecerna, relieving our supply situation temporarily, as Caesar began making plans to start offensive actions again. While the Legions were occupied in strengthening our defenses, the cavalry had been running regular patrols. There were clashes between our horsemen and the Pompeians on a daily basis, with both sides taking and inflicting casualties. Hopefully our turn would come to get stuck into the enemy, as the men were heartily sick of digging, but as usual, Caesar was not sharing what he had in mind with anyone, because if he had we would have realized that the digging had just begun.

~ ~ ~ ~

Now that we had more veterans salting our ranks, Caesar ordered us to prepare to move out and leave this camp behind. All we were told was that we were going to march to the town of Uzita, which was one of Scipio's main supply bases, with the twin goal of denying Scipio while relieving some of the pressure on our own situation. Scipio was marching his army out of his camp to array for battle every morning, but Caesar was not having any part of it, completely ignoring the challenge. I suspect that

Scipio was making this move knowing that Caesar was not likely to give battle, but needed a way to instill in his raw troops a sense of superiority, for that was what the Pompeian force was almost exclusively composed of in the Legions, raw *tirones*. If the rumors were true, many of them were pressed into service against their will. In fact, the Pompeians had been exceedingly heavy-handed with the local populace, so much so that once the natives finally accepted that it was indeed Caesar who had landed, and not one of his generals, they were coming in increasing numbers to ask for Caesar's protection from their supposed guardians. Like so many of the upper classes, Scipio, Labienus, and the rest of that lot had assumed that the natives would offer not just obedience but support, thinking that it was nothing more than their due. When it had not been as enthusiastically forthcoming as they thought it should be, these noblemen exacted reprisals against the populace. Now the leading citizens of many of the towns were coming to Caesar in response to the Pompeians' actions, with one of those delegations coming from the town of Uzita, telling Caesar that if he appeared before their walls, they would throw open the gates to the city. The problem was that we had to get there, despite still being significantly outnumbered, particularly with cavalry. The ground between our camp and Uzita, which lay slightly to the southeast, was an entirely open plain, with no undulations in the terrain if we were to take the most direct route.

With a force of infantry to block our way, Scipio could use his cavalry in the manner that we had encountered during the previous battle that had given us so many problems, thereby whittling us down. We would reach Uzita, but a trail of bodies would be a clear marker of our passage, losses that we could ill afford. Directly south of our camp was a line of low ridges, running roughly from the northeast to the southwest, with Uzita directly west of these hills. We left the camp at Ruspina under the guard of a few Cohorts, then began marching parallel to the coast, using the line of hills to screen our intentions from Scipio, whose own camp was perhaps a mile to the north of Uzita, directly blocking the natural line of approach from Ruspina. Moving south, we marched within sight of the sea. Once the bulk of the army passed the northern-most hill of the ridge, obscuring Scipio's view of our march, we turned inland. The hills were not much, yet given that the surrounding terrain was as flat as a table, it meant these heights commanded the valley that lay between the ridge and Uzita, so Caesar immediately ordered that we fortify the ridgeline. There was also a series of hilltops running the length of the ridge, which we were ordered to fortify as well. It turned out that there was an enemy outpost on the next to last of the hilltops to the south, a small force of Numidian infantry and cavalry that was scattered quickly. However, now our presence was no longer a secret.

As we worked, we saw the Pompeian force streaming from their camp to array themselves for battle. A large contingent of enemy cavalry detached itself from the main body, then came galloping across the plain towards us, meeting the fleeing Pompeian sentries a few hundred yards out on the plain from the base of the western slope of the ridge. The cavalry stopped briefly as the leader talked to the sentries, obviously asking about the size and composition of our force, then pressed on, heading towards us at a gallop. Caesar immediately saw an opportunity, because the enemy cavalry now at the base of the slope had far outpaced the rest of their army and isolated themselves. He sent our own cavalry, still on the opposite side of the ridge and out of view, circling around the southern end to get in the rear of the enemy cavalry. Helping our cause was a large farm building located at the base of the slope at the southern edge that further shielded our men, allowing them to circle all the way around to fall on the Pompeian rear, just as their horses were ascending the slope, forcing them to slow down. Our force slammed into the rear ranks of the enemy horse, catching them completely by surprise and it was only a matter of moments before a panic ensued as the men further toward the front became aware of the threat to their rear.

As they drew closer, we could see that the enemy force was composed of Numidians, Germans, and Gauls in almost equal proportions. True to their nature and as we had seen before, the Numidians broke contact to go galloping across the face of the slope to escape. The Germans and Gauls chose to stay and fight, where they were quickly surrounded, then cut down to the last man. The sight of this slaughter so infected the advancing infantry with fear that they turned en masse, fleeing back to their camp, running for their lives though nobody pursued. We stopped working to watch the spectacle of an entire army running for their lives without shedding a drop of blood, giving us a lift of spirits to see it.

While we were constructing the redoubts, Caesar, seeing that the slope of the hill was not much of an impediment to a determined assault, ordered a ditch dug about halfway down the slope, running the entire length of the ridgeline, which extended for more than a mile. This sounds like a great distance, and it is, but when you have several thousand men, all of them with as much experience at digging as we had, it is not as much work as it may seem. Of course, that is said as a Centurion who had not shoveled a spadeful of dirt in some time, so perhaps I am not speaking truthfully. Regardless, we dug the ditch, piling the spoil on the uphill side of the ridge to act as a further barrier should the Pompeians want to dislodge us from our position. One of the Legions was sent to build our marching camp on the eastern side of the ridgeline at the base of the hills. It was there that we retired at the end of the day, the men filthy and tired, complaining every step of the march back about all the work they had done. Century-sized guards were posted on each of the redoubts on the top to keep watch of Scipio's camp, but we were all certain that after seeing the display they had put on earlier, we would be sleeping soundly that night, and we did.

~ ~ ~ ~

The performance of Scipio's *tirones* convinced Caesar that it would be wise to put more pressure on the Pompeians, so at the evening briefing we were informed that we would be arraying to offer battle the next morning.

"I seriously doubt that he'll accept the challenge, but we must be prepared for that eventuality," Caesar told us. "To that end, we're going to treat this as if we are going to fight. You all know by now what I expect from the men and I know that you won't let me down."

I, for one, knew that the men were not going to be happy, not about the idea of going into battle, but that Caesar always expected the men to look as if they were on parade, with all decorations and plumes in place and in perfect order. That meant that after a hard day's work of digging, they would have a hard night's work of polishing and cleaning. Such is the lot of the Legions.

~ ~ ~ ~

We marched out the next day, climbing over the hill, then descending down to the valley floor, where we deployed into the *acies triplex*, aligning so that the center of the army was directly across from the town of Uzita. This meant that we were at the point closest to Scipio's camp, but he would have to align himself more or less in the same way to protect the town. As we approached, we could hear the sound of their *bucina* floating through the air, calling the Pompeians to formation. I must admit, however grudgingly, that it did not take as long as I thought it would for them to begin streaming out of the camp from all four gates, hurrying to form up across from us, while we had halted to dress our lines. Once that was done, we watched as Scipio's army arrayed itself. Unlike our own three-line formation, Scipio employed four lines, with his cavalry in the front line acting as a screen. With Scipio's army moving into position, the order was given to advance, but we only went another couple hundred paces before halting again, which is where we stayed. The Pompeians did not move either, as we began a now-familiar staring contest. Fortunately, we were too far away from each other for the men to hurl insults, so it was quiet for the most part, with only a low buzz as the men talked quietly while we waited.

Perhaps a third of a watch after we moved into position, the rain started, a ripple of curses reaching my ears as the men saw all the hard work with their plumes and leathers literally melt away. The blacking we used for our plumes started running, streaking the men's armor where the horsehair touched it, while the varnish on the leather dissolved after a few moments exposure. There would be a huge mess to clean up whenever we were done, which did not help the spirits of the army knowing what immediately awaited them. Still we stood, neither side moving, as it became apparent that Scipio did not have enough confidence in his army to go on the offensive. He did have the advantage of better ground, there being a gentle slope up to where the town sat, and Caesar was never one to fight on unfavorable ground if he could avoid it. The rain continued the rest of the day, through to about sunset, when we were turned about to march back to camp, sodden and miserable, our cavalry staying as a screen in the event the Pompeians suddenly took advantage of our retreat. We spent the evening cleaning our gear, the downpour continuing, turning the streets to a thick, sticky mud that clung to everything it touched, compounding our misery. At the evening briefing, Caesar informed us that he had decided that we would not repeat the tactic of the day. Instead, he wanted to extend the trenchline further south, basically lengthening the rest of the line all the way to the southernmost point where the slope started, wrapping it around to protect our left flank.

"At least the ground will be soft," Cartufenus said as we left the tent, pulling our cloaks up to try to block out as much of the water that was coming down so hard that one would think that the gods were simply dumping a bucket on our heads.

"If it keeps up like this, we won't be able to dig anything without it collapsing," I grumbled.

"I was trying to look on the bright side," he retorted.

We parted, heading back to our respective areas of camp, neither of us looking forward to the next day.

~ ~ ~ ~

The rain did not let up. Since we had not marched with our tents, leaving them behind at the camp in Ruspina, the men were forced to create makeshift shelters using their cloaks, fastened together in whatever manner they thought worked the best. When the weather was clear, it was fine, but now with rain, then occasional hail, falling without letup, the misery of the men was manifest. Regardless, we went out, doing our work extending the trench as Caesar had instructed, the men coming back covered in the sticky mud, then cleaning themselves by simply stripping down while standing shivering as the rain washed them clean. Cleaning their gear was not so simply done. In recognition of the conditions, I suspended inspections, knowing that we would have the whole Legion, or the part that was here on the punishment list, which would only further damage morale. The conditions were so bad, that men resorted to using their shields, with the covers on of course, holding them above their heads as they struggled through the mud of the camp. It was in this manner that we passed the next several days, neither side making a move. Because of the rain, we could not finish the earthworks that Caesar had deemed necessary, so there was nothing for the men to do but sit huddled under their makeshift tents and talk, and men with time on their hands fill it by gossiping about whatever situation in which they find themselves. That usually means trouble for the officers. In this case, the topic was Juba's approaching army, which was supposedly very close, in the men's minds becoming larger and more formidable as each day passed. The men talked about not just the elephants; the defeat of Curio at Juba's hands had built the Numidian king up into a formidable adversary while no amount of persuasion on the part of the Centurions seemed to sway the men back to the belief in themselves that is so crucial to winning. The rain picked up in intensity to the point that one night we could not even have our fires, forcing us to eat our meals cold, which only made matters worse. Finally, Caesar had enough. Calling a formation to address the army, he ordered us to assemble in the sea of mud that had become the forum of the camp. He wasted no time with any of his usual words of encouragement and expressions of pride in the job that we were doing, his displeasure evident in his words and bearing.

"As you all know, the king of Numidia is now within one or at most two days' march away and there has been much talk about the composition of the Numidian forces. Rather than keep you in suspense, I will tell you what our scouts have reported. Juba marches to Scipio with ten Legions, 100,000 light infantry, 30,000 cavalry, and 300 elephants. There, now you know what we're facing, so that should put an end to all the questions. You can believe me because I know what I'm talking about, and now that I have told you, if I hear any more talk about it, I'm going to put you on a boat and send you out to sea to fend for yourselves."

With that, he turned to stride back to headquarters, leaving the men standing shamefaced, but not a little worried.

"Do you think he's telling the truth?" Scribonius whispered to me as we slogged back to our area.

I told him I did not know, though I doubted it, even if I could not give a good reason why I felt that way. If Caesar's only goal was to shut the men up, he was successful, though his declaration did nothing to improve morale. Fortunately, the rain finally ceased about the middle of the next day so we went back to work extending the ditch, the finished portion now a moat from all the rains. There were a total of six hilltops that were part of the ridgeline and we had fortified all but one, the southernmost point. Meanwhile Labienus, who saw what we were about and understood its importance, had fortified it himself. To support this redoubt, he left Scipio's camp to build his own to the south of the end of the ridge, perhaps two miles from it. Making matters more difficult was the terrain itself, this last hill being separated from the chain by a steep ravine, the floor of which was covered with a stand of olive trees. In order to secure our position, that last hill had to be taken from the enemy, so Caesar sent the cavalry down into the ravine through the olive grove. Labienus had anticipated this move, actually setting an ambush, but his men panicked at the sight of Caesar's Germans and Gauls, so instead of attacking as a unit, they burst from their hiding spot further up the ravine in small groups, intent only on escape, and as a result were cut down. The rest of the Pompeians, seeing their comrades being slaughtered, turned to run up the hill with our cavalry in pursuit, not even stopping to make a stand at the top. It was in this manner we took the hill, which Caesar immediately ordered to be fortified in the same manner as the others. Now that the ridgeline was secure, we could begin the advance on the town, which meant more digging for the men. Caesar divided the army into two groups, one group digging while the other group stood in formation out a short distance in the valley in the event that Scipio wanted to stop us from what we were doing. This was when I began to suspect that Caesar still harbored a grudge against the 10th because we found ourselves digging again instead of standing guard, and it had happened too many times now to be a coincidence. This fact was not lost on the men either, and their muttered complaints were hard to stop because their officers heartily agreed with them. I suppose that it was harder on the men of the 10th because for so long we had been Caesar's favorite, so our fall from grace was more spectacular. Of course, none of the rest of the army held any sympathy for us, particularly the veterans of the 13th and 14th, who had their collective faces rubbed in our glory for longer than any of the rest.

Even Cyclops, a relative newcomer to the 14th spared me no comfort when we visited each other. "What do you expect? From what I've been told, your boys have walked around for years thinking that their *cac* doesn't stink like the rest of ours."

"For a long time it didn't," I retorted, though I knew how weak it sounded as I said it.

Cyclops just laughed. "Well, it certainly does now, and you can't blame the others for taking a little pleasure in it."

I stopped arguing about it, thanked Cyclops for the wine, then went back to our area.

~ ~ ~ ~

At about the same time that we took the final hill, Juba and his army finally arrived on the scene. While his army was not as large as Caesar had told us, it was still big. The number of elephants was of the most interest to the men, both for the obvious reason and because there had been considerable wagering on the number, so when the final tally was made whoever had picked 30 found themselves rich men. Judging from the sounds of despair when the number was announced, not many men did. To advance on the town, Caesar ordered two parallel trenches running from the base of the ridge towards Uzita, spaced widely enough apart so that the army could array itself between them. This protected our flanks while providing cover to move from the forts on the ridge to a forward camp that we would construct as soon as the trenches were completed. It was from the forward camp that we would besiege the town and be able to do so in relative protection.

At the end of the first day, a force of Numidians from Juba's camp came boiling out to fall on our cavalry, acting as rearguard for the rest of the watching Cohorts as they retreated to our camp on the other side of the ridge. However, our Gauls and Germans, after recoiling in surprise from the initial attack, turned about to rout the Numidians with heavy loss to the enemy. The next day the work on the entrenchments was finished, then without any delay we began working on the camp, situated just out of range of the enemy archers. Fortunately, the Pompeians either had not thought to bring or did not have any heavy artillery with which to defend Uzita, and now it was too late for them to get any inside the walls. Again, the men of the 10th were chosen for the work of building the camp, and I seriously thought of going to Caesar to ask him to relent, but almost immediately dismissed the idea. He had put me in this position because he trusted in my ability to lead the men in the manner in which Caesar thought was proper, so for me to go to him now would mean that I was unable to do so. Instead, I instructed the Centurions to crack down, literally, on those complaining the loudest and there were a few *viti* broken in the construction of that camp. The front facing Uzita was more heavily fortified than was our normal practice, with the turf wall and parapet made wider so that scorpions and ballistae would fit. This camp was our new home, though we marched back to the old one to pick up our meager possessions, returning to the forward camp after dark.

While we were working, Caesar was busy as well, but on the seas, as trouble had struck the fleet on its way back to pick up the remaining men of the army. One of the Pompeians, Varus was his name, attacked our vessels as they approached Leptis, scattering them and burning some of the transports, which fortunately were only carrying food, though it was badly needed. Caesar was given word of the trouble while he was in the main camp by the sea. Galloping off to Leptis, six miles away, he boarded his flagship and with a scratch force sailed out to confront Varus. Pursuing him to Hadrumentum, Caesar went into the harbor itself, recapturing a ship taken by Varus while setting fire to a number of the enemy's own transports before sailing back. The rest of the fleet arrived safely, containing the rest of the 10th, along with the 9th, so there was much rejoicing in the camp as comrades were reunited. Unfortunately, the happiness was destined to be short-lived, at least for the 10th.

~ ~ ~ ~

Now that the 10th was back together, Caesar took the opportunity to inflict the punishment he had been forced to defer back at the Campus Martius, calling a formation in the main camp the day after the reinforcements arrived. He had not informed me what he was up to, but I suspected that it had something to do with the mutiny. So did the men, who were subdued and uneasy as we marched the short distance over the hill to the main camp. The fact that Caesar was having us assemble in the main camp, away from the eyes of the enemy, was a hint that he did not want them to witness what was to happen. Coming with the rest of the 10th were the two Tribunes, Avienus and Fonteius, and they were two haughty young bastards, barely deigning to speak to me, a lowly Centurion, at least one who was not one of their toadies, in the limited number of watches I was in contact with them. There were a few of those, the kind that always somehow make their way into the Centurionate, usually because of pressure from their friends higher up on men like me. Sometimes the pressure is in the form of a threatened exposure of a secret that would prove damaging, or sometimes it is in the form of outright bribery. So far, I had been lucky in that I had not been forced to face such a trial. I knew that it would be coming if I lived long enough, but at least it would not be coming from these two, because as soon as we were assembled and we had gone through the formalities that are a ritual of the army, Caesar wasted no time, calling both of them to the front of the formation. Even through their natural arrogance, their unease and worry was plain to see, and for this, they had good cause.

Looking down on them from the rostra of shields that had been constructed, Caesar's gaze was cold, while contempt dripped from every word as he spoke. "Gaius Avienus, you instigated troops in the service of the Republic to mutiny, you plundered lawfully constituted municipalities, and you have been of absolutely no use to me or to Rome. In direct contravention of my orders, instead of embarking troops on your ship, you boarded your personal slaves and horses. Because of your misconduct, we are now short of men, and for this and all that I have stated you are hereby dismissed from this army without honors and directed to leave Africa today." He turned to Fonteius, leaving Avienus white with shock, shaking with shame and humiliation. "Aulus Fonteius, you too are dismissed from the army for insubordination and conduct unbecoming an officer in the Roman army."

Then it was time for a surprise, because Caesar then called three of my Centurions to the front of the formation, and I was happy to see that they were the two disgraced Tribunes' lackeys.

"Titus Salienus, Marcus Tiro, and Gaius Clusenas, the three of you have reached the rank of Centurion in my army not by merit, but by favor. You have not been distinguished for valor in war or good conduct in peace, and instead of being obedient and exercising self-control you have been active in sedition and in inciting your men to mutiny against their general. Therefore, I deem you unfit to command Centuries in my army, and you are hereby dismissed as well, to leave Africa immediately."

As soon as Caesar finished, the provosts who had been waiting stepped forward, two men surrounding each of the disgraced men. None too gently they were led away to their fate. While I was happy to see that one pressing problem was solved in a manner that would have been too difficult for me to accomplish, at least as far as the Tribunes were concerned, I was somewhat disappointed because I did not think Caesar had gotten everyone. I had really hoped that Celer would have been one of the men sent packing, but I would just have to let Scribonius deal with him. I must admit he was probably doing better than I had when I was in command of the Second. I now had vacancies in the Fifth, Seventh, and Eighth Cohorts respectively, and I began thinking of possible replacements. Caesar had nothing more to say; his message was clear and understood by every man in the Legion. My only hope as he stepped down from the rostra, then headed for the *praetorium,* was that now the 10th was no longer going to bear the brunt of his displeasure.

~ ~ ~ ~

All was not going well for the Pompeians, who had their own morale problems, as desertions were beginning to mount. The trenches we dug, particularly the one on the side nearest the enemy camps, served as a secure passageway for those wishing to desert, so much so that it soon became a well-traveled road heading one way towards our camp as first rankers, then officers, particularly in Juba's army came to our side. Their stories were all the same; they believed that the Pompeian cause was lost and they were getting on the winning side as quickly as possible. As was his usual policy, Caesar welcomed all those who came to our side, though we in the ranks took a more cynical view of these new converts to the cause. Perhaps it was in answer to these desertions that Scipio decided that another demonstration was in order, so two days after the Tribunes were cashiered, the *bucina* sounded the call that the enemy was in sight. We formed up quickly in answer, and as the men made themselves ready, I ran to find out what was happening. Scipio was apparently offering battle, forming up in a line on the far side of the city walls, using a small creek that ran behind the city as a barrier to attack from our army. We were ordered out into formation, and for the first time since the 10th had been formed, we were not posted on the right, but on the left with the 9th. However, it was not as further punishment, but because Scipio had deployed a large contingent of cavalry beyond his own right wing. He was obviously hoping to send them into our flank and rear, should we engage with the right wing. Because of this development, Caesar wanted his most experienced men on that side. Nevertheless, I have to say it was quite an awkward experience and it took us longer than I liked to get in place. Fortunately, Scipio did not seem anxious to come to grips, so we had no problems despite the delay. As we did the last time, we went to all the trouble of forming up for battle and we simply stood there staring at each other as the sun moved through the sky. It became clear that Scipio was hoping to tempt us to attack, using the creek and town as natural barriers to help bolster his defense, yet Caesar would not snap at the bait, making for another boring day. The men were allowed to sit in place and drink from their canteens as the time plodded by, each side eying the other while talking quietly.

About two parts of a watch after midday, there was movement on the enemy side, so I called the men to their feet, the cursing and moaning cut short by a few judicious whacks with the *vitus* from the Centurions. The enemy cavalry force that was to our left had begun moving towards us, while at the same time the right wing of the enemy formation, composed entirely of cavalry also started moving. As they drew closer, we could see that it was Labienus in the lead, obviously recovered from his fall, the men jeering the sight of the traitor. Their intent was clear; they were going to try to pin us while the other force circled around us, but Caesar was ready for the move. Our own cavalry, along with an auxiliary force, came pounding across our rear, heading for the marauding enemy, while Labienus' cavalry stopped just out of javelin range to dress their lines then make themselves ready for a charge, or at least acted as if they were. Our cavalry and auxiliaries went splashing across the marshy ground around the creek to throw themselves into the enemy, but as the Pompeian force was composed of mostly Numidian horse, instead of standing and fighting they broke contact, galloping a short distance away before suddenly stopping then hurling their javelins. Several horses were hit, as well as a few men but that was all the damage done, and once the enemy plan was thwarted, they seemed to be content to retire to their camps, as we did the same.

~ ~ ~ ~

We spent the next several days doing little more than improving the works around Uzita, although there were skirmishes between the cavalry every day. This gave me the time I needed to fill the posts of the disgraced Centurions, which I did in the more traditional manner of moving men up and placing the new Centurions in the Tenth Cohort. The best news, at least for me, was that Diocles had finally made it. Although he did not bring my baggage, per Caesar's strict orders, having him at my side helped matters tremendously. Poor Diocles probably did not feel that way, since there was a pile of paperwork that I had been neglecting that he was forced to spend all of his time finishing. The reason Diocles was allowed a spot on the ship was that while he was my body slave, he was also the Legion clerk, so it made my life easier in other ways.

Our supply situation was a never-ending concern, but word reached us of a large supply of grain in a village a few miles distant, stored in subterranean caves. Sending out a force of cavalry along with two of the Legions, they carried back all that they could hold, but left a goodly amount behind. Labienus learned of this expedition and that there was still a significant amount of grain left behind, so he apparently decided that he would set a trap for us when we returned. His plans were thwarted when some deserters informed us of his intentions, telling Caesar exactly where and how Labienus was setting the trap. Instead of confronting the enemy immediately, Caesar chose instead to wait several days. As is natural and to be expected in these circumstances, the men who were to spring the trap grew bored, and bored men get careless. After perhaps a week, the 10th, 9th, and 13th were ordered out to march to the ambush site, led by close to a thousand cavalry, each of the horsemen accompanied by an auxiliary pressed into service from the local populace in the manner of the Numidians. As Caesar had predicted, the ambushing enemy force was out of position and completely unprepared, so our cavalry fell upon them, immediately routing them while inflicting a few hundred casualties. The battle was over before we ever got there, whereupon we turned about to march to the village without even drawing our swords. We heard later that Juba crucified the men who survived our attack by fleeing. Retrieving the remaining grain, which yielded only enough for about three more days for the army, we returned to camp.

~ ~ ~ ~

The siege of Uzita was not yielding results, so after six weeks, we were told at one morning briefing that we would be moving operations, this time to a spot about 20 miles away near Aggar where there was supposed to be more food available. In the fourth watch the next night, we set fire to all the towers and other structures in both camps, then in a parallel column, with the baggage train on the far side of the columns, we marched away. We covered the 20 miles fairly quickly since the terrain in that part of the world is generally flat, interrupted by low hills spaced in such a way that they can be easily avoided. At the camp at Aggar, we were joined by the last two Spanish Legions, the 7th and 8th finally arriving after being chased about by the Pompeian fleet for a few days. It did not take long for Scipio and Juba to follow us, where they pitched their own camps about six miles away to the northwest, once again setting up in three camps. Our own camp was about two miles northwest of the town of Aggar. It was definitely a better location from a foraging aspect, the land lush and fertile. However, this camp was not in the best position for defense, so we were marched to a spot about two miles to the southwest, slightly closer to Aggar and on a low hill, providing a stronger position than the original. About two days after Scipio arrived, we were informed by deserters, who were coming to us in droves at this point, that Scipio was marching to a town called Zeta, some nine miles farther northwest of their camps, where there were supposed to be abundant amounts of wheat. Although the area around Aggar had offered up an ample supply of olive oil, figs, barley, and an amount of wheat, we were still lacking in the latter. Accordingly, Caesar decided that it would be a good opportunity not only to augment our supply, but to inflict some damage on Scipio at the same time. Zeta was about 14 miles distance from our new campsite, but Caesar deemed it worth the risk of a flank march past the enemy camps. Leaving a few Cohorts behind to guard our camp, we marched out at fourth watch. Moving quickly, we came upon Zeta to find that Scipio's men were further afield searching the farms surrounding the town, which at least allowed us to take the town without incident.

Before we could go hunt down the Pompeians out in the fields, our scouts came to report that we had in fact not slipped by undetected and the enemy was coming in force from their three camps to meet us. I think that our experience at Ruspina was still fresh in Caesar's mind, as it was in ours, and not wanting a repeat performance, Caesar ordered us to break off contact. Leaving a garrison of auxiliaries and one Cohort under the command of one of the Tribunes, Oppius I believe, we turned about and began marching back to camp, with 22 of Juba's camels in tow that the enemy foraging party had brought to carry their booty home. The men were not happy about being marched for half a day, only to be forced to turn around again. Still, nobody wanted a repeat of the ordeal at Ruspina, so they needed no urging to match the pace that Caesar set. At first, we had no opposition, until we were pulling even with the Pompeian camps, when the cursed Numidian cavalry led by Labienus and Petreius came boiling out from behind a low hill where they were waiting for us to begin harassing our rearguard, thankfully not us this time. Our own cavalry galloped to the rear, but closing with the Numidians as always proved to be as easy as grabbing and holding a wisp of smoke, even the men on foot who accompanied the cavalry proving too swift. The Legionaries in the rearguard had no better luck, dashing after the Numidians who were as nimble as ever, leaving panting, frustrated, and angry men to do little better than shake their fists. Naturally, our progress was now slowed as it was at Ruspina while the Pompeian cavalry began to flow around our marching formation like water, darting in just long enough to fling a javelin at us, which of course forced the men to remain constantly on their guard. The enemy auxiliaries were focusing their attention not on our men but the mounts of the cavalry, their missiles striking several of the horses, putting their riders afoot, most of them scampering to the safety of the formation. Very quickly, even our slow progress stopped as the shower of missiles continued unabated up and down the formation from all sides. It had turned into a hot day, and the men had not gotten the opportunity to refill their canteens, so soon what water they carried was consumed as the sun beat down.

The order to march would come, but we would only move a few paces before we had to halt again as the Numidian horse would swarm about us. Their volleys of javelins came so fast and furious that the men could either march or defend themselves but could not do both. More than a full watch passed in this manner and at the end of that time, we had not moved more than a hundred yards. Our cavalry was both exhausted and depleted as more and more men came running back to the rest of us without their horse. The enemy aim soon became apparent. They had no intention of closing with us, but instead would let the hot sun and elements do their work for them, pinning us without water for a sufficient amount of time to weaken the men to the point where the inferior quality of the enemy infantry was not a factor. Scipio's Legions had been shaken out into a triple line outside their camps, yet they made no move to intercept us, preferring to let the Numidians do the work of whittling us down. Finally, Caesar sent the order to withdraw the cavalry from the rearguard, putting the exhausted troopers in the middle of our formation, relying on the Legions to provide security. We resumed the march, except this time we did not stop despite the harassment, marching with our shields on our arms instead of strapped to our backs in the normal manner, as the enemy continued to pepper us with javelins. Unlike Ruspina, however, this time the men were more prepared and knew what to expect, so the panic that infected the army the last time was absent. The sun was setting, as once more darkness would aid in our escape, the Numidians able to harass us but no longer able to stop us now that Caesar had decided to move no matter what. We arrived back at our camp about a watch after sunset, and while the men were tired they were not nearly as discouraged as they had been at Ruspina, namely due to the fact that we suffered no deaths and only about a dozen wounded, none of them from the 10th. It was something of an act of the gods that kept our casualties so low, and there were a number of offerings made to Mars, Bellona, and Fortuna in thanks when we got back. But Caesar had seen enough, and as usual, he had plans of his own on the best way to combat the tactics used by the Pompeians.

~ ~ ~ ~

"There are elephants in the camp!"

I jumped to my feet, as anxious to see what was happening as any ranker. It was two days after our foray to Zeta, and Caesar had been hard at work with the army, embarking on a training regimen quite unlike anything we had ever endured before. Nobody was exempt, the most veteran Legions, like the 10th, training alongside the boys of the 29th and 5th. Caesar had grown as tired as we were of dealing with these Numidian troops, particularly our cavalry who were in danger of running out of horses at the rate they were losing them. To that end, we trained more like gladiators than soldiers, as Caesar instructed small groups of men in exactly what needed to be done to defend ourselves successfully against the Numidians. When was the right time to give chase to the enemy skirmishers and how far we should chase, when was the right moment to use our own javelins with a better chance of hitting someone than we had been doing previously. The elephants were part of this training, though it was obvious that Caesar had sent for the beasts some time before, since these were from Rome, or at least the peninsula. There were five of them, and they had been trained to perform in the shows put on for festivals and such, so they were used to humans, shuffling docilely enough through the gates, their great long trunks waving about as they sniffed the air, taking in their new surroundings. Men lined the Via Praetoria, their voices excited, acting more like children than hardened soldiers. I pretended to be indifferent, but even having seen an elephant before, they are still awe-inspiring creatures, and I wondered exactly what Caesar had in mind when it came to training. Thankfully, the boys of the 5th would be the ones doing the work with the animals, for which I at least was grateful. Very quickly Caesar began working with the 5th, getting them familiar with the elephants, making each man come right up to the animal to touch it, that event being the cause of much amusement with the part of the army that saw it as they conducted their own training. Many men had to be shoved by their officers to get within touching distance, while a few had to be threatened with flogging before they would reach out a trembling hand to touch the side of their particular beast. For their part, the elephants endured this patiently, obviously used to being the center of attention wherever they went, standing there with their tails switching back and forth, eating the fodder spread out for them to eat. It was a good thing that our supply situation had eased, since one elephant eats more than five horses, but they had to earn their feed just like the rest of us. For the next several days, the normal sounds of camp life were augmented by the trumpeting of the elephants as their handlers made them act as if they were going into battle. The men of the 5th threw their javelins, tipped with cork of course, at the animals, though I can't imagine that it was pleasant for the elephants even if the points were blunted. The cavalry horses were brought into the training as well, as they were even more skittish around the huge beasts than we were, so that it was not long before they became accustomed to the smell and sight of them.

We continued our own training, and the men, unaccustomed to the amount of running that we were doing as they dashed back and forth, would reach the end of the day exhausted, spending just long enough around the fire to have a quick chat with their friends before retiring. I attended the daily briefings, so I was present when envoys from a nearby village called Vaga came to ask for Caesar's aid, claiming that the Pompeians, Juba's men in particular, had been ravaging the town and its inhabitants. Caesar sent a squadron of cavalry along with a Cohort of the 7th to the town, but when they arrived, it was too late. Juba had slaughtered every man, woman and child in Vaga, leaving their bodies for the carrion birds to pick their bones. While the most extreme example, this was the normal manner in which the native populace was treated by the Pompeians. This should explain why we were constantly being approached by delegations from the surrounding cities, towns, and villages, offering Caesar aid in exchange for protection.

~ ~ ~ ~

Despite how busy we were, the traditional start of the campaign season was just beginning, so on March 21 under the old calendar, we held the lustration ceremony, consecrating our standards while asking the gods' blessing on our endeavors. It is a ritual of great importance to all of us in the ranks, from the lowest Legionary to the Primus Pilus, which Caesar knew and therefore made sure that the ceremony was carried out flawlessly, that the auspices were good and all sacrifices were performed in the proper manner. Caesar was Pontifex Maximus and had been Flamen Dialis, but I do not believe he was a particularly religious man, he just knew how important it was to others, particularly the lower classes. We Romans set a great deal of store in our religions, and are a superstitious bunch of people, so I believe it was this that made Caesar pay such attention to rituals and ceremonies of religion. One slight setback to Caesar's plans came with his recognition of something that we in the ranks had predicted, the failure of the locals to serve as auxiliaries supporting the cavalry. To remedy the situation, Caesar called for volunteers from each Legion, 300 from each to march in light order, ready to leap from the ranks to support our cavalry. It was the cavalry, which was severely depleted both in men and horses, that worried Caesar most, a concern that was shared by the rest of the army after seeing the results of every battle we had fought so far. After a few more days of training, I was called to the *praetorium*, where I was given orders to prepare the men to move. We were going to attempt a similar operation to what we did at Zeta, at the town of Sarsusa, about a day's march almost directly west of where Scipio had another supply of food. This town was supposedly garrisoned, so we marched out in force, leaving only a few Cohorts behind to guard the camp.

It was not long before Labienus and his cavalry came out of their camp to start their harassment, first falling onto the wagons that were following us, that would carry the grain back to our own camp. Then our newly formed group of men combined with our cavalry to catch the Pompeian cavalry flatfooted, inflicting several casualties before driving them off. We continued on the march, and while Labienus did not attack us again, he followed us like a shadow, keeping to a line of low hills to the right of our march.

We reached Sarsusa, finding it was indeed occupied with Pompeian troops, but the low walls were not sufficiently defended to keep us from taking the town quickly, where we put the entire garrison to the sword in retaliation for the outrages done at Vaga. The next day, we marched south to another enemy-held city, Thisdra, but this was too well defended to take quickly, and because the only available water was inside the walls, we marched back to our camp by Aggar. When we arrived, we found that the last of the reinforcements had arrived, another 400 cavalry, about a thousand archers and slingers, along with the remainder of the Legions, men too sick or injured to make the trip with their Legions when they came over, about 4,000 total, including about 200 men of the 10th who had been left behind. The army was now 35,000 Legionaries strong divided unequally among nine Legions, with about 4,000 cavalry and 2,000 missile troops, these being roughly evenly divided between archers from Crete and slingers from Rhodes and the Balearic islands. We stayed in camp for another few days, each side waiting for the other to make some sort of move. Finally, Scipio came marching out to offer battle again, this time choosing a spot near a town called Tegea that lay between Aggar and the Pompeian camps. The *bucina* called us out, where we quickly formed up into our own triple line, and we were placed back in our normal spot on the right. As was his habit, Scipio had chosen his ground carefully, on a gentle slope that we would have to climb in order to close with the enemy, which Caesar was not willing to do. Instead, we stood there as we had so many times before, each side waiting for the other to make a move. Scipio had posted cavalry on either wing, except this time he stationed them farther out than was normal. Then, after waiting for the better part of the day, Caesar sent some of our own cavalry charging at the horsemen on the left wing of the Pompeian line. The enemy cavalry commander responded by spreading his men out, with the obvious intention of allowing our force to charge into their midst, then enveloping them and cutting them off. To counter this, Caesar sounded the call for the 300 Legionaries from the 10th to dash out to support our horsemen, with Velinus of the Fifth Cohort in the lead. The sudden appearance of our men on foot, running swiftly with their javelins, which they jabbed up at the unprotected faces of the mounted men or at the belly of the horses, threw the enemy cavalry into complete confusion, as animals started rearing and lunging to try to escape the sharp points of our weapons. Our force pushed the Pompeian cavalry back closer and closer to the left wing of Scipio's infantry, who began shifting nervously about at the sight. Seeing an opportunity, Caesar sent the rest of the cavalry charging into the fray, churning up even more of a cloud of dust, the sounds of the fighting our only guide to what was happening. We could hear cries of alarm and pain as our horsemen, accompanied by our men on foot, pushed into the left side of the enemy formation. While we watched, the Pompeians started giving ground, their *cornu* sounding the recall. With their left wing fighting back our men, the rest of the Pompeian army marched back up the gentle slope all the way to the walls of the town. Their left wing staged a fighting withdrawal, our men only breaking contact when they got in range of the javelins of the waiting comrades of the left wing at the base of the walls. The men came trotting back to the formation, gasping for breath, but grinning and laughing, happy that the slope was strewn with enemy bodies, both horse and man. We retired at the end of the day, yet despite the limited success, the frustration at every level of the army was high, because it had become clear that we would have to find a way to force Scipio to come to battle. That night at the evening briefing, Caesar announced that we were going to change tactics and would be marching the next day. We would be marching to Thapsus.

The army departed at dawn the next morning, leaving a burning camp behind to let Scipio know we were on the move. Unlike other occasions when we would try to steal a march, this time Caesar wanted Scipio to know that we were leaving, taking no measures to hide where we were headed. Thapsus was the one city that steadfastly refused to join with Caesar, and it was the main supply point and naval base of the Pompeians. More importantly, it was the last strongpoint freely allied with Scipio and the Pompeians, so the fall of the city to Caesar would spell the deathblow to the hopes of the Pompeian forces. We arrived at the end of the day, making camp before starting on a contravallation of the city the next morning. Thapsus is on the coast, on a promontory of land with a huge expanse of marshy ground a few miles south. Because of the marsh and the contour of the coast on either side of the city, there are only two overland approaches, one from the west that squeezes between the coastline and the northern edge of the marsh, and from the south, also between the sea and marsh. The area of the city and open land hemmed in by coast and marsh formed a triangle, with the city at the apex of the triangle where the coast made almost a ninety degree bend from north to west. Caesar situated our camp equidistant between the bend of the coast so that our contravallation would extend from sea to sea while our camp would be roughly in the middle. The weakness of our position was that by blocking the two approaches, we would also be hemmed in and unable to forage, so it came down to a race to see what would happen first, whether we would take Thapsus or Scipio would starve us out. In order to keep Thapsus from being reinforced, a small, fortified camp was built astride the road leading to the city from the south, manned by two Cohorts. Scipio and Juba came following behind a day later, moving cautiously, rightly fearing an ambush, but Caesar could not spare the men from our work of entrenching, though of course, the enemy did not know that. Thwarted by the small fort blocking the road, Scipio first made camp to the south, while Juba made camp next to him. Then, with Juba staying in his camp and leaving a portion of his forces with Afranius in the other, Scipio marched through that same night to the west, swinging wide around the marsh to take up a blocking position to the north. Giving his men a rest of just a full watch after they arrived in position shortly after daybreak, Scipio then had his men start on a fortified camp and series of entrenchments, putting the entire army to work. Although Scipio had effectively blocked us in, by placing his troops in a small area that had such impassable barriers on either flank so that his greater numbers were meaningless, he had also outsmarted himself, as Caesar was about to demonstrate.

~ ~ ~ ~

The *bucina* sounded the recall, stopping the men from working on our own contravallation, summoning us back to camp. As soon as we returned, there was another call of the horns for the senior Centurions to meet at the *praetorium* immediately, so I hurried over with the rest of the Pili Priores of the 10th.

As soon as everyone had arrived, Caesar wasted no time. "We're going to take advantage of Scipio's error and attack immediately."

This caused some comment, but we quickly quieted down as Caesar gave us our dispositions. We would be on the right with the 9th, while the 13th and 14th would be on the left, with the new Legions in the middle. The 5th was not assigned a spot, since they would line up wherever the elephants were, and we were sent to hurry our men to make them ready for battle. We had done this many times before, usually ending up standing in place for thirds of a watch, while our cavalry saw most of the action, so it was hard to get the men moving with any urgency, but judicious use of the *vitus* got them going. We were ready in less than a third of a watch, marching out of the camp, then forming up in *acies triplex*, on the right wing, the rest of the army taking its place. The *cornu* sounded the advance, and we stepped off, the Centurions calling out the count while the Optios at the rear of their respective Centuries kept the men in line. The army closed the distance fairly quickly, so we caught the Pompeians still working on their camp. Their *bucina* sounded the alarm as their men went scrambling for their weapons, followed by what appeared to be mass confusion as they went running about looking for their standard bearers. Our front line moved into position approximately 300 paces away from where the Pompeian line formed in front of their camp, where we caught the first sight of the elephants lumbering into the spot designated by Scipio.

"I thought there were only 30 of them," Glaxus said, the worry clear in his voice. I had been thinking the same thing, but I did not want to sound bothered. As we watched more than 60 of the beasts move into position, I saw that Scipio was splitting the force into two, placing them on each wing.

"There are thirty." I tried to make it sound lighthearted, though it was hard. "On this side, anyway."

In fact, there were 32 of them on each wing of the Pompeian line. As soon as their disposition was seen and understood, Caesar ordered five Cohorts of the 5th to our side, where they formed up to our right, while the other half did the same on the opposite wing. The 5th got into position quickly, then the men were ready to go, as it finally became apparent that today would be different, that Scipio was done running and we were going to fight. Caesar was on Toes, riding across our front as he had done so often before, spending most of his time with the youngsters in the center, exhorting them to emulate the veterans and follow our example. The men of the 10th were ready to go, but the ground on the left wing was sufficiently broken so that it made it more difficult for the men of the 13th and 14th to get into position, so we were told to wait, which did not sit well with the men. As the moments dragged by, Caesar kept talking to the youngsters, while the men on the right, including my men, began talking more and more animatedly.

"Let's get going. We've been waiting long enough," a man called out, to which there was an immediate roar of agreement from his comrades.

I turned about to glare at the men, but it did not seem to have any effect. "Shut your mouths. We'll move when we're told and not a moment before," I yelled as loudly as I could.

"What's taking so long?" someone else called out. "Let's end this now!"

Another chorus of approval met this call, then something happened that I had never seen before. Without being told, a *cornicen* in the 9th, obviously heeding the urging of the men around him, sounded the call to advance. In perfect unison, as if the command had actually been officially given, the men of the 10th, along with the five Cohorts of the 5th, stepped off with the 9th. All up and down the line, the other Centurions and I began roaring at the top of our lungs for the men to stop, but none of the rankers paid any heed whatsoever. I was reeling with shock as I looked over at Glaxus who was nearest to me, and who could only give a helpless shrug. Cursing every one of them, their mothers, fathers, and whoever else I could think of, I ran to catch up to take my place at the front, wondering if this was my last day not only as Primus Pilus, but as a Centurion. I looked over to see Caesar staring at us in astonishment, yet he recovered quickly, turning to snap orders to his own *cornicen*, who sounded the general advance of the whole army, while Caesar galloped Toes to the front of the line. Turning to see if it had just been the first line to advance, I was relieved that the second line, while farther back than normal, was hurrying to close the gap. The third line was staying put, but that was standard, as they would only come rushing in at the decisive moment to break the enemy completely, or to rescue us if things should go terribly wrong. As we rapidly closed the distance, the archers and slingers assigned to our wing began loosing their missiles, making the elephants their primary targets, and a flurry of arrows and slingshot went flying at the beasts. After only a matter of perhaps two or three volleys, the first of the animals, trumpeting in terror, whirled quickly about, despite its massive bulk, to go stampeding into the poor men standing in formation behind it. Immediately following the last missile volley, the men of the 5th hurled their own javelins, then launched themselves at the now thoroughly frightened animals. Elephants are herd animals, so it was only a few heartbeats before the rest of the huge beasts were following the first one. The carnage they caused was terrific, turning even the hardest stomachs as they impaled men that they thought were standing in their way with their tusks, while at the same time stomping on others, turning them into a mass of jellied meat in the blink of an eye. The chaos was total, the air rent with the panicked screams of the men, along with the trumpeting of the maddened elephants as they went charging back through the gaps of the unfinished camp. Seeing what was essentially their protective screen disintegrate, the Numidian cavalry positioned on the far left simply turned to gallop away, without putting up even a token of resistance. Hundreds of men just on our side of the battle were crushed, as the men of the 5th went after the animals in hot pursuit.

Meanwhile, we stopped long enough to loose one volley of javelins before slamming into the already wavering men of Scipio's left. Dozens of men were cut down by our missiles even before we broke into a run while drawing our swords. The men of Scipio's left did not wait to meet our charge, turning to run, thereby sealing their fate even before we smashed into them. It is not much of a challenge to cut down a man from behind as he is running for his life; indeed, the only trick is to run faster than they do, which was not hard under the circumstances. The front ranks of the Pompeians turned to flee back into the skimpy protection of their camp, while the rear ranks were still standing in place, resulting in the inevitable jam of men, most of them closest to us still with their backs turned when we slammed into them. Some turned to try and fight; one Centurion, about my age, was trying to rally his men, and had succeeded in turning perhaps two sections worth about, forming them into a makeshift wedge. They were just getting settled, bringing their shields up as I went slamming into the leading man, relying on my larger size and weight to knock him backwards. He left his feet to go crashing back into the two men behind him, all three of them losing their footing. I was followed closely by men of the First Century of my Cohort, who wasted no time in thrusting their blades into the fallen men, while I reached out with my free hand to grab the rim of the next Pompeian's shield. I was taking a terrible risk of losing my fingers, and if my adversary had been experienced, I would have lost at least my fingers, if not my whole hand, but I had seen the look of wide-eyed terror above the rim of his shield so I knew that I was facing a scared *tiro*. Still, I was almost done for, only because when I yanked on his shield with all my strength, he simply let go, causing me to fall backwards, so that I tripped over the body of one of the first men we had dispatched. If one of my men had not caught me, I would have fallen flat on my backside and that could have been all for me.

"Easy there, Primus Pilus," I heard a voice in my ear as he used his shield to push me back upright. "It wouldn't do for you to fall on your ass in front of this bunch. It would make us look bad."

"We can't have that," I replied, reversing the shield that I had ripped out of the recruit's hand, grabbing the handle, then striking the hapless youth with the boss, sending him flying.

Without waiting for him to recover, I focused on my opposite number, the Centurion, who in a matter of heartbeats had watched most of his men be cut down, my own busy while I was falling about. I looked at him over the rim of the shield while my men spread out, surrounding him. Signaling them to hold, I lowered the shield a bit, but kept watching him closely. His face was a mask of despair, knowing that his life was measured in heartbeats at that moment, yet he held his blade in the first position, having picked up one of his men's shields.

"There's no need for this," I called out to him. "I have no wish to kill a Centurion of Rome, any more than you wish to die."

"How do you know I don't want to die?" he challenged, though he still dropped his shield a fraction as he talked.

"Because if you did, you wouldn't have waited. You would have already attacked. And died," I finished meaningfully.

"Maybe I'm giving you a chance to surrender," he replied, but while the words were truculent, the tone was not and I had to laugh, as did my men surrounding him.

I liked his spirit; a man who can keep his sense of humor when he is about to die is a good man.

Making the decision, I stood erect, signaling the men to lower their swords, which they did, some of them reluctantly. "Give me your sword, Centurion," I said. "You'll be under my protection."

He considered, and for a moment, I thought he would refuse, then letting out a breath, he reversed the weapon, offering it to me hilt first. "I'm Gaius Aspirius," he said. "And I'm the Tertius Pilus Posterior of the 6th Legion. I'm your prisoner, Centurion."

I looked at him in surprise. "You're in the 6th?" I asked, not sure that I had heard correctly.

He nodded. "That's correct."

"Then you were at Pharsalus. You're the part of the 6th that escaped."

Now he looked uneasy, but he still nodded. "That's also correct. Why does that surprise you?"

"Because I was with the two Cohorts of the 6th who fought for Caesar. I led them in Alexandria."

At the mention of the two Cohorts that had chosen to live by marching for Caesar instead of being cut down by Antonius, Aspirius' face flushed.

"They're traitors," he said harshly, and around me, I could hear the sharp intake of breath from the men, while as one their blades came back up.

I held my hand up. "They're only traitors if Caesar lost, but he didn't. Now you're the traitor. And despite your impertinence, you're still under my protection. But, Aspirius," I indicated the men around me. "You should watch your tongue. Saying that the men of the 6th who march for Caesar are traitors, you're saying that these men are traitors. That's not something they're likely to appreciate."

He opened his mouth as if to make a retort, but then thought better of it, saying instead, "You're correct, Centurion. I spoke in anger and for that I apologize."

I pointed to the rear, telling one of the men to escort him back to our camp.

He was about to walk away, but turned. "Whose protection am I under, if I may ask Centurion?"

"I'm Primus Pilus Titus Pullus, of the 10th Legion," I replied, and I was gratified to see by his expression that my name was known to him.

With that, I turned back to the battle, or slaughter, to be more accurate, and with the rest of the men, hurried forward into the enemy camp.

~ ~ ~ ~

The Battle of Thapsus, as it is called, was not a battle at all. It was a rout, a slaughter, and as complete and total a victory as any of us could have hoped for. The men of Scipio's army who survived the first onslaught turned to flee into their camp, yet only stayed there briefly, it becoming clear very quickly that there was no protection within the walls. They ran out the back gate, intent only on escaping to what they hoped was the safety of Afranius' camp. Except to get there, they had to cut across the marshy ground. Not surprisingly, slogging through the mud is slow going, so men got bogged down, sinking into the muck up to their knees then getting stuck, perfect targets for our men to conduct javelin practice. The cries and screams of men pierced through the body as they struggled helplessly to extricate themselves was almost continuous, the men collapsing once they succumbed to their wounds to get sucked under by the stinking mud. The men that managed to struggle through the muck then staggered the couple of miles to Afranius' camp arrived only to find that Caesar as always was a step ahead, sending the two Legions he had left in camp to assault the other Pompeian camps. Our men found Afranius' camp deserted, the occupants having run off to escape the fate of their comrades. Moving on, Juba's camp had fallen to our forces as well, so that the men fleeing the rout at Scipio's camp ran right into our two Legions who cut them down, slaughtering the enemy without any mercy. Now something happened that I offer as an example of what occurs when men have been laboring under the conditions and circumstances for as long as the men of Caesar's army. I do not make excuses; there is no real justification for what took place, but it should not be described without consideration given to the underlying causes. I will not deny that the 10th did its share of killing that day, especially in the moments after we entered Scipio's camp, and I also will not deny that many of the men that we cut down were trying to surrender. However, this is not only not uncommon, it is the norm when the bloodlust of fighting men is aroused, and the men that we slaughtered were for the most part men of the ranks like ourselves, and not any of the upper classes. When the remnants of Scipio's army that survived the escape through the marsh and the following onslaught at Juba's camp then ran to a low hill on the far side of the camp, where they signaled their desire to surrender, they were joined by a number of the occupants of Afranius' camp who were not combatants. These men were Senators and prominent equestrians who had aligned themselves with the Pompeian cause and they now called to Caesar for protection, offering their complete surrender. No doubt, they knew of Caesar's record of clemency and mercy so I suppose they had good reason to be optimistic that when Caesar arrived on the scene they would escape with their lives, if not their fortunes. It was just their bad luck that the men of Caesar's army were not in a forgiving mood. Too much had happened; too much misery, too much bleeding, too long away from their homes and loved ones. Even Caesar could not stop our men from exacting revenge for all their suffering, as the group of men who sought refuge on that hill asking for Caesar's protection were slaughtered to the last man. All told, Scipio's armies had scattered to the winds, but not before more than 10,000 of their number were killed, with the gods only know how many wounded. Around Scipio's camp, bodies were stacked on top of each other like pieces of firewood, which I suppose they were in a sense, since the Romans among the dead were to at least be given the proper funeral rites and be purified by flame. Our losses were laughingly light; a total of 50 men in the entire army died, with twice that many wounded, only a few of them seriously enough to be discharged from the Legions on pension. None of our dead were from the 10th, for which I and the rest of my comrades were thankful; there were few enough of us left as it was. Scipio escaped, as did Afranius, Petreius, and Labienus, along with a good number of the cavalry and some of the infantry. Not surprisingly, at least to us, we learned that the few veterans among Scipio's army, namely the 1st, and some of the 4th, had kept their heads, literally and figuratively, and were among the escapees. They headed to Utica, along with Scipio and Labienus, while Afranius tried to make it to Mauretania. Petreius left with Juba back to Numidia. Although the defeat of Scipio was total, it did not extend to everyone. The city of Thapsus still held out, under the command of a man named Vergilius, so Caesar turned his attention to the city. After returning to our original camp towards the end of the day, Caesar ordered the elephants rounded up, all 64 of them having survived, though some were hurt. One in particular had several cuts on its trunk that his handler had tried to treat with some tarry substance smeared on the wounds.

His presence was pointed out to me by Scribonius, who asked, "Did you hear what happened to that one?"

I said that I had not, and he relayed the story. When the 5th had attacked, running into the midst of the elephants, this particular animal had caught one of the Alaudae and it was down on its knees, crushing him. Seeing his friend in trouble, another man of the 5th ran up to begin poking the animal with his javelin. The elephant stood up, then reached down with its trunk to snatch up the man and begin waving him about in the air. The elephant only released the Legionary after receiving several whacks on the trunk with the man's sword, resulting in the deep cuts, the beast throwing him to the ground and knocking the wind out of him, but the Legionary's actions saved his friend.

"He's going to get decorated for that," Scribonius concluded.

"As well he should," I agreed, then thought of something. "But is that the civic crown? Or is it different because an elephant is involved?"

We pondered that as we watched the animals, their handlers deciding that it was better to be on the winning side, maneuvering their lumbering charges into position to take up a single line in front of the city walls. The message, at least as far as we were concerned, was clear, but Vergilius was apparently unmoved because the gates did not open. The day was growing late, so we did not take any action against the city, retiring to the camp to celebrate the victory while bemoaning the work that we would have to do to dispose of so many bodies. A double ration of wine was ordered, as Scipio's, Afranius' and particularly Juba's camp had been well-stocked with the liquid, the word in camp being that it had been ordered by Scipio in preparation for the victory feast he was planning on giving when we were defeated. Whether it was true or not, it made the wine taste that much better as we toasted our success.

~ ~ ~ ~

The next day Caesar ordered a formation in front of the walls of Thapsus. The entire army was being arrayed as a demonstration of the futility of further resistance. Caesar took the occasion to decorate several men for bravery, including three men from the 10th whose names were put forth by their Centurions and the man of the 5th who indeed did win the Civic Crown, elephant or no. Vergilius still refused to submit, so Caesar left three Legions, the 14th, 26th, and 28th to continue with the siege, then sent the 8th and 25th with Domitius to Thisdra, which was now held by Considius, who had left Hadrumentum. The rest of the Legions marched with Caesar to Utica, following the Pompeian cavalry, the only unit that had escaped the battle essentially intact. On the way, we came across a village that had tried to close its gates to the Pompeians, and paid for it by having not only their possessions put to the torch, but also the inhabitants then were thrown into the bonfire themselves. We marched first to Uzita, the town that we had spent so much time and sweat trying to take before we turned away. Yet this time, all it took was forming up in front of the walls for the gates to open. Leaving a Cohort behind, we marched north, veering back towards the coast, stopping at Hadrumentum. After Considius moved on to Thisdra, his replacement was not made of the same stern stuff as he, so we did not even have to form up for the commander of the garrison to throw open the gates. At both Uzita and now at Thisdra, the Pompeians, at least the upper classes, came streaming out, crying big baby tears, begging for Caesar's mercy, which of course he granted. The men had long since grown tired of Caesar's clemency, and truth be told, I was no longer inclined to argue with them about it, because I had grown weary of it as well. It seemed to us that it was all a great joke; a Pompeian would be caught, swear that he would not take arms against Caesar again, then laugh at us as he joined the nearest Pompeian force to strap on armor to face us once, twice or even three times more. While I had understood Caesar's policy in the beginning, it became so much of a joke that I thought it was actually more damaging than helpful at this point, so when the men groaned and rolled their eyes at the sight of the line of men waiting to kiss Caesar's ass, I did not stop them. At Hadrumentum, another Cohort was left while the rest of us continued our march to Utica, following the Pompeian horsemen and the trail of destruction they left behind.

~ ~ ~ ~

At Utica, Cato was in command of the city and its garrison. As we marched, there was much talk of what we could expect when we reached the city. Cato had been Caesar's bitterest enemy from before the civil war, and in my view and the view of most of the army, was one of the primary instigators of the war. Thinking about him gave me a pang, because Vibius was one of Cato's staunchest supporters. We had spent many third of a watch around the fire arguing the rights and wrongs of Cato and Caesar's respective positions. But as time went on, even Vibius had become less willing to voice his support for Cato, as more and more men died because of his implacable hatred of Caesar. Since Cato was in command, we had no illusions that the gates of Utica would be open to us, but the gods had other ideas. The cavalry fleeing from Thapsus, who slaughtered the people of the village we had come across, came next to Utica. Instead of being grateful for the refuge, they fell upon the citizens of Utica as well, killing a number of them before being driven off by Cato and his troops. The fighting with men who were supposed to be on their side so further demoralized the Utica garrison that even a man as uncompromising as Cato realized that further resistance to Caesar would be useless. As we learned later, Cato himself urged the remaining Roman citizens who had helped to fund Scipio's campaign to make peace with Caesar, a fact that surprised me a great deal. He might have helped the others to appeal to Caesar, but that was not an option for Cato. It was not because Caesar would not have offered his mercy, but precisely because Caesar would and a proud man like Cato could not bear to live with that shame. Once he had arranged his own affairs and then ensured that he had done all he could to prepare for Caesar's coming, Cato went off and opened his stomach. Apparently, he botched the job, being found by his slaves and friends, who stitched him up. That did not stop Cato however; as soon as he was left unattended, he pulled the stitches out. Then, depending on what version you heard, he either bled to death or actually pulled his intestines out, throwing them about the room. You can probably imagine which story was most popular with the men. In any event, Cato was dead when Caesar arrived at Utica, vexing him greatly. Caesar was not a vengeful man, but of all the Pompeians, he most wanted to see Cato humiliated, and his suicide robbed Caesar of that pleasure.

The gates were open when we arrived, a long line of supplicants waiting for our general to decide what to do, and we were slightly mollified to learn that he fined them a substantial amount to help pay for the expense of the campaign. We camped outside Utica as Caesar took care of his business, and it was while we were in camp those several days that we heard of the capture of Afranius by Sittius, who was brought in chains before the assembled army. There was considerable wagering in the camp about whether or not Caesar would show mercy to this particular Pompeian, though I refrained from wagering because I had heard from Diocles through Apollonius that Caesar was going to make an example of the man. Our general wasted no time; the next morning at formation, Caesar announced that Afranius was to be executed for crimes against the Republic, a necessary fiction I suppose. However, Caesar refused to allow the army to witness the execution of Afranius, which was extremely unpopular with the men, especially those who were in Hispania and had lost friends when Petreius so vilely betrayed them while Afranius stood by and let it happen. Caesar would not budge, and Afranius was executed inside the headquarters tent, with only Caesar and his generals as witnesses. Scipio had attempted to escape by ship, but he was run down by vessels that belonged to our friend Sittius. In the ensuing fight, Scipio drowned. Finally, the news reached us of the fate of Petreius, which was a bitter disappointment to all of us who had hoped that he would be brought before us in the same manner as Afranius. I had even planned on approaching Caesar in order to convince him that unlike Afranius, the army should witness the execution of Petreius because of his absolutely despicable deeds. We were to be denied that pleasure though, as we learned that Juba and Petreius, the former being turned on by his own people, had held a banquet, after which they fought a duel to the death. Petreius was the winner, whereupon he immediately committed suicide. As part of their revolt against Juba, the Numidians sent a delegation to Caesar promising the city of Zama, with Caesar sending a contingent of cavalry to hold it and putting Sallustius in charge of what was now a Roman province. Caesar was now done in Africa, all affairs arranged according to his desires, so it was time for him to return home to Rome. At the morning briefing the day after the execution of Afranius, Caesar stood before us, surveying his officers and Centurions a moment before he spoke.

"Now that Scipio has been defeated and I've arranged affairs here in Africa to my satisfaction, I'm returning to Rome. And the Spanish Legions, along with the 5th and the 13th, will be shipping to Italy to march in the triumphs I'm planning on holding."

I am not sure what else he said after that, because he was drowned out by our cheering. Not everyone was happy of course, but as far as we in the Spanish Legions were concerned, the chance to see Rome and march in a triumph was long overdue from our service in Gaul. I was grinning from ear to ear as I looked over at Scribonius, thinking he would feel the same way as I did. I would be seeing Rome at long last, while he would be returning home, yet Scribonius looked anything but happy at the thought. I shrugged then decided that if the moment were ever right I would finally ask him about it. In the meantime, I had some news to give to the men that I was fairly sure they would appreciate.

~ ~ ~ ~

As usual in the army, matters were not as simple as just packing the few belongings we had brought from Sicily with us then marching down to the docks at Utica. Moving six Legions, even under strength as all but the 5th was at that point is a massive undertaking, especially when the trip was in two movements. First, we would ship to Sicily where we would retrieve the rest of our property, then to Italy. As accustomed as I was to the slow progress, I was still in a state of seething impatience, because I had been told that we would be landing either at Brundisium or close enough to it that I could take only a few days to go see my family. I am afraid I took that impatience out on the men. After almost three weeks, it was finally our turn to land in Sicily, where we spent the next week packing up while the Centurions had their hands full adjudicating disputes of ownership and investigating the inevitable theft of the possessions of the men, guarded by supposed comrades who had bribed their Centurions into being left behind. Some of the cases were either so egregious or the men so inept that their guilt was clear, meaning that there were about a half-dozen executions and twice as many floggings while we were in Sicily. Thankfully, none were from the 10th. Finally, our day came to be loaded up and transported to the mainland, having marched to Lilybaeum from our camp the day before. We were on the quay at dawn. I went looking for the master of the fleet and I found him standing, chatting to some of the shipmasters. I had a question for him, and my patience had long since been exhausted, so eager was I to get to Brundisium, and I am afraid I was rather abrupt with him.

"Where are you landing us?" I demanded, not even bothering with the formalities of identifying myself.

He frowned, obviously irritated with my manners, but my Centurion's crest and I suspect my size kept him from being as rude to me as I was to him. "Paestum," he replied, and I cursed bitterly.

Paestum is nowhere near Brundisium; I had hoped for Tarentum, which would have allowed us to march straight up the Via Appia, but most importantly, was just a few thirds of a watch walk or less by horseback to Brundisium.

He made no attempt to hide his amusement at my unhappiness. "Why so upset, Centurion? You wanted to land somewhere else?"

"I was hoping we would land in Tarentum at the least or Brundisium most ideally."

I cannot say for sure what it was, but something in his manner changed immediately, giving me my first stirring of unease.

"Why do you want to land in Brundisium?"

"My wife and children live there," I replied.

His face turned grave as he shot a glance at the shipmasters around him, who looked equally grim. "That wouldn't be possible under any circumstances, Centurion," he said quietly.

My ears filled with a roaring noise as my heart started pounding so loudly that I was sure they could hear it.

I had to swallow more than once before I could croak out, "Why is that?"

"Because the plague has come to Brundisium. No fleet is landing there right now."

~ ~ ~ ~

I do not remember much of the voyage to Paestum, spending most of it in the captain's tiny cabin, sitting with Diocles and Scribonius, who did not talk. We had barely tied up at the dock when I leaped off, Diocles hurrying after me. Putting Silanus in charge of the Century and Glaxus in charge of the Cohort and the 10th, I hired two horses for Diocles and me, leaving Paestum no more than a third of a watch after the fleet arrived. Taking the Via Popilia a few miles, we turned off on the branch road that connected to the Via Appia, pushing the horses and ourselves without mercy. We stopped only long enough to change horses, grabbing a loaf of bread and some cheese that we ate on horseback. Poor Diocles was unaccustomed to traveling at the kind of pace I was setting, yet he hung on grimly to the mane of his horse, making no complaints, though he was never the complaining type to begin with. We arrived at Tarentum, passing through the city, stopping only long enough to change horses.

While I hired the mounts, Diocles sat in a tavern near the stables, listening to the talk, and when we had resumed our journey, told me what he had learned. "It's an outbreak of typhus and it's supposed to be very bad, Master."

Diocles kept his voice calm, but I could hear the strain in his voice, making me suspect that he had heard more than he was telling. Normally, I am the type of person who wants to hear the complete and unvarnished truth, no matter how painful or unpleasant it may be. But not this time, so I did not press him for details. We passed the remaining miles in silence, approaching Brundisium a third of a watch before sunset. In truth, we smelled the city several miles before we came within sight of the walls, the stench such that it reminded me of some of the battlefields in Gaul, Alesia in particular, which did not help my frame of mind. The traffic on the road was understandably light, and almost exclusively one way, those who were able having left earlier when the outbreak first started. By the time we arrived at the city gates, Diocles had vomited more times than I could count, but I was not in the mood to tease him about it as I normally might have. Besides, my stomach was lurching as well, though for entirely different reasons, having become accustomed to the smell of death long before. The city guard had clearly been hit hard as well, there only being two men still on duty instead of the normal six or so, both of them wearing sprigs of herbs pinned to their neckerchiefs which they had tied around their faces to block out the smell. As we approached, they examined the two of us, their surprise and shock clear when I made to ride past them into the city. Looking at each other in alarm, they both moved to block our passage. Looking down at them, I struggled to remain calm. While I was not wearing my armor or helmet, I was wearing my sword and the fact that it hung to my left told them my rank, which was how they addressed me.

"Sorry, Centurion, but nobody is allowed into the city until the plague is past."

"I've come to check on my family. They live here."

The older of the two, a short, stocky man who was running to fat, shook his head, clearly uncomfortable, but intent on doing his duty. Normally, I would not have faulted him for his devotion, but these were not normal times and I was not in the right frame of mind.

"I'm sorry, Centurion, but our orders are clear."

I do not remember making any conscious decision. In fact, it seemed as if my arm acted on its own, pulling my sword while the rest of my body urged my horse forward to get closer to the older man. In the time it takes to blink your eyes, the point of my sword was against the base of his throat.

"I'm coming into the city to check on my family. If you try to stop me, I'll kill you."

I did not speak loudly, pitching my voice so only he and his companion could hear. The guard was shaking with fear, while his companion held his own spear with the point upright, either too shocked or too afraid to try to stop me from threatening his comrade.

For a moment he did not speak, then finally managed to croak, "Very well, Centurion. You may pass."

"Thank you," I said, but I did not sheathe my sword or turn my back to either of them until we were a safe distance away.

The streets of the city were almost deserted, as those not affected had either left or had blockaded themselves in their homes to wait for the passing of the sickness. This was the same affliction that struck down so much of the army when we were camped in Brundisium before our invasion of Greece. I vividly remembered that some of the survivors were so weakened by the illness that they were unable to rejoin the army until we were in Sicily. Outside of some homes there were corpses, wrapped in whatever shroud the survivors could spare, waiting for collection. Those that could afford it paid for the proper funeral rites to be performed, so that on the south side of the city there were columns of black, greasy smoke that told the story of bodies being consigned to the flames. As we turned onto the street leading to my family's apartment, my throat was as dry as if I was marching for a day across the desert without a drink, but even if I could have had a drink of water, I doubt I would have been able to keep it down. Arriving in front of the building, I tried not to stagger as I dismounted. The windows of the building were shuttered, which was not unusual at such a time, yet it disturbed me nonetheless. I was more scared than I had ever been in my life as I walked to the stairway then began to mount the steps, thinking of the last time I was here and watching Vibi tumble down them. Even now, in the last years of my life, more than 25 years later, I cannot speak of those next moments. I will turn to Diocles to give his account.

~ ~ ~ ~

*In the relatively short time I had been with my master, I had never seen him in such a state as he was when we pulled up before the building where his family was living. He went to the steps, but stopped there for a moment before mounting them. He tried to open the door, but was unable to do so, the door obviously locked. He knocked, softly at first, then with more and more urgency. Still, the door never opened. He stood for a moment, and I did not know what to do for him. Suddenly he reared back, kicking against the door, which flew open with a loud crash. From where I was sitting, I heard a cry of alarm, and for a moment my heart leapt with joy before my brain recognized that the sound came not only from inside the house on the first floor, but that the voice was male. My master made no sign that he had heard, and stepped inside the door, his face set and white as he disappeared. It was a few moments before he emerged, his shoulders slumped as he descended the stairs and walked over to me.*

*"There's nobody there, and the place is cleaned out."*

*"Master, that must mean that they left like most of the others,"* I said, but my words did not soothe him.

He shook his head, and I could barely him reply, *"I don't think so."*

He turned and walked to the door on the ground floor of the building, and began banging on it. I was sitting on my horse just a few feet away, close enough that I could hear the stirring of someone inside, but the door did not open. Banging harder, my master called out loudly enough to be heard several streets away, calling the owner of the building by name and identifying himself. Finally, the door cracked open, only by a matter of a couple of inches and I could barely make out a pinched white face peering up at my master. It was hard to tell whether it was a man or woman, and I only learned by the sound of the voice that it was a woman, the wife of the owner, I presumed.

*"Salve, Centurion. You've come at a most unfortunate time, I'm sad to say. I'm sorry that I can't open the door, but my husband won't permit visitors."*

*"That's fine, lady."* My master's voice was calm and his tone pleasant, but I had been with him long enough to hear the strain underlying his words. *"I'm here to find my wife and children. Do you know what happened to them?"*

I do not know how many heartbeats of time it took her to answer, but if time has ever stood still, it was in that moment. Now that my eyes had adjusted to the darkness of the doorway and the interior behind her, I could see her more clearly, and on her face, sadness was plainly written and not a little fear.

*"I'm sorry, Centurion. Your family is dead. The plague claimed them all."*

At first, my master gave no reaction, just standing there looking down at her. I began to think that he had not heard her, though I did not see how that was possible. Then, without a word, his legs lost their strength and he collapsed to his knees, his head dropping to his chest. I leapt off my horse, taking a step towards him, then stopped, not sure what to do. The woman looked down at him, and I saw a withered, spotted hand reach out and touch his shoulder. Suddenly, it was as if a dam had burst. It began as a low moan, my master's body beginning to shake as if he had the ague himself, then he began to sob. The woman opened the door and stepped out, and I heard a man's voice angrily demanding that she come back inside and shut the door, but she ignored him. Kneeling next to my master, she wrapped her arms about his giant shoulders, and he leaned his head against her breast as his grief consumed him. I stood helplessly, then took a step towards them. She looked at me and shook her head, so I stopped as she murmured words to him as they both rocked gently back *and forth. They stayed like this as the last light of the day faded away, and it was only when it became dark that he began to stir himself. He climbed to his feet, then helped the woman up, but even in the gloom, I could see how unsteady he was on his feet, so I stepped next to him in case he needed help.*

*He had said nothing since his question about his family, and when he did speak, his voice was hoarse and barely recognizable. "Where are they now?"*

*The woman looked apprehensive now, though I did not understand why, but she obviously knew something I did not, given the reaction she got when she told him, "They were taken away and buried."*

*My master went rigid, his grief turning to anger as quickly as a bolt of lightning strikes. "Buried," he hissed. "That is not proper! You should know that. How could you have let them be buried?"*

*She shrugged helplessly, the fear in her voice making it quaver. "Centurion, we didn't have any choice in the matter. The urban Praetor issued a decree that all non-citizens were to be buried as quickly as possible."*

*"My children were citizens, damn you! They should have been given the proper rites! Now," his voice broke, "they're doomed to wander the underworld for eternity and I'll never recognize them!"*

*His shoulders began to shake as a fresh spate of tears struck him at this thought.*

*"Centurion, it was your wife's wish that they be buried with her," the woman said gently. "As I understand it, that was the way of her people anyway, wasn't it? To be buried? Besides, your children were Roman citizens, that's true, but weren't they also of her tribe as well? And if they were, then they walk with her now, in their afterlife, don't they?"*

*As religious arguments go, it would not have taken me long to dismantle it, but under the circumstances, I was only too happy to see that this brought him some comfort.*

*After thinking about it, he nodded. "Do you know where they're buried?"*

*She shook her head and replied that she did not, adding, "And you don't want to go to where they're taking the.....bodies, Centurion. I've heard that it's a very grim place and it wouldn't bring you any comfort. You should remember them alive."*

*"I hardly knew them," my master replied, and there is no way to convey the amount of sadness and pain those words carried. Looking down at the woman, he said, "Thank you for telling me and for your . . . kindness. Were our accounts with you in order? Is there anything that we owe you?"*

*She shook her head, saying that everything that had been owed was paid. With that, he turned away and walked past me to his horse, leaping astride it and gathering up the reins.*

*"Goodbye," was the last thing he said to the woman, leaving her standing there as I trailed behind him.*

*We rode in silence, retracing our route out of the city, the streets even more deserted than when we came, the sound of our horses' hooves echoing off the buildings. We exited by the same gate. Fortunately, the guards did not make any comment at our departure, for I believe they would have died if they had. Under normal circumstances, we should have been finding a place to sleep for the night, but I suspected that there would be no sleep for us this night.*

*A third of a watch passed, then two, and finally I could take it no longer. "Master, is there anything I can do?"*

*He did not answer for several moments, then finally he replied, "Yes. You'll never talk about what you saw back there. And I'll never speak of it again. My wife, my son, and my daughter are dead. There's nothing I can do to change that and there's no point in dwelling on it. This is the last I'll ever talk about them."*

*And he was true to his word. After that night, I never heard him speak of his family again.*

## Chapter 8- Triumph

I have little recollection of the journey back to Rome, and I doubt I would have made it if Diocles had not been with me. We returned to the army, camped on the Campus Martius, where the men were readying themselves for the first of four triumphs that Caesar planned for Gaul, Egypt, Pontus, and Africa. While the 10th would march in three of the four because of my time with the 6th, I would be marching in all four, meaning that Diocles was kept busy, making sure all of my uniforms and decorations were in order. The men were understandably in a state of high excitement, a state that I could not share, though I did try. Here I was finally at the gates of the city that I had dreamed of seeing all of my life, yet I saw none of the color and vibrant life that flowed in and out of the city all day. Finally, Scribonius showed up at my tent one morning after formation, informing me that he was taking me on a tour of the city, brushing aside my protests about paperwork. Entering the city was like entering another world, a place of constant noise and movement, full of people of all colors and sizes, every one of them seeming to be in an incredible hurry as they conducted what was obviously very important business. I had never seen so many slaves in one place before, and they were as varied as the freedmen walking about, each slave wearing the bronze placard around their neck that proclaimed to whom they belonged. The streets were positively jammed with humanity, the smell indescribable, a mixture of humans, animals, and the aromas of baking bread, spices, and the gods only know what else. It was all a bit overwhelming, but it was at least nice to tower above most of the people so that I could look around and take in the sights.

"Well, what do you think? Is it everything you thought it would be?"

I was not sure if I should be polite, since this was Scribonius' city, or be honest. I opted for the latter. "It's the dirtiest place I've ever seen. And it's a lot more cramped than Alexandria."

If Scribonius was disappointed or insulted, he did not show it. He just laughed. "It is that," he agreed, taking my elbow to point me down another street.

One of the things I found so disconcerting about the city was the seemingly haphazard way that the streets seemed to run, with no discernible pattern to them. I realized that the time I had spent in Alexandria, with its wide, ordered streets laid out in a grid, had set an expectation that Rome would be the same, yet it was not. Because we had come from the Campus Martius, the first great structure we encountered was Pompey's Theater, and despite vowing to myself that I would not act like a country bumpkin, I found myself standing there gaping at the sheer size and opulence of the place. It was a massive semicircular structure, with the stage positioned at the bottom of the semicircle. Scribonius told me that it had been built and dedicated while we were fighting in Gaul, during Pompey's second Consulship, and it had caused some controversy because building such a large theater as a monument to himself was considered sacrilegious. Therefore, to avoid censure by the Senate he erected a small temple to Venus Victorious at the top of the theater, looking down at the stage. He was not so concerned that he did not have a huge statue of himself erected and placed in the main entry hall so that all who entered had to pass literally under his feet. Of course, it was at Pompey's feet that Caesar was to be murdered, but we were happily unaware of what was to transpire. Leaving the theater, we headed to the Forum being built by Caesar, called appropriately the Forum Julii, to look at the temple to Venus Genetrix, the goddess from whom the Julii were descended, which was basically completed and awaiting consecration. This was going to take place during the first triumphal parade in just a matter of a couple days. The building was under guard, but since it was being watched by men of the 10th, they did not hesitate letting their Primus Pilus and Secundus Pilus Prior enter the temple, as Scribonius and I looked at each other, smiling like schoolboys who have managed to avoid classes that day. The temple had several alcoves, almost all of them empty at that moment, which would hold some of the booty taken by Caesar during his military campaigns, but only after they were paraded before the people of Rome as proof of all that Caesar had conquered.

As we looked around, Scribonius said something that had been rattling around in my own head, yet I had not wanted to say aloud. "You know, this temple belongs just as much to us as it does to Caesar and the Julii." Scribonius said this quietly enough, but I still caught myself looking guiltily about to see if there was anyone there to listen.

Fortunately, the temple was empty except for us.

"That may be true, but that's not something you want to say very loudly," I replied. "Still, you're right. But it belongs more to the men who won't be marching with us than anyone."

"Like Romulus and Remus," Scribonius whispered.

"And Calienus," I added, feeling a sharp stab of grief at the thought of our old Sergeant, which was immediately followed by a vision of a woman with flame-red hair, holding a baby on her hip.

I was horrified to feel tears start to fill my eyes, but if Scribonius saw, he had the good grace and sense to say nothing about it.

"So many of us gone," he said sadly, then we said nothing for several moments, each lost in our own thoughts.

Finally, I shook myself and said that we had more to see, so we left the temple, the guards at the entrance saluting us as we departed.

~ ~ ~ ~

By the end of the day, I was feeling dizzy and wanted nothing more than to return to the relative quiet and routine of the camp. To my ordered military mind, Rome was nothing but chaos and disorder, a maelstrom of sights, sounds, and smells that threatened to overwhelm me. While Alexandria is similar in population size to Rome, the Egyptian city is much more spread out, due mainly to the lack of hills to enclose the space in the same manner as Rome. We walked through every area of the city, save one, the Palatine, and although I wanted to go see where the rich folks lived, Scribonius refused to take me. At first he gave the excuse, plausible enough I suppose, that the sight of two men of the 10th Legion would not be welcome after what our men had done to the area, but it did not take me long to recognize that this was merely an excuse. Scribonius' reluctance was from some other cause, yet try as I might, I could not pry from him what it was, so I finally just gave up, much to his relief. We did go into the Subura, and I refused to believe that this was where Caesar had grown up, because it is one of the filthiest, dingiest places I have ever seen in my life. I could just not imagine that a man as high born as Caesar would have ever walked through the place, let alone live there.

"Just because a man is high born doesn't mean he has money," Scribonius explained. "In fact, until Caesar came along, the Julii had been poor for more years than anyone could remember."

I mused on this; perhaps this was why Caesar seemed to relate so well to people of my class. He had grown up with us, knew how we thought and lived. I mentioned this to Scribonius, and he immediately agreed that this was probably the case. Yet even knowing that Caesar had walked these same streets, I was anxious to leave. The buildings, if they can be called such, are built so haphazardly that most of them look in danger of falling over. Indeed, the taller ones leaned so precipitously at the top that they almost touched the building on the opposite side of the street, which would be leaning just as much. It gave the impression of being in a dark canyon, and I despised the feeling that I was going to be buried alive so much that I practically dragged Scribonius along until we left the Subura behind. Still, despite my happiness at returning to camp, I was glad that Scribonius had taken me on a tour, and I thanked him for showing me the sights.

"I'm happy to, Primus Pilus," he told me, always sure to address me in the proper manner when we were back in front of the men.

I was about to turn to enter my tent, but I could see him hesitate, plainly wanting to say something more. Feeling my stomach tighten, I was sure that I knew what he wanted to say, yet I also knew that it meant more to Scribonius to say what he needed to say than it meant for me not to want to hear it.

"Yes?" I asked in what I hoped was a pleasant tone.

Scribonius, who always seemed to know the exact right words for any occasion, was now fumbling about.

Finally, he said, "Primus Pilus, I just wanted you to know how sorry we are, and I mean the men and the officers, about Gisela and your family. We've made several offerings for their safe journey."

I looked at my friend, then for the second time that day, I felt the hot rush of tears threaten to unman me, but I managed to hold them back. "Thank you, Scribonius. That means a great deal to me." I turned to enter the tent, then turned back. "And thank the men for me as well."

With that, I walked into my private quarters, telling Diocles to bring me wine, and plenty of it. I sat alone with my thoughts for some time, ignoring Diocles as he came to light the extra lamps when it became dark, steadily draining the amphora of wine that Diocles had set on the table. Drinking it unwatered, it still did not seem to have any effect on me as it normally did and finally I gave up. Just as I was about to lie on my cot for the night, I realized I needed to answer the call of nature. Deciding that the fresh air from a trip to the latrine would do me good, I got up and left the tent. I had only gone a few steps when I heard a familiar voice.

"Titus?"

Whirling about, my hand clutched at my dagger, peering into the darkness towards where the sound came from, waiting for whatever happened next. A dark shadow detached itself from the backdrop of the edge of my tent then stepped into where the pool of light from the torch placed at the corner of the street pushed back the gloom. It was Vibius.

For several moments, we just stood there, staring at each other, before Vibius cleared his throat. "I just . . . I just wanted to tell you that I was very sorry to hear about Gisela and Vibi. I know how much you loved them both, and I grieve for you."

I did not say anything, just staring at him as my mind fumbled for the right words to say. So much had passed between us, and there was so much I wanted to say, but nothing came. Finally, seeing that I was not going to answer, he abruptly turned and began to walk away, stumbling a little in the darkness.

I was jerked out of my state of silence, and I called out to him. "Vibius, wait."

He immediately stopped, turning back slowly. As he approached, I realized that I did not know what exactly it was that I wanted to say.

At the last moment, I only managed a weak, "Thank you for your . . . just, thank you. That means a lot. Gisela always liked you."

"No she didn't," he replied immediately, but it was not meant in a mean-spirited way at all and we both burst out laughing.

"No, you're right. She didn't care for you that much," I admitted. "But it had nothing to do with you and everything to do with her."

"I know. She just didn't like sharing you. I understood."

"But, Vibi," I said, and immediately regretted it, as I felt my throat tighten up at the thought of my son, the namesake of my best friend, "he loved you. The last time I saw him one of his first questions was about when you were going to come visit."

And with that, I could not hold it back anymore, and I began to weep. Yet for some reason, I did not care about doing so in front of Vibius, even after all that had transpired between us. I think it had to do with the fact that I had seen him in a similar state after Juno betrayed him and married another man. Whatever the case, I was not ashamed. I had covered my face with my hands, so I did not see him step closer, and was surprised when I felt his hand on my shoulder, awkwardly patting it. I do not know how long we stood there, but it had to have been several moments before I was able to regain my composure. We stood there, looking at each other. I did not know what to say next, and obviously neither did he.

"Well," he broke the silence, "I just wanted you to know, that's all."

"Thank you," I said again, and there was really nothing more left to say, so we both turned away and walked away from each other into the night.

~ ~ ~ ~

The day of the first triumph dawned clear and bright, the men in a state of high excitement and spirits as they did their last minute scrubbing and polishing. I walked up and down the Legion streets, checking that everything was in order, listening to the men talk animatedly about what was to come.

"I tell you boys," Didius proclaimed, smacking his lips at the thought, "when we go marching by, the women will be wet as a September rain just at the sight of us. They'll be ours for the taking."

"Since when have you ever been interested in a woman that you didn't have to hold a knife to her throat or pay?" Vellusius shot back. Didius took this with his usual bluster of threats, which in itself had become so much of a joke that even Didius could not make them without laughing about it.

This was the tone of most of the conversations taking place throughout the camp as the men, most of them never having marched in a triumph, tried to guess what was awaiting them. Some of Pompey's veterans had marched in his last triumph, but there were very few of these men left, so we all were relying on tales of past triumphs told to us by any number of sources. All we knew for sure was our role; we would be marching behind the last of the wagons pulling the reproductions of the notable moments of the Gallic campaign, as the 10th, despite the difficulties between the men and Caesar, was given the place of honor at the head of the procession of troops. Just three days before the triumph, we were informed that the 6th, or the two Cohorts that had fought for Caesar, would be marching in the Gallic triumph by virtue of the two years they were on loan from Pompey. Their service had come towards the end of our time in Gaul, and they had been consigned to garrison duty, though they had seen some action quelling the rebellions that had punctuated our last years there. Still, it did not sit well with some of the men, as I heard them mumbling around the fires after the news about the injustice of it all. Fortunately, they were going to be at the end of the procession, since it would have caused a huge uproar with the other Spanish Legions if they had been forced to march behind men they considered latecomers.

Shortly after dawn, we were formed up on the Via Publica, with all the wagons carrying the booty and the animals to pull them, along with the prisoners, all of them bound in chains, with Vercingetorix in the same helmet and armor that he was wearing on the day he surrendered at Alesia. His physical appearance was shocking, at least to my comrades and me, who had been there and had seen him with our very eyes on that day. Even in defeat, he had ridden his horse tall and erect, his bearing as regal as any king who ever strode the Earth. Now, he stood chained to a pole erected in the bed of a wagon, only standing upright because he was chained so tightly that he could not sit if he wanted, yet his shoulders were slumped, and he was deathly pale. His guards had done their best to clean him up, but no amount of scrubbing could mask the stench of defeat, nor could the clothing of a king disguise his complete and abject apathy. I was looking at a man who was alive in name only, for whom death would be a sweet release. Despite all the pain and loss he had caused us, I still felt a pang of sympathy for the man. It was no way for a warrior of any stature, let alone one like Vercingetorix, to end their days, except that it was our custom to execute those prisoners not sold into slavery on the day of the victorious general's triumph for more years than anyone could remember, so this would be the fate of Vercingetorix. The rest of the prisoners who would be walking were in just as wretched a state as their former leader, and would shamble along behind the wagon carrying Vercingetorix, their chains rattling, making enough of a racket that it nearly drowned out the sounds of the horns and drums that would be playing marching tunes to keep us in step. As we formed up, the men stopped to gawk at the wagons carrying the scenes of the campaign that were constructed out of wood, plaster, and paint. There was a wagon depicting the siegeworks at Alesia, more of a huge map built in three dimensions, with a second wagon showing the surrender of Vercingetorix, the figures made of plaster but painted so well that they looked very lifelike. There was a depiction of our victory over the Helvetii, and of our battle on the Sabis as well. There were four wagons dedicated to the invasion of Britannia, with these the most elaborate and detailed by far. The prisoners were distributed among the wagons, those of each tribe and race walking in front of or behind the wagon, depicting their defeat, and I wondered how that must have felt. The group that I was sure would cause the most stir were the Britons, who had been forced to paint themselves with their blue paint, and spike their hair with lime as if they were going into battle and not to a life of slavery, or execution if they were of high enough rank. Leading the whole procession was Caesar, garlanded with oak leaves, his face painted red in the custom. It was supposed to be the blood of the bull sacrificed in the ceremony immediately preceding the triumph, but blood flaked off and was too dark, so some sort of paint was used instead. He wore a purple toga trimmed with a design of palm fronds embroidered in gold thread and he stood in a quadriga, the chariot pulled by four horses, while behind him stood one of his slaves, as custom dictated. The slave had two jobs, one to hold the garland of golden oak leaves over the head of the triumphing general, while whispering in his ear the reminder that fame was fleeting and that he was a mortal. Caesar being Caesar, he had to do things his own way, so he had chosen to wear the garland on his head. The gossip among the men was that it was to cover up his bald spot, and I think they were probably right, though I did not make any comment. Counting the wagons hauling the spoils from the campaign, all told there must have been close to 60 of them, so that along with all the prisoners and the army, the procession must have been more than a mile long. The horns sounded the signal to begin, then the 72 lictors that had been voted by the Senate for Caesar, the largest number ever for an individual in the history of the Republic, stepped off to begin the parade.

~ ~ ~ ~

The procession began down the Via Triumphalis, passing under the large wooden Triumphal Arch that was only opened for triumphs and which marked the official beginning of the parade, as the crowds lined the way 15 to 20 deep. The noise of their cheering reached all the way to where we were standing, waiting to move, causing an excited rumble of talk among the men, all of them eagerly anticipating the adoration of the people. Given the mass of prisoners, wagons, and animals, the size of this parade was similar to marching the army, although there were not quite as many animals or slaves this time. We would only be marching a couple of miles, but it still was almost a sixth part of a watch before the last of the display wagons immediately ahead of us started to move. That was our signal to make ready, so I gave the command to the *bucinator* to sound the appropriate call to attention, followed a moment later by the signal to march. Off we went, and the gods know that I am not exaggerating when I say that we made quite a splendid sight. Our plumes were all new, as were our cloaks, bright red and draped over our left shoulders, while pulled back over our right arms in the proper manner, the folds arranged as carefully as a patrician does his toga. Because it is technically illegal for any armed men to enter inside the *pomerium*, the sacred boundary of the city, we did not carry javelin or shield, though as part of the triumphant army we were allowed to wear sword and dagger. I do not understand the distinction, since a Legionary is as deadly with a sword as with a javelin, and when I asked Scribonius, all he could do was shrug and say that it had always been that way. That seemed to be the most common answer to every question about why things were done the way they were, but that had always been hard for me to accept, though I did. Every man also wore all of his decorations, polished and glittering, those of us with Civic Crowns wearing it wrapped around the crown of our helmets. Those men who had won the Corona Muralis or Corona Vallaris wore the crown in place of their helmets, making them stand out among their comrades and becoming the object of much attention and admiration, particularly from the females in the crowd. Because I was Primus Pilus, I was allowed the choice, since I had won the Corona Muralis in Alexandria, but I chose to wear my helmet so that I could wear my Civic Crown. I had won it saving Scribonius against the Helvetii during our campaign in Gaul, and of all the decorations I had won to that point, it meant the most to me.

The street we marched along was strewn with rose petals and garlands thrown for Caesar, along with a fair number of rotten vegetables and other refuse that were hurled at the prisoners. Of course, by the time we arrived, there was a fair amount of droppings from the animals pulling the wagons as well, so we had to step lively to avoid the refuse. Normally when we marched through a city, the men were ordered to look straight ahead and not speak to whatever civilians were lining the streets to watch us march by, a regulation that was almost universally ignored. However, during a triumph, the only real rule is that no man can break formation, so there was a great deal of banter between the men and the people lining the route, particularly the women. As the Primus Pilus, and because of my size, I had more than my share of attention and offers from the women, but I was not in the right frame of mind to appreciate the attention, though it was flattering.

We marched by Pompey's Theater, then turned onto what was called the Vicus Iugarius, and it was after we made that turn that the crowds grew in size and enthusiasm. It was at this point that the men launched into a song they had been working on for days, which I had heard more times than I could count by then. Still, I could not fight the grin as they began the song about our general and his legendary appetite for all things female, particularly those who happened to be married to other men. The ditty brought riotous laughter and shouts of approval from the crowd. As soon as this one was finished, they launched into another, this one aimed at the Centurions, particularly me, making fun of my size and some other things that I will not mention here. Despite being the butt of their jibe, I had to admit that it was clever and very funny, though I was not about to let them know it. We had not yet left the Via Triumphalis, when there was a sudden halt, though no command was given, almost causing us to march into the back of the wagons before I could get the men halted. All up and down the line, there were curses and shouts as men tripped over each other, though we did not have any idea why we stopped. It was not until we were done that we found out the cause. Knowing what I know now, I cannot help thinking that it was as bad an omen as could have happened. For no reason that anyone could discern, the axle on Caesar's quadriga suddenly snapped in half, throwing him to the ground. I know that over time the story has changed somewhat, that he was almost thrown out but managed to grab the side railing and keep his feet, but immediately afterward that was not what was circulating around the camp. At the time we had no idea, yet once we got started again, we noticed that the crowd along the Velabrum, where the incident had happened was much more subdued than earlier along the route, though we did not know why. Once we passed through the Velabrum, the crowds became their raucous selves again. We marched through the Forum Boarium, which Scribonius had shown me on our tour, where most of the meat in the city is sold. Even after being scrubbed by hundreds of slaves, the stench of blood and death was still in the air, yet that did not dampen the enthusiasm of the people any that I could tell. Many of the men standing along the route in this part of the triumph obviously worked in the market, as they were still wearing their bloody aprons, signs that they had been hard at work slaughtering the thousands of animals that would be consumed by the people who would be feasting. After leaving the Forum Boarium, we turned the corner, approaching the Circus Maximus. Although I did not think it possible, the sound of the crowd up to that point was but a whisper compared to the wall of sound that descended down on us as we marched through the wooden tunnel through which the racing chariots enter the stadium. Most of the equestrian class was seated in the Circus Maximus, their rank among their peers marked by how close to the track they sat. Scribonius had told me that the Circus had a capacity of 200,000 people, a number that I found hard to believe until I actually entered the stadium. The tiers of seats seemed to rise to the sky, with the people of my class filling the upper rows of seating, though they were little more than tiny specks to our eyes. They waved down to us, their motion making a rippling effect that was somewhat disconcerting, as if the crowd were some multi-legged huge animal that could not coordinate its thousands of limbs. The women seated in the first rows of seats were much more reserved than their counterparts out along the streets or in the upper rows, looking bored and as if they would rather have been anywhere but sitting there nonetheless. However, if you looked carefully, you could see their eyes running up and down the bodies of the men as they marched by, with a look in their eyes that told us that they were anything but bored. Their husbands seemed to be oblivious, and I was struck by a memory of when Gisela told me that if men knew what their women were really thinking at any given moment, we would sleep with one eye open, keeping them under lock and key every moment we were not around. She had said it when we were fighting, yet seeing how the high-born women were acting it made me wonder if she had been telling me the brutal truth.

We made a complete circuit of the track so that the people on both sides could see us march past, then looped back around, exiting the Circus on the opposite end from where we had entered, then followed the street that circled around the base of the Palatine. My ears had started ringing from all the noise, while I could feel the sweat soaking my tunic. Frankly, I was beginning to grow bored. Once the novelty of people throwing flowers at you, while calling you the embodiment of Achilles or Ajax or Dentatus wears off, it is a bit of a bore, if the truth be known. At least it was for me, though I was happy to see that the men did not seem to grow tired of it. For the men in the ranks, marching in front of adoring crowds, being wreathed in garlands and cheered was the payoff for all the years of marching, digging, fighting, and bleeding and it had been long in coming to them. We finally turned onto the Via Sacra, where Caesar, at the head of the procession, had already reached the foot of the temple of Jupiter Optimus Maximus. The wagons pulling the spoils continued past the temple to be taken back to the Campus Martius, while the prisoners were led away, most of them finally to be sold, except for Vercingetorix and others of similar rank and prestige. He was led to the Tullianum, the dungeon under the Gemonian Stairs, where he would be executed by being garroted. As we got near the sacred precinct and saw the huge temple that sits on top of the Capitoline, we finally got a glimpse of the crowning touch of Caesar's triumph. Lining the last several hundred feet on both sides were 40 elephants, 20 to a side, each one holding a burning torch, a most impressive feat when you see it. These were some of the elephants in Juba's army that were shipped back to Italy for just this occasion. Marching past, I will admit that I was a bit nervous as I wondered if the sight of men in Roman uniform marching past them would trigger some sort of memory of the battle, causing them to go crazy and stomp us into greasy red smears. Nothing happened though, and we marched past without incident, winding around the hill then circling back towards the Via Triumphalis. Meanwhile, Caesar made his offering to Jupiter Optimus Maximus, consisting of his garland crown, along with the ivy that had adorned the fasces of every one of his 72 lictors. The parade part of the triumph was over. However, the festivities were just beginning, as was the work of the Centurions.

~ ~ ~ ~

The second part of a triumph is a massive feast, and as was his habit, Caesar was determined that his one would be larger and more extravagant than anything the people of Rome had seen before. A total of 22,000 tables were set up, each table seating ten people, and that was just for the civilians. The army held their own banquet back at camp, a prudent measure to keep us separate from the masses, given the amount of wine that flowed. The fare was the most extravagant and exotic that the men had ever seen, rivaling what I had experienced at Cleopatra's banquet the year before. Platters of meats of every description, pastries stuffed with both meat and sweets, loaf upon loaf of fresh, steaming bread, along with fresh fruits and vegetables prepared in more ways than one could count. Truth be known, the bread was the most popular with the men, as more than one of them turned their nose up at the meats, which was fine as far as I was concerned, since it meant more for me. I had taken a lot of teasing over the years about my preference for meat over bread, but I had long since learned to shrug it off.

As the day progressed, the conversation grew steadily louder and more boisterous. It had not even gotten dark yet when the first fight broke out. It did not start with my men, though it certainly did not take long for the violence to spread to the series of tables where my men were sitting and I was not surprised that one of the first men to be knocked to the ground was none other than my long-time tent mate, Didius. Sighing, I looked over at Scribonius, who was still Didius' Centurion. He gave me a rueful smile and a shrug as he got to his feet to stride over to where Didius and another man were now rolling about in the dirt, as Scribonius administered a few whacks with the *vitus* that broke it up. This was the theme of the rest of the night: a few moments of drunken camaraderie, punctuated by flying fists and bodies rolling around on the ground, keeping the Centurions and Optios hopping from one brawl to the next. Even after all these years together, there were still grudges and disputes, some of them going back ten years or more, over gambling debts never paid, suspicions about cheating during dice or tables, or most commonly about a woman. As long as the men were sober and under our eye, these problems rarely flared into open hostilities, but with the wine flowing and the spirits high, fights were breaking out all over the place. In other words, it was a normal night of revelry and abandon and a good time was had by all, except for the Centurions.

The five days before the next triumph were devoted to games, again held on a scale never seen before in Rome. A wooden amphitheater was erected in the Forum for gladiatorial games, where hundreds of pairs fought, some of them to the death, the most notable being between a disgraced Senator who was slain by the son of a Praetor. There was a series of battles fought out, first between two groups of 1,000 gladiators per side acting as infantry, then between 200 mounted men per side. The blood flowed freely, and the crowds loved it, including the men who sat in the section designated for the army, these Legionaries attending according to the lots drawn every day to determine who could go. Out on the Field of Mars, a temporary stadium was erected where people watched athletic competitions featuring contestants brought in from all parts of the Republic.

But the best part, at least as far as all the men were concerned, was the news given to us at a formation the day after the triumph, where Caesar himself announced to us that he was paying off all that he had promised to the men, and then some. Each man was given 5,000 denarii apiece, or about 20,000 sesterces, while each Centurion received 10,000, except for all Centurions of the first grade who received twelve thousand. Primi Pili like myself received 15,000, which equates to about 60,000 sesterces. With this amount added to what I already had, I now had the 400,000 sesterces needed for a man of my station to elevate to the equestrian class. With the term of my enlistment ending soon, my future was assured. Yet, I no longer had any intention of leaving the army. That decision was made for me when my family died, and now I was not willing to leave the only other family I had. Unlike most of the men, I did not celebrate the news by immediately running out and gambling a large percentage of it away, or by attempting to drink the city dry. I did replenish my stock of Falernian, which cost me quite a bit more than usual because of the circumstances of so many people and so much money floating about, which inflated the cost.

All around the city, rivers of wine were flowing as the masses spent part of the 100 denarii that Caesar had paid to each and every citizen toasting his name. I believe that you could not have filled a Cohort with sober men, yet not everyone was happy with Caesar. It is easy to look back now to see the signs that would lead to the event of his death, though at the time, it seemed little more than sour grapes from members of his own class. It was only after the first triumphal parade when we had returned to camp that we heard about the negative reaction to Caesar's 72 lictors, although we thought it a perfectly reasonable thing to reward every man who had been a lictor with the chance to march in the parade. A lictor's term is only one year, so over the years, Caesar had many lictors, and not all of them were in the parade. Apparently, his fellow patricians and Senators did not see it that way, so there had been some grumbling about it. Of course, once Caesar heard about it, he was more determined than ever that every one of his parades would contain the same number of lictors. In fact, word was sent out to look for the rest of the men who had not been summoned to march in the first parade, though fortunately, none of them showed up, or there is no telling what his peers would have made of him marching with 90 lictors, or a hundred. Still, as far as the people were concerned, Caesar could do no wrong, and his name was toasted night and day. Finally, the day came for the second triumph, for his victory in Egypt, and for this occasion, I was reunited with the men of the 6th.

~ ~ ~ ~

The Egyptian parade was in some ways more elaborate than the first, but during this procession, I believe that Caesar made his first real misstep, because it was with the people and not the upper classes. The night before the parade, I made my way over to the 6th's area, where I found Felix, Sertorius, and Clemens sitting around a fire, talking idly about something or other. They appeared to be genuinely happy to see me. I had seen them briefly before, but since it was shortly after I returned from Brundisium, I had not been in much of a mood for small talk. Now I was sufficiently recovered, and I am sure the amphora of wine I brought along smoothed whatever awkwardness there might have been.

"How have things been with the men?" I asked.

The three of them looked at each other, then Felix shrugged. "Well enough. They were certainly happy about the bonus Caesar paid us, but they're all ready to go home, Primus Pilus."

I nodded, having expected to hear something like that, this now being a common refrain throughout much of the army, particularly the Spanish Legions.

"Well," I replied, "that's to be expected. But since those whelps of Pompey ran off to Hispania, we will be going home, I just don't think it's quite in the way that the men were hoping."

"We figured as much," Sertorius replied. He scratched his chin as he stared into the fire. "Truth be known, it doesn't really much matter to me. I'm not leaving the army."

"Neither am I," added Clemens. Felix remained silent, and soon we were all looking his way.

Catching our gaze, he shifted uncomfortably, then shrugged again. "I still haven't decided. What about you, Primus Pilus?" he asked me. "Last time we talked about it, you still weren't sure what you were going to do. Have you decided?"

"I'm not going anywhere," I said, mentally preparing myself for what I knew was coming next.

"I bet your wife's not happy about that. You probably won't be doing any slap and tickle for a while," Sertorius joked. I saw by the wince on Felix's face that at least he knew.

"You're right about that," I said as lightly as I could, for I truly did not want Sertorius to feel badly about something he had no knowledge about, so I changed the subject.

"The men are ready for tomorrow?"

"Of course, Primus Pilus," Clemens said a little stiffly, and I saw that I had offended all three of the men by even asking the question of such a veteran Legion.

"I knew they would be. Forgive me, it's just a habit."

We talked of other things for a while, then I took my leave, and I could see their relief at my departure. It is a funny thing about being in a unit. When you are finally accepted, you are as a brother to each and every man, but once you leave, something changes. Each Legion, each Cohort, each Century in the army has a life of its own, and that life continues whether an individual is present or not. When someone returns after an absence, even a short one, things have happened that the returning man is not part of, which makes him a little less a part of the family than before he left. The longer he is away, the more pronounced the effect, and I had been back with the 10th now for almost a year. I would always be welcome at their fires, yet I would never quite be a part of things the way I was when we were besieged in Alexandria, which made me a little sad as I thought about it. It seemed as if a large part of my life in the last year had been one of loss in a number of different ways.

~ ~ ~ ~

The parade the next day was not as long as the Gallic because there was a much smaller army marching, just the less than 900 remaining men of the 6th, along with the Gallic cavalry, the 28th and 36th having been left behind in Africa to fulfill different duties. While I was marching with the 6th and was technically the Primus Pilus, Valens had been ably filling that role since my departure, so I asked him to march in my spot while I marched at the head of the Seventh Cohort. The wagons carrying the scenes of the Alexandrian campaign were even more elaborate than those of the Gallic campaign, perhaps because the craftsmen making these had more time to work on them. The most spectacular was the scale model of the lighthouse that was complete with a small flame burning at the top in front of a polished metal mirror, just like the real one. The spoils from Alexandria were even more staggering than those of Gaul, at least in how exotic they were. Piles of golden crowns, chests containing mounds of gemstones of varying sizes, but all large, and all manner of riches were on display. Yet what caught the attention of the crowd even more than these were the animals, particularly the giraffes. These beasts are nothing if they are not 15 feet tall, and while their torsos are shaped somewhat like a horse, they have extremely long and spindly legs. However, what makes them fantastic is the length of their neck, which is easily the height of a man my size. Perched atop this long flexible neck is a head very much like a camel, while the whole thing is covered in brown spots over a tawny backdrop. Caesar had shipped 20 of the animals, but only six survived the voyage and ensuing captivity. It was these six that were pulled and dragged along the route while the people ooh'ed and aah'ed. Caesar had planned on using the water horse that inhabited the Nile, with which the men had such sport on the river cruise in the parade, but he had given up. They proved to be impossible to manage, however, not to mention that their smell was absolutely atrocious, so they were left behind. Still, it was not with the animals or the spoils where Caesar made his error; it was in his choice of prisoner to be the center of attention of that part of the triumph. Standing in a wagon, draped in chains was Cleopatra's sister Arsinoe, along with her tutor and general, Ganymede. The sight of such a young and seemingly innocent girl chained in the same manner as a man like Vercingetorix did not sit well with the crowd, and we could follow the progress of the procession by the boos and catcalls of the crowd as we marched. We knew that the crowd was upset, but did not know why until later, and it did not seem to matter that Arsinoe was not to be executed, just banished. The crowd did not like the appearance of Rome bullying young girls, no matter how deceiving that appearance may have been. There was not a man in the 6th who felt the same way as the crowd, but we had all been subject to her ruthlessness and cunning, and we knew her true nature, while all the crowd saw was a helpless youngster. Cleopatra had come to Rome by that time, and was living in a residence on the Janiculan Hill, though she was not allowed inside the *pomerium*, since she was a sovereign and no king or queen is allowed inside the sacred boundary. However, the rumor was that she had managed to slip past her guards and had come to the city in disguise so that she could watch the final humiliation of her sister and rival. I have never spoken of it until now, but I can say that this is not rumor; it is fact, because I saw her with my own eyes.

~ ~ ~ ~

We had just exited the Circus Maximus, about to turn onto the Via Sacra, when my eyes met a pair of dark brown ones, though the rest of her face was hidden by a veil, and I saw them widen in recognition and surprise for just an instant before she regained her composure. She was standing on the second floor balcony of what appeared to be a private residence, dressed as a common household slave, but if I had the chance to consult with her before she put her costume on, I would have pointed out to her that slaves did not wear veils in Rome. Fortunately, since she was above and a little way behind the crowd, nobody seemed to notice. I saw just behind her two large Nubians, dressed in short tunics and cloaks, designed to hide the daggers they wore under the robes. Our eyes remained on each other as I drew closer, so I could see the worry in hers, and I wondered how much trouble it would cause if I told Caesar that I had seen her. I am sure this was the same thought going through her mind as well, but making up my mind, I just winked at her while touching the side of my nose. Her relief was clearly written in those very expressive eyes, and I confess I felt a small thrill at being a co-conspirator with the likes of Cleopatra. As far as I was concerned, it was the least I could do for her. She had been very kind to a country bumpkin at his first, and so far, only banquet of state, for which I would never forget her, so her secret was safe with me. I could not wipe the silly grin off my face the rest of the parade, which I am sure the women on the route thought was meant for them, yet I did not really notice any of them that day. Once more, Caesar made his way up the steps of the temple of Jupiter Optimus Maximus, with his second garland, along with the ivy from the lictors to be given as offering. I could not help wondering if the god would grow tired of this, since there were still two more times to go and he would be receiving the same offering every time. Even the gods like a little variety, or so I think, but that is the way it has always been done, and therefore will be the way all the times in the future.

~ ~ ~ ~

For the Egyptian games, along with the gladiatorial contests, a large hole was excavated on the Campus Martius, then filled with water, making an artificial lake where naval battles were fought, using some of the ships from the Egyptian navy that were captured along with their crews, pitted against a small fleet manned by Tyrians. The Tyrians were chosen because they had refused to help Mithradates of Pergamum when he was raising a force to come to our aid in Alexandria, so their fate was to have some of their best young men chained to the benches of their ships and fight to the death for the enjoyment of Romans. The ships sailed all the way from Egypt and Tyre, then up the Tiber River to Rome. Finally, with the use of huge rollers and thousands of slaves, the vessels were manhandled across the open ground of the Campus to the artificial lake.

The endeavor had attracted a huge crowd of men from the army to watch, but the overriding sentiment was best described by Vellusius, who sniffed, "Well, we did that in Britannia and we didn't have any slaves to help us. It was all our sweat that did it. What's the big fuss about all this?"

With that, he turned away, followed by the rest of the men. I went with them as well; Vellusius was right. So much of what we were seeing constructed and done for this triumph that was done by slave labor in Rome had been accomplished by citizens in the army. I was noticing that I was picking up the attitude that most of the men, who in fairness had been in and around Rome for much longer than I had been, had about their fellow citizens. To the men of the army, our civilian counterparts were spoiled, soft, and incredibly lazy, and their attitude towards any type of manual labor engendered many a campfire discussion.

"They consider it beneath them, but it's fine for anyone wearing a uniform to work as hard as a slave," Glaxus spat into the fire shortly after our evening meal one night.

Scribonius was visiting, and Silanus was there as well, along with Balbus and Arrianus. There was a murmur of agreement at this, and I was one of those who agreed. Although I had not been here as long as the others, I had seen enough of the attitude to understand that it was indeed the prevailing one.

"It's a load of *cac* is what it is," Arrianus declared. "These civilians stick their nose up at us whenever we walk by, and you hear them making comments about what a soft life we've got sitting about in camp all day and night, just lolling about. Who do they think built this camp? Don't they know a slave never digs so much as a spadeful of dirt building our camps? Or that the roads they walk on and that carry all those goods from every corner of the Republic were made by us and by the sweat off our back?"

"No, they don't know that."

I smiled, knowing that Scribonius could always be counted on to provide the other viewpoint.

All eyes turned to him, Arrianus scowling at Scribonius, who was whittling on a piece of wood, a favorite hobby of his. "As far as the people are concerned, all of what you speak of happens the same way that it happens in the city, by slave labor. Nobody has thought to tell them differently, so as far as they're concerned, we're no better than they are."

"We're much better than they are," retorted Glaxus, raising another chorus of agreement. "We've sacrificed more, we've lost more friends than any individual citizen will ever have, all so that they can look down their nose at us when we walk by!"

"It's our own fault, really." Now I looked at Scribonius in surprise, while the others' reactions were a bit stronger. I had understood and basically agreed with what he was saying, but now he was going into territory where I could not easily follow. "Think about it like this. How many people did we enslave out of Gaul?"

"About a million," I answered.

Nodding, Scribonius continued, "And before that, how many slaves lived in Rome itself? Anyone know?"

We all shook our heads.

"I'm not sure either, but I think it was around 300,000, and I don't have any idea how many in the rest of the Republic, but my guess is all told there were at least 1,000,000 slaves. Now in the space of seven years, we doubled that amount. How many people did we put out of a job?"

"You mean that they're mad at us because we freed them from having to work?" protested Arrianus. "Why, they should be kissing the ground that we walk on."

"Do you really believe that, Arrianus?" Scribonius asked quietly. "How would you feel if you could no longer provide for your family because you were replaced by someone who works essentially for free? Not because you did your job poorly, but merely because you needed enough money so that your family wouldn't starve? Would you really be grateful about that?"

All eyes turned to Arrianus, who was smart enough to know that he was on the losing end. "No, I suppose not," he grumbled. "But it's hardly our fault we're so good at conquering people. What should we have done with all those Gauls? Thrown them back so we could fight them again?"

There was some laughter at this idea, as Scribonius admitted, "No, I'm not saying that necessarily. Honestly, I don't know what the answer is, but I do know that it's a little much to expect everyone to be happy with us for essentially taking away their livelihood."

~ ~ ~ ~

Another five days of celebration passed before the third triumph, this one for the victory against Pharnaces, and again, just the men of the 6th marched. For the Pontic triumph, there was not as much to display, only a few hundred prisoners, and unlike with the Gallic and Egyptian, there were no high-born or prominent men to execute, so Caesar attempted to make up for it with wagons loaded with the arms and armor of the Pontic army that they had discarded fleeing from Zela. One of the pictures portrayed Pharnaces running away in his chariot, which seemed to be very popular with the crowd, but the one I favored the most was not a painting as much as it was an inscription. Caesar had his by-now famous words, "Veni, vidi, vici" written on one large canvas, and it was this that led the procession of scenes. I had thought that by the third triumph, the enthusiasm of the crowd would have waned, but this was not the case. Pontus had been an enemy of Rome for years, so the record of their defeat brought much joy and jubilation to the crowd. Of all the triumphs we celebrated, this was the least controversial, which was good because the final triumph was going to prove to be the most troublesome yet.

~ ~ ~ ~

As far as the men of the army were concerned, the last triumph was a bad idea from the moment it was mentioned. While our conquest of Gaul, along with the defeat of the Egyptians and Pontics was straightforward, we had fought our own people in Africa. Supposedly, the triumph was celebrating the defeat of Juba, and Caesar did parade Juba's five-year-old son, also called Juba, though he did not have him wear chains and of course, he was not executed. He was actually treated very well, being raised as Roman. If things were left at that, there would not have been any problems, but Caesar could not content himself with only going that far. Several of the paintings depicted scenes that showed the assorted demises of Caesar's enemies. Scipio was portrayed drowning at the hands of Sittius, Petreius in his duel with Juba and subsequent suicide, but I think the painting of Cato was the most distressing to the crowd. Caesar had spared no detail, showing both Cato's initial attempt at suicide and the most grisly version of how he actually died. I have to say that whoever the artist was, he went to great lengths to show him pulling his guts out and throwing them about, so much so that even for a crowd as hardened to scenes of bloodshed as this, it was too much. The boos this time were loud and long, raining down on us from the crowd, causing us to look at each other with some concern. The crowd did not seem to be particularly inclined to violence, but with such a massive group of people, one never knew. I was marching back with the 10th, this time in my spot as Primus Pilus, so I was closer to the crowd and the expressions on their faces were ugly, their anger at the scenes that passed them by very raw and real. As we learned later, there was even more of a reaction from men closer to Caesar's class than from those lining the streets. As Caesar entered the Circus Maximus, passing along the benches that were reserved for the Tribunes of the Plebs, all but one of them came to their feet as custom dictated. The man who refused to stand was one Pontius Aquila, which Caesar did not like one bit. There was an exchange of angry words between them, though I did not learn what was said, but while Aquila was the most visible in his disagreement with what Caesar had done, he was far from the only one. Still, Caesar was the undisputed master of Rome and the entire Republic, while the dissenters were in the vast minority and their protests little but a whisper, so if you had told me then what was to come, I would have laughed. There was still work to do, for both Caesar and the army, while many of us would be going home again as we had hoped, just not in the way we had planned.

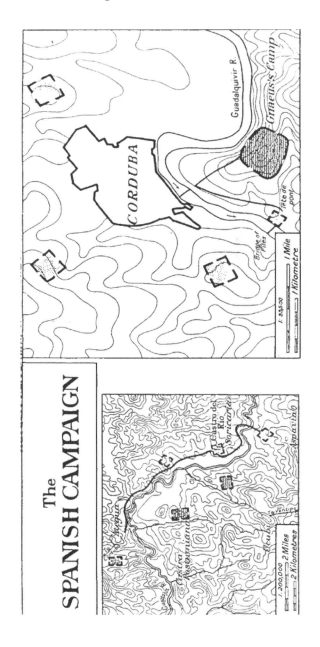

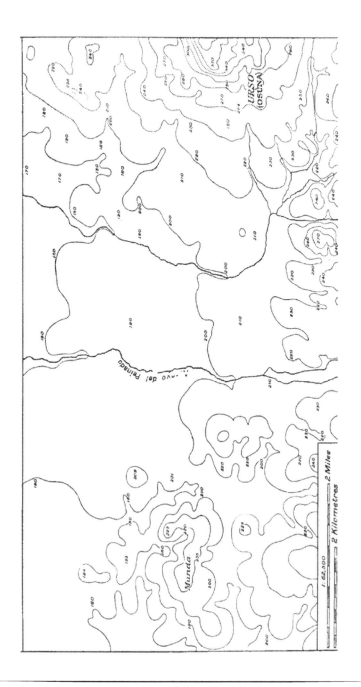

# Chapter 9- Munda

As the 20 days of festivities came to an end, it was not all good news for Caesar and by extension, the army. Pompey's sons had escaped to Hispania after Pharsalus, where Pompey was still revered, his name carrying much weight with people. Almost immediately, two of the Legions, the men of the 2nd and Indigena, promptly declared for the sons of Pompey. Not helping matters had been the behavior of Quintus Cassius, who Caesar left behind as governor of the province three years earlier. He had been governor in Hispania before that, and during his first term acted with great avarice and cruelty towards the population. Apparently, he decided to pick up where he left off when he came back. I will not enumerate all of his crimes, but they were many and varied, the common belief being that he was his own worst enemy. He had died some time before, yet the rancor and bitterness he left behind was sufficient to make people throwing their allegiance to the Pompeys an easy choice. Caesar had left the 21st and 30th behind in Hispania and there was a *dilectus* for the 3rd Legion so it was full of raw youngsters. Commanded by Pedius, he was co-commander of the entire force with Fabius, but the 2nd, Indigena and the 1st, which had escaped once again, from Thapsus this time, was composed of veterans. Therefore, Caesar sent explicit instructions not to engage with the Pompeians. The Pompey brothers, Gnaeus and Sextus, were joined by Labienus, who just did not have the good grace to die, along with a number of other vermin who had managed to save their skins in Africa. The Pompey name created a stir of excitement in Hispania, culminating in the city of Corduba declaring for Pompey because of the crimes of Cassius, despite the fact that both were dead. About two weeks after the triumphs, at the morning briefing, we were given orders to make the men ready to march to Hispania, an order that was not unexpected, given all that we had heard about developments there, yet it was troubling nonetheless. When I was relaying the orders back to the officers of the 10th, there were a number of looks exchanged between the Centurions, but for several moments, nobody said anything.

Seeing this, I decided to speak up, as I was sure that the men were reluctant to voice their feelings, though I knew they were there. "I can see some concern with this order," I began. "Anyone care to say why they're worried?"

For a moment, I began to think that nobody was going to say anything and that I had misread the situation. Then Balbus cleared his throat. I had expected this from either him or Scribonius, or perhaps Horatius, who was not shy about speaking up.

"It's just that we're marching back with all the other Spanish Legions," he said. I did not understand his meaning, so I bade him to continue. "The 7th, 8th, and 9th are now several years overdue for their discharge, and yet they're marching home."

"Have you heard anything?" I asked.

Balbus shrugged, clearly reluctant to say much more, but I was not about to let him off the hook.

He had opened his mouth, so now I stared at him until he finally replied, "Nothing definite, no. Just some grumbling about having to march home, but not being able to return to their families."

"They will, once we finish up with the Pompeian whelps," I protested, but the others were not moved.

It was Scribonius who spoke up next, and I knew that he was speaking for the rest when he said, "Primus Pilus, the men have been hearing that for almost three years now. I think that they're past believing that it will actually happen."

The rest of the men added their agreement to what Scribonius had said, as I found myself rubbing my face once more, trying to decide what to do about it. Some said that I should immediately send word to Caesar about what I had heard, yet I did not feel that there was anything specific enough that would warrant such a move. If I ran to Caesar every time the men complained about something, I might as well have brought my cot to set up in his headquarters. Besides, I reasoned to myself, Caesar had ears everywhere, so I had to believe that I would not be telling him anything he had not already heard himself. Once again, I was wrong.

~ ~ ~ ~

We packed up, marching away from the Campus Martius, the 5th, 6th, 7th, 8th, 9th, 10th, and the 13th, marching rapidly west. The first few days were tough on everyone, a month of celebration and debauchery taking some of the iron out of us so that we had more than the normal number of stragglers, some of them not making it to the nightly camp until well after dark. The days were starting to get shorter, though the weather held for the most part, although there were a few squalls while we were marching near the coast. Caesar was remaining behind in Rome to finish some of his legislative work, along with his continuing consolidation of power, or else it might have been even worse for us if we had marched at his normal pace. It took us more than six weeks to reach the border between the two Hispanias, marching into the camp of Pedius, Fabius, and the three Legions under their command. By the time we arrived, all the fat and soft living was marched off of all of us, including me. It was shortly after we arrived, with the men busy setting up their tents in the area marked off for the use of the 10th that the concerns of my Centurions came to fruition.

"Primus Pilus, you're needed at the *praetorium* immediately," came the summons from one of the Legionaries on headquarter guard duty.

I was about to give him a good thrashing because he had not announced himself properly and his salute was sloppy, but I could see that he was a youngster from one of the new Legions, probably the 3rd, huffing and puffing from running to find me, and completely scared out of his wits. Something was happening, so this youngster was going to escape a beating, though I do not think he realized just how lucky he was.

"What is it?" I snapped. "Why are you all out of breath like Cerberus is chewing at your heels?"

Gasping for breath, it took a moment before he could stammer out a reply. "I don't know, Primus Pilus. It just has something to do with some of the other Legions. General Pedius has called for all the Primi Pili and Pili Priores immediately."

"Which other Legions?" I demanded as I turned to grab my helmet and *vitus*.

"I don't know, sir. I just know that some of them have deserted."

I stared at him in astonishment, then quickly shook my head. He surely had it wrong, but I was never one to take my wrath out on helpless rankers unless it had some sort of value. Ignoring the rest of what he was babbling on about, I sent Diocles to round up the Pili Priores while I trotted over to headquarters. When I arrived, some of the other officers were already there, talking excitedly to each other. While some of the others seemed surprised, I noticed others with a look of resigned acceptance, and I hurried over to a small group standing in a corner.

"What's happening?"

The Primus Pilus of the 5th, a tough old bird by the name of Battus, gave a harsh laugh, but there was no humor in it. "You haven't heard then? Well, it seems that some of your fellow Spaniards have decided that they've had enough and are marching to join Gnaeus Pompey."

I said nothing, sure that he was just having some sort of fun at my expense, but then I saw the grim expressions of the other men around him.

Finally finding my tongue, I asked, "How many and which ones?"

"It looks like it's the 8th and 9th," Battus replied.

"And the 13th, looks like," a new voice added and I turned to see none other than Torquatus, old of the 10th and now the Primus Pilus of the new 3rd Legion.

"The 13th!" I exclaimed. "But they still have a couple years left on their enlistment. The 8th and 9th I can understand, they've been unhappy for a long time. But the 13th?"

Torquatus shrugged. "I don't have any better idea than you, Pullus, that's just what I heard General Pedius say."

"Where are they now?" Battus asked.

Torquatus indicated the area out beyond the front gate. "Formed up and marching away. They stayed just long enough for their Primi Pili to come tell Pedius what they were going to do, then left."

"Pedius should sound the call to arms and we should hunt them down and kill every last one of the bastards," Battus said angrily, as a couple of his own Centurions added their agreement.

While I understood his feelings, I knew that this was not a good idea, on a number of different levels. "And who's going to do the killing?" I asked. "My men?" I continued before he could reply. "The men of the 7th? Men who have marched side by side, bled side by side, died side by side? You really think that the men will be willing to lift a sword against some of their closest friends?"

"And relatives," added Torquatus, but Battus was unmoved.

"The men will do what we tell them to do, damn them," he stormed. "They take orders, and if the General orders it, and I hope he does, then they'll do their duty."

"Speak for yourself," Torquatus retorted. "I've got nothing but green youngsters. That lot," he indicated the cloud of dust marking the passage of the defecting Legions, "would take a lot of killing, and you should know that as well as anyone. And just because your boys took on some elephants, that doesn't mean that they're any match for those Spaniards."

Battus' face flushed with anger as he took a step towards Torquatus, who just stood there looking at him calmly.

Seeing that the situation was unraveling, I spoke up. "Battus, how many men are you willing to lose to keep them from marching away?"

Battus was still angry, and snapped, "As many as it takes."

"Then who will be left to fight the Pompeians?"

That finally got through to him, as his mouth opened and closed a couple of times before he finally shook his head. "It's just not right," he muttered.

In that I had to agree with him, but I also did not want the rest of the army to mutiny, which I was sure would happen if we were ordered to try and stop them from marching away. Fortunately, Pedius had come to the same conclusion, which he informed us about once we were all gathered. He could not shed any more light on why the 13th had thrown in with the other two Legions, telling us that a dispatch had already been sent to Caesar, informing him of the defections. There was nothing much we could do except go back to our respective Legions, and of course by the time I returned, the men already knew what had happened.

I called a meeting of the Centurions immediately; as soon as they were assembled, I asked the question that had been pressing on my mind since I had heard. "Do we have anything to worry about?"

I was vastly relieved to see that all the men seemed to be in agreement that we did not.

"I'm just glad that the general didn't order us to try and stop them. That could have been ugly," Scribonius said, and there was universal agreement about this as well.

"I don't think he ever considered it an option, though I can't say the same for some of the other Centurions," I replied, then I was struck by a thought. "And now we're suspect as well, because we're Spaniards like the 8th and 9th. You need to impress on the men the need for them to keep their mouths shut about what happened and how they feel about it, at least if they're sympathetic to their friends, which I suspect many of them are. The last thing we need is somebody from another Legion overhearing one of the men talking and having him accused of inciting a mutiny."

It was not the best way to run an army, but I did not want a bad situation to become worse, and the Centurions all agreed that they would keep a tight lid on the men for the next few days.

~ ~ ~ ~

While Sextus Pompey was holding Corduba, older brother Gnaeus had decided to besiege the town of Ulia, one of the few in the region that still held for Caesar, but neither Pedius nor Fabius wanted to move until Caesar arrived. So we waited in camp, doing little more than conducting weapons drills, not even going out on forced marches because of the threat of ambush. We did run regular cavalry patrols, using native levies along with some of the men who had marched with us, thus keeping apprised of the enemy movements to a reasonable degree. Caesar wasted no time, taking just 27 days to travel what it took the army six weeks to cover, outrunning even his cavalry, which trailed behind several days. He arrived in early Januarius of the old calendar, which by this time was so far off being aligned with the seasons that it was still mid-autumn. Word of Caesar's arrival spread quickly, and upon hearing it, a small party of elders from the town under siege managed to slip out to come to the camp, begging Caesar for assistance. In response, Caesar ordered three Cohorts of the 7th and three Cohorts of the 21st along with the same number of cavalry, under the command of a Tribune who had local knowledge by the name of Paciaecus, to leave shortly after dark, using the same route to enter the town as the elders had used to escape from it. In concert with that, Caesar ordered us to pull up stakes, then march on Corduba, the idea being that Gnaeus could not maintain a siege when his rear and base of supplies was under threat. As had so many of Caesar's enemies, Gnaeus did not credit the idea that our general could move an army as quickly as he did, so before Gnaeus knew it, we were camped on the southern bank of the Baetis (Guadalquivir) river, just across from Corduba. Now Gnaeus had no choice but to lift his siege, hurrying to the aid of his brother

Sextus. While Gnaeus was in the process of turning his army about and coming to confront us, Caesar put us to work building a bridge across the Baetis. There was already a stone bridge in place, but there was a fort guarding its northern side, which would have forced us to make a possibly costly assault, so instead, Caesar selected a site about a mile downriver to the south. We left a force of several Cohorts occupying a fort identical to the Pompeian fort on the north bank, the only difference being ours was on the southern bank, blocking Gnaeus' army from crossing the river to get to Corduba. The bridge we built was a makeshift affair, constructed of baskets filled with stones, which we sunk to the river bottom to act as pilings. It was one of the shakiest constructions we had ever made while marching for Caesar, though it served its purpose. We crossed the river, then Caesar immediately disposed us into three separate camps, placing one to the west of the city, one to the north and one to the east, with the river serving as a barrier to the south. The 10th occupied the camp on the eastern side, which took us until past dark to finish since we had to build a camp in the face of the enemy. This type of camp is more strongly fortified while requiring more men to stand ready in case of attack. About mid-day the next day, Gnaeus' army arrived on the other side of the river. Instead of immediately assaulting our fort and trying to force his way across the stone bridge, he chose instead to construct his own camp, siting it on a hill that rose up from the bend of the river that curved around the southern side of Corduba. This allowed Caesar to order a trench built that ran from our temporary bridge to our fort at the stone bridge that would allow us to send reinforcements to the fort under cover. The digging began immediately, and to Gnaeus' credit, he did see that he had made an error, so he sent out a force of men that he could spare from the building of his camp to try to stop the work on the trench. There was a sharp fight, but after some hot work, our men repelled the Pompeians so that work continued. As this project was underway, Caesar and his engineering officers were surveying Corduba, yet even from my limited examination, I was not confident that we would be able to take the city easily. I had visited Corduba as a young recruit, but I had been too green to be able to assess the city's defenses back then, not knowing what to look for. Now, almost 16 years later as I examined the approach and the walls on our side, I did not like what I saw. Fortunately, after his inspection, Caesar came to the same conclusion, so instead of trying to besiege the city, we spent the next several days trying to entice young Gnaeus to meet us in battle by forming up on the plain to the north of the city out on the open ground. The young Pompey was not biting, however; he was unwilling to put his mostly untested troops against the veterans of Caesar's army. While Gnaeus may have had the three veteran Legions that defected from our army, he clearly did not trust them, because along with the 1st and the

4th, on paper that was more than enough to face us with a reasonable chance. After a number of days where we marched out to offer battle, only to be rebuffed every time, Caesar gave the order to break camp, our next objective being the fortress town of Ategua. It lies a day's march to the southeast of Corduba, on the north bank of the Salsum (Guadajoz) River, a tributary of the Baetis, where there was reportedly a large supply of grain. In order to steal a march on Gnaeus, we were ordered to keep the campfires burning in order to deceive the enemy, so we left men behind in the camp to tend to them. We slipped past first Corduba, then the camp of Gnaeus, crossing over the makeshift bridge and marching through the night to arrive outside the walls of the fortress shortly before mid-day. While part of the army constructed the camp, the rest of us immediately began the contravallation of the town.

The fortress was on top of a hill with fairly steep sides, so we also began working on a ramp in the same fashion as the one we built against the Aduatuci those years ago back in Gaul that would allow us to roll a siege tower up to the walls. On the nearby hills surrounding the town there were a number of towers that Caesar ordered a section of men to occupy in shifts to watch for Gnaeus' approach. Finally, the weather began to catch up with the calendar, as it turned very raw, with driving rain and blustery winds. In order to combat the elements, we asked permission to build huts instead of using our tents, which was granted. They were rude shelters, and I for one did not think them much, if any better than our tents. Yet given the propensity of our leather tents to suddenly split after being subjected to soaking rains for more than two or three days, I suppose they were an improvement in that sense at least. We invested Ategua without encountering any resistance from Gnaeus, who as it turned out, at first, believed that Ategua was too strong to fall. Although some of his generals, and I suspect Labienus was chief among them, convinced him that underestimating Caesar's ability to reduce any fortress was folly, Gnaeus delayed further because he believed that the elements would provide a sufficient barrier if the walls did not. When Gnaeus finally realized that Caesar was indeed serious about taking Ategua, only then did he rouse his army to come in pursuit. Fortuna favored him by blanketing the area with a dense fog to cover his approach, preventing the men in the watchtowers from doing their job. During his advance, forward elements of his army stumbled onto one of the watchtowers and there was a sharp fight for it. All of our men were killed, the position falling to the Pompeians, while the Pompeians made camp at the base of the hill on which it stood. The next day, Gnaeus apparently felt that his position was not a strong one, so the Pompeian army marched past the town, crossing the river, then marching round to the southeast to take up position on a hill that put another one of his fortress towns, Ucubi was its name, to his rear to serve as his new supply base. On the southern side of the river was one lone watchtower that Caesar had ordered occupied. Once he divined Gnaeus' intentions, he reinforced this position, sending a full Century to guard it, which turned out to be a wise move, even if it meant that he sent one of my Centurions to hold it.

"I want you to send one of your best to hold the watchtower on the south side of the river," Caesar told me at the daily briefing. "Now that I've seen what the young Pompey is up to, I'm sure that he'll deem it vital to take that tower."

I knew that when Caesar worded an order in this manner, he already had someone in mind, so I asked him as much. Smiling slightly, he replied, "I was thinking that Scribonius is one of the most dependable of your Centurions, and he has a good head on his shoulders. Do you disagree?"

I shook my head, not that I would have objected even if I did. Caesar's nerves had been very raw lately, those defections opening an old wound, so it did not take much to rouse his temper, especially with matters concerning the army. I was just thankful that I actually agreed that Scribonius was the best choice, and I went to tell him. He and the First of the Second were ready to march shortly after Caesar gave me the order, whereupon I stood watching as my old comrades marched out the gate, calling to their friends, happy that they would be relieved from the monotony of digging for a time.

~ ~ ~ ~

That night, Gnaeus sent a Cohort-sized force against the watchtower. I was roused from my sleep by a man sent by the commander of the guard, who had heard the sound of the Century *cornu* sounding the call to arms. I quickly pulled on my armor, and then I woke Diocles, telling him to rouse the Centurions of my Cohort to get the men ready to march. I moved quickly to the southern rampart, though it was too far away to hear the sounds of the fighting but I stood listening nonetheless, next to one of the sentries and the commander of the guard, straining to see any movement in the darkness. After perhaps a sixth part of a watch, one of the sentries called out, then a moment later my eye spotted movement, slowly gaining form to become the figure of a man running towards the gate. As he got within hailing distance, one of the sentries offered the challenge for the day, which the man answered with the watchword, and I recognized the voice.

"That's Vellusius," I exclaimed, jumping down from the parapet to meet him at the gate.

He had just entered the camp when I reached him, panting for breath and unable to speak for a moment.

"Any old day, Vellusius," I grumbled, though I did not really mean it, just anxious to hear his report.

"Sorry, Primus Pilus," he gasped, and I saw his teeth, or what was left of them flash in the gloom as he grinned. "I guess I'm just getting old. Pilus Prior Scribonius sent me to report that our position is under assault from a Cohort-sized force, but that it appears that it's about to be reinforced by at least three more Cohorts. The Pilus Prior says that we can hold out for another third of a watch, but no more than that."

Sending Vellusius back to the Legion area, I ran to the headquarters tent to inform Caesar. He had also been roused by the commander of the guard, and was already in his armor when I gave him Scribonius' report.

Turning to one of the Tribunes, who was also in armor, though clearly upset at being roused from his slumber, Caesar rapped out his orders. "Go inform the Primi Pili of the 5th and 7th that they'll be needed after all. They will be ready to march in a sixth of a watch."

I realized I should have known that Caesar would be prepared for such an eventuality. The thought crossed my mind that Scribonius and his Century had been set out as bait. I stifled the feeling of anger welling up within me, partly because it would not have changed anything, but mostly because I did not know what I was angrier about, that Caesar had used my men or that I had not seen it coming. The men of the 10th were formed up by the time I arrived in our area, so we marched quickly to the southern gate to wait for the rest of the party that would be marching to relieve Scribonius. The waiting was difficult, not improving my mood any, as I strode up and down, cursing the 5th and 7th for taking their time to join us. Of course, they were doing nothing of the sort, but these were my oldest and best friends fighting out there and every moment that passed meant a better chance of one of them being wounded or dying. I felt the same way about all of the men of the 10th, and for the men of the 6th for that matter, but I had a soft spot in my heart for the First Century, Second Cohort, which I carry to this day, even for Didius. Caesar came trotting up, not using Toes, but one of his other mounts, then I heard the pounding footsteps and jingling of the two other Legions. I looked to Caesar, illuminated by the torches that are kept lit at the gates, and he nodded, indicating that we should proceed.

~ ~ ~ ~

We marched as quickly as the darkness allowed. As we got closer, we began hearing stray shouts and calls first, then came the ringing sound of metal on metal. Caesar ordered the 10th, since we were in the lead, into a double line of Cohorts, two Centuries across and three deep, which was somewhat unusual, but we would be attacking on a narrow front. The enemy was too busy with Scribonius' Century to notice us until we were almost on them. One of the Pompeian Cohorts sent to reinforce the original assault force had circled behind Scribonius, so they had their backs turned to us, barely having time to turn about when I ordered the *cornicen* to sound the charge. Night attacks are a tricky thing, but we were well versed in the maneuver, it being a favorite of Caesar's and one that we had performed many times. While the surprise was not total, it was enough, as the screams and cries of men being cut down informed me as we slammed into them. The Pompeians went from attacker to defender in the heartbeats it took us to hit them, and they now found themselves pressed between two forces. It was about a Cohort-sized force, their Centurions working frantically to get at least a couple of their Centuries turned about to face the threat we posed. Fortunately for us, these were not seasoned veterans, the chaos of a night attack ripping their cohesion to tatters, so it was just a mass of men flailing about, most of them doing more damage to the man next to them than to us. My men cut through them like stalks of wheat, it not taking more than a couple moments before the inevitable panic set in, the Pompeians dropping their shields then turning blindly to run away, only there was nowhere to run. They went just a few steps before colliding into the back of the men still facing Scribonius' Century, exposing their own backs to us and sealing their fate. Perhaps half of them managed to escape in the night by scrambling to the sides of the press formed by our two forces, while we slaughtered the rest of them. As we were taking care of the force to Scribonius' rear, the 5th had swung around to assault the Pompeians fighting the half of Scribonius' Century that he had faced in that direction, doing essentially the same thing that we had done, with the same result. All told, the Pompeians lost perhaps 300 to 400 men, though we did not stop to count the bodies. The rest of them fled into the night, throwing their shields and weapons away to lighten their load. Once things had settled down, I found Scribonius who was binding up a wound on his arm.

He saluted then said, "I guess this means that Vellusius made it back."

I grinned, hoping that he could see it in the dark. "Oh he made it. It just took him a while to get his breath back. Says he's getting old."

"Aren't we all," Scribonius replied, then said sadly, "Not all of us."

"What's the butcher's bill, do you know yet?"

"Not completely. I know of two dead and four wounded. One of them is Didius."

"How badly?"

His tone was grim. "Bad enough. It's his leg, but the muscle is cut almost all the way through and is hanging like a piece of meat. He'll need a litter."

This was indeed bad news, but I decided that I would bribe Caesar's surgeon to take a look at Didius to see if he could be fixed up enough to keep marching, since we were literally months away from the end of our enlistment. Nonetheless, the regulations were clear; the only way that Didius would get his full benefit was by serving his full enlistment. Because Caesar was the master of Rome and Didius one of his Legionaries, I was fairly confident that the regulations could be bent, but it was not a foregone conclusion, and I knew that if I were Didius, I would not sleep easy until the matter was decided. Better that we did not have to rely on Caesar, I thought, so spending the money was not an issue for me. The other man I was concerned with was Vibius, though I made no comment when I learned that he was unhurt. It was not all bad news, however; the only losses we suffered were with Scribonius' Century, the rest of the Legion with only a handful of minor wounds to show for the action. We marched back to camp, leaving the watchtower unguarded, Caesar saying that it had served its purpose and would be too much of a problem to continue guarding. This confirmed my suspicions that Scribonius and his men had been nothing but bait, and I simmered with anger at Caesar, though I was still not sure why. He had done similar things more times than I could count; I had never had a problem with it before, and he had used men of the 10th before as well. Perhaps it was that it was my old Century, with my oldest friends.

We did not have everything our way, however. The next night, Gnaeus managed to reinforce the small garrison inside the town by a stratagem of deception. One of his Tribunes, Flaccus, I believe was his name, had spotted the youngsters of the 3$^{rd}$. Recognizing them for what they were, once it got dark, he went alone to one of the sentry posts, and while pretending to be from Caesar, learned the challenge and watchword. Using that knowledge, he led a force past the youngsters, giving the watchword when challenged, leading his men into the town. Caesar was understandably angry when he learned of what happened, but because of the youth and inexperience of the men, he only had them flogged and not executed, as was his right. We continued the work on the ramp, the final piece before we could assault the city, but the work was slow going because of the weather and with the garrison reinforced, the Pompeians in the city could sally forth to try to destroy the ramp. Ironically, the weather that had been hampering our efforts also was an aid in keeping the enemy from setting fire to the ramp, so they would retire back inside their walls, frustrated in their attempts. In order to discourage their attacks, Caesar ordered that any man captured in their raids be executed in front of the walls, something that he had never done before, which I took as a sign that he was getting as tired and frustrated with the continuing resistance as we were. From our point of view, the matter between the Pompeians and Caesar had long since been decided. The refusal of the Pompeians to recognize that was not only pointless, but also criminal, because we in the ranks had no choice but to obey orders and to continue killing and dying. Because of their stubbornness, we were still huddled in thatch huts, shivering against the cold, worried about where our next meal was coming from, while men like Didius who had survived more fighting than any army in Roman history were being cut down. Now when Caesar gave orders to execute captured men, whereas at one point this would have been an unpopular order, we were now completely willing to carry them out. The fact that these were men just like us, who were only following orders, no longer made any difference to us, and since we could not take out our frustrations on the likes of Gnaeus, Sextus and Labienus, they suffered the brunt of our anger. The townspeople, seeing our treatment of the enemy combatants, began to fear that their fate would be even worse, so one day, perhaps a week into the siege, a lead slingshot was flung at the feet of a Centurion supervising work on the ramp. Since it was obviously not an attempt to kill the Centurion, he correctly interpreted that there was another purpose behind it, picking the missile up. Inscribed was an understandably brief message suggesting a surprise attack should be attempted, while giving the location, along with the expected signal, a shield raised on a standard. The Primus Pilus of the 30th Legion approached Caesar, asking that his Legion be allowed to conduct this operation, to which Caesar agreed. That night, the men of the 30th began tunneling towards the spot indicated in the message, working through the night, with the intention of attacking shortly after first light. The rest of the army was ordered to continue with their normal duties so as not to arouse suspicion. Given that we were now working on the ramp night and day, the work continued normally through the night. Unfortunately, the men of the 30th did not finish their tunneling in time to launch their attack when they had hoped, so it was perhaps a full watch after sunrise before the shield was finally raised to the standard. I do not know if the delay contributed to what happened, but the attack was a disaster. It started out well enough, as the section of wall that the men of the 30th undermined collapsed with a sudden roar and roiling plume of dust, taking with it a couple men unlucky enough to be standing on guard on that section of the wall. The First Cohort of the 10th was standing guard on the rampart of our camp, so they had an unobstructed view of the action. Accordingly, it was Metellus who pointed out the problem that I think was the main cause for what was about to happen. Even as the dust was still settling, the men of the 30th went running towards the gap opened in the wall.

"It's not wide enough." Metellus pointed to the hole and I instantly saw that he was right.

The 30th had not created a breach of sufficient size, a mark of their inexperience. Undermining a wall is a tricky business, because the tunnel has to be sufficiently small so that it doesn't collapse. Once under the wall, it has to be widened so that it takes a sufficiently sized chunk of the wall down with it when the pile of wood and rubbish that is stuffed in the space is set alight, so that at least a full section can enter side by side. They had not done this, so the resulting breach was only wide enough for perhaps half a section of men abreast to enter. This meant that it would not take nearly as many men to plug the hole to defend it as it should have, so very quickly the attack bogged down. As we watched, about a half Century managed to crawl up the pile of rubble to enter through the breach before their progress was stopped. The sounds of battle carried across the air towards us, and it was quickly becoming clear that our side was faring badly, the calls and cries growing increasingly panicked. The rest of the 30th could only stand helplessly outside the walls as their comrades tried to push their way into the town, yet after several moments, no progress had been made. By then, the defenders had rallied a substantial number of men to climb to the parapet to begin flinging missiles down on the heads of our waiting men. *Testudo*s were quickly formed, but not before a number of casualties were inflicted. While protected for the moment, the 30th could not stand there for any real length of time before their arms gave out and their shields dropped.

"They need to pull back. They've botched it sure enough. Now they just need to cut their losses," Varus, my Hastatus Posterior, said glumly, and I could only agree.

A few moments later, the *cornu* sounded the withdrawal. The 30th began moving backwards, staying in *testudo* until they were out of missile range, their retreat marked by the jeers and insults of the Pompeians lining the wall. Their shame was compounded by the fact that they left those men who managed to push their way into the breach to be taken prisoner.

"They're dead men," Metellus spat. "After what we did to those prisoners the other day, there's no way that whoever is commanding the garrison won't exact revenge."

Again, I agreed with Metellus. Happily, we were both wrong. For reasons we did not understand at first, the men of the 30th were not executed. It was only the next day when a deputation of the townspeople managed to sneak through the breach to approach our lines, asking to see Caesar, that we learned the reason. They were brought into his presence, and it was then that it was learned that the citizens of the town had intervened with the garrison commander on behalf of the captured men. They hoped that it would prove to Caesar that they were acting in good faith by coming to him to offer their conditional surrender. I do not know what terms they asked for, but whatever they were, Caesar deemed them unacceptable, sending them back to the town still under siege.

~ ~ ~ ~

It was about this same time that Gnaeus, realizing he must take some sort of action, moved across the river to build a redoubt closer to the town from which he could launch sorties against us, though with little success. His forces did briefly drive off one of our cavalry outposts before our horsemen rallied, in turn inflicting heavy loss on the Pompeians. Two days after the attempt by the 30th, the garrison commander Munacius rounded up a large number of civilians from the town, then taking them onto the parapet in plain view, executed them in the most barbaric fashion imaginable. Babies were tossed into the air to be caught on the points of spears, while women were defiled, then butchered while their husbands watched, all while we stood by helplessly. Supposedly, this act was perpetrated because of the intervention of the civilians with the garrison concerning our captured men and for the attempt by the town elders to surrender. Once killed, the bodies were pitched over the wall to lie in a heap in plain view of the army. We could not retrieve them to dispose of the corpses properly because they were within missile range of the defenders. What we learned later was that this was a diversion, albeit a bloody one, to allow a messenger from Gnaeus to slip into the town while our attention was occupied elsewhere. No more than one watch after the massacre, the army of Gnaeus left their camp to array for battle, while the gates of the town were flung open as the garrison made a desperate attempt to break through to link up with their comrades. Several sections of Pompeians carried hurdles to throw into our ditch, while other sections carried the long poles with hooks to pull down our palisade. Even more men carried with them bags of silver and other valuables, the idea being that they would strew these about once they had penetrated our lines, counting on the greed of the men to worry more about grabbing the loot than stopping the two Pompeian forces from linking up. As a plan, it was not bad, yet as is so often the case, the gods laugh at our attempts to arrange our affairs, especially in matters as naturally chaotic as war. This time, it was the refusal of Gnaeus' army to budge from their spot in front of their camp. In order for the plan to work, Gnaeus would have had to attack at the same time as Munacius' force launched their assault, yet for some reason, despite the fact that this was Gnaeus' idea and plan to begin with, he did nothing but stand there, watching as the garrison tried to fight their way through our lines. Naturally, they were unsuccessful, being forced to retire back into the town, though not without leaving a fair number of bodies behind, along with prisoners who were promptly executed in retaliation for what had happened to the townspeople. Our casualties were minimal, while the biggest change to the situation came about because Munacius now realized that he had been forsaken by Gnaeus, who in turn had resigned himself to the town being lost. The men of the garrison continued to fight, succeeding in burning one of the towers, but it was clearly a lost cause.

~ ~ ~ ~

The night after this action, Diocles came into my private quarters to inform me that one of the slaves belonging to Caesar's physician was waiting to speak to me. Knowing that this undoubtedly concerned Didius, I followed him to the hospital tent. No matter how many times I entered this tent my stomach always rebelled at the smells, suppressing a shiver at the sounds of suffering men, some of them mine. I followed the slave to where the physician was standing, a Greek with a suitably haughty demeanor, by virtue of his status and relationship to Caesar no doubt.

Still, his face was sympathetic as I approached. "Your man, Didius isn't it?" he began in heavily accented Latin, "He is faring poorly, very poorly indeed. His wound has become corrupt, and the rot has spread throughout his leg. Unless I remove it immediately, he will die, but he refuses to let me touch him until he has talked to you."

While the news was not completely unexpected, it was nonetheless disheartening to hear, and I asked, "How much of the leg do you have to take?"

"All of it," he said firmly. "Almost to his hip joint. In fact, if we go even another two watches without removing it, the corruption will spread into his internal organs and then he will die. Primus Pilus," he put his hand on my shoulder as he looked up into my eyes. "His life is measured in thirds of a watch right now, so say whatever you have to in order to convince him that this is his only course."

Sighing, I nodded that I understood, then stepped through the leather curtain that separated the most serious cases from the rest of the men who were recovering. We referred to that room as "Charon's Boat," the vessel that ferries us all across Styx to what lies beyond, and not many men who were carried into that room emerged alive. I bit back a curse, resolving to talk to the physician or the orderly to find out exactly who had moved Didius into Charon's Boat, knowing that this act alone was as likely to kill a man from despair at the idea that the medical staff had given up on him. It took a moment for my eyes to adjust to the gloom, then to find Didius, who was lying at the far end. It was quiet in here, most of the men being unconscious or so heavily drugged with poppy syrup to ease their suffering that they were already dead for all intents and purposes. As I got closer, the smell of his rotting flesh assaulted my nostrils, requiring a substantial effort of will to keep me from wrinkling my nose or making a face.

He was awake, his eyes wide and bright with fever, and not a little fear. "*Salve,* Primus Pilus," he said hoarsely. "Forgive me for not coming to *intente.*"

"You're on report for that," I said with a smile, pulling up a stool to sit next to his cot.

His breathing was shallow and raspy, and in truth, I was amazed that he was alive at all. His lower leg to just above the knee was black, oozing pus that was so dark green that it was almost brown, and I could clearly see the livid red streaks on his upper thigh that marked the fingers of rot steadily marching through his body, laying waste just as thoroughly and mercilessly as we had in Gaul.

Clearing my throat, I began. "Didius, I've spoken to the physician. The only way you're going to survive is if you allow him to take your leg, and to do it now."

"Noooo." His head thrashed back and forth, his tone so pitiful and wracked with fear that I found it impossible to remember that for many years Didius and I had been bitter enemies.

Putting my hand on his arm, I looked him in the eye, saying firmly, "Yes. This is what must be done, Didius, or you will die."

His mouth twisted bitterly, then he gave a weak bark that I knew passed for his laugh. "What does it matter if I die now? If he takes my leg, I'm out of the Legion and will have to live by the charity of others. I'll be dead in a couple months in that case, so what does it matter if it's now?"

I listened to him, not sure what to say. While Didius was right in that he would not be allowed to remain in the Legions, and that he had not finished his enlistment so therefore was not technically entitled to the pension and land that was due all of us, Didius had been marching as long as I had. He had profited from all the years in Gaul, Britannia, Greece, and Africa just as I had, not to mention the bounty that Caesar had paid out at his triumphs. It was inconceivable to me that he was destitute, and I said as much.

For a long moment, he said nothing, his expression one that I could not immediately decipher. When he spoke, I realized that he was embarrassed. "I . . . I lost most everything that I was paid over the years." He darted a look at me, then his eyes shifted away. "The dice haven't rolled my way lately. Fortuna's turned her back on me, that's for sure." He waved his hand in disgust at his rotting leg. "If this isn't proof of that, I don't know what is. Just a few weeks short of our enlistment ending, and this happens."

I sat there completely mystified. Here Didius was telling me that he had lost most of his fortune gambling, and that did not make sense. "Didius, that can't be true." I shook my head. "I can't count all the times that you told all of us who would listen about how much you had won, either at dice or tables, or whatever."

"Primus Pilus, you haven't spent much time at our fire in a long time," he said quietly. "That was certainly true at one time, but that hasn't been the case for a while now."

"What changed?" I asked, genuinely puzzled.

My question elicited a rueful laugh. "I stopped cheating." I stared at him, sure that I had misheard, but he only shrugged, looking away as he continued talking. "I just got tired of looking over my shoulder all the time. When you're gulling men, you have to be alert constantly and careful to hide your tracks. It wears a man down after a while, and I just got tired of it. So," he looked up at me, "I decided to go straight. Turns out that I was a much better cheater than I am an honest gambler."

I could not help laughing. For a moment, he scowled at me, then gave a weak chuckle. I put my hand on his shoulder then said quietly, "Didius, you don't have to worry. I'll talk with Caesar and make sure that you get your full pension, and I'll contribute enough to make sure that you'll never go hungry or want for a roof over your head. But," I pointed at him to emphasize my point, "you have to swear on Jupiter's Stone that you'll quit gambling."

Tears welled in his eyes, causing him to blink rapidly, but I pretended that I did not notice, and his voice was hoarser than before as he said, "I swear it, Primus Pilus." He reached his hand out, so I grasped his forearm, neither of us saying anything for a moment, then he let out a rasping breath and said, "Well, Primus Pilus, tell that Greek bloodsucker to get in here and do what he has to do. Might as well get it over with."

I stood and wished Didius luck, then went to find the physician, relaying Didius' permission for the amputation to proceed. If he was surprised, he did not show it, instead turning to one of the orderlies, telling him to make the necessary preparations.

"How long before he can have visitors again?" I asked, and he considered.

"Provided he survives, he should be able to see visitors in three or four days, though I don't know what frame of mind he will be in then."

I nodded that I understood, thanked the doctor while handing him a bag of coin over and above what I had already paid him and returned to my tent, shaking my head. Didius had gone straight, I mused as I walked down the street towards the Legion area. Maybe there was hope for all of us.

~ ~ ~ ~

The amputation went smoothly, or as smoothly as such an operation can go, I suppose, because Didius survived. He only had a few inches of stump left, and he was still very sick for longer than the doctor had foreseen, but the immediate danger was over. He would remain in the hospital tent for the next several weeks, as life in the camp went on as normal. About a week after the garrison attempted its breakout, a scroll was launched towards our lines from the town walls. When it was retrieved, it was from Munacius, offering his services to Caesar along with the surrender of the town. Caesar mulled this over for a day before accepting, so the town of Ategua became ours, where we hailed Caesar as Imperator once more.

~ ~ ~ ~

Gnaeus, having lost Ategua, began to withdraw southeast towards Ucubi in order to shorten his line of supply, which we had been disrupting with some success, while securing the town itself. Ucubi was south of the Salsum River, the walls of the town about three miles from the riverbank, so Gnaeus had his men construct an earthworks between the town and river in order to stop us from enveloping Ucubi the same way we had Ategua. We followed shortly thereafter, arriving on the northern bank of the river, making camp directly across from the Pompeian earthworks. Once camp was constructed, Caesar put us to work pushing across the river, building a series of redoubts that protected the riverbank while allowing passage back and forth across the river, which was shallow and had a rock bottom. As we worked, Gnaeus seemed more concerned with exacting reprisals against those he suspected of having Caesarian sympathies among the townspeople. Encouraging the citizens to inform on each other, he executed some 74 citizens who were identified by their neighbors as being aligned with us. What Gnaeus did at Ucubi was nothing new. In fact, one of the most powerful weapons we had were the actions of Gnaeus Pompey and his generals towards the local Roman citizens, who the Pompeians seemed intent on alienating and brutalizing, just as Scipio had in Africa. Not just the civilians bore the brunt of what I have to believe were their frustrations at being constantly defeated by Caesar. We were accepting deserters into our ranks in ever-growing numbers, and even taking into account the typical amount of exaggeration that a deserter will voice about their horrible treatment at the hands of their officers, conditions in the Pompeian army had to have been grim. I believe that the state of his army forced Gnaeus to pull up stakes yet again, continuing what had become a retreat, just about a week after we encamped on the river's opposite bank. This time, Gnaeus continued his easterly track, though moving further north to another fortress town called Soricaria, which was located farther down the river from Ucubi, but on the northern bank instead of the southern. This proved to be yet another mistake, because Gnaeus had ordered that the supplies kept at Ucubi be transferred to a fort about six miles almost directly south of Soricaria. I can only assume his reasoning was that he believed Caesar would stay on the northern side of the river to concentrate his forces on the Pompeian army at Soricaria, but as usual, young Gnaeus outthought himself. Perhaps he did not believe that Caesar would learn that his supply base was being moved to this fort, called "Aspavia" for the small village located there. Yet I find that hard to credit, given that it had to have been clear in the preceding months that Caesar knew a great deal of young Pompey's movements and plans, which he consistently thwarted. Now, instead of following the Pompeian army, we struck south to head towards the fort. For once, Gnaeus acted quickly, no doubt spurred on by the knowledge of the disaster that would befall his army if we captured his supply base. His hold on his army was now tenuous, as he was forced to resort to blatant lies, going so far as to take slaves, dressing them up in the uniforms of some of our dead to parade them in front of his men, claiming that they were deserters. Daily deputations were coming to Caesar from towns and cities, both in the region and in other parts of Hispania, claiming their loyalty to him. We learned from them that Gnaeus was sending letters to these locations where he claimed that, in fact, Caesar's army was trying to avoid battle and not the other way around. One of the men belonging to a deputation from one of the towns even brought the letter that Gnaeus had sent to their town, which Caesar read aloud to us at our morning briefing. By the time he was finished, most of us were doubled up with laughter, tears streaming from our eyes as we listened to the fantastic claims that Gnaeus was making. His army, according to him, was only growing restive because they so longed to lay into us, while we were cowering like dogs because Caesar's army was now full of raw troops. Gnaeus was claiming that the bulk of the army consisting of us Spaniards had demanded that our enlistments be ended and that we had returned to our nearby homes, leaving Caesar with several Legions worth of raw *tiros* that he had basically pressed into service against their will. The fact that this was indeed the exact thing that Gnaeus was doing made his claims even more outrageous, further proof just how far above his head command of an army actually was. The only thing that Gnaeus had been close to correct about was that the 10th's enlistment could now be counted in weeks, it being late March by this time, but nobody had gone home. Now Gnaeus was forced to confront this army of "raw" troops because he had effectively allowed Caesar and the army to get behind him, again.

~ ~ ~ ~

As Diocles reads my words back to me, I realize that I may be a little harsh concerning Gnaeus and his abilities. He was extremely young, and it had to have been a difficult proposition for someone of his youth to control not only his army, but his generals. All of them were old enough to be his father by a number of years, and all vastly more experienced than he was, particularly Labienus. The only thing that Gnaeus had going for him was his name, but because of his harsh treatment of the locals and the men of his army, the luster of the name was rapidly waning. Still, he chose to continue the struggle. Young he may have been, but he was legally an adult and certainly was smart enough to understand all of the ramifications of his actions. His army seemed willing enough to obey his commands when they moved to intercept us before we could reduce Aspavia, but still Gnaeus would not meet us in open battle, choosing instead to try fortifying a rocky knoll a short distance from the fort that would allow his men to fall on our rear when we besieged the town. Seeing the strategic value, Caesar gave the order for the 10th, the 7th, and the 5th to move from our place in the marching column, drop our packs, pull the covers off our shields, then move directly into battle, the objective keeping Gnaeus from occupying the knoll while taking it for ourselves. We formed up quickly and smoothly, in an *acies triplex* with the 10th on the right, the 5th in the center and the 7th on the left, then began the advance towards the knoll. Gnaeus, instead of detaching part of his army to move ahead of the main body as we had, was trying to maneuver his whole army to face our three Legions and beat us to the knoll. The combination of the sheer size of his army, along with the fact that most of them were raw *tirones* meant that the maneuver was mass confusion as conflicting orders were given to different parts of the army, causing Legions to march into each other, becoming hopelessly entangled. It was comical to watch, while we could clearly hear the cursing and frantic orders of the Centurions as the officers tried to restore order. In contrast, we were marching smoothly and quickly towards the knoll, as finally Gnaeus returned to his senses, the Pompeian *cornu* sounding the call that sent just three Legions from his army to meet us and try to take the knoll for themselves. As we closed, I strained my eyes, trying to identify the Legions opposing us, as the one thing that I, and I am sure the other Primi Pili, were worried about was if any or all of those Legions were our former comrades of the 8th, 9th, or 13th. If they were the ones facing us, I could not honestly say what my men would do. I remember thinking that if I was Gnaeus, I would have sent those Legions to take the knoll; almost as quickly I realized that he had to have the same fears that my counterparts and I did. Just as there was no way of telling what our men would do, Gnaeus had even less of a history with our former comrades to know whether they would fight us or not. In any event, it did not make any difference, as two of the Legions were made of raw *tiros*, the third being a native levy, none of them being the 1st, 4th, or the other part of the 6th. Their youth and inexperience was clear to see as their Centurions and Optios tried with only partial success to get them to maintain proper spacing as they approached the knoll. We were closing from opposite sides, but despite our superior speed of movement, the Pompeians had the advantage of being much closer to the knoll, so the Pompeians reached it first.

"All right, boys," I called out. "Looks like those kids over there want to make us work for our pay today. Let's push those bastards off that hill!"

The men roared their agreement. Shortly before we reached the lower slope of the knoll, I looked over to the center to see Primus Pilus Battus of the 5th signal the halt to allow us to dress our lines and catch our breath before we began the assault. The formation stopped as one man, the next few moments spent with the Centurions and Optios inspecting their Centuries, ensuring that the men were properly spaced. I walked quickly along the front, using the trick of looking diagonally across each Century to see if I could see the man on the other side of the man closest to me, grunting my approval when I could not see them. It was no surprise, but it was still gratifying to see men continuing to act as true professionals, despite being so close to the end of their time in the army. I moved to my spot at the far right corner of the first line, signaling to the center that all was ready on our side. A moment later, the *cornu* sounded the advance, the first two lines beginning their move forward.

~ ~ ~ ~

As a battle, it was not much to write about. The youngsters of Pompey's army tried to put up a fight, but they were too disorganized from the very beginning to be effective, so it did not take long for what little cohesion they had achieved to break down completely. As is always the case, almost all of the casualties we inflicted came when they broke and turned to run, our men hot on their heels, cutting them down before they went more than a few paces. The opposite slope of the knoll was littered with Pompeian bodies, while it took a few moments for the men to stop their pursuit and return to the knoll to begin fortifying it. There was a moment when we were vulnerable; if it had been Caesar leading the opposition instead of Gnaeus, we could very easily have seen the tables turned on us and been in real trouble. We built a redoubt on the knoll, finishing shortly before dark. The next morning, Gnaeus tried to take it with a force of cavalry, using a Legion in support, but we easily repulsed them while inflicting heavy losses. We were whittling the Pompeians down with every engagement, not just by inflicting casualties on them, but by the resulting desertions that inevitably happened after each defeat. Later in the day of the Pompeians' second attempt to take the knoll, a deserter from Gnaeus told Caesar that all of the members of the equestrian class who aligned themselves with the Pompeian cause were planning to desert *en masse,* then were betrayed by one of their slaves, Gnaeus putting them all in chains. After losing the knoll, and in the face of mounting losses and desertions, Gnaeus evidently decided that it was wiser to preserve his army than to lose even more men fighting for Aspavia. In order to do that, he broke his camp in the night then began marching again, this time towards the southwest. We did not follow immediately, as Caesar deemed it prudent to secure the surrender of Aspavia, which did not take long, the garrison commander having the same reaction as Munacius back at Ategua at being abandoned by his general. Once the fortress was secured, we marched off in pursuit of Gnaeus, who appeared to be heading for another large town called Urso, which was a good joke to us, because it had been one of the elders of Urso who brought us the letter which caused us such amusement. Gnaeus was in for a surprise when he got there, or so we thought anyway, but what happened just shows the lengths people will go to in order to appease a man who is marching at the head of an army.

~ ~ ~ ~

As Gnaeus marched, his army either took or destroyed anything of value in the way of food and supplies, including setting small farms and villages to the torch, making it easy to follow their progress by the lines of smoke rising in the air. When Gnaeus reached Urso, the citizens welcomed him, despite the oaths of their elders to Caesar to be loyal to our general. I understand why the citizens of Urso flipped back and forth so; it's hard to say "no" to a man with a sword in his hand. Nonetheless, it rankled. Gnaeus immediately put his army to work, using the same tactic of taking anything that might be of value to us, stripping the countryside of all usable timber. About six miles east of Urso was another fortress called Munda, situated on the highest of a series of hills that overlooked the plain between the town and fort. Gnaeus built his camp at the foot of the hill on which the fort sat, on the other side of a small stream that bisected the plain. We were approaching from the east, making camp for the night just a few miles away from the plain. The next morning, on the 17th of March, we were about to break camp and move to a better position, when the scouts assigned to watch the Pompeians came galloping in to inform Caesar that finally it appeared that Gnaeus was ready to risk all on one throw of the dice and do battle. He was forming up his army on the plain outside of his camp, so Caesar decided that it was time to end things with Gnaeus once and for all. The red standard was raised outside the *Praetorium*, followed by the *bucina* calls summoning the Centurions. Knowing that something was going on, but not knowing what, I passed the order for the men to stop breaking down their tents to don their armor and weapons while I went to the *Praetorium*.

"Pompey is offering battle, and I believe that this time he means to fight," Caesar announced as soon as we had all gathered in the forum.

He was standing on a makeshift rostrum, having already donned his scarlet cape, a sure sign that he planned on accepting the challenge. Caesar went on to give us our order of battle, putting us on the right, with the 5th on the left, placing the *tirones* of the 3rd next to them. Next to us was the 7th, with the men of the 6th occupying the center, along with the 21st and 30th. There was really nothing much for Caesar to say; we all knew what the stakes were, and what needed to be done, so we hurried away to prepare our men for what lay ahead.

~ ~ ~ ~

With an army as veteran as ours, it did not take long for us to shake ourselves out into the three-line formation in front of our camp. Across the plain, the ranks of Pompey's troops were just dark lines at the top of the hill on which the enemy camp was built. This hill was part of a small group of hills, the largest on which Munda was built. Once the men were in their spots and settled down, there were a few moments of delay while we waited for Caesar to make his appearance at the head of the army to give his speech. I took the opportunity to speak to the men, something that I did not normally do, but I had the feeling that we were at the true and final ending of what had become a four-year struggle, and it was happening literally days before the enlistments of the men of the 10th were set to expire.

"I truly believe that this is our last battle," I said to the assembled men, and I could see that while there were some who looked hopeful, just as many had an expression of disbelief and doubt at my words. Ignoring these men, I continued, "Our time together is almost up and it's been a long, hard and bloody road that we've traveled. Look to your right, and to your left." I waited as the men did so before speaking again. "Those faces you gaze at are more familiar to you than even your most loved members of your families. Some of you don't even remember what your mothers and fathers look like. I know this is true because I've heard more than one of you say as much around the fires. But for every face that you see, for every man that's here, we can all think of men who are missing, and there are almost two of the missing for every man that's standing here today." I paused as I felt a lump forming in my throat, and I could see that most of the men were similarly affected, so I knew that I had to finish quickly before I unmanned myself in front of them. "Fight for them today, just as you fight for the man who is standing beside you. Remember them," I finished, then quickly turned about to face to the front so that the men could not see the tears forming in my eyes.

The silence was thick in the air for a moment before someone started beating his javelin against his shield. In a couple of heartbeats, the rest of the men joined in, destroying the silence with the sound of a few thousand men honoring the dead in their own way. Caesar appeared at the head of the army riding Toes, his cloak billowing behind him as he trotted along the front of the army so that the men could see their general. A rolling cheer followed his progress as he started at the opposite end from where we were standing, then headed towards us. The men were still beating against their shields when Caesar drew near, whereupon they began shouting his name, adding to the din. He pulled Toes up in front of us, then sat there looking out over the men, his face set in what I recognized as his command face; regal, with a touch of arrogant contempt for the enemy. The men, even after all that had gone on between them and Caesar, still loved him, in much the same way a boy in his teen years can simultaneously hate and love his father. They had known nothing but victory with Caesar, and he had made every one of us richer than we had ever dreamed, even if men like Didius had pissed most of their fortunes away. More importantly at that moment though, was the fact that we had always won under his command, and we held no thought that this day would be any different. He let the men demonstrate their affection for several moments before he lifted his hand for silence, though it took a bit longer than normal for the men to fall quiet, causing some of the Centurions to lash out with their *vitus*.

Once they were quiet, he began speaking. "Comrades, today is the day for which we have been striving for so long now. We can end this madness today with one more effort. Can I count on the men of the 10th?"

The men roared their promise to give our general their all. He raised his hand again, then smiled down at us, the radiance of it reminding me why he had the reputation with women that he did.

"I knew that I could."

He turned his attention to me, our eyes meeting as he favored me with a nod of his head, then said loudly so that all the men of the leading Centuries could hear. "Here we are, Primus Pilus Pullus, together again. I remember the day I decorated you for the first time some 16 years ago. I told you then that I expected great things from you, and you haven't disappointed me. Will you give me great deeds again today, my giant friend?"

Knowing that his words were for the men as much as they were for me, I replied in a tone that matched his. "Yes, Caesar, you can count on me to do whatever is necessary to bring you victory." I theatrically drew my Gallic blade, raising it so that everyone could see it. "I will soak this blade in Pompeian blood or I will be carried off the field, I swear this on Mars and Bellona."

The men again roared their approval, as Caesar answered so that only I could hear, "Let's hope that it doesn't come to that, Pullus." He gave me a grin, started to turn away, then turned and asked me, "Have you ever thought of politics, Pullus?"

I could not suppress my surprise, nor my laugh as I replied, "Gods no. I'm sorry, Caesar, but I'm afraid that my stomach isn't strong enough."

He laughed giving a nod of his head as he galloped away to deliver his speech to the rest of the army. I sheathed my sword, shaking my head in amusement at the thought of me in a sparkling white toga, striking the orator's pose as I begged the masses for their vote. I would rather fall in the field than run for office, I remember thinking. I was about to get my wish.

~ ~ ~ ~

Once Caesar had finished his speech, the *cornu* sounded the call to advance, and we began moving towards the waiting Pompeians. When we reached the small stream, it became clear that while it was narrow, a strip of marshy ground on either side extended for several feet, which quickly bogged us down as we sank into the muck. Larger men like me were plunged mid-calf into the stinking mud as our cohesion quickly fell apart, men struggling to extricate themselves with each step. I anxiously watched the Pompeians, sure that they would see us in difficulty and try to gain an advantage by advancing on us while we were vulnerable, but they remained standing at the top of the hill. If the situation was reversed and it had been Caesar standing up there, I have no doubt that he would have seized the moment to strike.

Fortunately, Gnaeus was neither experienced nor bold enough, so we only had to contend with the sticky mud. It took several moments for us to negotiate the stream, then once on the other side, many of the men were covered in filth from where they had slipped and fallen. All of us were panting for breath from the exertion required to make it across. Caesar had moved from his accustomed spot in the center to ride at the head of the 10th, and seeing the condition of the men called a halt when we reached the bottom of the slope. There was a rumble of grumbling at the halt by some of the men, who had prepared themselves for the lung-bursting madness of the headlong assault uphill at that moment. They chafed at the delay, but Caesar had seen that we were already out of breath and wanted to give us a moment. There was an unexpected benefit as the Pompeians, mistaking our pause for fear of facing them, in turn moved a short distance down the hill towards us, closing the distance. Caesar snapped an order to his *cornicen* and the command to close ranks sounded, the men automatically tightening together, an order that I did not particularly agree with, because it was a blade that cut both ways. While it meant that our force was concentrated so the impact of our charge would be greater, it also meant that we would be more vulnerable to the javelins that the Pompeians were even now preparing to throw. We could hear the shouted commands of the Pompeian Centurions to ready the javelins, then saw their arms sweeping back. At the same time, Caesar's *cornicen* sounded the charge, immediately echoed by the other *cornu* up and down the line, followed by the verbal commands of our Centurions. I turned to the 10th as I drew my sword, bellowing out something, I do not remember what, then turned back to begin the charge up the hill.

~ ~ ~ ~

We had gone only a few steps when the Pompeians released their first volley of javelins, the air turning black with missiles streaking towards us.

"SHIELDS UP!"

Javelins slammed into our front line, in a flurry as thick as any I have ever seen and most certainly had been on the receiving end of, yet somehow I was not struck, despite not having a shield. Screams of pain added to the din of the assault, and I could tell by the sounds that we were hard hit by the volley. I turned to look, dismayed to see that my front line was absolutely savaged. It seemed that at least one out of every three men was either hit outright or had their shields pierced, and it was only the first volley. The Centurions and Optios were working feverishly to restore our cohesion and alignment, while in the instant of relative quiet before the next volley, I reached down to grab a shield from one of my men who no longer needed it. We continued up the slope, the second volley slamming into us, stripping more men of their shields and inflicting more casualties. However, instead of demoralizing the men, it made them even angrier, and a low growl began to issue from the ranks. We had waited to get closer before launching our own javelins, and when the *cornu* sounded the command, we unleashed our own volley, the shorter range meaning that our javelins did more damage, pinning men's shields together or even passing all the way through one man to lodge in another. Now it was the Pompeians' turn to cry out in pain and fear, eliciting a savage shout of delight from our ranks. The slope of the hill was steeper than it had looked from a distance, and I could feel my heart hammering against my ribs as I tried to catch my breath for the final charge. Not wanting to lose the momentum gained from our first volley, Caesar ordered the *cornicen* to sound the final assault rather than loose another, the men dropping their remaining javelin to draw their swords. As soon as all blades were out, we sprinted the remaining distance to where the Pompeians waited for us. I picked out a Centurion standing in his place then headed for him, and we slammed together with terrific force. My weight pushed him back, but only a step before he steadied himself as we bashed at each other with our shields, looking for an opening. All around us were the cracking sounds of shields splintering or metal ringing as blades struck, interspersed with the wet, sucking sound as someone found a fleshy target, followed by howls of pain or cries of despair when the wound was mortal. Men were cursing at each other as both sides poured out their rage and frustration, and at least this time we all understood each other. My opponent was highly skilled, so neither of us could gain an advantage. I was already winded from the sprint up the hill, and I fought back a sense of panic as our private battle wore on, feeling myself growing more and more tired with the strain. The Centurion that I was facing naturally was shorter than I was, but he was older, his skin as brown as old shoe leather and as tough from the looks of it. I remember that he had extremely thick eyebrows that pointed downwards above his nose, giving him the look of a man who was always angry, and now his eyebrows were almost meeting as he did his best to end my days. He was extremely quick, though I was just a shade faster, but I was wearing down while he seemed to be maintaining his strength. It was only one of those strokes of luck that gave me an opening, when the man next to him suddenly fell sideways, crashing into my opponent, causing him to stagger. For just an instant he had to move his shield arm away from his body in order to maintain his balance, but it was enough and I was not about to let the opportunity slip away. I thrust hard with my blade, held parallel to the ground, sweeping upwards to catch him just below the breastbone, the point punching through his mail. His breath whooshed out of his mouth, blasting me with the smell of vinegary wine and garlic, his eyes widening in shock as he gave me a look I had seen so many times before. He fell backwards as I recovered back to the first position, but before I could take advantage of the hole created, the man behind him stepped over his body and in perfect training ground fashion, lashed out at me with his own shield, sending a terrific shock up my arm. I grunted, not as much in pain but in surprise as I looked over the rim of my shield into the eyes of a youngster who managed to look terrified but determined at the same time.

"Not bad," I gasped. "But you should have followed up with a thrust."

Before he could say anything, I launched a flurry of attacks, my blade flashing as I probed his defenses while he desperately parried every one of my thrusts. Keeping him on the defensive, I did not give him a chance to try his own offensive move, then inevitably, he made a mistake as his arm started to weaken from the constant pressure I was applying. I could have killed him easily enough, but I was impressed by his determination, if not his technique, so instead of the point, I lashed out with the pommel of my sword, catching him flush on the nose, knocking him cold with a blow. He dropped to the ground as if all his bones had suddenly been removed, and I kicked his sword out of his hand in the event that he woke up. He was not going to have the women chasing after him anymore, not with his nose smashed flat, but he would be alive. I took a step back to catch my breath and to see how the rest of the men were faring. After a quick look to left and right, I let out a curse at what I saw; we were in serious trouble.

~ ~ ~ ~

The Pompeians may have been raw youngsters, but they were not giving ground, not an inch. They were standing toe to toe with the most veteran army in the history of Rome, giving as good as they got. I do not know what infused them with such a ferocious spirit to resist as vigorously as they did; perhaps it was the knowledge that this was the final battle and all would be decided, or that their backs were literally pressed against the walls of Munda. Whatever the case, we were not experiencing the kind of success that we had assumed would be easily achieved when we started up the slope. There was not much I could do at this point except try to set an example, so taking a couple of deep breaths, I blew the whistle for the third time to signal a relief change, then stepped back into the line myself. With our numbers so depleted, all of the Centurions had to make a decision about the best way to relieve their men. Some Centurions chose to have each man fight a little longer than he would have if we were up to full strength, thereby giving the relieved men more time to rest, while others chose to have their men fight for a shorter period of time but consequently giving each of them a shorter rest period. I chose to use both methods; in the beginning of the fight I let the men fight longer, then as time wore on, I shortened the fighting period. As Primus Pilus, I could have ordered the Centurions to adopt my method, but that was not my style of leadership, as I remembered how it felt to have every decision made for me by my ranking Centurion. Plunging back into the fighting, I took my frustration out on whatever Pompeian I could close with. Still, they refused to give ground. I was growing more and more tired, and so were the rest of the men. That is when it happened. I sensed more than saw that the numbers of my men around me were thinning. When I risked a glance to either side, my heart fell to my stomach. My men, the men of the 10th, the veterans most renowned in the armies of all of Rome, had begun to take that first, tentative step backwards, and if I did not join them, I was going to be quickly cut off and surrounded. I do not believe I ever cursed so bitterly and with such variety as I disengaged from the man I was facing, bashing him with my shield to knock him off of me before stepping backwards, taking care not to trip over the bodies of the men who had already fallen. By the time I had removed myself, the rest of the Cohort, along with the other Cohorts on the front line, had moved a few paces back down the hill to stand, panting for breath. The ground between the two forces was littered with shields pierced by javelins, fallen men, some dead, but most wounded, moaning for help or crawling back to their respective lines.

"What is the matter with you bastards?" I raged at the men, none of whom dared to look me in the eye, staring sullenly at the ground as their chests heaved. "They're children, for gods' sakes! You're letting yourselves be shamed by children!"

Nobody said a word, a good thing given my state of mind, as I might have run them through if they had tried to make excuses, I was so angry.

Fortunately, the Pompeians seemed almost in as much shock as I was, so did not press the advantage, contenting themselves to stand there hurling insults at us. The entire attack, at least on the right wing, had ground to a halt, while no amount of my scorn and threats could make the men move. That is when Caesar proved again why he is the greatest general in the history of Rome.

~ ~ ~ ~

There was a sudden commotion in the rear ranks of the Cohort, as I saw men moving aside to make way for someone moving up to the front. When I saw who it was, I could only stand and gape; it was Caesar, who had grabbed a shield from a man in the rear and was pushing his way to the front of the formation. Following behind him was his gaggle of staff officers, all of them looking panicked. Supposedly, it was from the danger posed to our general, though I suspect that a few of them had not been this close to where the real fighting took place in a long time, if ever.

Caesar was oblivious to the danger, and when he reached my side, he was visibly furious. "Pullus, what's happening here? Why have the men stopped advancing?"

I suddenly felt as if I were a *tiro* all over again, standing in front of Caesar stammering and shaking, not knowing what to say. In fact, I do not remember what came out of my mouth, and he did not appear to be listening anyway.

Instead, he ripped his helmet off, throwing it on the ground, then stepped far enough away from the front line so that he could be plainly seen by everyone. "Aren't you ashamed to let your general be beaten by boys?" he roared as he pointed up the hill.

None of us said anything, just remained standing there, panting for breath.

When he saw that his words were not having any effect, he turned to his aides, saying, "If we fail here, it will mean the end of my life and the ruin of your careers."

Then he turned and began walking up the hill, drawing his sword as he advanced. We stood there as if we were rooted to the spot, the shock of watching our general advance against the enemy alone turning us to stone. The Pompeians seemed to be in as much shock as we were, because all motion, all activity, all noise seemed to cease as every pair of eyes watched Caesar march up the hill. Finally, one of the Pompeian Centurions regained his senses, and I heard him give the command for his men to find some javelins, causing all of us within hearing to let out a gasp.

"He'll never survive," I heard one of the staff officers exclaim.

As the arms of the Pompeians who had found javelins swung back, I turned away, unable to watch my general's life end. I heard the whistling sound of the missiles, followed an instant later by the sound of them striking. I winced at the thudding sound of javelins striking the wood of his shield, but it took a moment for it to register that I had not heard the sound of iron striking flesh, nor any cry of pain. Still, I was reluctant to turn to see what had happened. When I did, I could not help gaping at the sight of Caesar standing there, his shield looking like a porcupine, the ground around him sprouting the still quivering shafts of javelins, while the man himself was clearly untouched.

"By all the gods, it's a miracle," someone shouted.

Miracle or not, none of us were willing to test the favor of the gods again, while Caesar's example served to move us to action when his words could not.

Turning back to us, the contempt on his face and in his voice was clear to all of us as he called out, "Well, what are you waiting for?"

~ ~ ~ ~

Shamed by our general, we resumed the attack, charging up the hill to smash into the Pompeians, our fury fueled by the laceration to our pride of seeing our general expose himself to such danger. We fought with renewed energy, and though they tried, the Pompeians could not stand up to our second onslaught. I lost sight of Caesar in the fighting, but I could hear him calling out to the men around him, as we quickly pushed a wedge into the Pompeian line. I cut down any man who tried to stand before me, in moments covered in enemy blood up to my elbow. I felt the fury building in me, reminding me of the first time it had happened so many years ago on that hill further north, and I welcomed the warming flush racing through me, feeling new energy that made me push even deeper into the midst of the enemy. I think that was my great mistake, the joy of battle clouding my senses to the point that I stopped being aware of the situation around me, so I did not see how far ahead of the rest of the men I was getting. Although we were now turning the tide of the battle, the Pompeians beginning to take the inexorable step backwards, they were not through fighting by any means, so a man my size, and a first-grade Centurion at that, made a target that was too much to resist. I suddenly became aware of enemy movement around both my sides. I then realized how far in front of the rest of the men that I was, but it was too late. I was surrounded by Pompeians, so that now I was not fighting for victory; I was fighting for my life. I heard the shouts of some of my men who saw me in difficulty, one of them shouting to me to hold on, that they were coming to my aid. A squat, ugly little man came lunging at me. As I whipped my shield around to deflect his thrust, another man who had worked his way to my left struck me hard in the side, forcing the breath from my lungs in an explosive gasp. The pain shot through my body like a bolt of lightning, but while his blow had broken some of the links of my mail, it had not penetrated. It was still a damaging blow, causing me to struggle to catch my breath, yet before I could recover even a tiny bit, a Legionary to my right saw his own opening. I sensed the blur as his blade flashed towards me, while I desperately whipped my own blade up in a sweeping arc, striking his just as it was about to pierce my side immediately below my ribcage, which would have disemboweled me. Instead, the blade deflected upwards. Although my counterstroke had robbed some of the force from the thrust, it still had enough power behind it to pierce my chest, just below the collarbone, the point driving at least two inches deep into my body. There is no way to describe the pain accurately, yet as bad as it was, the worst effect was that suddenly my arm all the way down to my hand lost all of its strength. I saw but did not feel my sword drop from my grasp. There was a roaring in my ears, yet even with all that noise, I heard the shouts of triumph from the Pompeians around me, though I was still not through fighting. I felt my legs start to shake as my upper body turned wet from the blood pouring from the wound, and I realized that I was going to die, that I was not going to achieve my goals, filling me with a despair I had never felt before. However, with it came a resolve that I would take as many of the enemy with me as possible, that I would die in a manner that men would be talking about around the fires for years to come. All I had was my shield, but in the hands of a Roman Legionary, a shield is just as much of an offensive weapon as a defensive one. Whipping it around, I twisted my wrist so that the shield was parallel to the ground. Because of my height, it was at a level so that when the metal edge struck the man who had stabbed me, it hit him just at the junction of his neck and shoulders. I had put all of my rapidly waning strength into the blow, and I was rewarded by the sight of his head spinning into the air as the stump of his neck spurted blood from his still beating heart, the body slowly toppling over to lie quivering on the ground. Before I brought my shield back to first position, the squat man lunged again, this time striking me low and hard, and as bad as the pain was from the first wound, it was nothing compared to the feeling of a red-hot poker being plunged deeply into my side. Now my legs did give way, as I staggered backwards, still weakly trying to defend myself by keeping my shield up, yet it had become too heavy for me to lift. As I fell backwards, I hit a man behind me, feeling his shield at my back, and I realized that the thrust that killed me would be from behind, the first and only time I would not have a wound in the front, making me want to weep. That is the last thing I remember, falling backwards against someone's shield with the darkness closing around me, the cries of triumph of the Pompeians ringing in my ears.

~ ~ ~ ~

My next memory is of opening my eyes to see the leather roof of a tent, the flickering light of an oil lamp making it seem as if the roof were dancing about. Within an eyeblink of regaining consciousness, an avalanche of pain emanating from my side and shoulder forced a gasp from my lips, my body spasming as if it had a mind of its own. Yet when I moved, it made the pain even worse and I passed out again. I do not know for how long this time. It was in this manner that I passed the next two or three days. I would regain consciousness for only brief moments before the all-powerful agony of my wounds rendered me senseless again. In those brief moments, I would hear snatches of conversation, and I thought I recognized the voice of Diocles, along with Scribonius, Balbus, and once I even thought I heard the voice of Vibius, yet I could not swear that it was he. During those short periods, a shadowy figure whose face I could never really make out would try to get me to sip some water or some concoction that tasted horribly bitter, which I fought, but thankfully was too weak to successfully ward off his ministrations. It was a world of shadows and smoke, where I would see my dead sister standing by my bedside, next to the one who still lived. Gisela came to visit, and we would talk and laugh as if she had never gone away. Once she even brought Vibi and my baby daughter to see me. I cannot lie, it was very pleasant and I remember thinking that if this was what it meant to be dead, it was not bad at all, particularly when compared to the wretched agony of those moments when I returned to this world. Slowly, the periods of time I remained conscious lengthened, but I was still too weak to talk so instead I listened and learned about my condition and what had happened at the battle. The first sign that I was regaining my strength was when I was able to turn my face to look at more than just the ceiling of the tent, though the effort left me with a pounding head and as exhausted as if I had just done a 30-mile forced march in full gear. That was how I learned that I was in my own tent, that I had indeed heard Diocles, who was sitting on a stool in the corner of the tent. I do not believe he ever left my side, as he was always there whenever I awoke. It was from the expression on his face, the exhaustion etching deep lines in his cheeks and the way his lips were pinched together, one of the surest signs that he was worried, that I determined just how grave my condition was. I finally was able to recognize the man who had been there to force water and medicine down my gullet, and more than Diocles' manner, his identity told me that I had one foot in Charon's Boat. It was one of Caesar's personal physicians, not his chief surgeon, but one of his top assistants; I do not remember his name. I suppose I was unconscious for so long that the two had become accustomed to speaking about me as if I could not hear, which most of the time I could not, yet I vividly remember the first exchange I overheard between them. They were speaking in Greek, but by this time, I had picked up enough to understand what was being said, though I still could not converse very well.

"Has enough time passed to tell whether my master will live or not?"

The physician's tone was not encouraging. Surprisingly, I was not particularly distraught by what he said, probably because of the dreams or visions I was having.

"The fact that he is still alive at all is a good sign, I suppose, but I honestly do not know why he is still breathing. In fact, I expect almost every breath he takes to be his last." He chuckled, but without much humor. "But I have been expecting that for almost a week now."

"But you said that since his bowel wasn't pierced, he had a good chance," Diocles protested.

I must say that news was a relief.

"No, I said that he had *a* chance," the physician corrected Diocles. "I never said it was a good chance. And just because neither his bowel nor his intestines were pierced, that does not mean that his wounds will not become corrupt. Indeed, I am worried about the wound to his chest more than to his side because the flesh around the wound is turning proud and the pus is no longer clear."

That explained why my shoulder and chest hurt relatively more than my side.

"I thought you got everything out of the wound. You said you were sure that you had gotten everything out of it."

"I did." The physician was beginning to sound irritated. "But that does not assure that the wound will not putrefy. Once I have done all that I can do, it is in the hands of the gods, and that is truly where the fate of your Primus Pilus lies. Do you know who his household gods are?"

Diocles assured him that he did.

"Then you should make offerings to them."

Now it was Diocles' turn to be indignant. "I have been, three times daily, and I've offered a white kid goat to the augurs when he recovers."

"Then you should sleep well, because you have done all that you can do."

"Don't I have a say in the matter?"

I did not recognize my own voice, which was little more than a rasping sound that could only charitably be called a whisper, the forming of words feeling foreign to my tongue, but the reaction of the two men was worth the effort. It almost made me weep to see the joy on Diocles' face as he knelt by my side, while even the physician looked pleased, impressed by his own skill, no doubt.

"Master, it's good to hear your voice!"

"It's good to be heard," I replied, but that was all I could muster as I felt my eyelids growing heavy, so I turned my head away and fell asleep.

~ ~ ~ ~

The wound in my shoulder festered, becoming corrupt, the smell so sickening that it made keeping down what little I could tolerate almost impossible. I was beginning to think that I would not survive after all, but then the physician attending me brought Caesar's chief physician along, and after a brief conversation, they talked to Diocles in low tones that I could not hear. I saw his expression change to one of disgust then he shook his head, but the physicians were insistent, so he left, clearly unhappy.

Only then did they turn to me, the man who had been treating me saying, "Primus Pilus, I think you know that you are in grave danger."

I did not answer, only nodding my head.

"The wound in your shoulder has become corrupted, and while it is draining almost faster than we can change the dressing, it is not improving and in fact is getting worse." He pointed to a series of red streaks radiating out across my chest and down my arm. "See those? That is a sign that the poison is moving through your system. Because of where the wound is located, cutting out the corruption is not an option. So," he glanced at his superior, who had remained silent, "we are going to use the maggot treatment. It is your only hope."

While I had suspected this was what he was going to bring up, it still made my stomach lurch. I had seen it used before, and while it was certainly effective, the men who had undergone the treatment had not recommended it. Diocles returned, his hands cupped together, his face wrinkled in revulsion and loathing at what he carried. It was not just the maggots themselves that I imagine he found so disgusting, it was how and where he found them. After a battle, in just a matter of three of four days, the air becomes black with flies busy laying their eggs in the rotting meat that is strewn about, so there is no shortage of maggots to be used. Nonetheless, plucking them from a rotting corpse is one of the more unpleasant tasks a man can undertake, and slave or not, I appreciated the fact that Diocles did so. He offered the physicians his harvest, and they peered into his hands, poking about before finally selecting three fat, wriggling specimens then bringing them to my bedside. Lifting the bandage, they placed the maggots in the wound, and the sensation of their movement in the hole in my flesh still ranks as one of the most unpleasant experiences of my life. Shortly after, I fell asleep again, my head filled with thoughts of worms eating my flesh.

~ ~ ~ ~

As disgusting and unpleasant as the experience of using the maggots may have been, it still proved to be effective. Barely two days later, there was a marked improvement in my condition as the red streaks subsided while the corrupted flesh was reduced, the maggots eating happily away.

The only problem was that the maggots became engorged on my rotten flesh so quickly that they had to be replaced every day, forcing Diocles to trudge out to the battlefield again and again, which he did without complaint. I finally improved to the point that I actually had an interest in what had taken place after I had fallen, so the physician finally relented, allowing some of the other Centurions to come visit, though they were ordered to keep their visits brief and no more than two at one time were allowed to see me. It was from them that I learned that our victory was total.

"Well, it's finally over," Scribonius told me as he sat next to my bed. Seeing my raised eyebrow, he gave a rueful laugh. "No, Titus, it's really true this time," he insisted. Continuing, he told me, "Gnaeus Pompey is dead; he was caught outside of Carteia and had his head lifted from his shoulders. His brother Sextus has disappeared, but he's just a whelp, so he won't be any trouble."

"Yet," I interrupted grimly.

My mental outlook was not the best at this point, I will be the first to admit. As much as I trusted Scribonius, knowing that he would not be telling me anything that he was not sure was true, this war had been going on for so long that I found it impossible to accept that it would ever be over.

Scribonius seemed about to argue, then simply shrugged. "That may be," he admitted. "But it won't be for some time; he's barely out of his teens, if he's that old." I was too tired to argue, and in my silence, Scribonius pushed on. "After you fell, the battle turned in our favor when the Pompeians finally broke. I don't know what you remember. They had started to fall back, but they were still fighting for every single inch of ground."

I nodded that I did indeed remember, the feeling of doubt and despair still very clear, the idea that we had finally met an enemy we could not defeat as fresh a wound in my mind as those of my body.

"Well, for some reason that nobody really seems to know, they suddenly turned tail and began running for the town." He shrugged. "You know what happens then. Still, a pretty good number of them actually made it into the town and made to put up a fight. Caesar put a stop to that pretty quickly, I can tell you."

"How?" I asked, only mildly interested.

I was finding that topics that had seemed of utmost importance to me just a few weeks before could now barely hold my attention. I remember wondering if this was a temporary condition, or if I had reached that point that many soldiers do, of complete apathy about one's situation, the clearest sign that it was time to get out of the army, before it was too late.

Scribonius grimaced, clearly uncomfortable with what he was about to describe. In a moment, I learned why. "To convince the garrison of his sincerity, he ordered us to build siegeworks."

"So?" I interrupted. "That's standard procedure. I don't understand why that would scare them off the walls."

"It wasn't the siegeworks themselves, it was what they were made of that convinced the Pompeians to surrender."

Now I was completely lost, and I said as much.

Taking a quick look around, as if hoping to catch someone eavesdropping, which would have been impossible since we were all alone in my tent, Scribonius continued. "We used the bodies of the dead Pompeians as breastworks. Every 50 feet we stuck the head of one of them on a spear, facing the walls, of course."

As hardened as I was at that point, I still had to suppress a shudder at the thought of what that must have looked like.

Seeing my reaction, Scribonius nodded. "Exactly the same reaction the Pompeians had. It didn't take them long to surrender after that."

"I can imagine," I agreed. I was struck by a thought. "And what of the other Pompeian generals? How many escaped this time?"

Now Scribonius' smile was unfeigned, though it bore more than a trace of malice. "Labienus is dead," he said with relish.

Forgetting how much it would hurt, I let out a whoop of delight, sending a stabbing pain through my body, but it was worth it. Of all the remaining Pompeians, Labienus was the man we hated the most, even more than Pompey's sons. Gnaeus' and Sextus' implacability towards Caesar we understood. Even if it had been indirectly, Caesar was the cause of the death of their father and the ruin of their own fortunes and future, but Labienus had been Caesar's most favored general in Gaul, and in our minds owed all that he was to Caesar. As we learned, Labienus did not see it that way, in fact viewing the situation in the exact opposite terms, that because of his brilliant generalship, Caesar had been the man to benefit more than himself. The fact that circumstances proved otherwise had not deterred him from being our most virulent foe. Indeed, perhaps that realization had fueled his hatred of Caesar and his cause even more.

"He was cut down outside the town, near the end of the battle as he tried to escape."

"I hope he suffered," I said fervently, and I meant it.

Moving on, Scribonius described Caesar's movements as he mopped up the last remnants of resistance, marching first to Corduba with most of the army, where he was faced by the 9th and 13th Legions. Although the 9th immediately threw in with Caesar, the 13th refused to return to the fold, so to speak, for which they paid a heavy price, the 13th being wiped out almost to a man, part of more than 22,000 more dead. Fortunately, these were the last major casualties of the civil war, as now Caesar was finishing his inspection of the remaining towns still in Pompeian hands.

Turning to other matters, Scribonius seemed to hesitate, and I struggled to sit upright despite the pain I still felt moving about, alert to the change in his demeanor.

Before he could begin, I said sharply, "What is it?"

Scribonius winced. "Can't you ever let a man work up to things in his own way?" he asked wryly.

"No, not when I've been lying here for weeks," I snapped, then instantly regretted my tone, but Scribonius and I had been friends too long for him to be ruffled by my bluster.

"The 10th has been discharged," he said, his tone as neutral as he could make it. I sat back, a flood of emotions running through me that I found hard to identify.

I cannot say that it was unexpected; we had been due for discharge some time, but I realized that the attitude of the men had infected me as well, with a deep-seated disbelief that the day would ever really come. Now it had, and I supposed that technically I was a civilian, as was Scribonius, and it was a very unsettling feeling.

My emotions must have been clear to Scribonius, who laughed. "Yes, it does feel strange, doesn't it?"

Turning my mind back to the men, I asked the question that had immediately forced its way to the front, and that was whether Caesar had honored his promises. For a moment, Scribonius did not answer, and my heart started thudding heavily in my chest. If Caesar had gone back on his word, for any reason, the implications were enormous and not just in the political sense, but personally as well. I had been Caesar's man through and through for half of my life. All that I had and all that I was I owed to him. My *dignitas*, such as it was, was as important to me as Caesar's was to himself, albeit on a much smaller scale. Still, it was the thing that I held most dear, so if Caesar had reneged on his agreement, my standing among the men, at least those who would elect to remain in the army, would be substantially damaged. Caesar would return to Rome, but I would be left behind to deal with the aftermath. All of these thoughts were racing through my mind in the instant it took Scribonius to answer, though the gods were only toying with me again.

"Caesar paid the men every sesterce he promised, along with the land he promised."

I made no attempt to hide my relief as I sank back against the pillows that had been arranged so that I could sit up.

I realized that I was shaking a bit from the tension. "Thank the gods for that at least," I said fervently, to which Scribonius nodded his agreement. "So what's happening now?" I asked.

"There's a new *dilectus* being held for all of the Spanish Legions. The 10th is being re-formed, with the men who are signing on for another enlistment being put into the first five Cohorts."

"How many have re-enlisted?" I asked.

"About 500 so far, but you know how it is. A lot of the men will try to be farmers for about a month or two, then realize that it's actually hard work, and they'll come running back."

I laughed, thinking of Crastinus, who had said essentially that very thing when he was recalled. Everything Scribonius had been relaying was standard practice, yet I felt a gnawing sense of doubt growing, which I found both disconcerting and puzzling, because I was not sure why I felt that way.

The source of the uncertainty came into my mind fully formed when I asked the next question, and I realized why I was feeling anxious. "So who's conducting the training while I'm recuperating?"

"Glaxus has been filling your role." Seeing my face, Scribonius added hastily, "But he and the men know that it's just temporary."

I grunted, not wanting to verbalize what I was thinking at that moment.

Moving on to the other topic that occupied my mind, I asked, "And who's been filling the empty slots in the Centurionate? I can't imagine that all the Centurions re-enlisted, so there has to be some scrambling going on right now."

Scribonius nodded, and there was something in the careful way he seemed to be forming his words that warned me that the surprises were not over yet.

"Actually, that's what I needed to tell you. Caesar is on his way here to make selections for the 10th since you're unable to do so."

"Who said I couldn't do it?" I was getting angry now, though I knew it was not fair to vent my spleen on Scribonius just he happened to be there. "How hard is it for me to review records and conduct interviews, even if it's from bed?"

Now Scribonius was looking distinctly uncomfortable, and he shrugged helplessly. "Titus, it certainly wasn't my decision."

"Then who sent for Caesar?" I demanded.

"I believe it was General Pollio."

I cursed bitterly, but I knew that there was nothing to be done for it now. "When is he going to be here?"

The only answer Scribonius could give was a shrug. "With Caesar, who knows? It could be next week, it could be tomorrow."

"That's a comfort," I grumbled.

As it turned out, it was four days. It was also the last time I saw Gaius Julius Caesar alive, though it was also the occasion for a first as well. Our last meeting would mark the moment when I first laid eyes on the young Octavian, who is known by a different name now.

~ ~ ~ ~

"Well, Pullus, is that any way to greet your general, lying in bed?"

The words and the man speaking them gave me such a fright that I tried to come to my feet, the sudden movement causing me to gasp in pain while making me dizzy.

Caesar's expression turned to one of alarm as he stepped forward quickly, putting his hand on my shoulder, pushing me back in bed. "By the gods, Pullus, I wasn't serious! Forgive me for giving you such a start."

"Of course, Caesar," I said, the sweat pouring down my face as I gritted my teeth to avoid showing how much pain I was in.

Even with my discomfort, I was more worried about Caesar's appearance than how I felt. He looked more haggard, more tired and careworn than I had ever seen him, even during the days of short rations in Gaul and Hispania. There were dark rings under his eyes, which looked like glittering pieces of ice. The skin on his cheekbones was pulled taut, while the lines around his mouth were crevices that seemed bottomless. Still, with all these physical signs, his manner was as energetic as ever, his voice still strong, though he was slightly hoarse. Once I settled back, Caesar signaled for a chair to be brought next to the bed. He sat down on it, regarding me for a moment with eyes that, as usual, missed nothing. Every time I was subjected to his scrutiny, I was sure that he could peer into the darkest recesses of my soul to see every secret that it held, even the resentment that I harbored towards him for some of the things he had done to the men of the 10th, the Legion I considered to be mine just as much, if not more, than his.

Finally, he spoke. "You gave us all quite a scare, Primus Pilus Pullus," he said this lightly, but I could tell that there was real concern there, and I was deeply touched. I bowed my head as I tried to compose myself before I spoke and Caesar, seeing my shame, continued speaking. "When I heard you had fallen, then was told how seriously you were wounded, I made several offerings for your complete and speedy recovery. I'm happy to see that the gods looked on not just my offerings, but those of all your friends and comrades with favor. Your death would have been a huge loss to Rome."

"Thank you, Caesar," my voice was husky with the emotion I felt and the strain of controlling myself. "I'm very thankful for your prayers and those of the men. I'm glad I could keep them from going to waste."

It was a feeble jest, but Caesar laughed heartily, as if I had said the cleverest thing in the world. "That makes two of us. You would be a hard man to replace, if not for your size alone." Turning serious, he continued, "And that's why I'm here. We have some decisions to make about the vacant spots in the Centurionate. I wish we could wait until you were fully mended, but unfortunately, we need to get the slots filled. I hope the work we need to do won't tax you too much."

I shook my head, seeking to reassure my general. "If you don't mind me doing it sitting or lying down, I can do whatever you need me to do, Caesar."

"It's your mind and experience that's needed here, Pullus. You know most of the men we'll be discussing more intimately than I do, so it doesn't matter whether you're standing up or lying down while we work." Standing up, Caesar finished with, "But I'll let you get some rest now, and we'll start in the morning. I have some other matters that must be attended to, and I'll have to leave for Rome in just a couple of days."

He turned to leave.

Without thinking, I blurted out, "It seems that I'm not the only one in need of rest, Caesar."

He looked back at me, giving me a smile that showed his fatigue more clearly than anything he could have said or done. "There's too much to do, Pullus. Once I've done all that needs to be done to put Rome to rights again, then I'll rest. But not before then."

And with that, he left me to continue his work.

~ ~ ~ ~

As promised, Caesar was ready to start work early the next morning, sending a litter to carry me to the *Praetorium*. When I saw the contraption, the thought of being carried through the camp on it so mortified me that I got to my feet, announcing that I would walk. The slaves given the task of carrying me to headquarters looked terrified, and I understood that in his usual thorough way, Caesar had given them explicit instructions that I was to be transported by this conveyance and not allowed to go under my own power. Caesar was not the type to threaten slaves with all sorts of dire punishment if they did not follow his instructions, but he did not have to resort to such measures to instill the belief that he would nail up anyone who did not follow them. In fact, there was a pile of bony hands in Gaul that bore mute testimony that showed their fear was not misplaced. Not wanting the thought of men nailed to crosses on my conscience, slaves or not, I relented, lowering myself into the litter while insisting that the curtains be drawn so that I would not be seen. This was a pathetic ploy on my part, given the damn thing was parked outside my tent in plain sight of the entire camp, but I had to do what I could to retain some sense of dignity. My largest concern was for the new *tiros*, who I had yet to lay eyes on and vice versa, since I did not want their first view of their Primus Pilus to be of me lounging about on a litter. It never occurred to me that none of the men, new or veteran, would view me as weak, all of them knowing how close I had come to death, along with my reputation in the army. Even with all that I had achieved, there was still a large streak of insecurity in my makeup, vestiges of that time when I was an oversized boy who crawled into his sister's bed for comfort during a storm. It is only now, here near the end of my days that I can even acknowledge that, when it really no longer matters. I arrived at the *Praetorium*, and here I flat-out refused to be carried into the headquarters building, insisting on walking in under my own power.

When I was announced into Caesar's office, he turned from where he had been poring over one of his endless scrolls with one of the scribes, his eyes narrowed at my now-gaunt frame moving under my own power. "I gave explicit instructions that you be carried here, Pullus," he snapped. "I hope for your sake, and the sake of those poor slaves outside, that you heeded my orders and didn't walk here from your tent."

Silently thanking the gods that I had read the situation correctly, I hastened to assure Caesar that the only steps I walked had been from the entrance to his office. Immediately mollified, he turned to point to a couch arranged with a number of pillows so that I could either sit or lie on it, ordering me to park myself on it, which I did without any protest. While I could now walk for short periods of time, the small distance between the entrance and Caesar's office had tired me out a bit, not much but enough to know that if I were to try standing for any length of time I would be faced with the prospect of keeling over at my general's feet. Settling myself on the couch, I chose for the time being to keep my feet on the floor; even being given leave by Caesar, I was still extremely reluctant to lounge about in front of my general. Caesar was finishing up what he was doing, which gave me the opportunity to examine the young man sitting quietly in the corner of the office. When I got a good look, my heart skipped a beat. I was looking at a young Caesar! He had the same brilliant blue eyes, the same strikingly handsome features, although as I examined him more closely, there was something almost feminine in his beauty that Caesar did not possess. I was struck by a wicked thought, that here was the kind of boy that men of a certain persuasion are very fond of, and I wondered if he would be receptive to their advances. I snuck a peek at Caesar, sure that he would be able to read my mind, and I was relieved to see that he was paying me no attention. Nonetheless, before he noticed me looking in his direction, I quickly looked away, returning my gaze on the young man. I got a second shock, because our eyes met, as he had obviously taken the opportunity to do his own examination of me when he thought I was not looking. I cannot help thinking now that the memory I carry with me today of the impression I came away with is colored by all that has transpired in the intervening time since that day. But where I was Caesar's man through and through from the first time we locked eyes those many years ago, I did not have the same feeling when I looked into the eyes of this young man, who I had deduced was the young Octavian. In fact, the more closely I looked, the more I realized that the similarities I had thought so striking on first glance were more superficial than real. Although he had grown his hair long to cover them, there was no disguising that his ears stuck out like jug handles. His chin was not quite as strongly formed as Caesar's, but the real difference was in the eyes. When you looked into the eyes of Gaius Julius Caesar, and he chose to reward you with the warmth of his gaze, there was no hint that it was forced, that there was anything that was not completely genuine in his affection and regard. With Octavian, there was a coldness behind the gaze, and I was struck by the thought that I had seen that type of look before, though it took a moment for me to put my finger on it. Then I remembered where I had seen that look, which I found very disquieting, because it was nothing human. Octavian's cool, unblinking stare reminded me of the cobras that the Ptolemies kept as pets as they sat coiled in the corner of the cages in which they were kept. I could only hope that my thoughts were not revealed on my face, though I have never been very good at that, but he did not seem to notice me recoil as he gave me a shy smile before looking away. The smile softened my heart quite a bit, because in that moment he looked like what he was, a teenage boy who was awestruck by his surroundings. However, as I was to learn, there was much about Octavian that was not what it seemed on the surface, and I realize now that he was anything but a star-struck boy. Fortunately, that lesson was down the road.

~ ~ ~ ~

Finally done with his other business, Caesar turned to me, ordering the slaves who hovered in the corners to move the table he had been working on next to my couch. "You don't mind if I stand while we work, do you, Primus Pilus?" Caesar asked me, as if I would even think to say that I did mind, but these little things that Caesar did that made him different from every other patrician I ever met. I shook my head, and satisfied, Caesar then turned to Octavian, beckoning him to stand beside Caesar. "Pullus, I'd like you to meet my niece Atia's boy, Gaius Octavius," Caesar announced.

Caesar's pride was obvious and to my eye, completely unfeigned, and I had enough experience with Caesar that I was sure I could tell if it was. I struggled to my feet to offer my hand, pleasantly surprised at the firmness of Octavian's grip, though the skin was soft and smooth, a sign that he had not been partaking of the military training that all fine young men are supposed to go through at his age.

"Young Master Octavius, it's an honor to meet you," I could not bring myself to call him "sir," so I decided that this was the least offensive alternative, but neither he nor Caesar seemed to notice or mind.

"No, Primus Pilus, the honor and pleasure is mine. You're a legend, and my uncle has spoken very highly of you."

Now, I am just as susceptible to flattery, perhaps even more so, than any man, and I felt my heart soften towards the boy, thinking that perhaps I had been harsh in my initial assessment.

"I was hoping that you'd be my guest at dinner tonight," Octavius continued. "I have so many questions about your experiences that it would take many, many thirds of a watch, but if I could have just a few of them tonight to at least ask the most pressing questions, I'd be eternally in your debt."

Oh, he was smooth, knowing all the right strings to pluck, and while I had warmed to the boy considerably, there was still something in me that caused me to hold back, though I still did not fully understand what it was.

"It would be my honor and my pleasure, young Master," I replied, then with those details seen to, Caesar indicated that I should resume my spot on the couch so we could begin our work.

~ ~ ~ ~

There were 35 slots in the Centurionate that needed to be filled in the 10th as it was brought back up to full strength, slightly more than half. In addition, we had to make decisions about how best to assign those Centurions who had decided to stay on for another enlistment. In the past, the usual custom was just to shift all the Centurions into the leading Cohorts until all the spots were filled, then bring in new Centurions, or men from other Legions who were looking to advance but could not in their existing Legion to fill out the rest. However, neither Caesar nor I were proponents of this method, no matter how entrenched in custom and tradition that it may have been. The problem, at least to our minds, was obvious. While the first four or five Cohorts would be led by experienced men, the rest of the Legion would be filled with green men at all levels. The more sensible approach would be to salt every Cohort with experienced Centurions, but there was a challenge with this approach, which was behind the reason why the system of promotion had been done in the manner it had been for all these years. With the old system, every remaining Centurion was almost guaranteed of a promotion, some of them jumping several grades at once. This enticement was responsible for the high retention rate of the Centurions compared to the rest of the men, but the rumors had already spread that Caesar would be doing things differently. As a result, several Centurions had come to me in the days before, seeking reassurance that if they chose to stay they would be rewarded with promotion, a promise that I could not give because I was not sure exactly what was going to happen. Caesar and I had enough discussions over the years that I had a feeling for his thoughts on how to handle this delicate matter, but since he had never given me any concrete plan before this, I was unwilling to stake my personal reputation on the outcome. Now, while we had 35 Centurions who had indicated they would stay, relatively few of them had signed their new enlistment oaths, choosing to wait to see how things turned out. It was a very tricky situation; while we had to do what was best for the Legion, we also had to keep the self-interest of the Centurions in mind, or we would lose the majority of the men who were staying on. Caesar decided that our first order of business was to arrange the disposition of the re-enlisting Centurions, before we began discussing candidates for the Centurionate. Next on the list were the Optios, who presented their own set of challenges, though not as pressing. As the scribes began laying out the scrolls containing the records of the Centurions, Caesar ordered some of the slaves to leave the room to fetch something. When they returned, they were carrying in a large board, with legs attached so that it stood almost like a wall. While I had seen Caesar use such a device to hang maps on, this board was different because it was painted with a series of columns and rows, each of which had markings heading each column. It took me a moment to recognize that the columns were the numbers of each Cohort, and the rows were for each Century. There were hooks attached to the board, at the junction point of every Century and Cohort. I was puzzling over this when another set of slaves walked in, each carrying a handful of tiles, which they set on the table. I looked at the tiles, and saw that they each had a hole in them. Finally, on every tile was written a name, the names of the thirty-five Centurions.

"I thought this might help make our task a little easier," Caesar explained. "I've always found that when I can see a problem arranged in a logical fashion, it helps me solve it more quickly."

I do not remember what I said, because I was still consumed with admiration at the genius of Caesar in thinking up such a contrivance. He had indeed made things much easier, but that only became apparent as we used his device, and once you saw it, it made perfect sense and you wondered why nobody had thought of this before. I suppose that is the sign of true genius, in solving a problem in the simplest manner possible, and in doing so making people wonder why nobody has come up with this solution earlier. The way it worked is that we would take the name of a Centurion, place his tile on the hook of the Cohort and Century that we thought would be the best fit for him and the Legion, then we would have an open discussion about our choice. General Pollio was invited to participate, which I did not mind, as well as some of the Tribunes, who were strictly enjoined from speaking. What we found is that rarely did a Centurion stay on the hook that he was initially given, as his relative strengths and weaknesses were discussed. It was in this manner that the day passed, although I found that I had to go from a sitting to a reclining position fairly quickly, and it became night, but Caesar showed no sign of stopping.

We had been taking only very short breaks to relieve ourselves, and it was during one of these breaks that Octavian approached me and whispered, "I'm sorry, Primus Pilus, but it looks as if our dinner will have to be postponed."

I laughed. "I would have warned you that you were being exceedingly optimistic about that," I agreed. "Once Caesar gets the bit in his teeth, there's no stopping him."

"So I'm learning." Octavian gave a rueful laugh of his own, then grimaced at the sight of Caesar waving us back to work. "But I'm learning a lot, and that's what's most important."

As we walked back to the board, Octavian, seeing that I was a bit wobbly, offered his arm. It was a sign of my fatigue that I took it without hesitation or complaint.

I thanked him, though I was also a bit surprised, not at the offer of help, but at what he had just said. "You plan on a career in the army?"

The doubt must have been evident in my voice because he looked up at me, and just for a moment I saw what I thought was a flash of anger.

Then it was gone almost more quickly than it had come, and he gave me a smile. "Not necessarily, Primus Pilus. Oh, I plan on doing my obligatory campaigns, but I don't believe that I'm cut out for a military career any more than you do." I could feel the flush rising up my neck as I began to stammer out some sort of protest, but he cut me off with a laugh and wave of his hand. "No, don't be embarrassed. You're absolutely right in your assessment. But I still find this all very fascinating, and I love to learn new things, no matter what the subject. Except Greek, perhaps." He made a face, and I saw the schoolboy emerge. This time I held my tongue, remembering how touchy young men are about their youth. "Still," he continued, "you never know when something like this will come in handy. Who knows, one day I may be in Uncle's position myself, and what I learned today will come in very handy indeed."

I was about to laugh at his hubris, but something stopped me, and now I am glad that it did. We had made it back to the board by this time, where there were just a couple of tiles left, but one in particular I had been surreptitiously shuffling back to the bottom of the stack, wanting to put off the decision.

At least, I thought I had been sly. "Pullus, it's time that you stop delaying the decision about where to put your friend Scribonius," Caesar said gently, proving once again that he did not miss a trick.

~ ~ ~ ~

I had been in an agony of indecision about Scribonius, who had told me some time earlier that he was planning on re-enlisting, no matter how things shook out. While I took that as a sign that he would accept whatever posting he was assigned, I still wanted to do my best for him. Since the rift between Vibius and me, Scribonius had become my closest friend, and he was one of only two of my original tentmates that was staying on. The other was Vellusius, who by his own admission would never be anything other than what he was, a Gregarius. Vibius had made his decision to leave the army the day he found out that Juno's husband had died, and as far as I knew, was already back home and married to her. Scribonius, on the other hand, I considered much smarter than I, and while he was not as good a fighter, he was an outstanding leader of men, and when all is said and done, that is probably the most important aspect of a Centurion's job. You can be the greatest swordsman in the army, or you can do vast sums in your head faster than the quickest clerk, but if men will not follow you willingly, into and through anything, then it is all for nothing. Perhaps most importantly to me, I trusted Scribonius with my life. So the question before me, while simple, was also damnably hard at the same time. Did I reward Scribonius by moving him into the First Cohort, and thereby into the first grade of Centurion, but in one of the lower Centuries, or did I keep him as Pilus Prior of the Second, where he had demonstrated that he was one of the best in the army at running a Cohort? While moving into the First was technically a promotion, the reality was far different. Being a Pilus Prior, even of a lower Cohort, gave a Centurion a certain autonomy that would be missing if they were commanding a Century in a higher ranked Cohort. Many times, operations, especially under Caesar, were of Cohort size, and that is one place where Scribonius had flourished, when he was in independent command, out on his own and away from my prying eyes. It was also a load off my mind knowing that I could depend on Scribonius to make the right decisions without running to me for help. For perhaps the hundredth time, I cursed myself for being too cowardly to discuss this with Scribonius before now, because I was afraid that he would give me an answer that I did not want to hear, since the truth was I was as close to decided as one could be to keep him where he was. I valued him too much as Pilus Prior for him to be Princeps Posterior, which was the post that was open in the First at that point, but I honestly did not know how he would respond. As I said, he had assured me that he would accept whatever posting he was given, yet I did not want him to resent me, and I also wanted him to know how much I valued his service and his friendship. Keeping him in the Pilus Prior slot, at least to my mind, was not exactly praise and reward. All these thoughts were going through my head as I fiddled with his tile, and I suddenly realized that Caesar, Pollio, and Octavian were all studying me. For the second time, I felt the heat rising to my face, Caesar's expression of amusement not helping any.

"It seems that you are on the horns of a dilemma, neh Pullus?" Caesar asked with barely suppressed enjoyment.

I swallowed my irritation at his seeming pleasure in my predicament, and nodded unhappily.

I started to explain my thinking, but he quickly waved me to silence. "I completely understand, Pullus, believe me, which is why I am so amused, I suppose. These are exactly the sorts of problems I've been wrestling with and I suppose that misery loves company. How do you show your regard for the service of a loyal subordinate when by rewarding them you put them in a position where they are in fact, less valuable to you? Have I described the essence of your problem?"

I had to suppress a wince as he spoke; when it was described so nakedly it certainly made it more unseemly, at least to my ears, but he had summed it up in just a few sentences, and I said as much.

Suddenly inspired, I asked him, "So what would you do in my place, Caesar?" There, I thought, see how you like it.

He did not bat an eye, nor did he hesitate, answering evenly, "Well, I think it's obvious, isn't it? You have to put him, or I suspect in this matter, keep him where he'll serve Rome the best, and I believe that's exactly where he is."

He looked me in the eyes, sending me a very clear but unspoken message. You can try to drop me in the *cac* all you want, but I will still come out smelling as if I had just come from the baths instead, his eyes told me as they danced with silent laughter.

"Do you agree with my assessment, Primus Pilus?" he asked with only slightly mocking deference.

Despite myself, I could not help but give a rueful smile as I acknowledged defeat. "Yes, Caesar. I agree."

With that settled, we moved on to the question of Optios, finishing the entire task shortly before dawn.

~ ~ ~ ~

With the question of who fit where on Caesar's great board, now came the hard part, which of course fell squarely on my shoulders, and that was telling the Centurions and Optios of their respective fates. Some of them would be ecstatic, some would be pleased, some would be indifferent, but it was the last category of men who would be unhappy that I was worried about the most. I do not know if it worked out that way by accident or not, but as I examined the list of names of the men who Caesar, Pollio, and I suspected would be the most disaffected by their posting, with not a little dismay I saw that many, if not most of them, were men who had not actually signed their re-enlistment papers yet. These were the men who had adopted a wait and see approach, which told me that there was a strong possibility that a fair number of them might opt for life on a farm rather than a posting that was not to their liking. Compounding the problem was that if a good number of the men actually did take the option to retire, that meant that we would have to look outside the Legion for eligible candidates for those spots, as we had already run through every possibility in the 10th to fill the empty spots. This was not all that unusual, but no Primus Pilus likes breaking in a Centurion from another Legion, for a variety of reasons. Every Legion is run a little differently, according to the tastes and whims of the Primus Pilus. I had a very specific way that I ran the 10th, and along with overseeing the training of the new *tirones*, I would have to make sure that the new Centurions were broken in as quickly as possible. However, if all of the men were from within the 10th to begin with, I would not have to worry about teaching them how I ran my Legion. If I had the added headache of worrying about Centurions who did not know how I ran things, my life would be that much harder. It was with this in mind that I went to the camp priests to offer up a white kid goat to be sacrificed to help ensure that this possibility did not come to pass. I am not particularly religious, but I figured at that point that it could not hurt.

After thinking about it, I decided that I would talk to the man I was most worried about first, and that was Scribonius. I was in my now-accustomed spot in bed, although I was sitting up with my feet on the floor when he was announced by Diocles, and he came in, helmet under his arm in the prescribed manner. Waving him to a seat at the table, I got up from the bed to sit next to him, pushing an amphora of wine in his direction.

He nodded his acceptance, then Diocles poured him a cup, of which he took a sip, his eyes narrowing in suspicion as he swallowed. "This is Falernian," he observed. "Which means that you're trying to soften me up for something. I bet I can guess what it is."

I bit back a curse; Scribonius had always been smarter than I was, and had seen right through my attempt to set a lighter atmosphere. "Fine," I snapped, angry at both him and myself. "Since you don't want to enjoy the wine, I'll come right out with it."

Even as I spoke, I could hear my inner voice screaming at me that I needed to curb my tongue and soften my tone. This was not starting out well at all.

I paused to collect myself, then plunged in. "Scribonius, I want you to know how much I value not just your service, but your friendship, which is why making this decision has been extremely hard."

Setting his cup down, he leaned back. "Go on," he said coolly, clearly determined not to make this easy on me.

"Ultimately, I have to do what's best for Rome, and for the Legion. I want you to know that it has nothing to do with your record of service, or my opinion of you . . ."

"By the gods, Titus. Are you trying to make this more painful for both of us?" Scribonius interrupted. Before I could say anything, he finished, "Just spit it out."

"I'm leaving you where you are," I blurted out.

For several heartbeats, he sat there with a blank look on his face, and I was struck by the idea that he did not take my meaning. "I mean, you're going to continue to be Pilus Prior of the Second."

Finally nodding, he did not speak, but reached for his wine cup, taking a deep swallow. As he lifted his cup to his mouth, I could see that his hands were shaking, and I was stricken with guilt, thinking that he was taking it even harder than I had thought he would. Then, he began making a choking sound, and now truly alarmed, I stood to pound him on the back, while signaling for Diocles to come offer aid. Before I could do anything however, his mouthful of wine went spewing across the table, as the choking sound changed into something completely different, though it took me a moment to realize. Scribonius was laughing, not just laughing, but guffawing harder than I ever remembered him doing before. Convinced now that he had gone completely insane, I looked to Diocles in alarm, who could only give a helpless shrug as we watched my best friend shaking and gasping for breath.

Finally, he gulped in enough air to speak. "That's the bad news? That I'm going to remain Pilus Prior?"

"Yes," I said cautiously, growing more confused by the moment. "I wanted to promote you to First Cohort like you deserve, but you're too valuable to the Legion where you are." Understanding was slowly dawning on me, and I asked, "You mean you're not upset?"

Scribonius looked at me in open astonishment, then threw his head back and laughed again. "By the gods, no. In fact, I was worried that you were going to do exactly that, promote me to the First. That would have been the bad news!"

I sat down heavily, pulling the wine to me and pouring my own cup full to the brim, thinking that I would never understand the way men's minds worked.

~ ~ ~ ~

I wish all of the interviews had as pleasant an outcome as the one with Scribonius, but that was not to be. Of the dozen Centurions who we suspected would be upset, our instincts were correct on every one of them, and out of the dozen, seven of them opted to retire to the land promised to them by Caesar rather than take what they saw as a demotion.

As one of them said angrily, "Why don't you just bust me back to the ranks and make me start over? That's practically what you're doing anyway!"

Then he stormed out of my office, trailing a string of oaths behind him. I had to go back to Caesar to report that we now had seven more spots to fill, a fact that made him none too happy, since it meant that he would have to postpone his departure until we found suitable replacements. Fortunately, he did not take his ire out on me, choosing some choice invective for the now-retiring seven men. Of course, while he was disappointed, he had also prepared for this eventuality, and I was presented with a list of candidates that Caesar's staff had prepared and told that interviews would begin the next morning. Some of the names I was familiar with, if only by reputation, and I had to admit, however grudgingly, that if all I had heard about these men were true, then Caesar had picked very well indeed. I decided that I would reserve judgment on that question until the next day.

~ ~ ~ ~

The candidates for the seven slots were all sitting or standing in the outer office of the *Praetorium* when I walked in. I had taken the litter but had stopped the slaves two streets away from the headquarters so I could be seen walking up. I was not willing to be seen in the litter by Centurions I did not know, whether it incurred Caesar's wrath or not, but he was busy inside and did not notice. There were 20 men waiting, and I nodded to them as I walked past to enter Caesar's office without being announced. Caesar and Pollio were standing in a corner, talking intensely in low voices, while Octavian sat in his accustomed spot, pretending not to be listening as carefully as he could get away with. I could see by Caesar's face that whatever Pollio was telling him was not welcome news, so I assumed it had to do with events in Rome, which were still unsettled as the city waited for Caesar's return. Once finished with their conversation, Caesar signaled for us to begin, then we called in the first candidate, a Centurion from the Sixth Cohort of the 15th as I recall. The day dragged on and on, but by nightfall we had talked to every man, and had made our final decisions. Thirteen men were disappointed, while we found the seven that we thought would best fit into the 10th Legion. It probably will not surprise you when I reveal that the identity of one of them was none other than my old tutor and brother-in-law Cyclops, who was going to become the Pilus Prior of the Eighth Cohort.

Since the business was concluded fairly early, Caesar turned to me and asked, "As this is my last night here, Pullus, I was wondering if you'd like to join Octavian and me for a light dinner tonight? It will be nothing special, soldier's fare, but I hope you would find the company an enticement."

Of course, I agreed, and the time was set for a third of a watch later.

~ ~ ~ ~

The dinner was as intimate as promised, with only Caesar, Octavian, and Pollio, and the fare was as described, though the quality of the bread and oil was of a much better grade, while there was more meat than was normal, which Caesar explained as we sat down. "I know that you're more partial to meat than most men, Pullus, so I took the liberty of having some prepared. Besides," he added. "You need to build your strength for the coming trial of getting the 10th trained up to standard."

I was touched, even though I knew that Caesar's motivation was not selfless or just for my benefit. The fact that he knew I liked meat more than most men was just another example of Caesar's difference; I could no more imagine a Labienus, or even Marcus Antonius paying attention to what a Centurion ate than I could see them sprouting wings and flying. Besides, he was absolutely correct, I would need every bit of my strength for the ordeal that lay ahead of me. Centurions are expected to lead from the front, in everything. While I would not go through the physical training, the thirds of a watch I would put in, expected to be everywhere at once, would tax my strength, even if I were fully recovered. As it was, I had progressed to a point where I could stand on my feet for perhaps a third of a watch at a time before I had to rest, while the periods of time I spent recovering were growing shorter, but I still had a long way to go. As we ate, the talk naturally turned towards politics, which I listened to with some interest, though I had nothing to contribute. The main topic was Cicero's tract about Cato, which Caesar was still angry about, and he announced plans to write an "Anti-Cato" in response to Cicero.

"Cicero is an old woman," Pollio opined, a sentiment I agreed with, but I was surprised to see Caesar shake his head.

"Cicero is a brilliant orator and legal mind, but he's an insufferable snob, and it's his snobbery that blinds him to what needs to be done," Caesar said as he unenthusiastically dabbed some bread in oil. It had always surprised me to see how little Caesar ate, for all his energy. Shrugging, he continued, "Besides that, he's still angry with me over my actions in the Catiline affair. He feels that I should have backed him in that awful mess, but he overstepped his authority, and I had no choice."

"At least he refuses to sit in the Senate. That's a good thing," Pollio said.

Before Caesar could answer, I saw Octavian shaking his head out of the corner of my eye, and so did Caesar.

Instead of answering Pollio himself, Caesar turned to Octavian. "I see that my nephew doesn't agree with this assessment, and I'd like to hear his reasons why he believes as he does."

We looked at Octavian, who had turned bright red, but his voice was steady and cool as he spoke. "There are many in Rome that say Uncle wants to make himself king, or at the very least he's a tyrant who intends on absolute rule. Because of that, I believe he needs men of distinction like Cicero in the Senate who are known to oppose him and not be one of his creatures. That's the best way to quell talk about any aspirations he may have about being king." He swallowed, looking at the rest of us through lowered lashes, and finished, "That's my opinion, anyway."

I looked over at Caesar, who was positively beaming as he looked at his nephew in approval.

Slapping his hand on the table, he exclaimed, "My nephew has it exactly right! As much as I may dislike Cicero's actions, I need him in the Senate, along with other men like him who aren't afraid to voice their dissent. I have no need to be king; being Caesar is enough."

While I saw the sense in what Octavian and Caesar were saying, I cannot say that I agreed. I suppose I was too accustomed to the ways of the Legions to think that having someone constantly carping and criticizing your every action could be good in any way, but I was not about to venture my own opinion. The conversation moved to other matters, notably Caesar's plans for some of the reforms he had determined must be accomplished if Rome were to survive. I very quickly found my attention wandering, so I have little recollection of what was said. While I was only faintly interested in politics, the one part of it that intrigued me at all was the human aspect, the relationships, and alliances that were forged as a result of political expediency. Matters of policy; how land was to be granted, how much a citizen should be taxed, rules for voting and the like were completely boring to me, so I contented myself with appearing to be interested while I gorged myself on the roast pork and beef as the others chattered away.

Finally, having solved all of Rome's problems, Caesar turned his attention back to me. "Well, Pullus. Octavian and I are leaving in the morning. While I want you to devote all of your energies to getting the 10th trained up to the standard I expect, you must also take care of yourself until you're fully recovered. Agreed?"

I did not see how it was possible to do both things, but I also knew when Caesar was not looking for an honest answer, and this was one of those times, so I agreed.

Continuing, Caesar said, "I expect that it should take about four months to get the Legion trained to a point where you can be ready to march to Rome. I plan on leaving for Parthia shortly after the Ides of March so I need the 10th to be fully provisioned and ready to leave with me. You'll need to arrive in Rome no later than the beginning of March. I know I can count on you."

"Yes, Caesar. We'll be there, ready to march. We may not be quite ready to fight, but we will be by the time we face the Parthians, I promise you that."

Caesar smiled, turning to Octavian. "The key to success in the field, Nephew, is to find men like Pullus and let them do their jobs. The minute I laid eyes on him when he was all of 16, I knew that he was going to be one of the best Rome had to offer."

He turned back to me, his smile even broader, as I felt my heart hammering in my chest.

"How did you know?" I gasped, and he threw back his head and laughed.

"I didn't, until now anyway," he responded, clearly pleased with himself.

The other two at the table looked bemused, glancing first at me then at Caesar. It was clear that Caesar had no plans on punishing me. As I thought about it, I realized that if he took any action against me, it would be as much of an embarrassment to him as it would be damaging to me, something his political enemies would use to make him seem gullible at best, and at worst, as being an accomplice in flaunting the ancient rules and customs of Rome.

"So, Pullus, how did you do it? It couldn't have been that hard to pass yourself off as the appropriate age because of your size, but you had to present proof of your age. I wouldn't like to think that the *conquisitore* took a bribe, though it's been so many years ago there's not much that can be done about it."

I shook my head, saying, "There was no bribe, Caesar. My father lied for me."

Caesar raised an eyebrow. "He must have loved you very much to do that."

I was thankful that I did not have a mouthful of wine because it would have been all over Caesar at his last remark.

Now it was my turn to laugh. "Hardly. He just wanted to be rid of me and this was the easiest way to do it."

Octavian asked, "Were you a younger son?"

I shook my head again. "No, I was the only son."

When I did not say anymore, Octavian looked about to speak again, but he was stopped by a shake of Caesar's head. I had no intention of going into any detail about the hatred my father and I held for each other, and I was suddenly struck by the thought that I did not even know if he was alive or dead. I assumed he still lived because I had not heard from Livia that he had died, but in truth, I did not know for sure. There was an awkward silence at the table, then Caesar spoke again, this time to Pollio, asking him about some details concerning Caesar's planned departure in the morning. I breathed a silent sigh of relief that nobody had pressed the matter about my father, and I soon got bored with the conversation. Finally, the dinner was over, at least as far as Caesar was concerned, as he stood, the signal for us to make our farewells.

Caesar clasped my hand, his other hand on my shoulder as he said, "Good night and goodbye for now, Pullus. I hope your recovery continues well. I have no doubts that the men will be trained to my satisfaction when they arrive in Rome. I'll see you in a couple of months."

I wish I could remember exactly what I said to Caesar that night, since it was the last time I ever spoke to him, but it was nothing memorable, and even more to my eternal shame, I never properly thanked him for his confidence in me, and for the rise in my fortunes that was due all to him. Diocles continues to admonish me because hindsight has perfect vision, but it really does not make me feel any better.

## Chapter 10- Fall of a Titan

Just as it had started 16 years before, the 10th Legion was reborn in a fury of toil, sweat, and frenzied activity, every moment liberally spiced with the cursing of Centurions and Optios. The only difference was that now my comrades and I were doing the cursing, while using the *vitus* on the hapless boys who had thought that joining the Legions would be a huge adventure and a lot of fun. To be accurate, my Centurions were doing the bulk of the work, since I was still much too weak to put in a full day, even if most of what I did was supervise under the best of circumstances. I was very judicious in my expenditure of energy, making appearances at places and times where I thought my presence would have the most impact, always in full uniform, adopting Crastinus' *numen* waving the invisible turd as my own. Now it was under my nose as I made my disgust at what I saw clear to the *tiros* shambling about trying to learn how to march and hold a weapon without stabbing themselves to death. To the rankers, I had to appear as if I were a son of Mars, not quite mortal but not a god either, something more than flesh and blood, a demigod who knew exactly what the youngsters were thinking at any given moment. I would suddenly appear while a Century was drilling, correcting a *tiro* with a poke of my *vitus*, or using my size to tower over some poor youngster. I had never been much for yelling, preferring to get my point across in other ways, but I had to be even more reserved than normal, because any outburst on my part caused my head to swim, and the worst thing that could happen was the sight of the Primus Pilus of the Legion keeling over in a dead faint. I am sure that the men knew that I had been wounded at Munda, but I gave strict instructions to my officers that the extent of my injuries remain a secret. The one factor in my favor was that I no longer had to worry about any challenges to my authority from any of the Centurions in the Legion, since they were all hand-picked by Caesar and me. Any man who I had even the faintest suspicion would pose a problem down the road either was passed over or sent to another Legion. Regardless, in the beginning, I could only manage to make three or four appearances a day, retiring to my tent after each to rest. The first week was the worst; by the time I would enter my tent, I would be shaking all over, my tunic as soaked as if I had gone for a swim in the river. It would be all I could do to remain standing long enough for Diocles and my body slave to remove my armor before I collapsed. My strength gradually returned, though I never took my health and vitality for granted again after that. I had always been robust and healthy, and in fact had never really been sick, other than a cold a time or two. In retrospect, I possessed the same impatience and barely concealed contempt for anyone I considered weaker than me that most men like me have, but this period of my life changed my outlook considerably. The training progressed in the same manner that it always had in the armies of Rome, though I found it interesting to experience the building of a Legion from the other side, as it were. However, I did institute some changes in the training regimen, but more importantly, and more unpopular were my reforms of hygiene and dietary practices. I put special emphasis on weapons training as, taking a page out of the manual as written by Gaius Crastinus, I selected weapons instructors personally, not confining my evaluation to men who were considered the proper rank, preferring to focus on ability to the exclusion of all else. This produced some grumbling, yet it was nothing compared to the howls of protest when I increased the ratio of meat to bread, particularly from the veterans salted into the ranks. I even got a visit from Vellusius, who was willing to risk incurring my wrath, gambling on his status as one of my original tentmates to avoid it.

He was right; I was more amused than anything, pretending to listen intently as he vehemently protested at the injustice of being forced to eat more meat. "We're not wolves, we're men. We need our bread," he began, and I could not resist the urge to have a little fun at his expense.

"So you're saying you would rather be a cow or sheep than a wolf?" I asked, stifling my grin at his obvious confusion.

"Cows? What do cows have anything to do with this? Besides, if you force us to eat cow for most of our meals, we might as well become one."

He beamed at me triumphantly, sure that I would at the least be impressed with his logic.

Instead, I feigned puzzlement, replying, "First, I've ordered that you and the rest of the men eat more meat, I never said what kind. Second, the reason I ask if you would rather be a cow than a wolf is because cows eat grain. Bread is made from grain, so you're eating the same thing as a cow when you eat bread."

Now he was completely flummoxed, and stammered, "I don't see what that has to do with us eating meat."

"Simply that if I were given the choice, I'd rather be a wolf, the beast that eats dumb animals like cows, than the beast that gets eaten."

"So, you're trying to instill in us the *animus* of the wolf?" he asked doubtfully, and I decided then that I would let him off the hook, so I beamed at him.

"Exactly right, Vellusius. I knew that if anyone was smart enough to understand, it would be you."

I rose, signaling that we were done, and he left, probably more confused than when he walked in, as Diocles gave me a mock scowl. "Master, you are a very evil man."

"That I am," I agreed.

The truth was that it had nothing to do with instilling any spirit of any kind in the men, and everything to do with their overall condition. It all came back to my newly found appreciation of my previous years of good health. As I thought about it, it seemed that I had always recovered more quickly from deprivation and exertions that lasted for long periods of time than the other men. If it had just been me, I would never have formed the belief that it had something to do with my diet, but the years in Gaul had shown me that men with similar eating habits as myself seemed to have the same recuperative abilities. Many a campfire discussion centered on the inexhaustible energy of the Germans in particular, who were renowned for their diet composed almost exclusively of meat of varying types, and how much effort it took to kill them. I did not, nor do I now believe that this was a coincidence, so when the 10th was reborn, I decided that it was the perfect time to put my ideas to work. While I had been Primus Pilus for several years by this point, the 10th had been composed of veterans, and I held no illusions about being able to force them to adhere to my new orders without a full-scale mutiny. With a Legion composed of about three-quarters young first-time enlistees, I saw this as my opportunity. Even so, there was quite a bit of resistance. The other change I instituted was not quite as radical, but in my mind was just as important, which was imposing stricter adherence to the need for frequent bathing. While it had always been army policy to provide baths at all but overnight marching camps, the enforcement of making men use the facilities was haphazard at best. Now I was insisting that during vigorous training cycles like we were undergoing at this point, all men would bathe daily, with exceptions made only for those who had guard shifts or were on the sick list. Vivid in my memory was the plague that swept through our winter camp that had claimed Remus those many years before. I remembered that Remus in particular was resistant to frequent bathing, and in fact would only do so when he was threatened with a beating by the rest of the tent. Finally, I ordered the Centurions to focus more on weapons drills than exercises such as forced marches, believing that with young men like the ones that now made up the 10th, the weeks we would be marching to Rome would knock them into better shape than anything we could do around the camp. My major concern was that these youngsters would be ready to fight when the opportunity came, and it was towards that end that I had the Centurions focus their energy.

~ ~ ~ ~

It is as at this point that it probably makes sense to name at least the Pili Priores of the 10th Legion for this second enlistment, along with the Centurions of the First Century. Of course, as I have already described, Scribonius was the Secundus Pilus Prior. The Third was led by Servius Metellus, who had been my Hastatus Prior, and suffice it to say that my initial impression of him as being a possible problem had been unfounded, though he was still as ugly as ever. The Fourth's Pilus Prior was Vibius Nigidius, who had been the Pilus Posterior and had in fact been running the Cohort in everything but name. These Cohorts were traditionally the first line of battle, although in reality it changed depending on circumstances, except for the First Cohort, which was always first. This meant that the Centurions leading them had to be the strongest leaders and best fighters of the bunch, and I was happy with them all. The Fifth Cohort was commanded by Marcus Trebellius, who had been the Pilus Prior of the Ninth, where I felt his talent as a fighter was going to waste. The Sixth's Pilus Prior was Servius Gellius, and he was the most junior of the Pili Priores, which did not sit well with some of the other Centurions, but next to Scribonius, I considered him one of the smartest men in the Legion. More importantly, he kept a cool head in battle. The Seventh had Titus Marcius leading it, a man only marginally less ugly than Metellus, but who was almost as good with a sword as I was. These Cohorts were the second line, and were almost always called on when it was time to turn the battle in our favor, or on those rare occasions when the first line was hard pressed and needed support. The final three Cohorts were the last line, usually only used as reserves and in the hottest fighting. The last three Cohorts were also somewhat ironically the Cohorts most likely to be sent on independent duties, such as holding forts or towns or going on foraging parties. So, while the men were not necessarily expected to be the best fighters, their Centurions had the opportunity to come to the attention of the Primus Pilus and Legates commanding the army by showing initiative and sound decision-making. The Eighth was led by my former tutor and brother-in-law Cyclops, while the Ninth Cohort's Pilus Prior was my old Pilus Posterior Marcus Glaxus. It had taken some persuasion on my part to get him to accept command of the Cohort, ultimately accepting my argument that it would give him a chance to shine that he did not otherwise have. Finally, the Tenth was led by Gnaeus Nasica and of all the Centurions, not just the Pili Priores, he was the biggest question in my mind, not because of any perceived weaknesses, but because I did not know him as well as I knew the other men. However, he had been highly recommended by a number of the other Centurions, including Scribonius, whose judgment I trusted implicitly.

In the First Cohort, I promoted Balbus to Princeps Prior; once I learned the source of Torquatus' animosity towards him, all doubts about his abilities and loyalties were put to rest. Next to Scribonius and Cyclops, I trusted Balbus the most, knowing that I could count on him to tell me things that neither Scribonius nor Cyclops was willing to tell me, no matter how much I may not have liked what he was saying. The new Princeps Prior was Marcus Laetus, up from the Fifth Cohort. The Princeps

Posterior had been Servius Arrianus, but he was one of the men who had decided he had enough, and in his place was his former Optio, Gnaeus Celadus. The Fifth Century also had a former Optio, Gnaeus Asellio, though he had been Optio in another Cohort, I forget which one. Finally, the last Century was no longer commanded by Gaius Varus, who like Arrianus had decided to be a farmer, the new man one Titus Vistilia. These were the Centurions of the new 10th Legion, who I believed at the time would be marching beside me into battle with the Parthians, and while only time and contact with the enemy would tell if Caesar and my judgment had been sound, I was well satisfied.

~ ~ ~ ~

Training continued apace, and I was pleased to see the men with barely enough energy to chew their food as they sat by their fires while I made my rounds. I had learned from Crastinus that the most important time in solidifying one's leadership over a group of men is in the quiet times in the evenings, aside from battle, of course. As Primus Pilus, I took on the role of the stern but loving father figure, letting my Centurions do the dirty work of instilling discipline. In the first weeks, I had been just as hard on the men as the rest of my officers, but now the time had come for me to soften things up a bit and in the evening, I showed my concern for their welfare. Because of my condition, I could only make an appearance at a few fires a night, yet I always tried to leave the men with a joke or word of encouragement. I knew that the men feared me by virtue of my rank, size, and reputation, but men follow best when the respect they have for a superior has some basis in affection as well. That I had learned from Caesar, and I found that I enjoyed the evenings immensely as I became acquainted with the men I would be leading. I admit that I also did not mind the looks of awe and admiration that the youngsters gave me as I talked to them. With the veterans among them, like Vellusius, I made a great show of camaraderie, sharing some story with their younger tentmates about the exploits of their older comrade, either during battle or during our off-duty time. I held my normal daily briefings with the Centurions, receiving their reports on the daily progress as what had been little better than a mob of men, was turning into a Legion worthy of marching for Rome. All in all, I was pleased with the progress, though there were one or two trouble spots, along with the inevitable number of troublemakers and malcontents that salt every Legion, the Didiuses and Atiliuses of this current crop. The latter would sort itself out in time, as the tentmates of the rotten apples would rapidly tire of the kind of attention their comrades brought on all of them, just as we had done with Didius. The former problems were what concerned me, and one area I paid attention to was the seeming lack of men skilled in other trades, because these men would become the *immunes* of the Legion, yet it appeared as if the recruiting officers had only signed up boys fresh off the farm, with very few apprentices or craftsmen in the bunch. Of particular concern was the lack of men with any skill at metalsmithing, because this is one of the most crucial jobs in the entire Legion, and at that point, we did not have nearly enough men to perform the kind of work needed to keep our weapons and armor in repair. We had more than enough strong backs by virtue of the farm boys, which would be useful when we had to build camps, roads and such, but without enough *immunes* it was not likely that we would even get to the point where we could march. We had been authorized by Caesar to bring all Centuries to the strength of 100 men again, like we were in the original *dilectus* of the 10th more than 16 years before, rather than the 80 of tradition. However, we had already culled more than five percent of that number, winnowing out the weaklings and men too dull to follow simple instructions, so I gave the order to bring the Legion back up to strength, but with skilled craftsmen instead of just any man who was otherwise qualified. To achieve this goal, I was faced with a choice, neither alternative being palatable, for different reasons. The first choice was to comb the countryside for qualified men and "persuade" them to join by force, if they were not willing to do so voluntarily. While I was not opposed to that in any moral sense, I knew from experience that men forced into service would be more likely to desert at the first opportunity, which meant that I had to explore the other alternative, and that was to offer enlisting men a bounty. The problem with that was that I did not have the authorization to take it out of Legion funds, and would have to go to General Pollio for permission, though that was only part of the issue. Money at that point was very tight, as Caesar had spent huge amounts of gold and silver in the pursuit of his aims, and now was determined to fix all the damage caused by years of civil war, as well as instituting his massive reforms. All of this took enormous amounts of money, and Caesar had taken pains to explain to me before he returned to Rome how important it was for me to make Legion funds stretch as far as possible.

I was now wealthier than I ever dreamed possible, and because I had been frugal, I had more money than I could ever spend in a lifetime, so I decided that I would use my own funds to provide a bounty of 1,000 sesterces for *immunes* of the second grade, and 2,000 for those of the first grade. Trades like tanning are considered second grade *immunes*, while smiths are of the first grade. While using my own money would solve the problem, it did not make me particularly happy, even with General Pollio's assurances that I would be reimbursed. I cannot deny that Caesar's tardiness in giving the men the bounties that he had promised was in the back of my mind, but ultimately the 10th needed these men badly, and fortunately, these actions solved that problem, as within two weeks we filled the empty spots with skilled men. The only problem was that my funds had been depleted by more than half, and despite Pollio's promise, I knew there was no real guarantee that I would ever see that money again. Fortunately, I was not only reimbursed, but Pollio ensured that I was repaid at ten percent simple interest. While I would like to think it was simply because of the regard in which I was held by General Pollio, by the time there were funds available for such matters, men like me had become very, very important to men like Pollio. But that is for later.

~ ~ ~ ~

As the day approached where we were scheduled to begin the march to Rome, the pace of training picked up, the men beginning to look more like Legionaries of Rome every day. I was almost back to normal, though my endurance was still not where I wanted it to be, while the wound in my chest had tightened into a knot of scar tissue that restricted my movement a bit, causing a dull ache at the end of the day or after a bout of hard activity. I had resumed my practice of a third of a watch of weapons training every day, stripping to the waist as I worked so that the youngsters could see the scars that I had earned over the years. I was definitely rusty, but before long the habits formed over the 20 years I had been training, starting when Vibius and I were barely in our teens with Cyclops as our teacher, came back. I must admit that it was a somewhat strange feeling to command the man who had introduced me to what it meant to be a Legionary, but Cyclops and I had talked about it, and he assured me that he did not have any problems with the arrangement. The one topic we did not talk about was Vibius, who I was sure I would never see again now that he had left the army, particularly since I decided that I would not be returning home to visit my sister and Phocas, mainly to avoid the possibility of running into him. While my anger towards him had cooled, it was still there, forming a hard knot in my soul that I did not want to rupture by coming face to face with him. The remaining time we spent in uniform after our confrontation at Pharsalus, we had the buffer of our separate ranks and the regulations of the army keeping either of us from spilling blood, although it would have been suicide for Vibius even to draw a weapon on a superior. If we were to come face to face now, neither of us would have that protection; I could easily imagine a situation similar to that time years before when Vibius and I had first come home on leave and we had taken our revenge on our childhood enemies Marcus and Aulus. It was Marcus and Aulus who had unwittingly introduced Vibius and me when we were boys and I came upon the two of them dumping Vibius headfirst into a bucket of *cac*. I had been a large boy, strong even for my size, so I thrashed the two of them easily, though Vibius had helped. After we had joined the Legions, we came home to visit for the first time, running into the two of them in the forum, where they had been up to their old tricks, except this time we were no longer boys; we were hardened soldiers. I still have some regrets about killing Marcus, and I believe the surprise at seeing the two of them contributed to my perhaps overwrought reaction. It was the memory of that day that was the basis of my decision not to go home before we began marching to Rome, although I was not about to give that as the reason when I wrote to my sister telling her that I would not be visiting. Instead, I fell back on the same excuses I had always used when I wrote to her, telling her that I would not be coming for a visit; that my job kept me much too busy. This time there was at least a grain of truth; breaking in a new Legion, especially one that was preparing to embark on a two-month march was a job that never stopped, as we were now little more than two weeks away from marching, although our destination had changed. Instead of marching to Rome, we would be marching to Narbo, where we would take ship to sail to Syria to meet Caesar and the rest of the army. The men had not been informed of this change, and I thanked the gods for the small blessing that the Legion was still too green to sniff out the news before we were ready to let them know. A long sea voyage is enough to make even veterans nervous, and we did not need to deal with a panicked bunch of youngsters while we were marching.

~ ~ ~ ~

There are moments that stay with a man, remaining as vivid as if whatever event being recalled happened just an instant before, no matter how many years and intervening memories have occurred in between. I was sitting at my desk, the Legion having arrived in Narbo, and was filling out ration reports the night before we were scheduled to board ships and start sailing, when Diocles entered my office, and he did not need to say a word for me to know that there was something terribly wrong.

"Master, you're summoned to General Pollio's headquarters immediately," his voice was choked with an emotion that I could not immediately identify, but the distress in it was plain to hear.

I looked at him in some alarm, my fingers tightening around my stylus as I tried to divine what was happening. "What is it?" I asked, more sharply than I should have, but his manner had triggered a sense of deep unease in me that was unsettling.

"I . . . I . . . can't say for sure Master. I wasn't told anything specific, just that you needed to report immediately."

I stood, signaling to him to bring me my armor, but he shook his head, saying, "The General's messenger was very specific that you didn't need to worry about being in full uniform, that you just needed to get there as quickly as possible."

My heart was hammering in my chest as I studied Diocles' face for clues, yet he refused to meet my eyes, which alarmed me even further. "What do you know, Diocles? What have you heard?"

He shook his head, clearly miserable, then I saw a glint of tears in his eyes. "I don't know anything for sure, Master. I just . . . I just overheard something, but I don't know what it means exactly."

"Then tell me what you overheard, Diocles. I'm not going to punish you."

He looked up at me then, and I saw what I thought was a hint of anger in his eyes, but his tone was as formal and correct as always. "That wasn't my fear, Master. It's just that I don't want to repeat something that causes you distress that turns out to be untrue, because what I heard was too horrible to even contemplate." Seeing that I was not going to let it go, he finished, "It concerns Caesar. Something has happened, but I don't know what exactly, just that it wasn't good. Now you really must go to see the General."

His words rang in my ears as I hurried to the headquarters building, my mind buzzing with the possibilities. I was one of the few people who knew about Caesar's falling sickness, having been in his office when it struck one time, yet somehow I knew that whatever had happened had nothing to do with any illness. By the time I arrived at the headquarters, my stomach was churning, my sense of unease only intensifying when I was waved immediately into the building, then into Pollio's office as well. Pollio was seated at his desk, but his face was hidden from me, his head in his hands, his eyes looking down at a piece of paper. He did not look up when I reported to him, and now I was sure that I was going to vomit all over his desk, such was my agitation. If only I had known that this was the best I would feel for some time.

"Caesar has been murdered."

I stood there, sure that I had misheard him, even though another part of me knew that I had not, as I waited for him to say more.

The room suddenly started to lurch about. I realized that it was now going to be a race between whether I threw up or fainted, so without asking permission, I staggered to a chair, sitting down heavily. "What exactly happened, sir?" I managed to ask.

He finally looked up. I could see his eyes were rimmed in red, and he looked suddenly old.

He was older than Caesar, though he had a vitality of a much younger man, but now all that life force seemed to have dissipated like smoke, and he spoke with a weariness that only comes when a man has lost all hope. "He was murdered," Pollio repeated dully.

I waited for more, but he said nothing for several more moments. "Sir," I prodded gently. "Can you tell me the details?"

Sighing, he indicated the letter in front of him. "He was assassinated in the Senate, the day before he was leaving for the Parthian expedition. He had some final details of business to go over with the Senate, and had called for a morning session. That was where his assassins struck."

"Who did it?"

He looked down at the letter, reading off the names of those vile bastards, whose deeds mark them forever as the basest, most despicable men in the history of Rome, if not the world. "Publius Casca and his brother; Ligarius; Cimber; Decimus Brutus; Cinna; Gaius Cassius," at this he looked up into my eyes, and through the pain and sadness I saw a great, burning anger, the same thing that I was sure was mirrored in my own expression, as he read the last name. "And Marcus Junius Brutus."

I gasped. "Brutus? Brutus was one of them? Why everyone was sure that Caesar was his father!" I exclaimed. Without thinking, I blurted, "If I ever get the chance, I am going to kill that cocksucker."

In theory, a man of my class had no business threatening violence against a patrician, but I was beyond caring, and besides, it elicited a ghost of a smile from Pollio. "You'll have to beat me to it, Pullus."

"So what do we do now, sir?" I asked. Pollio sighed, then gave a shrug.

"I have no idea, Pullus. I have absolutely no idea."

~ ~ ~ ~

I staggered out of the *praetorium*, not even noticing that the members of Pollio's staff who were in the outer office looked much the same as I did. Pollio and I had discussed what we should do about the news, jointly deciding that I would break the news to the Centurions, since there was no way that this kind of thing would stay secret long enough to arrange for a more formal announcement. When I came back to my tent, Diocles was waiting, and one look at my face confirmed that what he had heard from the slaves was indeed true. He burst into tears, the sight of his anguish then triggering my own flood, so we sat there for several moments sobbing like babies.

Finally regaining a bit of composure, Diocles asked, "What does that mean, Master? What will happen to you?"

His question caught me completely by surprise, because I had not had time to consider anything other than trying to absorb this cataclysmic change. However, once the words hung in the air, the implication of them threatened to crowd everything else out of my brain. What exactly *did* this mean, I wondered? I sat there pondering Diocles' question, my mind whirling with all the various possibilities. It was no secret whatsoever that I was Caesar's man, so depending on who stepped into the vacuum of power that could be a dangerous thing for me. On the other hand, as I thought about it, I recognized that as high as I might have risen from the circumstances of my birth, I was still a small fish when compared to men like Pollio, who had to be considered an even greater threat to the assassins, should they come to power. What made me dangerous was my position in the army, and the influence I held over my Legion. I would have been a fool not to recognize that, for that reason alone, I could be perceived as a threat. Voicing my thoughts to Diocles, he listened intently, then was silent as he thought about the problem. I had learned to value Diocles' counsel at times like this; his devious Greek mind thought in ways that were foreign to me, but were nonetheless helpful.

Finally, his face creased into a frown as some idea formed in his mind, then he said, "Perhaps there's a way to turn this to your advantage."

I looked at him in dull surprise; I was still reeling from the news, and truth be known, feeling sorry for myself. "How?" I asked, without much hope, or interest for that matter.

"You're in control of a Legion of Rome," he said quietly.

That got my attention.

I sat up straight as I thought about what he said, then I shook my head, "General Pollio commands the Legion, not me. I'm Primus Pilus, but I'm outranked."

"The General does command, but you control the Legion, Master," Diocles replied carefully, and despite myself I glanced around to make sure that we were alone.

What Diocles was saying might have been true, but at that moment, it was incredibly dangerous, as I was suddenly reminded of all those men who had just disappeared from around the fires; some of them were Centurions like me. Now I was getting irritated, because like all members of that pesky race, Diocles always seemed to speak in riddles at times when plain speaking is most useful.

The fact that he was taking precautions to protect me never occurred to me, and as usual, I gave my tongue free rein. "Stop circling about the subject like a vulture does a baby ewe," I snapped. "Say what you're thinking, that's an order."

Diocles' face reddened, but his tone was even and respectful as he spoke his mind. "Like it or not Master, you're in control of the Legion. General Pollio may command it, but the men will follow you, and I suspect that you know this to be true. That means that you have power, and over the next days, weeks, or months, that means that you have value to those that need help in achieving their aims. All that I'm saying is that if you value your skin as much as I do, then it would behoove you to make sure that the players in this drama are reminded of that fact."

I could see the merit in what he was saying, yet I was still unsure of where he was going.

Then, a horrible suspicion began to grow in me, and I looked at Diocles with new eyes. "Are you suggesting that if it looks like they're going to come out on top, that I should throw my lot in with the bastards who killed Caesar?"

I cannot express my relief at the sight of Diocles emphatically shaking his head. "No, Master, that's not what I'm suggesting. I know that you would rather fall on your sword than side with the men who murdered Caesar. All that I'm saying," he suddenly fell to his knees in a dramatic gesture, something I had never seen him do before, "in fact, I'm begging, is that you not declare your intentions should you be approached by agents for the assassins who come to feel out what side you'll take. Let them think that they have you, or at the very least that you're open to listening to what they have to say, or I'm afraid that you'll meet with an accident of some sort."

I gave a harsh, barking laugh, pointing at the scar on my chest. "In case you haven't noticed, I take a lot of killing. I'm not worried about the likes of Brutus, or Cassius for that matter."

"Well, you should be," Diocles said flatly. "You may be hard to kill, but you're not immortal. And they are very, very rich men, and you've just seen that they'll stop at nothing. Do you think you're better protected than Caesar?"

That caught me up short, I can tell you. I stared hard at Diocles, seeing him as if for the first time. We had talked about politics and the situation of the moment on several occasions, but he had never talked to me in this manner before. My respect for his shrewdness and ability to assess a situation in such a short amount of time went up immeasurably, because I knew that he was absolutely right. However, I do not think even Diocles knew just how right he would prove to be over the next months and years. It is with this knowledge that perhaps the fact that I recouped my outlay of cash for the *immunes* in such a relatively short time, and with interest, makes more sense.

~ ~ ~ ~

Taking a few more moments to compose myself, I dried my eyes then made attempts to cover up the signs that I had been crying, ordering Diocles to do the same before I sent him to summon the Centurions. While the tent of the Primus Pilus is large, cramming all 60 Centurions into it meant that the men would have to stand shoulder to shoulder, packed together like dried fish in a barrel. So while Diocles was gone, I moved all the furniture out of the way to make room, using the time to think through all that Diocles had said. I had never been good at hiding my feelings, but I realized that if I valued my skin, I would have to put on the acting job of my career when the inevitable visitors came to feel me out about my loyalties. In the beginning at least, I could not openly declare my feelings towards either side, until I had a better idea which way the winds from Rome were blowing. Perhaps the hardest part would be to disguise my outrage and horror at what happened to Caesar, but I knew that it was essential that I appear to be essentially unmoved by Caesar's assassination, viewing it as a political issue rather than a personal tragedy. By the time the first Centurions came filing in, my face was a mask and my emotions were stuffed away, and I was once again the Primus Pilus of the 10th, a hardened professional soldier of Rome, determined not to give the Centurions now arriving a clue as to what happened. Although I could tell that they knew something momentous had occurred, none of them gave any indication that they knew what had actually happened. Spotting Scribonius in the second group of men to enter, I waved him over to me. His face was a mix of confusion and concern as I beckoned for him to enter my private quarters, whispering that I would join him shortly. When Cyclops and Balbus arrived, I did the same for them. Without saying anything to the rest of the men, I entered my private quarters to face my three friends, pulling the leather flap that served as a door down to give us some privacy, keeping my voice low so that what I was about to tell them would not be overheard.

"I'm about to tell you why I've called this meeting," I whispered. "But before I do, I need to prepare you so that you don't give any kind of outburst that would alert the rest of the men before I'm ready to tell them. So brace yourselves." I waited for each of them to nod that they understood, then I told them, making my voice as emotionless as possible. "Caesar has been assassinated by a group of Senators."

As I watched their reaction, it struck me that this was probably what I had looked like when Pollio told me. To their credit, they did not give any kind of outcry, though Scribonius drew a sharp breath that probably sounded louder than it was, but still caused me to look over my shoulder nervously, forgetting that I had pulled the flap closed.

"When did this happen?" Balbus whispered.

"On the Ides of March," I replied.

"Two weeks ago," Scribonius said thoughtfully, his tone causing the rest of us to look at him carefully, as we all respected his ability to see things that the rest of us missed. "A lot has happened in the intervening time, no doubt. There's really no telling what's transpired and who's in power. Do you have any information about that?"

I shook my head. "The dispatch that Pollio received was apparently written no more than a few thirds of a watch after the murder."

Scribonius looked at me sharply at my use of the term. "Murder? That's a little strong, isn't it? I would think assassination is a more appropriate term," he said.

For a brief moment, my anger flared white-hot, my hand involuntarily reaching for my sword.

Then I looked at his face, realizing that he had divined the same danger that Diocles had. I let out a slow breath, nodding carefully. "Yes, you're correct, Scribonius. I spoke in haste, and in error. Caesar was assassinated, not murdered."

With that settled, I gave my friends time to compose themselves, then they followed me out to face the Centurions of the 10th Legion.

~ ~ ~ ~

"Caesar is dead. He was assassinated by members of the Senate on the Ides of March, the day before he was to depart for Syria."

It was as if the air was suddenly sucked out of the room, which I suppose it was in a sense, as 56 pairs of lungs drew in a breath simultaneously. There was just a heartbeat of utter silence before total chaos broke out as men shouted in despair, cursed the gods, or just let out an unintelligible moan. Shaking their fists, turning to each other, yelling out what they would do to the assassins, asking me for details, for several moments I let the grief and anger wash over all of us as each man dealt with the news that the father of the Legion had been struck down in their own way. Finally, I held up my hand for silence, but I was universally ignored.

Drawing a deep breath, I roared at the top of my lungs. *"Tacete!"*

For the first and only time, I was not instantly obeyed, and it was only the circumstances that kept me from lashing out at the nearest man who was still baying for the killers' blood.

Still, I was very angry, and made no attempt to hide it. "I said shut up now, you bastards! The next man to speak I'll flay and use his ball sac as my coin purse!"

That shut them up, as their looks of contrition and anguish extinguished the flames of my ire immediately.

These men were heartbroken, just as I was, and I had to let them come to terms with what had happened. "Brothers," I said with what I hoped was a sympathetic tone. "I know that you're hurting, as I am. You all know how much Caesar has favored me, how much I owe to him, and now to his memory. But we all have to be strong now, more than at any other time. The men are young and raw, and for most of them, the name of Caesar has been in their ears since they were born. They grew up on our exploits in Gaul, with Caesar at our head. Now this one constant fact of Rome is no more, and they'll be confused and frightened about what this means."

"What does this mean?" someone asked, and I felt the pressure of 59 pairs of eyes looking at me for the answer.

"It's too early to know," I said as honestly as I could. "The dispatch General Pollio received didn't give any kind of instructions, and it was apparently sent just thirds of a watch after the....event. As of this moment, I don't know what our orders are, but I plan on finding out."

It was not much, yet it was the best I could do for the moment, and I was relieved to see that the men seemed to accept that. "I've decided that rather than call an assembly and tell the men all at once, that I'm going to have you tell each of your Centuries. I think that this is the best way to handle it because I don't want a scene of mass hysterics."

As I expected, this did not go down well, but I was not going to be swayed. With that, I sent the men back to their Century areas, then sat down with Diocles and an amphora of wine, preparing ourselves for the coming uproar.

~ ~ ~ ~

The next few days passed in a blur, as I found myself going almost every third of a watch to the *praetorium* to find out from Pollio the latest developments. Dispatch riders came in a steady stream, not all of them from Rome, but from other parts of the Republic as the men who had belonged to Caesar sent missives back and forth, feeling each other out while trying to gather more information. First, we heard that Brutus and the other faithless bastards had been hailed as saviors of the Republic, that the people were acclaiming them as heroes, something I did not buy into for a moment, and it turned out that I was right. In fact, the reaction of the people was quite the opposite, as Brutus and Cassius in particular were now hiding from the masses. The people of the Head Count, my people, wanted to skin them alive and nail their hides to the Senate door, so the two of them were taking refuge in the Capitol. A couple of days after we heard this, word came that the two of them had ventured down to the Forum to mount the Rostra to give speeches justifying their actions, the reaction obviously not what they were expecting. The people did not tear them asunder, instead just standing there in complete and total silence. I can only imagine how unnerving that must have been, for either of the assassins or for the people watching. The eyes and attention of the people of all classes now turned to Marcus Antonius, waiting to see what he would do. When he took no actions against the assassins, I requested an audience with Pollio to get his opinion on what Antonius was thinking, because his inaction infuriated me, as well as the rest of the men. To us, it was clear-cut; no matter what I might say publicly, I viewed Caesar's death as nothing but murder, and for Antonius to sit by doing nothing to his assassins made no sense to any of us in uniform.

Clearly, I was not the only one missing my rest. Seeing Pollio, his eyes red from fatigue and sleepless nights, I recognized that the man was suffering from all this upheaval, as much if not more than we were. He was still seated behind his desk, and as it had become my habit, I did not wait for him to give permission, throwing myself into the chair on the opposite side of the desk.

"I believe Marcus Antonius is just being prudent," he told me, when I asked him about it.

"Prudent?" I asked incredulously, forgetting that Pollio was my superior for a moment as I let out a string of curses. Fortunately, Pollio was not the sort of officer who punished men for lapses like mine, particularly under the circumstances. "Prudent," I repeated. "What's prudent about letting the men who killed Caesar go unpunished? If anything, it would seem to me to be *prudent* for him to take action against them, since he was Caesar's man just as much as you or I."

I am not sure what I was expecting, but it was not the snorting laugh that Pollio gave. "Antonius is nobody's man but his own," Pollio said acidly, and I could see that he had no love for the man, no matter how popular he had been with the troops. "And while I don't care for the man personally, in this I agree with him. His position is too tenuous for him to take any drastic action against Brutus, Cassius, and the rest of them. And make no mistake," at this he leaned forward, pointing at me for emphasis, "it's Brutus and Cassius that matter the most, along with Decimus Brutus. And Trebonius," he sighed.

I found myself sitting upright, shocked to my core. "Trebonius," I gasped.

I had known about Decimus Brutus, which was something of a shock, but nothing like this. Gaius Trebonius had been one of Caesar's most loyal lieutenants, benefitting greatly from Caesar's patronage and support.

Pollio nodded wearily. "He didn't wield a knife, that much is true. But he kept Antonius tied up on some nonsense outside while the others did the deed. Yes," he sighed. "I'm afraid that Trebonius was in it up to his eyebrows. So you see," he continued, "that's another reason why Antonius can't just order the execution of any of the assassins, who by the way, are calling themselves The Liberators." Pollio laughed at this, though there was no humor in it. "The Liberators. What a joke. What do they think they've liberated us from? The Republic is dead as Caesar, it's never going to come back."

I must admit that his last remark disturbed me; like most Romans of my class, I could not really explain exactly what the Republic was, I just knew that it had been in existence for hundreds of years.

I also believed that it was the best form of government in history, though I could no more explain why this was so than I could sprout wings. "You think the Republic is finished?" I asked cautiously.

Pollio gave me a sharp look, clearly trying to determine if I had some ulterior motive. Such were the times that we were all looking at each other out of the corner of our eyes, wondering exactly what was going on in each other's heads.

Apparently, Pollio discerned that I was sincere. "Yes, Pullus, I do. The fact is that it was dead before Caesar ever took power, but the *boni*," he spat the term that the enemies of Caesar had claimed as their own, long before his assassination, "refused to accept that fact. Caesar's death doesn't change the reality, but I suspect that our Brutus and Cassius are only now coming to terms with that fact. And the jug is broken now; Caesar is dead, and nothing will bring him back."

"So you think Antonius is doing the right thing?" was my next question, his eyes narrowing as he thought about it.

"No," he said finally. "I don't think he's doing the right thing, I think he's doing the only thing that he can do under the circumstances. Until he solidifies his power base, and has a better idea of how much support Brutus and the rest of that bunch have, he really has no other choice."

"But the people are on Antonius' side, that has to count for something," I argued.

"That's true," Pollio conceded. "Pullus, don't take offense when I say this. The people of your class may have numbers, but they don't have money, and money is power. The patricians, and the wealthy equestrians, especially those who live outside of Rome, have the money, and therefore, they have the clout."

"I'm actually eligible for the equestrian class," I do not know exactly why I chose that moment to say this, other than my pride was stung by his words, no matter how true they may have been.

Pollio's bushy grey eyebrows lifted in surprise. "Really? I didn't know that, Pullus. Well, er, congratulations I suppose," he said awkwardly. "However, that really doesn't change things; however wealthy you may be, you're one man, and your riches are nothing compared to what the *boni* can marshal to further their cause."

I sighed; this conversation had given me a headache, yet I had to admit grudgingly that I saw Pollio's point, but I still needed some sort of assurance from him about Antonius' intentions, which he could not give.

"Ultimately, as I said at the beginning of this conversation, Marcus Antonius is his own man, with his own ambitions," Pollio finished. "He's going to do what's best for Antonius, no matter what."

~ ~ ~ ~

Pollio, of course, was entirely accurate, at least in his assessment of Antonius' motives. While the common people and the veterans of Caesar's army that had retired were grief-stricken, showing their sorrow by a spontaneous demonstration in the Forum and attempting to burn down some of the assassins' homes, Antonius took a conciliatory stance towards the men who called themselves The Liberators, even if nobody else afforded them that title. He issued a public proclamation granting the assassins amnesty, which was hugely unpopular in the army, while I found myself making offerings of thanks to the gods that I had such a green Legion under my command, for if it had been composed of Caesar's veterans, I do not know what would have happened. Even so, the men were extremely unsettled, while the tone was set by the remaining veterans, as whatever grievances they had had towards Caesar seemed to have evaporated with his death.

One night, I had Scribonius and Balbus as guests for dinner, and I broached the subject with them. "Do you think it's odd that the veterans are so worked up over Caesar's death after most of them mutinied against him?" I asked the both of them as I poured them another cup of wine.

"Not really." Balbus shrugged. "Whatever grievances they had with Caesar, ultimately they loved him as a father. I don't know how it was with your father, Pullus, but I loved and hated mine, all at the same time."

I had no desire or intention of discussing my relationship with my father with either Scribonius or Balbus, but I took his point.

Considering this, I then asked the both of them, "So what do we do? Do we let them talk, or do we clamp down on them?"

Scribonius frowned as he thought about it. Then, "I don't think trying to shut them up is going to work, it will just make them, the veterans anyway, more resentful. They need to be able to express their anger."

Balbus shook his head immediately. "I disagree. The youngsters are going to follow the lead of the veterans, and if you let the veterans continue to moan about Caesar, you set an example that will dog this Legion for the rest of the time these men are under the standards."

After listening to both, I agreed with Balbus, telling him and Scribonius to pass the word quietly to those veterans the most vocal in their anger that it was time for them to shut their mouths. I must admit I was somewhat torn about it, given that the men were just expressing my own feelings, but I knew that Balbus was right.

~ ~ ~ ~

Fortunately, a quiet word to a few key men was all that was needed and while the anger remained, it was muted to little more than a whisper around the fires. A few days later, at the end of April, we received word that Brutus and Cassius, no longer able to bear the pressure of constantly watching their backs and homes, had fled Rome, with Antonius aiding Brutus at least by passing a law that enabled him as urban Praetor to be absent from the city for more than the ten days prescribed by law. Antonius also introduced a law that abolished the office of Dictator, along with a measure that ratified all of Caesar's acts prior to his death, along with his proposed measures. However, it was on Antonius' say-so alone as to what Caesar had proposed to do and what he had actually begun implementing, since he had seized Caesar's private papers immediately after his death. The granting of citizenship to Sicily was one example, so in effect Antonius was every bit as powerful as Caesar in this respect. Oh, he was treading a very careful path and as time passed, and grudgingly I had to admit that Pollio had been right about Antonius, at least as far as what he was doing in the early tumultuous days after the assassination. As difficult a situation as it was, we still had to continue training the men, although we now had nowhere to march to, so we began incorporating day-long marches out into the countryside. Compounding our problems was that we had no idea when or where we would be marching, or who we would be fighting when we got wherever we were going. What all the officers feared was that we would be fighting against Romans again. Still, that did not keep us from training our men to the best of our ability.

~ ~ ~ ~

The next momentous event occurred when word arrived about the contents of Caesar's will. Once again, I found myself sitting in Pollio's office, but this time he was more animated than I had seen him in weeks, though not in a good way.

I had barely sat down when he waved yet another scroll in my face. "Do you know what this says?" he demanded. I assured him that I had no idea what it contained. "It's the contents of Caesar's will, or at least the most important parts."

We had been expecting to hear of it for some time before this, so it was not a surprise that we were finally receiving word about it, but what followed was not just very much a surprise, but a huge shock.

"Caesar's heir is named," Pollio continued, and I nodded, fully expecting to hear the name Marcus Antonius, since he was really the only logical choice.

I supposed Decimus Brutus was another possibility, but I was sure that his part as one of The Liberators notwithstanding, he was not a likely candidate.

Never in my wildest dreams did I imagine that I would hear the name that Pollio uttered, and so shocked was I that I made him repeat himself. "You heard me correctly. Gaius Octavius is Caesar's principal heir. His other nephews Lucius Pinarius and Quintus Pedius get a pittance, at least in terms of proportion, though they'll still be wealthy men, but Caesar named Gaius Octavius not only his main heir, but adopted him as his son as well, so he inherits the name, which in some ways is more important." Pollio smiled bitterly, "Though I doubt he'll live long enough to make any use of it."

I sat there, stunned, thinking that I just needed to learn not to expect anything to make sense so that I was not constantly having my head spin with all that kept happening. "Antonius will kill him," I blurted the first thing that came into my head, and Pollio nodded in agreement.

"I expect so, and I can't say that I blame him. I admire....admired," Pollio amended, "Caesar a great deal, but I think he did a great wrong to Antonius in this. And I think that in naming Octavius as heir, he has guaranteed that Roman will be fighting Roman."

Asinius Pollio was a good general. He was also a great scholar and a very wise man, one who was usually right about most things. In this, he was more right than he knew.

~ ~ ~ ~

While we were watching events in Rome, it was not as if there were not things going on in Hispania, courtesy of Sextus Pompey, who had managed to flee into the hills to gather together a group of die-hard Pompeians, but he was not much more than a nuisance. However, the fear was not what he could do at that moment, but that if he were allowed to go unchecked, he could gain strength and experience so that at some point in the future he became a formidable opponent. He was still in his teens, and he was smart enough to recruit men from areas that had been Pompeian strongholds for many years. One day I was called to the *praetorium* to see that there was a new face along with Pollio, and in thinking back, I do not know if I took an instant disliking to the man before he opened his mouth, but if not it was only moments after, when he did start speaking.

"Primus Pilus Pullus, this is Marcus Aemilius Lepidus. He'll be taking over command here, as he has been sent by the Senate to govern the province."

Pollio's tone was formal and correct, yet I had been around him long enough to know that he was not happy about this development. I turned to salute Lepidus, who I towered over by several inches, which was not unusual, but Lepidus was as narrow as he was short. He had little muscle on his frame, and a weak chin, which I have always found to be telling about a man's character.

He returned my salute with what I could only describe as indifference, then turned back to Pollio as if I was not in the room. "As governor and commander of the province, duly appointed by the Senate, I command you to go in pursuit of the rebel Sextus Pompey immediately. In fact, I'm surprised that you haven't done so before this, and it makes me wonder about your loyalty."

I could feel my mouth drop; this display of rudeness between members of the upper class, particularly in front of a subordinate, was something that I have never witnessed, before or since, but I learned everything I needed to know about Lepidus in that exchange with Pollio.

As for Pollio, his face turned purple with rage, though his voice was controlled, albeit just barely, his words clipped. "I can assure you, Governor, that I am as loyal a man as you'll find. Perhaps if you had spent much time in the field with Caesar, you would have been able to witness my loyalty firsthand, but I understand that Rome and its pleasures are hard to leave behind."

Now it was Lepidus' turn to splutter with rage, as he pointed a stubby little finger at Pollio and hissed, "I must remind you that you're speaking to a superior, in every way I might add. My birth and ancestors are impeccable, whereas you're nothing but an upstart and low-born at that."

And there was the nub of it, why Lepidus' name and deeds will only be a footnote in history. It was also why I and the other Centurions abandoned him later. As I said, he was a small man in every way, but he thought that he was a great man simply because of who he was and who his ancestors had been. Caesar's ancestry and bloodline was every bit as illustrious as someone like Lepidus, yet Caesar valued competence and intelligence above all else. He had accomplished more than any man in Roman history because of his farsightedness and open acceptance of men such as Pollio, and in a much smaller sense, myself. Lepidus was blinded to the abilities in others if their birth was not as exalted as his, and I was witnessing firsthand why he was never more than an annoyance and a bit of a joke.

The two noblemen were still ignoring me as they stood nose to nose, but ultimately, Lepidus had the rights of it, no matter how much both Pollio and I might have loathed him for it.

Finally, Pollio relented, while I was dismissed, but as I turned to leave Lepidus had one more nasty surprise in store for me. "Primus Pilus, I'll be inspecting your Legion in one third of a watch. Make them ready, and I expect them to meet my standards."

I froze in place; sure that this was some sort of jest on his part but as I was to learn, among his other failings, Lepidus had absolutely no sense of humor. Even Pollio looked shocked, as I looked to him for help. The men were training; some of them were out at the stakes, others were working on mending gear, the normal activities of a Legion in training. To expect them to drop what they were doing, get their uniforms, weapons, and leathers in the kind of condition that would stand inspection by not just a commanding officer but a governor, was a further demonstration that Lepidus had his head firmly deposited up his anal cavity.

"Governor, may I suggest that perhaps you postpone your inspection for a few thirds of a watch at least? Surely you'd rather rest after your long journey," Pollio oozed sincerity, their earlier differences apparently forgotten, but Lepidus was unmoved.

"Nonsense," he retorted. "You insinuated that I know nothing of military affairs, and I'll show you that nothing could be further from the truth. I will hold inspection in one third of a watch."

Pollio looked at me, then shrugged helplessly; he had tried, he was saying, but there was nothing to be done. As angry as I was at Lepidus, I was equally angry at Pollio, because it was his words that put Lepidus into this corner. His authority and knowledge had been challenged, so now he had to salvage some sort of victory. However, it would be at the expense of my Legion, and ultimately my career, for I had no doubt that as inept as Lepidus obviously was, he was determined to show everyone that he was some sort of military authority. The fact that he thought that he could prove his *bona fides* by holding a parade ground inspection was just an example of how little he actually did know, and all he would have to show for it would be half a Legion on the punishment list, along with a number of hugely embarrassed and angry Centurions and Optios. I saluted the both of them, executed a parade ground about-face, then stalked out of the headquarters.

~ ~ ~ ~

The inspection was every bit the fiasco that I expected. Ultimately Lepidus sealed his fate with not just the 10th that day, but after word of what he had done spread through the rest of the army, he earned the never-ending enmity of the Legionaries of Rome. My silent prediction of half the Legion ending up on the punishment list was off by a large amount; almost three-quarters of the Legion were found lacking in some way by Lepidus and his toadies, three loathsome little men who obviously wanted to curry favor with the governor. The whole ordeal took the better part of the day, and the only thing I can say that was positive about the experience was that it did more to unite the Legion than anything either any of the Centurions or I had done to that point. The one stroke of fortune was that Lepidus could not be bothered to stay long enough to witness any of the punishments that he prescribed for the men, which included about a half-dozen floggings for the more "egregious" offenses committed by the men, one of them being an improperly tied helmet strap, for which Lepidus ordered ten lashes, though he magnanimously announced to the sullen men that it would not be with the scourge. He claimed that he had pressing business elsewhere in the province and would be leaving in the morning, so for perhaps the first time in the history of the Roman army, not one man put on the list was actually punished, the matter being completely ignored the moment that Lepidus and his party was over the horizon.

~ ~ ~ ~

Pollio took leave just a day or two later, leaving me in nominal command of the camp until the return of Lepidus, a prospect that none of the Centurions found appealing, given what we had seen of the worm during his short stay. My biggest concern at that point was that with Pollio leaving, I would be in the dark about developments in the larger world, but he promised to keep me informed by messenger as he learned what was taking place. As much as Lepidus was personally despised, the one thing in his favor was that he was backing Antonius, though in real terms I did not think much of what he had to offer, since especially in those early days, Antonius was the logical choice for men like me and the other Centurions. By this time, Antonius had moved into Campania, where a large number of veterans of the 8th, 9th, and 10th were now settled. He had begun recruiting men for a period of service, though at the time he was not asking for a full enlistment. Supposedly, his biggest fear at that moment was Decimus Brutus, who under Senate authority had taken the governorship of Cisalpine Gaul, thereby commanding the 23rd through 25th Legions, which were now considered veterans. It was not until later that I learned that the real reason Antonius left Rome in the first place was because of his oppressive actions in the execution of a man named Amatius. This Amatius claimed to be the illegitimate grandson of Gaius Marius, whose name and memory still evoked a powerful pull on the common people, and after Caesar's funeral, he had supposedly made claims that he would kill Cassius and Brutus for the murder of Caesar. Antonius, with little if any evidence, arrested Amatius, then had him executed without a trial, which endeared Antonius to the Senate, but made him extremely unpopular with the people. When the people gathered in the Forum to protest, Antonius ordered some men from the 7th, who were stationed on the Campus Martius, to strike down an unknown number of citizens. This was the real reason he left the city to raise an army, because the people of the Head Count were now baying for his blood as well. Meanwhile, a rake named Dolabella had been named as Consul by Caesar, but our general's body was not yet cold when Dolabella turned on his memory, siding with The Liberators, making a number of speeches essentially blaming Caesar for his own death. Ironically, the other Consul for the year was none other than Antonius, but Dolabella and Antonius hated each other, meaning that any cooperation between them was bound to be non-existent. However, both of them were clearly attempting to curry favor with the Senate, though Antonius was trying to avoid going too far in his appeasement because of his very well-founded fear of Caesar's veterans seeing him as being one of The Liberators. What I found particularly confusing about all this madness going on was how the assassins so cynically followed Caesar's edicts, even though they had murdered him for his actions. As I mentioned, Decimus Brutus obeyed

Caesar's command to govern Cisalpine Gaul, while Trebonius did the same in taking the governorship of Asia, and Cimber took Bithynia, all of which Caesar had commanded. However, Cassius had been slated by Caesar to go to Syria, but for reasons I could not discern, the Senate actually blocked that move, choosing to send Dolabella in his place, while Brutus' governorship of Macedonia was given to Antonius instead. By taking command of Syria, Dolabella was also taking over responsibility for the invasion of Parthia, which I could not imagine any of the army slated for this operation was happy about. It was somewhere about this time that things became truly interesting, as a new player entered the stage.

~ ~ ~ ~

I received a letter from Pollio informing me that on the Nones of May, the young Octavius, now insisting on being called by the name of Caesar, which at this point nobody was doing, arrived in Rome to take possession and control of his inheritance. He had been in Apollonia studying and preparing for his duties as a Military Tribune, and he returned in much the same manner as Caesar did when his adopted father attempted to cross the sea to spur Antonius on to bring the rest of the army over when we were in Greece, braving a tremendous storm to come to Rome. That was the story anyway; as I have learned, sometimes to my chagrin, the line between what is fact and fiction when it comes to the man now known as Augustus is sometimes so blurry as to be invisible. Whatever really happened, the story of his courageous crossing of the sea in a raging storm evoked memories of his adopted father, which was undoubtedly welcomed by Octavian. He brought with him another Tribune, a man who I believe would be considered one of the greatest military minds of his or any other time, if he had been more ambitious and not so devoted to Octavian, young Marcus Agrippa. They landed not at Brundisium, but at Lupiae, a smaller port where he would not attract so much attention. He immediately made his way to a nearby military camp, where he passed among the Legionaries posted there, dazzling them in much the same way I suppose he had dazzled me by his resemblance to Caesar. The men there immediately swore their allegiance to him, and I am sure that it was as much due to that resemblance as it was to his status as the lawful heir of Caesar. Traveling to Brundisium, now accompanied by a substantial body of Legionaries, he made the same impression on the more sizable group of men stationed at the port, this being the primary collection point for the planned Parthian operation. It was at Brundisium that he made the formal announcement that he was accepting the bequest of Caesar, that he would henceforth call himself Gaius Julius Caesar Octavianus, and that he expected all men to address him in this manner. Another event took place, one that has been the subject of much discussion, the fact of Octavian's appearance at Brundisium coinciding with the simultaneous disappearance of the war chest that Caesar had set aside for the Parthian expedition. Nothing was ever said officially, but the grapevine in the army was of the strong opinion, in fact a certainty, that Octavian had taken it. I do not know exactly what transpired, but what I can say is that given the subsequent problems Octavian had prying his inheritance from Caesar from Antonius' grasp, he somehow kept finding funds to fuel his enterprises. I suppose it was inevitable that the two of them should clash; there can only be one First Man, and despite his youth and inexperience, Octavian was a serious contender for the title, if only at first by virtue of his adoption by Caesar. Whatever the cause, it did not take long for matters to become heated between the two of them. Pollio wrote to me that the very day Octavian entered Rome he went to Antonius' house, which ironically had once belonged to Pompey Magnus, and depending on whom you believed, either requested or demanded that Antonius hand over the cash portion of his inheritance, which Antonius had seized along with Caesar's papers shortly after his murder. Either Pollio had a source that was there, or his correspondent had a vivid imagination, because Pollio's letter went into great detail about the meeting. Antonius was extremely angry, according to this source, claiming that he had found the treasury empty, that he was using Caesar's funds to conduct public business, and was in no way enriching his own purse. He went on to point out that he was under no obligation to give Octavian anything since the will had yet to be ratified. I imagine that he thought that this would quell any ideas Octavian had, but for the first though not the last time, he seriously underestimated the young man. I cannot say that I blame him; Octavian was very young, while his precious good looks did him no favors. Even after spending time with him and getting a glimpse of his intelligence and the flash of iron that I had seen, I found it hard to believe that he could be a serious rival to a man like Antonius. However, I was not the one with so much at stake, Antonius was. By choosing to treat Octavian as a young boy and not as an equal and serious rival, he put Octavian in a position to do Antonius great damage, an opportunity that Octavian wasted no time pressing to his advantage. After his refusal by Antonius, Octavian coolly announced that his primary concern was the disbursement of the bequest to the people that Caesar had made in his will, so if Antonius refused to honor his adopted father's will, Octavian would, even if it meant using his own money. This is why I for one believed the stories that he had appropriated Caesar's war chest, because while his family was wealthy, the kind of money it took to pay every citizen the 100 denarii apiece that Caesar had promised was staggering. Antonius was outraged, and I have no doubt that this time his anger was real, because Octavian was spending his time in the Forum loudly proclaiming his intention of paying the people, while decrying Antonius for not abiding by the terms of Caesar's will. Not surprisingly, this put Antonius in quite a difficult situation, and coupled with his actions against Amatius, he was no longer the darling of the people, Octavian was. It was only through the intercession of intermediaries that an accommodation between the two was reached, although I do not believe anyone thought it would last very long. I am sure that the entrance of Octavian onto the stage was also behind Antonius' announcement that instead of governing Macedonia, as originally planned, he would be taking the governorship of none other than nearby Cisalpine Gaul. Suddenly, Antonius' official policy of no reprisals against any of The Liberators evaporated like a drop of water in the desert as he announced that he was marching with the approval of the Senate to punish the current governor of the province Decimus Brutus. Antonius at least tried to keep up the pretense of legality by going to ask for the Senate to enact the transfer of the governorship. Apparently, he did so at the head of almost a full Cohort of some of the veterans he had enlisted in Campania, so that most of the Senate, fearing that Antonius would do to them what he had done to the supporters of Amatius, stayed away from the Forum. However, Antonius was not to be put off; instead, he had one of his tame Tribunes of the Plebs issue an edict, giving the transfer at least the veneer of legality, no matter how thin. Most importantly for Antonius, and conversely for Octavian, it gave Antonius the legitimate command of an army of four Legions, including the 7th, while Octavian held no official post, and therefore had nothing, at least in terms of an army. He did have his name, which was enough for the veterans, most of them anyway.

~ ~ ~ ~

This is where things stood in mid-summer, when Octavian staged the traditional Victory Games for Apollo, held in the month that is now named for Caesar. A singularly peculiar event occurred during the games that further enhanced the popular belief that Caesar had become a god, indirectly benefiting Octavian as well. While the games were going on, for all seven days, a star bright enough to appear in the daytime appeared in the northern sky, low on the horizon but supposedly clearly visible at all times. It was widely believed that this was nothing less than the sight of Caesar's soul being accepted by the rest of the gods to become a god himself. I must say that, while I am normally an extremely skeptical person, I found it hard to ascribe any other meaning to this sign, because too many people saw it for it to have been the work of Octavian's agents. Even Scribonius, normally even more of a skeptic than I, was at a loss to explain it. I am not sure exactly when it happened, but somewhere in the progress of the games, Octavian produced the chair that Caesar had used to preside over the Senate. The chair itself had been gilded, along with the white ribbon diadem offered to Caesar three times by Antonius during the Lupercalia, which Caesar had refused. Octavian ordered both to be set up in the Forum as a tribute to his adopted father. Antonius, using his authority as one of the Consuls, refused to allow this to be done, which was hugely unpopular with the people, but he did not budge. Then, on the last day of the games, Octavian ordered that a statue of Caesar, with a star above his head to denote his status as a god, be erected in Caesar's temple of Venus Genetrix, the temple that Scribonius and I had visited shortly before its consecration. This drove Antonius into an apoplexy of rage, as he launched into an attack so vitriolic that some of his own Tribunes, commanders of his personal bodyguard no less, remonstrated with him about the harshness of his language towards Octavian. From all indications, this was the first that Antonius learned of the tremendous sympathy his own veterans held for Octavian, which shocked him to his core. Immediately recognizing that he could not afford to offend and alienate men whose strong right arms he needed to achieve his aims, he claimed that he wanted nothing more than to come to some sort of reconciliation with Octavian. All he wanted, Antonius claimed, was to be treated with the respect he felt that he had earned. It was agreed that Antonius and Octavian would meet on the steps of the Capital to make a public show of reconciliation, yet when Antonius made his way there, he was in for another shock. As Octavian approached from the opposite end, Antonius saw that he was surrounded in a protective cordon by Caesar's veterans, recognizing a good number of them as men Antonius had enlisted on his trip through Campania. His own men were sending a signal to Antonius that, though they might march for him, their hearts were with the young Caesar, for that is how they thought of him. Even if Antonius had planned on doing Octavian any harm, it had to be clear to him that not only would Octavian's supporters come to the young man's defense, in all likelihood so would Antonius' men as well. There was once more a public show of amity between the two, but the veterans were still not willing to trust Antonius, so after the meeting, they escorted Octavian back to his house. This show of support for Octavian by men who were in the employ of Antonius greatly angered the Consul, and I have to believe that it was this fact that led Antonius to accuse Octavian of plotting to kill him, using members of Antonius' own bodyguard. This accusation understandably caused a huge uproar, and in the interest of living however much longer the gods have deemed for me, I will remain silent on this subject, allowing you, gentle reader, to draw your own conclusions. Suffice it to say that none of this helped to soothe public fears that another civil war was not looming on the horizon.

~ ~ ~ ~

In our part of the world, on the other side of the mountains separating Hispania from Gaul and more importantly Rome, the men of the 10th were at least looking and acting like a Legion, though only the drawing and shedding of blood would determine if they were truly Legionaries. Pollio was off chasing Sextus Pompey around the hills, but much to our disgust and discomfort, Marcus Lepidus had returned, making a thorough nuisance of himself. The actions of this puffed-up piece of *cac* led to the first great crisis with the new 10th. Naturally, daily inspections became part of our routine, which meant that the punishment list was correspondingly long. At first, we managed to restrict the punishments to extra duties or monetary fines, although taking money from men who had yet to receive their first allotment of pay was an administrative nightmare that had every Centurion, or more accurately, their clerks cursing Marcus Lepidus. However, fairly quickly this was no longer enough for our general, as I found myself summoned to headquarters to face the little man, who looked even smaller seated behind the large desk of the commanding general. Standing before him, I wondered why Pollio, who was not that much larger than Lepidus, looked as if he belonged behind that desk while our current commanding general looked very much like a child who has sneaked into his father's office and is playing at being *paterfamilias*.

"Primus Pilus, I have summoned you here in hopes that you can explain to me exactly why you are intent on disobeying me," Lepidus began, trying to look severe, but only managing to look petulant.

Reacting more to the tone than the words, I immediately stiffened to *intente*, adopting the vacant stare and clipped tone of the perfectly correct Centurion addressing a superior who he loathed. "I'm sorry, General, but I confess that I'm at a loss as to the General's meaning. Perhaps if the General could explain what he's referring to I could be more helpful."

Lepidus gave a theatrical sigh as he rolled his eyes at one of his toadies who was standing next to the desk, smirking at me.

Despite knowing that this was all a huge game, I felt my stomach tighten in anger, yet things were about to get worse. "Such is my lot in life that I'm surrounded by imbeciles and idiots," Lepidus said. I had to fight back a laugh at the sight of the toady's face when he realized that Lepidus was referring to him just as much as me. "What I'm referring to, Primus Pilus," Lepidus continued with exaggerated patience, "is after more than a week of inspections, I have yet to see one good flogging, despite having a list as long as you are tall of men who have been found in gross violation of the standards of the army of Rome."

For a moment, I considered pointing out that a coat of varnish having a speck of dust on it was hardly a gross violation of anything, but I knew that it would do no good.

Besides, my mind was busy dealing with something else he had said, once again the evil *numen* that makes me say things that are better left unspoken taking over my tongue. "Sorry, sir, but I'm confused at your reference to a 'good flogging'. I don't think any man who's been flogged would refer to it as good. Sir."

I heard a sharp cough. Out of the corner of my eye, I could see the toady looking at the floor, clearly trying to suppress a laugh, and I thought that perhaps I had found an unlikely ally.

After all, Lepidus had called him either an imbecile or an idiot, I was not sure which. Lepidus, on the other hand, was not amused at all. "Perhaps if you took your duties a little more seriously instead of thinking of clever things to say, the men would not need as much of a flogging as they obviously do," he snapped.

Now it was my turn to get angry. "If the General is unhappy with my performance, he's free to relieve me at his earliest convenience," I said coolly.

"Don't think I wouldn't," he shot back, but we both knew he was lying.

Perhaps it is boastful of me to say so, but my reputation in the army was such that if Lepidus tried to relieve me, it would bring about too many questions that he would not want to answer. Every governor is corrupt, but Lepidus was even more corrupt than most of the men sent by Rome. Despite his overall stupidity, he was smart enough to know that taking an action as drastic as relieving the Primus Pilus would draw unwanted attention. Further, he had to know that I could be counted on to point those asking the questions in the right direction. He sat there glaring at me as I stood staring at a point high above his head, neither of us saying a word for several moments.

Finally, Lepidus cleared his throat as he looked down at some papers on his desk. "Yes, well, I don't believe it needs to come to that anyway. All that needs to happen, Primus Pilus, is that some men are flogged. That's not too much to ask, is it?" he gave me a grimace that I supposed passed for his smile, and it was all I could do to keep from gaping at him in open amazement.

Then, something clicked in my head, as I understood what was really taking place. Marcus Lepidus wanted to see men flogged, not for any other reason than he got some sort of satisfaction from the sight.

"Very well, General, it will be as you command. I'll make sure that you'll see some . . . good floggings, but I do have one request."

Lepidus' expression changed, and he sat back, his fingertips pressed together as he looked at me with unconcealed suspicion. "What is it?" he asked warily.

"Just that the floggings are done without the scourge, and just the lash."

His look of disappointment confirmed my suspicions. While I had not thought it possible, my loathing for the man increased tenfold.

He frowned, shooting a glance at his toady, then opened his mouth, but I cut him off, suddenly inspired. "Excuse me, General, but it's just that if we used the scourge, a fair number of the men punished would either die or be completely useless, and we're at a point in our training where it would be too much to expect to find a replacement and get them trained up to the proper level."

Oh, he did not like that one bit, yet even men like Lepidus had their limits and could not be seen to hurt the readiness and training of a Legion for his own personal satisfaction. Because that is exactly what would be spread throughout the army, and if it was common knowledge in the army it would not take long for it to be known in Rome, where the climate was such that it would make things very dangerous for Lepidus.

Biting his lip, he gave a curt nod, saying only, "Very well. That is all."

He dismissed me with a disgusted wave of his hand, not bothering to return my salute. I exited the office, trying to decide how I was going to get out of this mess.

~ ~ ~ ~

"He what?" Scribonius' mouth dropped open in shock.

I just nodded, pointing to his cup of wine to indicate that he should take another drink.

"We can't do that," Balbus said, his expression mirroring that of Scribonius.

This time, I just shrugged, replying, "What choice do we have? By the book, any man written up more than twice for any offense, no matter how minor, is subject to being flogged. Besides that, by tradition and custom, whatever the Legate commanding a Legion decides is as close to law as one can get, and this Legate also happens to be the governor." I shrugged. "At least he agreed for the men not to be scourged."

Balbus snorted in disgust. "That was big of him. Let's be sure and tell the boys who had a smudge on their buckle or their blacking smeared that at least they won't be scourged. I'm sure that will make them feel better."

"It should, because they'd probably be dead," I shot back, stung by what I perceived as their lack of appreciation that I had gotten at least that much of a concession from Lepidus. Leaning forward, I said intently, "Look, you weren't there. There was no changing his mind because this isn't about discipline, it's about that bastard getting some sort of sick satisfaction in seeing men striped bloody."

Balbus looked at me in open disbelief, while Scribonius sat back, nodding thoughtfully. "I had heard that about Lepidus. Apparently, he's a huge fan of the arena, and owns a stable of gladiators himself. But his interests don't stop there; supposedly he tortures his slaves for his own amusement."

Balbus looked at Scribonius in surprise, but I had long ago learned that my friend was a fount of knowledge about the upper classes of Rome, and he had always been right before so I saw no reason to doubt him now.

"So what do we do?" Balbus asked.

Again, all I could do was shrug. "We obey orders. Tomorrow we set up the frame in the forum, and some poor bastard is going to get striped."

~ ~ ~ ~

The next day, things went exactly as we had feared, except that it was even worse because there were a total of 20 men deemed by Lepidus to be worthy of flogging. There was an audible gasp every time as one after the other, the men under punishment were called to the front of the formation, name after name after name. I could feel the eyes of the Centurions boring into my back, but they had all been warned what was coming and cautioned against making any sort of display that would give Lepidus the excuse to have them punished as well. While I did not believe Lepidus would be stupid enough to try having a Centurion flogged, I was not willing to take the chance. So many men were selected that the punishment took the better part of the rest of the morning, with another problem presenting itself, though Lepidus offered the solution, thereby making things even worse. Each man was to receive ten lashes; with 20 men that was 200 lashes that somebody had to administer. Generally, a man from the punishment detail could inflict about 50 lashes before his arm gave out, and there were only two men per Legion, so for a brief moment I thought that either some of the men would escape flogging, or each man would only receive three or four lashes. Unfortunately, Lepidus had brought along a whole stable of men trained in the arts of torture and punishment, and he ordered these men to inflict the punishment. At the sight of the heavily muscled, scarred men striding forward to take their place by the frames, there was a low buzz of muttering that swept through the Cohort formations, and I could feel the hair on the back of my neck raise at the sound of a hugely angry Legion. As much as I understood and agreed, I could not allow this to continue, so I executed an about-face to glare at the men, none of whom could look me in the eye, and I was gratified to hear the noise come to a complete stop. Still, I felt the undercurrent of anger, worrying me that this was only the first day. Unless Lepidus realized what a huge mistake he was making, I was not sure that I could control the men, youngsters or not. I would be lying if I said that there was a part of me that did not want to control them, that would love to see them tear Lepidus into little pieces. That would not do my career any good, however, so I just had to hope that somehow the crisis that I was sure was coming could be averted.

~ ~ ~ ~

The punishment over, the men were marched back to their respective areas, while I scanned their faces as they marched past, my heart sinking at their expressions of open anger and disgust. Fueled by the veterans, who would no doubt be telling them that things had never been this way while marching for Caesar, or even for that bastard Labienus, the Centurions and I were sitting on top of a rapidly boiling pot. With that in mind, I called a meeting of all Centurions and Optios. Not wanting to have the type of discussion we needed to have in earshot of either the men or Lepidus' minions, we met at the small theater in town, with guards at the entrances to make sure that nobody could eavesdrop.

"You all know why I called this meeting," I began immediately, without any greeting. "We're dealing with a situation that frankly I'm at a loss how to deal with, and I'm looking for ideas on how we can contain things before the men revolt."

I stopped, waiting for someone, anyone to speak up, but the silence was complete, the men looking about for someone else to go first. After several seconds, I looked to Scribonius in appeal, but he shook his head. I insisted, waving my hand in a beckoning gesture while pointing to the spot next to me with the other hand, and finally, with a sigh, he stepped forward. I had no idea what he was going to say, but my hope was that having Scribonius speak first would break the ice and get the other men talking.

"I don't think there's anything we can do, really."

I looked at Scribonius in disbelief, furious that this was what came out of his mouth, yet he returned my gaze with a look that said, "You asked for this."

However, it did get the other men talking, if only to howl in protest at the idea that we were helpless. "We run this Legion, not Lepidus," someone shouted, and there was a roar of agreement.

I held up my hand, but it took a moment to get the men quiet. "Then how do we take back control of the Legion?" I asked.

"Make him realize that we're the only thing keeping the men from tearing him to pieces," I recognized the deep voice of Balbus, and I looked over to see him leaning against the wall, arms folded.

"How do we do that?" I countered, knowing that he had some idea already or he would not have said anything.

He shrugged, then studied his fingernails as he spoke. "I don't think that approaching him directly would do any good. He'd just get his back up like most patricians, then we'd be worse off than before. Is there any among his toadies who he listens to, who has some influence with him?"

I gave it some thought. I had seen that he seemed to rely on one man in particular, one of his Tribunes whose birth was not so high as to threaten Lepidus yet high enough that Lepidus considered him worthy to be in the same room. I do not remember the man's name, but it was his that I mentioned.

"Then I suggest that you approach him and have a word with him," Balbus said.

"And what if that doesn't work?" someone demanded. "What if it makes him angry? Then what?"

"Then," Balbus said calmly, as if he were discussing the next day's training schedule, "we kill him."

The fact that nobody batted an eye or raised even the tiniest voice of protest, no matter how half-hearted, told more about our hatred of Lepidus than anything else could. With that, the meeting adjourned, and I went looking for the Tribune.

~ ~ ~ ~

He agreed to see me. When I asked that the ensuing conversation take place only between the two of us and that he dismiss even his slaves he did not seem particularly surprised, giving me my first hint that he had been expecting some sort of meeting. Once one of his body slaves poured us each a cup of wine, the slave departed to leave us sipping from our cups, neither speaking for a moment.

Then the Tribune broke the silence. "Well, Primus Pilus, I don't believe that this is a social call. What is it that you wish to discuss?"

As usual, I preferred the direct frontal assault. "We have a problem, Tribune," I began, as he raised an eyebrow but said nothing, forcing me to continue. "It concerns the actions of General Lepidus and his excessive use of the lash on the men for minor offenses."

The Tribune leaned forward to set the cup down, his face revealing nothing. Speaking very carefully, he replied, "I'm not sure what you mean, Primus Pilus. Nothing that the Governor," he put special emphasis on Lepidus' civilian administrative title, which outranked that of ordinary General, "has ordered is outside the regulations or the customs of the armies of Rome."

"That's true," I conceded. "He is technically within his rights, but this is a young Legion, and he's using the most extreme punishment for offenses that haven't been administered for at least as long as I've been in the army. I can never remember a man being flogged for failing an inspection. Losing equipment, or failing to show up for an assigned duty, that's when a flogging is absolutely appropriate, but for having a smudged buckle?" I shook my head. "What happens when one of the men actually does something like what I just described? What's left?"

"Either the scourge or execution, of course," the Tribune said, laughing at my shocked expression. Looking down into his cup, I suppose in order to avoid looking me in the eye as he said this, the Tribune continued. "The Governor is a firm believer in the ancient and hallowed traditions of the Republic. He believes that discipline in the Legions under Caesar was lax, and that a firmer hand is required. Perhaps once your men realize this, they will put more effort into their duties in order to avoid punishment."

"With all respect Tribune, I don't think it has anything to do with the Governor's beliefs about the Republic. If it was, he'd be on the side of The Liberators, but he's not. I think it has everything to do with his enjoyment of seeing men weaker than he is suffer," I shot back.

The Tribune sat back, now looking me directly in the eye.

While I was expecting him to be angry, instead I saw the ghost of a smile. "Perhaps there is a grain of truth in what you say," he admitted. "But does it really matter why he does what he does? He's the Governor, and he has the law on his side."

"And I have a very angry Legion who the Centurions will find hard to control if Lepidus continues on this course," I countered, and now I saw a glint of anger in his eyes.

"That's a very serious statement, Primus Pilus. You understand what would happen if you and your Centurions were unable to control your men? At the very least the Legion would be decimated, and any Centurion who was found to not have done their utmost to stop such behavior would be executed."

"True," I granted, now it was my turn to lean forward to look him in the eye. "But Lepidus would still be dead, and I expect so would anyone the men thought close to Lepidus."

Nothing more was said for some time, then the Tribune sighed. "Understood," he said curtly. "So, what do you want me to do?"

"I've observed that Lepidus seems to respect and value your opinion a great deal." I saw no harm in laying it on thick, and he seemed to perk up a bit at the flattery. "I'm asking you to prevail upon the Governor to relax his punishment, not the discipline behind it," I emphasized. "We fully accept and respect his authority under the laws of Rome, and we don't expect him to ignore any violation of regulations, we're just asking that his punishment be more in line with the custom of more recent times."

"And what's in it for me?" he asked, not blinking. I suppose I should not have been surprised, but I was. "What do you want?" I asked cautiously. He laughed, I guess, at my naivety.

"Why, money of course," he said cheerfully.

He named a sum, making me fight the urge to pick up the cup and smash it over his head because of his greed. Instead, I agreed, while I was wondering how I would scrape up that kind of cash on short notice. Our business concluded, I thanked him for the wine, then returned to the Legion area to spread the news.

~ ~ ~ ~

As expensive as it was, the Tribune was at least as good as his word. While the next morning's inspection produced just as many men on the punishment list as before, this time the penalties were in the form of money and extra duties, something that Lepidus looked none too happy about. I could feel the breeze produced by the audible sighs of relief of both the rankers and the Centurions as the crisis passed. With that out of the way, we could return our minds and efforts to making the Legion ready to fight.

However, that is for later. Once again, I grow tired, and need a day or two to recover my energy. There is much more to tell about the struggle between Marcus Antonius, and young Octavian; more marching, more fighting, more bleeding and dying. Most importantly, a new Rome to be forged, a Rome breaking free of its past and becoming stronger and mightier than ever, thanks to the men of the Legions. Of which I am one, and will always be. Titus Pullus, Legionary of Rome.